Raves for *Treason's Shore*

"The fantastic fourth and final Inda fantasy is a superb ending to an excellent saga as the prime characters constantly must choose between personal desires and the kingdom's needs . . . Complex, with thriving cultures on land and at sea, *Treason's Shore* completes one of the best fantasy chronicles in years."
—*Midwest Book Review*

"Smith's battle sequences are convincing and her characters are interesting enough to make us care what happens to them . . . It's the travel rather than the destination that makes this such a good book." —*Critical Mass*

"The Inda books are everything you want from a fantasy series—an interesting, fully-developed world with several languages, environments, and cultures that are evocatively described, a complex but not confusing plotline with a number of unexpected twists, really well-written action scenes, and above all characters whose lives you follow and whose fates you care about."
—Diana L. Paxson, bestselling author of *Sword of Avalon*

"[The] beautifully-structured *Inda* series [comes] to a resounding conclusion in *Treason's Shore*." —*Strange Horizons*

And the novels of *Inda*

"The world creation and characterization within *Inda* have the complexity and depth and inventiveness that mark a first-rate fantasy novel . . . This is the mark of a major work of fiction . . . you owe it to yourself to read *Inda*." —Orson Scott Card

"Intricate and real . . . Filled with magic and glamour . . . Characters spring to life with humor . . . Complex and compelling." —*San Jose Mercury News*

"Many fans of old-fashioned adventure will find this rousing mix of royal intrigue, academy shenanigans, and sea story worth the effort." —*Locus*

"In this lively, accessible follow-up to *Inda*, Smith dares to resolve several plot lines, in defiance of fantasy sequel conventions. Smith deftly stage-manages the wide-ranging plots with brisk pacing, spare yet complex characterizations and a narrative that balances sweeping action and uneasy intimacy."
—*Publishers Weekly*

Also by Sherwood Smith:

INDA
THE FOX
KING'S SHIELD
TREASON'S SHORE

* * * * * *

CORONETS AND STEEL

TREASON'S SHORE

SHERWOOD SMITH

DAW BOOKS, INC.
DONALD A. WOLLHEIM, FOUNDER
375 Hudson Street, New York, NY 10014

ELIZABETH R. WOLLHEIM
SHEILA E. GILBERT
PUBLISHERS
www.dawbooks.com

First Paperback Printing, October 2010
1 2 3 4 5 6 7 8 9

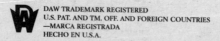

DAW TRADEMARK REGISTERED
U.S. PAT. AND TM. OFF. AND FOREIGN COUNTRIES
—MARCA REGISTRADA
HECHO EN U.S.A.

PRINTED IN THE U.S.A.

Acknowledgments

My heartfelt thanks to Hallie O'Donovan, Francesca Forrest, Kate Elliott, Shweta Narayan, and Faye Bi for their generosity with their time and insight in beta reading, to Tammy Meatzie for her patience and generosity in proofreading for me, and to Gregory Feeley for the title suggestion.

Anyone interested in extra information, there is a wiki full of Sartorias-deles geekery here: *http://s-d.newsboyhat.co.uk/* including a "what happened after" timeline.

It's difficult to pin down music that is close to what one hears, but there are three pieces that can provide a vector: the soundtrack of *Amistad*, "Chale Chalo," from *Lagaan: Once Upon a Time in India*, and "Azeem O Shahen Shahenshah" from *Jodhaa Akbar*, as well as some cuts from the Scottish band Albannach.

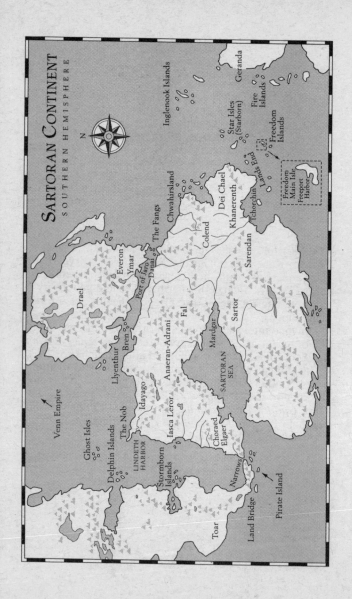

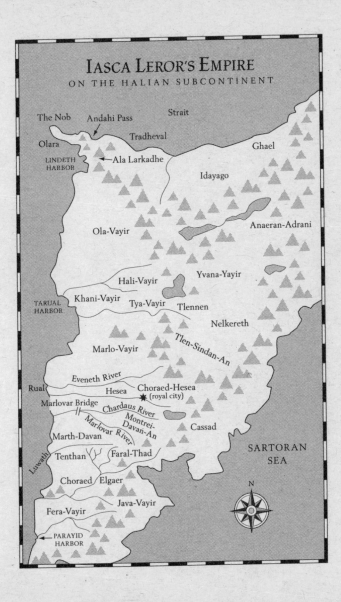

PART ONE

Chapter One

THE arched window over Tdor's bed glowed with the faint blue of impending dawn. She rose, pushing down the covers on the inside so no cold air would disturb Inda, her husband of one night. Inda slept on, an unmoving mound under the quilt.

Below, as the sun began to crest the eastern hills, Inda's mother, Fareas-Iofre, walked through the castle and to stable, courtyard, and garden as people shuffled out to begin their day. She spoke to each, requesting quiet movements so that Inda could sleep.

Many looked up at Tdor's bedroom window, smiling at the memory of Inda's wedding the night before. Others remembered how old he had looked on his long-awaited arrival home. Not old, no, but hard, though he had just turned twenty-one—hard and covered with scars. They picked up their tools with care, and spoke in lowered voices, if at all.

Tdor was too preoccupied to notice the unusual quiet. She stood for a short time, looking down at Inda's sleeping form. Her palm ached with her desire to caress him, but she knew he needed rest.

So she flung her waiting robe around her chilled flesh

and crouched down before the battered trunk that had
held her clothes since she had first come to live at Tenthen Castle when she was two years old. In the weak light
the trunk was barely discernable as a bulky rectangle; the
carved horse heads with tangled manes could only be felt,
not seen. Her fingers ran from those to the top edge, between the iron hinges. At the left end, the pattern of carved
leaves had been marred by a dozen or so rough notches,
gouged long ago. When Tdor left the castle nursery at age
eight, Fareas-Iofre had told her, *This trunk belonged to
Inda's grandmother. When she was a girl she made those
notches to commemorate happy days. It is now yours.*

Tdor had made notches on the right-hand side. Not many,
though she considered her life a happy one. But days when
the cup of light inside her heart so overflowed it seemed to
spill out into the world, those were the days she'd used one
of her wrist knives to make a mark of her own.

She ran her fingers over them, recalling each occasion.
The earlier ones seemed childish now, like the first day she
hit the target center with every arrow. The day she'd suc-
cessfully translated a whole line of Old Sartoran without
resorting to the gloss. The day she'd beaten Inda's cousin
Branid in a not-quite-friendly fighting match. After she
turned thirteen, for a long time she hadn't made any, not
with Inda away in exile for so many years, and so many
other bad things going on. During that interval she'd only
made two: the first on the day she left for the queen's training, and the second the day she returned (she thought) forever.

More recently she'd added another pair. One when her
foster-sister, Joret Dei—who had been betrothed to Inda's
brother until Tanrid had been killed—married a prince
over the mountains. The last one she'd made was after the
day she commanded a successful castle defense war game
the previous spring.

Tdor slid her knife from its wrist sheath and worked it
into the wood, slow and silent. It must be done now. In the
future when she touched it, she would remember kneeling
here the morning after her wedding ceremony, pooled in
happiness. Inda had come back from his long exile. He had
led the kingdom in battle against the invading Venn despite

terrible odds. He had regained honor and place—and he'd come home.

She pressed the blade deeply into the wood, then sat back to impress every detail into memory: the rough stone of the walls stippled with a faint honey color; her worn rug of green yarn, the dark green broken by the two lighter patches that she had worked in herself to mend worn spots—they hadn't found the exact green dye to match. The strengthening light glowing in the window began to reveal the two shades, once so annoying, but grown familiar, and then dear.

A movement from the bed snapped her gaze up. The warming light outlined the shape of Inda's shoulder, one relaxed hand, his brown braid with curls straggling loose. He slept on, so she continued her survey, breathing deeply of the familiar smell of stone, of horse, of mingled sweat. She cherished each, even the cold mottling the skin on her own hands as she gripped her knife.

I am so happy, Tdor thought, rising to her feet. The lightness of joy intensified to the sweet anguish of gratitude, making her giddy—almost afraid—as she looked across the room at Inda breathing deeply in the tangle of sheets.

Fear of a proximate threat was pragmatic; fear of the imaginary threat was just craven. She picked up her knives and her clothes and eased noiselessly from the room to run down to the baths.

The sun had appeared, shafting spangles over the gently steaming water when she forced herself to leave the hot bath. Inda's lover, Dag Signi, had obviously used her magic to renew the water-cleaning spells and whatever mysterious magic it was that took light and heat from the day's sun and hoarded it in the stones below the baths to keep the water warm. The familiar dank smell, strengthening slowly over the past year or so, was entirely gone.

Tdor consciously extended her gratitude to include Signi, the lover Inda had brought back with him. Tdor hoped before long that welcoming Signi within the family circle would be unconscious, as effortless as her own love for Inda.

Tdor was mentally ordering her day when she emerged from the women's side, walking at her usual brisk pace, and ran right into a tall, strong figure just emerging from the men's side. A flash of long, glossy wheat-gold hair, a beautiful hand gripping her arm to steady her: she looked up into dark-fringed golden eyes. "Tau?"

Each stepped back. Tau was mildly surprised to see Tdor awake; she was far more surprised to discover him dressed in his foreign clothes: a long vest over a loose shirt and narrow trousers rather than the ubiquitous blue coat worn by Marlovan Runners. "You're leaving? Does Inda know?" She flushed, hoping the question wasn't wrong. So much of Inda's life was unknown, even strange. "I mean—"

"It's all right." Tau uttered a soft laugh. "I'm leaving, and Inda doesn't know. Do you remember Jeje?"

Tdor smiled at the vivid image of the short, dark-browed woman her own age whom Inda had brought to the royal city when his exile had ended. Jeje had called herself master of a scout craft, which Tdor understood had something to do with boats. Jeje had been part of Inda's pirate fighting fleet. They'd only conversed once, but Jeje's pungent opinions and her matter-of-fact outlandishness had entertained Tdor immensely.

"I think I told you that she left us early on. Said she had a quest of her own, which I had assumed was to find her family. Late last night Jeje wrote to me by one of those magical letter cases." Tau tapped an inner pocket of his vest. "It seems she's found my mother. She won't tell me how she found her, or how my mother wound up where she is. It appears I'll be required to cross half the continent to discover what happened. And as Inda will not need me in the royal city, where he will no doubt find plenty of Runners far better trained at running than I, well, I may as well get started."

Was there just a breath of laughter, of self-mockery in his pleasantly spoken words? She did not look up. In the few weeks Tau had been among them, she had discovered that his expression—almost always mild and friendly—rarely changed.

"So here is a suggestion." Tau stopped on the stair. He held out a hand and Tdor stopped as well, looking up in surprise. "When Inda is bad in the mornings put willow-steep in his coffee."

"Willow," she repeated, and started down the stairs again. "But that's so bitter. And what do you mean by bad?"

"Wakes up with stiff joints. Mostly when the weather is wet—I don't know why. Not always. Don't ask him. He'll just say he's fine. Give him the willow. He won't notice, I promise you."

"He rarely noticed his food when small." For some reason Tdor's eyes stung. "He just shoveled it in. He was always planning what to do next. He organized all our games." She gulped. "It's so odd he never told you that. Talked about us. It's as if he wanted to forget us."

"No." Tau's voice was quiet, but resonant with conviction. "I think he missed his home so much he couldn't, or wouldn't, talk. But he's got you all back again."

But he doesn't have his home back, she thought as they passed through the children's dining room with its plain plank table and worn mats. *Home.* She cherished the dilapidations that had shocked Inda the day before. Though she knew she was happy—she was aware of the glowing cup inside her—the thought of leaving diminished some of the joy. But the royal city and their new lives were an unsurpassed honor, she reminded herself. Hadand was there. *I will be happy there, too.*

"How will you get to where you are going? You can't travel over the mountains now—winter is almost on us. It takes half a year to get through when the passes are clear."

"No more mountains!" Tau gave a soft laugh. "I thought I'd see if a ship or two miraculously survived the pirate attacks."

"Plenty of ships. No miracle."

They turned around to find Whipstick Noth, the beech-thin, tough, weathered Randael assigned to the Algara-Vayirs by the former king after Inda's older brother Tanrid was killed.

Amusement flashed through Tau as Whipstick went on. "Now't the pirates and the Venn seem to be gone, my dad tells me people're bringing out fisher craft and even trade ships they hid along the inlets until the troubles were over."

In the east, good manners required that if you overheard another's conversation, you pretended not to, and excellent manners obliged you to step out of earshot. Among Marlovans, Tau had discovered, if you heard it, you were a part of it.

"Maybe I can talk my way on board one, then. Work my passage." Tau flexed an arm.

Whipstick eyed Tau as they took up plates and helped themselves to fresh rye pan biscuits. The fellow was an anomaly here in Tenthen. Not so much his spectacular looks—though that was certainly a part of it—but his manners, his fine clothes, his outland habits, like teaching the steward to sew ribbon along the edges of the linens to make them last. But first he'd had to teach the weavers how to make ribbon.

You'd think, with those looks and his finicky ways, he'd be on the strut, but he hadn't been at all. More, he was tough. Whipstick had discovered that after his first offer of a practice session on the mats. Their strength was a match, but Tau always won because he was trained in some new type of contact fighting that Inda had learned while a pirate. Tau had used it fighting beside Inda at the end of the Venn War, where—according to rumors preceding Inda—the two of them had scythed down hundreds of Venn all by themselves, ending with the surrender of the commander himself. Whipstick knew how numbers of dead inflated with every telling, and he was waiting to discover the truth behind the rumors, if he could.

"You tell them who you are, that'll get you passage," Whipstick said.

Tau grimaced very slightly. It was brief, Whipstick almost missed it, and Tdor did; she was leaning against the prep table, staring out the window.

Whipstick realized Tau—for whatever reason—did not intend to tell anyone at Parayid Harbor who he was. Whipstick wouldn't waste time trying to argue. Instead, he sat down with his food.

Tdor turned away and joined the fellows as they all settled on the mats at the table. From old habit Tdor sat across from Whipstick. How strange life was! Ten years ago, she'd sat here one spot down to the left, across from Inda, with Tanrid and Joret at her right, the best end of the table closest to the fire. Then five years later, Tanrid was dead and everyone expected Joret to marry Inda (if he returned) and Tdor to marry Whipstick, who took to sitting in Tanrid's place, just because he could get up faster if called away.

Then Joret left to accompany Hadand, Inda's sister and a new-married queen, on a diplomatic visit over the mountain border into Anaeran-Adrani. Hadand had returned, but Joret stayed to marry the crown prince. Here at home, Tdor moved over a spot, again because it was easiest if she was called away.

Now Inda was back, and the rest of them sat here out of habit in the children's dining room; they still thought of themselves as the young generation because as yet there was not one younger.

Her reverie broke when Whipstick and Tau, who had been talking companionably, fell silent. The comfortable atmosphere had changed, and Tdor knew without looking up that Inda's Cousin Branid had entered.

He walked into the room carrying his plate, his eyes flicking back in forth in that anxious, snakelike way that made Tdor's innards tighten with dislike. Tdor had been shocked to overhear someone remark once that he was handsome. It was true that Branid was tall and he'd become muscular from his new devotion to drill. Alone of the Algara-Vayir blood relatives his hair had remained bright yellow, his eyes blue instead of the brown shared by Inda and his mother, but Tdor couldn't think of him as handsome. His features always seemed distorted into a perpetual pout when they weren't angry or sly.

She realized Branid had been standing there staring at them for several heartbeats. When Whipstick and Tau glanced up from their food, he forced a big grin. "Well, we should begin as we mean to go on, shouldn't we? I'm heir to the Adaluin now. Or will be when I ride to Convocation and make my vows."

Annoyance flushed through Tdor. She was about to remind him that this was the children's dining room, and the Adaluin hadn't sat in here for at least fifty years, more like sixty. But Whipstick just scooted down, leaving Tanrid's old place to Branid.

Branid flushed with far more pleasure than the situation warranted; Tdor's entire body tightened with resentment as he settled down, looking around with a smug, proprietary air at the room he'd been eating in all his life. "Why is everything so quiet? No one's at work?"

"They're at work," Whipstick said. "The Iofre asked

people to make as little noise as they could. To let Inda sleep."

The mention of the Iofre caused Branid to abandon whatever he'd been intending to say. Instead, as he broke his biscuit, he turned Tdor's way. "Inda needs sleep?" He grinned. "You wore him out, eh, Tdor?"

Scalding anger burned through her, so hot it made her ears tingle. At the sight of her blush Branid laughed with a knowing air that made her want to fling her platter at him.

But she controlled the urge, as she always had. She knew it was unfair, this reaction of hers: sexual jokes were common, even expected after weddings when the pair publicly go off together. She would even laugh if some of her friends among the guardswomen made the very same sort of joke later on. But somehow when Branid made them, with that insinuating tone, that leer, she felt as if worms had crawled into her clothes.

Don't make a fuss, she told herself. If you showed you were unsettled, or upset, he'd worry it like a castle cat with a trapped rat. So she pretended Whipstick had said it. "I did. Anyone want another biscuit?"

Her voice came out with only one quiver. Tau's brows lifted; Whipstick went on eating. Branid paid her no more attention, and then she realized what his real intent was.

Her answer didn't matter, it wouldn't have had she indeed thrown her platter at him. Even dripping with egg, he would have got to what mattered the most, as he turned to Whipstick.

He's going to start issuing orders, Tdor thought, and hate fired through her. It was only right. The title was now Branid's, after all these years. But she wouldn't stay to listen to him ordering Whipstick around just to be giving orders that the Randael now had to obey.

She whisked herself out, shook her half-eaten eggs into the pig pail, and walked out the other entrance, into the servants' end of the castle, though she wasn't swift enough to avoid Branid's voice, thick with triumph, "Whipstick, I'm thinking we should change the schedule around, so we can ..."

Tdor broke into a run to avoid that voice, stupid as it was. She burst into the great hall, which was usually empty, so she could get control, then stumbled to a stop. She was not alone.

The tall, fair-haired woman turned, and Dannor Tya-Vayir smiled. Tdor's heat of anger died down to a cold rock of resentment. From one horrible person to another: Mudface Tya-Vayir, who had forced her company onto Inda after his triumph in the north. Dannor had done her very best to lure Inda into setting aside his lifetime betrothal to Tdor and marrying her instead.

"How does it feel to be married?" Dannor's tone was so cordial Tdor was taken aback.

"Fine." Tdor strove to hide her wariness. When they were girls in the queen's training, Dannor had never once had anything good to say to Tdor. Ever.

"Where's Inda?" Dannor asked.

"Still asleep." Tdor pointed upstairs.

Dannor smiled, one shoulder coming up. During their girlhood, Dannor had never taken defeat well. But Dannor made no remark about Inda or his marriage. "Is this hall always so bare?"

Tdor flushed as she took in the holly and ivy garlands still hanging from the torch sconces, the ivy now drooping and withered. Except for the magnificent raptor chair on the dais at the far end, the hall really was very barren, though the previous night she'd thought the decorations festive.

Even though Tenthen Castle was—strictly speaking— no longer her home, a lifetime of pride kept her reply short. "Yes." And when Dannor turned her way, brows lifted, Tdor forced herself to smile, to be less abrupt. "We had a couple of old Iascan tapestries left over from the days when the Tenthens had the castle. Those tapestries were rotting, and we didn't like them well enough to reweave them. The Algara-Vayirs had one tapestry that I hear was a good one, but it got burned by pirates when the Adaluin's first family was killed. We've never had time or money to replace it."

"Why didn't you just make a new one?" Dannor asked.

Tdor sighed. "No one could agree on a design, then the tapestry weaver died of old age. No prentice, not after all the years of troubles. So the young weavers haven't actually made one, though they all say they know how to set up the loom. But times being what they were, and no one good enough at drawing to make the design, it never happened."

"That would make a splendid gift for the Iofre, then, wouldn't it?" Dannor asked. "I mean, if, say, Inda found himself wealthy in his new place as Harskialdna, and could fund one."

"That definitely won't happen." Tdor turned her back on the blank wall. It really did look bare, though she'd grown up used to bare walls. "Inda told me yesterday that the king says the treasury is empty."

Dannor waved a hand as though shooing insects. "Oh, they'll fill it fast enough. You watch. Evred-Harvaldar will squeeze the Jarls at Convocation, after speeches about triumph and glory. Men are all the same." She rocked back on her heels, and laughed. "But they look good in tapestries, if you know how to make them."

In their queen's training days, Dannor had displayed an ability to draw. She'd done it seldom, as Tdor remembered. Dannor had been far too busy bossing people around. But once or twice she'd picked up a chalk, and with a few quick lines sketched a goose stretching up into flight. Or a horse running through a field of high grass, mane and tail flying.

Tdor fought to overcome her dislike. Even Dannor's stratagem with Inda—attaching herself to him and doing her best to sway him into marrying her instead of Tdor— could be explained, if you looked at it from Dannor's point of view. Inda had not been home for almost ten years. For all anyone knew, Tdor would have been just as happy marrying Whipstick or even Branid.

Meanwhile, until summer Dannor had been a Jarlan, head of the household. During the recent war with the Venn her husband was killed leading a desperate charge in Andahi Pass, far to the north. Dannor had no children, so she would not be senior woman of Yvana-Vayir. Dannor could either stay and be under the orders of the new Jarl's wife or else go to her birth home, where she'd be under orders of her brother and his wife. No woman would want that unless she was fond of her family.

So it was time to return Dannor's generous acceptance of defeat with generosity. "Speaking of the king, you know Inda and I will have to leave soon. Probably even tomorrow. If you'd like an escort, you'd be welcome to come with us. We've extra tents."

Dannor smiled. "That is a kind offer. But I always liked drawing, and I've an idea for a tapestry. Why not sketch it out as a guest-gift for Inda's mother? I'll take a day or two to measure out the hall, then draw a design. As for travel, my Runner and I are used to moving fast. I get restless dawdling along the way you have to in cavalcade, dragging tents and gear."

"All right. Though if you change your mind, know that you are welcome." Tdor studied the wall as if trying to envision a tapestry there someday, afraid her relief would show. "I'm sure the Iofre would like some kind of commemoration. Even if it might be a generation or two before we can actually make the tapestry."

Dannor laughed. Her intentions were clearly friendly, but that laugh was so sharp a reminder of their teen years, Tdor turned away to hide a wince she could not suppress.

Tiredness was making her giddy, and anyway she needed to set about readying for departure and take some of the burden off her First Runner Noren, who she knew was grieving deeply at the prospect of leaving Whipstick behind. As Tdor bustled around a corner, she wondered if it would be better to talk to Noren, or to let her choose the time to talk—

"Inda!" she exclaimed as she nearly stumbled into her new husband. His scarred face looked so tired, so . . . what was his expression? She always used to know what he was thinking, but he seemed so remote now.

"Overslept." He gave her a sheepish grin, and she grinned back at him. That was her own Inda again. Joy refilled her being with light.

Then he looked around. "Where's Signi?"

Her face must have changed; Inda's smile faltered, and the biggest scar on his brow puckered as he stared at her, puzzled.

She clapped her hands together, rejecting the hurt of jealousy with a ferocious act of will. There was no more useless, no more utterly despicable an emotion than jealousy! *Now there are three of us,* she thought. *I have everything I want, just more of it.*

She smiled, and took his hand. "Let's go find her together."

When the Iofre finished her rounds of the castle, she discovered Signi out beyond the pigs' pen, whirling and dancing with slow precision. It looked a little like Tau's knife warm-ups, only with no weapons, no threat: the small, plain Venn woman became light as a leaf, sinuous as a cat, full of grace.

Signi spun to a stop and put her hands together.

"I saw movement." The Iofre opened her hands; Signi wondered if the Marlovans knew that this gesture was the old Venn sign of peace. "I did not mean to interrupt, or intrude."

"I am finished," Signi replied, and in her unremarkable hazel gaze, the lift to her sandy brows Iofre saw question.

"I asked everyone to let Inda sleep. He—I was shocked. He has changed so terribly. As if he's been gone fifty years, not ten."

The Iofre's voice was low. Signi saw her anguish in the tightness of her body.

"He is—he was . . ." Signi pressed her fingertips together, reaching for the right words. "I do not have the formal healer training. I also do not have the words in your language."

"Tell me what you can," the Iofre begged.

"During the worst of the battle preparations. And its eve. He was . . . coming apart in pieces. It is the only way I can express it. But his friends, they did not see. They laughed when he goes like this." Signi mimed rocking back and forth. "Or this." She wagged her head back and forth, her lips loose. Then looked up. "Not in cruelty. They are used to it, they are fond of Inda and his oddities. He must have done that sometimes as a boy, yes?"

"He did," the Iofre whispered. "In the early days I was watchful. I had a great-aunt, you see, who had begun life that way. But she never talked, nor saw you, even if you looked into her face, I was told. She would just give you lists of numbers, often relating to dates in history. These were always correct, no matter how far back they reached in time."

"What happened to her?" Signi asked.

"None of the healers could get her to hear them, so the family sent her to Sartor. To where they train the healer-mages. After ten years, she became a scribe. My grand-mother was sent by the family to see her. My great-aunt had come into the world enough to know people. She had a good life. But Inda has always known us. The healers had told my grandmother if a child starts life like that, imprisoned inside her skull, only love brings her out. When Inda was small, and I thought I saw similar signs, I told my people to help his mind stay present, with us. My nephew Manther was some-what similar. Both boys stayed ... present." Fareas closed her eyes, her old companions grief and regret seizing her in their merciless grip. Two mistakes she had made, she had de-cided after long, watchful nights: one, permitting Tanrid to thrash his brother into obedience just because everyone else did it. And her second mistake, permitting Tanrid to see Inda favored by everyone, and never telling him why.

Signi observed the closed eyes, the tight expression of inheld pain, and mistook the cause. "Perhaps he will re-cover, given time."

Fareas shuttered the emotions away with the practice of years. She must concern herself with the now. "I can talk to Tdor—no I can't. She is going to leave." The Iofre hesi-tated. Inda had been granted the highest honor in the land. And Tdor as well. Tdor ... "All these years she kept faith with her remembered friendship for Inda. I hesitate to say anything now, when she must get to know him as a man, and one with so strange an array of experiences—"

"Mother?"

Inda and Tdor stepped out of the kitchen door and into the truck garden. "Hold," the Iofre called. "We will come to you." She turned back to Signi, murmuring, "Evred-Harvaldar will surely look out for Inda's welfare. They were fiercely loyal as boys. Is it not still true?"

Signi's expression was impossible to interpret. "Yes."

Whipstick finished his breakfast as Branid issued his long string of orders. Unlike the Algara-Vayirs (which now in-cluded Tdor), Whipstick had had plenty of time to think about what Inda's promotion would mean to Castle Tenthen—and to talk it over with Noren, whom he would have married if she had not been a sworn First Runner.

Of course Branid would ride roughshod over those now under his chain of command, glorying in finally gaining the prominence his malevolent grandmother had tried to wrest for him all his life. But he did care about Tenthen, and Choraed Elgaer, though he had strange ways of showing it. Whipstick had decided how to deal with Branid long before Branid got his lifelong wish.

Let Branid strut. Order the men about. Whipstick would keep his temper and counsel the men to do the same, reminding them that Branid would all the sooner settle to the work that must be done. That was all that mattered, whoever gave the orders.

He did make certain of one thing, though, before he got started. As soon as he was done eating, he took Cousin Flatfoot, his Runner, aside. "I'm sending you to take Tau to Parayid. I'll give you my reports on what Inda told us about things up north to carry to my dad. He'll want to know. Then you introduce Tau to my ma. Tell her who he is, but tell her Tau doesn't want any fuss. She'll make certain he gets a good boat."

Flatfoot chuckled. "Done."

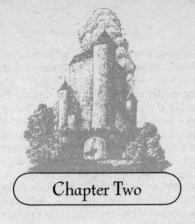

Chapter Two

AS soon as word traveled inward from the perimeter patrol outside Iasca Leror's royal city that the king's banner had been spotted, people put down tools and lined the main street behind the city gate. When low clouds rumbling overhead brought huge splats of rain, some ducked inside doorways, but no one returned to work or home.

At last the tower and the now-visible outriders exchanged the thrilling trumpet chords announcing the return of the king. The Bell Runners enthusiastically plied the ropes, and people surged from under cover to line the streets and began to shout and pound on hand drums.

"Evred-Harvaldar Sigun!"

"Evred-Harvaldar Sigun!"

"Evred-Harvaldar Sigun!"

The rhythmic shout gained volume as their young king rode through the city gates, tall and straight, his red hair darkened to the shade of his father's by the rain, color emphasizing his cheekbones. They cheered him and his men all the way to the castle gates, and only when he was inside did they go back to work in small clumps, everybody laughing and cheerful. Innkeepers promised to draw an ale for everyone (many knowing that that would begin an evening of festive largesse) to cheer the northern victory as they looked forward to the stories the returning warriors would tell.

Inside the castle courtyard Evred slipped from his saddle, leaving his Runners to supervise as the last remnant of his army—the King's Riders who guarded the city and castle—rode over to their barracks to dismount, unpack, and reunite with families for the promised liberty.

The warm splatters of rain dotting brown circles on the honey-colored flagstones began to merge as the young queen appeared, short like Inda, her wide brown eyes and unruly brown curls so much like his. But where Inda was broad in chest and shoulder, Hadand-Gunvaer was broad in bosom and hip. She and Evred clasped hands, and the tower sentries—men and women—sent up a cheer.

"Hadand-Gunvaer Deheldegarthe!"

Deheldegarthe: a fighting queen, one who had by her own hand defended the kingdom. It, like *Sigun* for the king, was the highest accolade—one that must be given, it could never be asked for.

The royal pair smiled upward, and as the rain abruptly increased walked inside together; Hadand observed her beloved's distant gaze and waited for him to return from wherever his thoughts had taken him.

The air was motionless and warm inside the tower, assailing Evred with familiar smells, comfortable smells, which were now free from the power to harm; his uncle and brother had receded to occasional distorted voices in dreams.

When he and Hadand reached his outer chamber, he discovered chilled wine-and-punch waiting. "Ah," he said on a long outward breath. "How good it is to be home."

"Your last report via the magic case stated that all is well in the north." Hadand dropped onto a waiting mat.

Evred sat down next to her and cradled the broad, shallow wine cup in both hands. "It is as well as can be expected. Ndand Arveas is there in the pass, holding Castle Andahi while Cama rides back and forth from Idayago to Ghael. We'll have to find someone to back her until Keth is grown, though she's strong enough to hold it on her own."

Hadand's lips parted. She longed to say, *So why don't you make her a Jarlan, and let her pick her own Jarl? Why can't women command castles?* It seemed so obvious—especially since it had been women who had held Castle Andahi in the teeth of the entire Venn invasion, down to the last one.

But now was not the time for new ideas. She had learned through letters from women across the kingdom that most of the men who had gone north to fight (those who returned) longed to resume the old ways, the comfort of tradition.

So she turned her attention to Evred even as he studied her. Out of a lifetime of habit, each tried to descry the inner workings of the other's mind: as children they had shared everything, but time and experience had built personal boundaries that were difficult to surmount, despite their best intentions.

"We'll have to establish watches all along the north coast," Evred continued, sounding tired. "Something like Flash's beacon system, which would have worked had there not been treachery from within. But I'm keeping our best dragoon captains up there, headquartered at Ala Larkadhe, since my twin cousins want to swap off yearly as Jarls of Yvana-Vayir and commanders of the northern force."

"Aren't they a bit young for that?" Hadand asked.

"A year older than I was when I was first sent north to command," Evred said wryly. "And yes, my authority was limited. So will theirs be, at first. They know Cama is under Inda in chain of command, and they report to him. They accepted it without argument. Good boys, both of them. Though Beaver never seems to stop talking."

Hadand said, "Will they keep swapping off by year?"

"For now. I hope by the time their cousin finishes here as a horsetail and can serve as Randael at Yvana-Vayir they'll settle it among themselves . . . if we do not have any more wars."

Hadand's brown, unwavering gaze was so much like Inda's—and yet not. Evred realized he was searching for Inda in Hadand's eyes. His emotions roiled until he locked them down hard. "To finish with Ala Larkadhe, the Morvende archive in the white tower was closed to me."

Her face changed from the tension of worry to comprehension. She knew what that archive meant to him. "Did the Morvende say anything?"

"Nothing. I permitted the archive to be used as a transport, which seems to have alerted them. But the closing was inevitable because I dared to lead an army to war." He tried, and failed, to keep the bitterness from his voice. "It appears that no one wishes to hear my reasons."

Hadand poured more punch, maintaining a compassionate silence. She perceived the effort he made to relax, to look up and around. "All seems well here."

"Yes. But we had no war to contend with." How it hurt her to see the effort he made; what could she do? She had worked hard to have everything just right when he came home at last, down to his favorite foods, now rapidly cooling.

He looked blankly at the biscuits, then up. "The war, yes. You must have questions. I know my reports were scant. Those magical boxes. I don't really trust them. And even if I could send a sheaf of papers instead of quarter sheets folded small, there remained the matter of trying to find the time to write on them."

"Indeed I have questions. Beginning with the Venn surrender. What exactly happened? I've heard several conflicting accounts, and Inda has never written to me. Tdor says he wrote only that he was still alive."

He frowned, yet she knew Inda was all right. Tdor had sent a message when Inda arrived safely home, that they were about to marry. And though Tdor had not written since, Hadand knew that nothing disastrous had happened, or surely, *surely* she would have heard.

"It was not really a surrender, though everyone believes it to have been." He spoke slowly, hesitating between words.

She breathed in relief. The problem was not Inda. Absurd to have thought it concerned him! "What exactly happened with the Venn? Are they really gone? So many rumors have run ahead of you, and like you say, your report was scant. I have it by heart now, I've read it so many times, trying to wring extra meaning from every pen stroke."

His smile was perfunctory. "Some of those rumors began just after the battle. I did nothing to interfere with them." Evred drank his punch down, then pressed his fingers to his temples, eyes closed. "It seemed to hearten the men to think that Durasnir, the Venn Fleet Commander, surrendered to

Inda. That he and Inda fought a duel. That he knelt before me and swore allegiance. None of those things happened. He asked for a truce, said that their king was dead, and that Prince Rajnir had to sail home to claim their crown."

"That was all?"

"There was one more thing. It was very strange. I don't know why I did it, but I asked if they were coming back."

"He'd lie about that, of course," Hadand exclaimed.

"So I thought the moment the words were out." Evred crumbled a rye biscuit without awareness of what his fingers were doing as he thought back. "I braced for threat or dissembling. Scorn, even. We heard none of that. You must realize first that we learned before the attack that the one we have to fear is the mage Erkric, who was using magic to aid the war. According to Inda's Venn lover, the Dag Signi—do you remember her?"

Hadand vividly remembered the small, older woman who had so kindly and quietly renewed all the castle magic spells for them, working all night while Evred and Inda raised the entire city to march to war. But Evred so distrusted magic that Hadand only signified assent without speaking.

Evred said, "She told us that Dag Erkric has attempted to strike a bargain with Norsunder in an effort to learn magic that will control minds. It is possible that he has done so."

"I find that more difficult to believe than anything," Hadand exclaimed. "You know how I've been researching magic ever since I could read, but I've never found mention of magic—in our present time—that does that. In the days of Old Sartor, perhaps. We thought it all figurative language."

"I have trouble believing it, too. I retained my distrust of Dag Signi to the end, but something that Commander Durasnir said seemed to corroborate ... well, you tell me what you think." Evred leaned forward. "He asked Inda if he'd ever met Ramis of the *Knife*. The mystery pirate who commanded the ship with black sails."

"The pirate who Inda said caused the rift to the sky through which the Brotherhood of Blood command ships were forced. I remember that." Hadand poured more punch in hopes of getting Evred to drink if he would not eat. "I always thought this mysterious Ramis was a, oh, a dream figure or something."

"Inda insists he's a real man. He met him. Spent some time with him in conversation. Anyway, Inda answered Durasnir. Told him that Ramis had said there were three men who were dangerous to Inda: Prince Rajnir, the mage Erkric, and Durasnir himself. After which Durasnir said, 'Two of us must obey.' And then he vanished by magic. Shortly thereafter, the Venn marched back down the pass, boarded their ships, and sailed away."

"Two of them? But that just means the commander and the mage must obey the king."

"Why did he not say so?"

Hadand's eyes narrowed, bringing Inda forcibly to mind.

She said, "You think the Commander of the Venn, your enemy, was *warning* you in some way? But that makes no sense. A threat I can understand. A warning?"

"If Dag Erkric truly does control their prince—now their king, surely—then the warning becomes clear. The danger we share is the threat of magic. Unfortunately Durasnir spoke in Sartoran, so of our people the only ones who understood him were Inda and Taumad."

"Well, what does Inda say? He could ask Dag Signi."

"They don't discuss the war. It's an honorable truce, and I understand that. As for Inda . . ." Evred touched a ring on his hand that she had never seen before. She did not often see his hands; though they were long and beautiful, he habitually hid them by clasping them behind his back.

"As for Inda, we did not talk to much purpose. He was either riding along the lines encouraging the men, especially the wounded, or else abstracted . . ." Evred paused, remembering the campfire conversations, painfully repetitive as Inda went over every move, almost every sword stroke of the fights he could remember. After a few weeks of that, Evred thought it a victory when Inda shifted from what he should have done to what he could have done.

Evred looked up. "We seldom had much time alone to discuss that."

Hadand did not ask why the two most powerful men in the entire kingdom couldn't send the whole army out of hearing if they did not want to walk apart. There were times when speech was insufficient, even impossible. She remembered the days following the Jarl of Yvana-Vayir's conspiracy: the vivid memory images, the long pauses when she couldn't remember where she was. Waking up in the middle of the night in a cold sweat, reliving the worst, and wondering if she could have done something to prevent it. Words had come with difficulty, if at all.

She nodded agreement.

He closed his eyes and faced southwest. "He's on his way." And at Hadand's questioning look said, "It's a location ring. Inda wears the other one. We used them in the Andahi Pass so we would not lose each other."

"So you trust this ring, but not the golden scroll-cases?"

Evred's expression was always reserved, but now it tightened.

He made an angry, determined effort to lock away the conflict of emotions. The golden scroll-cases had been bespelled by Dag Signi; the location rings had been provided, Evred strongly suspected, by Savarend Montredavan-An, otherwise known as Fox.

Evred knew Inda's loyalty to Iasca Leror—to Evred himself—was total. Yet Inda had somehow gained the personal loyalty of not only the Venn mage Dag Signi, but the potentially troublesome Fox, who now commanded Inda's old pirate fleet and who had, it seemed, rescued Inda from certain death at the hands of the Venn.

Evred flexed his fingers, watching the muted glint on the plain gold band as lightning flared in the window. He looked up to discover Hadand waiting, her gaze steady and unwavering. "The rings only convey direction, no words. And Inda's Venn lover had nothing to do with the rings. Yes, I know she's proved trustworthy, but what if her unknown, unseen friends interfere? How would we know? We do not see these mages—the Venn call them dags. We do not understand their powers. And it's not just them. What if some Venn warrior had killed Noddy early on and taken his case? He had it—I found it after he died. Inside his pocket were Inda's notes. The Venn could have got the plan right there. Sometimes I want to throw the lot of those gold things into the fire," he said in a low, savage voice. "I may yet, if I detect the merest hint of tampering. But I admit they are useful, especially with the north so unsettled. Fast communication is essential. Cama insists that the one thing keeping the Idayagans quiet is the prospect of Inda returning."

"Inda?" Hadand's memory of Inda was the smiling little boy of childhood. "How so?"

Evred looked away, his expression even more remote. "You did not see him in battle. Both sides spread rumors that Inda fights like ten men, that he cannot be beaten."

Evred paused at the sudden, unbidden memory. In the archive, he had read, *What you remember about someone teaches you more about yourself than it does about the other.*

When Inda performed his knife drills, his movements expressed humor as well as strength, grace as well as skill. Inda fighting to kill was an order of magnitude in difference, face purple and mouth a rictus, eyes cold as death, grunting like an animal as he unleashed that terrifying strength, and yet Evred had found that aspect of Inda as deeply stirring as all Inda's myriad moods and voices. If not more. How could desire and death be so close?

But Hadand did not know that. He did not want her to know it, and so he shook his head. "Never mind."

"At least we have peace."

"No. Now we have a respite. It remains to be seen for how long."

Hadand said baldly, to strip the moment of the possibility of sickening coquetry, "Since the word came that you had won and were alive, I have been drinking gerda leaf again."

Evred thought of a son, and Inda raising that son, and smiled. That smile caused Hadand to smile, and her heart to beat fast.

And so he came to her room that night. Afterward, Hadand, longing for the unthinking affection of their childhood days in the nursery, waited for Evred to offer to stay, now that the threat of war was past. Would he sleep in her arms as he had when they were children? But he rose and with unfailing courtesy wished her a good rest, then left. She was far too proud to beg him to stay and so stared up at the ceiling, dry-eyed. She'd wept herself out at fourteen, she told herself. Fourteen was the time for tears. Now she was a woman, a queen, and tomorrow there was work to be done.

The Fox Banner Fleet was not at all surprised to be attacked by a swarm of galley pirates from the islands east of Dei Chael. Fox had told the captains as much, saying that an attack would give Fangras and the newcomers—former privateers from Sarendan—some practice.

And practice they got: they found themselves surrounded by a combination of three fleets led by a pair of brigantines. After a short but very fierce fight, the pirates veered off as usual to vanish among the many small islands.

Nugget crept up on the weather deck of the Fox Banner Fleet flagship *Death,* trying not to cough.

The smoke thinned in the sleeting rain. She welcomed the sleet. It not only scoured the last of the smoke from her lungs, but it made a solid gray curtain, blurring *Death*'s battle detritus, and the deckhands busy with repair.

Her cap and jacket were soon as wet as everyone else's. She slunk around the mast and dashed for the binnacle. Her battle station was signals since with only one arm she could not pull a bow.

The *Death* plunged through low, pillowy fingers of smoke. Green waves slopped down the deck from a following sea. Barely visible a few ship lengths beyond the stern, the indistinct shapes of the rest of the fleet drifted in and out of the smoke, smears of red glowing between the cold gray-green seas and the low storm clouds. She sidled around the binnacle, peering over the stern rail—

Smack!

The slap came out of nowhere, catching her between one step and another. She thumped onto her rear and let out a squawk.

Old training brought her in a roll to her knee, good arm up in a block. Annoyance and accusation died in her throat when she recognized the tall, lean red-haired figure dressed in black looming over her. Fox! He'd come up quiet as a cat.

"Where—" He snapped out the word in a way that chilled her right down to the toes. "—were you?"

"I—" She looked around wildly.

Smack! He hit her again—the stinging hit of drill—and again she tumbled over.

"Stop that!" she cried, scrambling away. She looked around for support. There was Pilvig, her best friend. And right behind her, two of the newcomers they'd taken on from Fangras' fleet. Mates Nugget's and Pilvig's age.

But did they protest? No.

Fox was standing right over her again. She recoiled, scrambling back, and bumped up against the binnacle.

"You abandoned your station in the heat of battle," Fox stated. He looked terrible, his face smeared with soot and sweat, which emphasized the wintry ocean-green of his eyes, a bloody rag twisted around his right arm just above the elbow, another wrapping his palm. He smelled of smoke, sweat, and blood. The last time she'd seen him, he was leading the repel-boarder team when the pirate brigantines slid up on either side.

"You know what would happen to you in any navy, on any ship, abandoning your post in the heat of battle?"

"I can't fight," she wailed, turning to her friends for support.

But there wasn't any. Not from Pilvig, nor from Mutt, who appeared from the other side of the mizzenmast. "Can't you *see?*" She lifted her stump.

"Sock fights." Fox tipped his head toward the skinny half-Chwahir who always wore a sock on his arm stump.

Nugget opened her mouth to protest that he was *old*—maybe as old as Fibi the Delf—but caught a squint-eyed look of cold contempt from Pilvig.

Pilvig! Her best friend! Nugget scowled down at her toes. She was seventeen, taller than Sock now, she'd grown plenty strong—she was just *afraid*.

"You left Pilvig to do both flags and whirtler signal," Fox said. "That meant we were left to fight two ships before *Rapier* heard the whirtler. If anyone had died, that would have been your fault."

"No, they were already boarding—"

"Your. Fault. Get up."

"Why? What are you going to do? Don't thrash me—I *promise* I won't—"

"I'm going to smack you," he stated, "until you defend yourself. Get. Up."

Nugget was sobbing by now, a mixture of fear, shame, and betrayal. Out came his hand again, straight toward her face, and she snapped up her arm in a forearm block. Just like in morning drill. He hit her arm, nearly spinning her about.

His other hand came around for a side blow. She jumped back, her shoulder twitching—no hand!—but he brought his down anyway, just as if she had a hand there. She shifted her weight and her foot snapped up, almost instinctively, a move from the old days before her wound. She didn't connect, so he smacked her ankle. It stung.

His hand came at her again. And again. And again. When she faltered or tried to argue he slapped her. After she howled, "Stop it! I'm sorry!" he gave her a knuckle rap on the bicep of her good arm. That *hurt!*

He kept her working until she leaned against the binnacle panting, her good hand pressed protectively against her stump, muscles trembling with fatigue.

Fox said, "You've been out for drill every day, but you never scrap. That is going to change. From now on, you're going to scrap with me."

A soft whistle from the background and a snort.

"But—"

"And every time I hear 'but' I'm going to give you another watch on cleaning duty. Two watches if you start a sentence with 'But Inda always said.' You're already on the crew to rebuild the damage the brigantines' cut booms did to the jib, and to repaint the fire damage. Then you're going to be scrapping with me. An entire watch. Tomorrow, another one."

Everyone was gathered now, and not a single face gave her pity or sympathy.

Fox showed his teeth. "There is nobody on the seas who fights nastier than I do. And I'm not going to stop scrapping with you until you're the second nastiest. Get used to it."

The ship creaked, blocks rapped, the sea hissed down the deck at their feet, then poured away.

"Now go repack the signal flags."

He turned away. Shortly afterward the door to the cabin

slammed. The crew dispersed, some talking in low voices. But no one talked to her. Not even Pilvig.

Nugget gulped on a sob as the rain hissed down around her. She picked up the first signal flag. It was the same one she'd thrown down before she ran to hide: *Engaged with enemy*.

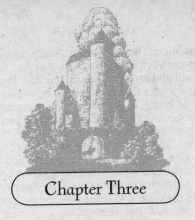

Chapter Three

SPREAD in two great wings, masts slanting like the pinions of raptors, the high-prowed Venn warships sailed toward the main harbor at Twelve Towers.

Not one of the people crowding the parapets, wall walks, and towers of the ancient city assumed it was accidental, this triumphant arrival on the first day of spring, which marked the turn of the year for the Venn.

So far north, each day's gain of light was noticeable, dawns and sunset often dramatic, if not stormy. A rare sight, the rising sun in a milky-pale sky behind the city; for many in the southern fleet who possessed spyglasses, it was a heartening sight after more than ten years away.

The southern fleet commander, Stalna Hyarl Fulla Durasnir, did not notice the weather.

For those watching from the walls and tower crenellations the complicated geometry of wind-curved sails were silhouetted against a dark western horizon, from which racing clouds tumbled, bringing yet another storm.

As they neared, the fleet peered hungrily back at Twelve Towers, so named for the twelve original ships that had gone a-viking in search of glory and trade. Finding no trade or prey, the twelve had sailed north toward what they thought was home. They'd found instead a rocky, grim coast and no humans anywhere: somehow they had ventured out of their world and into another. Faced with the immediate prospect of a winter that promised to be even less merciful than those at home, they'd dug in and built a city. Twelve ships, twelve towers, twelve clans in varying precedence. By the time those clans had renamed themselves the Oneli, the Sea Lords, the twelve towers had been reinforced into mighty, bastioned edifices on the surface connected by a single stone-patterned road that bridged the river; large as the towers were, they gave no sign of the far larger complex of domiciles underground joined by a system of tunnels.

Those onboard the ships, sweeping their spyglasses over the thick-walled imposing towers of pale gray stone, strained to pick out individuals from the clusters of mostly flaxen-haired heads. Already the wind had begun to rise, ripping across the gray seas from the snowy northern wastes, and hoods came up, some faces covered entirely except for the eyes.

From his position before the koldar, at which two strong men braced against the running current, Stalna Hyarl Durasnir stood in full battle armor, silver over white, his winged helm fitted over his long, thinning gray-streaked yellow hair. The rising wind whistled through the wires holding the wings in place and tugged at his sweeping white fine-woven wool cloak. He braced his feet on the surging deck, knowing that he was an object of scrutiny by all those gathered on the walls in the city.

With the steadiness of long practice he kept his glass aimed as the towers gradually emerged from the predawn shadow. There was the Anborc, the King's Tower, highest of all, reigning over the widest complexity of underground tunnels and dwellings. As he expected, the glints of color along the upper parapet resolved into the formal cloaks and hoods of Elders in the Houses . . . but not all twelve. He swept the gathering again, narrowing his eyes, and yes, two were missing.

Why? No, the question that mattered was whether the Elders had convened a Breseng, which would be a formality appointing Rajnir king. Not every House would deem it necessary to mount the walls to view the return of the fleet for that. If the Elders had invoked a full council, a

Frasadeng, that required everyone to participate in choosing a king.

And required a candidate for kingship to answer all questions put to him.

Durasnir spared a thought for Prince Rajnir, who sat in his cabin, Dag Erkric attending him. As the fleet neared the outer reaches of the harbor, fleet watched towers, towers watched fleet. The prince stayed hidden.

Durasnir swung his glass to other end of the visible part of the city, and leveled the sights on Sinnaborc, the Tower of Transgressors, or Traitors' Tower, where despite the racing wind, black specks circled high in the sky. Durasnir ignored the death birds, which kept vigil long after the bones of traitors chained to die of exposure had been picked clean. He stared at the blobs of light glowing around the tower: several new ghosts shimmering as the last shadows of night dissolved. As the first rays shot outward from the rising sun, the ghosts glimmered, paled, vanished.

Back to the central tower, the Saeborc, or Sea Tower—more important to Durasnir than Leofaborc, Tower of Concord, from whose towers those high in the council and the Hilda watched. The wind-flagged figures along Saeborc's upper and lower parapets were more distinct now: he recognized some of the wives of Oneli commanders and captains. His gaze slid past the occasional colors, and a handful in the unrelieved white of honorable mourning. Far more were dressed in the black of dishonorable death, either real or the symbolic death of being formally cast out.

Standing a little apart from the others, squarely centered on the highest wall, wearing black from head to foot, was Durasnir's wife, Brun.

So the sham begins, he thought.

This thought was shared, though he did not know it, by several of the women on the Saeborc wall, including Brun.

At the other end of the wall, a captain's wife with a glass pressed to her eye said in an undervoice to her companion, "I've got the flagship in view now. There's Stalna Hyarl Durasnir, with his glass turned up here. I think he saw us." She uttered a laugh, the wind snapping away the vapor from her breath. "I think he saw *her.* By the root, he's gone back into the cabin."

Both captains' wives turned their faces into the wind, now keen and cold, and surveyed Vra Stalna Durasnir, who stood alone, plainly wanting no company. "Brun Hatchet-Face was the first to wear black." The first one huffed a laugh; her breath froze and whipped away instantly in the keening wind. "He'll get an icy welcome tonight, you can be sure."

"At their age?" retorted her companion, with the superior confidence of a young wife. "That bed's been cold since the last Breseng."

"Halvir, their boy, is just turned five," a third said, from just behind. "And he wasn't a Birth Spell."

The two whirled around, then deferred as a tall, stout older woman took their place. The newcomer, whose cloak and long, tasseled hood were a stark black that emphasized her age-white hair, was wife to Captain Seigmad, Left Flank Battlegroup Captain, veteran of sixty years of service.

"You and your icy beds," Vra Seigmad pronounced, disgusted with their ignorance and presumption. She snorted as she raised her glass toward the ships surging in on the rising tide.

"There's *Petrel,*" the first woman exclaimed, peering past Vra Seigmad's shoulder.

From farther down the wall the waiting women gazed into the strengthening wind and named out loud the great warships as their smooth, arched prows resolved out of the fleeing night. The impressive formation—the horn of triumph—passed the Dragon's Claw that marked the outermost reach of the harbor, and the fleet tacked in exhilarating precision, the Battlegroup flagships in a row behind *Cormorant,* the others grouping behind in station. As the wind rose, sails loosened, brailed up and furled, magnificent in synchrony.

When the flagships vanished beyond the outward jut of the guard wall in order to dock along the Oneli jetty, the women withdrew inside, shutting inset doors tight against the sleet that began to tear horizontally across the gray-green waves. There were no windows anywhere facing west; the only doors giving onto the western walls were tucked inside bastions.

"Vra Seigmad must be berserk. Everyone's gone berserk! The Oneli in triumph when we all know they lost Halia?"

"Hatchet-Face in black makes sense," the young wife whispered, with a quick glance over her shoulder. "Friya Haudan herself witnessed Vra Durasnir throwing her scroll-case into the sea after word came about the loss of Halia."

"Ho!"

"Shh."

A quick look from side to side caused the young wife to look around as well. She'd forgotten the rumors about the dags' listening magic. Her own House dag was boring, she could not imagine him casting spells to spy on people or daring the gates of Norsunder in order to gain mysterious spells like was said about Prince Rajnir's Dag Erkric, who had to be seventy! An old dag, making up spells for warfare? It had to be rumor. How could a dag make war? Even the greatest of them could not bespell a sword to fight on its own or an arrow to loose itself from a bow.

What she definitely did not want was to catch the attention of the Yaga Krona, the dags who served as Eyes of the Crown. If they caught you spreading gossip during the Frasadeng, you could find yourself in the Hall of Judgment being fitted with an iron torc and given three years' menial service for contributing toward Rainorec. *The powerful can talk, they can even raise crowds, but you can't,* her mother had once said. *And even the powerful sometimes fall.* She'd made the gesture toward the north that everyone understood, no matter where you actually stood, to mean Sinnaborc and its infamous bloody tower roof.

Despite their furtive glances and lowered voices, the women's rapid exchange echoed off the stone walls with the peculiar sibilant clarity of sound in icy air, audible to anyone following ten paces behind. As Vra Seigmad was.

"So the senior wives will demand an accounting at the Frasadeng?"

"I'm certain that's what's going to happen. Why else wear black?"

"What I don't understand is why Hatchet-Face is throwing over her marriage. Stalna Hyarl Durasnir was not in command of the invasion. Stalna Talkar of the Hilda was." She twiddled two fingers, indicating "army."

"Doesn't anyone tell you anything out there in your faraway tunnel?"

"No one wants an iron torc and three years of scraping ice-mud from the streets for their pains."

"They only call 'treason' and 'Rainorec' on one another, those in power," came the scoffing answer in a lowered tone. "Here's what I was told. Stalna Hyarl Durasnir negotiated the defeat with the Marlovan king himself. The first defeat ever in our history."

The young wife snorted. "They can't send *him* to the far shore as outcast. Not a *Durasnir*. My mother used to say that Durasnirs don't use the Waste Spell because they shit gold."

"What I heard was Dag Erkric forced him into it."

"Then we'll never hear the truth. Who can gainsay a dag? All the talk about how he'll turn your brain into stone—"

"Shh! If you want to wake up iron-thralled tomorrow, just say *his* name when you walk into a spiderweb."

The young wife lowered her voice slightly. "But if Hatchet-Face parts with him, will she go back to her people? Who are they, anyway? I never heard that she was part of any of the Great Houses."

"She isn't. She was a scribe from a collateral family connected to Lefsan House. They own nothing."

"Lefsan? A Durasnir allied with a Lefsan? I don't believe it. They haven't put forward a king candidate at Breseng for a hundred years!"

"And you can count their captains granted helm wings on one hand. Even so. She and Durasnir met when he was a mere third son, born in a Breseng year."

"Oh!" Ordinarily this ancient history about old people would have been boring, but the fleet coming home, the rumors and whispers, even the Frasadeng made everything deliciously immediate.

The young wife wasted a heartbeat or two on the notion of the famed Fulla Durasnir being born a mere third son, conceived only because a Breseng year had come, from which the Houses would choose the next king candidates—though everyone knew how that law had been twisted by paid adoptions and other connivings as the great Houses struggled for supremacy.

Both women had grown up hearing about these struggles, but neither would have questioned the system that had governed their lives: every thirty years there would be a thirty-year-old king, young and strong, as the old king retired at sixty. Boys born that Breseng year were nurtured for fifteen years, at which time the future heir would be selected; the heir would then leave his family to live with the king and train for the next fifteen years. No king (or queen, selected by the women by different criteria) was permitted to have children.

The older wife enjoyed her position of superior knowledge, though she was scarcely more connected to the exalted Durasnirs than the young wife. "Like the others not picked that Breseng year, Fulla Durasnir was sent to sea, until his senior brother died in battle."

"I remember hearing something about a duel."

"There was talk about how and why the oldest son died in that skirmish over on Goerael. The second son died in a duel as the result of the talk. He won, but only outlived the loser by a day. And so Fulla was called back to take title and to marry. Vra Durasnir was his lover at the time—she was younger than you are, second assistant to the House Skalt—but he insisted on marrying her."

The younger wife was impressed. From a negligible family with no thralls to a House with maybe six homes above ground and below, an entire floor in one of the Twelve Towers, and at least a hundred born thralls, what a leap!

"And she was adopted into House Durasnir with the birth of Vatta, their first son. Who was killed in a sea battle just after the fleet was sent south."

The young wife did not explain that she had known Vatta, but she'd rejected his shy, awkward flirtations in preference to luring Prince Rajnir. You did not tell stories on fallen heroes, even sixteen-year-old ones.

The two reached the bottom of the stairs and joined in the crowds hurrying toward the tunnel decorated with silver and white mosaics that lay directly under the King's Road, leading to Anborc and the Hall of Judgment.

The young wife wanted to catch a glimpse of Prince Rajnir again. They'd had that passionate dalliance just before he was sent south to gain land for the Venn. She hoped that ten years and kingship would not have cooled his ardor; how fun it would be to become a king's first favorite!

Vra Seigmad was behind them. She'd listened to the two fools, gauging how much of the gossip was truth and

how much hearsay (and what that meant), head angled up
to catch the sound of footsteps following her. Surely Brun
Durasnir would be coming down behind her at any moment. And Vra Seigmad not only had a ring bespelled to
warn of magical spiderwebs, she knew how to keep her
voice down.

As she stared up the empty steps she brooded on the
protocol, which required those of the senior rank to speak
first in any exchange. The only way around it was if your
House was allied with the House of the person you wished
to talk to, but Durasnir and Seigmad were not House-allies,
despite the long friendship between individuals of two
generations.

Maybe because of that friendship? So many alliances
were forced on people, predicated on agreements between
one's rivals. But she could see no way to change that, especially now when every second person appeared to be looking over his or her shoulder for the shadow of Rainorec.

Rainorec: Venn Doom.

On impulse Vra Seigmad swung around and began
vaulting back up, grimly smiling as she moved her bulk
with the unflagging speed she'd trained with when young
and more lithe.

Venn got stout with age—in this climate, it was better
for health. But Vra Seigmad refused to let any of her added
flesh turn to flab. She bustled up the six or seven stair turns
as the air became more chill. When she gained the bastion
she paused and pulled her hood down to her chin, yanking
the cord so that it snugged at her neck, stabilizing the slits
over her eyes.

From long habit she shifted her body against the door,
knowing it would take all her strength to get it open.
When she'd eased it a handsbreadth, she peered through
and stared in surprise at the tall figure who waved
impatiently.

Vra Seigmad forced herself outside. The most dangerous conversations had to be held outside. Though the
House skalts all knew how to place (and to ward) what
were called spiderwebs, magical spells that somehow captured words spoken within spell-bounded spaces, everyone knew that the most powerful dags knew deeper, more
dangerous spells. They also knew that magical spiderwebs,

like the real thing, required physical boundaries. No one could bind one to the eternal wind.

"I hoped you would come forth," Brun Durasnir said. Her lips were already turning blue. "Thank you for heeding my message and wearing black."

Vra Seigmad clapped her gloved hands in a quick peace mode. "I hoped you'd find a way to tell us why."

Vra Durasnir bent toward her; it was getting harder to hear over the rising howl of the wind along the stones. "You have a scroll-case? What did Seigmad tell you?"

"He only wrote once. Said they lost. Never wrote again. I tried to find out more."

"Hold to it," Brun shouted. Her voice was faint. "Hold to it! Demand. An. Accounting."

She bent her head into the wind and fought her way to the door, Vra Seigmad following close enough to be whipped by her skirts and hood. Brun Durasnir held the door by main force so they could both slip inside.

Brun Durasnir raised a hand to halt Vra Seigmad there on the stairs, where she shivered, counting slowly nine times nine. They could not be seen together. Everyone would be whispering, trying to discover what they talked about. Everyone. And maybe even fitting words into their mouths in speculation.

Vra Seigmad was grateful to Brun Durasnir for sparing her that. She was also grateful for the water-repellent magic on her cloak and hood, the heat-retaining magic woven into the wool, as she ran down the stairs.

The tunnel leading to the Hall of Judgment was full of people, but as always, the moment people saw her black cloak and long hood with the Seigmad colors in the tassel, they deferred. She set a brisk pace, unhindered until she reached a group from Tharfan House spread across the tunnel and walking at a deliberately sedate pace. As the former Senior House, they still claimed precedence, and as there was no accepted king, Vra Seigmad must drop behind those long, arrogantly lengthened pointed hoods, the silken tassels of silver and white swinging to the backs of their owners' knees.

From long habit people's voices dropped when they entered the Hall of Judgment, which alone of all Venn buildings was not decorated with rich color. The groins curving up to hold the vaulted ceiling were bare white marble, reminding Vra Seigmad of clean-picked ribs. In the galleries sat ten of twelve senior House Hyarls, the Council of Elders, the Senior Guild Skalts, and the senior dags in sober blue. Everyone else ended up on the general floor. In this room the kings had spoken, but now the Council of Elders had declared a Frasadeng, a gathering of the Houses, and though everyone could speak, the horror of recent condemnations seemed to grip them all.

The only marks of bright color were the ceiling of blue stippled with ancient stars, and the banner of the golden Great Tree of Ydrasal hanging over the empty throne, nine and ninety handsbreadths tall. More subtle were the great blocks of marble building the dais in three steps.

Whispers ran round the room, quick as fire through tinder, when behind the dais the massive doors, carved into a semblance of a tree uncounted centuries before, began to swing open. The few whispers ceased.

Through the doors marched a row of Erama Krona dressed in neutral gray. White indicated duty to a king, black was reserved for a Blood Hunt. When they wore gray, they would answer only to the oldest king alive, who would speak for the Council of Elders.

And the previous king was alive, just short of ninety years old. Helped by gray Erama Krona, he walked out where he had last ruled thirty years previously, but he did not sit in the throne. There was a low curule chair after the old formal mode, cushioned for fragile bones.

The cold ring of iron-reinforced heels on stone brought everyone's eyes to the door. As the Erama Krona took up guard positions around the dais, out strode Prince Rajnir, dressed in silver armor over white, the only color the gold of the Tree on his chest plate. Flanking him to left and right were the equally tall forms of Stalna Hyarl Durasnir (also dressed in his battle armor, which glinted in the candlelight) and Dag Erkric, who wore the blue-on-white of the Dag of all the Venn.

The king said, his voice reedy with his effort to be heard, "Prince Rajnir, Breseng-chosen candidate for king. The council has convened the Frasadeng. In this chamber you are answerable to all, and all will be granted the chance to speak. It is for you to begin."

Prince Rajnir stepped forward, bringing his hands together and then outward in the sign of peace. He was tall and even at a distance the deep blue of his eyes was remarkable. His hair had darkened to the color of ripened corn, and the bones of his face had hardened, but otherwise he seemed the same young prince who had taken ship for the south years before.

"O king-father of us all," he said, his voice clear and strong; he used the respectful old mode. "Skalts and Houses, Oneli and Hilda. Dags, artisans, and people. Last the thrall. You have heard only that we return with empty hands instead of bringing the rich grains and the fine steel of the Marlovans. We would have succeeded. We nearly did succeed, so my commanders assure me."

He paused as whispers susurrated through the hall, amplified by the curved stone.

"But." Silence fell. "But we were betrayed by one of our own, in a traitorous action that broke all law and custom. Because of the actions of this traitor, many of our people died, and we reached an impasse. It was then that the news came of the death of the king, and I deemed it best to return."

Again a hissing of whispers.

Prince Rajnir lifted his chin. "The homeland must always come first. I made a vow to the Tree: once the Land of the Venn is again at peace, I shall sail to the south again to strengthen our force at Ymar, and from there we shall prevail."

The king bowed his head, then lifted it.

"Can you name this traitor who acts against the king's will?"

"I can." Prince Rajnir faced the Hall. "Born as Jazsha Signi Sofar, she was a family outcast before becoming a Sea Dag, known as Dag Signi."

Voices rose in exclaimations; the king lifted a hand, and one of the silent guards struck his spear on the stone three times, the sound cutting through the hubbub.

"I further call for a formal Blood Hunt, that this traitor may be brought before the seat of judgment."

The king said, "Prince Rajnir, have you witnesses to attest to the truth of what you say?"

"I so attest," Dag Erkric said, hands open, head bowed.

"Though this dag was one of my own. I witnessed countless acts of magic." His voice sounded tired, filled with sorrow. "You will hear them all when the time comes."

"I so attest," said a young dag favored by Erkric. "She interfered with our protective wards when we attacked the castle at Sala Varadhe."

His presence barely caused a stir; all knew he would speak at the command of his master.

But then Stalna Hyarl Fulla Durasnir spoke. "I so attest. I witnessed a single act of magic, one that lies outside of the duties of a sea dag."

This time the reaction was louder, and again the spear struck the marble.

The king raised his hands, palm out in the mode of it-shall-be. "Then with the concurrence of the Council of Elders, I will enjoin the Erama Krona to oath-bind a team to the Blood Hunt, and we shall reconvene when we have secured the accused."

The council spoke, one at a time, each saying, "Aye."

The old king put his hands together. "So be it."

Chapter Four

INDA, Tdor, and Signi set out from Tenthen Castle two days after the wedding. Everyone at Tenthen gathered outside in the cold to cheer and drum as the outriders blew the trumpet calls for a Harskialdna and Harandviar. Even the horses seemed excited, tossing their heads, flicking their tails, ready for the charge through the gate.

Inda raised his fist the way his father used to. It thrilled him with pride, but hard on that suffusion of pride was a strong pang of regret, even guilt. *Tanrid should be sitting here, fist raised in the signal.* Inda looked back, and his breath caught at the sudden, sharp longing to be standing between the gates, right where Whipstick was.

Tdor missed it. She even missed the silent pain to be seen in three faces, Whipstick's, Noren's, and in that of Inda's mother. She felt enough pain of her own as her moist eyes blurred the outlines of the women she'd grown up with, all standing along the sentry walk above the gate.

Signi's empathetic gaze observed Inda's and Tdor's expressions of yearning.

Then Inda opened his hand and pointed. He dropped the rein and his horse leaped into the gallop, freshly shod hooves clattering.

The rest followed. They raced through the gates, horns blowing, shouts carrying almost to the lakeside.

The ride in strict rank order barely lasted until the castle's towers were out of sight. With a long journey ahead, the first thought must be of the animals. Inda slowed up to talk to the Riders so he could catch up on their family news and share local war stories, as he'd had little time to do so during their frenzied preparations. He was relieved to discover that his pair of King's Runners, young men who looked absolutely nothing alike but happened to share the same first name (Ramond), had fit in with the Riders enough to be called by their nicknames, Twin Ain and Twin Tvei.

Tenthen Castle's concerns fell behind with the castle itself, except in Noren's heart.

Tdor thought ahead. From what she'd seen in the two days Inda had been home, people accepted that Signi was not an enemy because Inda willed it so. But that just made her a nonenemy, a Venn to be stared at when she wasn't looking, speculated about, and walked around when she happened to come near.

When it came time to camp, Inda and Signi sat down together in the unconsciousness of long habit. Well, that was better than Signi sitting all alone in her tent. As they ate and talked about the next day's journey, Tdor wondered what to expect in sleeping arrangements. Tdor had her own tent. Was that second tent the King's Runners set up for Signi or Inda? With Inda's return after exile her lifelong love for him had flared from the steady warmth of childhood into adult heat. When camp broke up, Tdor rose, hoping to have Inda to herself in her bedroll.

She had to fight the anger-burn of jealousy when Inda absently followed Signi into the other tent. Tdor heard the Venn's soft voice, "No, Inda. Tomorrow, maybe, but you should go in with Tdor first."

Inda came right out, grinning when he spotted Tdor. He took her hand when she held hers out. So Tdor knew she was not rejected, disliked, or despised.

Yet Signi was no mere habit. Over the stretch of days that followed, Tdor observed the tender, absent twinings of fingers, the way Inda unconsciously leaned against Signi when sharing a mat at campfire time. Those, like Signi's drifting gaze wherever Inda happened to be, those were signs of love. Since—so far, Tdor always resolutely reminded herself—she didn't want a favorite of her own, she was just going to have to learn to share.

As the journey progressed Signi made it her business to see that Inda shared his nights equally. And because Tdor noticed that the Marlovans tended to move around Signi as if she were a rock in the path, she made it her business to set the tone and topics of campfire talk so that subjects were not exclusive of the Venn dag. Most of the time these were successful, except for once.

"Fareas Iofre once brought us an Old Sartoran taeran. You know this word, right?" Tdor asked as the Runners collected the bowls to be washed and stashed.

Signi leaned forward. "It is the word for scrolls written in the ancient form of Sartoran." Her fingers gestured gracefully from high to low, indicating vertical script.

Tdor smiled. "Well, it turned out to have been translated by the Venn centuries ago, and we've always wondered if they changed a couple of words: 'dena Yeresbeth.' "

Signi's eyes widened. "That is Old Sartoran," she murmured. "There was no change by us. But we do not truly comprehend that phrase, except as a reference to the Blessed Three."

It was Tdor's turn for surprise. "Blessed Three?" *Blessed by who?* "Blessing" was an ill-understood formality also dating back before records were kept. Tdor had been taught that the meaning was akin to a formal approval from authorities beyond family or even government. Possibly beyond time and space, bestowed by beings such as angels. "Blessings are ineffable beneficence," Fareas-Iofre had said once, causing Tdor and Joret to go up on the castle roof on the first clear night in order to speculate which of the stars might be home to such beings.

Signi gazed into the fire, then looked up. "We understand 'dena Yeresbeth' be indicative of a Seer—the 'shape of clouds of light' is how the Sartorans described one who sees beyond the confines of the physical world." Firelight beat unsteadily on her face, the shadows shifting her contours to young and old, old and young.

Yet another surprise, more like astonishment. "You mean ghosts?" Tdor's mind jolted back to her wedding day, when Inda had said something about Signi and ghosts.

"Ghosts." Signi whispered the word, then gave a quick, stricken look Inda's way, the first time Tdor had ever seen her move inadvertently.

Inda stirred, his hand coming up to rub over his head in the gesture Tdor had learned meant discomfort, even distress. Tdor's lips were just shaping the words "I've always wanted to know about ghosts" but she quashed the impulse.

Signi made a quick gesture, half appeal, half aversion, as she said in a low voice, "Seers witness beyond the confines of the world. Some only See once, others are born Seeing a world we cannot perceive."

Inda chuckled, deep in his chest. "We call them madmen— or Cassads."

A couple of the listening Riders and Runners laughed, and someone swatted one of the Twins, who was connected to the Cassads.

Signi smiled. "Some of our people also regard Seers as mad. But most respect them, when the Seeing sheds light on the mysteries. You must remember that within our living history, as we call it—we have actual records, though few—the Venn crossed in their ships from one world to another. How can such a thing be possible? The questions are so vast!"

From there the talk ventured to perception, meaning, words shared across languages. Tdor schooled the riot of questions in her head, and introduced the topic of translation, and how words can appear to share meanings, but actually signify different things. Thus the bad moment passed.

Despite the unspoken cooperation of the two women, Inda was still troubled. His dreams had been uneasy for years; numbering among his familiar nightmares was a new one in which his canoe, running faster and faster over a widening river, pitched out into the air above a cataract. He'd wake up gasping and bathed in sweat, his body still tingling from the sensation of falling.

Two weeks into the journey, they camped early one afternoon as pounding rain washed across the countryside.

Inda helped with the horse pickets, leaving Signi and Tdor alone in the tent the Runners had just set up.

Tdor spread out the sitting mats as Signi laid the Fire Sticks and made the sign to start the flame. When she straightened up, she discovered Tdor watching her with an uneasy hesitation.

"What is wrong?" Signi asked. "Have I done aught amiss?"

Her own quick dismay forced Tdor into speech. "I—no. I, well, as it happens I don't have a lot of experience. With men. Never wanted it, really, though I had my chances, same as anyone. The thing is this. Inda has nightmares—we've all heard them. But more with me than with you." Her face burned. "Am I—"

"No, no! He has them with me, too, it's just that I know a trick for warding them when he first begins to stir. Let me show you," Signi exclaimed. "It is a healers' trick, taught me when I was a sea dag. If he becomes restless and wakens you, soothe him like this." She demonstrated in the air in front of her own chest, a stroking motion over the breastbone. "If you can catch him before the nightmare turns violent, you can sometimes send him back to sleep." Her expression was humorous and rueful. "It is also said to be effective in the comfort of babes."

The tent flap lifted, sending in cold, wet air to swirl and hiss in the fire. Inda entered, beads of rain on his head and coat. He smiled from one to the other, then plopped down on his mat. "What babe are you comforting?"

"You," Signi said, smiling. "Nightmares."

Inda grimaced. "I can't stop yelling out when I sleep. I finally figured out that's why no one wanted me down in the crew's quarters on the *Death,* when we had you as a prisoner. The fellows yapped about me ruining their sleep just before the battle. Camping in the mountains." He scratched his head, and raindrops flew off, hissing in the fire. "At least my memory is coming back. D'you know, I'm not mad at Dannor for sticking herself on us when we left Tya-Vayir, because I remember being angry at her. Otherwise I don't think I'd remember a single day of that journey. I can't remember the half of this year. Am I going mad?"

His joking tone did not hide his anxiety.

Tdor had slid her hands into the sleeves of her robe, and

she gripped her knife handles. "In the Old Sartoran texts, it was often said that the truly mad often think they are the only sane ones."

Signi made a sign of agreement, her small fingers graceful in the ruddy firelight. "To that I will add that war leaves wounds that are not visible, as well as those in flesh and bone. You are still recovering."

"I hope I recover fast. I have to be learning politics. Me! Isn't that a joke?"

"It will be if you don't review your history," Tdor said, hiding her fears for Inda. She knew from his childhood that Inda would hate smothering. He wanted a solution. If there was one. If there wasn't, well, better pretend there was. "So let's begin. We'll review some history."

That set the tone for the remainder of the journey. Inda was troubled by the gaps in his memory. He could not recover a single day from the long ride between Ala Larkadhe and Tya-Vayir, where they held the triumph, so he set himself to notice everything around him.

He was thankful when he recognized landmarks he'd seen as a boy traveling this road. During the evenings, after they'd named kings and battles, heroes and villains of history, the talk ranged freely over languages, ships, travel, and other kingdoms and customs.

Despite the steadily worsening weather, it was a calm, friendly journey, characterized by active good will. By its end, as expectations gradually fell into patterns, less often did Tdor have to make herself enumerate the reasons to be grateful, especially when Signi's trick of massage often calmed Inda back into sleep without him being aware.

At last the outriders came galloping back on a late afternoon under a lowering sky that, from the smell of the air, promised a possible first snow.

Inda turned to the others, grinning like a boy. "We can make it to the royal city if we take the remounts."

So they divided up. Inda, Signi, Tdor, their Runners and half the Riders galloped ahead, leaving the other half to accompany the servants with the camping gear and horses.

The sun made a brief, pale appearance just above the western horizon as they topped the hill before the royal city. The light was strange, the undersides of the clouds dramatically lit. They'd waved to the perimeter Riders, so it wasn't as if they expected to surprise anyone. A trumpet call at the main gate was their due, and the Marlovans straightened up in expectation.

To their astonishment, not one but all the towers rippled with brassy intensity the racing chords heralding a Harskialdna.

Inda flushed to the tips of his ears. The Marlovans all grinned in shared pride. Signi's emotions swooped. She could not blame them for martial ardor. She knew the very same was felt in her homeland.

Tdor and Inda guided their mounts into position behind the standard bearers, and everyone else assumed rank order. Signi dropped to the back as they galloped the last distance down the road and through the open gates.

People lined the walls to catch a glimpse of the famous Harskialdna, once a pirate and an exile, returned just in time to lead the Marlovans to victory. At his side rode his new wife, who would help the queen command the castle women. On the walls, on the streets, from the backs of head-tossing horses, men and women thumped fists to chests. The women were saluting Tdor, whose face flushed with a mixture of pride and embarrassment.

In all those cheering faces, in the trumpet calls and the salutes, Tdor saw herself reflected back as a Harandviar. This new rank, like her status as a wife, had become real. Had Inda felt real only after others believed he was real when he became a ship captain and then a commander? She could ask. Inda was home again, riding at her side, and they could talk to each other, instead of imagining conversations—something he'd admitted he'd done, too! Oh, could anyone be happier?

To greet his Harskialdna for his triumphal arrival at his new home, Evred-Harvaldar came all the way out to the castle gate, Hadand-Gunvaer at his side.

Inda dismounted into his sister's arms. "Well done, Inda. *Well* done," Hadand whispered, blinking away tears of joy.

"Welcome, Inda." Evred smiled briefly, hands clasped behind him. "You are betimes." And then, with oblique inquiry, "Do the Twins suit you, then?" He indicated the tall, thin, fair Runner behind Inda, and his partner, who was northern Iascan—short and dark.

"I like 'em. Ramond Lith reminds me of our Lith." A

thumb indicated the tall one. "You know, when we were scrubs. Ramond Jaya is quiet, like my cousin Manther. They get along with everyone."

Evred had not got the answer he sought. "You did not bring personal Runners from Choraed Elgaer?"

Inda shrugged. "Fiam never became a Runner, and Tau left the day before we did. So I was glad to have the Twins."

Tau left. Evred thrust away the sharp sting of disappointment. He'd also dreaded seeing Tau again. Now he need not think about that ambivalence. "Then the Twins shall be your personal Runners. Vedrid will get them a staff. Come upstairs. Let me show you everything before supper. We tend to eat quite late."

While he led Inda up the tower steps into the residence, his wife hugged Tdor with such strength Tdor's bones crepitated, but she just laughed and shook herself as Hadand extended a welcoming hand to Signi. Tdor smiled her way. Signi's light eyes flicked between the two, and her cheeks pinked. "It is good to see you again, Gunvaer-Edli."

"I understand I have you to thank for many healings and renewal spells." Hadand started up the tower stairs.

"I wish I were better trained in the healing." Signi's expression sobered. "There was so great a need."

Tdor grimaced, and Hadand caught herself up. The war between Marlovan and Venn. Yes. Shifting from that subject, Hadand said, "I sent orders for mulled wine and cider, soon as I show you where you'll live."

They reached the top floor and Hadand led them past the empty, closed-off guest rooms along the outer residence wing. The air was cold, the hall dim, almost dark. This castle in winter felt oppressive to Signi, though the others appeared to notice nothing amiss; she sustained a pang so strong it almost hurt, how much she missed the airy tunnels of Twelve Towers, lit by crystal glowglobes of gathered summer sunlight, the walls bright with mosaic knotwork patterns. Or in the poorer tunnels, painting.

Hadand took them to the center of the castle. "Here I am," Hadand said, indicating the queen's suite along the east wall, overlooking the inner courts. "Evred's over there." She swept a hand toward the western side, overlooking the academy, and beyond that the plains below the city walls. "This is the old schoolroom, which we use as a kind of catch-all. Those rooms opposite are for any royal children. And down here, opening onto the big tower, are the Harskialdna rooms."

The north end of the residence abutted the enormous north tower, ending at a strange right-angle jut: an older tower had been mostly obliterated when the tower and residence were enlarged, leaving an odd sort of cubby. Hadand led them around that corner to yet another hall, but that one was short. It held only the double doors to the Harskialdna suite. "You overlook the guard side from here," Hadand said, waving northward.

Tdor thought of the long, long walk between this end, the queen's rooms, and the area adjacent to the guard compound where the girls lived for the queen's training. "I'll need a horse," she exclaimed in laughing dismay.

"That, my dear sister-in-marriage, is why we call these people Runners." Hadand patted Tesar, her First Runner, on her shoulder.

Tesar, a tall, tough woman with corn-colored braids, grinned as Hadand indicated the double doors. Tesar gestured to Noren, Tdor's First Runner, and they vanished to see to the transfer of belongings.

"These used to be the Harandviar's workrooms," Hadand went on, indicating the row of three doors opposite the double doors. "And my poor Aunt Ndara used them to do the queen's work. But we've shut them off so we could use the furnishings elsewhere. No new wood; we have to account for even the smallest chair! There is lots of space in this suite, even if you only get one window in the main room. Which is right here."

She opened the double doors onto an oddly shaped room with a single slit-window set into an oval alcove up in the massive wall. That alcove was at the end of a narrow corridor with doors to either side, so at best it let in a narrow shaft of light. "Bedrooms here, here, and here—that door goes down to the guard side—and behind this door is your own stairway to the private baths. Runner chambers off every bedroom, and a wardrobe connecting here—or anything you want to call it," Hadand said, rapidly whirling them through a series of sparsely furnished stone rooms with doors that all seemed to bang into one another.

When Hadand saw Tdor's expression, she misinterpreted it. "Evred's uncle was hardly ever here. He slept down behind his office at the guard headquarters most of the time."

Oh," Tdor said, and went back to wondering if all three of them would have a bedroom, or if Inda had grown out of Marlovan custom and expected his own room and who would sleep there? Or would he have a bunk down in the guard area?

And what would Evred want?

These things raced through her mind as Hadand led her through the last bedroom to the main chamber again.

There she stood, hands on hips. "Those last two rooms are good for babies. When your children get weaned, I hope they'll spend their days in the schoolroom with mine. I love the thought of our children growing up together," she said, with a faint, self-conscious blush, and Tdor remembered that Hadand had been trying for a year to have a baby before Evred had gone away to the war.

The subject made Tdor uneasy. She was just getting used to the idea of being a wife. "So where is my office?"

"Over in my territory. It's not *that* far!" Hadand grinned. "Queen Wisthia, a dear and I'll always treasure her memory, wasted so much space when she was queen. Imagine a breakfast room, a music room, a sewing room, a morning room, in addition to the formal dining room and the study room we knew so well! Why can't you do all that in one or two rooms at most?"

Because she was caged here, Tdor remembered Fareas-Iofre saying after her single visit to the royal castle. *Queen Wisthia made an Adrani world within our Marlovan world, and found meaningful work, which probably made her feel less a hostage.*

Noise issued up from the stairway leading down to the guard compound, and a door banged open behind them. Evred and Inda entered.

"And here's where you live," Evred said. "Your main room is this one. Private rooms behind all those doors."

Everyone watched Inda as he turned around, taking in the stone walls of the oddly shaped room with its single slant of light coming down the narrow corridor with the inset window, the plain flagged floor. The only furnishings were a low raptor-footed table, a neat stack of old mats covered with crimson wool, and a bench between a couple of the doors. Signi, lingering at the back, thought she'd seen more comfortable prisons.

But Inda grinned as he turned around a second time, his coat skirts flaring out. "All this space! Hey-o, Tdor, come up in this alcove—there's a bench built into it. We can sit here and look out at the parade court."

"During your many watches of free time," Hadand said, and laughed.

Inda shrugged, hands out. "I'd be fine with a hammock and enough air to swing it in."

Only Inda was oblivious to the subtle reactions in his auditors. He marched to the main bedroom, peered at the inset window, and turned around to exclaim, "We can see the academy roofs from here, too."

Hadand opened the double doors to the hallway. "The mulled wine will get cold soon."

Hadand had glimpsed Signi waiting purposefully just behind Evred, so she slid her hands round Tdor's and Inda's arms and marched them off, leaving the question of work, Tdor, Signi, and who would sleep where back in the Harskialdna suite.

Evred checked at the sight of Signi the Venn waiting not two steps away, her face raised expectantly. Until now she'd deferred so expertly he'd scarcely noted her presence.

He suppressed a pang of irritation, a reaction that had grown far milder since the first day she'd been forced into his life. "You wish to speak to me?"

"Yes, Harvaldar-Dal." Her accent was almost gone now. "With your permission, I would like to make a journey around your kingdom. Renew the bridge and water spells."

Gratitude flicked into suspicion. No. It was possible she would send observation reports to her homeland, but she could do that anyway. She was a mage. He could send an army after her, but they could catch her only if she willed it. And she had done nothing to indicate she was a spy.

He waited until the reaction had cooled. "Did Inda request this service of you?"

She turned to study him. In a way her wide gaze, so infrequently encountered, almost hurt as much as Inda's, but for different reasons. But he sustained it as she said, "He did not. Perhaps you remember that I once explained how Inda found me: I was to go to Sartor for a greater purpose."

"To reveal the Venn system of navigation. I remember that. Has this changed?"

Her hand passed across her face; she did not hide her perplexity. "I don't think so. But I don't know. The last I heard, Dag Erkric was preventing our access to Sartor, or rather, having it warded. Until I know for certain that I will not walk into a magical trap if I go, I await more definite orders. Until then, I perceive there is work needed, and it is the kind of work that I have the training to do."

Evred let out his breath. One of the first and most pressing of the demands on him as king was to try to negotiate a return of the mages that the Magic Council of Sartor had seen fit to deny Iasca Leror. Then he would have had to find some way to pay them. "Thank you, Dag Signi. Thank you. And yes, you have my permission to travel through my kingdom. With my good will and my gratitude. I will write an order to that effect, but will you not stay at least for the Restday drum?"

She bowed her head in gratitude. The branches of the Tree connected to the great trunk of life, though individual leaves could not perceive their place in the whole. Here in this room had stood the only three people who carried a life passion for Inda. She would remove one of them for a time, so that the other two would the more easily discover an accommodation. In the meantime, she would do some good in the world.

Chapter Five

THE Venn had been gone a full month before the Idayagans finally emerged from their various retreats and
poked their way tentatively into the ruined harbor below
Trad Varadhe.

One of the sailors was a squint-eyed, skinny fellow in a
crimson knitted hat who claimed to be from Khanerenth
by way of the Nob. He dressed like an east coast sailor.
When cherished pieces of scouts, cutters, and even a couple
of schooners began to appear from burial in gardens, hiding places in attics and basements and caves and stables, he
pitched in to help in the rebuilding.

The ships had to be finished out at sea. The harvest was
in before the first schooner was ready to sail.

"Maybe the damn Marlovans will stick to their word and
let us go," the captain of the schooner said to those gathered on the dock, as out on the water his sons and nephew
led the work party in rattling down the shrouds.

"Sure haven't smelled them on the wind," one of the
other captains joked, which brought the expected guffaws
and some spitting over the rail.

"The One-Eyed Jarl is gone down south," someone else
reported in a knowing voice, though Camarend Tya-Vayir's

departure had hardly been a secret, and the subsequently increased patrols of his seemingly endless men underscored what would happen if Idayago tried any trouble while he was gone.

"Well, I'm for Bren," the captain declared, looking at those who'd brought their gear to the dock in hopes of being picked for the first ship out of harbor. "See what the rest of the world has been doing since the pirates tied us down. Right now there's enough north in that east wind that we should raise the Bren Harbor by New Year's if we sail on the tide. Now, who's volunteering? Because there ain't no pay this trip out."

No, but everyone with a hand up was hoping to make instant money buying long-needed goods and bringing them back to sell.

The captain chose first among those who had helped work on the ship, one of whom was the squint-eyed fellow whose broad forehead and pointed chin reminded one of a rodent. He'd worked hard but kept to himself.

They launched without the least trouble—not a whiff of a horse-tailed warrior or his mount riding down from the ruined castle or thundering over the hills above the harbor.

As the ship beat out into the open sea, the captain went through his new crew himself, learning names and skills.

When he came to the squint-eyed one, he said, "Don't tell me. You're a shipmaster. I saw the way you were runnin' that crew with the standing rigging. So you want to take the deck o' nights?"

"Suits me fine."

"Name?"

"Rat," said Barend. "Everyone always calls me Rat."

Inda woke to the echo of a shout. Warning?

He sat up, breathing hard. The room was cold. No, he was wet—salt spray?

"Inda." Tdor's voice was hoarse, and he had a vague sense of repetition. "You are here, in the royal city. There are no pirates. There is nobody named Rig. Inda? Hear me?"

"Tdor?" He caught himself before exclaiming, "What are you doing here?" He clawed a hand through his sweaty, tangled hair and mumbled, "Thought I was on Walic's ship again."

"Go back to sleep. Dawn will be here soon enough."

He flopped back and after a time his breathing slowed. He was asleep. Tdor lay awake, wondering if he was missing Signi more than he admitted—maybe more than he knew.

She hated the jealous feelings these questions stirred. *Poor Signi is gone, probably because of me, and here I am putting her between Inda and me in spirit.* She rolled out of bed; if her mind insisted on worrying at things it couldn't fix, it might as well concentrate on real work.

When Inda woke next it was from a vivid dream, so intense—the details so sharp, down to the color of the morning light stippling the stone walls of his room, and the smell of his green-dyed linsey-woolsey quilt when it first came out of the cedar chest in autumn—he believed he was in his bed at Tenthen. But the shapes and shadows in the lifting darkness confused him. He lurched toward what he thought was the stair to the baths below, slammed into a door he'd forgotten was there, and reeled back, a hand to his throbbing nose. He hadn't had that dream about Tanrid since he was on board the Pim ships. And wasn't there a worse one earlier?

Before she left, Signi had renewed the glowglobes. He clapped, and there was his enormous bedroom with nothing in it but the bed, behind him two doors, and another door on the adjacent wall. Three days here, and he still wasn't used to it yet!

He scowled at each door. The first led down to the baths, the one next to it to the next room, and the adjacent door to the main room. He had to get accustomed to this. His life had changed again, but it was a good change, full of honor. *He* was Harskialdna, not Sponge's uncle, and Sponge was the king.

So why would he have dreams like these? He wrestled into his clothes, ran down to morning drill, then to the baths. When he emerged he discovered new clothes waiting for him. He was still wearing the boots Cherry-Stripe Marlo-Vayir had grown out of, though they'd probably be replaced soon, too. He was supposed to dress correctly now, something he hadn't thought about since the days he was a scrub in the academy, lining up for inspection.

The academy! His mood lightened. Evred had said they would talk about the academy today.

While he walked rapidly down the hall, eating his breakfast on the way, Tdor found Hadand on the sentry walk above the court where the women did their own morning warmups.

Mistress Gand, wife of the academy headmaster, conducted the women's drill in the mornings. This job she looked forward to resigning into Tdor's hands as soon as the new Harandviar was ready.

"Why aren't we down there?" Tdor asked.

"I wanted you to see how I conducted drills, when I had to do it. Mistress Gand thinks it looks pompous to drill 'em from up here," Hadand said as the women whirled and leaped and posed below, knives glinting ruddy in the firelight. "But I like it up here. I see more. You being a Harandviar, you can be here, too, if you like."

"I'm used to drilling in your mother's style," Tdor admitted, watching the women sheath their knives and pick up their bows and thumb guards. "First in line, down in the court."

"Take aim," Mistress Gand shouted.

Hadand tipped her hand, frowned, and jerked an elbow; Mistress Gand bawled, "Get those elbows straight!"

Tdor had thought them good enough, but women straightened spines, aligned shoulders, flexed muscles and their form improved in a blink, straight lines from arrowhead to back elbow.

"Shoot!"

Strong and sure, the women loosed their arrows straight into the mark. "I think I'd better practice with her before I take over," Tdor said. "If I may?"

Hadand's brows lifted. "Hadn't considered that. I always think Mother does everything perfectly. But I can't believe Tenthen women are sloppy."

"Not sloppy, exactly, just not as sharp as what I'm seeing. Maybe we've worsened since the old armsmistress died, and we didn't notice." She'd been about to say, *I can take what I learn back and sharpen them up*. She wouldn't be going home again. Home was here.

They returned to the office at the end of the queen's

suite. "Settling in all right?" Hadand asked. "Do you need more Runners?"

"Not yet. I will when the new girls come for the queen's training. Right now Inda's and my Runners seem to bang into one another coming and going. Almost as often as all those doors."

Hadand laughed. "Is Inda settling in? Evred keeps checking that silly ring of his, then galloping off to make sure Inda's happy and has everything he wants. He's like a child with a new toy."

Another intense pang. *Least said, less to mend.* "Inda keeps getting lost. I forget he was never here. In the castle I mean. He said it's a relief that Evred keeps popping in on him and showing him which way to go, but he feels stupid, like Evred's his Runner, always having to point him the right way."

"I think Evred likes doing it. His spirits were very low for such a long time. Not just over the many deaths in that horrible battle, but the state of the kingdom and how long it will take to build it up again. If we can. And then there was the loss of that archive up north, the one he used to copy records from. The Morvende shut him out for being a warmonger. It's completely unfair—Evred went up there to defend us—but there is no one to complain to. I'm so glad to see him smiling again."

Tdor did not know what answer to make to that, so she turned her attention to the neat stacks of paper, and the several chalk boards on the T-shaped desk. "All right, we've been in this room twice, and you said you'd explain the details later. If you want me taking over, how about making 'later' now?"

"If you're ready, I'm ready. This is what we call the 'Files and Piles.'"

Tdor listened closely, touching each pile in order to fix it in her memory.

"Tomorrow it's yours," Hadand finished, dropping onto a bench and rubbing her cold hands. "You'll have to clap out the Fire Stick and take it with you if you work down in the women's guard office. Yet again the Mage Council renewed the kingdom's existing Fire Sticks without granting us a single extra. Again we all must make do, from king to cotter."

Tdor just shrugged. They had exhausted the subject of the unfairness of the world's judgment years ago.

The shutters had been pulled back, and the windows gave weak, watery light. Hadand frowned out at the wet walls and the women walking slowly along, heavy winter robes swaying just above their boot heels.

"Might I see the boys' academy?" Tdor asked. "It's the one place I haven't been."

Hadand smacked her hands on her thighs and stood up. "Now's the time for a tour."

A spurt of trepidation, habit from Tdor's teen years, surprised her: the rules had been very, very strict about girls setting foot on the boys' side. To be caught there was to be sent home in disgrace. Even Dannor hadn't dared to test that rule.

Dannor. As she followed Hadand down the back staircase, Tdor said, "Dannor followed Inda home. Did you know that?"

"Evred told me. He and I had a bet going whether or not Inda would ever notice she was trying to turf you out of your own marriage. That's astounding even for Dannor, thinking she could whisk away two generations of planning, like that!" Hadand snapped her fingers.

Tdor said cautiously, "She apparently thought Evred would make an exception. If she could glamour Inda into asking for it."

"Why?" Hadand looked bemused. "Oh, because he'd won a war? Yes, that's Dannor, all right."

Tdor scowled at the flagstones. Here they were at Evred again. Wouldn't it be best to tell Hadand about his passion for Inda? But if she did, what would that fix? Absolutely nothing. *There are two kinds of truth: that which enlightens and that which is only cruel.* "Well, maybe she's grown a little. She accepted the wedding without any of her old tantrums and when we left, she was planning a tapestry for your mother."

"She was always very good with drawing, I'll say that for her." Hadand led Tdor into the dank archway between the castle proper and the academy parade court; a party of Runners stepped out of their way, fists striking chests.

Hadand saluted back, and Tdor belatedly did. That, too, was something they seldom did at home. At *Tenthen.* This was now home.

Hadand paused, staring up at the mossy stones overhead. "I don't know why I dislike the idea of Dannor at Tenthen. Why did she even stay a day? What could she be after?" She snapped her fingers. "Tdor, it's so obvious! Why didn't you see it? Branid is going to have a title soon! You should not have left her there."

Tdor flushed to the hairline. "I did offer to bring her with us," she said, but she squirmed inside, hating the defensive sound of her own voice. She pressed her lips together without uttering the "What could I have done?" that would have followed, because she knew she could have done something—if she'd given Dannor a single thought a heartbeat after their one conversation. Yet another thing she could not say: *I was so distraught at leaving home—at leaving Tenthen—I had no room for anything but my own sorrow.* Relief flooded her. There was something she *could* say. "Inda made Branid promise not to marry without your mother's permission."

Hadand's face cleared. "And he's on his way here for Convocation, well out of Dannor's reach, so that's all right. Mother can be trusted to send Dannor back to Tya-Vayir under guard, if necessary, at the first sign of trouble. And she does make trouble—you should hear the horrible stories about her up in Ala Larkadhe, when Hawkeye was governor there. Poor Imand! But at least she'll be getting rid of Starand."

"You mean Starand hasn't ridden north to Idayago yet? And she a Jarlan in her own right?"

"I sent Tesar with a private message," Hadand admitted. "Begging Imand to keep Starand reined at Tya-Vayir at least through New Year's. Make her learn the duties of a Jarlan, by my command. This is why I need you, Tdor." She rubbed her temples. "There is so much to be done! Top of my list is to find a good couple to send back with Cama as Randael and Randviar, since the only Tya-Vayir cousin left is ten and about to come here to the academy. When he leaves he'll be the new Randael for Horsebutt. I need people who will be fair to the Idayagans, yet tough enough to keep Starand in order. Ndand Arveas will be the principal woman in the north. Between her and a strong Randviar in Idayago, we can keep the peace in the northern cities while Cama rides around keeping it in the countryside.

Ndand wrote to me just a week ago that the reputation of the Arveas women has had a very strong effect."

The thought of two hundred women and girls holding off the entire Venn invasion army for two days made Tdor go cold inside. "How do you search for such a person?" Tdor asked as they passed under the west parade court arch into the academy proper.

"Letters. Lots and lots of letters." Hadand wrung her right hand. "Which is why it's been taking so long. Great women have impossible husbands, or the best men have wives who don't fit my conditions. I might have to ride out myself to interview people. So you need to learn my job yesterday." She smiled. "Here we are. Inda's new realm."

So this was the academy! Tdor spun around, trying to take everything in at once. It was empty except for the caretakers putting up the winter shutters on the buildings.

"The smallest boys go here." Hadand pointed at the closest set of buildings to the castle. "We used to spy on them from one of the secret peepholes next to your own suite. Remind me to show you. I keep wondering if I should point them out to my children or leave them to be discovered." Her forehead tensed on the word "children." "Aldren seemed so big and terrifying then, and now—I think back—he was just a skinny boy. So unhappy. And so *angry*." She gripped her elbows. "Evred's father wanted his boys to be scholarly rulers, and Aldren just could not read. Such a small thing, but with such long consequences. Well, that and his uncle always telling him he could have anything he wanted because he was to be a king. This is where the twelve- to fourteen-year-olds live. You probably barely remember when Tanrid was that small."

Hadand talked on, showing Tdor the empty barracks and the mess hall and the practice courts. These latter were exactly like the ones behind the castle for the girls and women, but the barracks were so different. The light had strengthened into morning by then, and Tdor was astonished at the battered wood, the smudges of fingerprints high on walls above doors, where it looked like boys would leap and smack the lintel or wall just to be doing it.

"Here's where the cubs live. Those are the between ages." Hadand swept her gaze past the open windows with their scarred, knife-rutted windowsills. How like boys! She took in Tdor's wide-eyed astonishment and said wryly, "I brought Signi over here before she left. She did the spells on the buckets and baths while Evred and Inda were finishing dinner. Want to know what she said? *How very, very thin is the layer of civilization.* Do you think she meant we Marlovans are barbarians?"

Tdor shook her head. "No. She means all humans. Not barbarians, but ... she thinks we are our own worst enemies. At least, the humans living on the surface. She knows so much more about history than any of us. And she included the Venn in that judgment."

"I wonder what she'll make of the kingdom?" Hadand said, and sobered as they passed into the private court that belonged to the horsetails, the oldest boys in the academy. Hadand frowned at the empty courtyard, the low windows with the knife-carved sills. "Evred is glad she's gone. Not because he distrusts her, but because he thinks the Venn might want to come back. Something their commander said at the truce."

Tdor whirled, her face blanched with dismay.

Hadand raised a hand. "Maybe not yet. But they need land. Their Rajnir is young. Not much older than us. Maybe he'll be too busy rebuilding in the north and riding around being king to set sail our way again."

Then we don't fear for us, we fear for our children, Tdor thought as she looked at the heel-marked doors in the strengthening light, the battered chests and knife-blade-pocked walls. *Except they won't fear the prospect. They'll look forward to it, just like Whipstick and the others did. That's what Signi means, and she's right.*

But there was nothing she could do to fix it.

She and Hadand paced back, each lost in her own thoughts.

Chapter Six

THE prow of the Venn flagship *Cormorant* curved far above the dock, as arrogant as it was graceful, as a pair of men swung precariously about it, sanding and smoothing the figurehead. Warlike angled slants that vaguely resembled eyes dominated the prow's contours, emphasized by the gilding that glinted in the weak light.

The shape of the head reminded Brun Durasnir more of a snake; down the neck spiraled intricate knotwork; from a distance the effect was like strange stylized feathers. The skalts insisted the odd letters were secret runes from the days of the World Before, when the ancient ships wore the carved dragon heads that were only seen illustrated in very, very old scrolls.

A third man hung over the water in a sling, adding to the carving, as was done after each voyage. She wondered if there were runes for a failed invasion.

Her cart rumbled past the prow and down the graceful curve of the gunwales. Parties of men with a ship mage were busy examining each strake; they stopped when her cart drew near and put hands together in the sign of respect. Brun only lifted one hand, then peered up at bare masts, the muscles of her face braced against the cold wind as the oxen plodded steadily down the dock, the laden cart behind Brun creaking. She was aware of the names the younger women gave her: Hatchet-Face, Drakan-Prow, and the like. Her profile never had been beautiful, and middle age had emphasized the resemblance of her nose to a blade.

She relied on her grim profile now to convey the effect of an angry, prideful woman: her hood was thrown back as she sat next to the servant who tended the oxen. She knew that she was watched from the towers, watched from the other ships. Her bare face would be construed as pride in her moral superiority as today, the first clear weather they'd had since the arrival of the fleet, she brought her husband's personal belongings from Saeborc to the *Cormorant* to emphasize his being cast out of her house.

The oxen stopped, oblivious to the rain, and in silence Brun gathered the fine-woven folds of her black cloak about her, and then, with great ceremony, she picked up the small wooden box, carved with lovers' knots, that had sat on the bench next to her.

Those watching would assume it carried her marriage band inside, plus any other jewelry her husband had given her.

She mounted the steep ramp let down by the deck crew and stalked along the companionway to the cabin at the back, the box held in her gloved hands before her.

Her husband, Stalna Hyarl Durasnir, commander of the South Fleet, stood before the whipstaff, awaiting her.

The few sailors on duty remained at a respectful distance. Durasnir opened the cabin door and stepped aside. She walked in, and he closed the door, shutting out the curious eyes around the deck, and those watching from mast and tower.

The outer cabin, with its enormous table, now bare walls, and ancillary desks, was empty. The door to his private cabin stood open, the light dim from the inward curving windows.

As soon as he shut the door behind her she cast the box onto the bed and whirled around, poised.

"No spiderwebs." He smiled, the same pensive, almost shy smile that had caught her eye, and her heart, thirty years ago.

She flung herself into his arms. He crushed her close, his

arms trembling. A sob shook her frame—their lips met in a hard, searching kiss that tasted of salt tears—and then they broke apart, breathing hard. Her throat ached.

He hugged her again, and said into her rain-dampened hair, "Fulk Ulaffa himself went over this cabin just this morning, on the pretext of delivering a letter requiring my full testimony before the council."

"Ulaffa!" she exclaimed. He was not just one of the untouchable Yaga Krona, the king's dags, he was the chief of Prince Rajnir's circle.

"He is not Erkric's man. He never was, actually, but duty forced them to work side by side until Abyarn constructed walls of distrust between all branches of the tree of service."

So not just the military was fracturing. Not just the sea dags. The Yaga Krona itself! "I remember what you requested of me that day in Jaro. You said that Erkric might be spying on our scroll cases. And so, when I saw your code words after the invasion failed, I threw mine off a cliff as publicly as possible."

Durasnir grinned, looking younger for a breathtaking moment. "Gossip about that got all the way back to us. As I'd hoped."

Brun smiled grimly. "Should we be fighting?"

"Two of my ensigns are going to be drinking off duty tonight, each swearing friends to secrecy as they describe how you screamed at me about our stupid defeat by the Marlovans and hurled dishes when I attempted to defend myself."

Her smile faded. "And so? I do not really comprehend why we must have a false parting. Say rather, how our false parting can make any difference in what you once dreaded might happen."

"That my most loyal captains, with the best of intentions, would encourage me to take the throne? That has already happened, Brun. I will not have Venn murdering Venn in my name. In my heart I hear the skalt singing Slacfan's Song."

"*Cracks in the Tree, Thor-hammer ambition, The winds of discord, bring the Tree down,*" she whispered. "But it is not *your* ambition at fault."

"Does it matter whose? The loves we should have protected will still be dead."

She grimaced faintly. "At my age, I feel foolish saying such a thing, but people are laughing at us, Fulla." She was astonished when he grinned, reminding her of their son Vatta, dead at sixteen. It was a punch in the heart.

"I want them to," he said.

She had to pause and breathe deeply, in order to school her emotions. "I just do not see how making us figures of mockery wards Rainorec—" She tipped her head. "No, not true. Is it this, if your hot-headed captains hear gossip making you a figure of fun, they cannot use you as a banner to rally behind? But why is such a thing happening at all? Why should the prince be blamed for the defeat when he was not in command? I wish you had told me more before you left Ymar."

"But we were spied on so much. Then there was the . . . vagueness of my guesses. At the time, I just heard whispers about Rajnir's foolishness in making friends with that repellent Count Wafri. His growing tastes for the frivolousness of Ymaran entertainments. I did not want our captains trying to force me into opposition to him—especially if something were to go amiss during our invasion."

"You expected to be driven away by the Marlovans?"

"No. I thought we would succeed. But there were other aspects that disturbed me, and Brun, I was *right*. The truth is still not proved, but I fear it is worse, far worse, than I had ever guessed at the darkest moments." He kissed her hard, then let her go. "Brun, much as I want you, and have every day since we sailed from Ymar to that accursed invasion, no one will believe you are casting me to the shore if they don't see that door open as soon as my belongings are stowed below."

"What is to be done?"

"For now, we have to maintain the pose of parting, while you demand explanations for the invasion's failure—shout about how foolish our captains were to lose—get the women to make a noise, demanding accountings of all our captains. I trust by the time everyone is tired of it, we will know . . ." He frowned sightlessly at gilt carving around the bulkheads.

"Fulla! What? *Please* tell me."

His attention snapped back to her. "When I know the truth, you will be the first. Speaking of trouble. I counted only ten Houses on the walls, the day of our arrival. And ten in the Hall for Frasadeng."

"Loc and Hadna Houses tried to take the kingship. The bones of the young men lie atop Sinnaborc, picked clean after they endured the blood eagle. And the rest of the primary families are in thrall to First Tower until the new king is crowned and decides whether to show mercy or justice."

"I thought I saw new ghosts."

Her breath caught. Even in nearly thirty years of marriage, she had never quite accustomed herself to the casual ability Fulla Durasnir had to descry the mysteries. He could have been a dag, a skalt, or even a Seer, had he had the interest or training.

"If you cannot explain your concerns about Prince Rajnir, then at least tell me this before I go." Her gaze searched his face, so familiar and so dear, furrowed more than she'd remembered, though he was nigh sixty. But his countenance was keen as ever, and his grip strong. "Is Dag Signi truly a traitor?"

Signi: a vivid mental picture of the small, plain, earnest dag who—despite being turned down at the very last before becoming one of the exalted hel dancers—moved with such amazing grace. Who, on being passed over, had been so grief-stricken that she'd turned for comfort to Fulla, whose female friendships in those younger days often flared to ardor.

This flare had occurred when Brun was struggling with the illness of her first pregnancy. Dag Signi had been one of the few of Fulla's string of lovers to heed the old ways, and come to ask Brun's permission to lie with him. Brun had been impressed, and ever after the affair burned itself out, brief as they all were, she'd retained a fondness for the quiet, hard-working dag.

"No," he said. "She is not. I still don't understand why she was there in Iasca Leror. Sea-Dag Chief Valda did not tell me, and I only saw Signi the once. She did act against Erkric's doom-cursed meddling, in about as spectacular a way as any dag has contrived, probably for centuries. I was there, and it is known I was there, so I must witness."

Brun signified acceptance. "Where is she now?"

Durasnir knew about Brit Valda's great cause, but he had promised to tell no soul. That must include his wife. If Erkric thought Brun might know anything, he would find an excuse while Durasnir was gone on duty to tear her apart for information. "I don't know," he said. Which was true. Valda might have ordered Signi to leave the Marlovan kingdom for Sartor, or to remain there awaiting the signal that Sartor was no longer warded. But that quest was now a separate matter.

So he said, "This accusation is as much a surprise to me as it is to you. I had no idea it was coming. And I do not see what Erkric is about, but he has had months to put his plans in place—and it will be months, if not longer, before the Erama Krona's Death Hunt will find her."

Brun knew little about the inner workings of the Erama Krona. But one thing she had heard, they were forbidden to use magic on the Blood Hunt; they only used Destination transfers once they had secured their target. Like the hel dancers, their training was so secret, so consuming, no one—even Erkric—had yet corrupted them. They would refuse his offers of magical aid. Brun's mother had talked of a ten-year Blood Hunt that occurred when she was a girl.

Brun looked up in doubt. "If the Blood Hunt goes through Iasca Leror to find her trail, will that not cause more trouble?"

Durasnir made a negating sign. "By the time they reach Halia they will know the language, and how to dress to blend when they must. But they move only at night; if any one of them draws notice, it brings on him severe penalty. The Marlovans don't have our underground cities, with all the varieties of light that we do. Their kingdom is silent at night. No one will ever see the Blood Hunt—"

Three quick, light taps at his outer door. One of Erkric's spies had been spotted. "Brun, listen and be watchful. Be prepared for anything."

"What will you do?"

"Sit out here sulking until you forgive me." A brief smile. "And readying my fleet. If I am right, Erkric—Rajnir—needs to keep us busy. I suspect we may be sailing to Goerael soon, to reinforce West Fleet."

"His reasoning?" she asked swiftly as they walked into the main cabin.

"He has no reasoning." Durasnir made the sign of warding, and then bent, and gave her the truth, though he had meant to wait on proof. He pressed his lips to her ears. "He has no mind. He has been reduced to the shadow of a man. Every word he speaks is put in his mouth by Erkric, who I suspect wants us busy and out of his way."

Shock tingled painfully through her. But there was no time for questions. He opened the cabin's outer door and she was forced to step outside, her heart colder than the outside air.

"Here." Evred led the way into the series of rooms in the building perpendicular to the residence and the Great Hall. "This is where the herald-apprentices work. Each table is for the records of one Jarl, and the other old names are in the far room."

On their entry everyone paused, saluting. Evred laid his hand over his heart. Belatedly Inda did as well. He had to remember these things, he reminded himself, as Evred opened his hand in the signal freeing everyone to return to work.

Inda took in the neat stacks of old papers and scrolls on each desk. "What work?"

"Didn't I say? There's so much to discuss! Hadand and I resolved to verify Convocation oaths after last winter. Going through all the records is turning up all kinds of surprises. And not only from the recent generations, while my family has ruled. No one's ever read everything all the way back." Evred touched a battered scroll waiting beside others on a tray. "I mean to familiarize myself with every record back to before Savarend Montredavan-An's day."

"I thought none of that was written down," Inda exclaimed.

"Not here," Evred said, smiling. "There was no 'here' yet. This city wasn't ours. You Algara-Vayirs have early records from the days when you were just Algaras courting the Tenthens. The Cassads have the oldest records of all. Hadand discovered that the Cassadas queen who established the library—that is, she was a Dei, and only a Cassadas by marriage-adoption. Anyway, one of her projects was to send people to the old Marlovan skalts to write down the language, and what they sang to her to be written were the oath-songs. Since our forefathers had no script, that record is written in some kind of Sartoran dialect that was apparently adapted for communicating with the Venn over on Toar centuries ago. Ironic, yes?"

He touched the scroll again, then turned his thumb toward several fifteen- and sixteen-year-old girls from the queen's training who worked at a table by themselves, a carefully opened age-darkened scroll between them. "The girls are much faster at deciphering that, so Hadand and I decided to abandon tradition and let the girls loose on it. If they like it, and haven't a rank that requires them to go home, there's no reason why we can't go back to the old Iascan custom of having female and male heralds. It was my own ancestor, Anderle, who forbade female heralds, probably as a jab at the Cassads. All those quarrels are long gone and forgotten."

When he and Inda had regained the tower that connected the government building, the Great Hall, and the residence, Inda said, "Buck and Cherry-Stripe told me about Horsebutt and the guild taxes."

Evred snorted. "That's just covering arrows before the charge. Horsebutt knows very well he won't get anything revoked."

"And here I thought that explained government affairs." Inda looked rueful.

Evred laughed, just out of happiness. Inda was here at last. They would share home and work for the rest of their lives. The intensity of his joy really did feel like fire through his veins, just as the ballads always said. "Never mind that. Here's the truth. I need to stand up at Convocation and know everything about every agreement each Jarl family had made with the crown. Who owes what to whom, all the way back."

The joy tempered with the ready burn of anger. Inda was here, he must understand these things. "Sooner or later they're going to fling war damage in my teeth as an excuse for encroachment on crown rights." His voice was on the verge of trembling. He stopped at a window and looked out, working to get his voice under control, as thin rain began to blotch and then darken the stone. "It would be easier if we had a common goal. We had the Venn for so long."

Inda was appalled. "You want them to come back?"

"No." Evred struck a fist on the windowsill. The pain steadied him. "No. It would have been easier only in one sense. Not in the cost of lives. I have only to think of what we saw in the Andahi Pass to remind myself of that. War is a convenient fix for government problems if it happens somewhere else. To other people."

He turned away abruptly. "But that's my task. I wanted you to see this project. Downstairs in the annex are the council chambers and the guild secretaries."

Inda stared through the windows to the extreme end of the great parade court. He jerked his thumb at the government building behind him. "I used to wonder what was going on in there, when Master Starthend gave us a Rest-day punishment of sweeping the parade court. Remember that? Basna used to get everyone to guess how many flagstones lay in each section. Dogpiss was sure all the masters and guards snuck into those buildings to whoop it up with ale and gambling."

Evred half raised a hand in acknowledgment, then plunged up the tower steps at a rapid pace. Inda loped to catch up as Evred said briskly, "Now to your tasks. Retraining the guard, making some sense of where our forces are and who's left. I've been collecting all the reports, but there's been no time to read and tally. I'll give you as many King's Runners as I can spare, but I am already short. And we have so few candidates . . . To resume. By Convocation you must know who we have where and how many."

"Good. I like knowing that." Inda rapped his knuckles on the rough sill of an arrow slit as he passed.

Evred extended a hand toward the opening. "And finally, you and Gand have to set up the academy for next year. But before we get to that, when we rode away from Ala Larkadhe, I think we were too weary to consider what Durasnir said to us that day above the pass. But now we should begin."

Inda stopped on the landing. "I'm not sure I remember it all. That is, I do, but it's strange. Like someone was sitting on my shoulder, it wasn't me at all—"

He hesitated, remembering his ghost. He hadn't told

anyone but Signi about the ghost. It was gone now, so what would be the point?

But Evred was watching. "Problem?"

Inda smacked open the door and plunged out onto the sentry walk, from merely cold air to frigid. He thrust his bare hands into his coat pockets. "No. Just, the idea of being a Harskialdna."

Evred was surprised into a laugh. "You cannot possibly think that the entire army doesn't want you as leader. Did you know that the survivors of the Andahi Pass defense have taken to wearing red stones affixed to their ears?"

"What? But that's—" Inda stopped himself. It wasn't stupid. It was wrong, backward. He'd half regretted his ruby hoops ever since he'd poke the holes into his ears, yet he knew how the symbol worked. It set people apart after they'd endured something—it was a reminder—but most of all (and the reason he'd never taken his out) it created a bond with your fellow survivors. He could not understand *why* it worked.

". . . not many can afford rubies, so they use bloodstone, mostly, or garnet. And no hoops, as those are seen to belong to sailors. Can you tell me why? I never asked Barend."

"If you're shipwrecked, especially as a pirate, you can take the gold out and use it to get to a port. Or bribe someone not to send the local guard. A lot of sailors don't wear 'em as they mean *pirate* to many. Listen, I've been thinking, should I teach the boys the knife fighting?"

Evred's brows rose. "You won't be teaching. The masters can teach the boys. That would follow tradition. My father wrote that that distance gives us consequence."

Inda grinned. "How scared I was the first time your uncle spoke to me, right after Gand's wedding. He and I left the hall at about the same time, and he was probably just trying to be nice, in his own way. Let me yap on and on about the Marlovar Bridge tussle, like it was a major battle."

Inda laughed, and Evred forced himself to smile, though he strongly suspected that that meeting had not been coincidence. His uncle had never permitted coincidence: in fact, he wondered if he had hold of the missing piece of the puzzle of why his uncle had singled Inda out in the first place.

Inda thumped his hand against the stone wall, then

whirled around and began to walk backward. "So, you don't want the boys learning the double-knife fighting?"

"I thought about that. I'd rather you refine what we already use. From what I saw on the mountain, the double-knife fighting is only useful when you don't have shield and sword, which is expected in battle. I'm thinking you could teach the King's Runners, and we'll see how it works out."

Inda signified agreement, thinking, *I won't say anything about rubies in ears. But I'm not going to pay any attention to 'em, either.*

Under racing gray clouds, a small boat smacked through the white-capped, choppy waves outside Twelve Towers Harbor. It was two weeks after the fleet's return. Now they were sailing again, the fleet anchored beyond the Dragon's Claw in readiness.

Vra Seigmad tended the sail and her husband leaned his strength into the tiller. He was seventy-two, she was nearly that. Either of them could have ordered young, strong ensigns or servants to take Vra Seigmad ashore after her husband's curtailed liberty, but then they would lose this precious time alone. No witness but sea and sky.

They bumped and rolled through the splashing waves until they were midway between Seigmad's warship and the outer finger of Dragon's Claw, at which time she spilled wind from the sail, and he eased the tiller.

"Seigmad." She slowly worked her shoulders, wincing at the thin ice-shard protests of old bones. "Last night I thought I'd pee myself trying not to laugh when Fulla Durasnir ranted like a mad skalt. 'My captains and I have explained ourselves before the Frasadeng. We should not have to defend ourselves to our wives.' Heh!"

Her husband gave a chuckle. He sagged everywhere—she had braced herself against his not returning from the long southern campaign. But here he was, frost-haired, lined, but still hearty. "No buxom young Tharfan offering to marry me!" He struck his chest.

Though they laughed, they knew Parfa Tharfan wanted to father a Breseng boy, if Fulla Durasnir really would be divorced by his wife—but that was a sham. Further, a badly acted sham, to those who knew Durasnir.

She shifted impatiently. "Brun can't talk to me, not until she knows where all the spiderwebs are. Is that all the dags do these days, make ways to spy on us?" She struck her fist on the gunwale. "And Rajnir ordering the south fleet to Goerael? Either everyone has gone mad, or I've gone mad from the questions in my head that go without answer." She leaned forward. "First tell me straight what happened in the south."

He squinted at the flagships, all hives of activity as carts rumbled down the dock, full of supplies. "If the king hadn't died, we'd yet be on Halia. Probably sitting out in the ocean trying to plan a coastal attack in the west. The Marlovans are tough. More of 'em than we'd thought, if what Talkar reports of their trap in the pass is any indication."

She made a noise of disgust. "So why did Brun Durasnir get us wives in black and make us into fools?"

"Didn't you see young Dyalf Balandir?"

She spat over the side. "That for the Balandirs. Especially that boy. I never look at him, not since—"

"Never mind what he did to our boy. They're not boys any longer. If you'd paid young Dyalf attention, as you do to a diving death bird, you would have seen how he looks from one side to the other at every gathering. Hoping Durasnir will rebel while the kingship is in question, with Rajnir shadowed by defeat. Hoping we, the Oneli, will rise in Durasnir's name."

"And Dyalf Balandir would join, or fight against you?"

"Whichever gains him the most power."

She made a noise of disgust.

"Erkric is no idiot. He sees and hears all, through those spiderwebs. So he's commanded us to go put down the revolt in our colony on Goerael, though our ships are still gutted from carrying the Hilda, and all need to be heaved down and overhauled."

She leaned on her oars. "*Erkric's* command? Has the Tree fallen, making a dag into a king? With my own ears I heard Rajnir's speech before the empty throne."

"But we think those words were put in his mouth by Dag Erkric."

"So now tell me, what *are* these whispers about the prince? Was he a coward in the south? Did he lose the men's allegiance?" She waved her fingers as if shooing insects. "Or was your defeat really due to the interference of some sea dag?"

"Hah! Erkric had those dags playing warrior. I don't know the truth of what happened with Dag Signi, why Erkric would turn against her. I suppose the truth will come out when the Blood Hunt catches her. Durasnir is as talkative as stone about that. As for Rajnir, I can't explain it. In the old days, when we first took Ymar, he used to be with us, watching reviews. Training. Looking at the maps. Discussing. Now Erkric's got him walled by dags and magic. We never see him. Or if we do, the old soulripper is always around. And Rajnir speaks like a skalt in a hall—not just the speeches, which we expect, but all the time. Even when talking about sails, weather. Sounds practiced. We don't know how much of Rajnir's own thinking is in anything he does or says. Durasnir won't act unless there is proof that all can see." He thumped the oar against the gunwale. "So we think Erkric got the prince to order this journey so he can not only keep us busy, but to get Rajnir away from everyone's eyes. This talk of revolt, oh, there are always uprisings over there, nothing that the northern fleet commander could not put down. Even without his three best Battlegroups being sent to hold Ymar."

"Ymar found themselves an army?" Vra Seigmad exclaimed.

"No army. No navy. Rumor is the Chwahir and the Everoneth are talking alliance again, on their behalf. Anyway, Rajnir—Erkric—we all need the prestige of a win." His mouth soured. "Maybe then we will settle and resume life. That's what Fulla Durasnir says."

Blood flowing and lives ending, either in Twelve Towers or overseas, that's what a "win" meant. "So who leads us, if Durasnir will not? I would crawl on my knees through Thrall Gate and wear the iron torc around my neck until the Tree withers at the root, until the Great Serpent returns and swallows the world, if Abyarn Erkric is tampering with the prince's head, and we do nothing to fight—"

She stopped. *More war, either at home or at sea, is that the answer? Who is to blame here, women for proclaiming themselves honorable to expect their men to supervise the killing of other women's sons, or the men themselves for doing it?* So crazy a thought seemed treason, all in itself, and so she reshaped the question, "Why do we make war to keep peace?"

"I don't know." The furrows in his face deepened as he gripped his gnarled hands to the tiller, then he nodded up at the faint, but revealing twinkle of light up on the ramparts. "They're watching us from Saeborc."

She yanked the sail taut, and they sped toward shore.

Chapter Seven

SIGNI did not think she would need Evred-Harvaldar's permit-of-passage because she'd been regarded as next to invisible by his army during those long spring and summer months. And she prided herself on her ability to remain unobtrusive.

But that was before she set out alone into a kingdom too long under attack. At her first destination, a crossroads town called Hesea Spring, her offer of magic renewal was met with suspicious questions. Who was she? What kind of magic? Why hadn't they heard? Where was her escort—didn't the King's Riders keep watch on foreign mages? It wasn't until she brought out Evred's letter that brows cleared, voices eased, and much later there were even smiles and small stories about making do as people offered to share a meal and a place to rest.

So she was not surprised when, a day or so after she crossed the bridge at the border of Marlo-Vayir, a group of Riders came galloping up and reined in when they saw her. "Are you Mage Signi?"

"I am."

"Fnor-Jarlan requests an interview," the leader said.

She studied the faces of the men before her. Serious expressions. No anger, no threat. But intent.

"I will come."

"We have an extra mount," the leader said.

From this encounter she understood that word had traveled ahead; she had learned during the summer that the borders of the Jarlates were watched.

Twice before she had ridden through these gates. Both times the castle's people had exhibited high spirits and good cheer, though the shrill pitch of war fervor had buffeted her psyche on the last.

As they dismounted, the Riders did not talk with the freedom and laughter she remembered of the Marlo-Vayir liegemen earlier in summer, and the blue-robed woman who came into the court to meet Signi was polite but distant.

The once noisy castle was silent now, except for her guide's quiet footfalls. Signi felt closed in, as if the bare, honey-colored stones had absorbed sorrows that had little to do with the arrival of the winter chill. She no longer believed, as outsiders did, that Marlovans liked those prison-bare walls, but rather they just did not notice them.

As the silent Runner conducted her along the passage, she thought she saw faint traces of color up high here and there, and puckers in the stone, as of decorations removed by those driven from their castles several generations before. *The Marolo Venn forgot all the arts of stone carving in the centuries after they left us,* she thought. *And they forgot mosaic, which I had thought so much a part of our people.*

As soon as the door opened on Fnor's room in the main tower, the Jarlan threw down her quill and bustled around her table to greet Signi, hands out. Signi sustained another shock: Fnor seemed to have aged in the past half-year. Her face was thinner, taut, lines drawn by far too many days of distress.

"Thank you for coming." Fnor lowered herself to a mat, as Signi sat neatly across from her. "Thank you."

"What can I do?"

"It's Buck. Well, and Mran. Buck said you saved his leg from being cut all the way up to his hip. And you helped the army healer sew up him there." She jerked a thumb down toward her privates. "They all said you were a great healer."

"Buck is not healing?"

Fnor pressed her fingers over her lips for a moment. "No. Yes. No. I'm sorry. Cherry-Stripe's Runner was at Hesea Spring just after you did your magic on the baths. He was going to the royal city to ask Evred . . . Well. Let me start at the beginning. No. Hold hard. You're all muddy, and you have to be wet. Why don't you change into something warm? I'll bring up the meal I ordered soon's the outrider told us you were on the way."

Signi shook her head. "All that can wait. I will survive being muddy and wet a little longer."

Fnor drew her knees up like a girl, and wrapped her arms tightly around her legs. "The trip home was very bad for Buck. He didn't want the men to see him weak, I guess, so he never said anything, even when the roads jarred that stitching open."

Signi exclaimed, "That has gone unrepaired until now?"

Fnor waved her hand. "No, no, the castle healer sewed him up again, and tended all the wounds until they healed over. But that just added to the pain, d'you see? He's got a leg cut off at the knee, his right arm cut off at the elbow. And *that*." She whooshed her breath out. "He arrived home about the same time Mran started walking around looking like a ghost. Oh, she did her work. She always does. But you remember Mran. She's a Cassad, they're all strange. I grew up with her, but there's no hiding that Cassad nature." Fnor shrugged. "She was always like a summer bird, flitting around. Got that high voice, like a pipe. The old Jarl used to called her Bird-peep. Everyone loves Mran. But at summer's end she just . . . I don't even have the words. She went quiet and small, like a stunned bird. I thought it was the war, you see. And what happened to Buck. Then I thought she was worried about Cama, so I made double sure. Sent a Runner north. When she came back with word Cama was fine, Mran shut herself up for a day. Then she came out, apologized and went right back to work."

Puzzled, Signi said, "And so?"

Fnor sighed. "And so just a couple days ago Cama and his party galloped along our eastern border on their way to the royal city for Convocation. They have to get there early, on account of—" *The banner Liet-Harlan struck down rather than surrender to you Venn.*

She stuttered to a stop and blushed a fiery red. As Signi looked at her in silent wonder, Fnor continued in a rather hasty voice. "The important thing is, when they stopped, some of the Riders were talking, as they do, as half are related to someone who's related to someone else. Said that Cama and Ndand Arveas have fallen pretty hard for each other. Word spread."

Signi tried to understand the customs implied here. Mran was married to Cherry-Stripe, but marriage here compassed work and family more than it did personal relationships. "I remember that Mran and Cama were lovers," Signi said. "Did they part badly?"

Fnor jerked her hand flat out, as though pushing something away. "No, Cama would never do anything hateful. If you've been mates with someone and find someone new, you talk face-to-face with the old. First, if you can." She shrugged. "But Cama lives months away now, and he has to get to Convocation before New Year's Firstday."

"I think I understand."

Fnor looked askance, as if she didn't believe it; she was wondering why she'd even brought it up. It was just that Signi, though a Venn, was so easy to talk to. And Fnor hadn't had anyone to talk to about these matters.

"Well. Mran's a Cassad, like I said. They *know* things, somehow. She admires Ndand, who's an excellent woman. We always liked her. That helps some, and it will help more if he stops here on his way back north, after Convocation, and talks it out with her."

Fnor jumped to her feet and strode to the window. "I don't know what to do." She gazed down into the stable yard. The bleak winter sun shadowed her tense features and leached her blond hair to silver. "Buck's been so unhappy. He's a terrible patient." Fnor smiled faintly. "It's almost a relief to see him angry and impatient. Better than those early days when he just lay there, waiting to die. *Hoping.*"

Her chest heaved. Just once. Then her head dropped back, the muscles and tendons of her neck emphasized by the harsh winter sun as she fought to regain control.

Signi remained silent, sensing that comforting words

would be inadequate, even irritating. Fnor did not want comfort, she wanted a solution. But there wasn't one.

"But he didn't die." Fnor's mouth was crooked as she tried to smile. "We were too vigilant for that. So now he frets about Convocation. He thinks he cannot do anything here, so he should be in the royal city. To ride shield for Evred, in case Horsebutt tries something stupid."

Signi nodded, remembering the Jarl of Tya-Vayir, and the way he watched everyone when they were unaware. His expression had reminded her of Dag Erkric's, only this Jarl they called Horsebutt was far less competent. Everything he said seemed designed to put people on their guard, if not to offend. There was nothing subtle in his manner— unlike Dag Erkric's.

Fnor drew in a breath. "If he gets on a horse, I don't know if he'll make it back. Don't think he wants to."

Signi leaned forward. "What are you asking of me?"

Fnor returned to the mat and sank down. "He can't raise the staff. No matter how tired he was—even if he'd been at the distilled rye—he used to wake of mornings bannered for the charge. No more. When I try—" Fnor's palm turned down flat.

Traveling with an army had given Signi a thorough education in Marlovan slang. Her neck tightened with chill. The mechanics of sex were simple. Far less simple were the emotions behind sex. "I don't know what I can do. You must know I am not a trained healer. I learned a little over many years when I helped the proper healer aboard my ships, but I am a navigator."

"They said you did much for the men at Ala Larkadhe."

"I did some reading on healing in the Morvende archive at Ala Larkadhe, and what little I learned I put to use. But the archive closed before I made much progress."

"Please. Just talk to him?" Fnor kept her voice even, but her arms were locked against her taut body, expressing such unhappiness that Signi shivered in empathy.

"I will, if you believe my talking might be of any comfort."

Fnor brought her hands together, and Signi discovered that she did not mean later, after she'd eaten, bathed, and changed, but now. This moment.

She understood the urgency as a measure of the melan-

choly she saw in the faces around her as she walked with
Fnor to the room they'd set up for Buck. It was a large, airy
room, chosen so he could look out the windows and over-
see the stable and the guard training ground adjacent.

Even after the warnings, Signi was unprepared for the
gaunt, fretful figure on the pillows in the Jarl's bedroom.

All the shutters on the windows were wide. The light,
thin as watery milk, sharpened Buck's hollow features, the
wide black pupils in desperate eyes. His sun-brightened
horsetail, once hanging proudly down to the small of his
back, was gone. Buck had cut it off with a knife after a particularly bad night of bed-drenching cold sweats. His hair
hung in his eyes, tangled and darkened to the color of dirt.

"Dag Signi," he whispered. And to Fnor, "Did you tell
me she was coming?"

"No. She crossed the border just a few days ago."

Buck struggled against his pillows. Fnor reached out
of habit, then snapped her hands back at Buck's furious
glare.

Nobody spoke as he rolled onto his good elbow, and
batted pillows into shape with the stump of his other arm.
Then he pushed himself up, one leg moving for balance
under the quilt. The other leg lay immobile, the blanket flat
from the knee down. At last he dropped back against the
pillows in a semi-sitting position.

Signi approached. "Fnor-Jarlan asked me to see if there's
anything I can do."

"What can you do now that you couldn't do earlier?"
His voice would have been truculent if it had had more
force.

"I don't know," Signi answered, her gaze steady, her
tone quiet.

He remembered that quiet voice from the agonized
days when they'd tried to save his arm, how comforting it
had been. What comfort could she offer now?

She said, "I never studied the healing magics closely,
though I heard the beginning lessons, as we all do." She was
reluctant to admit that the implied level of human suffer-
ing that led to knowledge about such things as nerves, and
which inner parts would function if punctured and which
wouldn't, had driven her away from such studies. "But I
listened when your healer talked about his experience with

non-magical healing. May I put some questions to you on numbness, skin sensations, and the like?"

He made an impatient gesture of acquiescence.

In a calm voice she asked a series of questions. At first his answers were short, no more than grunts. Gradually he spoke more, if disjointedly, until Signi gained the impression of a once-active man whose purpose in life had been as mercilessly hacked apart as his extremities. His people assured him he could supervise (though his father and uncle were doing that just fine), he could train (though his brother had willingly taken on those duties in addition to his own), but in truth he couldn't even pour the wine for Restday drum.

When Signi was done with her questions, she said, "You could travel to a land where the healers have mastery over the deeper magics, though I do not know how much they could do. This I do know. Time does heal and strengthen. Especially if you help it by being as active as you can."

He dropped his head back, murmuring something unintelligible. She knew he was doing his best to summon up the words to thank her for what he regarded as nothing, so she slipped out.

Fnor was on her heels. As soon as the door was shut, she said, "Well?"

Signi's temple throbbed. It had been a mistake to come here. Buck had not wanted her intrusion into his shattered life.

So what could she say? "What I told him is true. Yet he sees what a Jarl must be and do, and he cannot be that and do that. He cannot see that you, all of you, value him as Buck, not just as Jarl. It is evident in the faces I see around me, in the care he's had, even in the room, with the bed positioned just so to catch the light."

Fnor's mouth trembled. "So I feared."

"And *you* cannot tell him. He will have to learn it on his own. Few people like to see themselves as a burden to those they love. Especially one whose own worth was bound up in being a leader."

Fnor's palm flattened in a sharp gesture, expressive of helpless agreement.

Signi put her hands together in peace mode. "I will retire to change." *And I will not make the same mistake with Mran: no intrusion that she does not invite herself.*

Fnor said, "Thank you, Dag Signi," braced her shoulders, and let herself back into her husband's room.

Buck jerked up on his elbow. He snarled, "Why did you bring her here? Now she'll blab that all over the world."

Fnor was not the most even-tempered of persons. She knew that. The old Jarlan had given her lengthy series of tedious and exacting tasks during her girlhood in order to teach her to curb her temper.

Now she drew in a deep breath, and held it until she could speak with composure. "No, she won't."

"So you made some kind of deal? Or she thinks I'm too pitiful even—"

"I didn't ask her, Buck. I wouldn't insult her that way." When he just cursed, a little of her pent-up temper escaped. "She's kept better and more important secrets than your problem."

Buck fell back against the pillows, his hair in his eyes. "Shit." He gave his head a savage jerk to fling the hair aside. "So now you know her secrets?"

"No. But I've heard from others what you should have seen right under your nose up north. Or maybe not you, but your rock-headed brother. All that healing, and before that, she caused a geyser to blow a city sky high? That woman is a *powerful* mage. Did Cherry-Stripe learn a thing about her? No. No one did. She keeps her mouth shut. Give me one single instance when she yapped."

Buck moved restlessly, his damp hair sliding into his eyes again. "Damn the Venn and her secrets. Fnor, there's no feeling in my prick, not after half a year. Everyone keeps saying 'Let it heal' but nothing's going to happen."

He looked away at the window, his mouth so unhappy all her anger was doused. "Maybe we need more time—"

He flung up a hand. "I've been thinking. You should take a favorite. I know I'm no good to you lying here. And I know my temper's been bad. You've been patient. You shouldn't be left with me, as useful as shit on a plate."

"Buck—"

"Go to the hot-house. Then come back and tell me about your fun. Maybe that'll cheer me up, if you find a good fellow to whoop it up with. But go find one. Fair's fair."

And watch you drink yourself to death as soon as you can find your way to liquor? They'd already hidden the knives after he'd off cut his hair.

She hesitated, trying to find the right words. She needed Mran, who was good with words, but even setting aside Mran's problems, instinct insisted that this conversation be private.

She had to resolve it on her own.

All right. The kingdom and custom only required there be a Jarl and a Jarlan. Whatever happened in your own rooms—or didn't—was yours to decide.

She'd discovered since her queen's training days that picked marriages, like Riders' and her bow guards and castle people, were pretty much like Jarl treaty-marriages. People married for all kinds of reasons, and those reasons could change. But as you aged, your duties changed, too.

As youngsters she and Buck had thought it would be fun to reserve sex with one another for after they were married. She'd had Vedrid Basna as a favorite—oh, those were good days. But they'd parted at her wedding, as agreed.

She lifted her eyes, not seeing the winter sky, but Vedrid's handsome face. The fire was still there, oh yes. And everyone liked Vedrid, even Buck. Vedrid would never marry—King's Runners didn't—and no one had reported that he'd picked a mate, so she wouldn't be interfering with another woman's life. Should she invite him back to her bed?

She looked down at Buck lying there, the wreck honor and glory had left of him. Her throat tightened. Maybe someday they could send him to Sartor, but she knew from writing to Hadand that there was no regrowing limbs even among the highest mages.

As for sex? Who knew. So what did she know? That Buck had never in his life had a favorite. Frequent sporting in his academy days and after, yes, but his heart had never gone to any of them. *Why are these things never straightforward?* she thought sadly. *Horses and dogs have it easier.* Then she caught herself up. She hated pity and whine as much as Buck did.

Honor. Buck had done his part, now it was her turn.

"Fair's fair," she repeated his last words as she sat down beside him on the bed. She took his sweaty, anger-tense fingers in her two hands. "You and I made a deal when we were fifteen—half our lifetimes ago. Didn't matter what anyone else did. Marriage was going to be a ride neck and neck for us." Her voice roughened. "It was a good vow, is how I see it, so I'm making it again. Just like we did before. Neck and neck means we go over the hedgerows together. Through the swamps together. We ford the river side by side. If one's horse throws a shoe, the other dismounts and we put it on together. And if the shoe doesn't stay on, we both walk the horses home."

His eyes squeezed shut, his mouth twisted. She pulled his head against her shoulder, stroking his damp, tangled hair. "Side by side, Buck. Wherever the road goes."

Chapter Eight

TAU'S trade ship skirted through The Narrows well ahead of the first ice and beat northeastward into the Sartoran Sea.

Tau was just getting ready to shiver through a night watch when he absently touched his golden case to discover the magical tingle that meant it actually contained a message. His third ever? Jeje had written twice, once to let him know she'd found his mother, and the second message had been even more cryptic:

> When you reach the market town that sounds like Shee-yov-han, you take the north road all the way to Elsaryan or Elsarayin, or however they spell it. Their letters are funny here, not quite like the Sartoran ones Inda taught us, and they pronounce it funny.

Typically, Jeje had not written back since. Tau fingered open the box. The note was in Inda's handwriting, seldom seen, his letters still schoolboy round: *My popularity has doubled*, Tau thought wryly.

> *E. was looking for you when we arrived. I don't*

*know what that means. I wish you were here. You see
things differently from me. Everything here is fine. In
the city. Even though there's no one attacking, the people like it when I do a sentry walk every night. T. or H.
come with me, sometimes E. when he gets away from
work. They asked about you.*

Tau looked up, and not for the first time sustained an
intense wave of . . . what was this? Regret? Unhappiness?
Definitely the desire to turn around and sail back.

He spent his watch pacing the ship and composing an
answer. As the sun made a bleak appearance over the distant juts of southern Halia, the mate of the watch shuffled
forward, squinted at the sandglass, yawned, then gave the
bell a *ting-ting! ting-ting!* Tau withdrew to the cramped
wardroom nook in the forepeak and pulled paper and pen
from his gear bag. Tired as he was, he wrote out his letter
while all the turns of phrase were fresh in his mind, stopping only to hold his fingers over the candle when they
began to go numb from the cold.

"*. . . Would you like me to remind you what ship gruff tastes
like, especially when the cook is glad-handed with the old
potatoes and pinch-tinklet with the cheese? Your army
slurry is a Colendi delicacy by comparison.*" Inda lowered
the paper. "The rest is mostly ship talk. It's probably fun-
nier if you know what the mizzen hatch is, and a capstan
bar."

He and Evred sat in the royal schoolroom, which Inda
had meant to use only to finish off reading the piled up reports of wounded still in lazaretto or released to duty. But
as the days slipped by he discovered he preferred this room,
with its four tall light-streaming windows overlooking the
academy, to the dark parlor in his and Tdor's quarters, or
the cramped, windowless old Harskialdna office down in
the guards' command center.

He waved the letter. "I'll skip the rest. Though it made
me laugh. I wonder why he wrote all that. Think he wants
me to miss being on shipboard?"

"Do you?" Evred asked, the humor fading into the familiar shuttered countenance.

Inda was getting used to that look and to the fact that he

just was never going to figure it out. He shrugged it away, and considered. *Did* he miss being on shipboard?

Evred scorned himself for the poison-spear of jealousy. Tau and Inda were not lovers. Evred had experienced that side of Tau in a way that Inda never would. And there had been no detestable demands, or assumptions, on Tau's part afterward. *I must accept that Inda had his own Sier Danas, undefined by any custom, but just as loyal. And Inda's loyalty is to me.*

"I do miss sailing," Inda said. "Sometimes. But would I go back? No." He threw his letter down. "My day makes Tau's look like a snooze in the hammock, and won't I tell him so!" The dawn bells began their unmusical clangor, and Inda jumped up. "Drill, and then Gand and I have to—ah, never mind that now. Listen, you'll be with those guild fellows about the ore, when I get back. Have any message for Tau?"

"No," Evred said.

Inda bolted out the door, his voice fading down the hall as he issued orders to the Runners waiting outside.

. . . & though Evred's day is much longer than mine he listened to your letter, & by the end he smiled. Hadand reports every time he smiles, because it's too rare. Especially with Convocation coming up at month's end.

In the fading light the Fox Banner Fleet sailed steadily northward toward The Fangs, at the extreme eastern end of the strait. Everyone was at battle stations. The smell of smoke from the firepots singed Mutt's nose as he stood forward on the bow of the *Sable*, glass pressed to his eye. His bow team crouched along the rail behind him, some rubbing their hands to keep them from numbing, others with their mittened fingers tucked in their armpits, their breath puffing in soft white vapor trails as the wind whipped the last of a sleet storm above the formidable line of round-hulled Chwahir ships ahead.

The Chwahir were silhouetted against the retreating clouds, obscured by slanting showers.

Mutt bit the inside of his cheek to keep himself alert. The long two days of battling this storm had left him exhausted and unprepared when the departing clouds revealed the battle fleet forming ahead.

At least I'm not on the *Death,* he thought as he swept his glass toward Fox's flagship, a long, low, lethal silhouette just in front of them. The *Sable* flanked the *Death* at the left, *Cocodu* at the right, the rest of the fleet spreading behind them in arrowhead formation, which had become Fox's favorite: he liked breaking lines himself, the *Death* being designed for speedy attack. The others, stationed in the widening wake, could either comb a line or combine to take on pairs of enemy ships, depending on how the enemy reacted.

Mutt thought he'd said those words inside his head. He held conversations with himself when pulling long watches at night. He discovered he'd spoken when a snort just behind alerted him.

"Bet Fox is in a real good mood," chortled Kanap, one of the *Sable*'s old crew.

"Less yack, my friends," said Captain Eflis as she strolled the length of the ship.

She was tall, blond, strong, with a ready smile. Her wide sash, bold blues and reds and yellows in her clothing, and her bristling weapons made her a familiar and dashing figure in the fleet. She and her first mate Sparrow sailed the fastest capital ship in the fleet. Mutt, serving as second mate so he could earn his way to captaincy, hoped to pick up their tricks for wringing extra speed.

Eflis doubled up her fist and thumped Mutt on the shoulder. "Eyes front, now. Let's see if our dish-faced friends want to come play."

Her tone went vague on the last three words as sails began to shift on the Chwahir vessels. Attention sharpened on the *Sable*'s deck.

"Looks like they're gonna haul wind," the lookout yelled from above.

"Naw. Has to be a ruse," exclaimed one of the bow team on the masthead just above Mutt.

On the *Death,* Fox expected absolute silence at battle stations. The rest of the captains were marginally more lenient.

But just as the lookout predicted, the sails shifted and the Chwahir fleet tacked southward, and began bucket-

ing toward the jagged line of mountains signifying their
homeland.

"Now that's odd," Eflis said finally. "We had the wind,
but they've got the numbers. And I've never seen any
Chwahir decline battle."

The lookout swung down to the deck, his lower face below
his knitted hat blotched with cold. "They was squintin' at
the *Death*," he said in the universal sea language known as
Dock Talk. "I seen the glasses on the flag's foredeck."

"Then they know who we are." Eflis peered under her
hand into the distance, the wind tangling her hair, then she
grunted. "With them, who knows why they do anything? So.
Mutt. Since we've been on watch and watch for two days,
I'm going to relieve everyone by stations for one watch.
Tomorrow we'll be back to regular. You go rack up and be
back at midnight, got it?"

Mutt yawned so hugely his jaw cracked. When he entered the swinging cone of light under the mainmast lantern, he checked at the sight of Nugget leaning wearily in
the waist, her good hand gripping her stump against the bitter cold. Mutt forced himself to pass on, though his heart,
tired as it was, beat the drum.

He dropped down the hatch and made his way to the
wardroom, where as second mate, he had a cubby all to
himself. This was supposed to be the first mate's cabin, but
as Sparrow and the captain were tight, they shared her
cabin. He kicked off his winter mocs, not bothering to see
where they landed, though he knew he'd hate himself when
it was time to waken.

He was trying not to think about Nugget as he climbed
into his hammock, but that meant he thought about not
thinking about her. He lay back, discovering how much his
body ached only as he relinquished his iron hold on over-
tired muscles. As he sank into the swinging canvas, he stared
at the faint blue-white light around the cloth that hung in
his doorway, the reflection from the glowglobe in the wardroom just beyond.

Nugget. He still did not know what to think about her.
Once she'd been the pet of the entire fleet, back in the desperate days under Inda's command, when they were going
after the pirates that had killed most of Inda's former crew.
Then they fought the Brotherhood, and Nugget vanished.

When she reappeared the spring before, the two years she'd been gone had turned her from a skinny ship's rat into a girl. With shape. A pretty girl with shape. But then she started whining, which they all excused because she'd been gone two years and thought they were all dead, because she'd lost an arm. Then she started scamping work. They still covered for her because this was Nugget, everyone's pet, she was alive, she was back—except for that arm.

Then she started hiding out, and lying, when they had to fight. And when Fox caught her at it, her friends had finally had enough. No one defended her. In fact (Mutt had seen it in every face) they'd been glad to see her catch it hot.

She'd been ignoring them ever since, except for glares, and they'd been ignoring her, too. Mutt was glad when the rotations between all the crews that Fox insisted on put him on one of the other ships. Nugget had been kept on the *Death* for the entire sail up the coast. Sometimes Mutt had heard the thumps of her private drill sessions with Fox on the deck overhead, and he knew how rough Fox was. No mercy. Ever.

Two days ago, she'd turned up for a rotation on *Sable*. She still didn't talk to anybody among the old rats from Inda's day, and nobody talked to her. But Mutt always knew where she was.

He closed his eyes . . . and jolted awake at the impatient tug of a crack-voiced ship's rat. "Midnight watch. Captain says tumble up."

"I'm awake."

It came out sounding like *mflmpguh*, but the rat was too tired to care. Mutt forced himself out of the hammock before he could give in to the almost overwhelming urge to shut his eyes again.

His head pounded as he hit the deck. The *cold* deck. His temper was as vile as the way his mouth felt. He felt around on the deck, found his mocs, jammed his feet into them, and made his way out.

His temper improved incrementally when a sleepy galley mate ducked out as he passed and pushed a hot mug into his hand. He didn't care what was in it, he just wanted the heat. Then the smell of freshly scorched coffee hit his nose, and he drew in a deep breath.

When he reached the deck without spilling a precious

drop, he slurped half of it down, ignoring the sting on his tongue. This was the good stuff Fox had negotiated from some traders a week ago, when they'd driven off another swarm of galley-pirates.

Really awake now, Mutt waved at Sparrow, who leaned at the binnacle, her eyes watering as she gaped with yawn after yawn, the chimes in her braids tinkling with the violence of each.

"I'm here."

"All yours. Stay on station, topsails plain. If the wind freshens, reef 'em."

Mutt ducked his head in agreement and gulped the rest of his coffee. When he blinked away the tears, Sparrow was gone.

Mutt paced around the deck, listening to the ship. He'd discovered during his years on the sea that each ship had its own sound, though they all shared a combination of wood and rope and block-clatter counterpoint to the wash-slap of the sea.

The lanterns at the mastheads swayed in rhythm, and the new watch looked as stupid as he felt. But the horizon was clear in all directions, except for the Fox Banner Fleet ships, the sky a scattering of brilliants against a black sky. All that remained of the storm were thin shreds of clouds in the distance, glowing faintly in the reflection of the almost full moon.

Almost New Year's week. He started to think about what might be fun to do when he realized that the sounds of rope and wood were not right. He looked up, peering past the intersecting lines and arcs of the fore-course with the square topsail above. Nothing. He moved past the bow and down the other side, looking up at the mainmast, where a shadow glimmered briefly then vanished behind the enormous curve of the main-course.

Mutt set the mug down on the capstan, ducked around the mainmast, and turned his head upward in time to catch a flicker at the extreme edge of his vision. He spun.

Nothing.

Then he realized what it had to be: someone was sky-larking. In the middle of the night! He paused, his body calculating the roll of the ship, then he dashed around the mast the other way—and there swung a figure.

It was swinging above the lanterns, whose glow made it difficult to see, but he knew something was odd. So he scrambled up to the masthead, where the topsail hand sat on a folded storm sail, head pillowed on knees, sound asleep. He dashed past—the ship was fine—and peered out, then his jaw dropped.

The figure had looked wrong because it—she—was upside down. As he stared in blank amazement, a slim girlish body swooshed out in a long arc and then, high above the deck, writhed in a way he'd never seen before and sailed out and around the topsail!

"Nugget?"

"Shut up." Her voice was barely audible above the sounds of the wind and sails and wood.

She swung around the other way. Now he could see what she had done; she had the rope wrapped around her legs and the crook of her knee in some way. She swooped down, her one arm extended outward.

"What are you doing?" he exclaimed, and the hand on the masthead woke with a snort.

"Shut up."

"Nugget, you are not supposed to be up here."

No answer as she swerved around again, *whoosh!*

"Nugget, there's no reason for you to be up here. You can't use a bow. You can't bend sail. Skylarking all alone—it's just stupid!"

"Shut. *Up.*"

She swooped out of nowhere, and her slim fist socked him on the arm. "Awk," she exclaimed as she spun away, then slammed into a brace, ricocheted off. Mutt realized he'd caught his breath, but she snapped her arm to her side, twisted her hips one way and her legs the other, and her arc changed.

"Nugget, if you don't stop that, I'll . . ."

He stopped, hating the very notion of snitching.

". . . you'll go shit in your hat."

He climbed down, angry, resentful, embarrassed.

And curious.

Headmaster Gand did not have his interview with the new Harskialdna for several weeks after Inda's arrival. He was gone to the mountain forges at Evred's request when Inda arrived, and on his return he glimpsed Inda from a distance from time to time, usually in company with young Evred-Harvaldar, sometimes trailing half a dozen Runners.

Gand scarcely recognized his former charge. As scrubs, the boys had been pretty much of a size, varying a little in family features, and more in style of learning. The only remaining resemblance to the boy Gand had eleven years ago seen toeing the flagstone line each morning for call-over while staring vacantly up at the towers was a pair of wide-set brown eyes and a head of unruly brown hair.

Those same brown eyes appeared in a scarred face abruptly one morning. During the winter, the academy's headmaster worked in a cubby in the row of rooms adjacent to the Harskialdna office. Gand rose and saluted, his manner grave.

Inda flushed to the ears. He saluted back, a loud thump to his broad chest with a hand even more scarred than his face, then pointed at the rumpled papers on the desk. "What's all that? Letters about the boys already?"

"Not the boys we've invited or who are returning. Most of these are letters from Jarls, or Jarls' men, interfering some way, on whatever pretext, most of 'em relating to the war." He tapped two letters. "These, just in yesterday, are about the pair of seniors from Hali-Vayir who ran away. You knew about them, right? Dressed as Runners and joined Buck Marlo-Vayir's men on the coast below Lindeth Harbor."

Inda pressed his heel palms into his eyes. "No. Yes. I think." Yes, there it was, a vague memory, but a memory: Evred just before they reached Tya-Vayir for the triumph, after a pair of Runners caught up with them ... *and the bodies were unrecognizable. But one of them had an armband letter in his gear and mentioned his friend. If the Venn had captured that horse, we would never have learned their identities.*

Inda looked up. "I take it I've got to write back. What does the Jarl want?" Another memory: Hali-Vayir, an older fellow, furtive in look, always standing just beyond Horse-butt Tya-Vayir.

"Wants to replace them with his own candidates. You and the king will have to decide that. The rest of these are

all crowding rein for us to take sons of their heroic Riders."
Gand swept his hand over the other letters.

"Because promotion comes through the academy." Inda
tucked the letters into his sash. "I'll ask Sp—Evred what he
wants to do about Hali-Vayir." He lifted his hand toward
the residence.

Gand mimed the gesture, then indicated the Harskialdna office with his thumb. "You're not going to use the
office?"

Inda rubbed his head. "Just until spring I'll stay upstairs.
I don't like that room. No air, no windows."

Gand looked wry. "The former Harskialdna chose it for
those reasons. He was always on the watch for spies."

Inda leaned against the table. "If anyone wants to spy
on me, they can come right in. We'll put 'em to work. Here,
d'you want to hear my ideas about what the boys will be
learning?" He grinned with the enthusiasm he'd shown at
ten. "I thought about it a lot. When I was running the army
on the road north. D'you see, they were sloppy, needed
work on . . ." He began to list a series of ideas.

Gand had spent half his life under the expectation that
if war came, he would lead the dragoons in the first line of
lancers. But the king had pulled him out of the field and set
him to teach boys, and when war was declared set him to
guard a castle at the border. During the next campaign, the
new king had pulled him back to teach boys again.

And here—miraculously returned and covered with
glory—was one of the first boys he'd taught.

A surviving dragoon captain from Gand's generation
had said of Inda after the Andahi battle, *He may look like
his skull's empty, but it isn't. You watch. He stands there at
the back of morning drill watching, but one of these days
he'll go up front, and start in with the "Do it like this," and
next thing you know, every muscle has turned to knots and
you can't get out of your bunk next morning. That's what he
did to us all the way up north.*

Gand held up a hand, and Inda stopped. "They're not
good ideas?" Inda asked, looking puzzled.

"You know they're good. Problem isn't with your ideas,
it's with the boys. Think back, Inda. Your year with me. How
many of you were serious about what you did after the first

few weeks? No, think past the punishments. You boys were serious about jokes, stings, getting away with extra sleep or less work, and with competition."

Inda grimaced. "So we were pugs and slackers. But isn't that what a change will do, get everyone thinking about the good of the kingdom?"

"In my long experience, the only time everyone is together working for a goal like the good of the kingdom is when there is an immediate threat or an immediate reward. Men or boys, Inda. This is all I ask. Give it a year. Watch them, listen to them. Get to know them and the ideas they bring here. What they have to unlearn before they can learn from us. Spend as much time with them as you will. Demonstrate. Impress them. But don't change anything until next year."

Inda's carefully, lovingly thought-out schedule vanished like smoke. Gand had been his ideal all those years, his standards Inda's. Inda was going to point that out, but he remembered himself as a scrub. How much of his later determination to keep himself to Gand's standards was because he wanted—somehow—to become worthy enough to be permitted home?

If he hadn't been exiled, would he be lazing around at Tenthen right now? *No, I still would have been in the war. But maybe not leading it.*

Then who would have led it? Inda grimaced again. Too much "what if." He forced it out with a breath. "All right."

"Good man." Gand gave him a sympathetic half smile. "You'll see everything differently, I believe, when we meet next year to have this conv—what is it?"

One of the King's Runners-in-Training had slammed the door open. These boys were taught to be quiet and unobtrusive on duty before they were ever sent out. Gand's irritation vanished when he saw the boy's eyes wide and stark.

"King wants the Harskialdna." The words came out in a rush.

Inda ran past the boy, jerked to a stop. "Where?" His hand came up before his face, the ring glinting. "Oh." And he was off again, leaving the Runner-in-Training to follow after.

Inda had never used the ring before, though Evred had

used his several times so far to find Inda. He skidded at intersections, hand before his face. The magical "snap" of the ring was quite distinct—more so than the internal tug that used to alert him to danger behind his head, when he'd carried the ghost of Dun the Carpenter, who (Inda only found out this past summer) had secretly been a King's Runner before he died defending Inda.

The ring pulled him splashing through the puddles of a recent storm, past the kitchens from which emanated the smells of baking rye bread and cabbage-and-rice rolls simmering in garlic, and up the old tower steps through a building Inda still got lost in. All the halls and doors looked pretty much the same to him; he tried to orient himself by the rooftops of the academy, when he could find a western window.

Up more stairs and to another set of rooms that he identified by the tables and papers as the oath project rooms adjacent to the archive. His frustration at getting lost burned away at the sight of Evred's wide green stare—green because his pupils had constricted to pinpoints. Next to him stood a tall, lean man whose gray coat was splashed to the thighs. Black curling hair, eye patch—

"Cama?" Inda exclaimed.

Cama struck his chest in silent salute, a corner of his hard mouth relaxing into an almost smile.

Inda turned from him to Hadand's somber, tear-stained face. Finally Inda noticed her outstretched hands, from which hung two rumpled, ragged-edged pieces of crimson-and-gold cloth splattered with brown dirt.

No. Inda had spent too much time around spilled, stained, dried blood to mistake the sight of it now. "What's that?"

Evred indicated a fourth person, whom Inda had glanced right past. This was a weedy boy of fourteen or fifteen at most, all awkward joints and knuckles, his unprepossessing face straining with his unsuccessful attempt to master awe and fear at being in the same breathing space as the king, the queen, and the Harskialdna, all at once.

"This is Radran. Connected to the Sindans and Tlens." Evred-Harvaldar opened his palm toward the boy. "He is the one who rescued the banner." He was about to say more, then thrust his hand toward the door. "Not in here."

Out they went, Evred setting a pace that had the boy trotting to keep up.

Inda fell in beside Cama. When Inda left Iasca Leror as a bewildered eleven-year-old, Cama had been a somewhat bigger, morose boy with a voice like a kitten's squeak. Inda had come back to find a tall, tough warrior who'd been serving as an unofficial Harskialdna in support of Evred's cousins, Barend and Hawkeye Yvana-Vayir. The first time Cama spoke, Inda had been startled by his voice, which seemed to issue from the depths of a rocky abyss.

"Banner?" Inda asked him, and then he remembered where Cama had come from, and his heart squeezed in his chest. "Castle Andahi?"

"Yes." Cama rasped the word.

Evred walked fast, leading the way down and down, stopping just inside the throne room. There he lifted his gaze to the high walls, the weak morning light slanting down through the clerestory windows onto the banners on the juts of the walls that formed the gallery, just below the windows.

Evred knew each banner. When they were young his father had taken him and his brother into the throne room to discuss the banners' histories, praising his sons when they could later name them off. Evred knew whose House each belonged to, who had carried it in what battle, and who had brought it back.

He turned to Hadand, whose uplifted face implored.

He gestured to the boy. "Radran. Tell the Harskialdna-Dal."

The boy's neck knuckle bobbed as he swallowed painfully. "Everything?"

Cama spoke across the banner in Hadand's outstretched hands. "Inda, the Jarlan sent Radran here up onto the mountain above the harbor. To count the enemy ships. He had a glass. He could look down at the castle. Saw the entire attack. Since he had orders and no weapons, he stayed put."

The boy trembled, swallowing convulsively, his lowered gaze stricken.

"Later—after the army marched up the pass—he sneaked down and retrieved the banner. Though the Venn still held the castle."

Inda whistled. "You went inside with the Venn in possession?"

"I know the castle," the boy mumbled. "Knew the traps. They were busy down below. The banner was on the gate-side sentry walk."

Hadand spoke for the first time. "Did you see her die?"

The boy's face blanched. "Yes. It was at the end." And because the adults all waited, he gripped himself hard, trying to keep his voice from squeaking. "At first they killed everyone soon's they could. But on the second day they brought Liet-Jarlan out onto the sentry walk. Took three of them, even with her tied up." He swallowed, his face slick with sweat.

Cama took pity on him. "They got her down, kicked her around. Then cut her arms off. Tied her to the counter-weight windlass for the inner portcullis."

Radran said, "They made her watch. When they brought out the last—" His throat worked, and his head dropped forward.

Cama finished. "The last three women, and one of the girls. They hacked them up, and when they were dead, they put out the Jarlan's eyes. Then they loosed her to run a knife gauntlet, but she dodged them and threw herself over the parapet. Cursing them all the way down."

Radran said grittily, "It's their blood on the banner. Hers and . . ." He lost his voice again trying to name them.

"And the last four," Cama said.

Hadand's eyes had closed, minute tremors running through her at each act of cruelty. Inda's recoil was equally subliminal, mostly signaled in the change of his color and his breath.

Evred gripped his hands tightly behind him, then turned away from those waiting gazes, and faced upward again. The banners were evenly spaced, chosen by his forefathers. He'd never thought to touch them, thought that they would hang there reflecting the glory of his family for centuries. All his early life he'd accepted that glory unquestioned. Now most of the banners seemed little more than boastful shouts after ephemera; this banner in Hadand's hands signified the fullest measure of loyalty and bravery. Even though the battle was lost. *Because* it was lost. It was hopeless from the beginning, yet each of those women and girls had fought to the terrible end in hopes of keeping off the inevitable just that much longer, keeping faith that he— Evred—was in turn keeping faith with them at the other end of the pass.

This banner was not a testament to Montrei-Vayir glory, but to honor, to faith in oaths to Iasca Leror.

He looked around, and knew his instinct was right. This had been the right place to hear the terrible history, and so it was the right place for the banner to come to rest. "That one there, by the throne. My grandfather brought back the Olaran banner he took from Ala Larkadhe. I think it has served its purpose. This banner will replace it. And at Convocation, we will sing Liet-Jarlan Deheldegarthe and all her women."

He saw in Inda's and Cama's faces, and in Hadand's and Radran's, that this was right.

Chapter Nine

INDA to Tau:

>   Today is New Year's Firstday. Did you know that? We never paid attention at sea. Evred had them hang up that banner I told you about. Cama told the Jarls what happened. Radran was with the Runners. E. thought Rad should have the honor of telling. I could see it, how sick it made him. Maybe only I could see it. I feel that way about what happened when I was Wafri's prisoner in Ymar. I don't want to say it out loud.

>   E. said R. could come here—he could be what he wants. He wants to be Cama's Rider. He told me he keeps having bad dreams the Venn ships will come back. He thought the dreams meant he was a coward. I told him two of my bad dreams. I feel stupid when people say "You? You are so brave," because I don't feel brave, I don't even know what brave is. Well, Cama is brave. Hadand says I am stubborn. She says she is, too, that we are a stubborn family. It makes sense to me. Rad said if he's a Rider, he will be ready if the Venn come back.

>   After they put the banner on the wall, we all made

*our oaths, me first. I was glad I had that practice be-
fore we reached Ala Larkadhe, when I became Harskialdna. Remember that? Barend's & my fight, just
like at Freedom. So I didn't stumble & make them
laugh. Cama was next, & he got a new name, to match
his territory: Idayago-Vayir. He also got the honor
accolade—he doesn't have to return for Convocation for five years. Only the old men remember the
old days when the king was a Sieraec and they had to
attend Convocation much less often, unless they had
business, or to be sworn. Horsebutt looked like he'd
bitten into a wormy apple. It was sadder when Cherry-
Stripe spoke for Buck & then Branid for my father.
They each got 2 year accolades, as did the Yvana-Vayir
boys. I was sorry I won't see Cherry-Stripe or Buck
for 2 years.*

*Debt day tomorrow. No duties for me. Then judg-
ment days. Evred changed his mind about telling me
what to expect. Now he wants me to listen, & after it's
all over, tell what I saw.*

*When I was small Tanrid told me Conv. meant Jarls
going to the royal city, spending a day or so saying
vows & paying taxes, then swilling & swaggering for
the rest of the week. Maybe watching the boys do exhi-
bitions so they could yap about how much better their
boy was than anyone else's. I thought Tanrid knew everything. He didn't know a horse fart about laws &
trade. They might be swilling & swaggering nights, but
days all the rest of that week is when the Jarls will sit in
judgment on each other. They wait a whole year to go
at each other, except when it's treason like Hawkeye's
dad killing the king.*

*Evred says we've got no treasury. Entire coast needs
rebuilding & Jarls will be like wolves on a fox. Fox. I
sure hope my plan with Barend works.*

*I read your last note to Evred. He laughed at that bit
about the sailor telling the other how to ride a horse.
Wooden horses, maybe. Laughing is good, T. says.
E. doesn't sleep, H. says. True. His lights are burning
when T. & I go to bed, & when I get up in the mornings, it's usually to find he's already out & about. I'll be
glad when Conv. is over.*

Remember Gutless, Walic's first mate? Horsebutt's grin reminds me of him. Same kind of mind? If you were here you cd. tell me. H. never stopped grinning when the Jarls spoke their vows. But made no trouble. Been a lick so far.

Inda's toes ached. He forced himself upright again. His place as Harskialdna was to the left of the throne, sword at hand. Purely symbolic, Evred had said: in the unlikelihood of an argument turning violent, the Guards would take care of it. But he wanted Inda there, a Harskialdna Sigun for all to see.

Inda was used to long watches on deck, though there he could keep moving. The problem was how intent he got in following the swift interchanges of debate. He kept unconsciously leaning forward until his toes cramped.

Branid, as heir to a prince, sat on the front bench next to Cassad, who was first in rank among the Jarls, with the quiet, anxious Yvana-Vayir twins on his other side. Branid had been so perfectly behaved that Inda'd scarcely been aware of him since his arrival two days before Convocation.

Branid stirred, looking uneasy, and Inda shifted his glance away. Weird, that, how you'd just feel someone staring at you even if you couldn't see who.

There was Cherry-Stripe on the Marlo-Vayir bench, arms crossed, a wicked scowl on his face that made him look older than Buck. None of the Jarls had made any fuss at all about the new oaths and their requirements. Hadand had said that the word about the oath project surely had spread all over the country. Tdor thought that the victory in the north was responsible. So debt day passed with each Jarl accepting his new responsibilities, and not a murmur.

But today?

Convocation's judgment day had begun with four judgment calls against Marlo-Vayir, three of them entered by Horsebutt Tya-Vayir. That had set off a shouting match of accusations of Tya-Vayir against Marlo-Vayir for owed horses, men, gear, damages—the accusations measured in the swing of the Yvana-Vayir twins' faces from side to side as they watched the older men brangle. Inda had stopped listening to them hectoring one another, waving papers from old archives, while Runners ran out and came back with corroborative (or corrective) papers from the project room, and Evred sat on the throne with his shuttered expression.

> *. . . I always thought the king could do anything he wanted. The Jarls all sit in judgment on themselves in anything but treason. & then they have to be present to see the king's judgment carried out. Never thought about what any of that meant. You never thought almost 20 fellows cd. sound like 60 wolves over one kill till you heard them yapping.*
>
> *I also thought it was simple, 1 man per territory, with 1 vote. But Nelkereth has a "guardian" instead of a Jarl, & can only vote on land or horse matters. Tlen-Sindan-An is supposed to be a single jarlate, but both Sindan-An & Tlen have 2 votes on certain things. Then for every vote the herald always calls out "Montredavan-An" & Evred has to say "In Exile." I can imagine what Fox wd. say to that. Well, Cama has to stand for his new territory & little Keth's. so he gets 2 votes. I can see how much Ola-Vayir hates that, at least as much as Cama's own brother does . . .*

Tau set Inda's letter down on the wardroom table and rubbed his aching eyes. The ship was pitching at every angle, sending the lantern swinging, which would make reading even good handwriting difficult.

Maybe he had better wait for daylight, when Inda's rapidly disintegrating handwriting could be read on deck. The light would be stable, even if the ship wasn't. But Tau wanted to get it all read, so he could take the intervening time to compose an answer intended for two.

Did Inda perceive that he was acting as a conduit for messages to Evred? *Laughing is good . . .*

The watch bell tinged, and the off crew thumped down the ladder into the wardroom, stamping and shedding snowy slush in all directions. Tau rolled up the letter and slipped along the companionway to his tiny cabin.

Tau threw himself in his hammock, wondering whether Evred was depending on Inda to send oblique messages back. Very oblique. Maybe it was Tau being too oblique? Evred probably didn't give Tau a second thought. "Want me to add anything? I'm writing to Tau," Inda would say. And Evred would say, just to please Inda, "Tell him the description of the green and purple lightning in that storm was interesting . . ."

Tau laughed, his breath freezing and falling. He knew better than to ascribe his own emotions to anyone else. But he'd taken a lot more interest in this almost nightly exchange of letters—answering Inda's scrawls with amusing letters he mentally composed all day—just to get back the gratifying message that *Your note made Evred laugh.*

By the fourth day, tempers were snappish. The throne room was bitterly cold, impossible to warm. Inda wondered if Convocation was deliberately held in winter. Sartoran tradition had established New Year's Week in winter, but who said Convocation had to be at New Year's Week?

Evred had said, *They all talk about how I should get chairs, or even mats, but I give them the bran gas about tradition. The truth? I found it in the one existing record written by Savarend Montredavan-An before my ancestor stabbed him in the back. He said making them sit on hard benches in the cold would get 'em through the business faster. It's certainly why we have benches in the boys' mess down in the academy.*

Cama Tya-Vayir, now Camarend Idayago-Vayir, Jarl of Idayago, had come south for three purposes.

First, to make his vows. That had been done. Second, to bring Radran before the king, so that he could give the queen the banner and tell its story as Ndand Arveas had requested—and apparently promised all the women in the kingdom. That he had also done.

His third purpose was not spoken to anyone. He watched his brother as the days passed. He talked with everyone, observed everything, making little comment except when his old friends pulled him into late-night reminiscence, and once, when Inda wanted to talk over some training ideas.

He kept silence during the brangles of Judgment Day, watching the Jarls' alliances form, split, and reform with Horsebutt trying desperately to gather an opposition to the king. Just to be doing it. Cama said nothing about that, either.

Then came the day of departure, and Cama would not be back for five years, unless something happened that required him to present himself before the king. He made the rounds of his friends, saying his farewells, but when the Tya-Vayir procession departed (for Horsebutt did not see fit to talk to his brother at all, much less bid him farewell), Cama rode out behind them, a sword strapped across his back, another at his saddle, and knives in sleeves, boots, and sash. He was alone except for two picked Runners flanking him, each as tough as he was.

The line of Runners behind Horsebutt Tya-Vayir shifted when Cama trotted past the column, looking fierce.

Stalgrid "Horsebutt" Tya-Vayir was in a furious mood. What an abysmal week. Every plan ruined, every coward running, just because that young fool Evred had that scar-faced pirate at his side—

A confusion of horse hooves behind him caused him to look round just as his brother rode up.

Cama flicked up a hand at the banner man. "Halt."

Horsebutt said furiously, "How dare you give orders to my men?"

Cama said, "You want this conversation in front of them?"

Horsebutt glared at his brother. Cama was alone, except for his two Runners, and Horsebutt had the maximum permitted Honor Guard, two flights.

But they were in sight of the castle walls, where no doubt that scar-faced pirate was watching.

Horsebutt struck his hand out in the flat-handed signal to stay, and urged his horse alongside Cama's, the snow crunching and squeaking under the animals' hooves, everyone's breath clouding.

Then Cama stopped. His voice was low and harsher even than their father's had been before he died, unmourned, in a duel with the Jarl of Tlennen just after the two led, and lost, a battle against pirates.

"I am now a Jarl. I am not your Randael. I am not under your orders, Stalgrid. We are equals, so I will say this once. If you make any more trouble for Evred Montrei-Vayir, then I will ride back down here and challenge you before the Jarls. You'll wish you were Buck Marlo-Vayir before I am done with you."

Cama turned away, kneed his horse, and thundered back to the royal city to fetch young Radran. And smiled: his three purposes were complete.

Stalgrid stared after Cama until he became aware of whispering behind him. He slewed in his saddle, glaring.

His personal Runner, used to his ways, urged his horse forward. "Message? Problem?"

"Nothing," Stalgrid said, hating Camarend, hating the pirate up there with the king. Hating himself. Because he knew he would never dare challenge Camarend, whom he used to kick into hopeless tears just because he could. "Nothing at all," he said bitterly. "Ride on."

From the towers the horns blew again, and the Tlen-Sindan-An and Tlennen Jarls rode out, now that Horsebutt was safely ahead. They looked splendid from above, banners bright against the smooth white-blue expanses of a heavy snowfall.

Inda was tired. His days had jerked between eternities of intense boredom while he stood motionless, and short bouts of angry, low-voiced arguing over minutiae between the Jarls, most of it started by Horsebutt. The evenings had been filled with banquets and too much wine.

The horns blew the chords for a prince's heir. It was his turn for relief as he watched Branid ride away.

Evred's head pounded from the effort it had taken to balance between all the demands: the individual Jarls as well as Jarls in group; the war reparations and the future; the constant friction of too many people interrupting the regular rhythm of the castle's life as they pursued their own concerns; and above all, above all, the long watches while he sat on that throne trying not to be distracted by the sound of Inda's breathing, the rustle of his clothing, the shift of a foot.

When the last banner had vanished beyond the snow-smooth hills Evred turned away abruptly. Inda waited, receiving no beckon or word. Evred sometimes did that, and Inda figured he was lost inside his head, reviewing the endless list of tasks that had been laid aside. He took off the other way, mentally sorting his own list of undone tasks.

Evred appeared again just before midnight as Inda was about to end his day with his sentry walk around the walls and towers. "Your observations?"

Inda had been thinking about them all along. In part, his
letters to Tau had been practice in organizing his thoughts.
He held up his gloved fingers, folding one down on each
point. "Branid was as confused as I was. The others were
taught things about treaties and laws we weren't. Cherry-
Stripe isn't an heir, but it sounds like Buck has been having
him share Jarl business for the past year."

"It's true."

"Took me about three days to catch up, figure out what
they were talking about. Branid seemed quicker, but Cassad and the others taught him over breakfast, Cama told
me."

"Go on."

"Well, overall everything seemed fine. No one yelped
about the oaths. Everything got resolved, except those two
questions of Horsebutt's from the first day, about who gets
the foals from the animals they had to loan the army according to treaty, and him insisting that the Marlo-Vayirs owe
him sixty-some animals. They kept postponing deciding on
that from day to day, and then agreed to wait for next year.
Even Horsebutt. Though I think that was because Cherry-
Stripe and Cama had . . . had . . ." Inda frowned, flicking his
earring with his fingers.

Evred was distracted by the guards they passed. They
all deferred and saluted, but many of them altered subtly when they met Inda's eyes: faint smiles, twitches of
shoulders. Like they wanted—expected—to be noticed.
"Ruby earrings? But Cama and Cherry-Stripe do not
wear them."

"I know. I asked Cama about that. He said only those on
the floor of the pass are worthy, and everyone agrees. Tuft
wears two, since he led. Hawkeye and Noddy would have
as well." Inda tipped his head. "Though I can't see Noddy
wearing earrings." He sighed.

They paced the length of the entire east wall before
Inda finally said, "They were on the strut without actually being on the strut. Everyone else acted like they were,
d'you see?"

"Moral ascendance."

"That's it. I'd forgotten the term, though I used to know
it even in Old Sartoran. Sponge, sometimes I think my
brains are leaking out. Saw moral ascendance in Tuft's dad,

and Tlen. Cassad. Everyone who was at the Venn battle or
had a son there."

Evred dismissed Inda's comment about brains as a joke.
He watched as Inda lifted a hand in salute to the sentries
who had backed to the battlements to let them pass.

Mentally Inda named them, and a fact or two about each.
He just about had them all by memory now. Good fellows.
Now that Convocation was over, he could go back to hoisting an occasional ale with them on a watch change. "So?"
he prompted, when Evred hadn't spoken. "Your turn."

"Here's what I saw," Evred said. "Horsebutt held his
tongue because he was aware that the older Jarls resented
his brother's promotion. In their eyes, Tya-Vayir got boosted
ahead of everyone else, though officially they are now two
families. Why weren't their sons given a command?"

"But the younger fellows didn't hold promotion against
Cama," Inda protested. "I think I would have seen that."

"No, they all thought Cama's promotion was his just
due, because he was a Sier Danas returned in triumph
from battle. Because of all he did in the north. None of
them resented Nightingale becoming Randael for Khani-
Vayir, same reason. Horsebutt saw this division between
young and old as a division between possible allies. He also
stepped back when I announced after the oaths that there
was a mage circling the kingdom to do the renewal spells.
I hadn't realized until I said it just how much Dag Signi's
generous offer would enhance my prestige." Evred finished
with that rare tone of self-mockery that always brought Fox
to mind. Fox and—

Signi. Inda grimaced at the surge of longing every mention of her name, every reminder, caused. He glanced
down into the torchlit courtyard where the evening watch
perimeter patrol was just riding in, snow clinging to boots,
horse gear. The night patrol's hooves diminished on the
clean-swept stones of the silent main street as they rode
toward the main gate, then out. "That surprised 'em," Inda
agreed, forcing his mind back to Evred's words. "So what
are you expecting next? From the Jarls, I mean. Not the
Sier Danas."

"That they will wait. There was a lot of 'Sigun' this year.
Whether it lasts or not . . . I think Horsebutt is going to be
the weathervane. 'Sigun' gave me a summer wind this year.

Maybe next Convocation will bring the east wind, especially if Barend cannot get us trade. I have to be ready. You don't see it yet, but all that about pasturage and who gets the foals is testing the battleground. If Tya-Vayir wins next year over Marlo-Vayir, then they can all start elbowing for more concessions."

"Why does Horsebutt need more of anything?" Inda stopped, smacking the wall with impatience. Snow flurried up into the air, and began to drift down; he turned away from that to search Evred's face. "He's got a good home. No money needs. None of the inland Jarls have coastal cities to rebuild, and you're doing all that anyway, right?"

Evred had turned away and began to walk, head down, torchlight flickering over his absorbed profile. When they reached the shadow of the bell tower, he said, "The Tya-Vayirs have hated the Montrei-Vayirs since the very beginning. That they have the smallest Jarlate was deliberate, I think, though no one set so direct a thought down in words. This I do know. Horsebutt will teach his son to hate mine." His breath hissed in. "And his young second-cousin who will join the scrubs this year to become his future Randael, since Cama is now promoted, will probably bring that hatred to the academy. The trouble will never end, and it's all because of a long-ago grudge."

He dashed through the tower entry and out the opposite door, speaking in a running undertone. "When we were boys I had no power. How I hated seeing injustice that I could not fix! Now I have power. Responsibility, too. I'm not afraid of hard work, it keeps me from—" He flexed his hands, then flung them behind his back.

From? Inda thought, jogging to keep pace.

"The truth is, I like power. I like walking into a room and seeing Horsebutt and that snake Hali-Vayir shut up and salute. And I really like knowing that I could order a full wing to scrag Horsebutt and they'd do it. But sometimes . . . I find myself looking for excuses . . ." He sighed sharply, his breath a faintly glowing cloud that vanished in the wind.

Evred stopped, and Inda caught himself against the wall, his boot heels almost skidding out from under him.

Evred stared westward over the academy rooftops, then said in a low voice, just audible above the icy wind, "There are two kinds of power. There's the obvious one of force, when you use your guards' swords to enforce your will on people. But the other kind is the power that people give you. It happened to me when I came home after my father and brother were assassinated. I did not try to take it, Inda. I rode home, I walked into the castle. The people were all gathered, and they gave it to me. With eyes, with fists here." He struck his own fist lightly against his heart. "They waited for orders, and when I spoke the orders, they obeyed. I did not have to use force."

The wind moaned, and Evred said, "You have to help me to remember that difference."

Chapter Ten

JEJE had been in a sour mood ever since she'd left Anaeran-Adrani, but this particular day made her previous gloom seem positively summery.

She hated this journey she'd set herself on. She could have stayed in Anaeran-Adrani, but wouldn't, nor would she tell anyone why. She'd been met with such kindness it just made everything worse. She couldn't even accept the magical transport token she'd been offered so generously because the only Destination near Freedom Island was in Khanerenth, and Jeje was sure she was doubly notorious there by now.

So here she was, trudging through mud, which she hated, in mountains, which she hated. The horse she'd been given had been stolen during a night she'd slept in the woods beside a road to spare money, though she loathed dripping trees. Great savings that turned out to be.

Now she was on the long winding road between Anaeran-Adrani and Bren, forced to hurry because some stupid outriders had galloped ahead to warn people that the hostel up at the top of the next plateau was going to be all taken up by a traveling royal.

Jeje had been ready to deliver her opinion of royals to

the outriders when she remembered from hard experience that merchants could be even sniffier. It was rich people she hated, especially when they slung around gold pieces in order to boot hapless travelers out of an inn or hostel just so they wouldn't have to listen to strangers slurp their soup.

"I suppose this royal would drop dead if a single female traveler asked for a bed," Jeje retorted in what she considered an attempt at compromise.

The first outrider was a skinny fellow barely of age. "Not drop dead, maybe. But we need forty-one beds, and the hostel says they can only make up thirty."

"So the rest of us are forced to sleep in the mud," Jeje snarled.

"You can ride on—"

"Do *you* see a horse?"

The second outrider just laughed, clicked to his mount and rode back down the muddy trail, but the first one gave Jeje a not-unsympathetic smile. "Been like this ever since the ships stopped going round. People have to travel with us." He slapped his sword. "Hostelries don't have enough beds, so we take our tents along. My advice? Get a job as an outrider. You get your horses free, and all you do is ride around wearing livery. You might have to sleep in a tent during the winter, but you get paid for it. And bandits don't dare attack big parties anymore. Not since the two biggest gangs took each other on and most of 'em either died or ran."

Jeje gritted her teeth. She knew she was being unfair— the fellow was just being friendly while carrying out orders—so she just lifted a hand in salute. The outrider returned a casual wave and galloped back down the road.

Jeje trudged grimly onward. Fog was another hate, she thought sourly as swirls of vapor lowered slowly from the blank gray sky, obscuring the red-soil hills and patches of dense forest on either side of the road.

She toiled up the hill, head bowed, debating whether she should just give up and write to someone via the golden case. Only what would she write? Inda didn't have magic. He couldn't do anything from wherever he was. Fox . . . She shuddered.

Tau?

She grimaced, her spirits now about as low as her icy, mud-caked winter mocs. It had seemed such a wonderful idea, to find his mother for him. The idea had come after she'd heard what seemed to be a clue in what Inda's betrothed, Tdor Marth-Davan, had observed.

But the longer Jeje had pursued it, the more convinced she'd become it was a bad idea. A *stupid* idea. Only her sense of fairness finally drove her to contact him, because he had the right to know. But she couldn't bear to see what he decided to do about it, because it was too easy to picture—

A crack of a twig was all the warning she had. She looked up to find a group of shabby figures slowly ringing her, each brandishing a weapon.

"Let's have your money," a man snarled.

First her horse, then a decent bed, and now this.

She threw back her head. "Come and get it."

"Hah! Mouthy, isn't she? Let's have some fun with this one."

One laughed, but another cut across, saying in a weird kind of Iascan, "Stop yapping and slit her throat. We have to hide the body before those toffs get up the road."

And they closed in.

She didn't even count the figures looming out of the fog, just dropped her gear bag into the slush and whipped out her boot knives, sending one to land squarely into the chest of the leader and the second into the closest attacker.

The first dropped like a rock, the knife in his heart. The second one stumbled into the fellow next to him so they fell, thrashing and kicking. Jeje snapped her fighting knives out and sprang between two attackers whose sword arcs were just right to—

Clang! Right into one another. She ducked under the blades, right hand slashing open one's gut, the other blade high, slicing across the man's face, which was the only visible flesh. As they recoiled she leaped past, blocked a down-swinging blade, using shoulder and leg to redirect the fellow's force toward the next nearest attacker. Smash, block, jab, whirl—it was just like fighting with Fox and the gang except she didn't have to control her strikes.

The jolt of danger flared into angry joy as the mountain robbers whooped, cursed, and finally yelped in dismay and stampeded off, dragging their wounded. She retrieved her boot knives, cleaned them off on the fellows' coats, and resheathed them.

Then looked around. Again. And kicked the snow, howling curses at the sky.

They'd retreated—with her gear bag.

She was yelling so loud at first she didn't hear the jingling and clopping of the royal cavalcade. So the newcomers were considerably startled to come on a short young woman stamping around in a circle, waving her arms and cursing. In the muddy snow lay three bodies. Surrounding them was a confusion of fresh prints and blood sprays.

"Is that Iascan invective?" A woman's voice.

Jeje was startled to hear her home language—with an Adrani accent. Out of the mist walked a tall woman in a beautiful yeath-fur cloak whose hood did not conceal all her elegantly arranged grayish-brown hair.

"Iascan," Jeje repeated, arms dropping to her sides. "You're Iascan?"

"Not quite. May I assist you?" The woman stopped.

"Too late. The robbers got my stuff."

"But they seem to have been driven off. Where is the rest of your escort? Chasing the miscreants, I trust?"

"I'm alone."

"Alone?"

The woman—and the guards—looked around again at the dead robbers and the blood spatters. Then the newcomer caught the faint, red gleam of a ruby at Jeje's ear and knew who this warlike young woman was.

"May I introduce myself?" She indicated a fine, well-sprung carriage behind six horses, which were stamping their feet and snorting. "My name is Wisthia Shagal, and I'm going north as the new Adrani ambassador to Bren. I haven't heard Iascan for a year or two, and this journey is so slow and boring. Won't you do me the favor of joining me?"

The snowy dawn silhouetted Bren Harbor and the city rising in gray-etched squares on either side of the river. It was just as large as Barend Montrei-Vayir remembered from his boyhood on the Iascan trade ships, before he'd been taken by pirates.

The choppy tide pushed the schooner past the islands in the bay. They signaled with the purple poppies of Idayago. The harbor signaled for them to tie up at the floating dock at the far end. By the time they rounded to, customs officials stamped back and forth in front of a small but doughty crowd eager for news out of the west.

It took all hands to secure the schooner fore and aft. Barend was one of the first up from the cramped crew's quarters, gear bag over his shoulder.

When he passed the captain down in the relative shelter of the waist, the customs officials had already surrounded him. "Yes, the war's over," the captain shouted in Dock Talk. "The Venn are gone! Marlovans savaged 'em! Destroyed our harbors before the vinegar-eaters even showed up . . ."

Barend jumped down onto the dock and walked away. A couple of the news-seekers tried to approach him, but he just shouldered past, letting the wind rip their words away. He'd heard far too much about the Kepri-Davans' terrible rule to be too resentful of the captain's attitude, but it hadn't been easy, listening to anti-Marlovan slanders during that long journey, made by people in no doubt their opinion was shared.

Barend hopped up onto the stationary dock and stumped to the quay. Despite the rising wind he stopped before an exquisite yacht, admiring the graceful sweep of the bow, the fine scrollwork, the sheathed blocks and gilding and clean rope straight off a rope-walk.

Snow began to fall thick and fast, turning darting figures to gray silhouettes. Barend splashed into an icy puddle, and nearly ran into a fellow. They both started back, and Barend yelled, "Where's the Five-Star office?"

The fellow roared directions, and Barend soon located the long, rambling building with the Fleet Guild banner painted on a sign. The wind wrenched the door from his numbing hands and smashed it into a wall.

He wrestled it shut and crossed to the inner door, which opened tamely into a warm damp fug that smelled like the crew's quarters of a ship in winter, when everyone has been wearing the same clothes too long. Stale coffee and the lingering aromas of spiced rice and crispy pan flatbread added pungency. He joined the end of the slow-moving line.

By the time he thawed out he'd shuffled forward a few
steps. Gradually the low murmur of voices resolved into
individuals. The Fleet Guild had obviously become a mariners' communications center. When he reached the front of
the line, he had gone from grateful warmth to sweltering.
He tried to ignore his discomfort, wondering how the messages people handed in so confidently were getting sent.
Had the Fleet enough money to pay the scribes to send
messages by magic, or had trade resumed?

"You in the red hat. Your turn."

A drop of sweat stung Barend's eyes, and for the first
time in weeks he snatched his grimy cap off, enjoying a
brief sense of coolness on his damp head.

Forgotten, Barend's ruby earring swung down against
his jaw.

The man tending the counter jerked upright, surprise
lengthening his face. Conversation stopped as people
flicked gazes from those round eyes and mouth to Barend's
earring.

"Fleet Master Chim?" Barend asked. "I've got a message for him."

The man behind the counter pointed a gnarled finger.
"You were with Elgar the Fox."

Which one would that be? Barend tried not to laugh.
"Yes," he said, seeing no reason to hide the fact, now that
he was away from the Idayagans.

Everyone began shouting questions at him, trying to be
heard over everyone else.

A burly man gripped Barend by the shoulder. "Did
Elgar the Fox take the Venn?"

Barend's muscles tightened. He was about to throw the
fellow off when an old voice, loud with deck-in-a-high-
storm practice, silenced them all. "Clear off! Clear yez off,
hear me?"

Barend swung around as everyone pressed back. This
scrawny old geezer with the balding pate and the braided
beard had to be Chim. He jerked a thumb over his shoulder
toward the stairs.

Barend gave in to another impulse. Keeping one's peace
for weeks in close quarters when everyone feels free to
slang your language, your customs and culture, does have
its effect. "What happened to the Venn?" he repeated. "We

Marlovans drove 'em off, that's what," he said, and chuck-led as questions, comments, and exclamations burst out be-hind him.

Two powerful sailors took a stance at the top of the stairs behind Chim, who led Barend to an office furnished with a cushioned chair, a table piled high with papers, and a bench. Barend dropped onto the bench.

"Zat true?" Chim asked as he plopped onto his chair with a creaking and popping of joints.

"Venn're gone." Barend jerked his thumb northward.

"How many yappin' mouths between you and this bat-tle?" Chim's expression was shrewd.

"I was there." Barend scratched his gritty scalp.

Funny, how little things can be gratifying. In this case the upward flick of Chim's bushy brows. Then he sat back. "What're you here for, boy?"

"Reopen Marlovan trade," Barend began cautiously. Chim snorted. "And?"

"We need some honest ships. To get started on that."

Chim abruptly switched to Sartoran. "You're a worse diplomat than I am. We don't have much time. No, I didn't send any message, but five or six of them downstairs are runnin' full-sail for the hill right now. If they don't have magic boxes. See, things've changed."

Barend sighed. "Inda told me to expect something like that. I know Jeje's pay fund must've run out in spring, but we were racing north to reach the pass before the Venn—"

Chim waved a hand. "Explain that later. First tell me what you're here for."

"To talk about trade, like I said. Now that Iasca Leror can trade." Barend hesitated, then figured, may as well go another step into the whirlpool, since it was already spin-ning. "I'm the king's cousin, which is why I know everything firsthand. Name's Barend Montrei-Vayir. I was ordered to contact the fleet Inda had in training. If they were here. On account of having not been paid since spring. Inda thought they might have gone out trading already, if news got out—"

Chim waved impatiently. "You want 'em for what?"

"Trade." Barend opened his hands.

Chim snorted knowingly, and Barend wondered if some-one had talked about that damn treasure after all. "Well, what you're more likely to get is your butt thrown into a dungeon. Prince Kavna is on your side, but the Crown Princess isn't. When Elgar slipped his cable at our meeting last winter—oh, you weren't there—"

Barend said with a trace of impatience, "Inda told me about it. Just after he captured Signi, the Venn navigator. Met you in some pirate cove west of here, just like you planned. He said he'd go spy out the Venn, send back word to you to relay to the fleet of volunteers Jeje had been training. But he had to slip his cable because there was some spy for your king alongside—"

It was Chim's turn to interrupt. "Oh, but Inda doesn't know what happened next, I dareswear. Nor do you. See, the king's spy must've reported by magic. Mistress Perran and I got back here to the harbor to find guards on every deck in Jeje's fleet. They had a choice, see: join the Bren navy or be hanged as pirates."

Barend cursed under his breath. "Then Jeje's fleet is gone?"

"It's now part of Bren's navy," Chim said wryly. "So here I be, Fleet Master of no fleet, and your Elgar the Fox has a warrant out for when he steps on shore. I'm afraid right now that's going to extend to you." A loud clattering below caused Chim to cock his head. "Damn. Magic boxes it was. I'd hoped we'd have a bit more time. Sit down, boy."

Barend leaned forward. "Give me one good reason why I shouldn't go out that window behind you right now."

"I know you could probably take most of 'em down." Chim stroked the braids in his beard. "Maybe even some o' ours will jump in and help. But are you going to want that fleet again? Because if you go killin' our people, may's well never come back."

"Aren't your guards coming to kill me?"

"Probably orders to kill if you fight," Chim said rapidly as thumping up the stairs caused the windows to rattle. "If you're dead the problem goes away. But see, she don't know yet but she's got a much bigger problem. Could say a weapon at the princess' throat."

"Talk." Barend stood poised, thin hands gripping the black hilts of his wrist knives.

"New ambassador from Anaeran-Adrani is Princess Wisthia Shagal."

"Aunt Wisthia?" Barend's eyes widened. "She's *here?*"

If Chim had needed proof that Barend was who he said he was, that would have convinced him. But he hadn't. He had been collecting information, very slowly, on his own.

He laughed, and at the expected pounding on his old door, cried, "Come on in! I hope you're bringing coffee."

Five or six men armed for battle crowded into the office, with more blocking the door.

The leader spotted the ruby earring and motioned the two biggest men to either side of Barend, one fellow grim and the other nervous.

Chim said in Bren's language, "Let me remind you this is Guild territory, and we made no complaints."

The leader said, "We're not attacking anyone."

"Good." Chim leaned back and his chair creaked. "So you can make yerselfs comfortable and lissen. Now. This here Prince Barend is on legitimate business. He's related to the new ambassador from the Adranis, the former Queen Wisthia of Iasca Leror."

The leader wavered as a third man came forward with rope. Barend's mouth thinned. The leader's gaze flicked from Chim to Barend's hands and up. "He's who?"

"This here's Prince Barend o' Iasca Leror. The Marlovan prince," Chim added.

Hearing his name and the words *Iasca Leror* and *Marlovan,* Barend watched the guard for reactions. Widened eyes, uneasy stances, lowered weapons had taken the place of battle-readiness.

He slowly dropped his empty hands to his sides.

The leader grimaced, then waved off the one with the rope, and the guards sidled into position around Barend. "Let's go."

Down the stairs they thundered, ink bottles rattling on tables in the lower room. The mariners crowded back as the guards marched their prisoner past the counter, through the doors, and into the storm.

Two big hands in fighting gauntlets gripped Barend's arms to make sure he didn't slip away, and enormous men pressed up on all sides, nonthreatening but not giving way and impossible to shift. Once when he was small, Barend had escaped his cousin Aldren's ready fists by hiding among the castle dairy cows. Trying to move among them was just like this, except cows' breath smelled sweetly of clover, and these fellows smelled of the pepper-spiced pan-bread and fried fish they'd had at midday. By now the snow was falling so thick and fast Barend couldn't see much farther than the broad backs in front of him.

The guards couldn't see, either. They tightened their circle, the Crown Princess' orders fresh in memory: *If the Marlovan pirate gets away, every one of you dies*.

No one relaxed until they reached the king's prison, divested the prisoner of his personal arsenal, and the iron-reinforced door slammed on him. The leader posted a double guard, and sent his orderly straight to the palace to dump the problem onto someone else.

Chapter Eleven

DOWAGER Queen Wisthia, now officially acknowledged as Ambassador of Anaeran-Adrani, stood at the window of her new domicile on Bren's Risto Ridge. Servants labored around her to turn an empty shell into a suitably impressive but comfortable representation of Adrani art and style.

She knew the promptness with which she had been invited to the palace and granted her accreditation interview was entirely due to the wary respect the neighboring kings and queens were according her nephew Prince Valdon, who was slowly taking the reins of Anaeran-Adrani's government that Wisthia's brother had left slack far too long.

Wisthia rubbed her thumb gently over her lower lip, which had chapped in the icy winter winds crossing the mountains. She did not want to watch what would happen to court life now that the fast, hard-living set around Lord Yaskandar Dei of Sartor had invaded.

Maybe she was too old, but while the hostesses of Nente were delighted to compete to attract the Sartorans, Wisthia had known immediately what had attracted that young predator's wayward attention. Or rather, who. She loved her nephew—and his serious, beautiful new wife, Joret—too much to see it happen.

So here she was, empowered to tackle the matter of ruined sea trade and the problems it was causing all over the continent. When the old ambassador had requested permission to retire, she'd considered his request an opportunity to get away from Nente and to do something useful.

Politically, then, she was off to a very good start. Personally? She thought back to the trip through the mountain pass, and her conversations with her surprising guest, Jeje sa Jeje. In Wisthia's long experience, people didn't like being questioned, but were always ready and willing to brag.

So you saw Nente, my brother's capital city? she had asked Jeje, who had given her name readily enough.

Yes. The glint of Jeje's ruby earring was a reminder of the fresh blood they'd just left behind beside the road, crimson against patches of snow. Jeje herself was no more than a dark shadow against the pale gray calendered cotton-flax lining of the coach. *Came from there.*

Jeje's voice was deep, with an attractive husky edge that reminded Wisthia of a great purring feline. It was a difficult voice to sift for emotional clues.

I trust they made you welcome, whoever it was you saw.

A princess named Joret. Jeje slumped back, thumping her arms across her front. *She—Joret Dei—treated me just fine. They all did.*

Wisthia remembered some of the gossip from her elderly aunt the month before, about how the courtiers had made a fashion of quoting Jeje's pungent commentary. They'd even competed to get her as a guest, the better to be entertained, except she'd refused to attend any court parties after one or two.

So you were not impressed with my homeland? But then you have traveled widely. Perhaps you have seen older and greater places than our city.

Jeje snorted. Then coughed, trying to hide expression of disgust. *I'm a sailor. What I see is ports, mostly. I liked your city, with those terrace things. Waterfalls. Roofs with tile patterns. Joret Dei made me welcome. But my business is done. Time to get back on board before I forget what a gaff is.*

Wisthia was experienced with far more subtle evasions than Jeje's. Though more intrigued as the days of their journey sped by, she could not get Jeje to talk about her purpose in traveling to Anaeran-Adrani. Jeje talked about anything and everyone except that, the more intriguing because Princess Joret had also kept silent about her visitor's business.

"Your highness. About the wall hangings?"

At the respectful but insistent voice Wisthia returned to the here and now, and turned her attention to the all important task of selecting the right wall hangings and chair coverings for her new home on Bren's Risto Ridge.

But she'd scarcely looked at half a dozen swatches of imported Colendi raw silk before yet another messenger yanked on the outside bell, sending an echo through the entire house.

She peered down through the shutters tightened against the earlier storm. She'd learned that official business came via Runners in royal livery of burnt orange, gold, and yellow. Then there were the liveries of aristocrats, the plain clothes with personal badges, the plain clothes with no marks, and finally the messengers in bright yellow, part of the city's scribe guild, who rounded the streets once each day.

This fellow below was more than ordinarily scruffy. He looked like an old sailor right off the dock.

Wisthia turned away, figuring he had to be there to see one of the new staff. The upholsterer and the three silk merchants waited patiently, hopeful smiles on their faces.

Once again she turned her mind to the fabric until interrupted by Jeje. "Queen?" When Wisthia looked up in surprise, suppressing the laugh Jeje's style of honorific never failed to raise, Jeje said, "I think you better come downstairs. Fellow's from Fleet Master Chim, and won't talk to anyone but you."

Wisthia smiled at the waiting merchants. "Will you pardon me for a brief time?"

Of course they would. She made a mental note to buy extravagantly as she followed Jeje out. "Should I know who this Fleet Master Chim is?" Wisthia inquired.

"The Fleet Guild is made up of five guilds related to

the sea," Jeje explained. "They formed up to fight pirates. Chim's their leader. He wouldn't send a message unless it was important."

"Take the Fleet Master's messenger to the kitchen and feed him. Let me get rid of these merchants and I will be right there."

Jeje vanished down the passage, and Wisthia slipped back inside, smiling at the merchants. "Now. Let's begin with the warm shades. Is straw still the fashion? No, I think I prefer this eggshell, such a soothing, subtle color . . ."

As soon as they left, she slipped downstairs, where she found the Fleet Guild messenger sitting to a princely repast with the pastry-maker's assistant as company, as the evening pastries were being layered. Jeje was nowhere in sight. "You are from Fleet Master Chim? I am Wisthia Shagal. What is your message?"

By then Jeje was almost all the way down Risto Ridge, running as fast as she could through the mounds of fresh snow that the sweepers were only beginning to shovel from the streets.

She reached the Fleet House just as the street glow-globes were being lit, which was the signal for many businesses to close up.

She tried the door, found it barred, and ran around to the stairway leading up to third floor where the workers lived. It was strange to be there again, smelling onion-crusted flatbreads fresh from the oven. Her stomach yawned as she dashed down the row of closed doors to the far end, where Chim had his two rooms overlooking the harbor rooftops and the masts bobbing beyond the quay.

She gave the old secret rap and was gratified when the door opened at once. Chim said over his shoulder, "Adrit! See who's here!"

Chim's wife bustled out, her face crinkling in mirth. Vyadrit Chim was no taller than Jeje, but twice her girth and strong as a tree. "Why, Jeje! Yez back!"

"Ye here about yer old mate Barend?" Chim asked.

"Yes." Jeje dropped to the low couch. "The fellow you sent to Queen Wisthia wouldn't give me details."

"I told him to use Barend's name to gain entry, but only talk to that queen, and he don't know ye." Chim gave her a quick report, ending with, "I sent one o' the youngsters t'sound the guards at King's Prison. Got the shut door."

Jeje glared at her pilled mittens, then tucked them into her armpits. "Did y'send a message to Prince Kavna?"

"Next thing. But I don't know if we can get through. *She*'s got him surrounded."

She. Crown Princess Kliessin was no sailor's friend, that much everyone in the harbor knew. Jeje grimaced.

Chim said, "Now, ye got my news, what's yez? What ye doin' back?"

"Did something for Tau. He has to decide what he's going to do about it. I left so he'd decide without me there. Thought I'd come here. Closest harbor. I was crossing the mountains. What with the pirates and the Venn rotting up trade while the local kings argue about who has to spend the money to protect all the trade going both ways through the mountains, turns out you either go with an army or get jumped. I got jumped. Met up with this queen and came with her the rest of the way. She's a pretty good sort, for a queen," Jeje added.

Chim whistled. "Good or bad, yez in just the right place if ye want t' help Barend. Help your training fleet and Elgar the Fox. The real one."

Jeje scowled at her hands. She had wanted to get on-board the first ship going east so she could regain Freeport Harbor and maybe even find the Fox Banner Fleet and *Vixen*. She'd had enough of kings, courts, and politics.

But Barend was an old mate from Inda's days. And Inda's first rule, right from the beginning, had been *We never abandon crew*. "All right. Tell me the details. Then I'll go back to the queen to see what I can do."

Out of habit Jeje took the shortest way back up to Risto Ridge and slipped in through the kitchen entrance.

Queen Wisthia's house was all lit up, servants coming and going. Jeje was surprised to find Wisthia pacing back and forth. On Jeje's entry into the main salon the queen whirled around, her eyes wide.

"You returned," she exclaimed. At first Wisthia seemed a plain woman, certainly no eye-catcher like the Comet, Tau's old lover, who had been reigning over Risto Ridge during Jeje's previous stay. But Wisthia's mouth could change from severe to attractive with just a curl, her eyes were steady and expressive, reminding Jeje unexpectedly of that red-haired king friend of Inda's back in Iasca Leror.

Jeje exclaimed, "Why wouldn't I come back?"

"Because not five heartbeats after you left Fleet Master Chim's messenger in my kitchen eating all our plum tarts for this evening, a liveried messenger arrived from the palace requesting your presence for an interview. Four armed guards accompanied him."

"Hoo." Jeje dropped onto a chair.

Wisthia took in Jeje's surprise and relaxed a little. Her instinct had been that Jeje, whatever her motivations, was no spy or conniver. "So. On our journey together you told me little about your reasons for traveling so far from the sea. I accepted that as your right, but now it seems your presence has disturbed the political waters. I need to know how, and why."

"Whatever's going on now has nothing to do with my mission in Anaeran-Adrani." Jeje clenched her fists. "It's from before. I'm known at the harbor."

"You seem to be known in several kingdoms," Wisthia retorted. The ironic shadow at the sides of her mouth jolted Jeje, again reminding her of Evred. "Here's my point. You are connected with Elgar the Fox, whose sinister reputation gives even Crown Princess Kliessin pause."

Jeje hunched, hands in her armpits again. "He was our fleet commander. Had nothing to do with politics."

"But politics appear to know him." Wisthia smiled. "Bren's royal court also knows, unfortunately, the general issues I'm here to discuss, the trade that I am enjoined to protect. I carried all that in my brother's letter when I gave my official presentation."

Jeje grimaced, remembering how uneasy she felt around Inda's king friend. She'd never met anyone who wore power like some kind of invisible cloak, like he did. And not in any obvious way. Wisthia kept bringing him to mind. "Are you turning me over to 'em? Or warning me to run?"

"Neither. You are now on what is officially regarded as Adrani ground. As long as you do not leave this house, you are safe enough. And when you leave it, it shall be as an escorted envoy."

"Huh?"

Wisthia tapped her finger against her chapped lips, then said slowly, "Over our first dinner during our recent journey, you favored me with your opinion of the rituals of diplomacy. Jeje, stop fussing with those knife handles in your sleeves and listen. I need to convince you that those embroidered robes, the carefully counted steps, the bows here, the succession of foods offered in this room and the ritual of exchanged words in that room, no matter how pompous it looks to you, is in every step, every fold of silk, every golden plate of tiny cakes, a way to deflect violence."

Jeje tried to hide her scorn. "I just don't see it."

"Think of it as a . . . a court dance. No, I see that doesn't work. Look, did your Elgar the Fox ever hold a parley with another pirate captain?"

"Inda wasn't a—"

"Pirate. Nonetheless."

"He did, but—"

"But nothing. Don't think about the differences. Think about how each side had to figure out who would meet whom and where, if they wore weapons. What each would do. They had to discuss it all and agree before the meeting, did they not?"

"Well, yes."

"So these rituals are all the results of discussion. If everyone performs his or her part, the other side knows what to expect. Negotiation can take place between enemies— well, between people with very different goals, let us say, because of those rituals. Do you see it now?"

Jeje pursed her lips, thinking back to the glimpses she'd had of courts at Nente. And the whispers about that cousin of Joret's, Lord Yaskandar, who broke àll the rules. "Not-quite-violence?"

She would think about that later. "I guess I've got it. So how do those rituals relate to me and you right now?"

"Because I think Kliessin is afraid of what kind of threat Barend's appearance brings. Don't think about what you know from experience, think about what your Fox Banner Fleet's reputation has been. Those rituals are the only weapon I have to save Barend's life."

"What?"

Wisthia brushed her hand down her robe. "And I am convinced that you must be the mode of delivery. As an envoy."

"That's what you said before. I can see the purpose, but I've never worn one of those fancy dresses in my life. Wouldn't know how to!"

"Never mind that right now. You come from Iasca Leror, you have the same accent Barend does. You also appear to be connected to my son."

"Your son?" Jeje stared. "Do you mean Evred?"

Wisthia smiled. "You see the resemblance, then? And everyone always said he looked like his father. People believe you connected with him, or rather to this mysterious young man Inda who, rumor reports, commanded the battle that sent the Venn back north. Something the rest of the world was unable to do during the last ten years. So we will use your reputation—and your connections—to our advantage."

Jeje grimaced. "How?"

"What if Inda sent you as envoy to meet me, let's say by a different route than my nephew? Yes. One over land, and one by sea. Thus the three of us may unite in representing Iasca Leror's interests in trade now that the southern world is emerging from the Venn yoke. Everyone in the southern half of the world is wondering who will dare to restore sea trade and what will happen. Let's take advantage of that."

"Me? *Envoy?* I don't know what to do!"

"There's nothing like practice. First the clothes. No lace and frills, you're from Iasca Leror. You'll have a robe like my daughter-by-marriage Hadand wears . . .."

In a newly redecorated mansion along the lower level of Nente's terraced city, a baroness drew a slow, deep breath of pleasure.

This affair is going to make me famous. Not just here in Anaeran-Adrani's court, but in Sartor, and maybe even beyond.

She savored it all, the words, the social triumph, and not least, the two beautiful creatures—beautiful without the arts of magical illusion—beginning a dalliance right under her guests' eyes. Because the gossips all agreed, no one ever turned down the mad, bad Lord Yaskandar Dei of Sartor.

It had taken six months to lure a brilliant flutist down from her mountaintop, and another six months of kingdom-spanning diplomacy and patience to coax her into the idea of combining her skills with those of the celebrated harpist from Sartor. But was anyone paying attention? The baroness smiled inwardly at the irony, when the rustle of silk and a faint, familiar scent of vanillin and musk warned of the approach of her chief rival.

The song ended amid a soft cascade of frescha petals. The guests stirred, many of the younger ones holding out cupped hands, and one young man throwing his head back so the silken petals would fall on his face.

A warm breeze lifted the petals, spiraling them into the air. A melody, patterned in dancing thirds, commenced a rise through the chords, minor to major, as the petals danced and swirled then looped and whirled toward the far arched door and away. There they were swept up by the silent servants who had spent all the previous day out in the conservatory along a high terrace, picking apart the carefully nurtured blossoms and carrying them down the mountain, layered in silk so they would not bruise.

The baroness was done with them; she did not know or care that her chief steward would pass them to her own daughter, who would dry them and sew them into little bags, selling them as sachets to use when winter clothes were laid away until next year.

Instead, the two rivals watched the petals dance around the pair in the center before whirling away toward the far door, driven by the skilled hand of the theater mage the baroness had hired for a stiff fee.

Then the duchess said, "I always appreciate a petal cascade." The word "always" drawled with faint emphasis.

The baroness enjoyed a thrill of loathing. So many things she could say! *You pretentious fool, everyone knows you married your position thirty years ago, but I was born a baroness.* Or, *Yes, Colendi cascades have been done and done again this past five years, but what else is there when the illusions of our young years are out of fashion, and everyone and everything now has to be real? We are limited to real decorations and to our real faces.*

The baroness's mouth soured. "I miss the days of illusion." She kicked a stray frescha petal, which promptly stuck to her slipper. She stepped on it, relieved the duchess had not looked down; a little story over morning chocolate about the baroness kicking and stomping would not ruin her prospective triumph, but it would make her look absurd. The baroness was already sensitive to the barely hidden smirks just because she was short and solid, her dark hair thin, forming a superficial resemblance to that horrid young sailor woman who'd sent the court into gales of laughter just weeks ago. "It was so much more exciting back then, never knowing what anyone would be."

"Or who," the duchess responded, flicking her fan out to catch an errant petal. It lay on her matte black fan, a perfect oval of creamy white with a touch of buttery gold at the edges. "Remember the night everyone came as the king and queen? They were prince and princess then."

"And beautiful, both," the baroness said on a sigh. "That was memorable." More memorable than a room full of the same two faces was her beloved at the time guised as the princess, and going off with one of the princes to enjoy a relationship everyone but the baroness had known about.

No, she would not be young again for the world, and she had never been beautiful. This new fashion for only the real—whom did it flatter but the attractive?

"Parties in our day were never boring," the duchess drawled, mellow in reminiscence. "I loved never knowing when I entered a ballroom if it would resemble the sky atop a mountain or a Morvende cavern covered in jewels or a pirate's den."

"Assuming pirates ever had the wit or taste to combine ancient Toaran tapestries with Venn vases and Colendi porcelain." The baroness chuckled, remembering that wild night. Odd, how taking on the semblance of the dregs of civilization had led to behavior that . . . well, best be forgotten. "The only limitations were one's funds and one's imagination."

The duchess pursed her lips and puffed across her leveled fan. The frescha petal spun into the air, then began to fall; the doorway glimmered as the hidden mage wove another net of magic to gather the last petals, and send them dancing on the air out the door. "So we are left to Colendi cascades."

The baroness opened her fan, but inwardly gloated: her party would be talked about forever as the night the wicked Lord Yaska met Joret Dei Shagal, Princess of Anaeran-Adrani, at last.

He'd been stalking her with delicate patience for weeks—accepting no invitations, but arriving to make calls just after her visits, or riding in the gardens when the ladies were out strolling.

Was it possible the duchess did not see it yet? Triumph prickled through the baroness as Yaska leaned toward Joret. He was dressed in muted gold to match the color of his eyes, the lining to his paneled robe the exact dark, dark brown of his hair, its golden highlights picked out in the candlelight. As a song ended and everyone stirred, he lounged forward to pluck a goblet from the tray being carried around, then resettled, his long hand resting near the princess.

Yes, the duchess saw. The baroness and her rival watched every single young person in the chamber track the movement of his hands.

Except for Joret Dei. She sat on her hassock in the center of the room, her back straight, her expensive silken skirts ruched forgotten around her, as she rested her chin on her fists, her steady blue gaze on the harpist as though the answer to the world's dilemmas lay just behind the music.

The duchess drawled, words etched in acid, "You realize he and his fellow raptors stooped on us only because Sartor has become untenable."

"I know." Below another song began, this one a slow, plaintive ballad in a Toaran counterpoint.

Yaska turned toward Joret, presenting a perfect profile.

"Until Servitude Landis dies and Lissais the Hypocrite reestablishes a bearable life for Sartor's court, the young courtiers have nowhere else to go," the duchess continued, amused.

"There is an entire world outside of Sartor," the baroness kept her gaze on that motionless profile.

Prince Valdon was not present—the word was the king

had sent him to see to something or other at the harbor. Was it accident that Yaska had finally accepted an invitation? Of course not.

"Their world—" A swoop of the duchess's fan toward Yaska. "—is court. In Sartor they are made to be servants to servants. Sarendan has no court, they're all fighting one another, or about to. Khanerenth's court is made up of merchants and the military pretending to have rank. The west is impossible, the rest of the east is too small and boring, except for the Land of the Chwahir, which has nothing we would recognize as a court, and he can't go to Colend."

Secure in the knowledge of her triumph, the baroness pretended she was not aware of the duchess' insult in telling her what she knew quite well herself. Her son, sent to Colend for seasoning, had reported in a private letter how angry King Lael had been to discover that his carefully selected garden of beauties had been competing for Lord Yaskandar Dei's attention right under the royal nose. Lael had suavely invited his honored and distant cousin to leave. She smiled. "I know."

"And anyway," the duchess finished, "Joret and our Valdon made a ring marriage last year, speaking vows of eternal exclusivity. We were all there. You heard them."

"I know." The baroness laughed. She liked young Valdon, and Joret Dei was astoundingly self-effacing for so beautiful a girl raised from foreign barbarity to a step from a civilized throne. Not self-effacing in a meek way. She was strong in a way that no Adrani courtier really understood, with her steel daggers, and riding around on horseback accompanied only by that grim, armed maidservant. Joret never raised her voice, nor was she rude, but somehow she had caused the entire court to superficially accept the presence of the sailor woman Jeje sa Jeje, peculiar as she was— and if they laughed, it was behind closed doors where the sailor Jeje (and Princess Joret) could not hear them.

A song ended, and Princess Joret tapped her fingers lightly against her palm in applause. Lord Yaska smiled down at her, whispered something, which won a smile back.

The baroness smiled. Really, young people would be young people, and the important thing was that everyone would be talking for years about how the affair began at her musical party.

Her hostess book lay ready to collect their charming scrawls on their way out, if the evening were memorable enough.

Now that is fame, she thought as Yaska leaned forward again to murmur soft words to Joret, his long hair brushing her shoulder.

Chapter Twelve

TWO weeks later Jeje followed a tall, stone-faced footman into the royal palace on the highest hill of Bren. They walked down a long marble hall with vaulted ceilings painted the gold of sunrise. The only sounds were their footfalls and the rustle of his burnt orange brocade tunic. Finally they reached a huge round room in which was an indoor fountain with water cascading down it in complicated arcs.

The footman turned his head slightly. The yellow silken tassel dangling from his tall brocade hat trembled as he murmured just above the splash of the fountain, "Wager you never thought to step inside this building, eh?"

"No."

"Last year I was sent down to watch your drills every month or so," he stated.

You mean spy. Jeje almost said it, but remembered Wisthia's last caution, *Words are now your weapons. Don't use them unless you must.*

So she shrugged, and the footman said, "Are you affronted that I speak? I assure you, the days of servants' tongues being cut out are long over. Though not on Toar," he added. "Dangerous ports, dangers everywhere, there."

Jeje's lips parted. A sailor! This king's spy in the stiff brocade and close hat was once a sailor! Again she caught herself about to rush into words. *Don't throw your knife on the floor, Jeje.* "Never been to Toar," Jeje said slowly. "Bad stories out of some parts."

"True enough. But everywhere has some bad parts, some good."

He's talking to me for a reason.

She was here after two weeks of evasive messages conveyed through third parties while the royal family was apparently at one of their other homes, supposedly for King Galadrin's health.

Wisthia had said cheerfully, *My brother—actually my nephew Val—has now made Barend and his proposal a top priority. He says he owes it to Cousin Evred for ending the Venn rule over the seas.* She'd sent daily messages from Prince Valdon to Barend via the royal palace, going along with the fiction that Barend was a royal "visitor." The messages were meant to be opened by all interested eyes: each day she begged him to attend her because they had so much of import to discuss and the rulers of Iasca Leror and Anaeran-Adrani would soon be asking about progress.

However, nothing happened until this very morning, just after dawn. As a brief storm lifted three fighting ships slid into the harbor, the foremost a long, low, knife-lean black-sided trysail known to sailors all over the southern seas: Elgar the Fox's *Death.*

Outside the islands the rest of his Fox Banner Fleet waited in blockade formation, at least twenty silhouettes, with the wind at their backs.

Quite suddenly an invitation arrived for Wisthia to join the royal family. Nothing about the king's health or other palaces. "And don't mention it, either," Wisthia had said as she walked around Jeje, critically inspecting the crimson-and-gold silk robe that they'd had made. "You take away a ruler's face, even in private, and they tend to throw the whole kingdom at you in order to get it back."

That's just why I hate kings, Jeje thought now. She kicked at the fine hem of her robe as she walked.

Still, she loved this outfit. Marlovan formal robes were

silk woven with cotton, but this was pure silk, otherwise it reminded Jeje of what Hadand had worn at that dinner. The voluminous black trousers, the golden sash at her waist, the high necked linen shirt under the long, billowing crimson robe all felt comfortable, and she liked the way they looked.

She met the footman's eye. He smiled wider for a moment, then faced front as they ascended a broad marble staircase about as wide as a three-master's foredeck. *He's telling you to watch wind and sail. So do it. Barend's life depends on you.*

Two more footmen in the burnt orange brocade and tall, tasseled hats stood before a door at the end of the hall. The door was a double one, carved with figures and symbols Jeje suspected had to do with history. Tau would know; the reminder hurt. She wished more violently than ever that he was here instead of her. He'd do everything right.

The doors opened onto a round chamber. A half circle of tall windows flooded with winter light. Around the windows and along the plaster-smooth walls someone had inset brilliantly colored mosaics of summer birds. They were interwoven in artful clusters, drawing the gaze toward crystal-faceted glowglobes in the white-and-gold domed ceiling.

If all this was supposed to intimidate, well, it worked.

Jeje walked slowly across the parquet floor—wood inlaid with a stylized ivy pattern—her attention shifting to the three people seated in chairs carved to match the tables and wall cabinets. The windows behind the three cast them almost in silhouette. She knew it probably wasn't diplomatic, but she raised a hand, shaded her eyes, and gave them a quick look over.

King Galadrin was short, round, and old, his gaze vague. Wisthia had explained that he'd waited until he was nearly sixty to get an heir as he'd wanted to postpone the kind of trouble he himself had caused when young. From two out of a series of consorts had come the princess and prince.

Prince Kavnarac was big, his expression welcoming. Jeje had been prepared to like him as he'd been Tau's friend; meeting his steady eyes, she felt as if he was silently encouraging her. Maybe he'd sent that sailor footman.

The princess was totally unexpected. Jeje had imagined someone even taller and more imposing than Prince Kavna, but Princess Kliessin was Jeje's own height, and they were built much the same, except Jeje carried not a whit of extra flesh—she was far too active for that. The princess showed the effect of little physical exercise and too many rich meals. She was beautifully dressed, her contrasting colors of yellow and blue joined by silken braid turning her solidity into gravitas.

"You come alone?" the princess spoke in Sartoran. All just as Wisthia had said. So far.

Jeje performed the bow she'd practiced. "Queen Wisthia is indisposed," she said, as rehearsed. "Sends her deepest regrets." It had sounded stupid to lie so obviously, until Wisthia explained that not only did it let the Brens know she knew they'd been lying about the king's health, it also gave room for negotiation. *Remember, I don't actually represent Evred. He probably has no idea I'm even here.*

Jeje was relieved when the king mumbled a few words of welcome, then turned to examine a golden bowl of nuts. A servant, unobserved until now, sprang to his side and began to crack shells.

"Please convey our best wishes for her recovery," the princess said with the kind of mordant sarcasm that reminded Jeje unpleasantly of Fox.

Out there on the harbor, yes. Why?

"Your ambassador presented her credentials as Princess Wisthia of Anaeran-Adrani," Kliessin said. "We shall continue to use the title she herself acknowledged."

Wisthia had prepared Jeje for that, too. Jeje bowed again. "I am Jeje sa Jeje, envoy from Iasca Leror. To us she is known as the Queen Dowager of Iasca Leror." *And wouldn't Inda laugh if he heard that "us."*

The reminder of Wisthia's relationship to Barend tightened the princess' tense face. "And so we come to your purpose here."

Kavna's hand had tightened on his chair arm, a gesture so subtle Jeje might not have noticed if the emerald in his ring hadn't flickered in the light from all those windows.

Jeje suspected he was trying to warn her to be careful, but she didn't need the warning. Except for the continuous crunch and crackle of breaking nut shells, the room was silent.

Kliessin said, "If you are an envoy from Iasca Leror, then presumably you will have firsthand information of events there?"

Jeje's palms were damp. She resisted the temptation to wipe them down her silken robe. "I was not at the battle," she stated. "Though I received almost daily reports from the Harskialdna's staff." Absolutely true. Tau was Inda's staff. The letters might not have been official reports, but they sure did cover exactly what was happening, almost as it happened.

Kavna said, "Then you can enlighten us as to what is rumor and what isn't?"

The princess' brows twitched together, and Jeje figured she'd wanted to control the entire conversation. But his question had nothing to do with policy.

Jeje said to him, "I think I can. They fought the Venn to a standstill in and around the pass between Idayago and the rest of Iasca Leror. So the Venn left."

Kliessin leaned forward. "Left. What does that mean? Surrendered? A truce? A hiatus?"

"They sailed away," Jeje said, as coached. "That is what I am permitted to say. For more information, you are invited to communicate with King Evred."

Kliessin huffed, almost a grunt. "No officials sent by proper channels—no ships until two weeks ago—yet everyone seems to know what happened. Only details differ. Some maintain that Prince Rajnir knelt at your Harskialdna's feet and laid his weapons down, others maintain that Fleet Commander Durasnir performed that role."

"For details, you must apply to King Evred, who was there."

Princess Kliessin waved a hand, brushing King Evred aside. "What I really want to know is how could his army commander be busy fighting the Venn and then a scarce month or two later be defeating pirates at various points around our southern seas?"

"I don't know anything about pirate battles," Jeje said stolidly, feeling the worst twinge of regret yet.

Kliessin sat back. "I note you did not attempt to claim that your Elgar the Fox commanded all these victories. *And* had time to sail about menacing people as the mysterious Captain Ramis."

"Him, I saw," Jeje said—her first unconsidered words. Her fists tightened. "He's not Inda."

Kliessin's eyes narrowed. "You saw this man? In person? Did he tell you who he was?"

"No. Never spoke." Jeje's brow lowered. "But I saw him'n Inda, side by side, at Ghost Island. At the battle against the Brotherhood, we saw the *Knife*. Big Venn warship with black sail. Ramis on the captain's deck. One eye, face all scarred."

"You saw a one-eyed man with scars," Kliessin drawled, her tone silky. "But you do not in fact know who he was, any more than you can furnish his place of birth, his antecedents, or anything else that time and money have not been able to discover. Facts that have been discovered about everyone else concerned, including your 'Inda.' I am relieved you did not attempt to convince me that he and the Elgar the Fox sitting out in our harbor are one and the same man. You were apparently there when Fleet Master Chim interviewed Elgar the Fox onboard his ship, with his red-haired captain standing at his side."

Jeje thought back to that day. Felt like years ago, but was just the previous winter. She recalled the long-nosed fellow Chim had termed a king's spy. "Inda and Fox are two men. The plan was for one to fight the Venn on sea and the other on land."

Kliessin smiled, then leaned forward again, gaze unwavering. "So you were in fact building a navy right under our noses? A navy waiting for a signal from Barend Montravair, or from you, who trained them, to rise and overthrow us?"

Jeje gaped. "To do *what?*" Astonishment was followed by an indignant squawk. "Why would anybody want to do *that?* I just told you, the plan was to fight the *Venn!*" Then flushed up to her ears. Images of being hustled straight out to execution—burning ships—war declarations galloping out right and left—made her insides hurt. Wisthia was supposed to be so smart at diplomacy, why hadn't she seen *that* coming?

King Galadrin watched his servant crack another shell, drop the nut onto a golden plate, and hold it out. He said quite mildly, "The only difference between you Marlovans and the Venn is that you don't have a navy. Yet."

Kliessin said, "My people watched you spending more time training those sailors in hand-combat than in boarding and repelling. We heard the rumors that you waited on a signal. When the message came for you and Taumad Daraen and Fleet Master Chim to meet your Elgar the Fox in a secret cove, we thought that was the signal."

Kavna smiled at Jeje. "But your Inda really did capture a Venn navigator, just as he'd promised. That wouldn't help him here, but it would against the Venn." Embarrassed and unsettled as she was, Jeje sensed that he was addressing his sister though he faced Jeje. "Then Inda and his fleet sailed to find the Venn," Prince Kavna finished. "Just like he promised Fleet Master Chim."

Princess Kliessin said in a more normal voice, "We never told the Venn envoy about the navigator. We did put Chim and the captains you'd been training to the question."

Jeje gasped. "Kinthus, I hope!"

Kliessin drawled, "I thought torture was the sport of you Marlovans."

Jeje was about to retort that she wasn't a Marlovan, but she clapped her jaw shut. *She's goading me to yap!*

Kliessin leaned back and let out a long sigh. "So far your story upholds the testimony of Chim and Mistress Perran. And we cannot—until there is a formal declaration of war— put foreigners to the question." Her regret was obvious.

Jeje's resentment spiked. *She's definitely trying to sting me to say more than I should.*

"The other thing that leads me to believe you is that your fleet pay ran out early last summer. Though I deeply resented the strain on our budget when we took over, especially as the pirate's and the normal mariner's idea of pay differ drastically. The lack of secret funds as well as the lack of orders suggested the fleet really was intended to fight the Venn."

Jeje was mentally wrestling with the realization that everyone, including Wisthia, had known all about the fleet being trained. They just had not known its purpose.

While Jeje struggled with these new insights, Princess Kliessin decided that she had heard enough. So far, the words from this clumsy excuse for an envoy matched what the troublesome Fleet Guild leaders had all said. She paused, wishing yet again that the Guild Council in Sartor would let her break this "Fleet Guild" (no true guild at all) and throw them out of the country. Instead, she had to stretch the navy budget beyond tolerance to support that raggle-taggle fleet of Chim's, and she had to pay an army of scribes to open, read, note, and reseal every one of those damn letters those would-be pirates sent out of the Fleet Guild. But her reward, if it was a reward, was as close to conviction as she could come that this mysterious Inda Elgar was as politically ignorant as he was militarily brilliant.

At least I'm saved the cost of a mass execution, she thought. *I will not tolerate pirates.* So . . . it was time for the raggle-taggle fleet to be tamed and run like a real navy. The advantage was that she gained ships for a navy far too small after the years of Venn control.

Kliessin smiled, and smacked her hand down on the arm of her chair. "Bringing me to my last question. If Elgar the Fox, who's never lost a battle *anywhere*, has not been training a navy under my nose, what is that black ship doing out in our harbor right now?"

Jeje thought, *I already fumbled. Though it didn't make things worse, another fumble might.* "That question by rights ought to go to Prince Barend—" (*Was* he really a prince?) "—and Queen Wisthia."

To Jeje's immense, almost dizzying relief, the princess gave a nod. "Well, then, perhaps our guest will have time to join us." Her voice sharpened, but Jeje had her tongue bowsed up tight.

The footman appeared at her side. Belatedly she remembered to bow, then followed him out, sternly quashing the urge to sneak a peek backward.

Down the stairs and past a huge fountain. Running water muted sound, that Jeje remembered from her days at the Lark Ascendant pleasure house. "Good job," the sailor-footman said as she paused at the fountain and dipped her hand in. "Many lives were still in the balance."

The water was shockingly cold. She wrung the crystalline drops off. "Chim said the people are in the Bren navy."

"That's what they"—a glance upward—"told *him*."

Another jab amidships.

"Oh."

They walked away in silence, and she returned to the heights in silence, sensing that she was being watched the entire way. *That's the end of my career as a diplomat. Soon's I report and have full dark, I'm gone.*

Chapter Thirteen

THE thud of footsteps outside the door brought Barend to his feet. His fingers tapped the locket hanging inside his shirt, though there was no reassurance there.

He backed to the corner, poised for action. If they were going to kill him, they'd have to do it right here. He would not march tamely out to die for some foreigners' entertainment.

The door swung open, and there were the guards. Looked like a flight of 'em. But they had no weapons in hand.

At the front stood a big, well-dressed fellow. "Your highness," this fellow said, bowing with grace. "My name is Kavnarac. I'm here to apologize for the misunderstanding and to escort you to Princess Wisthia."

Barend opened a hand, not sure what the proper protocol was around princes. Kavna's smile increased, but his gaze flicked aside in exactly the same way Evred used to signal that they might be overheard, when they were boys.

So Barend just said, "Food's pretty good here, but I wouldn't mind some variety."

Kavna laughed that laugh people give when they're trying hard for humor, and off they went, trailing all those guards. Kavna worked away at a boring conversation about

foods the continent over, with minimal cooperation from
Barend. The only real comment during the entire journey
through the castle, into an open two-seat carriage, down
the ridge, across the river, and up the other side was Kavna's sighing, "I would so love to go to sea."

The carriage stopped. With an apologetic air Kavna signaled to one of the silent guards accompanying them, who
returned weapons and gear to Barend as the prince said,
"I trust we will have a chance to speak at leisure. I look
forward to hearing some of your sea tales."

Barend hopped out. Kavna raised a hand and the carriage departed, leaving Barend before a fine house flying
three flags at the ridge pole—one of them Iasca Leror's
crimson and gold eagle.

The upper ranks of the city thus having seen the mystery man with the ruby earring taken by Prince Kavna to
the ambassador's, they were left to an evening's conjec-
ture as the prince returned to the royal palace.

Wisthia was also watching from inside the ambassa-
dorial residence. She came out on her doorstep to greet
Barend, sublimely unaware of the warriors stationed at in-
tervals along the street, and the shift in expensive curtains
in the grand houses surrounding them.

She led her nephew to her private salon.

There was the curvy furniture he remembered from his
brief visits during childhood, the low, cushioned chairs with
just enough back for support, and no thought to an assassin trying to sneak up behind. Curtains the color of the sea.
Rugs. In the corner, seated on more of the curvy furniture,
a trio of young women sawed and plunked away at the familiar deedle-deedle music.

He remembered his mother saying once, *Wisthia isn't
stupid. She works hard at that pretence of obliviousness.
That's her only protection against your father's suspicion.*

Barend shifted from his aunt's intense gaze to the room.
The only three people in earshot were busy making noise
that would keep anyone at a window or door from hearing
much. *The low chairs let you see all around. It's not attack
she's warding, it's eavesdroppers.*

Wisthia settled herself, observing her nephew as he took
in the room. Barend's triangular face evoked his murdered
mother so strongly that it hurt. But there was no time for

the luxury of private grief. "Prince Kavnarac nearly joined you in the prison for high treason," she said.

Barend dropped down next to her.

"It was only because of his sister's regard for him that he didn't. That," Wisthia added dryly, "and the fact that it would be foolish to, say, attempt to overthrow a monarch by issuing orders to a disparate fleet of former traders, no matter how well trained. Especially one you haven't paid in over half a year."

Barend cursed under his breath. "I never thought about that. What it must look like. Neither did Inda. He needed a fleet, and they were forming independently."

"They were fumbling around causing no problems until a pirate showed up and directed their fumbling into purpose. All without talking to the government, who really should have been approached first. *Do* begin to think," Wisthia invited cordially. "How you Marlovans see yourselves and how the world sees you couldn't possibly be more different. Now that we've dazzled them with stage-illusion, what are you really doing here?" She sipped the mulled wine her servants had brought.

Barend took a gulp of his and sighed as the warmth worked its way through him. "Trade." He spread thin, rough-palmed hands. "Evred needs trade. The harbor cities alone—"

"Barend." Wisthia laid two fingers on his wrist. "Why are you *here?*"

Barend grimaced. Inda had been firm about keeping the treasure a surprise. A secret, actually. They both agreed that Evred did not need another thing to worry about. There were too many dangerous ifs attached to the treasure, not the least of which was exactly how to turn it into something more useful than hoarded metal and stone.

He looked up. Here was just the person who could make it possible. If he could trust her. "First tell me your part in what happened after I was arrested," he said.

"Fair enough." She gave him a succinct account.

Barend smiled at the mention of Jeje and her opinions. When she was done he said, "Evred sent me to reestablish trade. Inda wanted to hire that fleet. To get us started."

"Hire how? Or should I say, with what?"

Barend grimaced. "The truth is, there's a treasure."

"Treasure," she repeated, taken aback. "What kind of treasure?"

"Pirate treasure. Mostly gold and jewels. Some in the form of coin, the rest in luxury things. Cups and plate and jewelry and the like. Piled up for years. Maybe generations."

"I did not think that pirates were the sort to save."

"Inda said a lot of it was the result of hiding royal hauls until the war fleets stop searching, but the pirate captain is killed, then the killer is killed, and so on. Somehow they always saved the book with the map in it. Until Ramis threw it in a fire. But Inda showed certain people where the treasure lies. They saw it—Inda described it."

Her brow furrowed. "How much are we talking about? A chest?" She mimed something square sitting on her lap.

"More."

"How much more? I can imagine a great deal, for example a set of boxes to fill this room."

"More."

"The *house?*" Her tone altered from shock to disbelief.

"Say three of these houses. But I don't really know how big this house is." He repeated what Inda had said of the cavern on Ghost Island. "A lot of it is underwater. I think we could fill several ships with it, maybe as many as a dozen."

Wisthia pressed her fingertips to her mouth. "In a way that's worse than the mystery fleet. I am very glad you did not talk about this treasure to anyone, and I'm even more glad Chim thought to reveal who you were before I did, so that diplomatic courtesy kept Kliessin from dousing you with kinthus and wringing your entire past from you."

Barend sighed. "Inda wants to use it to rescue the Iascan treasury. The kingdom's been pretty much shipwrecked by the embargo and war. I know all about going through proper channels to turn it into credit—"

"Barend. Try to see this matter through others' eyes. First, no Marlovan king has ever taken the least interest in diplomacy, with the result that you are profoundly ignorant. Dangerously so, because I don't think you know just how ignorant you are. Second, you bring that much gold into any harbor at once, and you'll throw the local economy into such turmoil you'll have not just that king astir—" She shook her head. "No, all that is for later. You don't even have it yet, am I right? That's what you wanted the fleet for. There is then time for careful—*very* careful—negotiation. Careful, and discreet."

She paused, thinking: *I could not be a proper Marlovan mother to you, Evred my son. But I can at least be a proper ally.* Out loud, "You may leave that to me. In the meantime, you are theoretically free—"

"Theoretically?"

"—though I notice Kliessin did not interview you herself. Surely you observed the armed guards everywhere? Perhaps your first step ought to begin with an act of good will."

"Good will? Aunt Wisthia, what's going on?"

"What's going on is a stalemate between all the players in the harbor—from sailor to king—and that pirate fleet squatting out there in the middle of the bay. Your act of good will might be to get rid of them."

"Pirate fleet? There are no more fleets . . . Oh." "Pirate" in everyone's view, perhaps, but the fleet's. "You mean Fox is out there. With the *Death*. How did that happen?"

She lifted her cup in salute. "The entire city is waiting for you to tell us."

Within a week after Convocation, Iasca Leror's royal city had resumed regular life.

The royal couple returned to eating dinner with the Harskialdna and Harandviar; it was the only time of day that Hadand could get Evred to sit down to anything but work. Though she could not get him to lay aside kingdom affairs even that long: he almost always brought up business.

At the end of that first week of the new year, Evred said, "Inda, you haven't begun teaching the King's Runners your style of fighting?"

"Waited for Convocation." Inda flattened his hand in negation. "Should I make it required? I thought we were going to run it volunteer. They have to unlearn so much."

Evred tapped on the table. Hadand had yet to accustom herself to the differences in Evred since he'd returned from the north. The Venn were not an immediate threat, he seemed pleased with the kingdom's progress, but he worked harder than ever, sometimes falling asleep at his desk.

He hadn't come to her rooms once since Convocation ended.

"If I give the order," Evred began slowly.

Inda poked a chunk of bread in Evred's direction. "If you give the order, they'll do it. Probably resent it, too. What's the necessity? Vedrid has been drilling them extra hard, and we know how many your Runner to Ola-Vayir took down before they killed him last spring. And he was old."

Evred knew why he wanted his men learning the two-knife style: because it had been developed by Fox Montredavan-An. Evred could not believe a Marlovan would design a fighting style superior to that taught at home and waste it solely on pirates. If Savarend "Fox" Montredavan-An came back with a force seeking to redress what he imagined to be the wrongs of his family, Evred wanted a force to meet them with equivalent training.

But he couldn't find a way to bring that up and not sound like his uncle, looking for conspiracies everywhere.

Hadand and Tdor waited, Hadand watching Evred's tense profile, Tdor's attention on Inda, who just hunched over his bowl, spooning up his tomato-and-cheese soup as if nothing was amiss.

Maybe nothing *was* amiss. Evred ceased tapping, then said, "Volunteers, then. And see how it goes. Open it to any who wish to learn. Will you begin it soon?"

"Sure." Inda's spoon waved in a circle. "Then I get someone to practice with." He grinned.

Tdor said, "What about us?"

Inda looked her way blankly.

"Women." She tapped her chest. "That fighting style is based on our Odni. Some of your improvements aren't any use to us, using men's different balance points, but a lot of it would improve our own performance. Does 'any who wish to learn' include us?"

"Why not?" Inda answered, before Evred could speak. "Everyone learns it on my ships. My former ships." Inda dropped the spoon into his bowl. "I know it's not custom for the men and women to train together, but why not begin? No harm in it that I saw when I was at sea."

Tap, tap, tap. Eyes turned toward the king.

"Run it as you will," Evred said, and they turned their attention to the rapidly cooling meal.

The next morning, the half-watch before dawn, Tdor walked down to the inner court set aside for the new lessons. The air was bitter; the cold leached through the soles of her winter boots and two pairs of the thickest wool socks. She was the only woman there, though all the King's Runners and a sizable number of the guard had turned out despite Inda's uncompromising insistence on the extra early time.

Tdor turned her back on the men. She was the Harandviar, and she knew no one would say anything to her. But she felt all those eyes. Most were curious, many were affronted: men learned attack, women defended. If women were here, was this new style really just fancy door-guarding?

Inda began the warm-ups without any ceremony. Most of these exercises were easy because they were designed for balance as well as strength. They were also meant to get their arms working as a unit, the way the women used their knives in the Odni. Tdor cast a glance at the torchlit lines of men when she whirled and kicked, arms in the first Wind defense. She was startled to see how difficult it was for the men to use their left hands. Most jerked the left forearm back into the habitual shield position.

When Inda motioned her to a place in the middle as demonstrator, there was no sound of protest.

And so it went for the next few days.

After a week, Inda did not just have Tdor demonstrate warm-ups, he asked her to show them proper form in sparring exercises. The first time was so disconcerting she almost stumbled, flushing furiously, but Inda's hands were steady and firm, his smile just for her. "Pretend I'm Jeje," he whispered, and she laughed, remembering the dark-browed young woman she'd liked instantly. And had missed when Inda returned without her.

By the end of the first month, more women appeared, though they kept to one side of the parade ground, the men ceding them the space wordlessly. Fewer men were there as well, as Inda had predicted, though all the King's Runners remained, from the boys in training to the older ones who mostly confined themselves to keeping records. He never said anything about who came or went, just taught whoever was there. Once in a while he'd choose someone out of the crowd and he wouldn't go easy and slow. He'd set aside his knives and use only his hands, becoming a whirl of gray coat skirts until the fellow was lying on the ice-cold stones, the side of Inda's stiffened fingers against the beating veins in his neck.

Tdor could not see what Inda saw revealed in these fellows' movements; the men looked uniformly awkward to her, as they tried with varying success to force long-trained muscles into new patterns. She suspected some kind of challenge from the ones he picked out, which Inda answered equally wordlessly.

By the end of two months, Mistress Gand and the female teachers at the queen's training had begun to join Tdor each morning. Hadand had ridden to Nelkereth on her promised trip to interview people for the coveted northern post or she would have been there as well. The Runners she hadn't taken were all there.

One morning they finished just as snow began to fall in earnest. Tdor walked away with Mistress Gand, who whacked her hands against her sides. "Fingers gone numb," she said. "Tdor, I'm seeing some adaptations we can make. The men seem to have learned that real power comes from the belly, but they still drive it through the shoulders."

Tdor had tucked her hands into her armpits. "Yes! I've been thinking the same, there's too much upper body in their version of the Leaps, they don't see how to use their hips—"

The women ahead parted wordlessly. Tdor broke off just as Evred strode down the passage toward them. He was rarely here for the drills—he trained with Vedrid and Kened, his First Runners.

"Carry on, everyone." Evred touched his chest in response to the thumps of fists against thick coats. "Where's Inda? I've a question."

"Went to guard side—" Tdor began, then remembered that magic ring Evred wore, and so did Inda. She wondered if he asked out of courtesy. This thought gave her that inward prickle of worry.

Evred made a polite gesture of thanks and walked on with hasty steps.

Mistress Gand was believed to be tougher than her husband by the girls under her exacting eye. Few of them saw the humor in her sun-bleached brows and lined face. "Venn on their way back?" she commented.

"I'll order lunch," Tdor returned. "I heard they like pickles."

Mistress Gand hooted a laugh. They parted, Mistress Gand to drill the women and Tdor to run upstairs to Hadand's office to attack that pile first.

So she was surprised when Inda appeared not long after, and kicked the door shut so hard the slam echoed in a sharp clap off the stone walls.

Tdor swerved on her mat, staring. She'd seen Evred angry several times since they'd come to the royal castle. He was frightening when angry, the way he turned to stone, his voice so soft you shouldn't be able to hear it, but you did, because of the precision of his consonants.

Since his return, she'd never seen Inda angry. Inda's anger startled Tdor into a laugh, though the impulse was less humorous than a weird thrill of uneasiness.

A glint of gold flickered across the office like a captured ray of sunlight. *Clank!* Inda's magical golden case hit the dull knife Hadand kept as an opener for sealed letters.

"Inda?"

He slammed his fist against the door. "Evred just got a note from Barend. You know, that locket thing they have." He smacked his chest. "Barend doesn't have one of these *damn* things."

"Should he have?"

"Evred didn't want him taking one. If he had, I could make even bigger mistakes," Inda exclaimed, and kicked the door frame. "Damn. Damn! I *knew* Fox hated us—that is, Marlovans—but I thought we'd resolved it all. I thought if I trusted him, then it would—oh, shit. It doesn't matter, I was just stupid." He booted a small stool, which skittered across the bare stone floor and clattered into one of the chests containing old orders and letters.

Tdor rose, her heart beating fast. "You're here, Inda. You must want me for something besides watching you kick apart my office."

Inda flushed red to the ears and stumbled to a stop. "I'm sorry, Tdor." He dropped onto the other mat.

Tdor sat down next to him as he clawed back loosened strands of hair with a shaking hand. "Barend wanted to know if I'd ordered Fox to Bren with the *Death* and the others. Of course I didn't!"

"Fox Montredavan-An is in Bren?"

"With my fleet! It's my fault. I told him about my secret plan—"

"What secret plan?"

"Oh, there's no use in explaining now. When I think how *close* we came to fixing all the problems . . . Damnation!" With his left hand he picked up the gold case and flung it with all his strength into the fireplace, where it clattered down directly onto the Fire Sticks. "What use is that thing anyway? No one writes to me, not even Tau anymore. Why did he stop overnight like that? Because I bored him? Jeje never wrote to me, not once. The only thing I brought about with these damn things was getting Noddy killed, and setting Fox onto Barend—"

"Inda. Inda, tell me what happened." She got up and used a wrist knife to poke the case off the fire. It had already begun to twist in the heat.

Inda stared at the ceiling, breathing hard until he got a grip on himself. "Barend's in Bren. Says Fox and the fleet showed up. So I wrote to Fox just now. Asked him why he went to Bren. Asked him what he intended to do there."

He tended to keep his right hand close to his side, especially after practice. Now it opened, and there lay a crumbled strip of paper. Tdor bent over Inda's palm and read the slanting letters:

I have yet to decide.

Chapter Fourteen

THE docks in Bren Harbor were deserted except for the roaming patrols of guards, all fully armed. On every single rooftop along the quay—warehouses, stores, taverns—guards roosted in the cold, snowy weather, bows to hand and a cache of arrows apiece.

Behind windows, people watched. They speculated to no purpose, worried, cursed, laughed, laid bets. Others threw up their hands and went on with their lives, some with a pirate-thumping weapon ready to hand, just in case.

The sinister black pirate trysail floated in the middle of the harbor, its consorts at either side, crews (at least a hundred spyglasses made certain) ready to flash sail at word or sign from the lone red-haired figure, dressed all in black, lounging on the captain's deck.

Through an entire day the spyglasses stayed trained on that ship. Not long after nightfall, a stir at the main dock brought word relayed up to the watch commander: "Woman wants to hire a boat to take her out to the pirate."

"What? This I have to witness."

Jeje never saw Barend. As soon as she returned from her interview, she skinned out of the fancy clothes, rolled them up into a ball (with some regret at treating silk with so little respect), and shoved them into her bag. She got into her sailor gear, pulled on the shapeless wool hat hanging by the door for everyone to use when going into the vegetable garden. Always scrupulous (according to her lights) Jeje left her old knit sock cap—too obviously a sailor's cap—in its place. Then she hefted her new gear bag and under cover of darkness slipped through the garden, over the back fence, through another garden, and into the street, walking anonymously past the patrolling guards.

She spent the night at Chim's, as the weather had turned too rough for rowing out into the harbor. Then there was the matter of the King's Guard having the entire harbor locked down. Chim sent word to a couple of his more trusty watermen to be standing by when Jeje reached the first perimeter.

"Who are you? Where are you going?" the sentry captain asked.

"I want to hire a boat." Jeje poked a thumb toward the hire craft floating at the dock. "Get back on board."

"On board what?"

"My ship."

"Which would be?"

By now she was surrounded. In the lantern light, naked swords gleamed. Not the time to be mouthy. "My ship's out there on the water—"

"Look at this," one interrupted, pointing under the terrible hat, where her ruby glittered in the lantern light. "She's gotta be the pirate Jeje. I think you better get the commander."

"I'm not a pirate." At the various shufflings, shiftings, and snortings of disbelief, Jeje sighed. "Look, no one wants any trouble. I just want to get back on deck. Princess Kliessin already interviewed me yesterday," she added.

The mention of the princess caused more looks and shuffles, then someone sent someone else loping off into the darkness as the warriors closed in around her, standing within sword length.

They stood like that, no one talking (Jeje wondering if she'd start a war if she asked the one who'd been eating fried onions not to stand on her toes) until the approach of running feet broke the circle. A tall, strong man with grizzled hair marched up. This just had to be the watch commander.

"You belong to yon pirate?" he asked.

"Yes." That was simplest. "I've been acting as envoy," Jeje said. "Saw the princess yesterday. Now I'm supposed to report back." She jerked her mittened thumb toward the *Death*.

Heads snapped seaward, then back. Another day she'd remember that and laugh. Now she just stood there, jaw jutted, feet planted, arms crossed, mittened hands gripping her knife hilts.

"Send her." The commander waved, his attitude adding *Good riddance.*

Chim's watermen appeared as if by magic, and Jeje, recognizing them, said loudly, "Got a boat I can hire?"

"Right at the dock," was the answer, hint hint, wink wink.

The commander rolled his eyes at this lumbering attempt at covert communication. If these people were sophisticated international spies, he was a Venn. "Row her out, and *you'll* report back to me before you run off to Chim," he added grimly, causing the would-be secret emissaries to deflate a little.

Onboard the *Death,* Fox had posted sharp eyes at the mastheads, watching the coast as steadily as it watched him. He'd expected someone to row out and demand his business; the long wait made him wonder what was going on inside the city. He was considering whom to send when at last a boat set out from the main dock, lanterns aswing at every heave of the oars.

"I think that's Jeje," Mutt yelled, his voice cracking. He was acting as lookout, and as captain of the foremast bow team. And then a triumphant aside to one of his cronies on the mizzenmast, "Nugget's gonna be *fried* she wasn't here t'see her first."

"She's too busy showing off for Cap'n Eflis," came the hoarse reply.

Mutt scowled into the darkness.

Fox was able to hear the sotto voce conversation going on over his head, but the time for absolute silence had passed. And Mutt knew it.

So Fox snapped out his glass, satisfied himself that this was indeed Jeje on her way through the night-black, icy waters. He said, "Signal the captains of *Cocodu* and *Rapier.*"

Then he returned to his cabin for the first time since dawn and sat down at the desk. Two movements were habitual: with one hand he reached for the desk drawer containing the gilt-edged black book, and with the other he touched the golden case. When his fingers tingled on contact with the gold, he shoved the drawer shut again. After months without any message, it seemed Inda had remembered someone besides his damned Montrei-Vayirs.

Fox, what are you doing in Bren?

Fox eyed the large, scrawling letters. It could be Inda's fingers were almost as numb as Fox's were now, but Fox read anger in those sloppy letters, and laughed. "I don't yet know, but you're not going to find that out," he said aloud.

Inda deserved to sweat. How stupid he was, to even consider throwing away ten generations of pirate treasure on those fool Montrei-Vayirs, whose own stupidity had run the kingdom aground in the first place.

Fox warmed his fingers over a candle, dashed off an answer, and tossed the golden case back onto the desk as Jeje's boat thumped up against the hull. On deck he discovered the older crewmates surrounding Jeje, some pounding her on the back, everyone talking at once.

Well aware of the spyglasses trained on them from the shore, Fox flicked a drifting snowflake from his arm and said, "Come into the cabin." And as soon as the door was shut, "Why did you leave Inda?"

"To find Tau's mother." Jeje glared around the cabin. Looking for signs of Inda, perhaps? No, Inda had never left any signs of habitation anywhere he'd lived, and she'd know that. Disapproving of the row of books on the carved shelf? The golden Colendi gondola lamps, or the astonishing silk wall hanging of raptors taking flight in the pale shades of dawn? All legitimate pirate loot.

Jeje eyed Fox's smile as he dropped onto his chair and propped a booted foot on the edge of the table. A knife hilt gleamed in the boot top, winking with golden highlights as the beautiful lamp swung forward, back.

"Well?" she said finally. "I'm waiting for your usual nasty remark about Tau. Or his mother."

"Don't tell me," he said derisively. "She's a long lost princess."

Jeje almost laughed out loud. Fox was interested despite

himself. She thought about what she'd discovered, and decided he'd have to ask. "No. That is, long-lost yes, princess, no. So where's *Vixen*, and who's in charge?"

"Right now, Nugget—"

"She's alive?"

"Showed up in Parayid. All but one arm. Instead, you might say, she'd armed herself with the conviction she was now everyone's responsibility to protect and defend." His smile turned nasty. "I've been thrashing that out of her since summer. Now she's teaching herself to move around the rigging, either to impress Eflis, or to show me up. Maybe both."

From outside boat calls:

"Boats, hai!"

"Cocodu!"

"Rapier!"

Dasta and Gillor had arrived from their ships.

Jeje turned her attention back to Fox. "She's playing in the rigging on *Vixen*?"

"No. Maybe. After she and two loudmouths rerig the scout and finish with some sail shifting practice." A snort of laughter. "She'll be back in time for dawn drill. It's for backchat on deck. We had a little brush with some of Boruin's former friends just off her old lair east of Danai, and Nugget acquitted herself so well she's got lippy." Fox shook with silent laughter as he glanced over his shoulder.

Jeje grinned. *Good for you, Nugget.* She hopped to the stern window and peered through the drifts of fog. The *Vixen* was only a faint silhouette, just emerging from the island's lee side, sails shifting with commendable speed. It would be a while before it tacked across the harbor.

Jeje fought off the strong surge of longing to see her scout again, and drew in a grateful breath of brine air, loving even the tang of wood-mold and slushy ice and a trace of hemp. No better smell in all the world.

The cabin door banged open and there were Dasta and Gillor, looking tough and weathered. *I wonder if I look land-soft to them,* she thought, then leaped up, laughing, to find herself squeezed in a rib-creaking hug by Dasta, and then by Gillor. Laughing questions, half-answers, a sudden, sharp, "Where's Tcholan?" to be reassured by, "He's in command of the blockade—guarding one end, and Eflis at the other. Even a floating plank won't get past those two."

Fox cut through the chatter. "Jeje was in the middle of her report when you interrupted. Do continue, whenever they will let you."

Gillor snorted and dropped onto the bench, Dasta preferring to lean against a bulkhead where he could see everyone.

Jeje smacked her hands together. "So good to be back! I hate land."

Dasta ducked his head, making a sympathetic gesture. "But you went to help Inda."

"She went," Fox drawled, "to discover Taumad's mysterious heritage. And seems to have found his mother. Behold my curiosity."

Gillor snorted even louder, though Dasta thought, *I'll wager anything that for once he's telling the truth.*

Gillor said to Jeje, "Was it true pirates got her?"

"One of Marshig's gang was holding Parayid. Got bored waiting for battle. Wanted to burn the town down for fun. She offered to trade herself for leaving the town be. Which is why Parayid was only partially destroyed, unlike some of the other harbors."

Dasta looked disgusted. "So she's now a Coco?"

Fox's brows rose in satirical question.

"Not her! That is, she agreed to be the captain's favorite, but just for a while. She hated the captain's habits of carving up crewmembers who'd made him mad. She asked him not to. When he wouldn't stop, she organized a mutiny. Wasn't hard, she said."

Gillor whooped for joy. "So she's a pirate captain? Why didn't we hear about her?"

"Because she isn't anymore. She objected to *anyone* being carved up. Which is what pirates *do*. So she proposed they become a pleasure ship. Hiring out to rich people who might like the danger of cruising on a real pirate ship. Nightly parties? Drink, dance, song, and fun? The pirates apparently were lightning-struck with the notion of being paid for sex. Naturally they intended to rob their customers blind as soon as the cruise was done, though she tried to explain that you didn't get return business that way."

Dasta guffawed. Fox shaded his eyes, but Jeje could see the smile in the corners of his mouth.

Gillor said doubtfully, "Were these pirates good looking?"

"My understanding was, no."

"Strange." Gillor slapped her hands on the table. "At least she wasn't killed. So why isn't Tau with you?"

"He's probably still traveling." Jeje jerked her thumb toward the rise of land. "Why are you here in Bren, of all places?"

Gillor shrugged. "Cruising the strait."

Dasta's thumb turned toward Fox. "Wanted to see if the Venn were really gone, and who was runnin' things in the strait. Bren being the best harbor for news."

Jeje looked skeptical. Why not settle in at Freedom Island for the winter and get the news from there? Something was missing. A quick look convinced her that whatever it was, Fox knew and the others didn't.

Dasta dug his thumbnail into the polished wood of the bulkhead, his brow perplexed. "I get you were finding Tau's mother, and I get that she's still alive, but I don't get your place in all that."

Jeje lifted a shoulder. "I met Inda's wife-to-be. She said something that made me curious. And, well, Inda didn't need me, not after he and his king friend put together an army. So I thought I'd investigate."

"Ah." Dasta's interest sharpened at Inda's name. "So is Inda really behind the rumors about the Venn—"

"How about later? I'm thirsty now, and—"

"Later'll do. Fox, are we leaving, and if so where to? If the Venn aren't coming after us, I wouldn't mind sailing back to Freedom to spend the rest of winter in comfort."

"Give it another day," Fox said.

Dasta and Gillor exchanged looks. They knew Fox was up to something, and eventually they'd find it out. Maybe Jeje would find out sooner.

They welcomed Jeje again and left; as the sounds of their departure thunked through the hull, Fox just waited, his expression derisive.

Jeje crossed her arms, glowering at him.

Water splashed against the hull, and the ship rocked gently. Footfalls on the deck became muffled: the snow was falling faster, masking the shoreline.

Fox broke the silence. "You were gloating, Jeje."

"I was not!"

"You were. I suspect you're itching to tell me that Taumad is a long-lost cousin of mine, but I figured that out years ago. That would make him the outcast of the western Deis—his grandmother disinherited because she skipped out of a duty marriage and ran off with my aunt."

"They were both supposed to make duty marriages, I was told. Skipped out instead. Good for them," Jeje added with trenchant emphasis.

"My aunt vanished over the border a week after my father was born, considering herself freed from the obligation of a duty marriage to produce an heir. That she was also disinherited doesn't mean much in my family at present."

Jeje sighed.

"So the sober branch of the Deis, fresh from their triumph at having their Joret turn up as next queen of the Adranis, unbuttoned about the family scapegrace, eh?"

"Could be you're right."

"And because the Adranis mimic Colend"—Fox's expression was more derisive than usual—"Taumad's mother flounced in expecting them to bow and smile, despite her having earned a living in trade. If you're a Dei, doesn't matter what you do, so long as you do it with *style*." He leaned forward. "And now you expect Taumad to take up palace life like he was born to it."

Jeje flipped him the back of her hand. "You are a shit. You know that?"

Fox laughed. "Yes, and so is my long-lost cousin. We're so alike, isn't that what you were going to imply?"

"You're not at all like Tau. He's actually got a heart."

"He's a Dei," Fox retorted. "They don't have hearts. They're just very adept at making you think they do. Is Barend in yon harbor?"

"Why do you need to know?" Jeje asked. Then, exasperated, continued, "Has Inda made some sort of plan? My magic letter case got stolen."

"Inda's got plans, yes. I believe he's sent Barend to raid the treasure on Ghost Island, and he was to get suitable conveyance here. Inda seems to have decided that we will squander that treasure on his childhood friends."

"*We.*" Jeje eyed him. "And you're going along with it?"

Fox extended a hand. "I'm here, aren't I?"

Jeje squirmed with uneasiness and distrust. She couldn't write to Inda to get the truth. Oh, but Barend could, couldn't he? Surely Inda gave him some kind of magical communication thing. "The Brens thought Inda's fleet we were training was going to be some kind of Marlovan navy. My guess is, they want to get rid of Barend. *And* us. If you send me ashore, I can report that we'll be leaving as soon as we have Barend. Then we can go do Inda's errand. How's that?"

Fox smiled. "I'll get Mutt to row you ashore. He's dying to give the back of his hand to that army glowering at us along the quay."

The next morning a triumphant Mutt returned with Barend.

The older hands were all glad to see Barend again, which surprised him. His squinty eyes were crescents of good will as he endured hearty buffets on his skinny back, and questions roared out that he hadn't a hope of answering.

"Good to be on deck again," he said, over and over.

"Shake the stink o'land!" and like pleasantries greeted him.

Fox stood on the captain's deck, smiling faintly. Mutt sidled looks around, determining with the antennae of the young that Nugget was not present, and turned in to his long-earned rest. Jeje, aboard the *Vixen* once again, and floating abaft the *Death* where she could see the captain's deck through her glass, eyed Fox's smile in distrust. There was nothing she could do, so she went back to working the scout craft's crew as they took it apart almost down to the keel, and restowed it, cleaner and squared to her satisfaction.

Snow started to fall in earnest, blanketing rigging, yards, and the deck. When the crew realized Barend wasn't going to tell them about his two years away, those who had to returned to duty, the rest retreated to the wardroom below where it was warm.

Fox stood at the cabin door, his manner one of waiting. *Better get it over with,* Barend thought, and walked in.

Fox shut the cabin door. "So Inda sent you to fetch the treasure, eh? Does he really believe gold is going to redress five generations of Montrei-Vayir blunders?"

Barend's hand moved toward his chest, then fell away again. He turned his attention to those angry green eyes. Either two years away had mellowed his memory of Fox, or Fox had got even tougher. And angrier.

Barend said, "You can set me adrift soon's we're out of sight of this harbor. I'll be about my business on my own."

"No, no," Fox drawled. "Wouldn't dream of it. Who better to get you safely to Ghost Island than us?"

Barend did not ask if that was an observation or a threat.

"You can have your old quarters." Fox extended a hand toward the captain's deck. "And your place. My shipmaster is presently with Tcholan."

Barend made a sign of agreement.

He waited through a couple of watches, until midnight. When the lights were out in the cabin, he slipped out to let down a boat. Despite his care, Fox loomed out of the darkness, and reached for him.

The fight was short and vicious. Fox wrenched every joint in Barend's body before, with calculated deliberation, he broke Barend's arm. His writing arm. Then turned him loose on the deck, all without a word.

Later—much later—when Barend was able to check his gear, he found the scroll case that Wisthia had given him was gone.

Chapter Fifteen

PRINCE Valdon of Anaeran-Adrani was unforgivably late to the Duke of Elsaraen's ball, but when you're a prince, you're forgiven anyway, even by a duke. He rubbed a finger over a floating strand of silk loosened from the embroidered pattern of leaves and berries on his sleeve. The turned-back cuff had caught against a place where a gilt flourish had separated from the wood carving around the carriage door. He sighed as he vaulted up the shallow marble stairs of the ducal mansion, the sapphires on his dancing shoes winking in the light of blue glass lamps.

Footmen sprang to open the front doors, which had been closed when the host and hostess went to join their party; the enormous foyer looked empty. The dragon-wing marquetry doors to the ballroom stood wide, inlaid fantastic patterns gleaming richly in the brilliant beeswax luminescence of two hundred candles.

The duke's gold marble ballroom had been built in a time when straight lines were unfashionable; complicated curves and vaultings led upward from turnip-top notched archways. The ceiling was midnight blue at the highest point, fading to pale blue at a marble ledge marked by carved festoons of gilt laurel leaves. The great chandeliers had been taken out. Two hundred candles formed a galaxy of tiny floats of cut crystal and mirror. A vigilant mage kept them in a slow pattern of movement, so it was like looking up at a sky full of dancing stars.

As Prince Valdon crossed the foyer, gazing through the twin archways of the door to those moving lights, movement on his periphery warned him that he was not alone after all.

Lord Randon Shagal had seen his cousin's carriage arrive at the royal palace earlier in the day. Assuming that Valdon would attend the ball as his wife was here, he had decided to get the worst over with.

On Prince Valdon's arrival he strolled out to intercept him.

Valdon paused, noting the ironic near grimace on Randon's usually pleasant face. "Trouble?"

Randon lifted a hand, tossing back the lace at his wrist. The diamond on his little finger described an arc of winking lights. "Yaska."

"Not you, too! Half the court has been writing busily to me about how he's been laying siege to Joret while I've been gone. Half worried, half gloating. What can I do?"

"Nothing." Randon shrugged elaborately. "No gloat, and no worry, either, but I thought you'd want to know going in."

"It was inevitable."

"So don't drink anything. That way you won't choke at the disgusting sight."

"It won't be disgusting." Prince Valdon gave his cousin a mocking smile, and kissed his fingers. "You know it won't be disgusting at all. Excepting only Elsaraen's new duchess, they will be the two handsomest people in the room."

They stepped inside. Valdon swept a glance over the glitter and gleam of gems and rich, bright fabrics of the dancers on the ballroom floor. At the very center, two dark heads contrasted with the whirl of color.

Footmen had run ahead to fetch the ducal pair, and here they were, smiling and bowing—the deep bow setting the pattern for the entire room full of people, including the dancers in the middle of the floor.

The musicians stopped, accustomed to the needs of protocol. Valdon straightened from his bow, lifted a hand, and the musicians recommenced.

He followed his host and hostess to the refreshments, answering their polite queries out of habit as he gave the floor another sweep. From this angle he could see down the ever dividing and reforming lines.

There they were. The sight of Joret's clean, straight movements, so unlike the fluttering grace of the courtiers, jolted him with sweet anguish. Every time he had to go away on duty journeys, he looked forward to the pleasure of seeing her on his return. His chest hurt. He tried to breathe.

Beyond her floating shades of rose and mauve and cream, Lord Yaskandar Dei circled, tall and elegant in those Colendi clothes made up of darkwood brown and a difficult-to-define shade that probably had some stylish name in Colend but reminded Valdon of antique pewter.

Valdon caught both their gazes. How different were those wide, long-lashed Dei eyes: his wife's happy smile below her blue gaze, and Yaska's slack-lidded golden challenge, about as warm as a pair of new-struck coins. *Go ahead and get half my court to wear those tight pants,* Prince Valdon thought as he flicked a hand in casual salute. *I'm not going to yip at your heels.* He had to admit the long paneled robe slit up the sides moved well if you had the shoulders for it, and though Valdon had rarely glimpsed the ocean, he was certain sailors did not wear hip-snug pants with those wide legs. They didn't look like you could sit down in them without serious damage where it would hurt the most.

A shift of silken fabric, a slight, well-bred cough, and he realized his fleeting look had turned into a stare. Yes, and everyone was aware of it. Damn.

"A glass of punch," Valdon said to the footman with the golden scooper poised over a crystal cup. "Thanks." And turned to the waiting duchess, who he knew would soon make him laugh.

Joret saw him catch himself, and smiled at her partner. "You were saying?" she asked.

Yaska found Joret's smile puzzling. So far, this delicate pursuit was not progressing according to well-practiced habit, but he would have been sorry to find even so distant a relation predictable. They were both Deis, after all. Even if the western branch of the family had gone regrettably provincial.

"Is this conversation or flirtation?" he asked, giving her a teasing glance.

"Whatever you like."

"Under the eyes of your husband?" The dance took them apart, but brought them back again. Yaska's smile was rueful. "A surprising twist that I have to admit I find delicious."

"Good." Joret's earrings glinted as she dipped under his arm; the corner of her eye quirked in amusement.

"Good?" His eyelids lifted in a semblance of surprise.

Wrists arched, toes pointed, they separated, pacing sedately down the dance. He was so used to being the center of attention he went on the alert only when it shifted elsewhere; she was aware of eyes everywhere, darting glances half-hidden by fans; in the lingering gazes of the two closest women Joret perceived their appreciation of Yaskandar's perfect combination of muscle and grace as he posed, turned, and bowed.

"And so?" he prompted as they pressed their palms together to make the dancer's bridge, his voice so low only she could hear.

Joret waited. The couple at the top of the dance minced down the line under the archway of jewel-decorated hands. Every nerve was alive, sensitive to Yaska's proximity: the silken swing of his hair, the whisper of fabric over long muscles, his breathing. His scent. The cat-tawny complexities of his eyes.

"And so?" he repeated.

She knew her palms were damp.

His hands were cool and dry, his clasp light.

She looked up, and he tipped his head, giving her a slow, intimate smile before turning away; from the angle of his head, she knew that he'd shot a questing glance in Valdon's direction.

When the dance brought him back to her side, he bent his head and, his lips a hairsbreadth from touching her ear, he whispered, "And so?"

He was being deliberately provocative, that she'd known from the beginning; the question was, who he was trying to provoke. "And so I'm glad you're enjoying our flirtation now that Valdon is here," she said, amazed at the tight spiraling of disappointment and hilarity within her. "Surely that ought to be plain enough."

"Shift your mind for a moment from your Valdon." The dance separated them.

She whirled around in a small circle, palm to palm with the laughing red-haired daughter of a baroness. Two weeks Yaska had been talking poetry with Joret, playing music for her (and he was very good, too), riding in company with her, dancing with her, racing over the hills on a garland hunt. Talking poetry and plays with others as she listened.

Once he began discussing the hidden meanings of the minor key flute flourishes that the Nare Daraen musician-spies put in the middle of traditional melodies. That had occurred during the bad old days when the Sartoran world empire was breaking up.

Most of the company had not learned this bit of history, but she had—and she noted the quick flash of eyelids betraying his surprise at her knowledge. She didn't know the flute-code as music, but as markings on paper; she did not tell him that Fareas-Iofre had trained the Castle Tenthen girls to use them in the coded letter writing that all Marlovan women used to a greater or lesser degree.

Joret knew that as Yaskandar entertained them with stories about how he and his friends used to put the symbols in songs just to flirt under the long, grim nose of the Sartoran queen, he was testing her. Not just her thinking, but her training.

Joret was intrigued and attracted; she liked the tingle when he brushed against her, the thrill of his brief touch. Amazing, how as simple a thing as attraction made the senses sharpen.

Now he was trying to seduce her right under Valdon's eyes.

Exasperation ran through her, chased by laughter. She could not understand Yaska's whim—it had to be whim—but it seemed related in some unfathomable way to how Valdon found it far more erotic to watch her perform her morning knife drills than to view a scantily clad fan dancer trained in the arts of seduction. There was something of competition here, and danger, and even a hint of restrained violence. As if part of the allure was the very act of restraint.

When the circle brought her back to Yaska she smiled. "But that's the point. I don't want to shift my mind from Valdon. Isn't that supposed to be signified by this?" She lifted her hand, where the ring glinted on her heart finger.

Step, step, whirl, step step, whirl, clasp of hands. She felt through the subtlety of his grip that he was aware of her sweaty palms. The dimple at the corner of his mouth deepened.

"The topic was just you and me," he said mildly. "And not in the context of marriage."

"I don't believe Valdon's inclinations run toward triangles."

His brows lifted as she turned under his arm. Once again he bent, and this time his lips just brushed her ear. "Do yours?"

"It doesn't matter." Skip, twirl, and back again. "Because his don't. Part of the ring vow is accepting each other's boundaries."

"I enjoy excellent wine—"

At least he plays fair, and didn't say porridge, she thought, a laugh bubbling inside her chest.

"—but I wouldn't make a diet of it."

The obvious response to such an obvious comment was to point out that he'd never tasted the wine of marriage, but surely he knew all that. Besides, the dance was ending and she wanted this discussion over before they parted; she'd discovered that prolonging intimate conversations in public was often taken as a signal for dalliance. *Time for Marlovan bluntness*. "I enjoy flirting, but I made a vow. I intend to keep it." There, that felt good—though she had to laugh at herself, knowing from childhood that the moral high ground always felt good.

But only if your auditor recognized you up there above them.

"What about family necessity?" he asked, and she tumbled down.

"Necessity?" she repeated, stung. Surprised to discover herself stung. *Have I come to expect everyone's devotion as my due?* "Well at least you don't chatter about love," she said, trying for balance.

."Love." He exhaled the word, short and sharp. "Acquit me of the tedium of hope-driven self-destruction."

The words were soft, quickly spoken. Her heart knocked against her ribs.

For a single thumping heartbeat she saw past his smiling mask to the tangle of anger and pain he hid behind it. The next heartbeat brought the conviction that she was not the cause, but neither was she the anodyne: his mask was in place again.

His gaze met hers during the three remaining encounters of the dance, clasp, turn, step, and bow. She sensed challenge.

The dance ended. At random she accepted the next partner who asked, and so the evening lurched along until at last Prince Valdon had finished his round of the older folks, answering questions and smoothing political ripples. He joined his wife for the last dance of the evening.

"We need to talk," she murmured as they bowed.

He waited until they were doing hands round, then it was his turn for covert commentary. "Please don't kill him in a duel. Would cause such a diplomatic mess."

She choked on a laugh. He smiled at her, aware of the court seeing her laughter, and set himself to enjoy the remainder of the dance.

At last it was over. They said their farewells to the duke and duchess, whose house was being packed by an army of servants as the tired guests drifted out; by the next evening the ducal pair would be on the road to their castle in the north.

"Shall we walk?" Valdon asked. "Or are your feet tired? You've been dancing all evening."

She chuckled. "That's not tiring. A full day and night of castle war games is tiring."

"Don't tell me you didn't have fun doing those war games." He waved to his carriage driver, who lifted his hand in salute then drove away from the best spot in front of the front steps; though the last to arrive, he always had precedence. He grinned, liking the royal pair and loving his job.

"War games were great fun." She laced her fingers with Valdon's, swinging their hands as they walked past the drivers and footmen in their various liveries standing about in small groups, chatting and drinking from flasks. One noticed them and hastily bowed, followed by the others, like wheat in the wind. Valdon waved a casual hand and they returned to their conversations.

The two paced to the end of the road, then started up the hill that curved around behind the ducal manse. Valdon gazed upward in pleasure at the sight of the peaceful stars overhead. Then he smiled at Joret, but her head was bowed, her attention on the bricks of the road. "You wanted to talk."

Her head lifted, her eyes a dense blue in the faint light from the top windows of the Elsaraens' manse, which was now just below the level of their feet. "I liked flirting with Yaska. I thought it was the same with him. But I had the sense he wanted more. He saved his question all these days, until you were watching. And I found myself disappointed by his motivations."

"Sex," he said, "is rarely easy, or simple, unless all concerned are agreed that it will be. Would you have that with Yaska?"

"No. And he didn't want that, either. That is, his goal wasn't just seduction."

"Do you know what he really wanted?"

"To compete with you, in part, and also, oh, a family thing. I hardly know how to explain."

"To preserve the Dei beauty and mystique by uniting with you just long enough to produce a child?"

"You knew?"

Valdon's smile turned wry. "Everyone talks about the Deis, you should know that."

"I'd always thought that a family secret. It sounded sensible when I grew up: from every second generation one child is picked to mate with a descendant of one of the other branches of the family. I knew about it, but never gave it a thought. My life was to be lived as Tanrid's wife. When I went on my home visits, that tradition of mating between the families was rarely ever discussed."

"So now we know what Yaska wanted, to bypass some Marlovan cousin of yours in favor of you. And you were disappointed?"

"I was disappointed that he really did not want me, in particular. Any Dei would do, and he was more interested

in tweaking you than in having me. What a salutary lesson!
Is that human nature, or just the arrogance of Joret Dei?
Here's a fellow I don't want, but I want him to want me.
Does that make sense?"

Valdon laughed. "Human nature."

"Well! Why don't I feel better? Anyway, what I wanted
to talk to you about is what happened right after I turned
him down."

He gripped her hand, listening.

"One day when I was small," she said in a slow, con-
templative voice, as their hands swung between them. They
made another turning, passing an old tower house. Through
an arched window just below the upward curve of the road
a young scribe was perfectly framed, sitting at a high desk,
bent over copy work. A lock of his hair lay against his
cheek, tangled with the fingers supporting his head as he
stippled a brilliantly colored drawing.

He passed from view, and Joret resumed. "It was the
height of summer. After a week of storm. The weather
turned hot. We girls went out to the river. I waded out in
the rushing water, so fast it tumbled I could barely stand.
The cold water pressing against me, the warmth of the sun
on my face, its light splashing over the water, all gave me
intense pleasure. I liked resisting the water, in not falling
backward to drown, in feeling the warmth of the sun on my
eyelids without opening my eyes to the sun."

"I see." He raised her hand and kissed it.

"But I am not yet done. Then a root caught at my ankle,
and nearly pulled me under. I had to fight to keep my
breath, to keep from being dragged under. I won, and flung
myself onto the bank, and that's when the clean air, the
bright sun, the rushing water were sweetest, because I'd
won the fight. For just a moment, Yaska let me see him for
real. He was far more attractive in that moment, but I still
would have said no. Knowing that was winning the fight.
Now I know my strength. It makes my vows with you the
sweeter. Now do you see?"

And he did. They passed quietly beneath the mossy
stone archway that had been built over the road to join two
of the old towers. Lights glowed in the arched windows of
the chambers above them. Just beyond, a gap piled high

with dismantled stone marked where another old tower had been taken down, to be rebuilt into a large, airy manse.

Valdon said slowly, "My attractions have always been fleeting. Until I met you I could walk away from any dalliance with mild regret, and no sense of risk, making me suspect that I will only love once. That makes my vow of fidelity to you easy to keep. But I have been preparing myself for the fact that one day, yours to me might ... not be worth keeping." His voice was light, but she felt his intensity in the grip of his hand.

"It won't happen." She gripped his hand tightly. "Because now I know what to watch for in myself, and I will not let my foot catch in the root. As for Yaska, he doesn't even know what love is. I cherish my memories of Cama Tya-Vayir, but even were I to see him again, I know the tumbling stream now, and the undercurrent, and the sun in the sky. You and I have made our house by that stream, and that's where I want to live."

He stopped, and right there in the street, between the tiled rooftops of one row of aristocratic houses and the closed doors of those on the slope above, he kissed her. A soft laugh from above, a hastily drawn curtain over a tiny window in an attic, revealed that they'd been seen, but neither cared.

They began walking uphill again; the palace spires were visible two switchbacks up.

"I had a talk with my father today." His voice lightened. "He agrees with what I did down south."

"The harbor guilds versus the trade?" she asked. Now that sea trade was starting up again, it seemed everyone had new ideas on how things should work from now on.

"Right. Joret, here's what he said. As soon as Queen Servitude dies—assuming of course she doesn't live to be five hundred, just to spite everyone—he wants to retire to our house in Eidervaen. Maybe tour other lands, like he did as a boy. Mother never got to see Sartor; she wants to go, too. That means you and I are going to be wearing the crowns. Figuratively speaking. I hate crowns. Do your Marlovans wear crowns?"

"Never saw one until I came here." She chuckled again.

"Back to the south." He grinned. "There was one more

item of business. Ever since I met you, I've tried a new
thing. I hadn't spoken of it before because I was not sure of
the wisdom of it—the first time I mentioned it to my father
he reacted in horror."

"Go on."

"It was your riding around with Gdand that caused me
to think of it. When I go myself to see to these problems,
I've begun leaving the carriage and livery and outriders.
They proceed as before, but the carriage is empty, driven
by one of the younger fellows. I put on plain clothes and
take to horse with just my own driver, who is a deedy hand
with a quarterstaff."

She laughed inside, enjoying this discovery; if their love
was a house, he kept showing her more doors to open.

"I ride around, and I see people I wouldn't otherwise.
I see *things* I wouldn't have. I spent a night in an old inn.
When I woke up early and wandered, I discovered a barn
where people were spinning glass. Did you know that
that wavery glass that you find in the countryside is spun
in plates? That's where the wave comes in. I used to love
looking at the world through that glass."

Joret smiled. "We made both kinds. Some actually prefer that glass, when the window just opens onto stone. It
can throw more splinters of light inside."

"I did not know. Well, anyway, speaking of your family.
It seems another of your relations has just crossed the border. I wore my plain clothes and spent a little time observing your relation while deciding what to do. Unlike your
decorative cousin Yaska, he exhibited no tendency to lead
a crowd of fast-riding, hard-drinking courtiers in making
trouble just to assuage their boredom. Before I left, he took
a job."

Joret knew exactly whom he meant. "I take it you had
him followed? Surely not arrested."

"Not unless he decides to raise an army."

Joret clasped his hands. "We both know where he's
going, and why. Will you let me handle this matter dis-
creetly?" Joret mentally rearranged her morning, knowing
that the duchess they'd just left, though equally tired and
about to embark on a long journey, would not deny her if
she called in private.

"I would like nothing better," he said with obvious relief, and kissed her. "I leave it to you."

The week after New Year's, when every hand aboard Tau's trader had been on deck through a day dark as night and a night made brighter than day by almost constant lightning, they were finally released in small groups to the waterlogged cabins to rest, as the ship sped through the spume and sea wrack of a departing monstrous storm. When they eased their fatigue-sodden limbs below they discovered that the mighty waves washing down the deck had broken both hatches. Water had poured in as the massive waves crashed down, then spewed out as they rode up the next wave. Most of their belongings had thus been swept out to sea—including Tau's golden case, which he'd carefully left in his hammock, along with his gear, in case the working of the ship's timbers let in water.

Just as the bitter east winds were beginning to weaken toward spring, they reached the northernmost bay of Anaeran-Adrani, where the captain and some of the crew had kin whom they had not seen or communicated with for years.

Tau thanked everyone, wished them a good journey, stepped ashore, and vanished into the harbor crowd. By day's end he had a job.

By the end of a week he'd earned enough money to travel. He bought a map and set out for the north.

Chapter Sixteen

WHILE Iasca Leror's royal city was gripped in winter,
Evred and Inda at last took their much-postponed
walk through the academy. They began with old reminiscences, talking over each other, breath clouding as they
laughed over their ten- and twelve-year-old antics. They
laughed even more as they slipped and slid on ice patches.
Then Inda asked about the years he was gone. Evred began
sharing memories as they approached the senior barracks,
which Inda had never set foot in.

Inda had begun to answer when they reached the door.
"... and you remember how much effort it took me to
learn something about those damned lances. I still don't
think I'd—ah. Here we are. I want to go in," Inda said, interrupting himself.

"It's empty. Nothing here," Evred protested mildly.

"I'm curious. I didn't get this far on Lassad's tour last
summer. He was—" Inda paused, reluctant to say *being
Smartlip*.

"Bragging," Evred finished. "I know. And I recall what
you said later that day. Look, Inda, you're going to find
flaws in all the masters. Try as I might, I could not staff the
academy with men like Gand, though I wanted to. There

aren't a lot of men like Gand—tough, wise, experienced, and able to teach. Horsepiss Noth is tough, wise, and experienced but he said he'd be terrible as a teacher. What makes him excellent for toughening up dragoons makes him terrible for dealing with boys."

Inda grimaced. "Didn't he thrash Whipstick when he had a broken arm? I didn't think twice about that when we were scrubs, but Whipstick couldn't have been more than ten."

"Yes. That was after the egg dance," Evred said, and Inda heard the regret in his voice. *Dogpiss.* "My father was very careful in selecting Gand, though his choice took everyone by surprise."

"I get it." Inda looked around, left hand on hip, right held close to his side. "I get it. Use the strengths, overlook the weaknesses. We did that with picking ship captains. I guess I thought things would be different at home."

"That we had a kingdom full of Gands for the asking?"

Inda laughed, and smacked his left hand against the lintel before opening the winter door. "Yes. Stupid, isn't it? If that had been true, everything would be different. Including you and me standing here right now."

He stepped inside, flung wide the winter shutters, and looked avidly at the battered walls, the warped floorboards, the low bed frames waiting for the old mattresses to come out of storage above the barns, where they acted as insulation for the animals all winter. There was no weight of memory to rein Inda's thoughts.

"Here's my question." He stamped numb feet on the bare wooden floor. "Gand wants me to wait on changes, but won't the Jarls sit up and howl if I don't change everything? At the banquets half of them were yapping at me about how I was going to make their boys stronger, better. Faster. What are they expecting?"

Evred leaned in the big window that opened into the coveted senior courtyard. He scarcely heard the question, so intense was the memory of sitting in this window, his favorite place during summer's still nights, golden light spilling onto the honey-colored stones below as the half-lit silhouettes of boys talked, drummed, sang, laughed. He could almost smell the dust and hay and the distant astringency of summer sage, so close was his younger self who'd sat here wondering where Inda was in the wide world and how to keep a vow of justice.

Inda seemed to think their memories were all happy. Evred gripped the knife-scarred windowsill, his gloved fingers next to a pair of initials shaped like a tree: that boy had been a year older. Rat Cassad's voice whispered in memory, after the losing battle against the Venn invasion just below Lindeth Harbor . . . *legs tendon-cut, arms smashed at the elbows. We found him on the shore with his own sword sticking up from his ribs.*

Evred turned away. "Tradition," he said finally, when he discovered Inda not just waiting, but still. He was so rarely still. Usually he rattled around and around whatever space he was in, pacing, rapping, thumping, but now he was motionless, that wide brown gaze as bright and painful as the summer sun. You did not look into the sun. "Tradition is important to us. Or so we say, but when I think about it, every generation has made significant changes from the one before, going back to when we first moved into castles. Now Hadand wants me to bring girls in as King's Runners."

Inda said, "Why not? You put girls to work in the archive for the oath project. Nothing terrible happened."

"I know. I know. It's considered an honor for families who will never inherit to have a boy invited into the King's Runners." He thought of that blood-stained, rent banner hanging over the throne, and said, "Who deserves the honor more than Hadand Tlen, the child who managed to bring what was left of the Andahi children through those terrible weeks?"

"I think it's a great idea," Inda stated. "Cama talked about her. Calls her Captain Han. You know how skimpy he is with the praise. I see this idea as a change for the better."

Evred's smile was pensive. "So you would think, Elgar the Pirate. As for the academy, the Jarls will all talk as if they expect their sons to come home ready for battle, but they'll be realistic. You could offer the older boys your Fox drills—"

Inda looked up quickly.

Evred snorted a soft laugh. "I know everyone's been calling your double-knife style Fox drills. I believe I'll survive the reminder of old family feuds. Especially since the

boys apparently think the name is related to the academy
Fox banner."

"Which also used to belong to Montredavan-An," Inda
began, but stopped when Evred paused by a bed frame,
drawing a slow breath.

"Noddy's?" Inda asked, the Montredavan-Ans forgotten.

In the distance the watch change bell clanged. Evred
said quickly, "He hated the sun in mornings. This was the
darkest corner. If I could reach down through time—" He
extended his fingers, but there was no tousled dark head
burrowed under blankets, just an empty frame and cold air.
"Let's go."

I'll never come here again, Evred thought, and closed
the shutters.

Chapter Seventeen

ON the first day of spring, all along the road Adrani
villages and towns aired their houses and put seedling
pots on windowsills, in the manner of the east end of the
continent.

Tau had crossed the broad expanse of Anaeran-Adrani,
finding its beauties and unwarlike life very much to his
taste. By the time he left the trade center Shiovhan, he was
aware that he was being followed, but he shrugged it off:
he'd deal with trouble if it came. He hired himself out to
share the driving on a northern-bound wagon train, having warned the team leader he would turn off at Elsaraen,
wherever that was.

One morning they plodded past a cracked plinth with
time- and weather-worn carved letters impossible to make
out. If he'd been alone, he would have ridden right past.
"There's your sign, you. It's old, old'r'n the moon," the
leader added.

The wagon train was slow and steady, so Tau flicked
his forehead in salute, hitched his modest carryall over
his shoulder, and jumped down without the oxen breaking rhythm. He trudged up the old road that seemed to
wind directly into the mountains. The road was edged

with white stone, arguing against poverty or some kind of isolated prison. It also argued against a pleasure house, as only a fool would build them out in the middle of nowhere and expect any business. But if his mother had for some crazy reason taken up her trade here instead of going back to Parayid, Jeje would have said so, for she approved of honest work.

He did not begin to guess at the truth until the road opened to a spectacular view of an old Sartoran eight-sided building with complicated arches and sun windows in weather-smoothed stone, enclosed by a "new" castle only a few hundred years old.

Tau stopped at a turn on the road and studied the old castle. The old sign, the well-tended terraced gardens visible in the valley below, the fine road, all gave evidence not just of wealth but of stability. One would think those good signs, so why wouldn't Jeje?

Tau's gaze finished taking in the vineyards on the north-facing hills and returned to the castle. A peculiar flutter behind Tau's ribs—not quite laughter—offered the most likely solution, one Jeje would hate.

With a pained smile, Tau descended the last way, and walked into the castle's forecourt. Servants came running out, stopping to bow.

Bows, and no word spoken yet.

Tau shook his head, following the one who indicated the way. The servant did not explain anything, by which Tau understood his mother would perform that office herself. She expected him to be surprised and pleased. The second servant relieved him of his carryall as if it were full of precious stones, and he was led up the stairs to a charmingly furnished parlor painted in a delicate blue, furnished with lyre-back chairs and low tables with half-circle legs. The walls and furnishings were edged with patterns of knot-work and stylized flower shapes.

His mother rustled toward him, arms extended gracefully. Saris was more beautiful than ever, dressed in pale blue, white, and gold.

"My darling boy! Here at last!" She enfolded him in a tender embrace.

She smelled wonderful—making him aware that he did not. She said nothing direct. She never had been indelicate.

With an airy promise that as soon as he was refreshed and ready, they would have a cozy chat, she left him outside of a beautiful suite, which included a tiled bath with a magically heated waterfall. Everywhere in this ancient castle lay evidence of her exquisite taste—and the wealth to indulge it.

He was clean and dressed in one of his traveling outfits when he rejoined his mother, damp hair spread over his shoulders, having been toweled and combed out by an expert. He had to admit he missed that kind of handling.

The cozy chat was not to be alone, he discovered as she brought forward a tall, gray-haired man by the hand. "Here is my son, darling." Her dark-lashed golden eyes lifted to the man, who was clearly besotted. "My Taumad."

And to Tau, "This is Ored Elsaraen, my darling. We were married last Midsummer Day."

Tau had noticed the ducal symbol by then: the white stylized lily of Colend, slightly altered. Gold lily for kings, silver lily for princes, white for dukes. He had learned that at his mother's knee, never questioning why he had to learn it.

"Let us go in to eat. You must be hungry," she declared.

Tau would have preferred to meet his mother alone first. She obviously thought her exalted rank a welcome surprise, but her bringing the duke into their first meeting was no mere flourish. His mother never did anything without purpose, to the smallest movement of her hand, or the way she managed her sweeping skirts. Art. Artful. *Just like me.*

So he followed the duke into a tower where a charming room of intimate proportion had been set up for dining, the dishes fine painted porcelain, the utensils gold.

The quiet, efficient staff entered after them, bearing trays whose contents were served with a finesse Tau recognized from his own experience. The room had only the one entrance, with no anterooms, even a discreet servants' door. This room was designed to be private. Interesting.

The servants left and shut the door noiselessly behind them.

"So! Tell us about your adventures." Saris poured out fine Sartoran steep for them all.

"Mostly sailing, and of late I was touring Iasca Leror."

"My poor boy," Saris protested. "It has to be the singular most boring kingdom in the world. How relieved you must

have been to hear from your Jeje once she discovered me!
She enchanted the entire court."

He did not miss the subtle question implied: *Why was
it Jeje and not you who sought me?* "How did she come to
find you, Mother?"

Saris laughed lightly. "Through my relations. The
younger generations aren't interested in old quarrels. So it
seemed I was to be permitted once again to use my family
name—"

"Which is Dei?" Tau asked, knowing he had the last
puzzle piece. The *what,* if not the *why.*

"—which I had begun to use again anyway. Once she
had the name, it seemed easy enough to find me. The family has always kept track of my movements, though I did
not know it." Saris spread her hands in a graceful gesture.
"I did send you a message as soon as I could contrive,
which probably still lies at Parayid awaiting you." She
tipped her head, her lovely mouth curling at the corners
just enough to dimple her cheek.

"I never went down that far. The harbors had no trade
during the long siege by the Venn, so I didn't think I'd find
out any more than I had directly following after the pirate
battle." Tau sat back. "I gather it's easier for the exalted
family to accept strays back into the fold when they come
with titles ribboned round their necks."

Saris did not deny it. She clapped lightly, then addressed
the duke. "You see, my dear. My son has my wit as well as
my taste."

The duke spoke for the first time. "You say you were in
Iasca Leror, Taumad. Is it true they threw the Venn back
into the sea?"

Tau turned the cup around in his hand. It was made of
thin porcelain. The painted clusters of berries gracefully
dotting the edges glowed like rubies in the sunlight. Like
blood . . .

He blinked away the unexpected memory. "In a sense."

Sarias fluttered her fingers. "Please, darling boy, let us
not ruin the peace of the morning with Marlovan rumors.
Listening to third- and fourthhand speculations in court
was tedious enough."

"For what it's worth, Mother, my testimony is firsthand.
I was there, in my modest capacity. The Venn commander

made it clear enough he had no intention of returning unless ordered to."

The duke's brows rose. Saris put her hands together and rested her chin daintily on her fingertips. "Firsthand, yes? The rumors did put you—in several amusing guises—at the right hand of the one they call Elgar the Fox. So do all these bloodthirsty tales really concern the little boy you brought home after your first sea journey? He was an appealing urchin, but I find it difficult to believe he could lead navies against pirates and hew down by his own hand hundreds of warriors without taking a scratch." She tipped her head. "Are you sure you are not being too modest? That his successes might have your brains as inspiration? You were very loyal to him, as I remember."

"Whatever brains I have do not encompass that kind of planning," Tau responded. "I have no ability in military leadership. I was never one of his captains. Just an errand runner. But of course a good one," he added mockingly, seeing her about to protest. He poured out more steep as he shifted the subject to one he knew she'd enjoy. "So, Mother, what is it like, being a duchess?"

Saris was never boring. She did not brag or revel in triumph. Her stories about the Adrani royal court were amusing and historically astute, but Tau sensed an undercurrent of question that strengthened as the meal came at last to a close.

His impression that she was observing him for a specific purpose grew when she invited him to join the company, for Saris had several court guests staying with her to whom she introduced her son. No titles or explanations, he noticed, just his name. His real name. "This is my darling son, Taumad Dei."

Taumad Dei. He needed time to get used to that.

As she led him to a chair and signaled to the waiting musicians, he sensed her disappointment in his lack of surprise, of amazement. He knew that everything, from the cozy meal to this gathering, had been carefully calculated, and that his behavior was being gauged. He sat back, appreciating fine music after months of Marlovan drums as the company exchanged civilized discourse, quick and full of wit and allusion. He smiled, but made no effort to join in.

On parting for the night, Saris caressed him, her voice tender yet a little exasperated. "Sleep well. I have many delightful activities planned for your enjoyment."

He was left feeling that she'd taken over his life again and was directing it like a play. He resented it with all his boyhood vehemence. That did not last past his thinking, with habitual self-mockery, *don't I do exactly the same?*

Tdor yawned as she opened the door to the Harskialdna suite. Late, low light slanted through the single window in the bedroom, deep in its alcove.

She walked in and up the three steps in the alcove to the stone seat adjacent to the window. She'd tried to make this window seat a favorite place, but in winter the window was too cold—the fire roaring in the fireplace did not seem to reach it—and in summer, the blazing sun would stream straight in, making it too hot.

She turned her back on the alcove and stretched her hands out to the fire. Inda lay on the bed, surrounded by a moat of papers. He looked up, his smile a blend of surprise and welcome that always filled her inner being with light.

He brandished a pile of notes. "Here are the last of 'em. By the first day, I'll know all their names. Then all I have to do is put the names to faces."

"What are all these other piles?" she asked, carefully moving one so she could sit on the corner of the bed.

"Reports from the north. Evred wants me to read all the patrol reports, every incident. Get a sense of what's going on up there. Look at that! For a fellow who hasn't read a book in almost ten years, I'm catching up fast."

"Not books." She touched the nearest report. "You're not reading books. You're reading reports."

"The difference being?"

She flipped a braid back. "You really have forgotten, if you have to ask. Books take us outside of ourselves. Reports just detail the world we know."

"Outside of ourselves." He repeated it slowly, and again. "Outside of ourselves."

Tdor sat beside him, concern escalating to worry. "Inda, what is it?"

He thumped his fist lightly on the papers. "Maybe that will do it. I need to read books again." He shut his eyes, so he could hear her voice. Faces didn't often tell him much—even Tdor's, now that they were grown and he had missed so many years of seeing her. But voices were always revealing, and her quick words, the rise in her voice meant she was anxious. That made him anxious. "I feel stupid."

"Inda! Where does that come from? How could you possibly think you are stupid?" She sounded irritated but not frantic—not as if she were hiding anything. Like a worry that he was losing his wits.

Cautiously relieved, he said, "I feel stupider than when I was young, reading with you and Hadand and Joret in the archive."

She sat up briskly. "*That's* easy to fix. The archive here is much bigger than at ho—at Tenthen. Read a good record. Where did you leave off?"

"Maybe I should just start over again. Do the easy ones, like that *Cassadas Atanhas* one. Meant for when you're five or six."

Tdor said, "That's a great idea. You're going to discover it's different, reading it now. We just thought of it as tedious language lessons, Iascan on one page, Marlovan on the other. Simple history. Now you'll get a hint of the queen who wrote it for her son so he wouldn't forget his Iascan side as he became a Marlovan. You'll see how words change, that she didn't pick 'atan' just because it's easy. She picked it because the sun was the Cassadas symbol, and 'setting sun' in the old, *old* days could mean more things than fading to darkness. She wrote another in case she had a daughter. It's all about archives, at least the words are, but the meaning is about how ways of life can be destroyed unless you keep records."

He heard her old enthusiasm, but there was a tightness to some words, and she spoke quickly. He opened his eyes. Tdor sat next to him, taut, almost not breathing, her entire body a silent question.

He put down his papers. "Something's wrong. You came in because something's wrong."

"Children," she said bluntly. "Have you thought about that? You and I."

"Oh." He looked blank. "No. I hadn't. I mean, someday, when we're, you know, old. Parent age." He waved his papers vaguely. "Though I know Evred told everyone not to wait the usual fifteen or twenty years. On account of the Venn. I wonder if he still means that?"

She said, "I think we could take our direction from Hadand and Evred. Except . . ."

"What? Can't you ask Hadand? I suppose I could ask Evred."

"Don't."

It came out too quickly. He dropped his papers, and now she had all his attention.

She wandered to the fire to warm her hands, while she scolded herself for speaking without thinking. She considered what to say, and what not to say, then turned around, to find him still waiting. "I don't think we should bring it up until Hadand and Evred say that they have a baby coming. By whatever means that works. I think it would be horrible for Hadand if we were first. Though she wouldn't say. But I'd know."

"You decide when," Inda said, and returned to his papers, relieved to postpone a subject that just seemed too alien. He had enough to think about.

Chapter Eighteen

THE windows of Castle Tenthen had been opened for two full days, as Choraed Elgaer enjoyed its first mild weather of the year. The spring scour-out was nearly done. Fareas-Iofre had left for last the job she enjoyed most, the dusting of each of her precious books and scrolls. She'd perform that task after her morning watch at her husband's bedside.

Jarend-Adaluin lay under a fresh blanket, his hair brushed, white against the creamy linen pillow covering. His breast scarcely moved with his light breaths. How tenuous was the connection between his soul and his body!

She stretched her hand lightly over his knobby one lying loose on the blanket. Sometimes he wakened at her touch.

There had never been passion between them, but there had been respect, consideration, friendship. He'd endured a long life full of disappointments, and she included herself among them, for she never could replace the one love of his life. But he'd said just before New Year's Week, during one of his lucid mornings, that one learns to redefine one's expectations when those of youth are denied. He'd come to love riding the countryside through all the seasons. He'd admired her wisdom and scholarship, balanced with unceasing care over Tenthen. And he was proud of his sons, who had been called to serve the king. Inda's return home had definitely roused his father out of the dreamworld, however briefly. Jarend said that his Inda becoming Harskialdna was the highest honor of all.

He had repeated that several times, though he did not always remember that the king was not Tlennen. She did not remind him that Tlennen had been murdered by Mad Gallop Yvana-Vayir's ambition. Jarend's loyalty to Tlennen had an emotional component difficult to define, but enduring.

Where will my soul go? he asked a few days later. *I used to want to join my Joret in death, but age sometimes clears your vision. She never wanted me. It was always my brother Indevan. He was beloved by us all . . . and loved his ease as he loved to laugh . . . I could never raise my hand against him . . .*

The Old Sartorans promise peace beyond the physical world, she had said. *Beyond sight, beyond hearing, taste, or touch, indefinable because we are bound by the limitations of life here. Some insist that once the soul escapes its physical bonds it vanishes into nothing, but if so, why would we think so often about what lies beyond, why do some catch glimpses, as if just around a corner we can barely at times perceive?*

He had smiled a little. *Around a corner,* he'd repeated. *I am content with knowing they are there, my father, my mother, the others, going back and back. Just around a corner.*

It was comforting, and the unsolvable mysteries of the universe did not preclude it. But try as she might, she couldn't see the corner. She couldn't see ghosts like Jarend did. She'd once thought only those who loved intensely could perceive ghosts, yet she loved her children at least as much as Jarend had ever loved his beautiful first wife, but though Fareas had tried hard for years to discover a hint of Tanrid anywhere in the castle, she'd had no success.

Was that because he had never liked being indoors, not from his earliest childhood? He'd done his duty—he was like his father that way—but he'd always been happiest outside. If he were a ghost—if human perceptions of justice existed beyond the realm of the physical—then Tanrid would be riding the borders through season after season, beyond the pain of winter's cold or summer's heat, accompanied by his beloved and faithful horses and hounds, all forever young.

The rightness of this vision seized her with poignant regret and longing and sweetness, all impossibly jumbled but all the more intense for the mixture. Her breath caught in her chest, and tears burned her eyes. If Jarend wakened, she would tell him her vision, in case it might comfort him as well.

Jarend lay so quietly in her blurred sight. A quick, sharp tingle through her nerves caused her to scrub her eyes against her wrist. The edge of her wrist sheath banged painfully against the bridge of her nose. She shook her head, then bent over Jarend. He was no longer breathing. Sometime during her air-dreaming he had slipped free of the leash.

She laid her hand on his thin chest. There was no steady beat of heart. Emotions chased through her mind, too swift to catch. She rose, her legs trembling.

Just outside the room Jarend's old Runner was carrying a basket of sun-freshened linens. "He's gone." Her voice sounded like someone else's in her own ears.

The Runner set down his basket very slowly. Fareas held out her hand, and they gripped their fingers together, then walked back into the airy room, now empty of life, to do what must be done.

Presently Fareas walked downstairs, not quite sure where she was going. Not sure even whom to speak to. Tdor now lived with Hadand and Inda in the royal city, Joret was gone over the mountains. Branid, scarce back a month from his first Convocation, was getting ready to ride out again on his first yearly border ride. And Whipstick had ridden out that morning to the forge.

She stopped outside Tdor's chamber, regret so intense she trembled.

Women's voices came from the workroom, where Dannor Tya-Vayir had organized the tapestry project. Fareas paused, fingers gripping her elbows. She felt uneasy around Dannor, though she could not define why. She knew the girls had never liked her, but Dannor had been the perfect guest since the wedding: first awake in the mornings, first to drill, and she had the eye of an artist. The tapestry would be as good as anything they could have ordered from Sartor back in more affluent days, and it would mean more, woven by their own hands on a loom they built themselves with wood taken from furniture donated from every castle family.

People change, Fareas thought as she looked across the room at the tapestry design on the wall, Inda so carefully sketched by Dannor (after plenty of advice from everyone) that even inexperienced hands at the weft would not blur those wide brown eyes. *Some change for the better. Some for the worse. Until the day comes when the last breath goes out and there is the greatest change of all.*

Feeling like some other woman controlled her body, Fareas walked into the workroom, where she discovered a volunteer crew of off-duty guardswomen stationed along the loom. Under Dannor's direction they endeavored to hold the sturdy linen warp yarn steady as they slowly rolled it onto the top of the warp beam.

Dannor stood back, head to one side as she eyed the handfuls of yarn, and Fareas' aching eyes slid past her to the design Dannor had made. There were the mountains of the Andahi Pass, Inda standing on a cliff with sword raised. Just below and to the right a tall blond figure knelt, laying a straight sword at the feet of a noble red-haired figure in Montrei-Vayir crimson and gold.

The women became aware of Fareas. They stepped back from the loom and saluted. Dannor whirled around, sidling a quick look right and left before she too saluted, her practiced, dimpled smile flashing.

"The Adaluin is dead." Someone else seemed to speak with Fareas's voice.

Exclamations—decent sorrow without much real emotion—brisk offers to see to the messages, bonfire, memorial feast, were like scattered flower petals. Fareas scarcely heeded them. Dannor's pretty eyes rounded, and her mouth formed a sorrowful "Oh." Her brow puckered, she pressed her hands together in a posture of surprise and sorrow. But her eyes, they were as watchful as Fareas' own.

The dizziness Fareas had done her best to ignore began to flicker at the edges of her vision and she sat down abruptly. The last thing she heard was Dannor's voice or-

dering steeped leaf, a blanket, a fan, then, for the first time
in her life, Fareas-Iofre fainted.

She was unconscious only for the space of a dozen
breaths, but she woke with a sickening headache. This
sign of weakness from the Iofre, whose calm strength had
seemed as unending as a river, upset the household as much
as the long-expected death of the prince.

Dannor had been a Jarlan for several years, ever since
her mother-by-marriage, the Princess Tdiran, died in a riding accident on the ice. She forced herself to keep her voice
sweet, and to make her orders into questions: "Don't you
think it would be a good idea to . . . ?"

By the end of the day, the servants were willing to take
her orders as the Iofre was put to bed, the funeral fire organized, the celebration feast in the process of being prepared,
and messages went out in all directions.

So when Dannor went in to see Fareas-Iofre, and in her
most caressing voice told the princess that Branid and she
wanted to marry, she smiled and waited for her reward.

Fareas-Iofre stared up at that lovely face. She had supported Branid's heirship because the new king had ordered
it. Dannor was related to one of the oldest Jarl families.
Branid must be married—on the surface everything was as
it should be—so what could she say but yes?

Chapter Nineteen

A succession of pleasant days passed in the low mountains of Elsaraen above the vineyards, during which
Tau rode, danced, listened, admired artistry in many forms.
Not all his mother's company was old. There were half a
dozen young people—four of them young women. All single, all aristocrats, all adept at being agreeable.

One of them Tau had met in Bren during the time he
lived under the guise of a pleasure house musician named
Angel. At first he'd expected affront. He'd been a hireling,
if a popular one. But he had forgotten the magic of rank.
She claimed him as a close acquaintance, though in Bren
they'd scarcely exchanged a dozen words.

As the days passed, he was aware of an increase in restlessness. This was a pleasant life, but not *his* life. He knew
why Jeje had left once she'd discovered Tau's mother in
Nente, married to a duke. Jeje had surely hated Nente and
its court because she hated the unearned privileges and
powers of birth.

She hated *kings*.

As Tau exerted himself to be agreeable, he debated
leaving. Only which way to go?

At length he became aware that his mother was expecting someone else. A woman? Matchmaking, to bind him with the ribbons of family and connection?

That night, he sensed a subtle air of triumph when they gathered for dinner. He said, "I think it's time for me to move on."

"Taumad." Saris regarded him in dismay. "Why? Have I disappointed you in some way?"

"Mother, I have had a wonderful time, but I feel the need to get on with my life."

She did not start an argument with the obvious *Cannot you make a life here?* "Please. Give me a morning of yourself, then. Just the two of us."

It would be churlish not to agree.

And so, the next morning, Tau performed his drills in his enormous bedchamber for the last time. When he emerged, his travel gear packed, he found he found his mother waiting with a breakfast set for two in a charming room of pale yellow.

She welcomed him with genuine warmth, but he sensed intent, as with dainty grace she heaped his plate herself, giving him a generous pile of fluffy wheat cakes and pepper potatoes with cheese crumbled over them. Then golden eyes met golden eyes. "Would you like to inherit a dukedom?"

Tau dropped his gaze to the gilt-edged porcelain cup as she poured him freshly steeped Sartoran leaf. He lifted the tiny cup and breathed in the complicated scents that evoked spring fields, mountain wild flowers after a storm. Summer.

When he opened his eyes, she was still waiting for his answer. "Your duke would adopt me, old as I am?"

Your duke. Her only acknowledgment of this clumsy hint at her motivation for her rise in rank was a faint pucker above her brows. He took that in, thinking that she was playing a role. She'd taught him that the life of art required one to live the role of the artist.

But her faint air of regret made him wonder if she did care for her duke in her butterfly way.

"Alas, no." Her tone was cordial as she brushed her fingers over her waist. "His future duke or duchess is here. But if we present you at court, my husband's rank, our name, and your manner and mode will bring you a range of possibility. I can name two charming single women who will inherit ancient duchies. I will admit there are few others who combine charm and wit with birth a suitable match for ours, but we could send you to Colend. You would not like Sartor now."

"Aren't there already enough Deis in Sartor?" Tau asked, laughing soundlessly. Then he leaned forward. "Mother, I appreciate your offer. You've always been generous with me."

"I'm glad you said that." It was almost a retort, but her tone was too pleasant, her smile too fond. He sensed he'd hurt her. "I trust you will honor me with your reasons for leaving."

Few could manage such a request without sounding either pompous or provoking. But he did hear the challenge in her lack of question.

"You know how much difficulty I have had with expressing my true thoughts." He frowned at his crumbled biscuit, not wanting to sound accusatory. He'd never minded running around naked as a small boy, but he had always hated the adults' well meaning examinations of his every action, idea, and motivation, discussed endlessly as if he was a pet on display. He'd learned early to hide his thoughts—but all this his mother knew as well as he did.

"My reasons have to do with experience. What I've done. What I've learned."

"Please go on," she said.

"Thank you for bearing with me. I broke my habit of silence with Inda and Jeje. As much as I was able. But Jeje is somewhere in the world and hates writing. And Inda . . ." *Has Evred between us.*

Evred. Tau sat back, nerves tingling. He would not discuss Evred, but he could examine his impulse there. "Well, Inda's busy being a Marlovan Harskialdna, which is about five men's worth of work. So I've gone back to my old habit of talking inside my own head."

She tipped her head, her manner attentive.

"It's easy to say that people ought to be taken as they are, without pretence, or rank. That was why you and I fought so much when I was young. I resisted the roles we learned to play. But civilization—order—seems to be predicated on playing roles, and the more rank one has, the more levels of the pretence."

"One might say, the greater need for privacy. But do go on."

"There's privacy to protect one's true thoughts from what one says and does while among the others, what the Colendi call the court mask. Then there's protecting one's life."

"Ah."

"I think I've figured out social hierarchy. It's the agreement to advance or withdraw in order of rank, because no matter where we are, we humans can't seem to get away from rank. Somebody has to be first, so either we fight for it, or agree by other means. Face, manners, protocol are the other means."

He looked up. Saris indicated he should continue.

"You did try to tell me, but I guess I had to learn it on my own. See it at work outside of life in Parayid. So my first experience in the world was shipboard. Rigid hierarchy. No face, but there is protocol as well as force. On board, the captain has as much power as any duke."

"I was wrong in predicting you would return to me within half a year."

"I almost did. After two months. But then I met Inda." Tau shook his head. "Never mind, the subject was hierarchy, and the context my leaving your fine home, and your generous sharing of it. My first storm convinced me why the hierarchy aboard ship worked. Everyone knew what to do, and command was mostly based on experience. My next hierarchy was that of pirates. Based on speed. Skill. Above those, savagery. After that, Freedom Island, where rank was a complex net of naval successes and favor of the harbormaster. In Bren, I was back to aristocrats and entertainers. Then I was with the Marlovans, whose rank is less dependent on birth (though it is certainly present) than on military prowess."

She had listened patiently. "Your conclusion?"

"The worst are pirates, a distortion of civilization."

She smiled. "They are at their weakest when they assume the trappings of civilization."

"I know that you were taken by pirates."

She laughed. "You could say, in a manner of speaking, that I took them. But I will not bore you about my experiences while you are making a point."

"I don't know that it's worth making." He spread his hands. "I can respect rank based on merit. I have trouble respecting the unmerited supremacy of birth rank. When I looked beyond the dazzle of wealth, fine clothes, and houses, the brilliance of art and intricacies of fashion, I discovered that in any other hierarchy other than a royal court, one does not have to suffer fools and defer. Pirate leaders are savage, but not stupid, or they don't last long."

Saris' amusement verged on laughter. "Do you consider yourself free from snobbery?"

"I'm a vile snob," he retorted. "I was raised to be." And when her eyes narrowed, "My personal hierarchy ranks people according to wit and skill. Style. And power. And so I'm leaving. Mother, why did you give me the education of a prince? That's not a requirement of the sex trade."

Saris set down her little gold bread knife. "Walk with me."

She opened what had once been an arched window, scarcely more than an arrow slit. Someone had knocked out the stone to floor level, widening the window just enough to permit passage. A door of mullioned glass had been fitted in, the central muntins worked around colored glass in a pattern of twining lilies.

Tau followed his mother out onto a narrow parapet. The stone was pale gray, the crenellated edges of the wall weather-worn. This was the oldest portion of the castle.

She shaded her eyes with her hand, gazing over the terraced valley, where people moved about tending the grapevines. In the distance, a carriage rolled along the road, pulled by four horses. Her gaze drifted past and came to rest on a pair of horseback riders proceeding up the steep hill at a sober pace; they vanished round a cliff. Ah.

"Let us return to the matter of masks." Saris smiled at her son. "You'll probably remember, if your memory is as clear as mine, that I taught you all about how humans mask emotion. That we in the pleasure houses see people not just unclothed but unmasked. Desires bared, emotions unhidden."

"I remember. But—"

She held up a hand, her smile wry. "How long before you discovered how wrong I was?"

"When I was taken by pirates. Later when I worked at

the Lark Ascendant. I learned that some don't take off their social mask even if they remove their clothes. Pretence is among the lineaments of desire, just like anywhere else."

She laced her fingers together tightly. "My mothers warned me, when I was small, but like you, I thought I knew better than they. What did old people know? Then they died within two weeks of one another before I turned fifteen. I knew enough to run the house, and inside I was queen. Everyone deferred to my so-called wit and wisdom."

"What happened?"

"I discovered the real world when my house was burned down. I still prevailed, but my life was ... difficult for a time."

Tau held out a hand in appeal. "I'm not going to rail at you for my upbringing. I know I couldn't raise a child well. And you were about the same age I am now when you were raising me."

"I realize now that I was lonely, but at the time I thought to create the perfect being," she admitted. "And my intention was to send you as an elegant weapon against our family in Sartor, who'd had the temerity to drive my parents out. You were not surprised when I told you our name. How much of the rest have you figured out?"

"That we're tied in with the Montredavan-Ans in some way, that there was probably a runaway match, and that there was some sort of disgrace or I would have been claimed by cousins years ago. And you kept changing our name."

Saris nodded on each point. "A runaway match indeed. The Marlovans were angry because a missing Montredavan-An bride upset their marriage treaties, and the Deis were upset because my mother had been chosen to mate with a distant cousin she loathed. Both girls were disinherited. Not that that presently means anything for the Montredavan-Ans. But for the Deis, the worst crime of all is acting contrary to family decree. The Dei family, in their own view, (as you have probably discovered) transcends mere governments." She dusted her fingertips together. "So they are raised."

"So you resumed one of the names you were entitled to when you married"—*your duke*—"his grace?"

"Yes. With the Deis everything is fine, and you are welcome to as much of their attention as you want. I never met any Montredavan-Ans, and what little I've heard makes me disinclined to pursue their acquaintance. I will never lay claim to their name."

"I've met a couple of them. Back to why you raised me the way you did."

"Can't you guess it? Well, no, you don't have the crucial piece of information yet. The runaways ended up in Colend for many splendid years. Thence to Sartor, full of art and style. They were initially welcomed by the eastern Deis, probably as a snub to my family; the western Deis. They set up in the pleasure business, bringing the newest Colendi arts to it. Unfortunately, this was just when the current queen was beginning her reign of austerity, and to counter it—she was ruining business—they used their popularity to begin to interfere in politics. I can tell you more if you really want to hear it, but they were invited to leave and not return."

"Ah. So they returned to Iasca Leror, and set up in Parayid under a new name?"

"Exactly. They were very old before thinking about an heir. The Birth Spell gave them me. Our success by then was known up and down the coast, all the houses with pretensions copying our styles to varying degrees and becoming social centers. I was raised to resent the pretensions of the Sartoran Deis and thought the best revenge would be to send you back to Sartor one day as a prince in every way superior to them."

"Revenge?" Tau gave his soundless laugh.

"You were to break hearts, then snap your fingers under their noses. Or carry off the most wealthy and prominent of them. The choice was yours, you were just not to reveal who you were until it was done." She chuckled. "Well, I was very young and arrogant, I must confess."

"So you will not raise your heir the same way you raised me?" He indicated her middle.

"No. I believe in retrospect I told you too much far too young. There was no chance for discovery, to emotionally comprehend the facts I required you to learn. But I only comprehended that after you were gone."

Tau almost laughed. "Had you planned to tell me who I was before sending me to Sartor?"

"Oh, yes. You were to outwit them, you see, and out-match them at their own games. See beneath their masks." An airy flick of fingers from an arched wrist. "You know what is said of us in the histories: *Deis are kingmakers though never kings.*" She smiled. "Let us finish our break-fast in peace."

They slipped back inside and finished their meal, each feeling far better about the other than they had expected.

At last she smiled. "May I make one last request?"

It was lightly said, and she did not move, but he sensed that this next surprise was also planned. Maybe everything had been planned. Exasperation drove out regret: dealing with his mother was like walking in a maze of mirrors and glass. You think you've found the path at last, then walk smash into an invisible deflection.

"Of course," he said, because of course he could not say no.

"Stop in the blue parlor on your way." She rose and shook out her skirts. "It's the little room where you were first brought." She kissed his brow and rustled out.

A short time later he opened the door to the blue parlor, and then stood on the threshold, stunned into speechlessness.

Chapter Twenty

J ORET Dei caught herself up first.

"Where is Her Grace? The footman said she was coming." Joret narrowed her eyes, offering a friendly smile. "You will be her son Taumad, am I right?"

It took Tau a few long breaths to gather his wits. Was this how people felt when they saw him? But what did people *see*, besides pretty features? His kin-cousin Joret Dei was even more beautiful than Saris in a way that had nothing to do with youth. There was no mirror maze in Joret's dimpled smile or dark-fringed blue gaze. There was no vestige of artfulness in her exquisite features or dramatic coloring, no studied grace in the straight limbs clothed in the plainest of riding outfits. Her hair was braided up into a coronet in the style of the Marlovan women when at work; she did not hide her thoughts as her expression changed from doubt to gravity and then interest.

"I–I don't know what to say," he muttered finally, awkward and unsettled.

"You don't have to say anything. I rode up here to El-saraen on her invitation, and I did want to meet you. I just did not expect it to come about so suddenly. Where is the duchess, and why did she send you alone?"

"I don't know." Tau made a rueful gesture. "I still don't understand why she does some things." And then, the humor fading, "You rode all this way to meet me? I trust you don't believe I'm here to make trouble."

Her mouth deepened at the corners. "You haven't met the Sartoran Deis yet, have you?"

"No. But I heard some gossip about the one my age. What was his name, Yaskandar?"

"Yaska *is* trouble." She shrugged. "But then all of us are. That's what I've discovered. Even when we don't mean to be."

Tau was about to say *You weren't,* then remembered the gossip from the other Marlovan Runners about how Evred's older brother, Aldren-Sierlaef, had chased this Joret clear around the Marlovan kingdom. In a sense, the violent change of government could be laid at her door. And was, in some people's minds. Yet she had not intended any of it.

"Is the entire family . . . like us?"

"Yaska could be your brother, though his skin is darker than yours. Not as dark as mine. His hair is almost as dark as mine as well, but your eyes are exactly the same pale brown that people call gold. My mother had your light eyes, but a long nose, and hair the color of mud. My cousins have large blue eyes, round cheeks, and button chins."

"So we don't all spring out as miracles of beauty."

Her chuckle was deep, in her chest, not the least like an artful court titter. "No. Though the older generation values beauty first and fame second. You had better be prepared. Both branches of the Deis will probably come wooing you, breathing sincerity and talking up the life of art, because they want to preserve the family legend by cross-matching distant cousins."

He wiped his arm across his brow, an instinctive gesture his mother had worked hard to train out of him when he was small. "I still don't know what to say," he admitted. "I went to sea to get away from art. By the time I was ten, artful had come to mean artificial."

Joret said, "Yes. I understand. Though I wouldn't have before I left Iasca Leror and came here to court."

"Marlovans, I've discovered, are often brutal, but seldom artificial."

She did not deny it. "What did you learn about art, and artfulness, at sea?"

He made a self-deprecating gesture. "There are few worse bores than those who go on about their past."

She gave a short laugh. "I'm not bored."

"Oh, it took capture by pirates to convince me that artfulness was not necessarily deceit or deviousness, and being open about one's intent was not necessarily admirable. On the other hand, you did meet Jeje, am I right?"

Joret smiled. "Yes, when she came to Nente looking for your mother."

"She and Inda are my proof that words, thoughts, actions can all match and yet be admirable."

"The word is integrity."

He sighed. "I grew up thinking that word actually meant 'the ability to be convincing.'" He opened his hands. "I don't intend to stay in this kingdom. Or is this conversation in some sense a mark of distrust aimed at my mother." It wasn't a question.

Joret gestured upward, toward the rest of the castle. "Your mother told me before she left Nente that politics are tedious and fatiguing, the running of a business made large. When she returns after the birth of her child, she promised me the extent of her ambition is to transform a stagnant, fractious court into something with its own style, instead of mimicking Colend. I begged her to try, because I can't do it."

Tau paced to the window and halted, fingering a wind chime hanging before a closed window. "I'd thought of going to meet Jeje, since she did not wait for me."

Joret thought back, uncertain whether or not to share one of Jeje's remarks. Though nothing had been said about confidence, it had felt like one: *Tau needs to be needed.*

Joret picked her words with care. "She went north, I believe. Said something about taking ship at Bren Harbor."

Tau's head lifted. "I wonder if that means Inda's fleet is in the strait." Though they had never met before this day, he was comfortable with her. It wasn't just their shared family, he sensed that they shared similar experience. "Another discovery I made at sea was a taste for danger," he said slowly, and sure enough, she did not bridle or mime horror. Just gave a sober nod. "But I've faced enough of it to want my efforts to be for a purpose. I could rejoin the fleet and fight pirates. Getting rid of pirates is a worthy goal. But anyone can do it. Pirates are predictable. They will always choose bloodshed over wit or art." He swung around. "Do we Deis all think alike?"

"I can safely promise that we do not. Just before he left to go yacht racing, Yaska defined love for me as 'hope-driven self-destruction.' "

She was startled when Tau stilled, eyelids lifting. She went on to finish, but she wasn't sure he even heard her words, "I don't think I've ever heard anything more alien to my thinking."

He turned again to the west window, hands now behind him. "You once were part of Inda's family. You must know the new king."

"Evred?" Joret did not hide her surprise at this unexpected turn. "I saw him very little, actually. You must have seen how enormous that castle is, and the girls had their own enclave. But my first meeting with him was quite memorable."

"What happened?" Tau undid the window latch and flung the casement wide.

Joret said, "Nothing extraordinary. He was about thirteen. Maybe fourteen. I was fifteen. I'd just arrived for the queen's training. Sponge—that's what they called him then—he was sitting in the tack room mending a headstall. He'd been doing that all winter. He looked just like his father, so sober and intent on his work. Older than his years. But then Hadand told him that Inda had arrived, and he leaped up, and his face changed into a boy's face. Full of joy. I've never in my life seen such a transformation. He dashed out, running so fast he crashed into a wall. But he just laughed and ran on."

Tau struck the back of a chair lightly with the flat of his hand. "Hope-driven self-destruction. You would think that a fellow with Yaska's looks, his wealth and taste, would be at the pinnacle of happiness. But such a narrow view of the variety of emotions that we group under 'love'—what happened to make him so angry?"

"Pain." She opened her hand. "I saw it. For scarcely a heartbeat, but it was there."

Tau rapped twice on the table, then turned his back to

the window. "Yaska can sail around the world in an effort to outrun his anger, or he can fight a duel and find his troubles ended for him. No one else is dragged down his avalanche. But what if he were in a position of power? Would his self-destruction spread out into the world?"

Outside the open window a bird chirped, then flitted off in a quiver of wings. "I don't quite know how to answer that," Joret said finally.

"It's all right." Tau smiled. "I think I do."

Traditionally the Marlovan academy's first callover for the scrubs of ten or eleven years of age was held in the castle's main parade court.

This was because some of the boys were sent by Riders who had never been to the royal city and did not know their way around the academy, which had no signs. The main parade court was easy to find, the main entrance lying beyond the massive archway between the biggest wings of the castle, housing throne room and great hall, respectively.

The traditional first callover was at noon, for the same reason.

Evred permitted himself few indulgences. One he'd anticipated for half a year was watching Inda preside over the academy's first day. He'd organized his schedule around it, even though Inda had steadfastly refused any parade or ceremony. "I'm just going to watch," he'd said. "And only the scrubs. Big boys I'll talk to when I go over to teach 'em."

Evred set aside his tasks as the midday bells began to clang. He waved off his Runners, ran upstairs and down the empty hallway of the royal residence.

The jut where the new wall met the old tower just outside of Inda's suite ended in an awkward cubby. If you pressed your face up against the uneven wall, you would discover a finger's width of an old arrow slit, imperfectly covered. The castle children had long used it to spy down into the parade court.

Evred reached the cubby, then halted, fury lancing through him. He was not alone after all.

At the sound of his footfall the figure crouching there turned. It was Hadand. She smiled up at him. "Do you

remember your first callover?" She faltered, expression
changing from pleasure to question. "What's wrong?"

The suddenness as well as the intensity of his fury unsettled him. It was his own fault for indulging emotion, which
was dangerous at best, betrayal at worst.

The people who had legitimate reason to be here were
Inda's sister, his wife, his lover. Evred was none of these.

"Headache." It was true.

"Inda's down there, I saw him earlier. But he's not
dressed in his coat. He looks like a stable hand. Is that on
purpose?"

"Yes. He doesn't want to be noticed unless he decides
he has to be."

As she obligingly knelt, giving him access to the upper
portion of the spy hole, he leaned into the small space without touching his wife, whose intimacy he'd avoided since
Convocation. The prospect of touching anyone—of being
touched—was too much like thrusting his hand into a fire.
The only solution was work.

Thirty-six small boys stood in two ragged rows, the cold
east wind snapping the proudly worn smocks, some old
and worn, others so new they were stiff as canvas—most
castle people the kingdom over believing that the first requirement of clothing for children was sturdiness. They
all wore riding boots. You could tell at a glance who had
inherited from a brother or cousin by how badly the boots
fit.

"Who's the master? He's new, isn't he?" Hadand asked.

"Landred Askan. From Inda's and my own class. Inda
and Gand decided that the masters all had to have fighting experience, to prevent obvious trouble. Askan was at
Olara."

"Oh, smart idea."

On the parade court, Landred Askan stood before his
first group, studying the faces. An instant's vivid memory
of Master Gand—now Headmaster Gand—surveying
him and his scrub-mates made him take his time and really see those faces. Was there one like Kepa? Like Inda?
Like Cherry-Stripe? Like Smartlip Lassad? He could hear
Lassad in the distance, yelling at a group of newly arrived
ponytails.

"Most of you know some of the rules," Askan said, try-

ing to gather their attention and hold it with his voice, just
like Gand did.

About half straightened up. Two smirked knowingly.
One stared up at the sentries on the castle walls.

"First, nobody has rank in the academy. If you're appointed a riding captain, it's for a single game. If you are
appointed more than once, don't assume it's because you're
the best. Sometimes the worst get extra chances in hopes
they improve."

The two smirkers laughed. The others, hearing a
laugh and no wands whistling through the air, chuckled
belatedly.

Gand was right, Askan thought. *Don't watch their mouths,
watch eyes and hands.* He tried not to let his own gaze slip
sideways to where Inda sat on a barrel next to the empty
pegs for horse harnesses. Most of the boys hadn't seen him
yet, or if they had, they'd ignored him, for he wasn't in a
coat and his hair was just clubbed, like the stable hands'.
But two boys had spotted those swinging earrings. Keth
Arveas sent frequent peeks his way in hopes of being noticed. The other was Dauvid Tya-Vayir, who stiffened, face
tight with scorn. *Those scars, that has to be the Harskialdna,
the one Uncle Stalgrid says is the king's claphair.*

"The second rule you know," Askan continued in a
louder voice, and felt their attention snap back to him. "Its
that Ains and Tveis are now mixed. The training is the same.
Now, time for your first callover, once I see two straight
lines. You will call me Master Askan—" Flash of memory:
Cherry-Stripe, so tall back then, piping, *YOU can be Lan.
The horsetails are calling ME Cherry-Stripe.*

Askan shook away the image and began the callover. He
knew their names of course, and had memorized the reports
on the boys' interviews when the King's Voice gave them
their invitation. Now to match description to presence.

"Arveas-Andahi."

Keth grimaced, unused to that weird name. He stared
at the ground, shuffling his feet, as all the rest of the boys
turned to stare at him.

And Askan knew he'd lost them. Their attention had
gone to the small boy on the end whose hair was already
turning brown under the sun-bleached top layer. Two or
three made noises; Askan's fingers twitched. Already reach-

ing for his wand? Gand had been able to control them with
just his voice, and after a week just with his eyes ... failure ... what to say? Not a threat, not two heartbeats into
their first day—

Footsteps on the flagstones. Inda had left his barrel.

A small boy in the back gasped. "That's the
Harskialdna!"

Sudden silence. Evred and Hadand were too far away to
hear, but they could see from the sudden stiffening of the
boys that something had happened, and then Inda strolled
out to take up a stance beside Lan Askan.

"Arveas-Andahi is a new name." Inda tried to make his
face stern. He badly wanted to laugh, not at the subject, but
at himself. *Here*. Standing over these pups like ... like he
didn't feel just a year or so away from being a pup himself
at times. "Do you know who gave it to Kethadrend?"

He's the Harskialdna, the boys were thinking, with various reactions. Dressed like a stable hand, but look at those
scars. Those were really pirate earrings!

Dauvid Tya-Vayir was pleased he'd guessed right and
figured the next threat (because every man was either a
threat or a lackey) would be Headmaster Gand. Uncle
Stalgrid had said about the Headmaster, *Just a coward who
stayed behind to teach little boys how to ride, when his dragoon wing was fighting in the north.*

Inda said, "The king gave Keth this new name because
the name Arveas will be honored through history. The
other new Jarl is now Camarend Idayago-Vayir. His boy
will one day stand here and hear that new name at callover.
See? So your scrub-mate there had no choice about having
a new name. In foreign lands, names and land can be different. In Iasca Leror, the Jarl shares his name with his land.
It's a sign of responsibility."

One of the boys was hopping up and down.

Inda said, "Yes, I know my family is the exception, but
we're also not Jarls. That's because the Algaras made a marriage treaty with the Tenthens of Choraed Elgaer before
we Marlovans moved into Iasca Leror. But my forefather
put Vayir to his name because the king asked him to."

The boy stopped hopping, looking warily convinced,
and Inda wondered if among these boys there were versions of himself and Evred who would be making historical

speculations during hay-pitching duty. "Arveas-Andahi is also a kind of invisible banner. Have any of you seen what a castle's like after the Venn have been there?"

The tall boy said, "I saw a harbor. After pirates. At the Nob. M'dad's dragoons fought 'em when they came back."

Inda said, "This would be worse. Keth, how many of your blood family lived?"

"None."

"How many of the Riders lived?"

"None."

"How many of the castle women?"

"Only Aunt Ndand. Because she was sent away with me."

"What was left when you and your aunt got back to the castle?"

"Nothing . . . blood. Smoke. Then the Idayagans attacked us." Keth studied the ground.

The only sound was the wind snapping the pennants. The listeners wrestled with shock and envy. And scorn, on the part of Dauvid Tya-Vayir: *Uncle Stalgrid said it's all just brag.* However, Aunt Imand had said, *Believe it.*

Inda said, "The Venn could come back. And it might be you on horseback, facing them. Any of you. You're here to learn what to do about it. So let's see two *straight* lines. Let's see your attention on Master Askan."

Hadand watched Inda gesture casually toward Askan, then the boys stiffened into two perfect lines. "How did my little brother gain that sense of authority?"

"You haven't been watching the morning drills?"

"Boys are far, far tougher to manage," Hadand said. "Isn't that why your masters take sticks to them?"

Below, Lan Askan dismissed the boys for what would be their only day of liberty all year. They shot out of the court, some looking back at Inda. At the far gate, tall, gawky older brothers waited to sweep their Tveis off to Daggers Drawn, the academy boys' own tavern, to be fed and lectured. Most of them crowded forward hoping to be noticed by the Harskialdna, and why was he there with the brats, of all people?

Dauvid walked alone, eyeing Keth, who was the center of a crowd. He hated that. *I'll scrag him first. Uncle Stalgrid said, you get respect faster when they know who's strongest.*

Inda watched them all go, then discovered tough old Gand at his shoulder. "Not bad. But you'll get a real sense of the year tomorrow at the shearing."

Inda grinned. "Was looking forward to that!"

Gand rubbed his jaw as they paced across the parade court in the other direction, toward the guards' side. "You ever spent time around an apiary?" he asked presently.

"No," Inda said. "Only thing I remember about the bees at Tenthen was that I didn't like 'em any more than they liked us."

"Bees and small boys don't mix well," Gand conceded. "Neither knows how to give way when they want to be in the same space. If you did spend time around them, you'd learn that the bees' hum doesn't always sound the same. Beekeepers can hear trouble in the hum. Sometimes weather, sometimes other things."

Inda opened his hand.

"Here's what I've found. The shearing is sometimes like the bee hum. You get a sense of the year ahead in their faces, the noise they make. How they act."

Inda remembered that the next morning, when the academy except for the horsetails—who could be there but traditionally held themselves aloof—made a long double line in the big training paddock. At the far end, the staff waited with their scissors; the masters stood in lines behind the boys.

Everyone straightened up when Inda arrived, which made him want to laugh, so intense was his memory of running down that line. Back then these small, scrawny pups had seemed enormous and frightening.

Askan's voice rose beyond the gate, which opened, and the cubs and ponytails gave a shout as the scrubs stumbled in. Down the line they staggered, eyes wide, mouths open, propelled by many hands. Those who fell were foot-nudged into rising, except for one boy who seemed too stunned to move. A huge ponytail hauled him to his feet, laughing, and the boy plunged on, the braid he was about to lose flapping on his skinny back.

All was noise, laughter. When the scrubs were gone, the masters divided their charges to begin the first lessons of the day. Inda found Gand and said, "Well? What did your bees hum?"

Gand snorted a laugh. "They'll be a handful."

Chapter Twenty-one

WHEN the signal-mirror flashed from the mountains heights above the Andahi Pass, the woman on duty at Castle Andahi's south tower ran straight down, shedding rain at every step.

She burst into Ndand-Jarlan's office, her eyes enormous. "Jarlan-Edli! King's Rider in the pass," she exclaimed.

Ndand suppressed the lurch of fear followed by self-mockery. "Probably some new instructions for Cama." She forced herself to shrug though she knew that Cama had one of those necklace things that the king wore, which sent messages instantly. They'd use that, surely, if something terrible happened.

Not that the king could do anything from months' hard ride away, but he and Cama both labored hard never to be taken by surprise again. She waved at the young woman, one of the new arrivals who had been sent with the new horse herd. The lookout retreated to her duty.

Ndand tried to get back to work, but found it impossible, so she prowled around the office, which was as close to the same as Liet-Jarlan's as she could contrive though the former furnishings had either been destroyed or taken by the retreating Venn.

Ndand's own bedroom had changed, so as not to remind her of her happy years with Flash. How weird life was! No sooner had she made everything be as different as possible, than the desire to remember every detail of those good years intensified.

Cama understood. When he stayed over, they slept in his room, not hers. She could hardly articulate why—during her marriage with Flash they each had many lovers. Flash couldn't possibly have existed without lovers—he was just that way. And he'd always been friendly and welcoming to hers—the ones they didn't end up sharing. *I loved him, too, when I was a horsetail*, Cama had said. *We all did.*

She sank down onto a bench and had her cry. She'd got used to those. She just missed Flash so much! She'd taken to talking to his ghost, though she couldn't see one. But just the idea that he might be there, smiling over her shoulder, watching over the home he had come to love . . .

The messenger was Vedrid, Evred's pale-haired First Runner. That meant a message of royal importance. But Ndand and Vedrid knew one another. He pretended not to see her reddened eyes, and she pretended that nothing was amiss as she opened the door to his knock.

"Cama is doing his rounds in Idayago," she began.

"My business is with you." Vedrid smiled. "With you and one Hadand Tlen."

"Cap'n Han?" Ndand gasped. She turned to the Runner who had brought him. "Run and fetch Cap'n Han."

Flash's great-aunt-by-marriage, Ingrid Tlennen, appeared. The Andahi castle people had been glad when she showed up with a herd of new horses and a selected group of seasoned men and women, some with their children.

Everyone knew that Ingrid Tlennen had held Tlennen Castle in the bad old days when brigands had tried to cross the plains of Nelkereth and steal Marlovan horses; she had defended Tlennen Castle not once but several times. She had brought many of her tough relations from Nelkereth, including her sixteen-year-old niece. Her grizzled husband, the former Jarl, was the new Captain of the Arveas-Andahi Riders. They had retired when Hastrid Marlo-Vayir did to make way for young Jarls to serve a young king, but retirement had not really satisfied them. He, too, felt young again to have real work.

"The girl will be along quick," Ingrid-Randviar said in a gruff voice. "You'll pardon the dust and dirt, Herskalt?" She used the formal term for King's Voice, asking a question without asking.

"I understand," Vedrid said. He did not add, *I'm not here as Herskalt, just as a Runner.* So he *was* here as the King's Voice, then.

Hands smoothed clothing, twitched sashes straight, all of it unconscious as they awaited what had to be news of great importance.

Before he could speak a cluster of girls clattered in, their high voices piping shrilly. That is, most talked, but the one who talked fastest was the most shrill. Vedrid picked out the shrill voice from the pack of girls. Where their skinny arms and legs, their sun-bleached flaxen braids were much alike, this one's limbs were already forming into slender grace. Self-conscious grace, he noted, as she caught his eye and made a little business of fussing over her hair and clothes.

In contrast, "Cap'n Han" was indistinguishable from the others, a wiry small girl just starting to lengthen into coltishness, with a steady pair of light-colored eyes in an unremarkable round face. "Did you want me?" Her heartbeat pulsed in her skinny neck.

Vedrid said formally, "Evred-Harvaldar and Hadand-Gunvaer unite in sending this message to your guardian, Ndand-Edli, and to you, Hadand Tlen." The child's face paled at the sound of her formal name. "You are invited to present yourself to the royal city to train as a King's Runner next spring. Will you be twelve by then?"

Han trembled. She flicked her thumb up, unable to speak. The other girls squealed and screeched, jumping up and down. The pretty one also squealed and jumped, but with a sidelong, speculative glance toward Vedrid.

Why *her?* Lnand was thinking. *Why does Han get everything? I'm a leader, too!* As soon as she could (for Ndand-Jarlan was about to send everyone back to work so she could write a letter to Hadand-Gunvaer before presiding over a meal in honor of the Herskalt) she sidled up and said in her sweetest voice, "We're all so glad for Han, especially those of us who helped her so much last year during the war. Poor Han!" An affected laugh. "She almost . . ."

Lnand had been watching Han as she spoke. She wasn't even sure she dared refer to the fact that Han had wanted to throw a bratty three-year-old off a bridge. Well, not quite, but *almost*.

Han gave Lnand one of those *looks*. Lnand tossed her braids back and ran off to fetch some seed-cakes. That stupid Herskalt wasn't listening anyway.

Ndand gave the girls a little time to get over their excitement then said, "So no one has anything to do?"

The children knew that voice. They didn't stop to answer—Cap'n Han included—until Ndand-Jarlan snagged her by the sleeve and kept her back.

"You should hear this part," she said to Han, distracted for a moment by the child's serious face. But her mind was too busy with questions to ponder it. "What does that entail? Are we to send dispositions? Keth didn't have any. We still don't have much."

Vedrid said, "The Gunvaer-Edli says that all that will be supplied. You have only to get her to the royal city next spring. She can travel with Kethadrend when he goes to the academy. Until then, she is to work hard on her skills, including her Old Sartoran."

Old Sartoran? But Han didn't know any! Liet-Jarlan had only taught the Runners that. Gdand had learned a few lessons before the attack. Since then, the girls hadn't had any reading lessons. They'd all been too busy cleaning the castle, restoring it, and training in defense.

Cap'n Han's dismay caused Ndand to chuckle. "She'll know plenty by next spring."

"So this is what you do," Inda said.

As the fifteen- and sixteen-year-old boys watched, he demonstrated the aggressive feinting arc with the right hand and how the left came around to strike the opponent who had just shifted to avoid the feint.

The academy ponytails' court was cramped, the boys crowded together. It still didn't leave much space. So Inda hopped around to face the other way, becoming the opponent. "The right hand comes here." He pointed toward his face. "Now, we usually block, and he knows that, which is why you walk right into that left hand, and the horsetails dump you right on your butts. And laugh," Inda added, his tone as bitter as the ponytails all felt, though for different reasons.

For them, the matter was nothing more (or less) than the age-old arrogance of horsetails. Inda was annoyed because the few horsetails who'd stuck to the special lessons (all of them had come the first weeks, then fewer each succeeding Restday) seemed to be using what they learned to better their scragging techniques. Already there'd been two broken arms and several sprains, but because they all insisted they'd fallen down, the masters officially took no action.

Inda went down on one knee. He angled his body, left hand up and right jabbing straight toward the imagined enemy gut. "Down he goes instead." He got to his feet, then surveyed the faces. "What? It's not that hard."

"But we never fight on our knees," one expressed the general doubt.

Inda sighed. "Why not, if it works? Is it better to take a punch in the gut and listen to 'em laughing about what weeds you are?"

"No . . ."

A sudden confusion of shouts and cries halted the lesson. Inda straightened up, and the ponytails shut up, eyeing him as he became the Harskialdna in some way they couldn't even define.

Inda's annoyance fired to irritation. He'd worked this out carefully. The horsetails were on a three-day war game designed to sweat some of that swagger out of them. The cubs were doing an afternoon of ride-and-shoot. The scrubs, the only ones given liberty this Restday, were supposed to go with Askan to Daggers Drawn.

But the high, angry voices coming from the knife practice court were definitely scrubs.

Inda turned back to the ponytails. "You've got liberty. Better use it wiser than the scrubs over there."

He vaulted over the two low fences and dashed around the rock wall dividing off the courts where steel weapons were permitted.

And here they were, sure enough. A cluster of small boys froze in place. This was the place duels were held these days. In the center stood the duelists, one short, with sun-streaky brown hair, the other already gaining bone and muscle, with pale yellow hair and a fierce blue gaze. For the fifth time this season, Keth Arveas-Andahi and Honeyboy Tya-Vayir.

Dauvid Tya-Vayir, Inda corrected himself as he glowered at them. Keth was a heartbreaking reminder of Flash, and Dauvid strong and hard-boned like the Tya-Vayirs. Dauvid's scowl was a twin for Horsebutt's expression, a unique combination of arrogance and petulance.

"Stables," he said to the ring around the combatants. "The stable hands will enjoy their Restday liberty. You boys will groom and feed all the cubs' mounts when they come in. Then the stalls."

Mouths dropped open in dismay. One began to whine, "But *we* didn't—"

"That's not enough work?" he asked, and they took off.

"You two," Inda said, "are going to be sweeping the parade court together."

Keth blinked rapidly, struggling against tears. One cheekbone was rapidly swelling, and the knuckles on both hands as well. His clothes were awry, imprinted with dirt from the flagstones. Honeyboy, who loathed the nickname as passionately as his aunt and uncle had loathed being called Honeytongue and Horsebutt, scowled.

"It's his fault!"

"Now."

"But he keeps—"

"You want to sweep all the barracks, too, Tya-Vayir?"

Keth had run off in the direction of the storage shed. The Tya-Vayir boy flung himself after, cursing under his breath.

Inda started back in the direction of the headmaster's office, where he knew he'd find a gathering of the masters who had liberty.

Askan dashed around the corner of the wall of the senior courtyard, and stopped him. "Another fight?" he asked. "I walked them all over to Daggers Drawn myself."

Inda said, "As soon as you were gone a dozen of 'em slithered back to have their fight, just like they see the big boys doing." He told Askan what he'd done. "You know what they were fighting about?" he asked. "I didn't let 'em tell me. I wanted Tya-Vayir to see that they were getting the same treatment."

Askan flung out his hand as he fell in step with Inda,

palm down. "Tya-Vayir will have convinced himself that you gave Arveas-Andahi preferential treatment by the time we gather for Restday Drum no matter what anyone says. He arrived convinced that he'd be unfairly treated, and everyone else favored."

Inda smacked the seniors' wall. "Horsebutt."

Askan flipped up the back of his hand, then looked around guiltily.

Inda also looked around. They were alone. "At least the scrubs aren't putting one another in the lazaretto."

"Not like our year, eh?" Askan said, rapping his knuckles lightly against Inda's ribs with one hand, and with the other, touching his eye where Cama wore his eye patch.

"Maybe I shouldn't be teaching any of the boys the Fox drills. Only if I don't, when do they learn? What is it I'm doing wrong?"

"Nothing," Askan exclaimed, hands outflung. "They're just a pack of brats. Not a brain to share between 'em."

Inda didn't make any response, but he asked the same question of Headmaster Gand later on, after the boys had been dismissed from Restday Drum. The cubs and ponytails, tired from running around in the hot sun chasing flags, retired to their barracks to while away the time until the Daylast bell; the scrubs were turning out their barracks to scour it down and restore everything before sweeping their court on Askan's orders.

"They all knew what was going on, even if they didn't get into it," Gand said. "In the meantime, they see that everyone gets equal punishment."

"Because of Horsebutt," Inda said.

Gand opened his hands. "His father was just the same, and the old Randael almost as bad. Grandfather rumored to be worse. Are you certain you don't want to thrash those boys?"

Inda grimaced. "You can, if you want. I just can't do it." The thought of thrashing anyone always brought nightmarish flashes of Wafri and his tortures, something he never told anyone. Fighting, that was different. Someone tries to kill you, you kill him first. But thrashing some small boy who can't defend himself? *Fox does it, and they don't come out the worse for it,* Inda thought bleakly, feeling even more incompetent than he had earlier.

Gand took in that lowered gaze, the unhappy mouth, Inda's loose hands, and said, "Another thing about the Tya-Vayirs. Not all, but most. They had a knack for making everyone seem smaller and meaner and worse than they actually are."

Inda pressed his fingers to his eyes. "I thought there would be some Cama in that boy."

"There might be yet."

"He just looks at me with that sneer. 'The King's Claphair.' I know what caused that first fight. Keth trying to defend my honor. It's . . ." He kicked the wall. "It's funny, but it's not funny. The worst of it is, when I asked him, that boy didn't even know what a claphair is! Seems to think it's what we used to call a bootlick!"

"Horsebutt has that much of a sense of what's right," Gand said, unperturbed.

Inda got to his feet. "And I was going to reorganize the entire academy, from dawn to dusk, turning out . . ." *Turning out boys as tough and trained as Fox's boys and girls in the fleet.* Inda left, feeling like a failure.

While he was trudging back toward the pile of work awaiting him in the Harskialdna office, his sister Hadand entered Tdor's office with a paper in hand.

Tdor looked up from a pile of exasperating tasks she'd put off for days. How many mattresses to reorder against next year and how many to try to repair in order to coax them through another year, shifting the night patrol around for three women who'd got sparring injuries, squabbles between two they'd intended to send north to reinforce Ndand-Jarlan's women. Would they grow out of it, or would they be another problem if both went?

Tdor threw her pen down. "I saw your northern Runner ride in through the gates when I was going down to drill this morning," she said. "Good news, I hope?"

"Good, and . . . odd. So far, Honeytongue—er, Starand has been on her best behavior up in Idayago," Hadand said. "She loves Idayago and has taken to wearing their dresses. Eating their food. Some of the local women have been courting her favor, for whatever reason, and you know she'd love that."

"If courting her favor turns her sweet, I hope they court her forever," Tdor said. "Odd?"

"Fnor writes me that recently Mran started having nightmares about children and Venn and getting lost."

Tdor was taken aback. "Mran? Children? So Buck and Fnor have given up on having an heir?"

Hadand stared out the window. "No, Fnor says they don't talk about that at all, not even the prospect of trying the Birth Spell. But Mran asked if Inda got any letters, or messages, from Dag Signi the Venn."

Signi. Tdor's fingers busily straightened the already straight pile of papers as she remembered Inda's occasional wistful questions about where Signi might be, what she might be doing, why didn't she send a letter. It didn't happen often, but each one made Tdor struggle against envy all over again. She was ashamed of that. *I know Signi went away because of me.* "Dag Signi? What could it mean?"

"I don't know, except the Cassads are strange—they have dreams that turn out to be true—some even say they see ghosts. But you know that."

Hadand stood in the doorway, looking down at the paper, her profile so unhappy Tdor stared in dismay and wonder. "Speaking of heirs, I stopped chewing gerda," Hadand said at last. "It turns my stomach, and Evred seems to work through all watches, except when he falls asleep in his chair."

Tdor tried to think of an answer, but Hadand walked out.

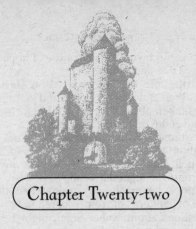

Chapter Twenty-two

THE fierce summer sun was just setting when Fox's fleet spotted the jagged teeth of Ghost Island on the horizon.

Exclamations of relief sounded around the ship, for they'd had to navigate by the sun-tracker, always dangerous.

Barend, at his place behind the binnacle, stayed silent as he swept the glass over the horizon.

Two days after Barend's arm was broken the fleet touched land, where the *Skimit* awaited them, having arranged for supplies. Barend lay in his hammock unable to move.

Over the following half year, as the fleet made its way west, practicing ship maneuvers to integrate Fangras' independents under Fox's exacting eye, they touched land once more, at Llyenthur, on the other side of the strait.

During those months, as the sun steadily regained its southern heights, Barend's arm healed without mishap—it had been a clean break—and he took up his job as ship master as if nothing had happened. As soon as he could, he resumed deck drills, and by the time they were sailing west into open ocean, he no longer favored that arm.

Now Ghost Island's dragon teeth resolved into separate

islands. Under an azure sky rapidly darkening into night they were met in Halfmoon Harbor by a stone-faced contingent of armed islanders, their fast little boats covered by steep-roofed structures with leddas mats laid over them. They could shoot fire arrows from behind those and stay out of harm. They might not defeat a fleet of twenty-odd capital ships and racing schooners, but they could inflict a great deal of damage. And the only place to resupply within months of sailing was right here.

It did not take much to imagine the harbor, now slowly lighting up with twinkling glowglobes and lamps, full of armed citizens determined to protect their freedom.

The same old woman who had met them on their first arrival, half a year after their defeat of the Brotherhood of Blood, stood in the bow of the first boat. Her challenging frown was accentuated by ruddy flickers of lanterns. "Why are you here?" she called up. "We only trade with the Delfin Islands. We will not trade with you."

"We're pushing west." Fox leaned over the *Death*'s stern rail. "Looking for trade. Need to resupply, repair. A little liberty."

"You may have three days, and you will be permitted ashore only if you are not armed." The old woman's voice rasped with distrust. "We permit that much because you did nothing untoward before. But we see that your former captain is no longer with you."

"He retired from the sea—"

The woman cut across Fox's speech. "Do not trouble us with what may be lies. We cannot prove your words either way. We liked this Inda Elgar. He kept his promises. You must prove to us you will keep yours. Three days. Without weapons. Without any trouble from your crew, or we will rise against you all."

Lanterns had been lit on the *Death* by the deck crew. At the wheel, Mutt watched a muscle in Fox's jaw jump. *Ooh, trouble,* Mutt thought. Fox had been nastier than ever these past few months, ever since he'd decked Barend. On the other hand, the entire fleet was in the best fighting shape it had ever been.

But Fox only said, "Three days it is. And there will be no trouble from my crew."

"Fox will kill 'em if they sneeze wrong," Jeje observed to

Dasta. She'd sailed the *Vixen* up the side of *Cocodu* away from the *Death,* then climbed stealthily aboard to observe with its captain.

"How d'ya sneeze right?" Dasta muttered out of the side of his mouth.

She snorted. "Ask Tau that. If we ever see him again. Me, I figure it's right if you don't sneeze into my soup."

From the *Vixen*'s deck Nugget stared up impatiently. Jeje had left her at the tiller, which meant Nugget couldn't hear the talk. That annoyed her. She just *knew* something was going on, but no one would tell her *anything*.

She yanked up the glass, balanced the tiller against one thigh, and glared through the lens at Mutt, there at the wheel on the *Death*. They still were Not Talking, even though she'd made sure he saw her kissing Captain Eflis. So much for his vows of friendship, and how Inda's ship rats would always be together, just like Inda and his original ship rats.

While Nugget brooded, Dasta said through stiff lips, "What's he going to do about Barend?"

He and Jeje turned their attention away from the island boats, which were retreating rapidly in the capricious breezes, leaving the capital ships to wallow more slowly behind the *Death*. From where they couldn't see Barend.

Jeje kicked a barrel with her bare toes. Once Barend had got out of his hammock, a sling all fixed up for his arm, Fox had refused to let him make ship visits. *Your friends can visit here. Anything they have to say can be heard by me. There will be no misunderstandings that way.*

It hadn't taken much effort to guess what problem lay between Fox and Barend, not when Ghost Island was mentioned.

Treasure.

Jeje and Dasta had talked aboard the cutter, figuring that Inda had told Barend about the treasure and maybe sent him to get some of it to help back in the Marlovan kingdom. Jeje told Dasta how worn out everything there was—and that was before the big battle with the Venn.

Dasta muttered, "I hope Fox isn't going to kill Barend. Throw his body to rot in that damned cavern alongside the pirate skeletons."

"Not while *I'm* there, he won't," Jeje growled.

"So what do we do? You can't fight Fox and win."

"I can't alone. But he can't take us all. We have to stay united," Jeje retorted.

"You and I can't take him together, either. So do we bring people in?" Dasta grimaced. "Seems to me the more people know, the more they'll go crazy after gold. Just like Fox."

"I don't think Fox's crazy after gold. Why else didn't he take it when he had the chance? No, I just think he doesn't want Inda to have it. That's why he's so angry at Barend."

"Is that what's going on?"

"I think so. Nothing else makes sense."

"And that does? Shitfire. I wish the damned islanders had burned that damned book before Inda ever got here." Dasta's usually pleasant face was grim.

They would have been surprised to discover that roughly the same thoughts were going through not just Barend's mind but also Fox's.

Barend stood silently at his station behind the binnacle. He hadn't spoken to anyone for weeks, except when necessary to deliver orders. He blamed himself for what had happened; he should have known Fox would figure out his purpose. He should not have come on board. He should not have tried a sneak that night. And he should not have left Aunt Wisthia's golden scroll case—given to him so he could keep her apprised of his progress—in his gear. Of course he'd asked Fox where it was, and of course Fox had asked, "What case?"

How many times since had he laughed at himself and Inda, closeted there in Ala Larkadhe, each thinking himself so smart, so far-seeing? *Get the gold,* Inda had said. *Turn it into trade,* Barend had said.

We were idiots. No. We are idiots, Barend thought, watching the harbor close in. He was alone, for he refused to try raising a mutiny with the gold as reward. Just how many would be killed if he tried that stupidity?

He also refused to write to Evred via the locket, which was still hanging around his neck. Evred could do nothing. Knowing about his fool cousin's foolish actions would only increase his burdens. Barend must take care of the situation himself. Or die trying.

*   *   *

Fox paced restlessly on deck. He was angry with Inda, angry with Barend, angry with Dasta and Jeje. He knew they hadn't yapped *yet* about the treasure to anyone else, but how long would they hold out?

If only they wanted it for honest purposes, like buying a tavern. Or a castle. Or wasting it on a year-long orgy. He could stomach just about any motivation except a reward going to the soul-cursed Montrei-Vayirs. He hadn't eaten for days because his gut burned with fury.

Jeje had slithered the cutter to the far side of *Cocodu*, which meant she was head-to-head with Dasta now, and thought he didn't see her.

He didn't think they were stupid, or desperate, enough to loose the secret in order to raise a mutiny. True he'd be dead if he was wrong, but they had to see that the fleet would promptly turn on itself. Fangras and those others had wanted one thing out of Inda: wins. They would never loot a treasure and take the gold tamely to wherever it was Barend had appointed . . .

Ah, no use in arguing inside his head. Time to act.

"Signal, Pilvig."

She backed up a couple of steps from that venomous glare.

"*Cocodu, Vixen* captains, meet on shore." Then Fox turned Barend's way. "You, too."

He turned back to Pilvig and issued a stream of orders to be signaled. Then he went back to his cabin to prepare.

When the tide turned as the sun sank, the fleet had anchored and liberty boats were lowered.

Barend climbed silently into the captain's gig and dropped in the bow. Fox settled into the stern sheets as the gig crew picked up their oars. He kept his glass to his eye, watching as he checked the lantern-lit liberty boats swarming toward shore. The sailors sat soberly, the signal orders having been explicit about what would happen if they did not keep order.

When his gig reached the white sands of the shore, he leaped out, Barend behind him. Dasta and Jeje waited, backed by Gillor. Just beyond them, Nugget marched past Mutt, nose in the air. Mutt slouched, knowing he wasn't wanted, but the other young mates had wheedled him into staying to find out what was going on.

"Go away," Fox said to Mutt.

Mutt was glad whatever had hit the ground back there wasn't sticking to his feet. Nugget flounced ahead, chin up, swinging the long silken fringe of the scarf she had taken to winding around her stump. Mutt loped after her, heels kicking up arcs of fine white sand.

Gillor remained where she was. Her frequent glances toward Jeje made it clear she knew there was trouble, but not exactly what.

Inda hadn't told Gillor about the treasure, but that did not mean she hadn't guessed. She returned Fox's gaze, flushing in the bobbing lantern-light of the last straggling sailors as Fox flipped his fingers at her. "Go get drunk, Gillor," he said.

"Why can't she stay?" Jeje snarled, arms crossed.

"Because I'm not going to discuss my plans until she's gone."

Gillor flipped up the back of her hand in a not-quite-humorous gesture, then stalked toward the city, the last of those on liberty.

When her blue silk shirt was just a pale starlit blob against the silhouetted buildings, Fox said, "At dawn we'll take *Vixen*. See if it's still there. Then discuss the next step."

"You mean, kill us all at a comfortable distance from these townies?" Jeje jerked her thumb over her shoulder.

"How long would I get away with that? Use your brains, Jeje," Fox snapped back impatiently. "You and Dasta vanish and they'll all be howling with questions. The choice I see is between some sensible plan—which has nothing to do with pouring gold down the Marlovan rat hole—or just breaking the secret, come one come all, sit back, and enjoy the merry bloodshed and greed."

"Inda needs it," Barend said.

"Then Inda should have come and got it," Fox retorted. Barend shut up.

"Dawn? Here? Agreed? All four of us? If you insist," Fox drawled, "I'll emulate Inda's heroic gesture and leave my weapons behind when we go over to the island."

"Do that," Jeje snapped.

"Oh, shit," Dasta exclaimed. "I hate this. Yeah, dawn, but as far as I'm concerned, let 'em all have it. Or better, we just sail away and leave it. Like we did before. I don't like what that gold is doing to *us*. If we give out the secret, half the fleet will be dead by morning. More."

"It might not even be there," Fox reminded them. "We don't know for certain that our little excursion went unnoticed. Or that someone local had not read that book and found out that the last of the pirates who'd been stationed on the island to kill anyone who landed had all hunted and killed one another."

"Leaving it to the ghosts." Jeje chuckled.

There were nods and grunts of agreement, then they all turned away. Fox and Barend walked up the shore side by side, neither speaking.

Jeje and Dasta joined Gillor, who had waited at the edge of the beach where the brick terrace began.

"Why aren't those two fighting a duel?" Gillor asked, jerking her chin toward Fox and Barend.

"They're Marlovans." Jeje snorted. "You *know* nothing they do ever makes any sense."

"Right. So this doesn't happen to concern Inda's clinking bags that day you all came back in the *Vixen* just before the storm, does it?" she asked, when Barend and Fox were well out of earshot.

Jeje sighed.

A corner of Dasta's mouth turned up. "I'd say, my promise was only to Inda. So if you were to, oh, show your face at dawn, why not see what happens?"

"Huh." Gillor snorted. "I might at that."

Mutt caught up with Nugget just before reaching the edge of the main road. "I can show you where to go," he said tentatively. "Since you never saw this place."

She tossed her hair back. "I thought I'd wait for Eflis."

He walked away.

She waited for the space of three breaths, not believing he was just going to leave.

"So much for you keeping your promises," Nugget yelled.

Mutt stopped, his shoulders going tight. Then he kept walking.

She pounded after. "You're a liar. And stupid!"

He turned around at last. "Go howl at Eflis, if you're so in love with her." He walked on.

When Eflis and Sparrow caught up, there was a woebegone Nugget, teary-eyed, waiting. Eflis held out her arms, and Nugget threw herself into them. "You can bunk in with us," Eflis said, running her fingers through Nugget's curls as the girl sniffed and pressed against her.

Sparrow remained silent.

Jeje and Dasta stayed in a pleasure house on a narrow street. They met outside just as the sun began to lift in the east. Dawn came fast this far north.

At the intersection they found Gillor leaning against a wall from which she could see the shore as well as both ends of the street. She'd propped a foot behind her, and she was honing one of her knives on a whetstone. "Mornin'."

"Seen anyone?"

"Not a soul. Or, none of ours. *Vixen*'s out on the water, bowsed up tight." She tipped her head seaward, where bare poles of the fleet's landing craft gently bobbled on the rippling water, *Vixen* and the fleet in the middle.

"Barend?"

"Didn't Fox make him rack up in the same place he stays?"

They all turned their heads toward the top of the hill, where the huge Pirate House stood. Lights gleamed on its lower level. Someone had obviously moved in since they were here with Inda.

On their first visit, Fox had dossed in an inn directly across the street from Pirate House so he could watch over Inda's comings and goings. He had to be at that same inn; they all knew he avoided pleasure houses when possible.

"I still don't know if he likes men or women," Gillor commented as they trod up the steep street.

"Neither. Snakes," Jeje cracked.

Dasta hooted with laughter, and Gillor said, "Jeje, that's disgusting."

"For the snakes," Jeje returned, her low, husky voice almost bass.

They all laughed, then ventured increasingly ridiculous ideas of Fox's style of wooing. Not that it was easy to imagine an amorous Fox. The raillery, however funny, sent a pang through Gillor.

They reached the inn, and Dasta volunteered to go roust

the laze-offs. Jeje agreed, with some regret: her preference would be to kick Fox out of bed, but she suspected that would be a very brief pleasure, and likely her last.

She and Gillor remained outside, talking low-voiced out of regard for the bedroom windows open just above. They jumped when Dasta reappeared, eyes wide and furious.

"Barend's up there snoring like he's going to sleep for a week," he whispered, almost strangling in an effort to keep his voice down. All of them were mindful of "making trouble."

"Sleepweed, you think?" Gillor asked. And on Dasta's nod, "Why would he swallow that?"

"Because I don't think he did. Not by himself. Fox did it to him. Fox is gone," Dasta added.

Chapter Twenty-three

INDA began climbing up into the stands around the parade court, for this was the first day of the Summer Games. The middle section of the middle stone bench was not marked off in any way, but everyone left that space empty. That was where the royal family sat, and everybody knew it.

Half a dozen steps up Inda paused, one foot resting on the next stair. People stopped behind him until there was a line of impatiently shuffling spectators. A quick, covert whisper "The Harskialdna" riffled back down the line. No one yelled or elbowed; one, then two people eased around him, and when he just stared witlessly up at that empty bench, people flowed around in twos and threes, filling the rest of the stands.

Inda had been caught by the memory of his watching that bench when he was ten: how looming and inscrutable the king and his brother seemed, seated with a thin woman with a triangular face Inda barely recalled. She was Barend's mother, the Harandviar. Tdor's title. Following hard was a flood of memories: the dust, the snapping banners, the excitement of a shared secret tempered by the frequent and heavy-handed warnings from brothers not to expect any audience, or praise, and definitely no accolade, assuming the Royal Shield Arm was even there. Tanrid's brown eyes as he shaded his eyes against the sun. *Father almost never comes the year he has to ride back for Convocation. Last Games he didn't even come though it was alter-year.* At the time Inda had thought Tanrid said it so Inda wouldn't get unrealistic expectations, but now he wondered how much hurt had been there.

If only he could talk to Tanrid!

The intense longing jolted him back into the here and now. He started up the steps. All spring and summer seemed like an unending stream of reminders of expectations that had turned out to be impossible. Everyone said that the academy was running fine. It didn't feel fine. He knew he could command battle. He made a plan, he led from the front and used all his wits and strength until not an enemy stood around him.

Teaching boys?

Inda reached the royal family seat, remembering that the Royal Shield Arm, as head of the academy, was the one to decide if the boys would get the accolade. How had he managed to forget that? No. He had not forgotten. He had just never thought about what it meant.

He dropped down beside Hadand and Tdor, who were talking in low voices.

Evred arrived then, causing a stir among the Runners waiting with the trumpets and the boys impatiently nudging and wriggling beyond the corral gates. Evred sat down next to his wife, his profile tense.

Inda leaned across the women and punched Evred in the arm. "Evred.Hadand. You're going to have to tip me the signal if you think they'll get the accolade."

Evred rubbed his jaw. "Better not than too often."

Inda sighed. What was too often? But Evred had his wall-face on again, he stared straight ahead, fists on his knees.

Hadand realized something she'd been peripherally aware of for half a year: Inda was the only person who crossed in and out of that invisible space Evred surrounded himself with. Inda didn't even seem to be aware of it. But Hadand could not imagine anyone else daring to hit Evred on the arm.

She shook away the thought. "Remember to listen to the crowd around you. If they really expect it, they are usually right."

Inda leaned against Tdor and muttered in a whisper, "I want to give the brats the back of my hand."

Tdor stifled the impulse to remind him that the stands were filled with families of the boys. "They think it was a great year," she said. "You have to have seen that at the banquet last night!"

She'd had to attend the Summer Games banquet for the Jarl families the years she was here for training. The tense atmosphere of those long ago banquets and the geniality of the previous night's could not have been more different.

Even Evred had seemed more relaxed while chatting with Horseshoe Jaya-Vayir, here for his last Summer Games: his son and nephew would go to the guard for their two years once the games were over.

"It wasn't a good year," Inda said under his breath, gaze beyond the waiting Runner with the horn. "Fox would've had them all trained."

"Fox," Tdor retorted, "would just get rid of the Honeyboys and the rest of the troublemakers. You have to take Jarls' sons, whatever they're like."

"Inda. Fist up," Hadand said out of the corner of her mouth. Inda hastily raised his fist to signal the official start to the games.

The boys cheered, some drumming on the temporary railings set up for the horses. It felt so strange, after all those years of wishing he was down there with the boys. What a laugh on himself!

Tdor gave him a mockingly severe look. "So you'll have to revise your methods for next year."

"Had to every day."

"So did I," she reminded him, as below, the seniors took down the makeshift gate and began to bring out the horses for the scrub shoeing.

Inda watched some of the senior boys execute riding tricks on the horses' backs. "But your girls aren't brats."

"Some of them are," she countered. How to express the truth? "I think you expected the boys to be like you. If you're not going to beat them into instant obedience, then you have to expect they'll have their own motivations. Ideal

training might be ideal for ideal people." A shout went up
as a senior did a handspring from a horse's back to the next
horse, and she raised her voice slightly. "Hadand and I were
talking about that this morning just before inspection."

The shout died away as the seniors ceased showing off
and tied the animals to the rail.

Inda drummed lightly on his knee, sighing as the scrubs
ran out and lined up squirming and nudging. "Yeah, they're
good when I'm there, but when I'm not, Honeyboy was
slanging everyone, including me. Keth got into fights all
spring. The horsetails scragged the ponytails. I keep trying
to be Gand, but it doesn't work." He nodded at the waiting
bugler, who played the call.

The scrubs promptly started struggling, scrapping, shoving, shrieking, as people in the stands laughed or shouted
encouragement.

Hadand said, "Inda, where are your wits? Those boys
love you. They will do anything for you!"

Tdor was aware of Evred listening silently. "Your
mother told me something before I left. Since I was about
to be training girls I don't know, unlike at ho—at Castle
Tenthen, where I've known everyone all my life. She said
unless there's immediate danger, two things motivate the
young: competition and desire for attention."

Evred joined the conversation, though he did not
look away from the scrambling boys on the field. Inda
was surprised Evred could hear over the noise around
them. "There are worse motivations than game wins and
stings."

Hadand leaned past Tdor. "Here's another thing, Inda.
The boys act out because they want your attention. They
never wanted Gand's. They're too scared of him."

Inda made a skeptical face. "They're not afraid of me,
yet everyone keeps saying I have a rep for being rough and
tough?"

"You're rough and tough on the battlefield." Tdor
chuckled. "Their fathers and uncles and relatives have told
them that. You never scrag anyone just to strut, and also,
they can tell you like them. Gand grew up perfecting that
dragoon disdain. You just never think about what your
face says."

Inda waggled his fingers. "Maybe we need a mirror in

our rooms so I can practice. What's a Gand face, anyway? How about this?" He slitted his eyes, twisted his mouth into a sneer, and stuck out his jaw.

Hadand waved at him in amused disgust, then turned her attention to the field.

"Looks like you got burrs in your drawers." Tdor elbowed him. "Pay attention."

The little boys were halfway through the shoeing. They were busy competing each for himself, just like the boys had been doing for generations. And yes, it *was* really funny to watch as they rammed into one another, dropped shoes. *Splash!* Honeyboy Tya-Vayir pushed Harstad Tvei into the closest horse trough, and laughter rose up from the audience. Inda did not see a hint of shock or disappointment that these ten-year-olds weren't fast and competent.

"I guess I expected more out of them. I guess . . . I don't know, somehow it feels like me being judged down there, that if they laugh it's at me."

"Boys," Tdor stated, "are going to laugh. And so do the girls. If children can't laugh at their elders, how can they expect to do better? We laughed before things got dangerous. I missed the laughter afterward."

Inda found no answer, but the boys' fooling around disturbed him. *This is why the Harskialdna stays distant,* Inda told himself, sitting back and trying to look serious. *Next year will be different—I won't teach 'em anything they can use on each other.*

The day rolled toward its end, the boys' skills neither demonstratively better or worse than any of the other years Evred had sat in these stands or watched from the gates. But the general atmosphere carried a qualitative difference, less sharpness, less of the old undertone of anger. As far as he could see, he was the only one aware of it.

Evred tested his observation over the next few days, without discussing it with anyone.

By the last day of the games, he knew that Inda was at the center of the new atmosphere, though Inda himself was not aware of it.

It was clearest at the siege, the most popular event of all, during which the queen's girls defended a ramshackle building hammered together for the horsetails to attack. The boys mounted a clever enough attack, a three-pronged assault in which the feint was unclear, sending the girls running back and forth.

But the girls' running was to a purpose, not just frenzied dashing about. On a whistled signal the girls leaped out, each with her target, and the big horsetails hadn't a hope of defending against the practiced Odni sweeps and falls.

One, two, three, the boy captains of each group were sat upon, wriggling and cursing in futility, and the boy commander was surrounded by determined girls ready to treat him likewise. Seeing his forces thoroughly routed, he raised his hand in surrender, and the packed stands cheered wildly.

Hadand and Tdor grinned at one another. As the four walked toward the residence to change for the last banquet for Jarls and their offspring, Tdor said to Inda, "I think that was the funniest thing I've ever seen."

Hadand leaned over. "Showed the boys just how useful those drills are."

"Too late," Inda said. "They aren't getting 'em next year. What a bunch of pugs!"

Hadand stopped, and put a hand on her brother's chest to halt him. "Inda, those boys have been killing themselves to master their double-stick and lance and arrow-shooting from horseback, just to impress you. They can't use any of that on these sieges."

"But they could have learned to be fast with their hands," Inda retorted. "They never took the Fox drills seriously."

Tdor and Hadand exchanged looks. For generations the women had kept the Odni from the men because the purpose of it was to be able to take a bigger, stronger man by surprise.

Well, things had changed, and men were learning it.

"New things take time," Hadand said.

"But old things—like competition between boys and girls—make changes go faster." Tdor smiled as the girls departed, hooting, calling insults, and laughing. The boys eyed the girls, some uncertain, flushed and grumpy at their total defeat. Others pretended affront as an excuse to tease and flirt. "You watch. They'll be more serious next year. Not because anyone that age sees how the new ways might be a help in the future, but because next year, the girls won't be able to laugh at them, ha ha."

Hadand chuckled as Inda rolled his eyes.

Evred slipped away, leaving the others to the fathers who, in praising the year's games, were all really fishing for praise for their boys and girls. That was now Inda's and Tdor's job. Evred had only to preside at the last banquet, then the noise and interruptions of the Summer Games would be over.

He was surrounded by people demanding his attention, from whom he detached himself with the privilege of his rank. His head ached with the unexpected impact of memory. He'd been watching the Summer Games for years, but somehow, sitting there with Inda an arm's length away had brought their own year so vividly to mind: Dogpiss, laughing in the sunlight . . . Noddy slouching along, cooing to the horses as he led them to Mouse Marth-Davan . . . Flash's laughter. The horsetails, looking so old then, but so horribly young, all lined up at the corral rail: Hawkeye, Manther, Buck. His own brother. All either dead or cruelly maimed. How sharp was the knife of memory! His head throbbed with it.

He had to be alone before he could trust his public face again.

Shaking off the last of the crowd, Evred took the Runners' side route into the castle. When he reached the quiet of his own rooms, he glimpsed a blue-coated silhouette at the window, and had a single heartbeat's warning before he recognized those shoulders, the long wheat-gold tail of hair.

"The privilege of a Runner is to enter and leave without fanfare," Tau said, turning around and smiling. "I trust I did not break some rule of which I was unaware?"

He came to me first. Not to Inda. Why? The war-drum tap of Evred's heartbeat had changed for a blacksmith's hammer. "No." He entered the room, so the sinking light from the window fell on his face.

And saw shock widen Tau's eyes. Evred shut the door with his own hands, then put his back to it.

Tau said, "When one sees people every day, change is usually imperceptible."

Evred's wits had flattened on the anvil. "You are making an observation about me?"

"You've aged ten years. Twenty."

Evred flushed, then turned away, a hand half raised.

"You've never talked to Inda," Tau ventured further.

Evred turned back, a sharp, angry movement. His face had thinned, emphasizing the bones; the creases Tau had seen between his brows and bracketing his mouth during the previous summer were beginning to etch into lines.

Tau gave a half laugh. Here it was again, that thrill of danger. "You have more power than anyone I've ever met. I could feel it coming upstairs here, the rings of guardians you've put between yourself and the world."

Evred's lips parted, then he stilled, shutting himself off. Tau watched it happen: the man was gone, leaving the closest semblance of a stone effigy humanly possible. He could feel the effort it took.

"You had a purpose in returning?" Evred asked, in the effigy's flat voice.

"Yes," Tau said. "To see you. Oh, Inda as well. And Hadand. And everyone else I met and befriended previously. But I've been thinking about you all through this past year. I even found myself trying to talk to you through Inda's letters last winter, before my golden case got swept overboard in a storm."

Evred had gone to the desk, his tense hands fussing purposelessly at the neatly stacked papers there. "Inda wondered why you had stopped writing to him."

"I even brought a justifiable reason to return," Tau said, and thrust his hand into his gear bag, which crackled promisingly. "About a dozen of the latest plays, because if any kingdom needs a theater, this one does. With your permission I will put myself to work."

Evred said, "How?"

"Volunteers. My theory is that your Marlovans will be more willing to try something new if they have a hand in its creation. But that's my public reason. My real one is . . . you."

Evred opened a hand, a wary rather than promissory gesture. "Is it I or the kingdom you intend to benefit from your presence?"

Tau ignored the sarcasm. "I am discreet, and I observe things. Like this aura of distance, almost of threat, that surrounds you like a lightning bolt about to strike. No one truly separates heart from head except at the cost of sanity.

You've become so angry that people feel it as soon as you enter a room."

Evred had not moved, but the armor of aloofness was gone. His voice was soft with menace. "You think I'm malevolent? Or just insane?"

"You will compass both if you keep denying normal human emotion."

"And you are my cure?"

"You have to be your own cure. What I can offer you is the chance to laugh. To shed some of the passion you work so hard to deny. You *know* that's not sane or healthy, Evred."

Infuriated to the point of nausea, Evred briefly closed his eyes. The rushing in his ears was back. He walked to the window and looked down without really seeing the great parade ground, where wanders were busy magicking away horse droppings, others busy with brooms to catch up the bits of straw and splinters of wood. "Get out."

"I'm going to give my greetings to the others, then maybe find a likely tavern and sing for my supper," Tau said. "I told Vedrid I'd take that last room in the guest wing, the one before the middle tower. It has the most private entrance."

He went out, shut the door, and leaned against the wall for several whickering breaths. He was drenched in sweat.

Well, that went . . .

Abandoning that thought, he bathed, changed, then went to hunt the others down one by one.

They were all happy to see him in their individual ways: Hadand flushing up to her hair, grinning like a girl when he bent to kiss her hands. Tdor smiled, and Tau wondered if it was hope or relief he saw in her quiet countenance. Inda was distracted, surrounded by several Jarls, Runners, and men Tau would soon learn were academy masters and assistants. Kened and Vedrid, as well as his old friends. Tau knew he was going to need an entire day for each of them. But he'd find the time.

He gracefully declined Inda's offer to attend the banquet, and went into the royal city to visit the taverns again.

When the midnight bells rang he was waiting in his room as promised, and when Evred knocked just once a short while later, welcomed him in.

Dauvid Tya-Vayir and his escort reached home just as the harvest season began. The worry about what Uncle Stalgrid would say was so familiar Dauvid was not aware of its grip tensing him. It just was.

The Riders stayed in the stable to take care of the mounts. Dauvid paused to greet the dogs leaping up to lick his face and thump against his legs, tails batting the air. Then the two Runners brought Dauvid inside. They were passed along until they found Uncle Stalgrid out in the field, where he could see with his own eyes that no one sneaked an extra basket away at shift change.

The air was hot, full of buzzing insects; in the far fields, voices drifted faintly, singing old Iascan harvest songs.

"There you are," Uncle Stalgrid said. "I've received no complaints of you. No praise either, but that's as usual. No bootlick of Evred Montrei-Vayir's is ever going to bestir himself on your behalf. Did the claphair strut his battle stories?"

"Not much. Boys asked, but—"

"Any changes from what I told you to expect?"

"Just, we got taught some of the Fox drills, but everything else—"

"Pirate tricks. What use is that in honorable battle? Well, the claphair is trying to win the favor of the boys, that's obvious. What dishonorable name did they stick on you?"

"Honeyboy."

"I hope you fought whoever did it."

"Yes. That is, I think—"

"Break their teeth? You have to break teeth, or they don't take you seriously."

"No, I—"

Uncle Stalgrid's eyes widened. "You what? Were afraid? Of the boys? Of King Willow? If you're afraid of a smack or two, then I'm going to have to waste the winter season toughening you up again."

Dauvid braced for the expected smack. It was too hot for much more, and Stalgrid wanted to keep his eye on the harvest, so he sent Dauvid away.

Dauvid's head hurt as he trudged back to the castle, where he found the women in the far yard, pumping lake water in to soak the flax.

As soon as she saw him, Aunt Imand beckoned and took him inside. "I promised your mother you'd get food and drink first thing," she said, and while he sucked down cold water, she pulled a knife from her wrist, sliced some fresh bread for him, and stuffed the bread with cheese and smoked turkey.

She stood over him while he ate, and when he was done, she said, "What did you learn this year?"

He told her, a jumbled rush of words divided equally between bragging and complaining about lessons, the Fox drills, scragging, the fights he got in, who won, who lost, who cheated. He hated the name they stuck on him, Honeyboy.

"There's worse," she said. "There are far worse names."

Dauvid had been afraid that he'd end up Dogbutt because his uncle was Horsebutt, so he did not argue. "How's my cousin?" he asked, referring to Horsebutt and Imand's baby.

"He's got about ten words, and just started walking."

"Should I be teaching him something?"

"Next year," she said, with a pensive smile he did not understand. "There's time. Soon's you're done, you go to the armory. The scythes always need sharpening."

Chapter Twenty-four

THE first sliver of the rising sun sent golden ribbons of light from the east to the captain's gig that Fox sailed alone. Directly south, Ghost Island blocked the stars, a dark mound against an equally dark sky.

As the freshening breeze lifted the gig's sail, the strengthening light and increasing proximity gave the mound texture, color, and finally dimension, its features sharp and clear in the pure morning air.

Fox glanced back. A thin, faintly glistening white line began to coalesce between him and the main island. It lay too low to be a white squall, which was good, but he'd never seen a fog form so rapidly.

Wait. Yes, he had. Signi the Mage had once made one by magic when Inda's small fleet stumbled into the entire Venn armada.

Damn.

As the wind kicked up he leaned into the tiller and sped toward the island. There was the rocky promontory, and the three trees twisted round one another.

He sailed into the cove, its tranquil water a deep aquamarine. His wake rilled out, disturbing the mirror-smooth water.

Fox anchored in as close as he could, flung his boots, socks, weapons belt, and wrist sheaths to the beach, then dove from the rail. The air was already heating up. The water was just cool enough to be refreshing, waking him up from his all-night sail.

As he waded ashore, the light changed subtly. Drifts of vapor veiled the mountain above and wreathed through the feather-edged fronds growing in profusion right down to the edge of the sand. Fox sniffed the air. The familiar salt tang of the sea surrendered to the complex aromas of vegetation growing, blooming, and rotting, enriched by pungent spices, sweet fruits, and fragrant flowers. The thick foliage rustled, but Fox figured the cause was hidden birds and animals. Not ghosts. He had to admit that ghosts seemed to exist, perceivable to some, but no one had ever claimed they could do anything but drift about. Fine. They could drift all they wanted, if that's what kept the people on the populated island away from this one.

He climbed onto the sand and sat down to pull on his boots. He belted on his weapons, checked the fit of his boot knives, then started up the trail.

He still did not know why he was here. What was he going to do once he'd determined that the treasure was intact? Fight all comers? He cursed under his breath as he walked, the familiar rage seething in his gut.

Halfway along the trail to the waterfall that hid the entryway to the treasure cave, the crawling sensation of being watched had settled into conviction.

He reached the last bend before the waterfall. There waited a man dressed in white shirt, riding trousers and boots. His hands were bare, his brown hair tied back. He was seated on a rock, his attitude one of patience.

"Good morning, Savarend." The man smiled in welcome.

Dasta and Gillor, being the tallest, half carried the groggy Barend down the hill to the shore. No one dared to speak until they were out of earshot of any locals.

When they reached the sand Dasta, Gillor, and Jeje started talking at once.

Barend just winced, shaking his head woozily. Jeje realized she'd never seen the color of his eyes, they were so squinty. He paid no attention to the others' questions.

Jeje ran straight into the low breakers and swam powerfully out to the *Vixen*. The others followed, keeping a firm grip on Barend, who was thoroughly awake by the time they all heaved themselves up over the rail onto *Vixen*'s deck. Moving fast, they got the anchor up, the mainsail raised and sheeted home, and began skimming out to sea.

Jeje took the tiller, which prevented her from kicking and punching everything in reach. "I'll kill him," she kept saying over and over.

Gillor rolled her eyes after the fifth or sixth repetition, and slipped below into the cramped living space to poke about the tiny galley. She laughed when she thought about how furious Nugget would be to discover she'd missed a possible adventure. Eugh. Maybe it wouldn't be an adventure but a slaughter. Fox would not like being chased.

Gillor located the stash of Sartoran coffee beans, now half a year old. If they lived through whatever was going to happen next, she'd buy new beans, she promised herself. The local coffee was the best she'd ever tasted.

She snapped the Fire Stick into flame, set water to boil, then vaulted topside. Barend sat on a coil of rope, water dripping off his nose onto the deck. Dasta was handling sail, Jeje at the tiller.

"Barend, if you do want to get trade going, it just came to me. You could get a fleet o' traders. Sail these islands, buy up the coffee now't the Venn are gone. The Venn used to get it all, selling it to merchants along our coasts at a stiff price. Then they slapped their tariff on top of that."

"I know," Barend said without glancing up. "Thought of that last summer, when Flash was grinding his last—" He turned his head to the side, then shook it, fingers brushing the air as if pushing something away.

Gillor hunkered down directly before him. "You were *there*. Marlovans against the Venn. Weren't you? Jeje gave us a report on what happened, but she didn't see any of it."

Barend squinted up at Gillor. "Yeah. I was there."

"And you're going to be just like Inda, aren't you?" Gillor exclaimed, throwing her hands wide in exasperation.

"What *is* it with you people? Someone will come along and kill you if you talk about your past?"

"You didn't see 'em die," he said to his interlaced fingers. "I don't mean crew. Or warriors. Or Venn. I mean friends. Kin." He squinted up at them. "Don't you remember how many of Inda's first crew Walic killed before Inda was brought aboard? Did Tau talk about that fight? He was a jabberer, but he never talked about that anywhere I heard."

"He only did once," Jeje said, elbow hooked round the tiller. "Right after the mutiny. And I think he did only because he'd had wine on top of two or three days of no sleep. And just to me, because I knew 'em, too."

Dasta eyed the sagging mainsail, then raised the jib. As he worked, he called over his shoulder, "What I want to know is, are we going to jump Fox? He broke your arm, Barend. Your call, is what I'm thinking."

Barend snorted. "Nah. I should've seen that coming."

Jeje snarled, "He's a wolf's arse."

Barend waved impatiently. "Could have been worse. I figured out a heartbeat too late he wasn't pulling back, but that was all he needed. Made sure the deck crew all heard the snap. How much trouble do you think that warded?"

"He's a pig's butt," Jeje stated. "I'm sick of him calling the plans. No more. He can't fight us all. If you are squeamish, just help me get him down. *I'm* going to be teaching *him* a lesson for once. He'll be in his hammock for a year."

"And that solves what?" Gillor sat back, eyebrows lifted.

"Fog coming." Dasta pointed at the slowly tumbling white line obscuring the other islands.

"Great. Watch us sail in circles."

"We won't sail at all." Dasta flipped up the back of his hand at the sagging sails.

Gillor swung to her feet. "Well, my water's boiling. At least we'll have coffee."

Fox stopped at the head of the trail, leaving five or six paces between the seated man and himself. Drifts of fog obscured the jungle, which had gone oddly silent.

Fox addressed the man. "You're familiar." His hands

flexed once, then he crossed his arms, fingers within reach of the hilts of his knives.

"By sight, perhaps." The man's Marlovan was accentless. "You and I have never conversed. But I know who you are. *Life, death, and power, that is all there is.* Is that not the wisdom you attempted to inculcate in your friend Inda? Or was it sex, money, and power? Perhaps it was youth, beauty, and liquor?"

Fox flushed.

"Reducing the range of existence to three elements does impress the young," the man observed with mild amusement.

Fox's heart thumped like a war drum. "If you had the eye patch—which anyone can wear, I realize—and the purple scarring I'd say you are Ramis. Not, it seems, of the *Knife*."

"The ship is here. On the other side of the island. We will discuss it presently."

Fox flicked his fingers toward the waterfall. "After discussing what first? The treasure?"

"What do you intend to do with it?"

"Why," Fox drawled, shifting his stance to readiness, "do you need to know?"

"I already know. I want to hear you articulate your reasons. Ah. I forgot how very young you are. I see that you need convincing in the conventional manner. Are you always so predictable, Savarend? Never mind. Come on." Ramis sat there, hands on his knees.

Fox flushed at the indulgent tone, for the first time in his life feeling like a scrub. It just made him more angry.

Ramis sighed. "Do you not solve all your problems with violence? Here I am, willing and ready. I'll even give you a little needed training. You should appreciate the offer."

Fox no longer heard the scratching of little claws on branches, or the rustle of fronds. No soft-throated murmur of birds in the underbrush. The world unaccountably had gone silent as that eerie fog drifted overhead, etching the foliage faintly against the blank white sky.

The ground crunched under his heels, his blood rushed to the beat of his heart. He was real. Was this man real?

Fox sprang.

That was his last offensive move.

From the moment he reached the other he was on the defense. Ramis was a full hand shorter, and no stronger or faster, but he was unnervingly prescient. Fox tried a series of increasingly nasty tricks in rapid succession to find a block or deflection or counterstrike waiting. Each exactingly graduated to be more painful than the last.

But Fox did not give up, though his senses swam and his body was wracked with agony. He *never* lost! He had to fight harder.

Finally the world whirled and he crashed to the ground, bones jolting. He blinked until the red dazzle faded.

He lay pinned, immovable, Ramis smiling down into his eyes. "Shall I break your arm?"

The fog pressed round the *Vixen*, thinning and thickening in slow undulations. The four sat on the deck, eating a breakfast made up of the odds and ends left over from their long journey. The wind had completely died. The sails hung slack, the scout wallowing with no vestige of way. They sipped Gillor's coffee at leisure and, after a half-year's wait, got caught up on one another's news at last. Gillor gave Jeje and Barend a detailed report on the fleet's actions since Inda had left for Iasca Leror. Jeje was amused by the discrepancies between Gillor's succinct account and the tangled, emotion-charged, highly exaggerated narratives Nugget and Mutt had given her. From there they passed to gossip about Freedom Harbor, as related by Fangras and the new fleet.

Jeje was just composing herself for a nap (grab 'em as you can was her firm rule) when Dasta, who had been frowning skyward, cut through the conversation and pointed. "Look up."

Obediently they turned their eyes skyward, which was flat white except for a thin pinpoint of brightness.

"That's the sun," Gillor said. "So?"

"So it's the same place it was before the fog closed in," Dasta said grimly. "It hasn't moved."

"That's impossible," Jeje stated.

Barend shook his head slowly. "It was impossible to see a hole ripped between sky and sea after the fight with the Brotherhood. But we all were there, and we saw it."

"Time has *stopped?*" Jeje asked. "Why?"

Nobody answered as seawater splashed against the hull.

Ramis held Fox immobilized and waited for an answer.

Shall I break your arm? That couldn't possibly be a reference to Barend. "No." Fox discovered that his lips were numbing fast.

Ramis lifted his hands and moved away, leaving Fox to roll painfully to a crouch, and then—it took effort—to his feet.

He touched a careful finger to his mouth, which was beginning to swell. His teeth ached. He couldn't even remember the blow, but he tasted blood; he'd bitten the inside of his lip.

Fox's head pounded sickeningly. Up close Ramis was a hand shorter and looked maybe ten years older. His lack of conventional threat or posture somehow made him seem all the more menacing. "What now? The black door to Norsunder?"

"Why should I exert myself?" Ramis dropped on his rock again, one foot propped on a hassock-sized flat stone, fingers laced loosely around his knee. "It appears to me that, given another few years, you will make your way there on your own."

Fox recoiled, the reaction too swift and too intense to suppress.

"When," Ramis asked, "does the use of violence shift from moral imperative to convenience?"

So the arm question had been deliberate provocation. Fox wiped the back of his hand over his bleeding lip. "When does a Norsundrian have anything at all to say about moral imperative?"

"You will discover"—Ramis flicked his fingers outward—"that discourse on questions of morality is a favorite amusement in the Garden of the Twelve."

"Implying that I am on my way there?"

"That right now is up to you," Ramis said, palm up. "If you catch their interest, you will find yourself summarily invited. As soon as you cease to be entertaining, you cease."

"To . . . ?" Fox asked, knowing that Norsunder lay beyond time. Therefore, presumably, beyond death.

"Exist. Memory by memory. Wit by wit. Your identity stripped away in thin curls." Ramis made a sharp gesture, like the flick of a blade. "And savored as each is consumed."

Terror crowded inside Fox's chest. He knew he was outmatched. All that remained was pride. "So get it over with."

"My warning? I am not constrained at the moment to act as agent of invitation." Ramis' voice was unremarkable, his countenance not expressive, yet Fox suspected his choice of words was not idle. That he had been so ordered and had so acted.

Ramis whispered a word, traced an arc in the air that glowed. Ramis stepped through. Fox was drawn inexorably after him. He found himself standing on the deck of a ship he'd only glimpsed twice.

They were alone. Fox took in the gold leaf along the rails, the beautiful rigging and pure black canvas of the sails, as new as if the ship had launched yesterday. Fox had heard that magic transfer was a wrenching experience, but he'd felt only the briefest sense of unbalance, no more than a lee lurch in mild weather, and the strangeness of passing from the warm, spice-redolent air of the cliffside waterfall to this cooler, shadowed bay with the sun on the other side of the isle.

Ramis led him into the spacious captain's cabin. The bulkheads under the ceiling were edged with fine-carved fretwork in complicated, overlapping circles composed of three curved arms. Those circles were interlocked in triangles, two low, one high, and then the pattern reversed. A marquetry tree wound and wound upward along bulkheads in twists from the inlaid deck, its many-wooded grains pleaching around the stern windows and ending in leaves of vein-embossed gold.

The Tree of Ydrasal appeared again in a gnarled candelabra with nine branches ending in candleholders. The candelabra was built into a shelf above a desk. Over the captain's table hung a chandelier of intertwined branches into which twenty-seven candles would fit.

Fox had studied the Venn. He recognized in these silent signs that this craft had once belonged to a Venn king. He yanked open the door to the cabin and gazed down the length of the deck to the prow. Instead of coming to a vaguely shaped figurehead with mere slashes that resembled eye sockets, the prow rose to an elaborately carved dragon's head, slanting eyes at either side, the long, scaled jaw parted. That dragon's head had not been on the prow after the pirate battle.

Fox whirled around. "Dragons. Did they exist?"

Ramis looked amused. "I never saw any. They were here thousands of years before my time. But sources that were unfortunately burned while I was elsewhere indicated that they were present in this world, though they did not originate here. They came to an agreement and vanished again, taking the more innovative and creative people out of what later became the Land of the Chwahir."

As he spoke, Ramis opened one of the many small, carved doors in the desk, and took out a book bound in fine blackweave edged with gold.

Dragons were forgotten. "That's my book," Fox exclaimed.

"Yes." Ramis tossed it to Fox, who caught it and just barely concealed the impulse to clutch it protectively against him. "I read it last night. You write with vividness and precision. The battle at the Narrows was particularly well done. Your memory agrees with my assessment of the end."

Fox rubbed his forehead, then looked up. "You scragged me, then forced me here to tell me you approve of my writing?"

"I brought you here because this cabin is warded in space and time. The spell will not last a hundredth of the time it took to set it up. I am here to exhort you to carry on with that project. It seems worthwhile, unlike most of your other endeavors."

Fox kept rubbing his head. Trying to think made his head ache more. "You're serious." His voice cracked on a laugh and his head ached. "You really want me to write down all my battles? For whom?"

"Your descendants."

Fox was not ready for that topic. "Norsunder lies outside of time. I suppose that means you are far older than you appear, which would explain why no one was able to discover any of the details of your birth."

"True. The guise was necessary and effective."

"And no doubt fun," Fox jibed. When Ramis did not deny it, "So do you know the future?"

Ramis flicked his fingers again, a negating gesture. "There are beings in this world who do not experience time and physical space the way we humans do. Magic can shorten distance, though it takes effort. To move ahead of the sun's measure can be likened to swimming in amber, and one's clarity of vision is roughly equivalent, probably because of the possibility of change."

"Yet you say I'll have descendants?"

Ramis opened his hand toward Fox's book. "For whom have you written those accounts?"

"Myself."

Ramis waited.

Fox turned away, gazing blankly out the stern windows. The quiet water was azure. Faint rays of sun struck glints off the water, veining the cabin with shifting light. "If I have a son," he said slowly, "then I do so knowing I condemn him to the same meaningless existence my family is condemned to."

"How has your life been meaningless, except as you deliberately chose meaningless actions?"

Fox turned away from the window.

Ramis had taken a seat at the table and crossed his arms, head at a skeptical cant. "You cannot possibly be implying that life is meaningless because you are not king of Iasca Leror."

Fox flushed. Treachery by the Montrei-Vayirs, who called treason justice—his father's slow suicide by pickling his brain—all those old reasons kited through his mind. "Meaning," he said finally, the word twisting with derision. "My family is living proof that concepts such as *honor* and *justice* do not exist except as conveniences for self-justification."

"You, like everyone else in existence, are living proof that human beings are capable of both justice and injustice. We are also proof that both have consequences that ripple outward through time, through space." Ramis indicated the book. "While you brood on your captain's deck over your notions of treason, your mother, sister, and betrothed are striving to provide justice over the land your family still retains."

Fox grimaced. "Marend is still there?"

"Yes. Whom would she marry, with so many young men in your homeland dead?"

Fox paced the cabin's perimeter, then stopped to examine more closely the carving of interlocked circles around each candleholder in the chandelier. "It was that bad? Inda wouldn't say. Now he doesn't write to me at all."

"Inda," Ramis said, "*talks* to you."

Fox did not ask how he knew. "Not by letter."

"You will not see one another again?"

Fox whirled around. "You don't want me to write my battles. You want me to write Inda's," he accused.

"I don't *want* you to do anything," Ramis replied. "But you already began." He indicated the book.

"Writing out Inda's battles was a mental exercise." Fox threw the book down on a table inlaid with stylized dragons winding in a circle, heads to tails. "Seeing if I could lay out in sequence how he perceives the chaos of battle, and how he organizes it. Listen. If anyone was to draw the attention of your Garden of Twelve, it would be Inda."

"That was a possibility for a time." Ramis's eyes narrowed to an inward focus. "You know what Inda dreamed about last night? Rig's death onboard Walic's ship."

"I don't know who Rig is."

"Do you remember the first one of Inda's crew Walic had killed? He wouldn't join because the pirates had murdered his brother in their initial attack."

"All I remember is making sure Inda didn't betray himself, and us."

Ramis closed his eyes. "Inda's nightmares," he said in a musing voice, "fall into three categories. The boyhood ones, the pirates ones, and a new category has added itself after the recent battle. In most of the pirate nightmares, he sees accusation—condemnation—in Rig's face because he was helpless to save any of the crew." Ramis opened his eyes. "If you hadn't stupefied him with that blow to the head he might possibly have saved them. He would most likely have touched off the mutiny he organized half a year later."

"I know that." Fox turned around. "Are you blaming me for cracking his skull to shut him up?"

"I'm telling you why he lost the interest of Norsunder. If he'd led a mutiny that day, taking Walic's flagship and thence his fleet—" A lifted hand. "He was stupid with pain, but he just looked stupid to Norsunder's witness onboard that ship. The witness lost interest and left, as she considered Walic and his mates to be too petty for use. Even the Brotherhood of Blood didn't want Walic. Inda's subsequent wins appeared from a distance to be accidents, largely because he did not follow up on them in the traditional manner, by building a pirate empire."

Fox pressed both hands to his head. The conversation had turned from unbelievable to absurd to . . . what? To a blurring double view of what had been real, and what someone had apparently worked hard to make appear real to Norsunder's "idle eyes." "You want me to tell the truth? How can I? All I know is my own experience."

"I just told you something that Inda has never told anyone," Ramis said. "If you find the need, you will have access to what I saw. And heard."

Memory by memory, wit by wit. The sound, and finally the sense: this man was a mind-reader. He won the fight because he really did perceive every move before it was made.

A mind reader. So, that meant . . . "You're a soul-eater?" Fox barely got the words out. He did not even try to hide his sick fear. The fellow could read it as easily as he'd read the book.

"No." Ramis made the negating gesture again. "Only one of the Host is. Some do try to match that, ah, dimension of cruelty, but enough about them. What do you intend to do about the treasure?"

"What's the use in asking? You're obviously going to tell me what to do, and even I can see that there is little I can do to stop you."

"When I exert my will, you will know it," Ramis observed. "You can do anything you want. You can kill those four in the scout craft out in the bay right now—"

"Four?"

"—or you could force them to leave the treasure and take your fleet down the strait to Ymar, where the Ymarans and the Everoneth are gathering with the rest of the Fleet Guild alliance to determine who is going to control the strait once they throw the last of the Venn out. The Chwahir are on the way."

Fox did not know what question to ask first.

"The protective ward is fading. We must finish. It is time to see the end of that treasure. Far too many have died because of it. Therefore, if you choose to fall in with Barend Montrei-Vayir and Wisthia Shagal's plans, there will be a reward. Not for you. But for your descendants, someday. Every coin or artifact you bring out of that cavern to be carried back to Wisthia Shagal will cause another gold coin or artifact to be brought beyond time to a place I will one day tell you."

"That's impossible," Fox exclaimed. "How can you promise all these things? How can you *know* these things? How can you prove any of what you've told me is actually true?"

Ramis smiled. "The young man the Marlovans called Noddy Toraca made Indevan Algara-Vayir promise something just before he died. Inda could not hear it. What Toraca said was 'no more war.' Tell Inda that."

"But—"

"Just remember what I said." Ramis struck his knuckles on the table holding the royal candelabra of an ancient Venn king. "This vessel will await you. If the Venn return, I suggest you take it into battle. You will discover it has unexpected virtues."

"Battle?" Fox repeated.

Ramis laughed soundlessly. "What was old Savarend's first rule of bad government? A rule his assassin was careful to destroy."

Fox repeated automatically, "When you cannot control your own people, you send them out to fight someone else." He said on an outgoing breath, "The Venn. They're coming back."

"The situation right now is very fluid, but the one who took seeds from the Garden knows the cost if they do not bear fruit."

Fox remembered Inda and Signi explaining about the Venn dag Abyarn Erkric, then dismissed him. The important thing was that the enormous army necessary for such an invasion—a second invasion—could not be marshaled, supplied, and launched from Venn. It was too far away. They had to be closer to make the jump to Halia. Then coordinate the attack, which would have to be from every harbor at once, as a concentrated strike in the north had not worked. So that meant—

He looked up, ignoring how much that hurt. "The Venn only hold Jaro Harbor in Ymar. Are they coming to retake the strait?"

"Right now it's just reinforcement on the way," Ramis said. "They expect an easy win for this small force. They count on it."

The dark scintillance began to coalesce around Fox. He snatched up his book, then he found himself at the waterfall, but this time he was alone.

Jeje had scolded and nagged the other three into making a plan for dealing with Fox. When the fog dissipated before a sudden, driving wind, they sailed toward Ghost Island, putting the finishing touches on their plan.

All of which vanished like the fog when in the slanting light of sunset they found Fox waiting on the shore for them, blood crusted on the side of his chin, a spectacular black eye forming. He leaned against a rock with a semblance of his usual negligence, but the four were far too experienced not to see how much effort it took him to stay upright.

"Who got to him first?" Jeje asked the air.

"And how?" Gillor rubbed her knuckles.

Fox moved stiffly down to the water line as they brought the rowboat in. "I just came from the cavern. Everything is there, untouched. My suggestion is this. We send Fangras and his fleet down to Ymar, where Chim and his allies are forming to jump on the last Venn outpost."

"What?" Jeje demanded. "How'd you know that?"

Gillor shrugged. "Makes sense. If the Venn are gone, the strait will be up for grabs."

"The Venn aren't going to be gone for long," Fox said, gently feeling his swelling face and wincing.

This time, they all exclaimed, "What?"

"I don't know any more than that. We'll pick up information when we reach Bren. Chim will know where we can find the alliance. Right now, we'll keep our five capital ships here. Load up, buy coffee for trade. Extra barrels to hide the gold in. Load our capital ships and some of the smaller ones with hand-picked crew. And we'll follow on after the fleet, with a side trip to deliver the gold to Wisthia Shagal."

"Empty it?" Jeje said, and whistled.

"I suspect you'll be thoroughly sick of the amount by the time you're done carrying it." He laughed silently, then winced. "Speaking of sick, orders will go out to the entire fleet: collect fish oil as they sail."

The four exchanged glances, and Gillor gave her expressive Fal shrug. If he'd gone mad, at least it was a madness a Fal could appreciate.

Jeje scowled. "You gonna tell us what happened?"

"No," Fox said.

Barend opened his hands. "Then let's get busy."

Chapter Twenty-five

"THE Council of Elders is reconvening the Frasadeng tomorrow at noon, and all in service rank are required to attend," the young messenger wearing the white of Anborc said to Brun Durasnir the next morning—or what passed for morning when the windows still showed dark. "The accused traitor has been found."

Is this accident, coming the very day after the return of the fleet? Brun Durasnir thought. Instinct was sure: nothing was accident. There had been no announcement the night before at the council gathering celebrating the triumphant return of Prince Rajnir and his commanders.

A full day before the convening? Why? The messenger was not the one to ask. She dismissed him and returned to her tasks.

The low winter sun, gaining strength every day, had just emerged from the southern horizon when one of the *Cormorant*'s ensigns appeared at the command quarters in Saeborc to leave Fulla Durasnir's formal summer uniforms and take his freshly aired winter gear back to the ship. He said nothing, but there was something in his gaze, and the careful way he laid the heavy linens and silk in her arms, that caused her to speed to their room as soon as he was gone and to sort through the clothing.

And there, rolled up in a shirt, was a single strip of the archivist's paper that she used to mark scrolls, with a single rune drawn on it.

She twitched it into a twist, tossed it into the stove vent under the sleeping platform, then carried on with her tasks.

A short-glass before midnight, she checked to see that her son Halvir was peacefully asleep in his bedchamber. Then she went into the wardrobe room against the cold west wall, and took from her oldest trunk the long scratch-wool gray cloak of a thrall. Her skin crept as she shrugged it over her own cloak, though it was clean and had never been worn by any thrall. Her own mother had used it to punish her when she was young. She had kept it as a disguise and as a reminder.

Symbols make seeming real, she reflected as she yanked the hood over her face, and then pulled heavy gloves over her house gloves: life inside the tower, expected of the commanders, meant endless cold drafts from nowhere during winter that the house dag never seemed to be able to ward.

It was good to walk where the silent ones had to walk, she thought as she slipped down the thralls' narrow stairs, where pairs of thick wooden clogs waited. She thrust her fine shoes into a pair of the clogs. There had to be thralls—she understood the order of things—for who would do their work if there were none? The lowest branches of the Tree gave support to the higher reaches, everyone knew that, and to walk for a time where thralls walked reminded her not to be brusque with those who could not answer back.

She eased through Saeborc's Trallagat, the thralls' entrance to the abandoned Hilda annex. Icy air found the chinks in her clothing as she ran up the steps to the side door that gave onto the narrow causeway beside the King's Road gutters, where thralls must walk so their feet would not defile the tablet-patterned stone of the road.

Even wearing three layers, she gasped when the wind struck her full force, trying to flense her flesh from her bones as she bent into the wind.

She had confidently expected to be alone, and so she was surprised to discover shrouded figures here and there, some carrying burdens, all bent into the wind. *So I will just be one more of them,* she thought, and toiled grimly toward the bridge.

On rare good days, the distance from the Saeborc to the bridge over the river, midpoint along the King's Road, was but a few steps. In the fierce, numbing wind of winter, it seemed longer, but terrible as it was, this plod into the wind was preferable to the thralls' long staircase, covered with moss, that led to the frigid, dank old tunnel under the river, and then the long climb upward again. From the number of those abroad, most clothed in gray, others thought so, too, causing her to wonder if they were all thralls. *I must not see conspiracy, just because we have lived in an atmosphere of it. We have regained order . . .*

The King's Road was customarily only used for ceremony, or to be strolled on during the rare pleasant summer evenings, when people would light the ramparts with candles and walk about talking and sipping the sharp, heady triple-distilled bristic. The exception was the Blood Crowd, when a condemned traitor was taken in full view of the city, who could vent their anger for their betrayal before the application of the knife on the top of Sinnaborc and the slow expiration under the waiting eyes of the death birds.

Her heart lurched. A Blood Crowd? Were the burdens some bore baskets of stone and ordure? She lengthened her steps, while keeping her head low.

Thin, ragged clouds obscured patches of brilliant stars as she peered northward along the road, shifting her eyes away from the lone pale tower of Sinnaborc at the terminus. If you ignored the Sinnaborc, the north towers looked like fingers reaching toward the sky: the massive Saeborc at her shoulder the thumb, the pairs of towers on either side of the road forming a cupped hand reaching upward.

This was the shortest way to the abandoned tunnels that once had belonged to the Hilda, before a king in the previous century had tried to shift power away from the Oneli by giving the Hilda autonomy and their own annexes off Leofaborc.

She bent farther into the wind, stumping in the awkward peg-heeled clogs over the icy stone of the bridge toward the southern curve of the King's Road. Far below the covered bridge corridor, the river plunged in a roar over the stones to empty into the sea.

She turned her head sideways to peer past Skalts' Tower toward Leofaborc, and beyond that, Anborc in the distance. The three smaller House towers were obscured from her view, which meant no one who might be braving their western ramparts could see her, either. And if they did, they would see only a humble thrall, head down.

One more peek, up the smooth western face of Skalts' Tower: no one visible on its rampart. She left the gutter for the old pathway down to the rocky point from which people had viewed the ships along the single pier for centuries.

To the right, the viewpoint, to the left, the old Trallagat.

She stamped into the mossy old tunnel as echoes of the surf roared over the rocks below, then hissed outward again. In her day the young had often met here for assignations. Here was where she'd first trysted with Fulla when she was just a scribe and he a third son about to be sent south.

A scrape, followed by the ice-tinkle and squish of a step from the other end caused her to halt. Then the footsteps approached rapidly, as someone whistled a single soft note. She ran forward, heedless of mucky puddles, then fell into Fulla's arms. They ripped their hoods up and kissed with all the passion of youth.

When at last they broke apart, he said, "Did anyone say anything to you last night after we met at the gathering?"

"No. No one is interested in our reconciliation. We're old and boring." She added dryly, "Our parting was interesting as long as they could laugh about our cold beds, or speculate whether you'd choose a wife from another House and whether you would set aside Halvir in favor of a new son."

Durasnir snorted, his breath a brief pale cloud in the cold, dim blue light. "Erkric noticed I did not go home with you. I want him to think affairs remain cool between us."

"Why? What happened in Goerael?"

"First tell me what has been happening here."

She said, "Nothing. People are quiet, going about their lives. Except for glancing over their shoulders in fear of spiderwebs, which has become habit for us all."

"Like steps in the hel dance, when they use their slippers to make the patterns in the sand on the floor," he observed.

"You are so used to their beguiling movements, at first you do not see that the sand-patterns have changed."

He so rarely used figurative language she was surprised, and wondered if he'd been sipping bristic to ward the cold. She said slowly, "As you predicted when we began our farcical parting, the council has accepted that Prince Rajnir will be declared king. The skalts have made much of your triumphs on Goerael under his leadership—"

"Triumphs," he repeated scornfully. "Triumphs! They all ran and hid, except for a mad few. On Goerael, Rajnir never said a word without Erkric at his side. I never spoke to Rajnir except to receive orders, and Erkric stood there to watch me receive them. I tried to contact the northern commander. I also tried to hold conversation with my captains, but at every turn there was one of Erkric's dags. Their being able to shift around by magic gives them the advantage. That and their spying webwork."

"Why?" she asked. "I thought all that must end, now that the old king is all but forgotten, and everyone looks to Rajnir as our next."

"Listen: there is more. Erkric caused Rajnir to assign each of the commanders a dag for an aide, but these are nothing more, or less, than personal spies."

"A personal *spy?* A *dag* as a spy?" She made the sign of warding; the world, which had seemed safe (once she'd accustomed herself to the lack of private speech in her own home) had again cracked into madness.

Durasnir bent his head, whispering into the rough wool of her hood. "Ulaffa was able to accomplish one thing. My spy is our old friend Dag Byarin. Now, I cannot tell you for certain that he works against Erkric. In their own ways, I suspect, the dags not committed to Erkric's cause face as much danger as we do. I am careful to say nothing before Byarin that he cannot report to Erkric. And in his turn, he does not see me anywhere but where I say I am. So right now, I am asleep on my ship." A brief smile. "But I am summoned to the Frasadeng for the treason trial."

"Bringing me back to my question. Why? No one blames Rajnir for the failed invasion. It is past. The talk is all about Goerael. Because you told me to speak to no one for fear of spiderwebs, and because my contacts among the old queen's household were dispersed to the far corners of

Venn, I cannot write for information. I am left with these unanswered questions."

"There is no talk about Rajnir? No suspicion?"

Brun exclaimed, "How many times must I say it? All I hear around me is a wish to return to the old ways, to order."

Durasnir gripped her arms. "You forget magic. By brandishing Signi as a traitor, Dag Erkric will convince the council, and the Houses, and the people, that his own actions were unquestionable."

"But what is the need? Rajnir will be proclaimed king, and his first act will be to name Erkric Dag of the Venn. What more is there?"

"Magic, as I said. Until now, magic has been used according to strict rules. What I did not tell you before was this: during the invasion, Erkric began breaking those rules. He still did not win, but he might have, had not Dag Signi, or someone else, interfered. Not in defense of the Marlovans, but directly counter to Erkric's actions, which were nominally in our favor, but only when gaining him power."

"Nominally?"

"Some dags died. By magic, it is said. Again, I don't have proof. Ulaffa, head of the Yaga Krona, does not have proof."

For the first time, the possibilities of unchecked magical power broke on her mind, making her feel sick with apprehension.

Durasnir sensed it in the tensing of her body, and went on deliberately, so that she would understand. Now that Erkric thought he was in reach of winning—that Durasnir was isolated even from his wife—he could share his burdens with her once again.

"These actions will give Erkric powers that none of us—Oneli, Drenga, Hilda—with all our training, can withstand." Durasnir let her go and massaged his temples with his gloved hand. "I pondered long while I was at sea and tried to put together the leaves to show me the shape of the limb. How does this sound? Whatever the truth behind her actions, with this trial, Erkric can make Signi the focus of hate so no one questions what he himself has done. Also his forcing Dag Signi into the position of traitor makes it look like dags are answerable, when in truth *he* isn't." He gripped her again.

"So Dag Signi is no traitor?" She thought of the furtive figures abroad at night and added, "I think a Blood Crowd is being formed."

"That would be on Erkric's orders, I have no doubt. As to Signi's guilt or innocence, I do not know. The single time I saw her take action, both our people and the Marlovans were swept aside by a mighty geyser." Durasnir felt his wife stiffen in his grip, and he said, "No, I don't believe she's a traitor."

"By the Tree," she whispered, appalled. "Does this mean that you and the dags will permit Erkric to put an innocent woman on that tower to suffer so hideous a death? Because no treason trial has ever ended but with a death!"

"What can I do? Start a civil war so that more die than just this one?" His voice roughened with grief and deep betrayal. "Do you think I want to see her thrown to the tower stones and her lungs pulled through her broken ribs?"

Brun's voice was low. "If you stand by and let it happen, believing she is innocent, then all your efforts to ward Rainorec were for nothing. Nothing! For Rainorec is already here."

She walked away.

The steady tang of the alarm bells smashed Cama out of sleep. He rolled out of bed, cursing when his bare feet hit the cold stone floor of the mostly bare guest chamber at Castle Andahi.

The door slammed open. Ndand Arveas strode in, bow strung, fingers fastening her quiver over her shoulder with the absent speed of practice. "Pirates sailing into the bay. Looks like five of 'em. Big ones."

"Damnation," Cama exclaimed, hopping on one foot as he tried to get his clothes wrestled on all at once.

Another time Ndand would have laughed at the sight of Cama flailing around, black hair hanging everywhere, sleeves and trouser legs tangling. But the memory of sudden threat from the sea was far too sharp for that.

As Cama flung the shirt down and concentrated on getting his legs into the trousers, she ran out through the sentry walk door. Her voice rapidly faded, "Cap'n Han! You get your girls on the high wall . . ."

Cama plunked down onto the bed, and pulled on his dirty socks from the day before rather than hunt for new. Then he grabbed his shirt and coat in one hand and his weapons in the other and bolted downstairs for the guard barracks.

The five capital ships were the *Death, Cocodu, Wind's Kiss, Sable,* and *Rapier.* The scout *Vixen* sailed on station abaft *Death.*

The sails brailed up, anchors splashed, and *Death*'s gig lowered over the side.

Barend dropped down and sat forward, peering through his glass at the castle limned with early morning light. The landslide was still there, greenery dotting the upper half. A high stone wall had been built across the lower half, and a sentry path led up and down. No one would hide up there to shoot down onto the castle again.

Cama ran out the front gate. Barend grinned at the sight of his hair hanging down to his waist, his coat open over an unlaced shirt. Cama looked more like a pirate right now than pirates did, as he brandished his weapons toward the shore and shouted unheard orders to rapidly assembling men.

Above him, Ndand stood squarely, arrow already nocked, her women taking position along walls and towers. Why? There was nothing on the roads, or the heights. . . .

Oh. Barend realized for the first time that his old friends thought they were under attack from the ships.

From the stern sheets, Fox remarked, "You say these people will welcome you?" His drawl masked the tension he felt not from threat, but from extreme ambivalence.

"Forgot they can't tell the difference between a Venn or an old wine-barrel caravel. Why, I'll wager anything they think *we* are *pirates!* Stay here," he added, chuckling hoarsely, as the sailors lifted their oars and the gig rode the small waves up onto shore. "I'll go up alone."

"If they shoot you down I'm going to crow," Fox warned.

"You won't last long enough," Barend retorted.

Fox had to agree. The castle's assembled defense had been fast and excellent. No, really it was superlative, though he wouldn't admit that out loud. *So are you listening, Ramis?*

No answer, of course. Fox had taken to sending mental comments to the air, though there was no sense whatever that they were heard outside the confines of his skull. In fact, by now he would have been convinced that the entire episode with Ramis was a bad dream, except for the bruises and aches that had lingered for days. *Probably deliberate reminders, right?*

No answer.

The castle defense waited for Barend to reach the broken ground directly below the outer curtain wall, the worst possible ground for an attack. The sight of armed Marlovan women on the walls, bows drawn and ready, gave Fox an unexpected twinge of regret.

Barend walked into the ground deliberately strewn with the broken rock of ruin, his hands held up at shoulder height, palms out.

Cama had finished strapping on his weapons, then found his eye patch in his coat pocket. He yanked it impatiently round his head, then pulled the watch captain's spyglass out of his hand, put it to his good eye, then slapped it back into the surprised man's hand as he yelled, "It's Barend!"

Up on the wall, Ndand lowered her bow. "That's Barend?" she called down. "Why's he dressed like that?"

Barend had begun loping up the shingle toward the castle. Cama took off as fast as he'd been as a boy, and they met just below the small bluffs where the soil ended and sand began. The entire castle was at the ready; they watched in bemusement as the Jarl and the fellow in the crimson shirt, deck trousers, and black sash laughed, whacked each other on the back, then started back toward the castle, still laughing.

"Stand down," Ndand called wryly to the watch captain, who signaled to the Rider with horn at the ready.

Taut bows were unstrung, battle-ready lines dissolved into chattering, stamping knots of people, many complaining about the cold that had abruptly set in the week before after a long, lingering late summer.

"What are you doing with pirate ships?" Cama asked, swinging around to regard the sinister silhouettes riding in the bay.

Barend said, "Those are Inda's. The black one is the second one he took."

Cama whistled. "He took that thing away from pirates when we were running around with wooden sticks, thinking ourselves so tough being horsetails?" He shook his head.

"How are things here? Settling 'em down?"

"Some. It's partly the rebuilding. We don't have any money to pay the locals like Evred wants done, so we've been piling up a debt. They don't believe we'll pay it. Then there are those who don't want to do anything but fight. They lurk up in the hills, watching for a chance to scrag us." His teeth showed briefly, a white flash in his dark face. "Scrag *me*. You'd think there's a bounty on my head, except no one up here has any money, either."

"Well, that money thing is why I'm here," Barend said, and when Cama swung around in surprise, Barend cast a furtive look about. They were some two hundred paces from the retreating guards. "That's actually why Inda sent me. Those ships are crammed with pirate treasure."

"Even the little one?" Cama shaded his eye from the sun now sitting just above the coast.

"That one has the best stuff. Cups studded with diamonds, jewels probably looted from the ships of kings. The biggest one, there, is full of Sartoran twelve-siders. The idea is to send it to Evred, for use now. The rest is going east to be turned into trade paper. Listen, if Evred likes this plan, you're going to have to arrange for wagons and fellows to make sure it gets to the royal city."

Cama stroked his chin. "I've got Nightingale's golden locket as well as the golden case thing. But Evred doesn't want us using those for important communications."

Barend asked quickly, "Nightingale all right?"

"Randael in Khani-Vayir now. Cousin's old. Asked him to give up being King's Runner. Nightingale's running the jarlate. Married Hild Sindan."

Barend remembered the young woman who'd been a watch-commander at Ala Larkadhe under Tdiran-Randviar, and he gave a grunt of approval.

"Who've you got in that boat?"

"Gig crew. And Fox Montredavan-An."

Cama turned all the way around, but all he saw was an indistinct figure in dark clothes. Was that red hair? "Bring 'em in." He whirled his hand in a lazy circle. "We'll get some breakfast into 'em while we make our plans."

Barend loped back toward the shore, and Cama rejoined Ndand to tell her he'd invited them to breakfast so Barend could share his overseas report. The rest he saved until they could be private. Neither of them had forgotten the poet-spy Estral Mardric.

Barend reached Fox. "Talk over breakfast."

Fox's tough, hand-picked gig crew turned his way. He waggled his fingers at the castle, and faces lightened with anticipation.

And so, after eleven years, Fox Montredavan-An set foot again on what was now Marlovan land.

"This is Castle Andahi?" Fox peered around as they started up toward the castle. "Looks like a new landslide. That is, new enough. Part of the war?"

"Yes."

Fox snorted. "You're almost as gabby as Inda."

"Everyone lost too much to want to talk about it. Especially Ndand. She was sent south by the Jarlan, leaving the women to defend against the entire Venn army. Not one woman survived, but they held the castle for a crucial couple of days."

Fox's faint smile tightened to grimness. The damage was revealing, if you knew how to assess it. The new rock fitted and plastered into old walls, the makeshift gates. Fox slowed, examining the silent testimony all around him as they passed the first curtain wall. Those were massive gates, the hinges and chains new. How had the Venn brought *those* down?

He eyed the pair coming to meet them. Cama was tall, black-haired, and Fox identified under the black hair and the body that seemed to be made of whipcord and steel a bone structure akin to his own. The Tya-Vayirs were cousins to the Montredavan-Ans back six generations, but then most of these Vayirs were cousins if you went back far enough.

Cama gave Fox a speculative head to heels sweep through his one eye, then deferred to Ndand, a plain Marlovan woman with corn-colored braids who gave a brief introduction; Barend said, "This is Fox. Fleet commander."

As Cama and Ndand led the way inside, the gig's crew

were taken off by a couple of Runners to the guard barracks, where they would try to outdo one another's war
stories.

Fox looked around. The castle, though clean, was sparse
in furnishings, and all those were new. The walls and ceilings still bore scorch marks.

Ndand sneaked another glance at the tall fellow in
black who had come with Barend. It was unsettling how
much he resembled the king, yet was dressed like a pirate.
"Fox." She knew she'd heard that name before. It was a
common enough nickname for Marlovan redheads.

That was it, he spoke Marlovan.

They sat in the dining alcove, which was a bare room
with only the usual low table and plain-woven mats. Fox
hadn't sat on a mat to eat for so long that this, too, felt
strange.

The food was the same food Fox had eaten in childhood:
pan biscuits of rye, cabbage rolls, root brew and water to
drink, for castle people never had alcohol at early meals.
They had far too much work ahead of them.

The talk at first was mere chatter, and he left Barend
to it. Weather, sailing versus riding, wherever do you buy a
crimson silk shirt like that? They shifted to questions about
people, and Barend was just getting to the "So how's . . ."
which are so tedious if one doesn't know any of those
named when a small boy with unruly short brown hair
erupted into the room.

"Barend!" he yelped.

"Keth." Barend grinned and gave the boy a friendly cuff
as Keth bent to pinch a biscuit and dunk it into the honey.

"Use your knife," Ndand scolded. "It's not manners,
dunking in the table honey."

"Takes too long to clean." Keth made a face. "And he
isn't company, he's just Barend. Oh." He took in Fox, from
black boots to earring, then addressed Barend. "I'm in the
academy now. See my short hair?" Keth proudly flicked the
wisps around his ears.

Barend had never been in the academy due to his father's prejudice, but Keth didn't know that. "How'd it go?
How's Ind—the Harskialdna?"

"The horsetails call him Pirate," Keth said with that
carefully offhand importance meant to impress. "He started

training them, but stopped. We used to sneak up on the rooftop and watch. Hoo, he's fast. No one can whup him, the guards say. Some of the boys gave me lip on account of my name, and Honeyboy Tya-Vayir lipped the Harski-aldna, you know, behind his back. 'He's a claphair! Talks old-fashioned, calls the stalls our pit, sounds stooopid!' So I got into some dusts, but I won. Most," he amended.

"You'll win more if you get out to the yard," Ndand hinted. "And get in some overdue practice."

Keth started out, then paused, eyeing Fox again. "You a pirate?" he asked doubtfully.

"Yes." Fox's smile was white-edged, and Keth backed up a few more steps, uncertain, then beat a fast retreat to brag to the rest of the castle children.

Cama shut the door and engaged the lock-latch.

"Claphair?" Barend asked. "Kind of young for that."

Cama snorted. "Changed meaning again, to what we called being a lick, in our day. Although I got word it's changing again, coming to mean someone's bullyboy. Inda's just too tough to make a convincing lick."

They all laughed at that, then Ndand said seriously, "Barend, Keth reminds me of something. This castle is full of orphans. The countryside is full of orphans. I've got at least three youngsters right here who want to go to sea. Parents used to be seafaring, before the pirates and the Venn put a stop to that. Can you take some of them on?"

Barend slid a look Fox's way to receive a slight shrug. Fox wouldn't say anything either way about taking Marlovans. "Sure. You know we might be heading toward battle."

Cama snorted. Ndand opened her hand. "Can we promise there won't be any more fighting here?"

No one had an answer to that, so Cama said, "Now, what's this about gold?"

Barend gave him the details, and Cama—knowing how much Barend hated writing—said, "I'll report to Evred. Why don't you take Fox around the castle?" And then, to Fox, "I know who you are. Inda taught us some of your double-knife fighting on our way up to face the Venn." As Ndand gave a small gasp of recognition, he asked, "Will you drill us before you leave? Inda kept saying you're better than he is. I find that hard to believe."

Fox just shrugged, and Barend said, "He is. Hand-to-hand, anyway. Ndand, how much are we interrupting your day? I remember my way around. I can give him a tour. But he wants to know about the battle, and I left before I'd heard everything."

Ndand thought of her full day of tasks, weighing those against this unexpected encounter with Shendan Montredavan-An's mysterious brother. Fox had been with Inda, who, everyone said, was as gabby as a rock about his pirate days. "I'll take him around," she offered. "Why don't you stay with Cama. In case Evred has questions."

"Good thinking."

Evred's ring brought him to the headmaster's office door, and he paused at the sound of laughter coming from within, not just from Gand and Inda, but from many men. Ready anger burned through him and he slammed open the door, but there were no forbidden bottles during duty watch, there was no heady smell of ale or wine. Most of the masters were there, plus several instructors—the boys were all home by now. Evred then spied the chalkboards in everyone's hands, and realized that they were quite properly tallying the end-year evaluations.

It was so unfamiliar, that laughter during duty time. But it couldn't be wrong, because he could see that the work was getting done.

The men stood, saluting, smiles cooling to sobriety in all the faces, even Gand's. Inda's smile had faded to concern, then mute question.

"Carry on, Gand." Evred opened his hand, wondering what they saw in his face. "Inda, a moment."

Evred was speaking in that soft voice, the one Inda hadn't heard since just before Tau came back. Inda rolled a glance toward Gand only to have his own question mirrored back.

Shufflings and throat clearings rustled in the room, the masters returning to duty as Inda followed Evred out. As soon as the door was shut he began, "Look, if you don't like Tau running the Fox drills with your Runners, I can—"

Evred flat-handed his words aside. "I told you to do what you like." His expression eased slightly. "I notice that just about all the training girls have joined in the last few days since you sent him down there. And most of the younger men have come back."

Inda chuckled. "That's what Tdor told me."

Evred stopped in the middle of one of the practice courts, out of earshot of the sentries endlessly patrolling above. "Inda. What's this about a treasure?"

Inda whistled. "Did Barend write?"

"He is with Cama. They have five ships filled with gold in Castle Andahi harbor."

Inda flashed a wide grin. "It was meant to be a surprise."

"It is. A surprise."

Inda gazed into Evred's face, puzzled by the intensity he could not define. He could feel it, but not define it. "We kept it a secret. Only F—a few of us knew. Barend and I weren't sure if we could actually get any, so we didn't want to add to the load of things you already had on your mind."

Evred held out a thin strip of paper, covered with tiny handwriting. "Cama says here that Barend intends to unload one. The rest is going to Bren, along with barrels and barrels of island-grown coffee beans, to my mother, to be turned into credit. That is, if we agree."

Thank you, Fox. "You decide. The treasure is for you," Inda said, hands spread. "And for the kingdom. What else is it good for?"

Evred realized at last what he'd been seeing so gradually over the past eight months: the atmosphere of friendship among the masters, the sense of fun among the boys in the academy. It was a mirror of their academy days in the scrub barracks, when Inda was their commander in all but name.

They are loyal to Inda. Not a sworn loyalty, one demanded by honor and duty. It was another kind of loyalty, one freely given, perhaps even unaware. Just like when they were boys. Yet that bond had proved to be as strong as oath-bonds.

Evred struggled with far too many shocks. It had happened so gradually that only now could he see that the men were loyal to Inda in the way that Evred's uncle had so wanted the armed forces of Iasca Leror to be loyal to him. Uncle Anderle had wanted it badly enough to expand the academy to include brothers, so everyone would come under his training. They had come out loyal to the kingdom, but not to him.

So . . . this new attitude was new, it was real, but was it a problem?

Evred looked down at the paper in his hands, but did not see the painstaking words. *The men are loyal to Inda, and he is loyal to me.* No king could have a better command chain. Ever.

Inda waited, scrutinizing Evred for a sign of reaction. Was he pleased? Displeased? How could he be displeased?

"It will fix many things," Evred said slowly, thinking: *A king with such loyalty would be a fool not to use it to the kingdom's advantage.* He hated the thought of Inda leaving; he'd made it impossible for Inda to return to Choraed Elgaer, but that was to protect Inda against the pain of divided allegiance. There was no such problem with the north, and who would be better to guard that gold, and to convince the Idayagans to settle down at last? *It would never occur to Inda to use the gold, and the men, and carve out a kingdom for himself.* Gratitude, tenderness, the prospect of a day without hearing Inda's quick step, without seeing his rolling gait, without feeling the heat-spike of his sudden grin, hollowed him to the spine.

Once Inda had recoiled from his touch. "Many." Evred whirled around and walked away, leaving Inda standing there puzzled.

Chapter Twenty-six

NDAND and Fox toured the castle. At first she was carefully neutral as she gave a well-trained field report. But by the time she got to Liet-Jarlan's orders sending her with Keth and the children, and what they'd found there, her voice had deepened with emotion. The damage in high ceilings, old storage rooms, and stairwells was an effective illustration.

Ndand herself was an ordinary Marlovan woman, fair-haired, strong, with the swinging stride that came of years of training. When she whisked herself through a narrow access and ran up the stairs Fox hung back to watch her move. The flare of attraction—awareness—made him laugh inwardly. Wasn't *her* that stirred him. Had he been forming the younger women in the fleet to be Marlovans in all but speech and clothes? He knew the answer. How Inda would laugh!

At the end, they stood on the tower where the little girls had defended against the bungled Idayagan attack just weeks after the battle in the pass, and once again she spoke in a swift, detached manner.

Then crossed her arms. She'd been wondering how to introduce the subject of his sister, to ask if he wanted to send a letter home. She looked doubtfully into that hard, sardonic face, then decided if he wanted to write a letter, he was quite capable of asking for it to be sent. Meanwhile, there was that old treaty to think of. Weren't the Montreda-van-An men forbidden to step outside their border on pain of death? They could only go to sea.

But there was nothing to prevent her from writing to Shendan herself. "Fair trade?" she asked, smiling. "How about telling us some of the pirate stories Inda wouldn't?"

"What would you like to hear?" he returned.

At the end of the tour, Cama and Barend were waiting upstairs in the Jarlan's office.

Barend said, "Evred agrees. One ship offload, but we're to keep it all here. Pay off the debts in Olara, Lindeth, and Idayago. But right now sit tight. He's going to send Inda north with a force to protect the dispersal."

Cama rubbed his jaw. He'd never thought Evred would let Inda out of his sight. Ever. "I like that. Hope he sends him with a few ridings of dragoons. Hills are full of fellows spouting about freedom, but what they want is a fight, and loot. Not work."

Barend patted his chest, where the locket hung inside his clothing. "Evred knows that or he wouldn't be sending Inda."

Cama grunted. "The last holdouts of the Resistance will hate us paying up. It's over money they keep trying to stir trouble. Bound to be a try for the source once we start handing it out." He grinned, tapping the folded paper on the desk. "After Inda oversees the delivery of the gold, Evred wants him to spend the winter riding around looking dangerous."

As the others signified agreement, Cama observed Fox listening in silence. Strange. Here in Castle Andahi was the mysterious Savarend Montredavan-An. No. That old treaty was precise about what would happen if a Montredavan-An set foot on Iascan land outside their border. So here was the second Elgar the Fox, who had a hand in defeating the pirates that had scourged Iasca Leror's coast for so long.

Cama grinned. "Come on, Fox, let's you and I roust

up the guards' lazy butts and give the boys in the hills a show."

A Runner went to summon the off-duty men, and the two walked out to the expanse at the back of the castle, which was mostly grass, surrounded by the communal kitchen gardens.

After a drill that left them sweat-drenched and panting, Fox put them in pairs to spar. At the last the two commanders sparred as the others circled around, yelling and hooting.

Fox saw Inda's style in Cama's attack. What Cama hadn't had time to learn in trickery he made up for with speed, strength, and an unrelenting determination to win.

After a particularly bone-rattling fall, as Fox helped Cama to his feet, the latter pinned him single-eyed. "Ever lost?"

Fox huffed out a laugh. "There's always someone better. Always."

The evening passed congenially, the talk mostly sea battles as opposed to land warfare. Fox enjoyed himself. He was only aware of irony as he rowed back to the *Death* to sleep—he had felt at home among these fellows.

The next day was spent unloading the *Death*. Fox had bought up every barrel on the islands, most labeled for coffee, others for wine. He spotted at least three suspicious glints from the heights round the castle as guards and sailors alike rolled the barrels—coins packed with sand so they wouldn't clink—up the shore to firm ground, to be piled on wagons and driven into the castle, then thumped down into the newly redone cellars.

By nightfall Fox's ships were asail again, Barend with them. They would stop at Bren before continuing down the strait on the last of the western winds. There they'd join up with Fangras and the rest of the Fox Banner Fleet to discover who was going to control the strait.

Tdor could always tell when Tau was spending the night with Hadand by the scent of hot chocolate that lingered in the hallway outside the queen's suite.

Tdor paid attention to the royal castle's ways in her effort to make it home. During the summer, if she opened

certain windows in the Harskialdna tower, a northwest
wind could be sent all the way down the long, long hallway
of the residence's upper level, cooling the air.

In winter, though, no one wanted a bitter wind, so the
windows were shut and the air moved more slowly. She
could sniff the hallway watches after people had left and
name what they had been eating. She could even figure
out who had been there, if the air had stirred little, and the
person used bath herbs. Like Tau. The air always smelled
faintly like summer wherever he was or had been.

She paused outside the old schoolroom, which had become Inda's office, and also outside the dining room.

She paused with a hand on the door latch, listening to
the voices inside. Two male, one female. Tau's laugh, so
musical. He sounded like he was singing when he wasn't.
No, that was wrong, he didn't warble, or talk like he was a
Herskalt giving orders. The quality of his voice had music
in it, somehow.

Then there was Evred's quiet voice. It sounded so different now, he didn't cut his words off, and it had been a long
time since he spoke in that frightening whisper. He even
laughed. The first time Tdor heard that, she was surprised.

Evred laughed now. Inda had said, "Tau's good for
Evred."

Tdor could see that, but she couldn't understand how
showing up with bruises at breakfast could be good for
anyone. She still didn't understand how some liked rough
sex, but she already knew that Whipstick and Noren had
also liked it that way—she had even heard laughter as well
as crashing furniture back in Tenthen, when the summer
caused all the windows to be open.

Sex. She lifted the latch and opened the door, hoping to
leave the subject behind her.

Three faces looked up in welcome. Evred spoke with
his habitual courtesy, but his gaze seemed distracted; Tdor
wondered if Evred was already missing Inda as much as
she was.

Sex again. Or rather, passion. That reminded her of
Signi, and she turned her attention to Hadand, who had
also been so much happier since summer. From the number of chocolate-scented mornings outside Tdor's office, it
seemed like Tau spent most of his nights with the queen.

How did Hadand manage? How did they all manage
without anyone getting jealous? Tdor bit into a warm biscuit, eating mechanically as she considered love. Evred was
not in love with Hadand, though he loved her; Tau didn't
seem to be in love with either of them. If he loved anyone,
it was Jeje, judging from how his voice changed when he referred to her. Evred didn't love Tau like he loved Hadand.
Passion? Not like he had for Inda, not nearly as intense,
you could see it just in the way he turned his head when
either of them spoke.

Signi and I love Inda, and he loves us both. Tdor
squirmed, hating the thought that love was the cause of
jealousy, because that made love the enemy. *The same thing
that is wrong with me when I look outside the window, and
my heart eases when Signi is not seen on the road. I hate that
thing, I repudiate that thing. I just wish she'd get back soon,
so we can settle how our lives will be. How long does it take
to go from castle to town to bridge? Everyone says we have
fewer of them than other kingdoms—*

Inda banged through the door. Once again the three
looked up in welcome, their expressions so characteristic.
Evred's quick smile that then smoothed out, Tau's careless
grin, Hadand's fond, abstracted welcome.

"Everything's ready." Inda dropped down next to Tdor.
"Horses being packed now, men forming up. I'm here to
grab a bite." *Plunk!* His spoon splashed into the porridge.

The others talked around Inda, as usual. The conversation became general, mostly about travel with winter nigh,
as Inda bent over his bowl and ate as fast as he could.

Tdor turned back to Evred, who had resumed his polite
face. She thought about those quick, almost hidden smiles
at Inda when he ate, head down, like a puppy. Tdor wondered if she had the same smile. Did love make people's
habits dear? And did liking make them invisible? Because
Hadand and Tau looked away, but it wasn't deliberate.
They just did not seem to notice the familiar soft clack and
slurp of Inda at a meal, so very much a contrast to Tau's
neat manners.

So did that mean, if you didn't like someone, would their
habits make you begin to hate them?

Inda ate as fast as he could, his thoughts galloping headlong. He couldn't believe the treasure plan had actually

worked. Pleasure, question, annoyance—he had given up on writing to Fox. He didn't even know if the damned scroll case had survived being pitched into the fire. He'd just have to wait until he reached Cama to hear news about the Fox Banner Fleet.

As soon as the last bite of porridge was inside him he grabbed up his honey-smeared rye biscuits to eat on the long walk to the stable, and cut into the others' chatter. "I'm ready to ride."

Evred rose. "I'll meet you in the stable. I've something to give you. Let me get it."

He left, and Hadand followed him out.

Tau reached across the table and clapped Inda on the shoulder. "Keep a sharp eye. You sure you don't want me riding with you?"

"Tau, Evred's sending an entire wing of his toughest dragoons with me. If eighty-one dragoons can't keep me alive, nothing can. Unless you've learned some tricks I don't know."

Inda looked around in what completely failed to be a covert manner, but since his sister and Evred were gone, it didn't matter. He lowered his voice. "Besides, I think you are making them happy."

"That's what I'm here for." Tau's light gaze drifted Tdor's way, then he raised a hand in salute and left.

Inda wondered what he had missed, then forgot that when Tdor leaned toward him. "I will miss you, Inda," she said. Her voice had hurt in it.

He mumbled, "I'll miss you, too." He felt awkward. It felt so stupid to say things they both knew so well. Did other people feel better after saying obvious things? Damned Wafri and his torture—the days of his efforts to pry out Inda's thoughts and memories were long gone. No one was doing that now—he was surrounded by people he trusted and loved—but sometimes he felt ... pried. He couldn't even say how.

Then Tdor bumped her forehead gently against his, and all his thoughts fled. She only did that when something was important, and she knew he might not like it.

"Inda," she whispered. "Will you do something for me?"

"You know I will. If I can."

"When you're with the Idayagans, will you remember manners? Your mother taught us well. You didn't have to remember when you were a pirate, and you don't now. Because you are home. But all those people will be watching you. You are being all of us. You see?"

Inda flushed. "I—" There was nothing to say. It would be a lie to protest that he ate with manners when he didn't remember how he ate. He never thought about how he ate, except what a waste of time it was when he was so busy. How often had he wished you had a door in your stomach so you could unlock it, shove the food in, and lock it up again, and go on your way. "I will."

"Thanks. Let's go."

Hadand was waiting outside. Inda said, "Hadand, I'm taking that book with me, *Cassadas Atanhas*."

"What? But I thought . . ." Hadand shrugged as they walked downstairs, Inda between his sister and his wife.

"I've been falling asleep over it for half a year. Don't the guilds have a rule, no work after Daylast bells?" Inda joked. "Wish that extended to kings and their shield arms. I figure there's no work waiting in a tent at night, so I'm going to try reading then."

Noise filled the stable yard as Inda's column formed up behind the banner bearers, horses flicking ears and switching tails and whickering at one another as men walked around and talked. The only one aware of this double layer of communication was Inda, who was still trying to catch up with learning horse ways after his long absence. How instinctively the men communicated with the animals while gabbling with the other men.

Then Evred was there, his fist held out, fingers curled down. Puzzled, Inda held out his hand, and looked down in surprise when Evred dropped something onto his palm. Oh. One of those magical locket things.

"Use that to communicate with me," Evred said, and gave him the catch words.

There were five lockets all told: two had belonged to the former Harandviar, and the king had had three. Signi had changed the magical catches, so all five could communicate.

Evred had never used the bloodstained one Captain Sindan had worn until his death until now.

Inda flung the chain over his head, dropped the locket inside his shirt, and forgot it as he took hold of Tdor and kissed her, hard. She responded just as hard. Their noses bumped and they laughed unsteadily.

Tears made his form glimmer. She blinked them away as he mounted his horse. Inda looked back, grinning as he lifted his fist, then pointed.

As the horns blared and the thunder of hooves rumbled all around them, Hadand turned to Evred, lips parted.

But what she saw in his face as Inda rode out stopped the words, stopped light and sound and sense, cold.

Chapter Twenty-seven

L IGHTNING hissed overhead.

The violet glare branched across Signi's vision in a reverse image of her eye's veins.

She shivered, stretched out her arms, and when cold water trickled inside her sodden clothes, she shivered again, and forced herself into hel-dancer breathing. Her hands must be steady ...

The sun's daily retreat to the north had begun to bring the bitterness of winter again, here in the southernmost reaches of Iasca Leror.

She had saved the south for last because of its relative proximity to Sartor. If she were to receive any word or sign from Brit Valda, Chief of the Sea Dags, she must carry on with her original quest.

But there had been no word. There had been no sign.

There had only been increasing evidence for the past couple of weeks that she was being followed. No, *hunted*.

She had learned how to travel silently, at night, to do her magics within doubled wards out of the sight of locals. She liked thinking of people waking to the surprise of renewed heat for their baths, the cleanliness of their water, of bridges strengthened. But she had to get food, so she

limited her contacts and always told outright lies, claiming
each time to be a trader, a weaver, a potter.

She had crossed the country in zigzags, creating no pattern, but now, as she reached the end, the pattern must be
evident: there were few unrenewed places left.

And so, despite her crazy path and all her care, the trap
had closed around her.

Signi pressed her hands over her eyes. But there was no
escape from the images of the family she'd met just yesterday, their friendly faces, their generosity last night as they
invited a lonely traveler to join them in their meal; the children's anxious hope as she sampled the nut-cake they had
made themselves—

Last image: the children lying dead inside that house,
their parents beside them. All with their throats slit, killed
with such speed they never knew the silent, shadowy Blood
Hunt had entered their living space before they'd tumbled
into death.

The Erama Krona adhered precisely to ritual when on a
Blood Hunt. These deaths had been a warning. From now
on they would kill everyone who aided her, whether the
victims knew they were aiding a fugitive or not.

Signi had fled straight into the storm, running most of
the night. She sensed that dawn was not far off. She must
find somewhere to hole up for another long day.

Her days of mage renewal were done. She had her
greater duty before her surely, but if so, why had she not
been warned that there had been a Blood Hunt called out
against her?

There had been no message from Dag Valda since that
day on the tower at Ala Larkadhe, when Signi had declared
she would take a stand against Dag Erkric.

I will not be able to ward you, Dag Valda had warned,
but Signi raised the water anyway, in a desperate attempt
to prevent slaughter. Had Valda abandoned her, then? But
she must not assume.

She flexed her cold hands, envisioning a bubble around
herself, the protective ward advancing outward a fingers-
breadth at a time. So—

Ah! She held the spell, one hand gripped to aid her mind
in two simultaneous tasks as she laid another spell over the
ward. And another. On the last, as she whispered the spell,

she moved outside the ward. She had to feel her way for her eyes were dazzled by magic.

One more, and there! The ward lay like a bubble, invisible to the outer senses but discernable to a mage. Let them all assume she was inside it. She'd laid several different protections inside of it. That ought to take some time to dismantle, in case rigid tradition had been broken, and the Yaga Krona had been sent on the Blood Hunt as well. Erkric had become adept at breaking tradition while seeming to uphold it.

Signi felt her way into the young stand of green ash at the river's edge. Lightning flared again, mirrored harshly in the river water, the back-flash firing the slanting raindrops to crystal.

She left the ward at the river's edge and crept over the tangled ground under an old willow, then toward the cottonwoods and silver maple, all interlacing sturdy brown fingers overhead.

She eased around the ice-rimed puddles of low ground, stepping on the netted roots of water arum, four different types of water lily, and pungent sting grass as she made her way toward the gently rising slope—

Pain whipped into nerves, bones, muscle, flinging her to hands and knees. Lightning? No—

Hard hands yanked her to her feet. Someone twisted her arms behind her with such viciousness her shoulders shot red agony through her, weakening her knees. Someone else caught her up by the neck of her robe, and when her head dropped back, a young voice, guttural with hatred, uttered, "Traitor."

A warm splurp in her eye: he'd spat in her face.

Her hands were chained tightly. Someone else pulled cloth around her head, gagging her mercilessly so the sides of her mouth stretched wide, her tongue pressed back almost into her throat. Then a hard blow rocked her head on her neck.

"Enough."

Instant release of the remorseless hands sent her staggering, and she fell face-first into the swamp.

At least it cleans the spit off. Her mental voice chattered like the clatter of bones inside her head as she was yanked to her feet, her legs chained.

Erama Krona clad in the black of the rare and terrible Blood Hunt pressed in close. One by one they activated transfer stones, the last pulling her away and through space to drop her, staggering, on a Destination platform.

Someone released the grip on her chains. The Erama Krona flowed around her and away, two slightly apart, she saw with a heart beat of pity. The Erama Krona were forbidden, under threat of terrible penalty, from speaking or making personal contact outside of orders while on the hunt. The depth of moral outrage that would cause them to pay the cost was a message of warning far more dire than the actual violence they'd done to her.

The loosened chain thunked, rude and abrupt, against the knobs of her spine. Hands yanked her up, set her on her feet. When she began to fall, they held her up, fingers prising into her muscles and tendons.

Her throat spasmed, her tongue stirred horribly against the gag. A knife was thrust up behind her ear, shearing locks of hair. She jumped, then stilled as the knife sawed twice. The gag fell away.

Her lips had cracked from the extreme tightness of the gag. Blood leaked into her mouth as she struggled to get her tongue to partner with her lips again in the shaping of words. She coughed, hard, terrified her own silence would condemn her. "I—" There was her voice, like the squeak of a bat flying around one of the southern mountains. She had shared a cave once with bats. They were shy creatures, so beautiful in flight.

She was force-marched through Anborc's Trallagat, the Gate of Thralls, where the born thralls, or those indentured to service as retribution for misdeed, came and went. The Erama Krona forced her feet into heavy wooden clogs so that she would not defile the marble floors on the long walk to the Hall of Judgment, with its lofty ceilings of serene blue, painted with stars that their ancestors had remembered from the night sky of a world long gone.

To the dais, raised three upon three layers of marble, blue, gold, and white, where the throne sat, void of kingship.

Signi jolted into the now. Her eyes stung with dribbles of mud, blurring the surrounding Erama Krona: not those of the Blood Hunt, whose oath had been fulfilled. These were dressed in gray, which meant there was yet no king.

There was yet no king.

She felt the impact of the hall full of gazes as the Erama Krona positioned her in the middle of the first step below the dais, her chains clanking unmusically.

She was forced around to face the Losveg Skalt, face obscured by the mask of Law. Though Signi's eyes blurred and stung, she had been trained to observe muscle and movement, the flow of color in faces, the way people breathed. The woman's malignity was as palpable as a blow.

"You are summoned before the Frasadeng." The voice was strong and precise, meant to sound neutral, above human concerns. But Signi, sensitive to the subtleties of human expression in body and voice, recognized Dag Nanni Balandir, aunt to the new young Hyarl Balandir. She'd been one of the House Dags, possibly even the king's House Dag during the years Signi had been sailing in the south. She had been one of Erkric's protégés when they were all young.

"State your identity before the Frasadeng."

Not for Signi the simple "My name is" that seemingly all had a right to, a dignity she had claimed before the Marlovans. Here in the homeland she must stay with the strict truth, though it shamed her. But then shame was her shroud this day.

"I was born Jazsha Signi Sofar."

"What is now your name?"

"My name is Signi. I am a Sea Dag."

"Explain to the Frasadeng why your name at birth and your present name differ?"

"My mother declared me family outcast when I failed to achieve the last level of the hel dance, as had she and her mothers before her. Since I shared her personal name, I deemed it better to relinquish that as well. I earned my place in the world as Dag Signi."

"You, Dag Signi, outcast from the family Sofar, are accused of betraying your people by acts of magic, causing death and destruction to our warriors, and bringing about the failure to carry out the king's will."

Signi trembled inside, though she forced her muscles to a semblance of calm. There is a quality to every silence: this was the skull-ringing density of high emotion, of emotions as well as voices pent up. It was the silence of hundreds of people in close proximity.

"When did you decide to commit treason against your homeland?"

"I never committed treason."

"Did you raise a water spout by magic to drive out our force from taking the city of Ala Larkadhe?"

"I raised a water spout to prevent any more deaths."

"Did you remove protective magical wards and tracers from the tower at the city of Ala Larkadhe that were placed on order of Prince Rajnir?"

"I removed wards that would throw a stone spell around any who inadvertently crossed certain places, as stone spells against innocent people directly contravene our vows." Her voice shook with her effort to be heard.

"Did you break protective wards placed at the castle located at the north end of the Andahi Pass?"

"No."

"Did you break protective wards on the heights of Andahi Pass?"

She did not even try to hide how startled she was. "I did not."

"Did you remove tracer wards from any of these locations?"

"I did not."

The Losveg Skalt looked down at her papers, and then up. "Who did? You are permitted to speak if you can prove your innocence."

"I witnessed no such actions," Signi stated, and despite the cold, and ache of the heavy chains and the iron gall chafing her throat, she was angry at the absurdity of these accusations.

On they went. Signi locked her knees to keep from falling, and her voice sank lower and lower. Disbelief at the falsity of these accusations caused her just once to lift her head. The council sat like stone effigies, revealing little. Prince Rajnir was not even there. But she sensed a hidden intensity in Dag Erkric; she was too bewildered, in too much pain to understand much beside the fact that she was being accused of things that she had not done, she could not have done. Had anyone done them?

A flicker of memory, barely more than instinct. Then the Losveg Skalt said, "Did you place tracer wards on the communications scroll case belonging to Dag Erkric?"

"No." But Signi knew who had.

The shock of memory made her dizzy and she swayed.

White-haired, beak-nosed Dag Agel of the House Dags lifted her voice. "Losveg Skalt. We have increasing difficulty hearing the answers of the accused."

Signi scarcely heard, she was barely aware of Dag Erkric walking directly past her, the only notice he took of her was to keep his robe from touching her. He made obeisance to the old king, and then spoke in a tone too low to hear.

Signi shut her eyes, struggling to remain upright. *Brit Valda bespelled Erkric's scroll case; she told me herself. And . . . did she not say that she had tampered with some spells on some gates? I don't remember . . .*

Signi swayed and forced herself to hel dancer balance breathing. The rushing sound in her head resolved into whispers and shuffles.

The Losveg Skalt stated, "It has been deemed appropriate to break at this point."

Mercy, from Dag Erkric?

No, there was no mercy in that hateful gaze. The angle of his chin, the corners of his mouth: that was triumph. Instinct coiled, cold and terrible, inside Signi.

The Losveg Skalt went on. "The accused denies all accusations, and we cannot administer kinthus to a dag. Therefore we must call forward all who witnessed the actions taken by the accused. We shall reassemble three days hence at dawn. Take the accused to Sinnaborc."

The Tower of Transgressors. The name, the words, whispered through the Hall.

Signi did not see half the council stir in protest, for she was accused, not condemned, and half sit back in satisfaction. She had closed her eyes as a pair of Erama Krona, dressed in gray, took up a stance on either side of her.

If she did not walk on her own, she would be dragged.

The guards led her back to the Trallagat. She trembled from the hurt of familiar smells—stone and the sea and the spices of home—and the familiar slant of the sunlight.

These sensations hurt more than the bindings, for the pain was deep inside. But she braced her spine. Something far worse than the poignancy of homecoming was nigh.

More Erama Krona fell in behind her, the reverse of an honor guard.

Traitor's Gate opened only for one purpose: to display criminals accused of crimes against the Venn. There was the cart to conduct her along the King's Road, with a single low rail meant to keep her within while giving full access to her from all sides. One of the Erama Krona clapped an iron circle round her neck, the torc of the thrall. It was connected to a heavy chain, which was fastened to the cart rail.

The iron weight of the chain thunked across her back. In the bitter air her wet clothing began to freeze, creaking faintly when she jerked. She nearly lost her balance, and fearful of falling on her bound hands and breaking a bone, she braced against the chain.

Then, deep enough to vibrate through bone and stone, the enormous Campan Drak—the massive bell of alarm, of judgment—sounded thrice. Fashioned of iron plate dipped in melted bronze, it took nine men to set it in motion. The sonorous ring echoed from tower to tower all the way down the long road, announcing "Here passes an outcast."

The armored horse began pulling the cart.

Only once in her life had Signi trod the King's Road, with its fine pale stone fitted in the same pattern as the tablet-weave of formal clothing: when she had been accepted as a dag.

The cart began to roll on its iron wheels, jigging and swaying past Anborc, toward the mighty egg-shape of Leofaborc, Tower of Concord on the west, with the Skalts' Tower beyond it. Along the eastern side three smaller towers rose, still bearing the names of their original Houses.

The low murmur of angry people sundered the cold air, both sides of the streets full of those who braved the impending weather to deliver verdict: a Blood Crowd.

"Traitor!"

"Treason!"

"Cast her out!"

"Let her fly the blood eagle!"

"Put her on the tower for the death birds to pick her bones!"

Signi fell to her knees on the splintery boards of the cart, face raised to the cloud-tumbled sky.

Soft thuds hit her shoulder, her ear, her arm, releasing the sick-sweet smell of rot. The hurled chunks came fast and accurate, exploding over her with the sharp, stomach-scraping stink of ordure: dog, horse. Human, even: some there were so enraged they had deliberately squatted down to make waste just to fling at the traitor.

Crack! Pain shot through her temple from the impact of a rock and from the solid wall of shouted hatred. Small warm gobs signified people who darted close enough to spit. Not people—crowds roused to riot laid aside humanity— see them as the dart of serpent, flicker of tongue and jet of venom, and there the raucous claws, spindle-stab beaks of death birds wheeling above the Tower of Transgressors . . .

Tumultuous thunder kindled an outcry, and down came needles of hail.

If I am blamed yet know myself blameless, then someone stands behind me, using me to shroud the truth.

The cart jolted up: the King's Bridge, between Skalts Tower and Saeborc, once her home. The clouds parted, just long enough for her to see the first of the emerging stars, a giddying gleam, then sharp as a flint strike it was gone, and a rock, larger than the others, knocked her head forward into the cart rail. Harsh rose the rallying cry; her eyes were blinded by splintered lightnings of pain, followed by a thin rain of blood.

Past the remaining towers. Here thralls sent by Tower Families pressed forward to discharge their loads.

What did the Great Sanbrigid of Sky-Drakan say? I will not leave life with my heart embered in rancor, though my body be iron-garner. Memory must be her armor, her shield. Brun Durasnir's kiss of peace, Fulla Durasnir's affection when both were young. And there, steadfast and tender, Inda smiles, tousled hair light-stranded.

The cart jolted to a stop. Rough hands jerked her out, and guards walked her through the Traitor's Gate and into the white walls of the Sinnaborc, the Tower of Transgressors, at the northernmost point of Twelve Towers.

The Campan Drak again tolled thrice, the deep, harsh iron sound reverberating off cold rock and through her bones as they forced her up and up to Execution Cell.

Chapter Twenty-eight

LATE the second of two sleepless nights, between two long, crashing cracks of thunder, Brun Durasnir heard her door open. She half rose, pulling her knife from under her pillow, sliding one foot to the rug of her sleeping platform. She'd begun sleeping with a knife since the days at the Port of Jaro when the Venn had been warned of the pirate Elgar the Fox sneaking into Ymar with assassination as intent.

"It is I."

"Fulla?"

They had to wait for another crash, and Brun wished (as she did every winter) that her position did not require sleeping in the Saeborc. She missed their comfortable underground home, with its warm flow of air, mosaic walls, the green things growing in each room under the all-color crystal lights. But above all the quiet.

As soon as the roar juddered down to a rumble, he murmured, "Erkric believes I took the fleet to sea to ride out the storm. The ships are out there, right enough, but I am here. I've been hiding—never mind." He parted the curtain and stepped up onto the platform to sink down on the bed beside her, pulling the curtains shut to keep in the slightly warmer air from the vents under the platform.

He smelled of stale sweat, of tension, of a man who has not eaten in far too long. Desire and tenderness made her throat ache and her eyes burn.

"Brun, all our earlier surmises are wrong. No. We were right, but not completely so. Ulaffa believes—and has convinced me—that Erkric's real target is not Dag Signi at all, but Brit Valda."

"Brit Valda?" Brun controlled the urge to exclaim "Impossible!" She rapidly considered what little she knew. Brit Valda was the head of the Sea Dags, whom she had seen only once or twice. A small woman with a nest of untidy gray hair, she was almost as old as Erkric. "I thought she was dead."

"She vanished. With good reason. I wish I dared take the time to tell you everything that Ulaffa reported of events I had not known about during the invasion. It would take too long, and avails us nothing. Just know this. Valda did her very best to deflect Erkric's attempts to make dags into warriors. Not only that, but she succeeded in tampering with his scroll case, and among her discoveries—she told me herself, the day of the surrender, but I'd forgotten it in the face of everything else—there were five missing doses of white kinthus the week the king died."

"Does Ulaffa know?"

"Yes. But he cannot find proof. The king's Yaga Krona sealed the king's suite in Anborc, and of course the king's death was investigated by Anborc House Dags. Dag Agel personally led the inspection. She reported to the Council of Elders convened at the time that she found everything as it should be. They might not believe Ulaffa now. He was not here in the homeland; he was with us."

"The king's rooms were sealed by Nanni Balandir," Brun whispered. Dag Balandir had been the king's personal dag.

"Exactly. Reputation for formidable magical knowledge, probity . . . and being Abyarn Erkric's foremost student."

Durasnir could not see his wife in the curtained sleep alcove, but he guessed from the sound of her breathing the direction of her thoughts. "Ulaffa has to talk to Dag Agel," he said. "The risk is that she will not only disbelieve, but will deem it correct to report such a conversation to Erkric."

Brun took his cold fingers into her warm hands and rubbed them. "Dag Agel is known for her honesty, but she is also a traditionalist. She wants to restore us to the good days of our foremothers and -fathers."

"Ulaffa says that the Frasadeng is not investigating a traitor so much as attempting—"

"To blame Signi for everything, so her death will bury the problems. As you said before."

Thunder rolled, sudden and loud. The east windows flickered with manic purple light.

"Brun, Erkric was using magic from *Norsunder*. Valda also discovered that he'd taught death magic to Dag Mekki. There is no proof of that either: Dag Mekki is under a stone spell for twice eighty years."

"So why blame Signi? Were Signi and Valda even together?"

"Yes. That is, I only witnessed it once, that day on the tower top at Ala Larkadhe."

"Are you going to tell the council that?"

"I will avoid it any way I can. Here is the third thing: Ulaffa says that Valda is the only one strong enough to fight Erkric. Erkric knows it."

"I don't understand. Erkric is older than we are! What good can such scheming do? It would make more sense if he were Rajnir's age!"

"You forget Norsunder lies beyond time. Its mages are ageless. Erkric seeks to gain that type of power. He will rule through Rajnir, who at times is like a ghost, without will or awareness. Erkric will rule through the next king, and the next—*damnation*." He looked down; a knotwork ring on his forefinger glowed an evil, dull red. "I had better go."

"Fulla, are you plotting something?"

His breath hissed out; before he could answer, she said steadily, "Tell me what I can do."

"There is little that we can do, at least now," he whispered, a wraith against the pale stone walls. "But we watch and wait. Stand ready for anything."

Execution Cell in Sinnaborc tower was empty of furnishings and made entirely of stone except for the iron of the doors and manacles. They'd left Signi shackled to the wall with her arms apart so that she could not perform magic.

She lost all sense of time. Meals were a humiliation involving her head being yanked back and plate scrapings poured in her face to swallow, choke on, or dribble out. The first couple of times she tried to retain a modicum of personal dignity by refusing, but by the third time hunger forced her to gulp and gobble as best she could.

She felt the brush of magic keeping the air just warm enough so that she was not in danger of freezing. There was nothing to be done about her squalid clothing, but she could work her shoes and stockings off, a task that used up time. For a while she just rubbed her bare feet over the stone, over and over, trying to get that sensation to mute the itching, crackling, rancorous stench on the rest of her. The chain's chastising length permitted neither a full stance nor lying on the floor.

Her path had narrowed to survival. She sensed Erkric's will behind the cruelty; even if her body finally failed, as flesh must, she was determined that her will would remain a pole star to his: he had wrenched all meaning from Drenskar, he had spat upon the Tree with his false words, he had flung filth upon its leaves with his ambitions. And he had taken light from the path with his actions. Her light must come from opposition: she would not rail with hate, she would not fight and destroy, and above all, she would not betray her own vows.

If the truth requires my death, so be it. Surely, surely, for my own soul, Ydrasal's light will shine the way beyond the world.

At long last the door rattled and creaked open.

She kept her eyes closed as her arms were loosed from the wall to fall as dead weights to her sides. But only for moments; just as the painful tingles of returning circulation began, her hands were yanked behind her and shackled, to prevent her from doing magic. She was taken down and down and fastened into the cart.

Again the crowds were gathered in the frigid air under low clouds. This time most watched in eerie silence. Fewer objects hit her.

She did not look up at all, even when the cart stopped. She opened her eyes half a heartbeat before a bucket of ice melt pitched squarely into her face. She fell backward onto her bound arms, gasping; the chain on the iron collar was yanked short, snapping her head back. She struggled to draw her trembling legs under her, but they had gone numb below the knees.

Another bucket sluiced over her, and yet another. Three more, until the surface filth and grime had been dislodged enough so she would not foul the air of the Hall of Judgment in Anborc.

Once again she had to wear the wooden clogs of the thrall and was chain-led to the Hall of Judgment.

Dag Erkric came in through the king's door just after she was brought to the center of the dais. He halted, staring down at her, and terror shocked her nerves. His parted lips, the wide eyes, dark pupils, the fast breathing of bitter triumph: here was a desperately angry man.

"You lie, traitor. The dishonor you brought upon all dags can only be expiated on Sinnaborc's roof."

"Dag Erkric," the old king admonished.

Dag Erkric pressed his hands together and bowed. "Forgive me for speaking to the accused. It is not just the Venn who have been betrayed, but me personally, as the sea dags were under my eye, and I failed to see the rot at the root of the Great Tree."

He returned to his bench, and the Losveg Skalt rose, papers on her slate. She turned toward the old king, who raised a hand. The Losveg Skalt's masked face lifted as she surveyed the packed, silent hall, then she said, "We shall begin with testimony from witnesses. Then the accused will be examined so that the council may compare the witnesses' testimony to the claims of the accused."

Silence.

"We call forth Dag Ulaffa."

The old dag shuffled forward, looking old, tired, and frail.

"You will state your name and place before the Frasadeng."

"I am Fulk Ulaffa, raised in House Brac. I am Chief of Prince Rajnir's Yaga Krona."

"You were under direct orders from Prince Rajnir to aid the warriors' preparations in breaking the siege at the northern castle at Andahi Pass?"

"I was."

"You also made a transfer token so that Stalna Hyarl Durasnir could witness the progress of the battle?"

"I did."

"How did that come about?"

"The Stalna requested it from me. I conveyed his wish through Dag Erkric, who obtained the prince's permission. I fashioned the token and sent it to the Stalna to use."

"Did you prepare your token to send Stalna Hyarl Durasnir to the tower at Ala Larkadhe?"

"I did not. I prepared it for the ancient observation platform called by the Sartorans an *atan,* there at the heights. I assumed that that would be the best place from which to observe the progress of the invasion. As I know little about military matters, I was not aware that it was not in fact a good placement; it was far too high."

"Did you ever see the accused?"

"Only once. After the battle had ended."

"Did you personally witness the accused performing magic?"

"I did not."

"Did you ever transfer to the white tower at Ala Larkadhe?"

"The day after we received orders to cease and retreat. Dag Erkric conveyed orders from the prince to investigate while our forces were withdrawing from the pass."

Signi braced herself. Now was the time for Dag Ulaffa to mention Brit Valda. But Ulaffa remained silent, awaiting the next question.

The Losveg Skalt looked down, rattled her papers, then said, "When you investigated the tower, you were able to discover the accused's identity through magical tracers, which enabled you to determine that the accused had committed treason via magic, raising a great water spout."

Signi gripped her fingers together behind her.

Ulaffa bent his head, then finally said, "No."

"No, the Dag Signi did *not* magically raise a water spout?"

The old dag raised his head. The only sign of emotion was a slight quiver in his jowl, and the gleam of moisture in his eyes, but his voice was strong. "She did. According to the tracers."

"Will you explain your contradiction, Dag Ulaffa?"

"Yes. My understanding is that treason is an action that jeopardizes the kingdom."

"Treason," Dag Erkric spoke up from the bench behind the throne, "is an action in aid of one's enemies. It is an act that violates one's allegiance. It is an action against the will of the king."

Ulaffa looked up. "To the Erama Krona the king said, *Bring the Marolo-Venn, the lost ones, back to us with their lands.* He did not actually order us to conquer them. That was Prince Rajnir's desire. Furthermore, the oath of allegiance we dags make requires us to perform magic to the protection and service of the Venn. By her action, Dag Signi saved Venn lives as well as Marlovan, for subsequent questioning of the Battle Chief furnished the fact that no one died in the flood."

Signi scarcely dared breathe. She was certain that Valda had said something about Ulaffa as an ally, but she could no longer remember. That might only have been a dream.

Noise rustled through the hall. One of the Erama Krona struck the floor with a spear butt until silence fell.

"Did you witness Dag Signi giving succor to Marlovans after the battle?"

"After the battle, yes," Ulaffa said. "I did so see, when the prince ordered me to investigate, the day after the battle." Beads of sweat glittered in his grizzled hair.

"This action does not constitute treason? Giving aid and comfort to enemies?"

"We dags are sworn to protect life. Not just Venn life, but all life. This vow is the reason we do not learn the skills of war."

A whisper, but a ring of the spear butt from the Erama Krona again caused silence.

"The aid was given after the horns of retreat were blown, and no sword was raised by either side. No warrior aided by Dag Signi rose to attack our men."

"Why did she not offer aid to our fallen?"

"I do not know, but I observed that among the Marlovans there was no healer mage at all. For our men, we had one per Battlegroup, plus their assistants. The greater human need was among the Marlovans, by ninefold times nine. And the halt had been called, so it could not endanger our men to aid the fallen among the Marlovans."

"We are finished with you for now, Dag Ulaffa. We call forth Southern Fleet Commander Hyarl Durasnir."

The southern fleet commander rose from his seat beside Dag Erkric as whispers again rustled through the hall. Durasnir wore full battle gear, his face far more lined than Signi remembered. He did not once look her way.

"As you are well known to all assembled here, you may be brief in stating identity and place," the Losveg Skalt said.

She might have meant that as an obscure compliment, or maybe only to save time, but Durasnir used his deck command-in-a-thunderstorm voice to roll out his name, title, and Oneli rank. It was impressive; most sensed his righteous anger and wanted to speculate about the cause.

When the last echo of his voice faded, the Losveg Skalt said flatly, "The Dag Ulaffa has explained that your transfer token took you to another location, yet you encountered the accused on the tower at Ala Larkadhe, by accounts some two weeks' travel away."

Erkric stilled.

"The site chosen by Dag Ulaffa did not afford a close enough view," Durasnir said. "It might afford a fine view for a mage, but for military purposes, it was useless. I had been told that what the Sartorans call an *atan* would transfer to the tower."

Signi leaned forward, her chains clinking slightly.

In the gallery, the dags whispered. Signi caught a note of longing, even envy in the word *atan*.

The Losveg Skalt said, "So the records show. We sent a dag to test this transfer from tower to *atan*. They report that the tower archive is closed."

Durasnir gestured. "I know nothing about that. It functioned at the time."

The Losveg Skalt turned Erkric's way.

Dag Erkric said, "The archive was open, and the *atan* transfer functioned, when I attempted it in my investigation previous to our landing in the north."

The Losveg Skalt rattled through two papers, jerked one forward, then addressed Durasnir. "In your military opinion, did this water spout prevent our people from taking the city as ordered?"

"Only for the duration of the flood," Durasnir stated. "Drenga Battle Chief Vringir could have taken the city once the water was spent, but Commander Talkar issued a new order for him to lead his force to the harbor to secure it."

"The Oneli Commander speaks the truth," Commander Talkar said from the side, where he sat, stiff in his armor and battle gear, his winged helm on his knee.

The Losveg Skalt turned back to Durasnir. "You saw the accused perform this magical action, raising the geyser."

"I did."

"Did Dag Signi state her purpose for her action?"

Durasnir said, "She did not speak to me."

The Losveg Skalt fussed with her notes again, then jerked her chin up. "She was there on the white tower of Ala Larkadhe when you arrived to witness the progress of the attack?"

"Correct."

"Did she at any time indicate why she was there?"

"She did not."

"Did you ask?"

"I did not."

"So you just stood there in silence, the two of you? The commander of the southern fleet and a sea dag missing for half a year?" Sarcasm crisped the Losveg Skalt's consonants.

"There was a little talk, and events required our attention."

"What did you say to her on first seeing her?"

" 'I thought you were dead.' No, I believe it was, 'They said you were dead.' "

Whispers—even laughter—were swiftly silenced.

"Her response?"

"She asked if I had come to witness the fighting."

"And you said?"

Durasnir paused, frowned, then looked up. "We exchanged a little talk about the progress of events, and I do not trust myself to remember the exact words with any accuracy, for my attention was on the field below. I was there to witness the battle, and our forces were preparing to enter the city."

"You did not ask where she had been for half a year?"

"No. It has never been my place to question those in the other services."

"You did not ask what she intended to do?"

"No."

"When Dag Signi began her water spout, did she say anything to you?"

"She did not speak to me at all. When she began to do magic, I deemed it best to transfer."

"And that is the last time you saw Dag Signi?"

"Correct."

Signi's sight flickered at the edges, and she remembered to breathe as a few whispers, sharp and clear, were quickly silenced. Erkric looked up, a sharp movement revealing impatience, anger.

The Losveg Skalt's hieratic tone blurred into haste as she spoke the formal words that dismissed the fleet commander, and called forth two dags, Erkric's followers. She bade them stand opposite Signi. Then she gestured to the Erama Krona.

Signi's heartbeat thumped in warning as she was flanked by the guards who brought her forward to the witness stand and held her there.

Then began a long list of accusations of magical actions. After each the two dags were asked if they had witnessed the result of a magical act. They testified to it before Signi was called on to admit to having performed them. Signi could feel how the questions had been formed to hide the true cause of Valda's actions: by deft wording, her defensive measures blurred into Erkric's offenses.

He is condemning me, spell by spell, for Valda's actions in thwarting his Norsundrian magic.

Signi denied each with all her dwindling strength. Her arms throbbed with red pain as the Erama Krona held her upright; she could no longer stand on her own.

She braced for the conviction, or thought she was braced, but there was a yet another horror waiting.

The Losveg Skalt said, "The testimony of the witnesses proves that these actions occurred. The council agreed that in the event of your denying having performed them, you prove the truth of your words by naming the person or persons responsible."

And there at last was the true purpose of this trial.

Signi was too weary to raise her head. This trial was not hers, though she stood accused. On trial was Brit Valda, whom Erkric dared not name because he did not know how much she knew, he did not have her in hand, and because her actions had all been taken directly against him when he had twisted the tree of Ydrasal into the clawing, soul-devouring dragon of Rainorec by claiming that his orders all came from the prince.

Cold to the bone, Signi knew what must come: execution, public atonement not just for Erkric's secret deeds, but also for Valda's secret attempts to thwart him. Because of this last, Signi's path was clear, though cruel. She must not speak, she must not betray her vows.

"I repeat," the Losveg Skalt stated, louder. "Can you name the person or persons responsible?"

Valda is the only mage who can withstand Erkric.

Signi made an effort that took all her remaining strength, and raised her eyes to the golden banner of Ydrasal. Through the sheen of tears in her burning eyes, she saw past the gold-worked, much-repaired banner tree to the Great Tree beyond it, twelve branches intertwined above the rising sun, the whole coruscating with pale fire.

And its reflection glowed in her face.

He seeks to make my bones warp and my blood weft, but I will not betray my vow to laws above political boundary.

The great laws were the weaving of civilization. And so Signi gripped the spindle of sacred light and spun pain and degradation away, threaded by the frantic beat of her heart.

From above, and around, came whispers: *Vision . . . she is a Seer!*

Signi was beyond hearing, but Erkric wasn't. The light that seemed to radiate from the banner, or from beyond the banner, shafted down to touch Signi's filthy face, and the whispers that made clear how many saw it, pierced him with needles of pain. That light *must* be merely a mere trick of the glowglobes, a stray reflection from somewhere outside.

Too many stirred, faces raised in wonder and awe and even fear, to sustain the comfort of that assumption. So here he was, witnessing a Seeing at last, but he was not the Seer. Bitterness roiled in his stomach. What a waste! Proving, he thought, that such things were random trickery on the part of the unseen. The visions of the Yaga Ydrasal, the inward eye, belonged only to poets and to the insane, who were often indistinguishable from one another.

"Do we wait all day for the accused to answer the question?" he asked Ulaffa, just loud enough to prod the Losveg Skalt, who stared at Signi with her mouth half open behind her mask.

The Losveg Skalt jerked her attention back to the moment. "Dag Signi! I ask you a last time. Will you name the person or persons responsible for performing the treasonous magic that you deny performing yourself?"

Signi started and looked around in weary bewilderment. Those closest witnessed in the bracing of her thin body under its weight of chains, the tension inscribing lines in her face, her acceptance of the burden of time, place, and situation.

"I witnessed no treason," she stated, because that was the truth. In the resulting outcry, her low, exhausted voice was nearly inaudible. "I never committed treason."

In the following uproar, Erkric struggled to remain outwardly impassive, to mask his wrath. He knew what those words meant: she *did* know whose will and skill opposed his. She was rejecting the offer of mercy he had so carefully designed to come as relief, release, at the end, when she gave him Valda.

Let's see how brave you are alone with my Biddan. He will wrench Brit Valda's secrets from you, one cracked joint and bloody strip of skin at a time.

Chapter Twenty-nine

DAG Agel had not mistaken the old, old signs, almost unnoticed on the lintel above the archive door: a tiny white stone. When they were all young magic students, they used to arrange meetings in the archive by those stones. One above the emerald-eyed dragon meant dragon hour, when the twelve-hour glass was turned: midnight. A stone above the carved and gilt sun meant midday, and one above the moon meant the nine-glass hour, or nightwatch.

Her heartbeat sounded loud in her ears as she passed into the stillness of the old archive. Four levels up, a storm pounded the coast, evidenced only by a faint quickening of the channeled air vents in the public corridors. Here in the oldest archive the air slowly changed every decade. Longer.

She carried her candle, causing it to stream and waver, making the gilt scrolls worked into the mosaic patterns appear to leap and jiggle. She did not clap on the glowglobes, for those were too often bespelled to capture evidence of who trespassed these spaces these days.

She had checked for wards herself.

In the oldest chamber, where the fragments from their long ago past were preserved, there was a stir of blue robe, a glimpse of silver, grizzled hair, and Fulk Ulaffa came forward, holding his hands out wide.

Dag Agel set the candle down on a scribe's high writing table and held out her own empty hands.

"Thank you for meeting me." Ulaffa's voice was husky with exhaustion and defeat.

Agel's lips tightened. "Is this trial the end of our way of life? Do you not see how the distrust engendered in us as dags is going to shadow us far beyond the problems we are facing now?"

"At this moment," Ulaffa said, "I do not see myself surviving the problems we face now."

Agel raised her hand in the hearken signal, a silent reproach.

Ulaffa said, "Yes. I know I sound facetious. Agel, maybe it is time for our purpose to be examined, and not just by us, but also by those we swear to protect. You and I both remember Abyarn Erkric as an earnest and dedicated dag. Perhaps you still see him that way, yet."

"I did, but the more I ponder how life has changed by incremental degrees over the past fifteen years, the more I perceive his hand causing these changes. We were not so afraid of one another then, so wary in our daily steps. We did not distrust what we were told. We accepted one another's dedication to Drenskar, we recognized one another on the golden path, even if our branches diverged."

Ulaffa breathed out slowly. "Yes. Yes."

"So. There are two items that you and I must resolve."

"You investigated the kinthus in the king's chamber?"

"I did. The records all matched everyone's testimony. But then I brought the king's healer down to the clean room. He cooperated willingly. We went through all the events. When we got to the night of the king's death, his account was just a little too smooth, too devoid of . . ." She groped for words. "I hardly know how to explain what I heard. It was as if he repeated someone else's experience, not his own. So I tested for traces. And found one. The merest hint of magic, so subtle I would not have found it had we not been in the space where no magic at all is performed, vigilant as I was."

Ulaffa leaned forward.

Dag Agel's aged face furrowed with distaste, and fear.

These words were difficult to say. "Fulk, his mind had been tampered with. He had no actual memory of that night, and was not aware of this lack of memory. All his previous memories of eventless days had taken its place, and he did not know it. How is that even possible?"

"Have you visited the prince, as I requested?"

"I have not. There is no getting near him: his own guards have strict orders from him not to permit access. They insist it is for his safety. But . . ." Dag Agel looked away, ashamed. "I summoned the laundry thrall and had him submit to kinthus."

Ulaffa nodded; thralls had few rights.

"And what he told me about the prince during private times is profoundly disturbing. He no longer reads or debates. He is not even lying with women. He just sits in the dark, as if dreaming." She drew in a steadying breath, but it did nothing for the churn of her insides. "We hold to tradition, because it gives us order and meaning. When our traditions are twisted to an end we cannot see . . . well, the House Dags have fractured even worse than the House Hyarls. Oh, I need time to think."

"We do not have that time. We must rescue Dag Signi. Dag Erkric did not obtain what he really wanted, which is the whereabouts of Dag Valda. I think—I believe—Erkric will contrive a way to send the Biddan to her."

"He can't." Agel's body tightened, almost a flinch. "It's the law . . ."

"You and I both know that the moment Rajnir becomes king, Erkric will *be* the law," Ulaffa said. "Further. If he can submit a dag to torture, then where can he stop? Will you be next if you cross his will publicly? Will I?"

Agel made the sign of Rainorec. "Nowhere, yes, and yes. But Ulaffa, if she vanishes, there will be riots."

"There will be riots if he executes her. Too many people who have no cause with any of us saw her sustain a vision the other day. No dag created that light, though we all saw it. It takes no discernment to descry that most from high to low degree believe her testimony now."

"I know," Agel said, and let her breath out slowly. It did nothing to relieve her tension. "Dag Egal thinks that if this gathering had not been **a** Frasadeng the riot would have happened then. And of course the Erama Krona were out in force, so everyone stayed peaceful. But they were all talking."

"They do not know the truth. I do," Ulaffa stated. "Those accusations he made against Dag Signi were mostly his own actions. *He* taught Dag Mekki death magic. We know that we cannot bring someone out of a stone spell, but I can take you to the mountain height where Mekki is going to move with the slowness of ice over the next century and a half; you will sense Valda's signature in the trace magic."

Dag Agel knew that Valda would not put a stone spell of that magnitude on a fellow dag without just cause. And by acknowledging that she knew it, she had to take the next step, and acknowledge that she had crossed the bridge between Erkric's side with its semblance of order and law and Ulaffa's cause, which seemed to overthrow the rule of law.

Ulaffa said, "We are agreed that Dag Erkric has twisted the laws to his own ends politically. He is not going to stop working to gain control of *us*."

Agel dropped her hand, and rubbed her fingers. "Then you must act. And I will cooperate."

In the darkness of her cell Signi struggled to reconcile herself to a terrible death, light and love and sense ripped away by pain and humiliation until the death birds picked her bones clean.

She was startled by sounds outside the door. Before the rattle of the lock had come at dragon hour and first watch—after supper and before breakfast—when they came in with the bucket of plate scrapings soaked with spoiled vinegar to be poured into her face.

But the man who entered did not carry a bucket. He bore a tray with a glowglobe set on it, next to rust-streaked metal rods and probes and pincers.

Terror closed Signi's throat. She closed her eyes, and forced herself into hel dancer breathing.

The man said, "The pain will cease as soon as you tell me where Brit Valda is, and what you know of her plans."

Signi closed her eyes as cold fingers gripped her wrist. She recoiled, then frantically tried to resume the protection and control of hel dancer breathing. But she was so very cold, so tired.

Chains rattled as the man chuckled. His breath stirred

her hair as he leaned close. "I've always liked locks and puzzles. People are puzzle-locks. You take them apart piece by piece. And you find the secret inside."

A pricking poke at a fingertip, then hot, searing pain through her entire body, radiating from her fingernail.

"Just the outer locks first. Everyone always needs to be convinced of my truth, before they unlock theirs for me." He did not sound angry, or even passionate; at first his complete lack of emotion was more frightening than what he did.

That rapidly changed.

Another thrust, endless, deep, remorseless: the high keening from somewhere matched the rhythm of the burn in her throat. And now she had to learn about pain, how very many shades and intensities it encompassed. Pain came in colors, in burning, rusty, acid tastes: it distorted sound, even when one was not screaming one's throat raw.

The instructive voice went on with the lecture. "With so many women it is the face. Young ones, usually. With men, it is what cannot be seen. For you? The agent of doing, not of being, we begin with the hands . . .

"Just give me a location . . ."

Her senses billowed with red clouds and clashing metal and voices that made no sense as Biddan finally broke her tenuous mental hold, and discovered in her babble that she knew far more than anyone might have guessed.

Secrets are power. Now his passions kindled at last, to possess secrets that even Erkric had not guessed. In probing and twisting and wrenching for more, more, Biddan failed to grant her the mercy he'd promised. Intent on his acquisition of power, his questions blended with her shrieks so that he failed to notice the opening of the door.

A hand on his shoulder caused him to start. He whirled, the tool shedding drops of blood. Fulla Durasnir picked up one of the waiting tendon-slicing knives and wielded it to knock aside Biddan's slow, late blocks. With his other hand he seized the torturer by his hair, then ripped the blade across Biddan's throat.

Body and knife dropped at Signi's feet, a lifetime of pain-bought secrets bleeding out.

Durasnir gazed in horror at Signi. The other part of their plan would not work. She would grip no knife today, maybe never again. But he could, and did, catch some of her blood on his fingers and smear it over the knife for those who would investigate.

His two most trusted ensigns had undone the manacles by then.

Signi fell forward into someone's arms. Her inflamed, crusted eyes blurred with odd lights and shadows.

Then a familiar voice whispered, "Phew! What a wretched stench! No, lean on me."

"Brun?" Signi whispered, then gasped. New colors of lightning ripped through her as Brun gently shifted her in order to take all her weight.

"Is he dead?" Brun asked, her voice orange with hatred.

Signi peered wearily down at an empty, lifeless hand. "He had once a mother," she breathed.

"More shame to her if she'd grieve over such a son," Brun stated, and kicked the dead man in repudiation. "Now, I'm going to pick you up. It's time to leave."

Signi's hands fell to either side of her, throbbing with glowing-coal red heat. Steel blue shards of agony jabbed her shoulder joints and her knees buckled.

"She's got to touch the key." Durasnir's words were burned mint.

"I can't. Lift my hands."

Durasnir pressed the key against Signi's manacle-galled wrist, then dropped it to the ground.

"There. I don't know how mages can tell who touched a key last, but these were my instructions." Durasnir's voice buzzed.

Brun tightened her grip on Signi. "Now let's go." Her voice vibrated with a beehive hum.

"We'll run point." Durasnir had moved, his voice shading to willow-bite. "Can you manage?"

"Yes. Halvir is heavier. She's nothing more than bone and cloth."

"And skin and blood." Signi breathed a laugh, or almost a laugh. It tasted of rust and mold, and her words buzzed, too. "Brun. Is there danger to you and to others in my being taken away?"

"No," was the brisk answer, with only the faintest betraying tremor. "There is right now a . . . hole in the guard.

Erkric did not want the Erama Krona hearing what the Biddan did to you, so they have been posted elsewhere this night. Fulla and Ulaffa will make certain no one else sees any of us. Erkric's own precautions will work against him. And I very much fear that you are going to be accused of the murder of this pig-midden in your escape." Brun spat on the dead man as she passed.

Brun carried Signi the same way she carried her son Halvir, trying to avoid touching Signi's wounds. Signi's breath keened, causing Brun's innards to clench.

Down the stone steps she passed in the wake of her husband, and then set out at a swift pace along the cold stone tunnel.

Brun was afraid Signi might pass out and never waken. "Erkric is desperate to discover Brit Valda's whereabouts. Did you guess that?"

"Yes," Signi whispered, as red pain billowed up her arms, lapping at her eye sockets.

After the length of two tunnels, they reached the first underground level. The cool white stone arches led off in three directions.

"We wait here." Brun's voice turned blue and pine-scented as she gently set Signi down on the ground.

From her clothing she brought out a long knife, one not used since her training days.

Signi looked up through bleary eyes. Thoughts flitted through the murk of her mind, quick and silver minnows of remembered sanity. She remembered that Brun, when young, had been an assistant archivist. When had she learned to carry a knife? Probably in Ymar . . .

"Ah!"

Fulla Durasnir, his ensigns, and a dag arrived at a run from the tunnel leading to the next tower.

The dag bent to trace a square on the stone floor, whispering the while. Then he straightened up and motioned Signi into the square.

The Oneli commander and his wife each slid a hand under Signi's armpits, gently lifting her within the circle. Each felt the sharp ridges of Signi's bones under their fingers.

Signi made one last, great effort. "Will you be safe?" she asked her rescuers.

"If Ulaffa's spells work," Durasnir said. "You leave that to us. Your job now is to survive."

His buzz-voice voice had gone gourd-hollow, rattling like bones in the winter wind. He brought his hands together, and performed the low obeisance of honor. Brun, the ensigns, and the dag performed the same bow.

Signi's eyes blurred. The mage made the transfer signs, and Signi fell out of the world then back in again. She staggered into Brit Valda's waiting arms.

Chapter Thirty

THE white tower of Ala Larkadhe formed out of the
haze of early winter. Inda gazed up at it, remembering smells, sounds, sights from that summer. Sometimes
memory was overwhelming. He recognized the place the
army had camped when he'd been made Harskialdna; they
stopped there to water the animals. Inda paced over the
grass, trying to remember it all exactly. There, the two fires
had been set. Barend was here, the command tents there.

Inda smiled at the memory of the fight. A few of those
tricks he had invented in their early days as marine defenders, but most of them were Fox's, from their winter at Freedom Harbor, when they were drawing independents to
them in order to fight the Brotherhood of Blood. Their real
practice sessions had been on the hills, the staged "drills"
on the docks full of such trickery . . .

Inda looked at the winter-dead grass. The memories of
those days seemed so very long ago, like they belonged to
another person as well as another time. That sensation—
being so distant from himself—made him uncomfortable;
it made him feel split into different Indas.

He walked away, though he knew that physical distance never gave him mental distance. So he'd keep mov-

ing as fast as possible. He wished he had Tdor to talk to. He wished he'd see Signi. He'd thought they must meet on the road, but they hadn't. Instead, everywhere he saw evidence of her magic. Silent reminders of Signi, without her presence.

"Ready?" he asked his Runner on duty, short, quiet Twin Ain. "Let's ride on."

Valda half carried Signi into a tiny ship's cabin. The deck below Signi's feet heaved and rolled as Valda stripped the disgusting garments from her and eased her into the gently steaming water of a wooden bathtub. Signi hissed as the water searched every ulceration and cut. For a time the colored pain shapes crowded her vision, and she withdrew into her breathing, concentrating on the length and quality of each breath. Gradually she became aware that the billowing red breaths permitted her smooth, silken green ones, if she just did not move.

"Signi? Don't sleep in the water."

It took an effort to open her eyes.

On the other side of a small cabin Valda grimaced, her face turned away as she dunked Signi's clothes into a magic bucket. "Phew!"

For the first time the cleaning magic did not just glitter but flared and crackled with weird blue sparkles. The clothes came out innocent of the filth that snapped away to the ground from which it had come.

Valda ran up onto the deck to lay the clothes in the sun, and when she returned her worried face smoothed just a little when she saw Signi's eyes open.

Signi floated in the herb scented bath, her bandaged hands resting on the towels Valda had hastily folded along the edges of the tub.

Valda did not know where to begin, so deeply was she disturbed. *Begin with something good,* she decided. *It's little enough, alas, alas.* "It must have seemed all Twelve Towers were out in the Blood Crowd, but they were not."

Signi's eyelids flashed up. "My . . ."

Valda's cracked-crow voice tasted of pure water, and shone the silver of truth. "Your mother was locked in her rooms at Skalts' Tower. In the west window of the senior dancers' floor burned all nine candles in her Tree, there

for all to see. You have your name again, Jazsha Signi
Sofar."

Signi's eyelids closed over the burn of tears. Though
her skull ached almost as much as the rest of her, memory
welled up, pure and clear, giving her the intricate carved
candelabra in the family chamber of her early home, lighted
on special days—sometimes one candle, for a birth day.
Sometimes three, for an achievement. All nine for great
events. She had worked hard not to think of that candelabra extinguished after she had been outcast.

A deep breath, green veined with red. "Thank you."

"Now, you must drink this. It's listerblossom, with tincture of poppies." Valda brought Signi a cup of pungent
liquid.

Signi's first impulse was to resist. Everyone knew that
tincture of poppies gave a false euphoria that would, if you
drank much of it, turn into craving and then worse pain.
But dags could not take kinthus in any form, and oh, to be
free of pain for just a short time . . .

She gulped it down, and in the time it took to breathe in
and out, a cool blue-white cotton-blanket formed between
her and the steady boil of agony.

"You saved my life, Jazsha Signi Sofar," Dag Valda said,
making a formal bow. With each word the strange distortion faded, leaving her voice in proper proportion. "You
were willing to give yours to save mine. I will honor you all
my days for what you did."

Signi opened her eyes, and smiled a little, though tears
ran freely. "You do not have to bow to a bathtub."

"I will bow to the gutters running with the filth that
dropped off you. To the blood you shed in keeping my
name and secrets from those with evil intent." Valda made
another deep obeisance.

"I did betray you," Signi whispered. "At the end. If the
questioner had not died, Erkric would know everything."

"Which is why the questioner died," Valda returned.
"Ulaffa said to me that he himself would not withstand
torture long. We dags never trained in giving and receiving violence and pain, and even those with a great deal of
physical courage rarely have sufficient defense against such
desecration of being."

"Desecration of being," Signi whispered. "Yes."

"But you protected me in that travesty of a trial. And I heard about the glow of Drenskar in your face when you stood below the Tree in chains. Signi, not one of our dags performed magic. There was no known signature in the air, though all felt the magic. Erkric himself spent a night and a day testing and retesting, along with others. Ulaffa said he knows not what is more disturbing, the idea that some presence beyond human ken was there and acted, or that some mage with skills far beyond our ability to trace was there and acted. Compelling, do you not think?"

"I can't think at all," Signi admitted, her voice tremulous.

Brit Valda sat back on her haunches, wondering yet again if that shared experience had been caused by Signi Sofar's innate grace. So few had grace. Valda knew she didn't. *Is the difference simply an absence of anger?* Valda thought. *I am angry.*

She'd been angry all her life, ever since her mother abandoned her, pretending Brit was someone else's, just to hide her birth as a thrall. So Brit could have a future. But that was too simple: Signi was also an outcast yet she did not stay angry.

Was her lack of whatever spark the hel dancers sought a lack of anger? That was too simple as well—and beckoned to the comfortable but deadly road of self-justification. *I am angry, and I know anger is seldom a tool to be trusted. But it gives one vigor, and that can be put to use. So be it.*

"How cruel my heart abraded that day, to witness from my hiding place how you were the target of every piece of filth, every flung stone, meant for me. But I had to stay hidden. I still must! Abyarn Erkric knows what I did. More important, he knows I am aware of his intent, and his covert actions in service to that intent. He spent a year trying to track me down—using dags—while the Erama Krona was hunting you. I had to go into hiding, but I put that time to good use, seeking the oldest archives in the world, to discover ways to ward Norsunder's magic. Though three times I was just ahead of him, and once just behind him. We were on a thousand-year-old treasure hunt, he and I, each totally alone, with only trace magic as clues and warnings."

Signi said, "So there were wards keeping you from communicating with me?"

"I can't tell you how tangled were the traps laid for any-one who tried to contact you! He'd had it all planned out, you see, by the time the southern fleet reached the home-land. Your geyser merely gave him his excuse. He knew that you went south with your Inda. That—and trying to use you to find me—were his real reasons to pursue you."

Signi would have winced, had she the strength. "The old plan, to capture the king of the Marlovans? That is in force?"

"No, not publicly. But secretly, Erkric was pursuing it, once he succeeded in tampering with Prince Rajnir."

Signi understood. "I see! He did not want people hear-ing . . . about his plan for the Marlovan king . . . and then looking askance at Prince Rajnir."

"He put tracers on the Erama Krona Blood Hunt sent after you, without their knowledge or permission. So by the time Ulaffa and I discovered that you'd been found, the wards were up."

"I felt them." Signi's voice was fading. "Too late. I did not seek past. My own. Magical traces."

"More disturbing than Erkric's misprision is how each action is claimed to benefit Drenskar and yet each more deeply forswears our moral center. Even Ulaffa had for-gotten Erkric's plan against the Marlovan king. And I dared not remind him, lest he think the political advan-tages outweigh the moral. The Marlovan king, under Er-kric's control, could order that vast army launched against the continent in our name. *Think* of the devastation!"

Signi closed her eyes. "Inda . . . would he—yes, he would do it. Though it would probably kill him."

"He's the King's Voice," Valda said, sitting back on her heels beside the tub. "He is sworn to obey. That's proba-bly saved him from Erkric's attentions. That and Erkric is desperately overworked." Valda tapped her scrawny chest. "Since I could not save you, I used the time they chased you to ward the Marlovan royal city. I mirrored Erkric's own spells. He will never break those wards. As long as that king stays in his city, he's safe from Erkric."

Signi breathed again.

Valda straightened up, one hand to her aching hip. "We all make warding signs against Rainorec, but how many un-derstand what it means? It means our people are betrayed by our own customs. Erkric has found it far too easy to take our laws and twist them toward evil ends while speaking the names of everything we hold honorable and right."

Signi tried to speak, but her lips had cracked again, and she tasted blood. Even with the blanket of herbs, darts of pain reached her, faint warnings of what was to come when the herbal effect wore away.

"What is next?" she whispered finally.

"Frin of Loc House sent this salve by Brun Durasnir." Valda picked up an open shell on which something pungent glistened. She leaned over the bath and began to anoint Signi's remaining wounds, which, now clean of the crust of infection, bled sluggishly. The salve was cool and soothing.

"You must vanish," Valda said. "No more magic at all. Not the smallest spell, so that Erkric will never again be able to trace you. You will rest and heal. When you can hold a book and pen, I will rely on you to help me with my search through magical archives. I cannot do it alone, and still monitor Erkric's movements."

Signi's brow eased slightly: she had something to do.

"When you are sufficiently healed, then this ship must vanish. You must land and hide."

"Where?"

"I suggest you take advantage of my wards and go back to your Inda. But Signi, it is only for a time."

Another blow. It took all Signi's strength to speak. "The plan. Sartor. It still holds?"

"Correct. We have not given up our plan. If we can get Sartor to listen, our gift might go a long way toward redeeming the Venn in the eyes of the world. Erkric still has his spy wards around the Destinations we use to transfer to Sartor, but as soon as we can deflect him, we will attend to those. And then send you the signal, the milkweed again."

"Where will you be?"

"I plan to keep him so busy that you will be able to go to Sartor unmolested." She leaned down and kissed Signi's bruised, scraped brow.

Signi summoned the strength for one last question. "How can. You keep. Erkric busy?"

"I have several plans. You are going to help, as I said. While you are healing, you will be going through the ancient records I stored in these chests." Valda reached behind the tub and touched two heavy wooden chests, so old the carving was worn and blurry. "You are going to find me the spells to break Erkric's control over Rajnir's mind."

The relentless flood of memory reached high tide when Inda rode through the gates of Ala Larkadhe. Everywhere he looked reminded him so vividly, so viscerally, of Noddy and Hawkeye busy with tasks, of Buck striding back and forth, whole and laughing, it was like seeing ghosts. He knew they were not ghosts in the sense that others talked about and he'd seen so briefly once. These were memory ghosts, ones he carried with him, who came alive in dreams.

Inda tried to wall the flood of memories and ghosts by concentrating on the cold stone of the new garrison, the smells of baking pan bread and simmering cabbage rolls, the long, vowelly Iascan accent punctuated by the quick, sibilant Marlovan. But those things, too, were reminders of his previous stay.

Then Beaver Yvana-Vayir came bounding out to greet him, his distinctive square chin, his dashing smile so strong a reminder of Hawkeye that Inda grimaced.

Beaver rushed into words. They'd been sweeping, cleaning, repairing, and practicing for days, so that the King's Voice would be impressed. Beaver had been there a year— at New Year's his brother would ride north and they'd switch, and he'd be a Jarl ... what Badger had said ... what Cama said on his last visit ...

Inda defeated the memories enough to take in the people standing stiffly on their best behavior while Beaver chattered on and on, mixing in questions and comments with his report. They looked and sounded anxious for approval.

So he looked around to find things to approve.

Everything appeared as expected. Inda saw all the signs that Beaver was a careful commander, doing the best he could despite the lack of funds. The faces surrounding Inda seemed content enough, yet by the end of the tour of inspection, Inda had a headache, and there was still a banquet to get through.

Get through it he did, mostly by just lifting the wine cup and pretending to drink. He didn't like heavy wine at any time, but when his head ached, the smell made his gut churn.

He knew he'd have to make a speech. Gradually he became aware that they wanted a story from the battle at Andahi Pass. Not the entire thing, he realized as unsubtle hints were dropped, before or after looks sent Beaver's way. They wanted the story of Hawkeye's Charge, which Inda had not actually seen.

But he knew enough of what had happened to describe it in the terms people loved to hear, full of honor, glory, courage in the face of certain defeat. And at the end, Hawkeye dying with the words "Sing me" on his lips, following which they all stood and sang the new version of "Yvana Ride Thunder," the younger men drumming on the table with such verve the dishes jumped and clattered.

Then at last it was over. Beaver staggered off, muzzy with drink and singing with several of his riding mates. Inda longed for bed, but he had one more duty. He sat there wishing he could just send one of the Runners, except he had promised Evred he'd see to it himself. And they were riding out at dawn.

So if it was going to be done, it had to be now.

He got up and wound his way through the departing guests to the side of old Tdiran-Randviar, the tough old woman who commanded the women defending the towers and walls of Ala Larkadhe.

"Inda." Her voice was like a crow's squawk, her tone wry but not disapproving. "You did that well. Almost would believe you were there."

"I did see the end of it," he said, which was almost true. "Tdiran-Randviar, Evred wants me to visit Fala, Hawkeye's mate. See with my own eyes how she's doing." Inda hoped the woman would say Fala was well and living far away—anything so he wouldn't have to go.

But Tdiran's chin jerked up, a gesture of approval. "He's a fine boy, Evred is. Like his father. Those young hounds, Badger and Beaver, have their mother's nature, so Fala's doing all right. You'll find her tucked up just beyond the north wall, at the apiary."

Apiary. Bees—Gand—the academy. Inda shook away the reminder, resigning himself to a long walk, or else the trouble of getting a horse saddled up and prepared. He opted for the walk, hoping the night air, cold as it was, would clear his head somewhat.

He gestured to the Runner on duty and, guiding himself by the flickering wall torches, trod the narrow streets until he reached the north wall, and then, with a salute to the men and women above, he and his Runner walked through the gate. For a time the only sound was the crunch of ground beneath his and Twin Tvei's steps.

Inda sniffed the air as he walked, senses on alert. Maybe it was just being alone for the first time in so long—alone, that is, except for his Runner. But he felt he was being watched.

He checked his surroundings carefully. Now he was thoroughly awake. The steep rising land revealed nothing in the time it took to sink the city walls behind a rocky hill, and to spot the round cottage belonging to the city's beekeeper. A huge yard with a small, domed construct of some sort made indistinct shadows; as Inda crossed to the door, he realized that the beehives shared their space with a kiln.

That gave him just enough time to suspect what he was to find when the door opened, the light from inside silhouetting a short, stocky male figure. "Who's without?"

"Inda-Harskialdna," Inda said. Strange, how he still felt odd saying his rank, like he'd taken it from someone, no, more like he pretended to be something he wasn't. "I was sent by Evred-Harvaldar."

The light made a halo around the bright hair of a tall, thin woman in Marlovan robes and trousers. "Come within," she said and smiled in welcome, from behind the stocky man.

Fala was probably ten years older than Inda, round of face and pale of eyes and hair, characterized by a dimpled smile that had once been merry, but was now more pensive. "Welcome, Harskialdna-Dal." She used his Marlovan title, but spoke in Iascan.

"Inda is all right," he mumbled, wondering what else to say. He had a wallet of gold pieces, but Evred had been specific: *Only if she seems to need it. Don't insult her if she's found a new life.* "Um, Evred wanted me to ask how you were."

She smiled again. "How very like him. Here, come

within. Would you like some mulled wine to chase the cold away?" Then her eyes narrowed as she observed the tense brow and faint wince of a pounding headache. "No, maybe listerblossom steep?"

"If you have some," Inda said gratefully as he took in the round room, which was fitted up with an odd mixture of northern furniture and Marlovan low tables and mats.

"I have plenty," she said, not telling him that she'd kept a supply against Hawkeye's heavy drinking during the days when Dannor, Hawkeye's wife, had lived among them. Those days were gone forever. "In case the bees take against me in jealousy."

She indicated the mats. Inda sat down. The man also sat down; he neither spoke nor smiled. His skin was nut-brown, his thin hair dark, reminding Inda strongly of Jeje, which made him feel even more off balance. The man was probably old Iascan—oh, of course. Olaran, this far north.

Fala filled the silence with cheery chatter. She introduced her new mate, Kaz the beekeeper, talked about bees and pottery, said that Beaver was always sending over delicacies, as times had been lean for everyone.

Presently Fala brought the steep and Inda gulped it down, ignoring the burn to mouth and nose. "Oh, that's good," he sighed. "Thanks."

Fala made a gesture of sympathy. "We heard you were coming. Some think you're coming up with fire and sword, others to change all the commanders about."

Inda waved a hand wearily. "No, nothing like that. I'm supposed to ride around and look tough. Evred and Cama think that'll keep the peace. Idea being, we've had enough war."

The words were out before he remembered that Kaz was not a Marlovan, then he shrugged internally. Wasn't like "keeping the peace" was any military secret.

Fala laughed. They talked a little more about riding, winter, and how nasty the pass could be if it iced up. Then Inda rose to take his leave, Fala charged him with a greeting to Ndand-Jarlan, and he and Twin Tvei left.

But not alone. They were aware of being followed within ten steps. The Runner had hand to sword and Inda to the hilts in his sleeves as they turned.

"A moment." The voice was unfamiliar, the accent the slow Iascan of the north.

Inda paused, Twin Tvei taking up a stance at Inda's left, a little behind.

The light from the window outlined a short, stocky figure. "Kaz?" Inda asked, as the man stopped a couple paces away.

"You came just to ask about her," Kaz said, after a pause.

"Yes."

"Your king sent you. To ask about her."

"Yes." Inda reminded himself he was the King's Voice, and he was here to make peace. He had to remember not to slurp his soup so the locals wouldn't despise him and through him all Marlovans. So if a local wanted to stand here while the night got colder and tell Inda what he'd just been doing, well, that seemed to be part of the orders, to listen.

Kaz shook his head, then stepped a little closer. Twin Tvei's right hand already gripped his sword. His left drifted to his sash near the hilt of his knife, and Inda, arms crossed, had his knife hilts in a throwing grip, but Kaz's head was bent, his gaze on the ground that he couldn't see.

Finally he looked up. "We didn't want you," he said. "You Marlovans. But you're here. And some think the old king was far worse. Idayago, I mean. Tried to annex Olara, same as you people. But wouldn't rebuild the Nob after the first pirate attack, in the early days."

Inda was not sure what to say in answer to yet another statement of what they both knew, so he just said, "Yes."

Kaz let out his breath in a sharp hiss. "You're going to keep the peace, you say. Some rumors say you'll rebuild the two harbors."

"That's right," Inda stated, still patient.

Kaz snorted again. "Elbow Jink. Ambush forming. They'll take you from above." And in a low, swift voice, "Some might say I'm a traitor, because Zek na Zek is Olaran. But I don't like him. Never did. He's a bad leader, worse than Mardric ever was, and he'd make a worse king, him or his mates."

Kaz marched back to the apiary.

Inda started back, mentally calling up his memory of

the Andahi Pass, studied so intently before the battle. He remembered Elbow Jink as one of the first tight twists on the narrowing road, a day or two up the pass from Ala Larkadhe. Sheer cliffs on either side.

He and his men had already relaxed their guard while riding, seldom donning uncomfortable helms, shields hung at the sides of their saddles instead of strapped on their arms.

An attack from above was unlikely to kill them all unless the Resistance had gained an army of expert shots and all were crowding up there along the cliffs, but all it would take would be one very good shot to nail Inda.

"Damn," he said, and Twin Tvei opened his hand in agreement.

$$\text{Chapter Thirty-one}$$

INDA climbed to the top of the goat trail and looked around the clearing behind the cliffs above Elbow Jink. The muddy, trampled clearing had been camped on for days, maybe a week or two. The Resistance had learned from the Marlovans, planning an ambush from the heights, but they hadn't learned to set perimeter watches. *Either that* or *their leaders couldn't get anyone to sit out the fun*, Inda thought as he motioned his dragoons to spread out.

Some thirty paces beyond the scree protecting the clearing sat the Idayagans. They had ranged themselves along the very edge of the cliffs above the pass, weapons to hand.

Paulan Ebetim and his men scarcely noticed the cold that they had been complaining bitterly about until that morning, when, at last, their lookout watching the pass had galloped below. That was the signal: the Pirate and his Marlovans had been sighted!

And there they were, riding around the sharp curve at extreme range. Their horses plodded up the muddy switchback with heads low, harnesses jingling, the echoes up the stone cliffs tinkling like coins falling on ice.

A few of the watchers noted the mostly bare yellow heads of the riders, here and there a knit cap, and exchanged gloating glances. The Marlovans did seem to have their shields to hand, not tied behind them, but from the way they joked back and forth in their wood-snap, wolf-growl language, they clearly suspected nothing. Perfect targets.

Paulan Ebetim ignored the whispered cracks his men exchanged. He did not share their confidence of an easy win, not since Zek the Ropemaker's "I'll be right back" had stretched into two days. Zek and the rest of the Olarans had all had brief but necessary errands, Paulan had discovered the previous day. There were none but Idayagans here for the ambush, something the younger men had crowed about—good riddance—but that left Paulan very uneasy.

It didn't do to bring up some kinds of worry. People were too quick with words like "coward" and "fear" and especially "traitor" if they didn't like what they were hearing.

Paulan gripped his bow, tested the snapvine, discovered it had loosened yet again in the sodden cold. He bent over the bow to tighten it again, glad to have something to do with his hands, but he'd just begun the task when a whisper ran through the others: "They're in range!"

They slapped arrows to bows.

The horsemen finished rounding the curve and the front one with the banner rode directly below the Idayagans.

Paulan leaned out over a boulder, trying to descry which one might be Inda the Pirate. They all looked pretty much alike in those gray coats when seen from above.

"Pick your man—" His voice rasped, and he fought the urge to cough. The middle of the column was now directly below. "Shoot."

A heartbeat after the bows twanged, the shields below flipped up, and the hissing arrows thumped and clattered harmlessly against them.

Paulan scarcely had a moment to think *They knew!* when there was noise from behind him. The ambushers whirled around as gray-coated Marlovans advanced, their scar-faced leader saying, "Surprise."

Just before New Year's Week, Cama sat down to his desk, and laboriously wrote to Evred-Harvaldar:

> *Inda just arrived here at Castle Andahi. Ahead of a blizzard. Animals up to the chest by the time they got*

past Robbers' Cave. Inda says he reported to you the
attempted ambush at the mouth of the pass above Ala
Larkadhe.

   Inda brought along Paulan Ebetim & his gang.
Ebetim's been behind most of the west end assassina-
tion tries on me. Ebetim says the Olarans set him up.
Inda says he thinks Ebetim is sick of living in the hills.
People aren't so generous with handouts anymore to
Resistance. Ndand told me the Idayagan women are
saying, "Get work. We had to." when the Resistance
men come around begging food and gear.

   Ebetim said to us he'd rat out Zek the Noose if
he knew where he was. He & men are in the lockup
with the gold. Inda sent dragoons up our old path. His
guess was Zek would want to strike one of our signal
houses again before winter closed in, if he did any-
thing. You know Inda. "That's what I'd do." When he
says that, he's usually right. I thought Zek would be
in Lindeth to winter over. We're waiting to hear which
of us is right. I'll put the men on rock quarry duty for
half a year, same as always. What do you want us to do
with Ebetim?

New Year's Week, and Convocation, had passed before
Evred replied. Cama had got used to that; he'd carry right
on around the question until Evred had thought it out.
Nor was he surprised when (after he'd sent a second message, saying that Inda's dragoon flight had returned, having
caught the Olarans exactly where he'd predicted they'd be)
Evred wrote, "Let Inda decide."

Sitting in the makeshift jail down in Castle Andahi's
cellar, Paulan Ebetim had gone from terror to resignation. They'd separated him from the rest of the men, so he
had no idea where they were, or if they even lived. He'd
heard rumors that the Marlovans didn't take prisoners, so
he braced himself to be dragged out before an assembled
army to be put to death. At least his family was up the coast
at Olara, where they wouldn't find out until it was over.

Then day after cold, wearying day passed with nothing
to do but watch the slow march of light reflected through
the iron bars of his door from somewhere beyond the barrels and barrels of wine and coffee the Marlovans had

stored. He couldn't smell the beans—he figured the peculiar dark island wood of the barrels was too close-grained for that—but he sure could smell ground coffee drifting down from the kitchens directly above the cells. The smell was a kind of unexpected torment, though he was grateful for the warmth from their bake ovens.

After two weeks of no company, no talk, and food twice a day, he gathered enough courage to complain about the terrible food to his guards. "Is this slop some kind of torture?" he asked in careful Iascan.

The old man who'd brought the tray dumped the tray on the ground. "You eat what we eat." He slammed the door behind him.

After half a watch, Paulan realized that this was all he was going to get. He scraped up the spilled food. As he munched grimly through the now cold rye bread and the congealed oatmeal with dots of sticky honey—none of which tasted better for the wait—he wondered if they were forming up for the execution now.

But more days passed with no change in the routine (or the food), and then, without any warning, they came for him. "What now?" he asked when two guards, the old one and a young one, jerked him out of the cell.

"Harskialdna," the old one said.

When Paulan was brought before Inda, the smell of old fear sweat rising off stale clothing brought Inda right back to to the time he was a prisoner in Ymar. He tensed, fighting the urge to squirm. He hated the memories, hated the idea of prisoners, but these fellows hadn't attacked on the cliff, they'd all thrown their weapons down while their leader just stood there with his mouth open. Inda couldn't kill a bunch of terrified, unarmed men.

The followers had been put to work like lawbreakers, but this Ebetim was supposed to be a leader. So here Inda was, stuck with a prisoner, and Evred had told him to do whatever he thought best. Whatever Inda thought best was to pretend Ebetim didn't exist, except he did. The dawn and sunset guard rota had "feed prisoner" written on the watch commander's list of duties.

He eyed the wretched man. "Zek the Noose had a good plan. You were supposed to kill us, and when Cama and his boys ran up the pass, they'd drop on 'em from above, from our own beacon site. Good plan. But not good enough. It's never going to be good enough—none of you have the training. Do you really want to fight until you're all dead?"

Paulan waited. Everyone made speeches, it seemed. Mardric had loved making speeches. Zek, too. People in command made speeches, and because they were commanders, you had to listen—you couldn't tell them to shut up like you could your mates. Especially when you were a prisoner.

Paulan had shut his eyes against the sharp angle of sunlight coming in through the window behind the Pirate's head. When the silence had gone on too long he jerked up his hand to shade his eyes and discovered that the Pirate was waiting for an answer.

Paulan recovered the last few words and said hastily but with feeling, "No."

"You really want to live?" the Pirate asked. He had brown eyes. They were wide. His face was too scarred; Paulan couldn't tell if his expression was some kind of trick—if he was playing with the prisoner or he was asking a real question.

So stick to the truth and keep it short. "Yes."

"Right. Then we're going to put you on the next trader going out. You learn a new trade. And never come back, because if you do, you'll go up against the wall."

"I don't know anything about ships," Paulan said. Then wished the words back inside his throat.

The Pirate snorted. "Neither did I, when I was put on one. But one thing about ship life is you learn fast."

He waved a hand, and Paulan was hauled summarily away. Inda said to the grizzled Rider Captain, the former Jarl of Tlennen, "See to it he's not put on an Idayagan trader."

The captain thumped his fist to his chest and withdrew, taking the prisoner problem away. Inda got up from the Jarl's desk. At least Zek's assassination team had fought; these other fellows like Ebetim, throwing down their weapons before a truce or a surrender, how could they ever expect to win? They weren't warriors, they were playing at being warriors. Paulan Ebetim had spoken with the flat weariness of disillusionment.

"Maybe I should change the plans," Inda said to Cama. "See what you think."

As they talked they walked downstairs, through the hall where the children were practicing. Radran supervised the smaller boys and Captain Han Tlen the little girls as everybody worked through knife drill.

"They're not going to execute that Idayagan horse apple," Radran said, his face sour. Then, louder, "Do it again," to the waiting eight-year-olds.

Han scowled down at her feet. She admired Radran, and liked him, except when he talked about torture and killing. Though she wanted all those Venn who had killed her family and the Jarlan dead, dead, *dead*—and the Idayagans who maimed or killed someone's dad or brother or cousin, too—she didn't want to *talk* about it all the time, especially about flogging away their flesh and laughing while they screamed.

Radran had stopped doing it so much after he came back from the royal city, but he'd started again when the Harskialdna arrived, bringing that Olaran Resistance leader. Nobody knew what to do with prisoners. If people attacked, you killed them or drove them away. If people were brought in having done something wrong, you punished them. Not much of that, as Cama-Jarl hated flogging; he thought hard work much better, so mostly they were chained together and put to work on the stone-shifting gangs, rebuilding the walls. There'd been an abrupt drop-off in cut purses and the like since they'd begun that.

They didn't do that with Paulan Ebetim because he was a Resistance leader.

Prisoners, especially a leader, meant torture, Radran had said, grinning with glee. But days passed. Now, whatever the Harskialdna had decided, it wasn't on any execution, or they'd all hear the bell for gathering in the court. Han was relieved. She didn't want to hear Radran's bitter disappointment, so she said to the girls, "Shooting practice."

"But it's *sleeting* out there," Lnand protested, hands on her hips.

"So the enemies will wait around for a nice day if they attack?"

"*They* won't even *see* the target." Lnand pointed at the

little girls, who promptly began shrilling, "We can, too! We can, too!"

"Then they may as well learn. Right?" Han said over their squealing.

"I'll take them," said sixteen-year-old Ingrid.

Lnand whirled around, making a dramatic start. Han jerked, then hated showing that much reaction, because she despised how Lnand yapped on and on about how being startled gave her nightmares, After All They'd Endured During the War.

We didn't endure anything, Han thought. *Our mothers did.* She didn't say that, either. She hated talk about any of it.

So she ignored Lnand, as usual, and stepped back so that tall, calm Ingrid Tlennen could take her place. Ingrid was from Nelkereth. She'd helped to bring in the horses for Castle Andahi the spring before, as the Venn had taken all the Marlovans' horses after killing the defenders.

All the younger girls admired Ingrid. She was fast with bow and knife and had won all the competitions at the Summer Games her first year at the queen's training. She'd only had the one year, because she and her family were sent north by Hadand-Gunvaer.

Lnand marched away, nose in the air. Han knew she should go out and practice as well, but she lingered near the accessway, peering into the garrison's command center. As she tried to pick out the Harskialdna from all those gray coats and swinging horsetails, she remembered when Ingrid had arrived. They heard them first, hundreds of horses galloping down the pass toward Castle Andahi. She remembered Ndand-Jarlan standing on the south wall, looking up the pass, smiling despite the dust rising halfway up the cliffs and the pungent smell of the herd on a warm day. Han remembered that smile because she'd felt it, too. She and the other children had run around screaming, just because it felt good to run hard and to yell until her throat burned, because no Venn could hear, no Idayagans would shoot; she felt *safe* that day.

She'd felt even safer when the Harskialdna appeared just a few days ago. It was like someone had dropped a rock into a pool, only instead of rings going out they came in to circle around him, and no matter where he went, he was the center of everybody. You could hardly see his face because he wasn't tall like some of the men. You could hear his voice. He had a nice voice, Han thought. It was a deep voice, but he didn't sound husky and rough like Cama-Jarl, he sounded like he was almost going to laugh.

A rustle and quiet step next to Han caused her to look up. Ndand-Jarlan stood next to her. "Something wrong?"

"No. Just . . . watching *him*."

Men shifted, some clattering off in the direction of the stables, obviously having received an order. Others had broken into small knots, but Cama-Jarl and the Rider Captains stood around Inda. ". . . and we ride around looking strut. Me in the front, so if they want to take any more shots, well, there I am, and I'll be glaring around as if we'll strike 'em dead if they so much as fart. You, too, Cama. But you get your toughest dragoons into civ, and *they'll* take the wagons over the pass and up to the Nob and to Lindeth. If you and I go with those wagons, everyone suspects there's something else in those barrels. But if you and I ride around looking like we want a fight, all the talk is about us, and who would bother traders?"

The group closed up again as the knots shifted, and they could no longer hear Inda's voice above the hubbub.

"I remember when he and Flash were ten," Ndand-Jarlan said in the slow voice grownups used when thinking back. "Flash came home full of stories about him. Inda changed the rules on the scrub shoeing. Inda commanded the games. Flash talked about them all, but mostly Inda, then the next summer Inda was gone, and the next thing we heard was he had taken over a pirate ship soon's he left us and had pirates running away at the gallop."

"When he was eleven?" Han asked, remembering that big, frightening-looking black-sided pirate ship a few months back. "He took over the *Death* when he was my age?"

Ndand-Jarlan chuckled. "That's what they say. You can ask him, if you like."

The thought of speaking directly to Inda-Harskialdna made Han's tongue dry. When she was ten, she had command of a few children, and four had died because she hadn't kept control. And she almost, almost, pushed a baby off a cliff. When *he* was ten, he was commanding the boys

at the academy and the next year a pirate ship, and she just
knew he never almost pushed any babies off a cliff just because they stank and yelled.

Han slunk away, determined to practice harder. But beneath that determination guilt and failure gnawed at her
heart.

Chapter Thirty-two

IT was inevitable that Bren Harbor was more interested in the reappearance of the Fox Banner Fleet than in the cargo they carried.

To their immense surprise (and widespread disbelief) the narrow-hulled, rigged-for-speed pirate ships were actually acting as real traders, the colorful Captain Fangras declared. What's more, they brought islander coffee, the first anyone had seen in many, many years. The king's customs officials who went on board (watched with intense interest by most of the spyglasses in the harbor) could smell the cargo before they inspected it. Chim arranged for a warehouse, the Fleet Guild in association with the Adrani Ambassador set up accounts, the barrels were offloaded, and the fleet sailed away—with Cooperage Guild Mistress Perran in company.

Chim was aware of the general disappointment that this infamous fleet had tamely turned trader. He kept his opinion to himself, especially his uneasiness at the fact that Captain Fangras had already known about the alliance forming off Ymar at The Fangs, which everyone had worked hard to keep secret. But when asked how he knew, the wily old independent (pirate, rumor insisted) just said, "Fox told us."

"Right." Chim snorted. "Ye best take someone from the Guild along to show you where the alliance is meetin'." *And to explain your presence to the others*, was implied.

So, when two weeks later five more of the Fox Banner Fleet appeared, there was somewhat less interest, except in the black-sided trysail *Death,* which always drew the eye.

Spyglasses watched the *Death* for sight of its captain, but no one paid the least heed to the boats and boats of coffee and wine barrels Barend off-loaded from the five, or even in the chests brought out of the little scout ship. *Those contain islander spices, packed in sealed ceramic jars,* Barend told the boat crews: Gillor and Jeje had personally rubbed several eye-wateringly pungent spices into the wood.

The *Death* stayed in harbor for two tides. During that time Fox actually left his ship. Spyglasses tracked him as he rowed around his ships on inspection, apparently unaware of the intense interest he caused.

But then he clambered back aboard the *Death* about the time the last cargo boat was dispatched to the warehouse. Two tides after his inspection was finished they sailed away, Barend having asked Chim for the location of the massing force. Once again Chim said, "How did you know? Only the Fleet Guild has been told."

Barend shrugged. "Ask Fox. See if you get any more of an answer than I did."

Chim didn't waste the time rowing out to the *Death*. He knew he wouldn't get an answer.

He showed Barend where to go on his master chart, mentioned that Perran had sailed ahead to clear their way. *I smell trouble,* he thought, as he watched the wicked low, rake-masted ships beat out of harbor into the harsh east wind. He just hoped that the trouble was meant for the Venn still holding Jaro Harbor.

Captain Mern Deliyeth, head of Everon's branch of the Fleet Guild, hated pirates. She had spent her entire life scrupulously obeying laws and rules. Land laws, trade laws. Ship rules.

So the sight of the Fox Banner Fleet arriving to swell their forces was more troubling than welcome. And when the rowboat splashed down from Fangras' wall-eyed *Blue Star* turned out to have a tall, stout woman seated in the stern sheets whom Deliyeth suspected was the Cooperage Guild Mistress everyone knew was a friend to pirates, she knew the woman was sent for one purpose: to cajole, wheedle, and outright lie, to get the allies to accept the pirates. Why?

Perran had not wanted to come on this journey, but Chim had talked her into it. "When we were behind bars, you were the only one Kliessin listened to. People like you," he'd said to her.

Perran'd had to acknowledge that. She and Kliessin had found common ground faster than she'd dared to hope, in spite of the long, tense period she'd been kept waiting in an anteroom, tall footmen on guard.

But within moments of climbing aboard the Everoneth flagship, Perran and Deliyeth each got that prickle of antipathy toward the other.

They tried to fight it. They knew they should work as allies.

Perran eyed the tall, gaunt Captain Deliyeth, who (it was said) would not eat until her crew was fed, which had not always happened during their long history of evading the Venn. From a distance she'd admired Deliyeth, but in person, all the little signals the eye takes in, some conscious, some not, convinced her that the Everoneth captain was judging her—and finding her very much wanting.

So Perran spoke with more warmth than she usually did, smiled as hard as she could, in an effort not to show her distrust, which fast grew to dislike.

And Deliyeth found her efforts affected. Even worse, she suspected she was being jollied, if not lied to, by this well-dressed, stout woman obviously used to easy living. This caused her to stiffen, and to speak in a clipped, wary tone. Why should Perran lie? Deliyeth found it too easy to come back to the question of piracy.

Though she, too, was aware of the importance of the alliance, and so she did her best to communicate with Perran. "I understand that you and the Bren Guild feel that this ... Fox Banner Fleet has turned to trade. But there remains the visual evidence. Not one of those raffees and trysails is built for trade. Only navies and pirates run long narrow ships, and those people did not get those ships by legal means."

"They took them from pirates," Perran said, keeping her voice calm and smooth. "You will have heard nothing whatsoever of them attacking traders. Not since they formed up into this fleet and began flying that banner with the fox face on it."

Perran's false tone sounded condescending to Deliyeth, who had never been an attractive woman, and years of weather and worry had grooved her narrow face into a habitual frown of reproof.

They stood at the rail, looking at the low, rakish ships lying in the water near their compatriots as boats plied back and forth. "I don't accept rumor as truth," Deliyeth said slowly. "But the persistence of rumor has to be taken into account. One of the rumors we heard over and over is that the leader of the Fox Banner Fleet was a Marlovan. The same one who destroyed one of our own allies and caused the Venn to exact terrible retribution against Ymar."

"I've heard that rumor as well." Perran softened her voice, smiled. "But I find the stories about one fellow burning down a city single-handed too fantastic to believe."

Deliyeth took her words as sarcastic rebuke, and reddened. "It wasn't a city. I saw with my own eyes the destruction of Limros Palace. As far as we have been able to ascertain, the Marlovans have not only extended their empire over the west end of the Sartoran continent, but they beat back the Venn they descended from. *Like father, like son,* the saying goes. You cannot call it mere rumor that both peoples seem set on empire building."

"No," Perran said, in a make-peace tone.

"Therefore it makes sense that this Marlovan pirate no one could beat is looking to create a seagoing empire."

"We don't believe that," Perran said steadily.

"So I understand. Well, whatever happens in Bren is your business. But I want it made clear to them that we will fight alongside them if we must. We cannot defeat the Venn without numbers and training. But if they try to land in any of our harbors, we will meet them with fire and sword."

"Fair enough." Perran waved for the boat crew to move beneath, so she could disembark. There was no use in staying.

Deliyeth couldn't help adding, as Perran climbed down

into the boat, "Do not be surprised if you meet with the same from my allies."

Unfortunately, she was the one surprised when her misgivings were not shared by the coalition of Sarendan independents. They welcomed Fangras' return.

And so did the Chwahir, which was an even greater surprise.

She watched the ship visits through her glass as the independents and the Fox Banner captains traded news. *Where the Chwahir approve, trouble follows,* Deliyeth thought.

Until the Fox Banner Fleet arrived, the captains had agreed to meet aboard Captain Deliyeth's own flagship to plan the attack. Deliyeth heard less planning than arguing.

Everyone agreed that Ymar's main port, Jaro, was the most important at that end of the strait.

They agreed that this was the reason the last remaining outpost of Venn held it.

They agreed that the small but effective fleet of Venn warships that had appeared to reinforce Jaro when the winds had changed that summer had to mean more were coming.

The Venn themselves had put out the word that they would return in force. But the long summer season with its driving west winds had brought no more Venn. That fact, coupled with rumors of the Venn defeat by the Marlovans the summer before that, had caused this gathering: Deliyeth knew that despite all the trumpetings about freeing the strait from the oppressors, everyone wanted to make sure no one else got control of Jaro.

What they couldn't agree on was how to get rid of the Venn once they drew them out into the water. No one wanted a land battle, as rumor had it there were far too many Venn warriors left in Ymar.

The flat-faced, black-haired Chwahir insisted they fight in battle lines, because they always fought in line. The flamboyantly dressed east coast independents wanted to try running attacks, which might work against a haphazard fleet but not against Venn. You didn't frighten Venn by sailing down their sides shooting fire arrows. They sent their swift, maneuverable raiders to surround *you,* and next thing you knew, you were either dead or floating in the water, hoping the undersea folk didn't drag you down and put fins on you.

The half-a-dozen determined Ymarans, whose entire kingdom was on the verge of rising in a last and desperate attempt to win free of the Venn yoke, watched everyone. They had not had a good navy for two generations, the last two queens having relied on trade and diplomacy to ward off trouble.

This unwarlike policy, all knew, had drawn the Venn to occupy Ymar as their first step in taking all of Drael. So the Ymarans were forced into alliance with Everon, which still had a semblance of a navy—mostly converted fishers that had taken refuge with the rest of the Fleet Guild off of Bren. The rest had been burned or taken outright.

But the alliance refused to accept Deliyeth as commander. "You never won anything," one of the independents said bluntly. "All you did was hide."

In the two weeks after the arrival of the Fox Banner Fleet and its five flagships, four meetings were held, each breaking up when no one could agree with anyone else. Angry captains rowed back to complain to subordinates, and as soon as the sun went down, sent unlit rowboats back and forth to confer secretly with allies.

Then the rakish, black-sided trysail *Death* appeared with four other capital ships sailing on station as exact as any navy could wish for, the fast little scout *Vixen* just aft of *Death*.

Deliyeth watched the pirates brail up with a well-trained flash of sail—and hated how rowboats splashed down from every one of the allied flagships. Though they all rowed toward her, as they had been doing, she knew before they converged that leadership of the allied fleet waited somewhere in the air for that hard-faced pirate captain to take.

Cold late-winter light rippled over the plain bulkheads of her cabin as the gathered captains argued, reasoned, pointed, thumped, redrew their favorite battle plans on the slate, and smacked gloved hands on her chart depicting Jaro and the coastal inlets and islands surrounding The Fangs.

Deliyeth glared at the Fox Banner commander, a tall, black-clad, red-haired tough with a blood-red ruby hanging from his ear. A *pirate* trophy, flaunted before law-abiding people. He had spoken scarcely a dozen words since his

arrival on deck, and all those had been greetings or acknowledgment of introductions. But as soon as the meeting
started, Deliyeth noticed irritably how all the others turned
his way as the Chwahir admiral Halog issued a stately reit-
eration of her old argument in her slow, difficult Sartoran.
*At least no one accepted her as commander, either. Every-
body hates the Chwahir.*

As soon as Halog was done, one of the Khanerenth captains thumped the table. "You can't fight in line, they got
those big three-masters with those prows. They'll just run
you down!" Then he turned his head, and gestured to the
pirate. "Tell them, Fox!"

Silence inside the cabin made the outside sounds distinct: the thump of feet on deck, the creak of masts and
clack of blocks. Water whoosh-splashed along the hull and
in the distance, a first mate bawled orders onboard one of
the alliance fleet's vessels lying a cable's length away.

Captain Deliyeth watched in disgust as everyone waited
for Fox to speak as he gazed at her chart. She said, "I don't
recall ever hearing that *you've* fought Venn on the sea."

"Haven't," Fox retorted. His Sartoran was excellent,
though the consonants were clipped in the manner of the
Marlovans. "But I've seen them drilling. Their Battlegroups
are twenty-seven ships. They travel in line when they're on
the sweep, but form up into the arrowhead if they go on
the attack."

He leaned forward, picking up the chalk. When no one
objected, he pulled the slate toward him and used the
sponge to wipe away Deliyeth's own carefully drawn plan,
which was a last and desperate attempt to please everyone
by having them attack in groups. Only who would go first?

Fox sketched three inverted triangles forming a larger
inverted triangle, and then those triangles, in triplicate,
formed into yet a larger triangle, all sailing in such tight
formation they would be as effective as a real arrowhead
in cutting enemy battle lines. "This is what we will see. The
Venn were so well drilled they stayed on station no matter
how bad the weather, so that attempting to cut between
them could get you rammed as well as surrounded."

Deliyeth and Halog both had to concede.

"This is how their Commander Durasnir defeated us in
your year 3903," Halog said. "We had nearly won, but our

forces did not hold line." She indicated Deliyeth and herself. "Chwahir and Everoneth separated, each leaving the other to first strike in combing that formation."

"You can't comb an arrowhead like combing a line," Fox said. "What we call threading a needle. You'll find yourself surrounded, and while you're desperately putting out the fires they pinpoint all over your ship, their marines board fore and aft."

No one argued. While no ships boarded by the Venn had survived, the older Chwahir and Deliyeth herself had witnessed this tactic. They had only survived by outrunning their chasers.

"The one advantage we've got is when we have the wind, we are much faster." Fox swept a hand over the chart. "We have to use that."

The Chwahir just sat, watchful dark gazes moving between the speakers. The Khanerenth captains cut in with "Hah!" "That's right!" The Ymarans whispered.

"My suggestion is to adapt their tactics. We send a line to cut across upwind of them, laying down a heavy smoke layer. Then we send our fastest ships in a modified arrowhead to wedge between their first and third groups, using fire heavily so they won't want to close. We're adept at using fire, and even Venn can't see any better than we can in smoke. If they stay too tight, they might ram one another."

Captain Deliyeth shifted uncomfortably. *Pirate tactics.* Ship battles, when necessary, were board and carry. Those were the rules of the sea. You didn't kill unarmed civilians, and if someone surrendered, you either put them overboard in their longboats, or treated them decently until they paid their ransom or the king traded them for something he wanted.

But the Venn killed everyone onboard and took the ships to be remade in their own fashion.

"We want them to break formation," Fox continued. "If they do that, we can take them piecemeal in squads. They have bigger ships, but we've got the numbers. And speed."

One of the Chwahir said, "They have the raiders."

"So we set our small craft on the raiders, teams of three to one. For now—and this is why we need to act fast—we have the Venn outnumbered."

"Though their capital ships are bigger than anything we

sail." Commander Halog spoke, nodding slightly at Fox. "They know we are out here. We Chwahir will attack their guard ships around Jaro. Draw them out."

That gnarled old woman hadn't given Captain Deliyeth that much cooperation in weeks of talk.

Deliyeth said, "I concur that the Chwahir can draw them out, as they have the biggest fleet among us. But who is going to lead this wedge aimed between the Venn arrowhead vessels?"

Fox's eyes widened. "Didn't I say the fastest ships?" He laid his hands mockingly to his chest and opened them out.

The captains cut glances sideways at each other, making little movements of shoulders, hands, heads; a consensus reached without a word spoken.

Captain Deliyeth forced her voice to neutrality. "Then let us depart at once. I smell spring coming off the land, and that means we won't be able to trust to the east wind staying steady."

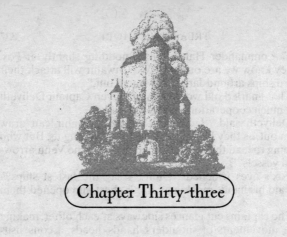

Chapter Thirty-three

"RISE up, Capn'nan!" Keth Arveas-Andahi whispered, shaking Captain Han. "We're riding out *today!*"

Han snorted and sat up in bed. Cold air touched the side of her face, and she wiped her mouth against her shoulder. She'd been awake worrying and hadn't meant to fall asleep. Somehow it had happened, but the way she felt, she'd slept maybe a glass or two.

The girls' dormitory was icy cold, most burrowed in their blankets. Han scrambled out of bed, the cold stones jerking her into wakefulness.

"Meet us downstairs soon's you're dressed." Keth ran out, his new boots clacking on the stones.

Han scowled at her new gear bag, packed and ready. She hurried with her travel clothes down to the bath. Afterward she met the rest in the mess hall, where nearly the entire castle was gathered to see them off.

The Harskialdna was everywhere, joking and laughing with men and women, even the children. Ndand-Jarlan surprised him with a fierce hug just before he sat down to the table and whispered something that caused him to laugh.

The men sent up a shout that rang against the stones above, smoke-blackened from the fires of the battle of

summer 3914, or the Fourteen, as the Marlovans had begun
to call the Battle of Andahi.

Han scarcely noticed what she was eating. The time
had come, and even more than before she veered between
pride and shame, as most of her friends gave her little me-
mentos they'd made, and the adults whispered how proud
they were of her. Those whispers made her feel worse, and
she was glad when they mounted up and rode out the south
gate.

The ride up was slow, mostly accomplished single file, as
the sides of the pass were still piled high with snow. Each
morning the children stamped the frozen runnels of snow-
melt, enjoying the tinkle and crunch. Those first few days
Keth and Han stayed together, neither daring to impose
their scrubby young selves on the dragoons who had been
riding around with the Harskialdna all winter.

But by the end of the first week, Keth had begun daring
a question or two, and when he didn't get swatted down for
his temerity, he'd taken to riding with the men.

Han rode behind the King's Runners, staring at their
blue-covered backs and wishing she dared to talk to them.

As Inda rode slowly up the pass, he thought about how
good it felt to be going home, leaving behind a job well
done. A job that had been fun. He chuckled from time to
time, relishing the memory of his and Cama's strutting
ride all over the north. Why couldn't life always be that
fun? They'd never tired of retelling the old jokes from
their scrub days, but even more fun was that competition
to outdo the other in frost. One day Inda managed to get
fourteen weapons distributed about his person before taking horse. Though the prick of knife blades in odd places
was annoying, he'd almost laughed aloud at the faces gathered alongside the road to watch them ride.

That was how he gauged their success, the fact that
people would down tools or walk out of the houses and
line the road to watch them ride by. That meant word was
spreading. So he'd stop the men at a crossroads, and either
he or Cama would call out some ridiculous order—"You
men! You were talking in column! Time for a thrashing!"
and they'd stage a weapons drill, one of the flashier ones.
Or they'd make a lot of noise taking sticks to the men's
backs, pretending to use full strength, while the men gri-

maced and grunted. No one ever laughed in column, but at night, around the campfire, they gloated exactly like academy scrubs after a successful sting.

Inda's favorite sting, he decided, was the one the day they reached the foothills of Ghael, somewhere near the place he knew his brother had fought his first battle. *Next batch of law-breakers you get around here, I want a wall built on that ridge. Hundred paces high! So I can see the ocean from it.* Cama didn't even smile. *But what if the ocean isn't in view?* Inda roared, *Then they take it all down, go to that mountaintop up there, and rebuild it.*

The glum faces were sometimes broken by expressions of disgust, but never disbelief. And it worked. Runners came back with reports that no one lined the road to see the wagon train with the plainly marked second best coffee and wine (the Marlovans keeping the best for their own use, the civ-dressed wagoneers were to let drop at inns) heading toward the two harbors to be sent out for the Marlovans' new efforts in sea trade.

Word ricocheted back once the supposed wine turned out to be gold. This was the week before Inda decided it was time to ride for the royal city. Cama had said, "You know that's going to bring out the last of the Resistance, the ones turned brigand. I'm going to send ridings of dragoons as escort for a while. Maybe they can even flush the last of 'em out."

Yes, it was all good, and Inda looked forward to reaching the royal city in time for the first day of the academy. He looked forward to making Evred and Tdor laugh when he described all the details of that preposterous ride.

The only memory that sobered him was his lack of success when asking here and there if anyone had seen a small, sandy-haired mage. No one had.

His mood stayed good until they reached the top of the pass, where there was no sign of the sea of blood that had soaked the ground that terrible day. No sign of ghosts, of pain and anguish, except in memory. Inda did not have to glance at earlobes for the telltale blood-red glitter to see which of the men had been present that day. They were obvious by the way they looked around, tight-shouldered as if braced for attack. He wouldn't stop there to camp, even though it meant making their way down around two or three bends in fast-falling dark.

Light snow began to fall when they camped at last. They set up their tents around a massive fire ring made by putting together all their Fire Sticks. It was against tradition, but the dragoons liked the circle. Inda liked being able to talk to people instead of sitting alone in his tent.

Keth's high voice floated above the lower buzzes of the men. Inda grinned, then checked around for the other child. As usual, she sat a little apart from Keth, a skinny scrap of a girl who never spoke anywhere in Inda's hearing. When she looked Inda's way she reminded him just a little of Testhy of the pale brows, one of his early ship mates. One who hadn't stayed with them. Testhy had had the same shifty manner, as if he had a secret.

"Food's up." The welcome shout from the cook tent brought everyone to their feet, the two children first. Inda stayed where he was. One good thing about being a commander, you didn't have to stand in line. Your Runner did, and he was sure to be served first, so he didn't stand long. The food got to you hot.

Inda had been very careful in Idayago, but habit is hard to break. Here among his own men, instinct caused him to hunch over his bowl and begin spooning the rice balls into his mouth. Two, three bites—there was that sense of being watched—he remembered his promise to Tdor and jerked upright, his face flooding with heat. Sure enough, there was that girl staring. He gave her a sheepish grin.

Han went cold and hot all at once. The Harskialdna slurping! Then hauling himself upright as if Liet-Jarlan had stepped from beyond death and smacked him across the back of his head for ignoring manners. And then he turned red, like . . . like . . . *anyone else*.

He was *human*.

Inda said, "Food too hot?"

Han jumped. Then she looked uncomprehendingly at her untouched bowl, her skinny shoulders hunched up to her ears.

"Are you all right?" Inda asked.

Her face crumpled, and she sucked in her breath, holding hard on the last thin layer of self-control.

"Ho." Inda set his own food aside, and reached over to

ruffle her hair, much as he had comforted the homesick ten-year-old scrubs at the academy.

And that cracked the ice.

"I–I–I . . ."

"Something wrong, cub? Can you tell me?" His voice was kind, which caused the dammed flood to break free at last. She began to sob without sound, deep, wracking sobs that shook her skinny frame. She had just enough will-power to turn her back on the camp, and from that Inda understood that she did not want an audience. Inda set aside their food and guided her out of the light, nearly tripped over a flat rock, turned and sat on it instead, pulling the girl down next to him.

When she could breathe again, it all came out. Everything. Inda had heard the story of the Castle Andahi children from Cama, who had been giving and receiving reports for enough years to remember details. But this time Inda heard about it from the child's view: the terror of hearing her family killed by the Venn. Not knowing if she and the other children were hunted. Having part of her command run away—straight into death.

And finally, the most severe test of all: a desperately unhappy three-year-old who nearly got herself thrown off a cliff. By the way Captain Han halted and hastily corrected herself, Inda suspected that she was not alone in the impulse, but she forbore mentioning anyone else. She had been in command, it was her burden to bear.

She was exhausted when she finished, her voice so low it was difficult to hear. "And so, I think, if the king finds out, he'll know I'm not good enough to be a King's Runner."

"How did you come to that conclusion?" Inda asked. "The King's Voice was Vedrid—surely he didn't say anything of the sort to you."

"I never told anyone. About almost throwing Rosebud off the bridge. Ndand-Jarlan . . . Cama-Jarl . . . everything was so terrible . . ." Captain Han gulped, her breath shuddering. She said to her pilled mittens, "I can't ever be as good as you. When *you* were twelve. Eleven! You commanded pirates."

"*What?*"

Heads in the camp turned. Inda waved, and they turned away again. Inda said, "When I turned twelve, I was crying in my hammock missing my home and trying to remember the difference between a jib and a gaff."

"But . . . all those s–stories. I remember. What they said. R–right in front of you. At the dinner, New Year's."

"I don't remember."

"With the Idayagan merchants and mayors. The big dinner. When that fat man talked about you commanding ships when you were no older than Keth, and he pointed right at Keth, and you and Cama were smiling."

Inda snorted. "If any of us Marlovans ask me about what happened to me, I answer with the truth."

She shivered at the sound of that "us Marlovans."

"But the Idayagans, well, here's why I didn't. The king ordered me to ride up here and act tough. He and Cama thought that if I didn't deny those wild stories, then people would settle down, they'd think we're too tough to fight against anymore. We want them to settle down. No more fighting, people getting killed."

"Oh."

"So I was riding around on the strut, see. So if those Olarans or Idayagans say I commanded the Brotherhood of Blood when I was six years old, well, I'm not going to say no. But when I was twelve, I was just like you, sent to a new life. Learning. Only you got picked for this new life in the royal city because you followed orders the best you knew how. Right?"

"Right." Captain Han gave another sigh, but this time of immeasurable relief.

Inda had been ignoring the earrings until then, and he certainly hadn't meant to do any such thing until the words came out. "When we get light, I want you to get one of the Runners to poke a hole in your ear. You wear a ruby there—I have a couple extras in my gear, left to me by Barend. When people see your earring, they'll know you survived that pass. You followed orders. That's the Marlovan way."

A week after spring's first thaw, the perimeter riders up on the ridge behind Piwum Harbor reported seeing Whipstick Noth riding at the head of the green-and-silver banners of Algara-Vayir.

At noon Horsepiss Noth, King's Dragoon Commander,

came out of the harbor garrison to welcome his son, whom he was surprised to discover in command of the border riders, instead of the new Adaluin of Choraed-Elgaer, Branid-Dal Algara-Vayir.

Since the bell had just rung for the noon meal, Noth took Whipstick into his modest house adjacent the newly built barracks.

A gaunt woman burst in, grinning as she enfolded her son in a hard hug. "Senrid!"

Whipstick grimaced. "Aw, Ma. What have I done?"

"That's the name I gave ye. It's how I think of ye in my heart." Marlovan his mother was, from the knives in her sleeves to the calluses on her fingers from years of archery, though she still spoke with the coastal Iascan accent she'd been born to. "I'm glad to see ye, but I didn't expect to. Where's young Branid? He looked mighty fine trotting through here last spring, mighty fine."

Whipstick thought back a year. Branid had indeed looked like a ballad hero Adaluin at the head of the Riders, young and blond and strong, laughing in a way that reminded many of his cousin Tanrid. Branid had been happy then. He had the rank he'd been raised to think belonged to him and was newly married as well, to a handsome woman of rank, one he liked.

Whipstick jerked his thumb over his shoulder. "Branid sent me instead."

"So ye can come see us, then. Good! Now, when will ye marry? Give me grandchildren?"

Whipstick's smile faded. Noren had gone to the royal city. And he just didn't want to marry anyone else. "I'm in no hurry."

"Your boys would have a place at the academy," Horsepiss said. "Your service is owed that."

"As if Inda wouldn't see to it personal," Ma Noth said, flipping her hand at her husband. "How's life with the new Adaluin and Iofre? Why isn't he riding? Though glad I am to see ye."

Whipstick rocked back on his heels, thinking. Branid had left Whipstick in charge of Tenthen while he relied on Captain Vrad of the Riders to show him the route through Choraed Elgaer. What to say? He thought of Vrad's bitter accounts of stupid orders, like running the horses until they were nearly wind-broken just because the countryside was boring. The extra drills ordered if Branid heard laughter in the column because he was convinced they were laughing at him behind his head. Most of all, how he'd angered the men on what should have been a good ride, because he wouldn't listen to how Jarend-Adaluin had always relaxed discipline while the men were alone on the road. Branid didn't even try to learn any of the names of the scattered people who housed them along the way. He didn't listen to their yearly reports, just grandly said to write it all down to be handed to the king when he rode to Convocation.

That had been Vrad's report. Branid's had been as different as night from day: how boring it was, just riding around for six months while every day got hotter when it wasn't thundering, how stupid the people, all whining about hardship and begging for things he was sure they could make themselves, how slow the horses and how badly disciplined the men.

"He wasn't raised to the ride," Whipstick said finally. "As for Tenthen, while he was gone, the carts arrived with all Dannor's furniture from Yvana-Vayir. Grand stuff it was, but Badger and Beaver Yvana-Vayir didn't want it."

"Their wives didn't," Ma Noth commented.

"Maybe so. Now they've got them a fine palace up there."

Horsepiss made a spitting motion over his shoulder, and his wife thrust her hands into her sleeves. "And?"

Whipstick leaned back, staring through the window at the gray sea. "When they're not arguing, she keeps him up there the whole day. I guess that's good. Then they're out of the way. But when he doesn't fall in with her wants, and he's as stubborn as she is, they fight like a couple of wolves."

"So she doesn't run him?"

"Not anymore. First, after they were married, yes. He was happy. Gave people things. Liked to be thanked, liked to surprise people. Get praise. That's all right. It was good for everyone, but *she* didn't like it. Said he was raising expectations—the people were taking advantage of a new Adaluin—if he gave them things they wouldn't respect him."

"Expectations of what?"

"That's what he asked, and when she started giving

the orders, beginning with no more gifts, well, that's when
the fights started. We all heard them, they didn't shut the
windows, and we were all in the court, at drill. I think she
wanted people to overhear. So they'd feel scolded, too. I
don't know." Whipstick grimaced. "She said they'd expect
to snake out of duty. Expect him to pay for things they
should do themselves because they'd think he was weak.
You know how much he'd hate that."

Noth whistled.

"She doesn't cross Fareas-Iofre, but she sure does run
the other women, especially anyone Branid dallies with, or
tries to, when she's locked him out of the bedroom after a
fight. She stopped running castle drills soon's the weather
got cold. The tapestry, too. She even lies abed for Restday
drum, although no one says anything, because the people
like Fareas-Iofre handing out the bread. And Fareas-Iofre's
out in the drill yard every morning now, gray-haired as she
is. Back on schedule, too, instead of whenever *She* decides
to get out of bed. That's what they call her, *She,* after she
had young Jdar flogged for telling them about 'Mudface.'
She went through the whole house, questioning everybody.
Jdar took the blame just to end it."

Horsepiss Noth shook his head. He'd never liked being
called Horsepiss, but he'd learned early that if you laughed
and took it, the worst name became a banner. If you raised
a ruckus, then they used it behind your head and felt they
had some kind of power over you.

"The Iofre-Edli knows order comes of schedule," Ma
Noth observed.

Whipstick shrugged. "Branid's granddam always said
order comes of knowing your place. The prince commands,
people obey. Prince *is* order, so he can do what he wants
when he wants. Well, Dannor's just the same."

Horsepiss shook his head. "That's bad. Then if you flog
the men for lying abed, you're punishing them for doing
what you do."

Whipstick turned his thumb up. "Branid yells when he
takes a stick to a man's back, 'I'm the prince! You owe me
obedience!' Men don't like that. Vrad came to me just last
week, before Branid told me to take the border ride this
year. Said his wife got an offer as a bow captain at Fera-
Vayir, and they said they could use him. I think it's just to

get away. Jdar is going with them. She says their old headstall maker is getting slow."

Horsepiss said, "Vrad is a fine Rider captain. He'll be a
loss."

Whipstick flicked his thumb up. "So, here's the thing. I
didn't send any report to Inda over the winter, not with
him all the way north. But Flatfoot says he likes the reports about Tenthen, no matter what he's doing, he drops
everything to read 'em. He'll be on the road home from the
north by now, and I expect if there's nothing waiting when
he gets to the royal city, he'll send someone to us. Should I
tell him what I just told you?"

The Noths both said no.

Horsepiss added, "Inda's the king's man now."

Ma Noth said, "You'll just worry him, since he has no
hold over Choraed Elgaer. The men respect you, you'll
just have to find a way to get things back to rights. Maybe
Branid will wake up to his duty when he has to report to
the king."

Horsepiss finished, "No one ever said being a Randael
is easy." He clapped his son on his thin, bony shoulder. "I
hope you'll have better news for us come next spring."

Chapter Thirty-four

INDA and his company arrived, horns blowing the charge. It would have been dashing except for the pools of snow melt that slowed the horses to a sluggish pace. The riders were mud-splashed, the animals almost unrecognizable.

Evred awaited them in the stable yard. "Go to the parade court," he said, after a swift glance at each face. "Vedrid here will take the new Runner-in-Training in charge, and Hadand is going to introduce her."

"I'm two days late!" Inda protested.

Evred laughed. "They're all lined up waiting for you."

So Inda urged his tired horse along the narrow passage from the royal stable through the mossy archway between the Great Hall and the throne room. He had to duck his head low.

Keth followed, but as soon as he was through he walked his horse to the back. A year of the academy had given him a vivid picture of what the bigger boys would say of his riding out front with the Harskialdna.

One of the masters had already summoned a stable hand, who took charge of Keth's horse, and Keth joined his mates, muddy as he was. He ignored the covert whispers out of motionless faces and the nudges on either side. He knew they were hoping for a tale of brigands or desperate Venn spies instead of roads that had turned to lakes.

Up front, Inda looked at the expectant faces, from the big boys nearing adulthood to the little boys poking and whispering in the back. His tired, annoyed horse, having smelled the stable and then unconscionably been bustled by his rider to this flat area full of two-legs, shifted and tossed its head.

"Here we are, ready for another year." Inda lifted his voice. "I don't care what you think of one another, you are not the enemy." The last word echoed off the castle walls. "We've got enough enemies outside the borders. But last year you were too busy fighting one another to listen to me. So I'm starting over. I'm going to watch your regular drills and practices and see how hard you work before we have any more extra training. And if you don't want the extras, that's fine. I know your dads didn't have them, and Marlovans are strong. I know it, you know it, our enemies know it. But one thing's for sure. You start scragging each other again and there won't be any extras for the academy. Just for the boys—and, uh, the new girl—over in the King's Runners-in-Training. What you'll get is drill."

Angry whispers buzzed through the boys in anticipation of the loathsome swagger of those pugs and turds in the King's Runners training. They thought themselves so tough....

Sudden quiet as Gand strolled out to join Inda.

"You boys get over to the stable. Let's see if any of you can lift a lance after a winter of slacking off," he said genially to the horsetails. "Rest of you, line up for the shearing. As soon as the Harskialdna-Dal returns to us, we'll begin."

Inda laid rein to his animal's neck and it promptly trotted back to the royal stable yard, where Inda vaulted down and tore off to the baths.

The shearing was no longer on his mind. He knew they'd wait, since they'd already waited two days. Though it was not his business, he wanted to see Han Tlen introduced to the King's Runners-in-Training. After traveling in her company for weeks, he'd grown fond of the child, who re-

minded him strongly of Tdor at that age. They even looked
a little alike—something about their long, earnest faces.

Vedrid had taken her off to the queen's training buildings so she could bathe. While Han took the fastest bath
of her life the Runner Vedrid had sent her new uniform,
which was pretty much like her old clothes, except in Runner blue.

Vedrid gave her a hasty tour of the main portions of the
castle on the way back, explaining as he went. It was kindly
meant, but she was totally bewildered by the time they
reached the annex perpendicular to the Residence Wing,
which housed the Runners.

Inda caught up just as they walked into the big main
room set aside for the youngsters in training to work and
play. All the Runners-in-Training shared these quarters,
and some of their training, the King's Runners separating
off for more rigorous work when the others were on stable
and sentry duty.

So Han found herself stared at by many new eyes. All
the Runners-in-Training were lined up against the walls,
boys on one side, girls on the other.

The King's Runners against the far wall. All boys.

Hadand stopped Vedrid and Han just inside the door,
and said with a smile, "Welcome, Captain Han. Because
you're the first girl to train as a King's Runner, you've three
choices: bunk with the girls in queen's training over on the
other side of the castle adjacent to the guards, in a little
room to yourself where the queen's staff lives, or with the
rest of the King's Runners, who are all at this end, nearest
the archive."

Inda knew how she'd answer that.

"I'm used to bunking with everybody under fifteen at
home," Han said. "I don't want to stand out. I mean, anymore than I already do."

Inda grinned as he stepped to the doorway and peered
between Hadand's and Vedrid's shoulders. He wanted to
see Han welcomed by Goatkick Noth and the rest of the
boys, the best of whom he'd learned to know during the
long march north before the Venn attack.

Instead, they stared at her in silence. Vedrid took her
down the row, naming each, and as Inda watched those co-

vert, resentful peeks at that winking ruby in the girl's ear,
he wondered if he'd made a very bad mistake.

Two weeks later, the first outland messenger arrived from
the eastern border. This year, among the messages from
Anaeran-Adrani was one from even farther away, all the
way from Bren.

> *Evred, my dear son,*
>
> *I trust by now you have been apprised by your
> cousin Barend of the exertions I am making on your
> behalf. With this missive you will find seven letters of
> credit, each from different banks. With Barend's per-
> mission I have engaged Iascan traders who have been
> out of business for years. They carry a guild sved from
> Barend and me, and, armed with it, are sailing for the
> islands to begin your coffee trade; I convinced Barend
> to send some to the Nob, as he wished, but to sell the
> bulk here, as you will gain three times the price anyone
> in Iasca Leror can pay at present.*
>
> *Events are turbulent, with alliances making and
> breaking over the question of Ymar, its independence,
> and how to protect the strait. There is no use in telling
> you the latest news as it will be half a year old when
> this reaches you.*
>
> *Barend tells me you are still relying on those love
> lockets that I brought as a bride-gift for your aunt. My
> son, I entreat you to overcome your distrust of scroll-
> cases. You can afford the price of trustworthy ones
> now. You need a trusted venue that does not limit one
> to a handful of words.*
>
> *You also need an envoy to see that your interests
> are represented as every royal voice talks about free
> trade but strives for precedence. Sending a messenger
> over the mountains for nearly half a year and then
> waiting another half year for a response isolates you
> more thoroughly than the Mage or Guild Councils
> possibly can. I say this because no one outside your
> border understands Marlovan, and what people do
> not understand, they tend to ascribe the worst moti-*

vations to. Your envoy must not only act for you, but must explain you to the rest of the world.

You now have what your grandfather wanted: control of every harbor on Halia. That means you not only control customs, but I suspect what is more important to you, communication between guilds. I'm sure it suits you to keep contact with the world confined to four harbors, maybe five, but does it suit your kingdom?

I know only you can answer that, but consider how much of an advantage it would be for you, your kingdom, and for the world if you were to send to me an envoy who can speak on your behalf, someone with skill and finesse. Prince Kavnarac, among others, insists that the ideal person would be Taumad Dei, who we understand traveled back to your kingdom to visit his friend Indevan Algara-Vayir. If this is so, I hope you will speak to him.

   Wisthia Shagal
   Dowager Queen of Iasca Leror
   Princess of Anaeran-Adrani, Ambassador to Bren

"Remember, the audience is here," Tau said, waving a hand toward the benches across the front of the old stable annex being turned into a theater.

On the bare stage (a flat square made of the wood of the former stalls) his players lowered their weapons and turned his way. They shuffled and coughed and looked around; Tau could feel them struggling to remember what he'd spent nearly half a year teaching them: *play-acting is not real.*

"You're forgetting your audience. Angle toward me. And when you fight, you strike the other's weapon, not his body. High, low, high. Stadas, you aim for the head. Tama, you duck, then swing for Stadas' feet. Stadas, you—"

"Leap, then the handspring, I remember. We just thought it was too slow, we'd put some muscle into it. Make it more exciting." Stadas was a tough young ironmonger with a fine singing voice and a hankering for drama.

"If you're fast, it'll be exciting enough, without nearly decapitating the rest of the players and knocking down the flats." *Again.*

He didn't say it, but they all heard it.

The fellows squared up to resume their mock duel. Tau had tried hard to convince them that mock duels could be just as exciting as real ones, if you planned them out and practiced. Not until he'd begun to use the word "drill" did they comprehend the concept of rehearsal. Drilling your play? Now, *that* made sense!

Then they'd balked at the older ballads, because, as one put it, "Nobody wants to ride all the way to Ola-Vayir just to borrow the first Jarl's tunic. Everyone says old Ola-Vayir's a horse apple."

Tau had been astonished that it was so difficult to get across the idea of theater, of representation. But at nights, when he dined with the royal pairs, he'd seen in Tdor's face how accepting new ideas came in degrees as he described his daily efforts. Didn't matter that the elements of theater—mock battles, words put in heroes' mouths—were already familiar from ballads in play form. These elements had never been put together.

Hadand was enthusiastic, Tdor interested, and Evred inscrutable but he listened, so Tau tried to make his reports entertaining. He strove to hide his increasing frustration at the Marlovans' resistance to such seemingly simple ideas as planning the actions so that the audience could see, instead of standing face-to-face on the stage "Because that's the way people really stand." Then there was the conviction that the painted flats (because there were no stage mages here) simply had to be exact in every detail lest some House take insult and declare a feud.

Within a week after assembling an enthusiastic body of volunteers from the closest taverns, Tau had quietly put away the plays he had so carefully selected while in Anaeran-Adrani. Everyone seemed to want a play by New Year's Week, so he'd decided to adapt one of the ballads everyone knew. Easy, right?

After rewriting the play script every single night for another two weeks, he'd gone back to the simplest types of plays, the ones that turned on a story everyone knew, with the players making up their own lines or using ones from ballads. He'd decided to approach written plays by degrees.

As the players recommenced their exchange (galloping through their words in the syncopated rhythm of ballads,

despite Tau's attempts to coach them out of it) and happily
hefted their wooden weapons for their favorite part of the
play, the door creaked on its ancient hinges.

When Evred's First Runner Vedrid entered, Tau knew
this had to be a royal summons. Scarcely a watch after the
mud-splashed Runner from the border mountains had
been seen? Not good.

The players launched into their mock duel. Vedrid stood
beside Tau in silence, watching the mock duel until the end.
When the two stage Jarls fell to arguing about who got the
better-looking strikes, Tau flicked an interrogative glance
at Vedrid. "Summons?"

"When you have liberty."

Tau understood that there was no emergency—but then
he would not be the one summoned in an emergency. That
would fall to Inda.

"All right," Tau cut into the argument. "Put together a
fight you think is both fair and exciting. The rest of us will
meet on the morrow."

And while the others began talking over one another in
their efforts to share their ideas, Tau slipped out.

A short time later he was ushered into Evred's private
study with no one else at hand. Evred was busy at his desk;
inevitable were the marks of tiredness under his eyes, but
his countenance no longer exuded lethal tension.

Evred sat back and tossed over a heavy rolled paper
with the remains of the royal Adrani seal affixed to it.

"Read that."

Tau sat down in the wing-backed chair, and looked at
the signature first. Wisthia Shagal? *Evred's mother.*

He read the letter through twice then laid it down. "And
so?"

"First, I had no idea you were part of the Dei family. I
thought we knew them all, except for the ones in Sartor.
There was a rumor in one of my father's letters about runaways from treaty marriages, but everyone assumed they'd
gone east."

"And came back. And had my mother, who had me."
Tau lifted his hands. "I found out the summer after I left
here. Does it matter?"

"You are oath-sworn to no one, as far as I am aware,"
Evred observed, avoiding the question.

"True."

"I understand that you do not see yourself as Iascan, much less Marlovan. Now, perhaps, I understand why." Evred touched the name *Dei* on the letter.

"I grew up without awareness of the family name."

"You did not tell anyone."

"Arrogant as it might sound, I still wanted to be accepted or rejected on my own merit," Tau said, shrugging. "I take it your mother's suggestion has gained your approval?"

Evred's brows lifted. "I don't have anyone else to send. Vedrid has twice been outside the border, but I promised him he would never have to leave again. And I don't know how well he'd do negotiating with these people."

Tau thought about Bren's court scene, the spies, innuendo, lies, and crosscurrents of ambition and intent. Then he shook his head. "It would be difficult."

"So permit me to ask what experience you have had with trade negotiations."

"I was often put with the purser when they discovered my facility with languages," Tau said. "After the Pim ships were lost, Kodl frequently had me as well as Testhy on hand when he dealt with captains and cargo. Later on, Inda relied on Barend and me to handle all our trade matters, such as they were." He smiled. "Turning pirate loot into ship repair and supplies is probably not what most would consider training for the stately pace of international trade, and yet I saw enough while in Bren to convince me the two are not so far removed as one might think."

"This Prince Kavna seems to think you would do well." Evred looked wry. "I would not be inclined to take the recommendation of some other prince had I not my mother's assurance as well. So. Do you have any questions for me?"

Tau knew the cost of that. "What did your grandfather want? Regulation of trade, besides military control?"

Evred's face closed, and Tau watched him struggle with a lifetime of secrecy. He waited.

Evred said at last, "The question is not merely one of control, though that is a part of it. You can see how much simpler things are with one rule rather than competing interests, the most successful often the most corrupt."

"Ah. Your Iascan guilds," Tau guessed. He knew from

growing up in Parayid Harbor that the Marlovans had pretty much isolated the guilds to prevent them from being in contact with the rest of the world.

"The archives are filled with dire tales of corrupt guilds bringing down thrones," Evred said. "Changing prices at whim for political ends. When we Marlovans came to Iasca Leror, the first treaty was with the Jarls, of course, but the second was with the guilds. Their business goes through us."

"And northern trade was limited to the Nob and Lindeth, once your grandfather took Olara. I know that much. So, I take it you want to open the kingdom to world trade again?"

"It will go through my people in each harbor. Everything honest—everyone pays according to the same standard. No bribery or secretly doubled fees for this person and cut rates for that friend."

Tau had no doubt that Evred meant exactly what he said, which was more than he'd allow many other monarchs. "A sound policy. What would be my role? Listen to royal gossip, follow world affairs, and reestablish guild contacts?"

"Does that not constitute a sufficient start?"

Evred was not issuing orders; their relationship was anomalous. Tau liked it that way. Evred had learned to tolerate it, which Tau thought a good sign.

But below that, another truth: Evred was willing to send Tau away. *So much for believing myself indispensable to a king and a queen.* He knew just how much Jeje would laugh at him for that. *Have I the Dei ambitions after all?*

No. The truth was personal, not political. Evred's accession to power had deepened those wells of reserve that, when he broke free and surfaced, made the resultant ardency as incandescent and dangerous as lightning. And about as brief. Tau knew himself addicted to those moments.

"I can do that." Tau forced a smile, an easy voice as he added, "It sounds intriguing." And when Evred made a wry grimace at the word play, Tau laughed. "How do we communicate? Do you really want half a year between letters?"

"It suited my ancestors." Evred pinched the skin between his brows, his tone dry. He sighed. "But it seems to put us at a disadvantage. So address the question to my mother."

It was late when Tau reached Hadand's rooms.

Hadand welcomed him with her customary calm practicality, but, like Inda, she could not hide the expression in her eyes. "You are going to be missed by more people than just me," she said.

"So you heard I was leaving?"

"Evred showed me his mother's letter and said he had asked you to serve as his Voice over the border."

Tau smiled. "Marlovans! I use my own voice, but I'll represent his interests."

Hadand frowned a little. "Do you understand what representing the King's Voice means?"

Tau waved a lazy hand to and fro. "I understand your military chain of command. It seems the only way to force your formidable captains not to take things into their own hands on a whim. I'm sure Evred will not be issuing any military commands through me. I certainly won't have a small army of armed dragoons to enhance my prestige, as I am traveling quite alone. And I prefer it that way," he added when he saw her about to speak. Then he tipped his chin toward the window. "I was just at the theater. Thought I ought to explain why I would not be there. They still seem to want to continue, though on their terms, not mine." He made a face in self-mockery.

"I know you don't consider your theater a success." She gave him a crooked smile. "Maybe we Marlovans will come to it in time. When I was in Nente with Queen Wisthia, I came to realize how much training is required just to learn how to watch a play."

And when he laughed, she crossed for the first time the boundary they had each observed so scrupulously. When they were together they had talked about everything except Evred.

But Hadand was hungry for the kind of insight she knew Tau could give. She sensed he was unsettled, maybe even upset, so she said tentatively, "I think Evred will miss you, too."

Yes, he was upset. Tau glanced back over his shoulder, the mockery pronounced. Then he walked around the room, the lamplight glimmering in his neatly queued golden hair, a bright contrast to the dun stone, the dark-wood low tables.

"If that is true, why am I leaving?" he asked finally and perched on the windowsill, his profile illuminated by torchlight. "He doesn't trust me now because his mother told him my family name? I don't know if that's worse or better then losing his trust by my own effort."

Hadand clasped her hands over her knife handles hidden in her sleeves. "Tau, he doesn't trust *anybody*. Except Inda."

"He trusts you."

"No, he *wants* to trust me. And Tdor, and to a certain extent he trusts Cama and his cousins and others to diminishing degrees. He has trouble trusting women because we hold secrets apart from men. Oh, I've thought about it and thought about it, and as near as I can figure his distrust goes back to when we were young, and he started discovering that we had secrets, but he couldn't see why. And I hadn't told him. He respects me, but he must have decided that my first loyalty lay with Aunt Ndara and my mother, not with him. Which wasn't true, it was just that I'd promised them. So that leaves one person."

"Inda," Tau said, looking away.

Hadand said, "I know what you all hid from me, but I saw Evred's face when Inda rode off to Idayago. It was stupid of me not to have seen it before. It's Evred's nature; I should have expected him to fall in love with my brother."

"There are all kinds of love, Hadand. Have you considered that some of Evred's passion for Inda might be the more intense because Inda's blind to his feelings?"

"Except he's *always* loved Inda. Ever since they met as scrubs down there in the academy. They didn't even use the word love, except for foals and puppies and their favorite foods. And I think it happened because Inda trusted *him,* without question. Without calculation. Without ambition. And this was ages before either of them had any interest in sex."

Her unhappiness strengthened his conviction that he'd failed not just Evred, but Hadand as well. *Sex is sex,* his mother had said once. *Do not look for it to be a solution to anything but desire.* Salutary! He said, "And then Inda left. Did his passion for Inda become a habit, or a dream that was easier to maintain than dealing with real people?"

"I don't think so. In Evred's family they're all like that. You should hear the stories about his great-great-aunt, and her ride across—oh, now I'm being a bore. As for Inda, yes, he's blind . . . *selfish*. He expects everyone to love him, and they do." Hadand's voice trembled as she prowled around the room, fingering her belongings. "At first I thought that when Inda got back from the north, I'd take him to task for his blindness. I thought, if Inda gave Evred a night, just once, maybe the . . . the power of anticipation would at least end."

Tau made a movement of protest. Hadand said quickly, "I know. After I got my own feelings out of the way, I saw just how much Evred would hate that. Who wants a pity tumble? That's why I haven't—" She smacked her hand against the wall in exactly the same way Inda often did. "But that road leads to thinking oneself a victim. There are no victims where there was no attack. Inda doesn't like men for sex, and Evred knows it. I love Tdor dearly, but I don't want to crawl into bed with her. We're made the way we're made, and anyway, Inda has Tdor *and* Signi—when would he have the time for Evred, too? He'd have to spent his nights hopping from room to room, unless it would occur to him not to leave one of his women out, as they got along so well when Signi was here, but oh, no—"

Tau concentrated on the rapid flow of words, the tremble in Hadand's voice and the disjointed thoughts convincing him that the real issue was not Inda's selfishness in not sleeping with both women together. "Tdor would hate a threesome," he observed.

Hadand tapped her fingers on the knife hilt in her other sleeve, the angry flush fading from her cheeks. "I know."

The calm in her voice, her honest gaze caused him to broach the real subject. "Evred would hate a threesome."

"I know." And again she struck the wall. "I've been wishing that you and Evred being together would some-how come to include me. He hasn't come near me in a year. I think he's relieved that you spend your nights with me when you're not with him. Then he doesn't have to."

"Have you asked him?"

"No. I used to wait outside his study for him to end
working, and I'd fall asleep on my feet. He'd always worked
hard, but this working through nights began around the
time that Inda and Tdor came." She rolled her brown eyes.
"And didn't stop until you returned and made him stop.
How long did it take me to see what everyone else seems
to have known?"

"First things first. I don't think a threesome would ever
happen, whoever the third was. Not Evred. One at a time
is about all he can bear." Tau grinned. "Threes only work
if the connections go equally all ways." And because she
was too close to the devastating discovery that her brother
unwittingly had the place in her husband's heart that she
would never have, he said with a mild air, "And it can be
lots of fun. Four, now, that's even more rare, but it can be
quite fun, too."

"Four? You've sported with four people?" She laughed.
"You're joking with me. How would that even work?"

"I've done it. For triple pay, I should add. People being
made the way they are, one must be agile as well as imagi-
native, but even so it's almost impossible to avoid a knee
smacking into a nose. And there are always way too many
feet."

She chuckled, and as he described some unfortunate
instances illustrating the impracticalities of human design
versus imagination, she finally gave way to gusts of laughter,
then wiped her eyes on her sleeve. Her anger was gone.

"No, I'm not fair to Inda," she admitted. "Everyone
loves him, and he loves everybody, but he doesn't expect it.
It just *is*. He just doesn't see how Evred's feelings are—"

"Unswerving."

"I was going to say unyielding. Sometimes it frightens
me, how *intense* Evred's love is. And his trust. Maybe because they are both so interdependent. I just wish . . ." She
shrugged, her mouth bitter. "He'd hold me. But as much as
he'd hate a pity tumble, I'd hate pity hugs."

"Evred knows nothing about affection, because the only
person who gave him any was you, then you stopped. Yes,
yes, I remember what you told me, and yes, he stopped
coming to you for comfort. Whatever his reasons were, they
no longer hold true, do you see? He has no defense against
tenderness, just a lifelong dearth of it. With me, he can shed

passion with violent play because I can take it and give it right back. I hope it's done him some good, despite the fact that he's sending me away."

"Maybe he's afraid to think so," Hadand said, with that narrow gaze so much like Inda's when he was evolving a plan. "He would see that as dangerous weakness."

"Could be." Inward laughter accompanied Tau's thought, *I sound so all-knowing.* "I just hope that when I'm gone he'll be sensible and go back to the House of Roses."

Hadand looked down.

Tau stepped away from the windowsill and took her hands. "I need to get my things ready. I'll ride out well before morning. Prevent awkward leave-takings. Here's my second thing. If you want your beloved in your arms all night, then you'll have to make your wishes clear. If you ask with no attempt at guilt, you will not get pity."

She backed away, hands pushing out. "I can't beg."

"So don't beg. But ask. Pity is not the only emotion that brings people together when the fire doesn't burn for both. People who grew up with no affection seldom know how to offer it. You cannot force the fire to burn, but you can teach people tenderness."

He kissed her and left.

He was gone before the sun rose on a new day.

That night, Evred was surprised when Hadand did not part from him with her friendly "Good night," as had become their custom, but invited him into her bed.

He stood there looking down at his hands, thinking of all the work he'd set aside for the night watch. But he chanced to look up, and there was Hadand with her own hands pressed together in a way he had not seen for a long time.

An unpleasant wash of guilt chilled his nerves. When he drew in a cautious sniff, he did not catch the distinctive astringency of the gerda root that women took when they wished to conceive a child. So she had stopped drinking the steeped herb and he had not been aware.

He looked up gravely and said, "I have been remiss. I beg your pardon."

Remiss? There was no sense in arguing the word. She would take him as he was, just as she'd promised when he'd come home to find his father dead and offered himself, saying *All I ask for myself is truth between us*.

And so he came to her bed once again. Afterward, when he customarily rose to depart, she said, "Please stay, Evred. At least try, just to rest, like we did when we were small."

He hesitated. Hadand asked so little of him. He assented, and to his surprise, he did fall asleep, and stayed asleep through the night, waking just before dawn to the comforting stroke of her fingers through his hair, just as she had done when they were children.

Chapter Thirty-five

JEJE braced the tiller against her hip as she eyed the two faces before her.

Mutt and Nugget glared at one another, bodies leaning into the slant of *Vixen*'s deck.

Jeje flicked her gaze down the length of the scout. Three of the five new ship rats were busy forward, chattering with one another as they tended sail under the direction of Loos Fisher.

The allies had waited until they had a strong, steady wind out of the northeast, but at dawn, when the Chwahir sailed across the front of Jaro Harbor shooting fire arrows at the anchored Venn fleet, the wind had inexorably shifted, bringing rain.

First things first. "You two," Jeje said, "are going to sit here tending stinking fish oil unless you make a truce. And convince me it's real."

"But he's been acting like a—"

"But I'm first mate now! Fox says, after the next battle—"

"I'll deal with Fox," Jeje cut in. "He's let the two of you divide up the old ship rats in your stupid feud. Maybe he thinks it's funny. I don't. You're going to get along, or it's fish oil duty. I don't care how good you were in that attack off Llyenthur, or how much you think you deserve a jump."

They did deserve a jump—a promotion—and they had been good when a blizzard had driven the Fox Banner Fleet to the north side of the strait, and ships swarmed out of the old Venn-rebuilt harbor at Llyenthur to attack them.

Mutt sidled a glance at Nugget. He was still amazed at what she'd done, swinging around upside down from *Sable*'s tall masts, switching from line to line with a coil or two around her knees as she used her single hand to whap enemies from above.

But he wasn't going to say so, not after the way Nugget had been strutting on *Sable,* with Captain Eflis laughing and cheering her on between loud, smacking kisses.

Nugget fumed every time she thought about how amazing Mutt had been, commanding the *Skimit* so that it knifed between two of the attackers with a handsbreadth to spare, cut booms out to rake the rigging of the biggest one. Why hadn't *she* been on board, in the tops?

Oh, she was glad to have been on *Sable* when those two galleys boarded from either end. She'd discovered that a belaying pin was as good as a knife. Maybe better. With a knife you had to slash fast because you were swinging and had nothing to brace against, but whacking a wooden mallet on the skull of somebody trying to gut a shipmate sent you arcing away fast, if you knew how to control the arc. And she did. After all that practice, she did!

That knowledge brought her chin up. "If *some people* think they're too good for *other* people who might have made some mistakes, well, I'm not going to talk bad about *them*, like *some people* do to others."

Mutt scowled, sure there was an insult somewhere in all that. Jeje ignored Nugget and gauged the speed of the lumbering Chwahir roundhulls doing their best to get away (slow) the Venn in their formidable arrowhead (fast and getting faster), and her own speed (very fast). Though she was the fastest craft in view, she might not be fast enough for this crazy maneuver.

She checked the choppy gray sea, the cloud-streaked sky, and the arched prows of the Venn warships just emerging from a band of heavy rain. They looked like plunging dragons with wings outspread. "Right. Get out the flat pans. You two are on oil duty."

"Oil!" Mutt protested. "The ship rats can do oil!"

"Eflis promised me I can—"

"If," Jeje said as she tightened her grip, "you yap any more, it's going to be for the next five battles. We're coming up on *Death* next, so I can report. Shall I have Fox put you two in the hold instead?"

The sounds of two scampering pairs of feet were her answer. Jeje swung round. *Vixen*'s tiller vibrated in her grip, sending shudders up through her bones and skull, making her grin so wide her teeth chilled. It was more exhilarating than wine or sex or fire to be at sea again, driving every stitch of sail to that trembling point between speed and disaster, running against a clear enemy, and, best of all, she was aboard her beloved *Vixen* while doing it.

It would be beyond best if Tau were here, but she was used to that wish. *He'll be back. Just like the sun. I have to make sure I'm alive to see him.*

The sky changed dramatically as a last, determined winter wind tumbled under the warmer air of spring and once again the Venn were shrouded by thick rain.

The roll and thump of barrels recalled her attention. From just forward of the mast a few paces away, on the other side of *Vixen*'s enormous, curving mainsail, came Nugget's voice. ". . . no, they can't just suddenly appear. If there were hundreds of Venn, well, Fox and Eflis would have seen them coming up the strait."

"But th–th–they c–c–came s–s–suddenly at Tr–tr–ad Var–ruh–ruh–adhe." The boy's intermittent stutter was always worse when he talked about home. "C–c–come dawn. Th–there they were. On the wuh–wuh–water. Far as you could s–s–see."

For a moment everyone, including Jeje, considered how that must have felt that terrible morning. Then Jeje sniffed and swiveled to eye the seascape as the wind whined a steady note in the rigging. If it shifted around to the south . . .

Nugget said, "The Venn woulda had to come down last summer. You can't sail a fleet against the east wind."

"But *we* did," one of the older rats said.

"That's tacking," Nugget instructed. "Haven't you

learned anything? Our sails can tack back and forth, north side to south side, but the Venn? When the wind's strong enough, they can tack and tack, but they get pushed right back to the west."

"So why do they have the square sails?" the older boy asked.

Nugget was quite certain he'd been taught, but she remembered her ship rat days, when she paid attention to maybe one in five things the oldsters droned on about.

She also loved showing off. A trifle self-consciously, she said, "Those big square sails are best at deep water sailing. They rig different because they sail different. We can get much tighter up into the wind but we have to hug the coasts. You go deep water, and next thing you know, people are singing 'Leahan Anaer,' only you don't know it because you're lost at sea."

Mutt straightened from tying down a shallow iron pan on an ironwork support, and saw the tight-lipped fright in the stuttering boy's face. Did his family sing the 'Leahan Anaer' for his parents, vanished somewhere at sea between pirate attacks and Venn? He was the one who'd been crying at nights. No wonder the Marlovans wanted to be rid of him, Mutt thought impatiently, then he moved away from the pans, goaded by memories of his own.

"If they tried coming up the strait in winter, they'd wallow worse than those Chwahir tubs," Nugget went on, always glad to have an audience. "I sure hope the wind doesn't veer anymore'n it has. Look at the pickle-butts shifting to cut 'em off if they turn southward out to sea."

"*W–wuh–we* have *h–h–horses*." The boy seemed to find comfort in that. "*Much* faster than shuh–shuh–ships."

"Well, they're no use at sea," Nugget pointed out.

Jeje heard a chuckle from Viac Fisher as he tested the tautness of the sail and grinned. The tall, tough, hawk-nosed Fisher brothers had become *Vixen*'s regulars. They were Venn-descended Gerandans—which was why Inda renamed them "Fisher" for their earlier trade—but Jeje had discovered they'd never been loyal to their ancestors. In fact, they had only just stopped the habit of spitting over the rail whenever the Venn were mentioned.

Loos Fisher called from the mast, "*Death* just a finger off the bow." He dropped lightly to the deck.

Jeje swung the tiller, the Fisher brothers shifting sail without having to be told.

The Fox Banner Fleet had been hiding on the west side of the rocky promontory away from Jaro Harbor; the rest of the alliance lay far to the east. Jeje hoped.

Now the *Death* was in the lead, tacking hard to the southeast. Jeje jinked southward to intercept *Death*, and the wind hit with a smack on the other side of *Vixen*'s hull, nearly lifting them out of the water. The Fishers whooped and the rats shrilled in delight and alarm. With the wind abaft, *Vixen* was practically flying.

A tousled fair head popped up from below a moment later. "Are we sinking?" cried the youngest, sister to the stutterer.

Jeje laughed as she peered through her glass and spotted the Fox Banner capital ships hull up on the horizon. "No." She smacked the back of her thigh. "Got the wind right where we like it! Gotta report what I saw."

Nugget ducked under the mainsail yard, her frizzled cloud of sun-bleached hair blowing back from her brow. "Think he'll let us thread the needle?"

"Might have to," Jeje yelled, though she knew that being forced to sail between these tight, disciplined Venn meant they'd end up as fireships. Nobody believed they could outfight the bigger, well-drilled and disciplined Venn warships.

They had to get to the weather side of the Venn.

On the *Death*, two men reinforced Fox at the helm. They watched sea, sky, and horizon as the *Death* surged forward, masts aslant. If they kept the wind amidships they might make it, but if the oncoming storm veered to blow from the southeast, even fast schooners couldn't sail straight into the wind.

Barend ran aft, his sharp-boned face ruddy from the brisk air and occasional splashes of water from the surging sea. Despite the cold he had a crimson kerchief twisted around his broad brow to catch the sweat. He'd been driving ship and crew to their limits since they emerged from hiding beyond the promontory west of Jaro Harbor. At dawn it had been all hands: luff, reef, jib-sails in and out, sails belling, tightening, flashing in near synchrony, Fibi the Delf bringing the best out of *Cocodu* to match Barend's demands of the *Death* as they fought to get between the chasing Venn and the Chwahir, as promised.

"Damn Chwahir are slow," Barend commented, peering eastward—straight into cloud and rain.

Fox finished the thought. "Won't matter if our loyal allies are in position. Signal! I want *Vixen*—"

"Already here," Barend commented, glass to his eye. "Look behind you. She's flying in on us there on the weather beam."

Vixen ranged up on their lee side shortly after.

Fox leaned against the stern rail, smiling down at Jeje, whose dramatic line of black brow made her mood clear. "Well?" he prompted.

"The Venn are in that band o' rain, hot after the Chwahir. We'd better put on some speed." Jeje scowled eastward. Was Deliyeth out there, or holding back?

Barend cursed as he tipped his head. "Wind might shift to the southeast."

"Then why are we waiting around?" Jeje's deep voice roughened. "You already got Fangras shifted, I just saw that comin' up. We better get ahead, or we're all going to have to thread the needle. Give me *Sable* and her pack o' schooners, that way you can use Fangras to protect the Chwahir's sterns if Deliyeth hangs back to see if we get cut up first."

"You think so too, eh?" Fox lifted a shoulder. "Take Eflis, then. She'd like nothing better than to attack an entire squadron of Venn with only your little boat as backup."

From her position abaft *Death,* Eflis watched *Vixen* through her glass. The scout slanted at a dangerous angle, speeding so fast white water arced a lacy feather behind. Eflis could barely make out the small crew standing at the high rail to stiffen the scout a bit more, the barrels of fish oil they'd been gathering for months lashed behind them.

Jeje did not slow when she neared, just cut across the bow, then splashed down the weather side. Jeje yelled up toward the captain's deck, "They're in that rain! We gotta top the needle, thread it if we can't make it!"

Eflis let out a whoop, then called to her flag mid, "Signal! All my ships, arrow formation, on me! Barrels at the ready!"

Crew swarmed above, putting on every stitch *Sable* could carry, in a long-practiced maneuver that made this the fastest capital schooner in the eastern seas. Eflis whooped again as the deck lifted under her feet.

A sweet tinkle of braid chimes—Sparrow was there. Not just there, but wanting Eflis to know she was there. Sparrow usually moved around noiselessly.

As the *Sable* plunged into the white-topped waves, sending cold spray down the deck, they stood shoulder to shoulder, Eflis laughing aloud as she tended the wheel herself. When it came time to fight, she'd roam the ship as she always did, but now, she needed to feel the pull of wood and wind and water, taking *Sable* to just the edge of snapping a mast, or broaching to . . .

Vixen sailed past the stern. Nugget's curls streamed as she kissed her fingers to Eflis, then cut her eyes to the right to see how lean, dark-haired young Mutt was taking her extravagant gesture.

Eflis flickered her fingers from the wheel to wave back, then gripped the spokes again.

"Eflis." Sparrow's voice was nearly lost on the wind.

"Aw, Sparrow, you know why she's doing that." Eflis laughed. "A few kisses, me teaching and her flirting, isn't that fair exchange? Heyo, look starboard. Venn prows coming out of the cloudburst, what a tight formation."

Sparrow's hands tightened on the binnacle awning. How alive Eflis was, how strong, how beautiful! At fourteen Sparrow had been a runaway, talking herself aboard a suspicious trader as a deck scrub. Two attacks later, she ended up wounded on the shore of Khanerenth, where she met Eflis, whose family had lost everything in the revolution. The girls had taken to pirating in revenge against the new king.

Sparrow never thought about the future; life with Eflis had seemed like endless youth, love, adventure lived at a dashing pace under the threat of sudden death. Then one summer morning she'd been shocked by the lines crinkling the corners of Eflis' eyes, the faint blurring beside her mouth and under her chin revealed in that clear light. Time and age were even more inexorable than enemies, because no matter how fast you moved, how well you drilled, you could not fight them.

"It does mean something." Sparrow was surprised when her voice went unsteady. "Kisses mean something."

Eflis flicked a round-eyed glance of surprise, then another, longer glance. "Sparrow? You're not carrying a hate for young Nugget? You *know* I don't mean nothin' by any of 'em, boys or girls."

"Nugget's not the cause. Only a result." Emotion swelled, difficult to define, to catch and hold. "She's young, young as we once were."

Sparrow had always distrusted words. On Toar, where she had come from, people used words as weapons, or as art, for mood, for gain. For fun. Not for the truth.

"But we aren't young anymore," Sparrow said, her voice husky. "Time's against us . . ."

Eflis had been intently watching the angle of the fast-moving armada of Venn ships angling in on the weather side as they pursued the fleeing Chwahir. Her mind streamed with images that flitted by too fast to form full thoughts: wind shifting with the storm brought Venn out, Fox miscalculated? Get there in two waves, maybe Fox figured on that, *why does Sparrow hate time?*

"What are ye wantin', love?" Eflis turned her head. "Deck! Weapons at the ready. Torches at the ready."

Out on the water, the triangle steadily shrank: the Chwahir the base, their round-hulled tubs blundering straight downwind. The Venn in pursuit formed one side of the triangle, and racing close-hauled to the breaking point to intercept the Venn were *Vixen* in the lead, the *Sable* and the Fox Banner Fleet all in a line.

They had to cross in front of the Venn to make the plan work or their smoke would just blow across them, and their allies—supposedly coming up from behind The Fangs from the east—would be seen and pounced on by the Venn.

"Topgallants," Eflis called.

Frightened looks were sent her way; this breeze was too high for three levels of sail.

Eflis kicked off her shoes and spread her stockinged feet on the deck, testing the vibration from keelson to the masts. If they carried away a spar from the press of sail, they'd die. No second chance: the Venn were distinct now.

"Arrow crews aloft!" she cried when the topgallants were sheeted home.

Sable jerked twice, trembled, then up came the bow. It plunged down, sending a wash of water down the deck. Those with torches braced with one hand, the other held up to keep their flames alight. The sail crews scrambled to ease the weather helm—the gathering of water on the lee side which could slow them down.

The ship responded like a sea bird taking flight.

Two cableslengths ahead, *Vixen* had just crossed the tip of the Venn wedge, barely beyond arrow range.

"Screens!" Eflis yelled, and the netting dropped, tenting them, blurring the sea, sky, enemy, and friend alike.

A faint crow from the scout ship carried back, despite the whipping wind cutting across the beam at a sharp angle. Eflis leaned her entire body into the wheel, holding, holding . . . her feet began to slide . . . "Brace!"

Sparrow and her ship master sprang to each side, adding their strength to keep the helm steady despite the massive forces of water and wind torquing the ship from different angles.

"Steady," Eflis shouted as arrows began to zip and hiss through the air overhead: the Venn were not aiming at crew from their extreme range, they were trying to puncture the drum-taut sails in hopes the wind would shred the canvas and the ship would turn up into the wind and founder. "Ready about!"

The command was unnecessary: everyone was in position, hands to the line. Each leaned unconsciously forward, stomachs tightened in an effort to speed the *Sable* a little faster . . .

And the schooner knifed past the point of the Venn arrow. For a moment they stared straight into the enemy formation in all its power. Those great warships, the towers of sail, everyone on station—and this was considered a small reinforcement? *If we ever have to face their entire navy . . .*

Eflis left the thought unfinished. As soon as she caught sight of the starboard side of the Venn flagship she spun the wheel. "Helm down," she yelled, easing the wheel.

Her sail crew, practiced after years of tight maneuvers, eased off the jib sails as the spanker boom hauled amidships.

"Helm's a-lee!" Eflis cried, loving this moment when the

ship was poised in the turn, a desperate situation even without an enemy aiming straight for the hull.

Foresails thrown aback, yards braced up sharp.

"Haul taut!" Yard arms swung. Sails thrummed and bucketed, fighting the line of crew using their entire bodies to get the sails snugged up tight. The little speed *Sable* had lost was made up in surges as each sail filled, held. Now they were running along the outside of the Venn, the wind on the forward beam, spars rigid.

Eflis laughed for joy. "Fire away!"

Already the intense whiff of rotten fish oil whipped past from the *Vixen* ahead; streamers of blue-tinged dark smoke drifted toward the ships forming the tip of the Venn arrowhead.

Along the lee rail Eflis' crew touched their glowing torches to the shallow pans of fish oil, and blue flame rippled and roiled, sending fingers of smoke that increased rapidly into a stinking billow that drifted toward the Venn, obscuring them from sight.

Eflis' fleet followed her in a snake trail, bow to stern, as barrels of oil, hoarded all winter, began to burn.

As the smoke increased, so did the stink, and Eflis turned her nose into her armpit, laughing despite stinging eyes.

"Allies weather-beam. But not very fast," Sparrow said.

Eflis faced eastward into the wind, where—*at last*—the allies appeared, black nicks in the gray cloud, still hull down.

A faint, weird blatting of horns carried down the wind.

"Here they come!" the lookout shouted.

Eflis didn't have to peer into the smoke to know that the Venn had sicced their fastest raiders on them. It was time to walk the deck. Eflis flicked a smile at her ship master, a solid old smuggler she'd met when she first took ship. He stationed himself at the wheel. Eflis grabbed up her cutlass, swinging it to loosen her arms as she leaped down to the deck.

Sparrow followed; she often fought shield beside Eflis. If Eflis died, she had privately vowed that it would be because Sparrow herself had fallen first.

"I'm wanting an anchor against time," Sparrow said, as tiny flickers of fire appeared out of the reek.

"What?" Eflis stuck her fists on her hips, grinning. "Sparrow! Have you been at the wine barrel?"

"If I die." Sparrow's lips tightened. "You'll get all I have. If you die then I will go with you."

Eflis cupped the back of Sparrow's neck, the chiming little braids sliding past her fingers to tinkle against Sparrow's collarbone. She gazed into Sparrow's wide, unblinking dark eyes, the tension shaping those eyes, then kissed her. "So we gotta live."

A weird whirtling sound, like the ululation of coyotes, from high above: a screamer arrow from *Vixen* signaling attackers.

"Defenders to the rails! Fire teams, more smoke! Torch the barrels!" Eflis thumped the helm. "Give us a stagger!"

The first Venn loomed out of the smoke, indistinct and dangerous: a steady stream of arrows zapped across, most fouling on the net, but not all. A short cry and a member of the bow teams above fell dead to the deck. The water teams sprang to drag dead and wounded away as bow teams shot with disciplined speed.

The ship yawed into a stagger and pulled away from the powerful Venn raiders who fought against the wind.

"Smoke!" *Sable*'s defenders lit more pans, sending foul-smelling billows of smoke over the Venn.

Crack! A raider emerged from the murk and rammed the stern. The crew staggered, many fell but scrambled up into defensive lines, weapons gripped tightly. Horn-helmed Drenga swarmed over the stern, roaring; the pair of girls at the bow kicked over their barrel of oil just as the Venn reached it, which sent the enemy skidding and sliding just before *Sable*'s defense team smashed into them.

The Venn were big and strong and well-trained, but they were human: they also hated chain mail at sea and could be hacked up like anyone else. *Sable*'s crew, drilled relentlessly by Fox, fought with vicious pirate tactics. The fight surged back and forth, both sides slipping in the slick, fetid oil; with merciless precision the Venn bow teams picked off defenders in the tops, but the defenders shot with unerring accuracy the moment a shield slipped.

The Venn hacked apart four of Eflis' old shipmates, two more dropped from arrows, the defense line wavered, some looking to their captain—what next? what do we do? Eflis vaulted over the capstan to hit the Venn leader feet first.

Then she clenched her cutlass in both hands and swung in attack, her fury rallying her defense line.

Venn and defenders pressed in, writhing with effort, blood-splattered as they hacked and stabbed. The Venn's superior mass gradually gained footing. They were poised to break through and run down the deck, but a large shape slid up on the weather side, stealing *Sable*'s wind. It was *Cocodu* come to the rescue. Fifty figures swung over and dropped onto the deck, Dasta at the lead.

"Hullo, Eflis! Smell the pickle juice?"

He dashed by, his fighters shrieking as they attacked. The Venn began to fall in rapid numbers under that murderous, howling onslaught. When all were dead, *Cocodu* took station behind *Sable* and it, too, began to send blankets of malodorous smoke across the water, obscuring the Venn.

Eflis sat abruptly on an upended bucket. The moment her sword arm dropped the nicks and cuts she'd taken began to sting and throb. She waved old, braid-bearded Collza, her healer, off. "Crew first . . ."

And then she saw Sparrow lying on the deck, her chime-woven braids fanning around her head. Her right arm was held close, her clothes dark-soaked with gore.

Waves of glitter and dark danced in Eflis' eyes as Collza and his aides bent over her.

The lookout screamed, "Here they come, straight off the bow!"

Eflis lurched to her feet, swept up her weapon, shoved one of the aides out of the way.

Collza looked up irritably, then his face changed when he saw the death wish in his captain. " 'S all right." His voice was a dry croak, but he strained to be heard. "She's alive. Bad cut along the ribs. Knot behind her ear. Alive, cap'n!"

Eflis spun away, dizzy with relief. Someone held out the dipper from an ensorcelled bucket. She gulped down water.

Two, three steps forward and a pair of Venn scouts sailed down either side.

Before the first one could close with *Sable,* the pirate trysail *Wind's Kiss* loomed out of the murk and rammed straight into the scout, sending splinters tumbling through the air.

Then Tcholan roared an order from the trysail's captain's deck, and *Sable*'s helmsman spun the wheel, sail crews hauling yardarms around before the two ships could collide. That left the other Venn scout sailing between the schooner and the trysail—right into a hailstorm of fire arrows.

"More a'coming!"

Eflis ran forward, waving her cutlass overhead. "Boarder repel team, to me!" Over her shoulder, "Signal for backup!"

The flags jerked up to the foremast, but Jeje had already seen the *Sable*'s situation and sent up the signal flags, drawing anyone in the Fox Banner Fleet who was near and not already in a death duel themselves.

As was *Cocodu*. They all saw Dasta go down defended by his crew. Jeje turned fiercely burning eyes aft to meet the angry gazes of Mutt and Nugget.

"Go!" she yelled.

They'd already prepared. The ship rats were left to tend the foul smoke as Nugget expertly whirled a hooked rope, sending it high into *Cocodu*'s rigging. She whirled up, knife out, and began swinging about, slashing down at Venn from above.

Mutt lunged from the rail and scrambled up *Cocodu*'s side, then *Vixen* was past, sailing across *Cocodu*'s bow so Jeje could see in the other direction . . . and find *Death*.

On the *Death*, Fox smacked the glass to his eye, cursing steadily at the dark, the smoke, the lack of—

A wash of rain and the glow of fires cleared briefly, and— was that a gap to the west? But one could hear whirtlers with the fleet spread out in a line, obscured by smoke and attackers.

Here was *Vixen* racing under his lee.

Fox remembered Inda saying, *You look around for Jeje and she's always right there. Sometimes I think she knows my plans before I do.*

Jeje peered up. Were those tear tracks on her face or sweat? "Chwahir aren't far," she shouted, her hoarse voice carrying over the noise. "If they tack north of west, they could squeeze the Venn through that gap."

"Go tell them." Fox waved a hand, revealing a rip over the back of his arm and the ruby gleam of blood.

Jeje knew him well enough by now not to mistake that

drawl for indifference. He only drawled when he was in a white fury.

"Loos! Make sail for the Chwahir flagship."

The Venn were outnumbered by a magnitude of three, but that knowledge just increased their ferocity.

A detachment chased the slower Chwahir. Fox led a line to the rescue, watching impatiently through his glass as the Venn *drakans* closed in pairs on either side of the Chwahir, using their cut booms to sweep the rigging. The weakened shrouds inevitably caused masts to topple and fall, leaving the ships helpless against the Venn raiders following on, crowded with crews of Drenga poised to board fore and aft.

Fox motioned his bigger ships to surround the Venn raiders before their Drenga could board the Chwahir.

Though most of the allies were smaller than the *drakan* warships, they were also faster or the Venn might have finally driven them off. The cost would have been even higher than both sides paid had not the Venn commander sent a message by scroll-case to Oneli Southern Fleet Commander Durasnir. He woke to the news that the reinforcement was vastly outnumbered. Were they to fight to the last man?

Durasnir had no intention of losing any more of his Oneli or Drenga to futile efforts. "Send an order at once to disengage and to withdraw all the way back to Nathur, at the west end of Drael. Await orders."

The wind remained steady in the east, which enabled the Fox Banner Fleet's oily smoke to so befoul the Venn they could only find one another via their navigators. Fox's allies then began systematically surrounding the Venn and setting them on fire.

Blurp, blurp, muhooooghhh! From across the water the Venn signal horns sounded like bulls in pain.

The signal caused a shift: longboats lowered over the sides of the burning Venn ships, and men dropped in. Abandoning ship!

Fox sent a whirtler up to cease fighting, but only his fleet obeyed. Some of the allies harried Venn until they nearly smashed on the rocks, the Chwahir tried to set fire to the retreating longboats, and when those were too fast, sent arrows into the men crowding them.

When the last of the Venn vanished into the smoky darkness, the allies began to form up in a ragged line behind the mass of burning ships. Aboard the Chwahir ships and the Fox Banner Fleet, discipline was temporarily gone as the noise of triumph spread throughout all the allies. They'd won! They'd beaten the Venn!

As Jeje carried Fox from ship to ship on inspection, he watched his allies silhouetted against the fiery glow of smoldering war, small figures dancing about.

When Fox returned from his tour of the Fox Banner Fleet, he found the *Death*'s crew was busy cleaning up damage under the narrowed eyes of Barend, who walked back and forth.

"Report?" Barend asked.

Fox surveyed the *Death* from deck to masts before he spoke. "*Swift* needs a tow. Bad damage, and there's maybe a quarter of his crew still on their feet. Swift himself is unconscious, not sure if he'll live to morning. Leg smashed when he led a team warding a Venn cut boom. Four of Fangras' followers sank. Fangras died just after I climbed on board, crew mostly dead, but I sent over the boats of survivors from *Catspaw* and *Wolf Wind*." He paused, hand tight on the rail. "Fibi the Delf died, along with her repel boarders, but they held just long enough for *Silverdog* to get there. Dasta's still alive. Barely." His voice dropped, for he liked Dasta. "If he makes it to morning, he might survive. Though I don't know if he'd want to." He lifted his voice again, aware of all the listening ears. "Prepare for sail." He vanished into the cabin to tend his own wounds and change his clothes.

When the decks were clear, the ship steady under a goose-winged mizzen and a reefed topsail, Barend dismissed the off-duty watch to sleep or celebrate. Several of the younger members began dancing on the capstan as others banged wooden mugs on the deck, the rail, the longboats in time to raucous singing in two or three languages.

Barend walked to the captain's deck, rubbing his neck. Evred's locket had vanished during one of the fights, leaving a gash where the metal chain had ripped his skin. When he saw blood dripping down his hand, he twisted his sash around his palm. The sash was ruined anyway.

Fox emerged from the cabin, looking about with faint approval at the gradual reappearance of order. "Well?"

Barend moved to the stern rail, sweeping his glass in a circle.

Fox turned his way. "There's only one reason the Venn would retreat like that."

"I suppose you aren't going to say 'Because they were beaten.' " In the golden glow of the distant fires, Barend's smoke-smeared face was wry.

Fox lifted his chin. "Custom maintains they fight to the death except when ordered to retreat and regroup. That means they intend to come back for another fight."

Barend's eyes widened, reflecting the many fires spread over the sea. "Tonight? Tomorrow? Half their fleet is in flames."

"I don't know when." Fox tipped his head back toward their own fleet. Not a single ship had escaped damage. "I want to think it through. Let's set sail for Freedom Island before Deliyeth and her good citizens get the bright idea of ridding themselves of pirates next."

Barend leaned on the rail, fingering his neck. "Not arguing. I'm all for Freedom Island. We can repair and rebuild. Yes, and train. But what are you going to think out? You know what the Venn will do next?"

"No idea. Except that they're sure to have a defense against smoke ships next time. Have to think out how Ramis has been right about everything. So far." He'd told Barend a little of what Ramis had said, when he showed him the *Knife*, waiting in a secluded cove.

Barend's thin brows shot up. "He can see into the future?"

"No. Said he can't. I believe him. It's more that he knew where the pieces in the game would move."

"So?" Barend winced and rubbed his neck. "What? You want to figure out the next move?"

"I'm going to figure out the game."

Chapter Thirty-six

ABYARN Erkric's teeth ached. When the ache built to little licks of flame through the backs of his eyes, he consciously unclenched his teeth and loosened his jaw.

Below, silken ribbons described sinuous patterns in the air as the black-clad hel dancers tumbled with eerie grace, lithe figures shrouded to be genderless as they were supposed to be invisible. The symbols they twirled and fluttered and flashed signified place, time, mountains, water, wings, castles. Ships. Above them, the rich, sonorous voice of the unseen skalt intoned the long verses that the audience saw enacted below.

The king sailed out a-viking, crossing world to world . . .

Erkric checked the king, in whose unblinking eyes tiny reflections leaped and twirled. Erkric had sat through "Drakan Cross Worlds" more times than he could count, but it was safe. And it made sense for Rajnir to request this recital. Kings liked it, everyone knew that: it supported kingship, order. *What could be more steadying than the origins of Venn glory?* he thought as a group of the black dancers leaped through the air behind the captain of the *drakan* fleet, tiny streamers in their hands indicating the Golden Path across worlds.

There must be no repeat of the Loc disaster. His teeth clenched again when he thought of that recital, presented the month after Rajnir's coronation. A ruinously costly performance in verse and dance, wild with thunderstorms and deluges, dragons descending out of the mountains, the words rife with fire and steel: the spectators had been struck into amazement at the time. And when it was over, scarcely had they left Loc Hall, their hoods over their faces, than they began whispering about Rainorec.

He could not blame Loc House. You could not suborn the hel dancers or their skalts. If you asked for a new recital, they gave you a new recital. You paid for it, but could not dictate anything beyond the cost. Loc House had spent ten years' income to celebrate the new king; they had not intended trouble, not after their Hyarl flew his blood eagle on Sinnaborc the summer before the southern fleet's return. After which they all submitted to having their hair cut off, and iron collars fitted round their throats while they waited for Rajnir to be crowned king. Their only desire was to do the new king honor. Every one of them had abased him- or herself most abjectly before the throne, wearing their iron collars and coarse shit-brown thrall tunics, begging for pardon.

Rajnir had to show mercy, or the rest of the Houses would have whispered even more. It was traditional: the new king was offered a great entertainment by those restored to their former glory. Heeding tradition was comforting, it signaled strays returned to the fold, the establishment of proper hierarchy and order.

But the spiderwebs revealed the truth, whispered in halls and behind hands: *The hel skalts and dancers harbingered Rainorec for the new reign.*

Three months a king and already there was trouble. Ever since that damn woman escaped . . .

Pain shot through Erkric's jaw again when he remembered Biddan's bloody corpse. Erkric had been desperate enough to risk making contact with Norsunder, a terrible risk and an even more terrible cost, in case they had taken Biddan's soul, identity, memories. Had Jazsha Signi Sofar talked before she killed Biddan? Why had the torturer let her loose? Was it part of the methods that Erkric had never wanted to hear any details of?

But all Yeres of Norsunder did was stand there in the gateway to the Garden of the Twelve and laugh and laugh, her laughter still ringing in Erkric's head when he woke from the resulting faint, with blood crusted in his ears. And nothing to show for his effort.

He stirred impatiently. Though he had access to the king's chambers at last, how could he get the old magic dismantled, and his own spells put in place? He had not counted on having to constantly mind Rajnir, and keep him away from everyone else, plus see to the enormous load of king's duties—not to mention the queen's duties—as he'd fended off the Houses' offers of royal partners. Who would have thought the damned people would have so many civil cases built against one another waiting for a queen to judge?

A buzz against his hip: scroll-case. A warning shot through him. He never let the thing out of his sight or physical contact anymore. He still did not know how much that damned Valda had learned . . .

Leaning back to keep Rajnir between himself and any prying eyes among the Hyarls in the first tier, he eased the scroll-case out of his pocket. He thumbed the catch and stared down at the paper lying in it.

> *Jaro fleet lost. Durasnir sent order to retreat, fall back to Nathur to await further orders.*

Pain again. Erkric unclenched his teeth. Another disaster. And Durasnir issuing orders! Of course it was within his realm of duty, but those "further orders"?

Those must come from the king. Not from Durasnir, whom everyone watched. He spoke the right words, but were they empty? Yes, they were empty, Erkric thought in disgust. The more people gabbled about Drenskar and Honor and Ydrasal, the more they meant for everyone else to be observant. Or to hear them being observant.

There were two threats to Rajnir's kingship: Valda and Durasnir.

Erkric knew with a liar's conviction that the southern fleet commander's oaths and promises were empty. You say what you have to say and watch for weakness.

Unfortunately, dig as he might, Erkric had not found a

scrap of evidence of Durasnir taking part in any treasonous talk or he'd be picked bones up on Sinnaborc by now. Durasnir was so powerful there had to be not only treason spoken, but believable witnesses to hear it. There could be no more disasters like Signi Sofar's trial.

Durasnir was suspicious. Erkric was certain of that from the stiff manner in which Durasnir handled himself around the new king, an astonishing contrast to his avuncular, even paternal, fondness for Rajnir in days of old. Erkric was also certain that, just as much as he needed proof against Durasnir's treason that would be strong enough to convince the Houses so did Durasnir seek proof that Rajnir was not himself.

Erkric turned his attention back to the stage, but he did not see the black-clad men and women symbolizing the *drakan* ships crossing worlds. Irritation made him long to be alone. So much to do! He needed to be three people: one to guard Rajnir and provide the signs for suitable responses, one to be alert to the machinations of Durasnir and his like, and the third to remove the old wards over the king's rooms and replace them with Erkric's own. If only he could get Rajnir away . . .

Away. Out of the Twelve Towers. But it could not seem a retreat because a young king desiring isolation right after his coronation would be seen by all as an act of weakness, of hiding. His leaving the Twelve Towers had to be perceived as an act of power.

If only Goerael would contrive another uprising! But things there were disgustingly quiet—

As Erkric gazed impatiently at the fluttering ribbons symbolizing the Golden Tree, an idea bloomed. Oh, what could be more perfect? Just as the first king crossed the world under the banner of Ydrasal, so the new king would restore his empire under the Royal Banner.

The king shall go a-viking, just as in days of old.

No one could fault that, not even Durasnir!

Erkric could shift back and secure the king's suite (which would supposedly be sealed) while he was thought to be in Rajnir's shipboard cabins. It had worked quite well during the attempted invasion—about the only thing that *had* worked.

With a pleasure inverse to the irritation of the past three

months—the past three years—Erkric envisioned the throne room, Rajnir seated on the throne in white and silver beneath the banner of kingship, the Golden Tree. And Stalna Hyarl Fulla Durasnir kneeling on the stone of the dais, bending his stiff neck before the invisible torc of the king's will as he became Oneli Stalna, commander of the entire fleet.

How long did it take to ready the southern fleet when they went south the first time? Erkric thought back to the chief shipwright saying to the old king, "It will take three years to properly equip ships and men . . ."

I'll give him one year to raise the entire navy.

That would keep the troublemaking Houses busy, and in a year's time—a quiet year for Erkric, so he could concentrate on what must be done—there would be a magnificent launch under the Golden Tree banner. Then the Oneli could spend another year—or two or three—regaining what they never should have lost in the first place.

Erkric chuckled.

And if a fleet commander couldn't somewhere along the way suffer a heroic death in battle, what good was a glorious war?

PART TWO

Chapter One

FNOR saw herself in a dream.

She was a child again, looking out the window of her small bedchamber at the deep blue of twilight, yet the sunlight poured in golden shafts through the window, warm as milk, glistening like a beeswax candle flame.

"I am dreaming," she thought, and in the dream she wept.

The sunbeam brought a stream of memories charged with wonder: the cool water steeped with herbs poured through her hair after a good scrubbing, drenching her with the scent of rain-fresh leaves; the warmth of the sun on her cheeks and neck while she crawled determinedly through chin-high young summer grass; the pleasant buzz of her skin while quiet, patient hands rubbed rough toweling over her.

"I am a babe again." But she was not a babe. Instead she saw a babe, heard its kitten noises, smelled the sweet scent of a baby's head . . .

"Fnor."

The image broke, and she drifted upward through layers of blue cloud, up and up until she broke the surface, and opened eyes that stung with tears.

Buck looked down at her, his sun-streaked yellow hair hanging tousled around his shoulders, his one hand gripping the rope they'd rigged over the bed. "Fnor?"

Question without question. "Did you dream of a babe?" she asked, a chill prickling the backs of her arms.

Buck's eyes widened, his pupils dark. "I can hear it," he whispered. "The spell."

Fnor closed her eyes, and there were the words, just beyond hearing, but she knew, she *knew,* if she put tongue to them, they would come.

"Let's tell the others." She laughed, and sat up. "You or I?"

"Tell Cherry-Stripe. He'll rouse the house." With practiced, unthinking habit Buck swung himself to the side of the bed, where his crutch rested against the bedstead.

"Good idea." Fnor ran barefoot toward the door leading to the bath stairway, then paused and looked back. "Put on your House tunic."

Buck's head canted in question, then he flashed a quick, rare grin. "Are you going to put on your House robe?"

She laughed to see him happy. Resignation he'd achieved, after a long and determined battle. Sometimes moments of contentment, after a small victory, such as crossing the castle with no help but his crutch. Staying on horseback with the aid of the saddle the Runners had spent an entire season making and remaking.

She said, "I shall indeed put on my House robe, since I won't be lying in that bed in nightgear." She paused, afraid that daylight and sanity would take away the dream, as always happened to dreams, and indeed, the scraps of image vanished, but the joy remained. "You and me—we're going to . . ."

She groped toward her stomach, then turned her hands out helplessly, not sure how to express it.

Buck said, "Get ourselves a baby." And shook his head in wonder. "I know it happens. But I can't understand it." Clack-hop, clack-hop, off to the men's bath.

She took the fastest bath of her life, but when she strode into the hall, still braiding her wet hair, she discovered everyone nearly ready, some still running about. Even the oldsters were in festival moods. Women brought out herb-stored baby clothing, and old Hasta Marlo-Vayir—who had ridden over to the castle two days before to help Buck look over the yearlings—proudly helped carry from storage the wooden cradle his sons had slept in.

The sun was strengthening over the castle, the air warming to summer heat as everyone gathered in the hall before the dais.

"What do we do? Where do we do it?" Buck asked, hitching himself up the steps.

"You take hands." The stonemason's wife motioned Buck and Fnor together. "You take hands, and you'll feel the baby come when you finish the words."

"Come?" Cherry-Stripe asked, pausing on a step just behind his brother. "From where?"

"The air."

"Ohhhhh," everyone breathed out the word, and Mran grinned, her thin, triangular Cassad face catlike with happiness.

Fnor closed her fingers tightly around Buck's single hand, and Uncle Scrapper set the cradle below, for added good measure. Cherry-Stripe stood so close to Buck he breathed on his shoulder, just in case Buck needed balance, though he seldom did anymore; after a quick look around, Buck cleared his throat, his eyes on his wife. He, too, had had a strange dream, mostly memories from boyhood, then false memories of Fnor with a great belly. He'd known even inside the dream that that was false, that Fnor had never been pregnant.

Whoever made this babe, he's welcome, Buck thought, because he was so certain it would be a he—girls were rare in his family. He had no Marlo-Vayir aunts back three generations. If Fnor had taken a lover and chewed gerda—and Buck had once tried to talk her into it—that babe would not have been his blood. But it would have been his boy or girl just the same. And so would this one, wherever it came from.

The words whispered inside his head and he repeated them, Fnor's voice higher than his, echoing the words. And then the air over their hands snapped with light shimmers, just like the ensorcelled buckets when you dipped something into them, and Fnor gasped, her body feeling just for a moment as if someone had pushed her through a window, but there was no pain.

Buck almost fell forward, he was so surprised to feel weight on his hand.

He was not aware of Cherry-Stripe's steel-band fingers gripping his arm as he stared down at the naked baby boy wriggling in Fnor's stiff hands. Fnor stared, mouth agape.

"Don't drop him, now," Mran said briskly.

Fnor clasped the babe to her bosom, and shook with a sudden, deep sob.

Buck's stare was as stark with fear and wonder as his wife's. "He's got Uncle Scrapper's ears." He pointed to the tiny earlobes, miniatures of his uncle's.

"What do I do?" Fnor asked, looking around wildly. "I don't have milk!"

"You will, if you suckle," the stonemason's wife said. "Or you can use a wet nurse."

"Mran asked me to come inside," came a voice from behind the crowd of servants, Riders, and Runners.

People parted, and there was a farm wife, her new babe cradled against her hip.

Fnor had refused to ask about these things because it hurt too much. Now she looked around bewildered, amazed, so full of joy she laughed, and then sobbed again, wiping her eyes impatiently on her shoulder. The unfamiliar little weight resting against her breast moved, and her hands tightened.

"Name Day dinner tonight," Hasta roared, still plenty strong in voice, if raspy. "What're ye going to name him?"

"Hasta, of course," Buck said, and his father reddened in pleasure. "That is, Hastred."

"You better show me what to do," Fnor said to the farm wife. She nicked her head toward Buck, his brother, and Mran. "Show us all."

"Let's get him dressed first," said the guide.

"Where'd he come from?" whispered Cherry-Stripe. "How is it possible?"

Buck just shook his head. He stared at those familiar earlobes, and the straight brows so much like Fnor's, until tears blinded him.

He was unaware of the slight, acrid stink of burning drifting in the air, but the kitchen people weren't. "My biscuits!" the baker cried and whirled around.

But her son appeared through the back entrance. "Burned," he said, in his slow, precise way. "Burned to hot rocks."

Which was how the new baby got the nickname that stuck to him all his life: Hot Rock Marlo-Vayir.

Hadand did not get the news of the new Marlo-Vayir laef until the end of summer; Fnor was afraid to write letters until she was sure the baby would not vanish the way he had come, even though she could see that the stonemason's sturdy boy was still very much extant, especially when he chased the hens in the yard.

Hadand told Tdor, after some time alone to get control of the sharpness of yearning and jealousy. Fnor had described everything, including the strange dream. Hadand forced herself to concentrate on each word, though the hurt was profound. She had no child, and no dreams of a child, though she was again grimly downing gerda each day.

Evred continued to come to her, though intermittently; there were still the nights he fell asleep at his desk or he closed himself in his suite. *Just not the right time,* Tesar, Hadand's First Runner, said recently to Hadand after she woke up to discover she needed to use the Waste Spell for her monthly courses. Another missed chance.

But she was young, strong, and very busy, she told herself briskly. In the past, clan chieftains (then kings) didn't even think about heirs until their forties to prevent young strong sons from wanting their fathers' place before their fathers were ready to give it up. She had plenty of years ahead, and the later the better.

Then she went out to tell Tdor.

Tdor listened while getting ready to join Mistress Gand in monitoring the progress of teams of girls trying to sneak into the castle. They sat in the highest tower watching the girls' progress through glasses. Tdor had declared all tunnels off-limits, an order whose reception she had observed closely. Some girls were surprised. Most heard it indifferently or semaphored question around, *What tunnels?* But a few had revealed sharp disappointment and Lies Ola-Vayir, young cousin to Starand, had looked around shiftily, encountered Tdor's gaze, and studied her fingertips. *Some-*

thing to remember, Tdor thought. *If there's ever trouble in this city, it won't come from an army trying to batter down the thick walls. It will come from inside.*

Out loud, she said, "Fnor Marlo-Vayir has a son."

"Huh." Mistress Gand swung her glass the other way. "There's Lendan, coming across the roof. Just as I thought. Fnor, eh? Hope she has a girl next. I'd like to see Fnor's girl here."

No one says that about the Ola-Vayirs, Tdor thought. *How much of personality is in blood and how much in how we are raised?*

At watch's end Tdor made her way to the Harskialdna suite, where she found Inda hunched over a book. Before she could speak the bell high above them clanged, echoed soon by all the city bells. Two clangs, and then Inda said, jerking his thumb at the western window, "Look. Sun's already setting at Lastwatch bell. I can't believe summer's near done and it's time for the Banner Game." He set aside the book. "Summer Games! They'll go home, and before we know it, time for Convocation. This year has gone so fast! I wasn't there for Convocation last year. This year Buck will come," he added with satisfaction. Then he paused, gaze distant.

He moved toward the door, as he often did just after sunset if he didn't have duty. Tdor knew where he was going and why, and usually left him to his tour alone, especially as half the time Evred encountered him somewhere along the long sentry walk in order to converse privately.

But the tilt of Inda's head, the pucker of the scar across his forehead, caused her to say, "Want company?"

His smile was enough of an answer. They left by their private tower entrance. Inda's way of dealing with all those doors had been to have some of them taken off so they didn't bang into one another. Since it was just the two of them living in the front part of the suite right now, it worked all right.

As always, that reminded Tdor of Signi. She stole a quick look at Inda, who walked with his head down. There was no logical connection, but the heart makes its own logic: she sensed in Inda's pensive mood that Signi was on his mind, though the Venn mage had been gone a year and a half.

Maybe his mood was because she'd been gone a year and a half. "Inda? Are you unhappy?"

"I've never been happier," he said, hands flicking outward. "Not since we were ... little." The words "at home" had been consciously excised from speech by them both, but they had yet to stop them from forming inside the head. Though they'd nearly vanquished the habit. *Home is where your heart lives,* so said the songs, and they knew they were very happy. "The worst problem I have in the academy is Honeyboy. Maybe the fault is mine, not his, because Gand says 'Begin every problem as if it's new,' and I do. No dragging in all the stupid stuff he did last year, or last time. But it doesn't work. And I keep trying to find the ... the Cama in him, and he just stares at me like I'm yapping Dock Talk. Maybe Fox would do better—"

"Except he can get rid of the Honeyboys," Tdor put in. She tried not to resent Shendan's mysterious brother. She knew it was not Fox's fault that Inda made these comparisons and found himself wanting.

"I know, you keep saying that. True, too. Maybe that's it? Our marines were there because they wanted to be. Academy, so many are there because they're sent."

"You wanted to be in the academy." Tdor remembered how scared she was on Inda's behalf, especially after all Hadand's dire warnings about Evred's horrible uncle. *How true they were, too.*

"Yes, I wanted to be there. Well, but Kepa wanted to be there, too, so that horse won't run."

"You know you can't reduce everyone to a single motivation."

"I know. Speaking of idiots, some of the horsetails are single-minded rock brains, but Lassad's gonna run 'em hard on the game. Knock some of the strut out." He threw his head back. "Never been happier except for a couple of things. You know this problem." He pointed ahead, toward the annex.

They'd walked briskly along the sentry route, saluting men on the outer walls and women on the inner. When they reached the annex perpendicular to the Residence Wing, they paused and looked into the open window, golden-lit, on the opposite side of a private courtyard. The third floor was the long recreation and study room shared by the King's Runners and those training to be scribes and heralds.

There sat little Han Tlen, alone as always. From their vantage, Inda and Tdor could see her busy translating from a scroll. The ruby in her ear winked blood red.

That end of the room was crowded with King's Runner boys studying, wrestling—Inda and Tdor recognized moves from the Fox drills—gathered around something on a table. One boy sat cross-legged on another table, practicing his drumming. They could hear the counterpoint called "second gallop" through the open window; the King's Runners-in-Training played counterpoint to the Guard drummer for Restday.

No one went near the isolated little girl.

At the other end, the scribes, boys and girls, were busy with their own pursuits. Mostly they stayed with their own gender, except for a couple of study groups, and one big, fast, noisy game of cards'n'shards.

"Hadand says she never complains," Tdor said with a sigh.

"I know. I ask Evred about her every week." Inda turned his back on the windows. "I think I hate these earrings," he said suddenly, so low she had to lean down to hear him. "I hate them because I don't understand why people look at them and see glory. I see a . . ." He gestured vaguely. "A glory-shaped hole. In the hole is death. Noddy. Rig. Dogpiss, even. Death, and that stink up in the pass. The only worse thing than that was the stench off Boruin's burning ship. Why can't I see glory? Why can't I feel it? Everybody says I'm at the center of it, but . . ." He jerked his head up, grimacing. "Tdor, am I whining?"

"No." Chill wrung down through her nerves, and her voice turned husky. She cleared her throat. "I don't know why they don't remember the terrible things the way you do, but I think the way they see the earrings has something to do with leadership. They look to you to keep them safe. You don't have that comfort."

"I think sometimes glory has something to do with sex." His head was low now, his voice embarrassed. "Fighting to win."

"You find pleasure in killing?"

Tdor tried to hide her horror, but Inda heard it in her voice. He began walking fast. "It's more the fighting. You don't hold back. You risk everything, so it feels good to be the strongest and fastest, to *win*. The burn is the hottest in the worst battle."

"Could it be a proportionate relief that you are alive so far?" she asked, working hard to comprehend.

"And sex." Inda huffed out a sigh as they dashed through a tower sentry station. "I don't always feel that way. A few times. Last one, on the cliff above the pass, though there's still something wrong with my memory. I felt like two men, because Dun was there. No. Three. Like somebody crowded my mind aside and took over my arm." He flexed his right hand, and winced.

"Inda, that's horrible."

He stopped, right there in the middle of the sentry walk. "The mind thing? Or the sex thing?" He peered anxiously into her torch-lit face, then looked away. "I know the sex feeling when you're fighting ... killing ... is wrong. But it's there. Not just me. Seen it in battle. Not everybody. Some are just scared. Angry. Determined."

Tdor hesitated, the words of rejection, of horror shaping lips and tongue. She felt herself poised on the edge of some new idea—maybe important—but it would not come, and she was so afraid to hurt Inda with the wrong words. She said slowly, "I won't claim that women don't feel desire with fighting. Maybe some do. I just don't know any. Haven't read of any, though I have read accounts where the anger to defend, to get revenge, felt good after something they'd otherwise think sickening, coming on it cold."

"Well, anyway, it hasn't happened since that day on the cliff. The sex burn or the mind thing. When me'n Cama had a few brushes up in Idayago, it was just work. I tried to make it fast. I guess it's different for everybody. Fox once said that winning a fight is better than sex." He sent her a quick look as they passed under a burning torch, and when he didn't see revulsion, just a somber sort of puzzlement, he added, "I keep looking for answers. In the books I've been reading. Trying to read. I'm so slow! I read much faster when I was little. Maybe my brains have leaked out after all." He was walking fast again.

"You used to skim," she said, no longer trying to hide

her worry. "And then you'd ask me to gloss 'em. Don't you remember? Or you'd listen to Joret and me talking. You learned a lot by listening, and then you'd read it. Don't you remember?"

"I remember you explaining things to me." Inda rubbed his eyes, then flung his hands out and dashed around a corner. She lengthened her strides to keep up. "I also remember that I didn't stop and think all the time, like I do now. Think and think, when I read something, and I look back at what happened in my life . . ."

She said carefully, "Have you asked for recommendations for your reading from Evred?"

"No. I don't talk with anyone about the glory stuff. Well, Tau, sort of, once. Fox, a little. And now you. Nobody seems to see it the way I do. Think I'm being, eh, modest, or something. To Evred Marlovan glory is important, somehow. I think, with him, it's all tied together with oaths and king matters." His voice lowered more, scarcely a whisper. "It's too important to Evred. Maybe because he's a king."

Tdor wondered what Inda heard in Evred's voice. But she did not dare ask. If Inda found out about Evred's feelings he'd struggle with remorse and obligation—two things Evred would hate. Evred already felt like a banked fire when Tdor was in his presence. Sometimes she had this disturbing fancy that Evred did not incinerate before their eyes only due to extreme exertion of will.

Inda shook himself, then plunged through a tower entrance. He flicked a salute to the duty captain, and then he burst out the opposite door, Tdor moving fast to keep up, though both knew that problems walked right along with you.

Tdor said, "Is Signi your second thing?"

"Yes. Evred called me in this morning. Said he got a Runner from Jaya-Vayir." Inda pounded his left fist on the battlements as they passed. "Took some time because they thought at first it was brigands."

" 'It'? She's not *dead*?"

"No. That is, no one knows. *Her* body wasn't found. There was a family. Throats cut. Everyone thought it was brigands, but ones with a weird sense of decency since the bodies were all straightened out, clothes smooth. Nothing taken, far as they could tell. Eventually someone put that together with a corner of Jaya-Vayir that never got magic renewed. The Jarl sent his best men to ride around, and they figured out Signi had been in the region around the time the people were killed."

"They don't blame her, I trust!"

"No, but they think her disappearance is related. Maybe brigands got the drop on her. Took her for her magic knowledge. Nobody knows. Anyway, Horseshoe's kin got some mage apprentice from Sartor to come and finish the renewals—supposedly the Mage Council doesn't know. Evred had to dispatch a smacking big fee— what it would have cost to do the entire south—but at least it's done."

"Inda, I am so sorry." Tdor felt sick.

He turned up his palm, and as sentry women approached, he said, "Here's what we plan for this year's Banner Game . . ."

When Dauvid Tya-Vayir got home from his academy season, Uncle Stalgrid demanded an accounting as always. As soon as Dauvid said, "Wasn't so bad, this year. The Harskialdna says we're almost—" Uncle Stalgrid knocked him down.

"I don't want to hear that claphair's damned opinions," he roared. "Especially out of your mouth!" He punctuated with smacks all his reasons why the king and his pirate shield arm were stupid so the boy would remember who was Jarl of Tya-Vayir. There'd be no traitor like Camarend growing up here, despite that damned academy. Horsebutt would never let Dauvid go back if he dared, but he was afraid Evred would make some excuse to send dragoons to camp in Tya-Vayir as a punishment. So Dauvid had just better remember who was Jarl in Tya-Vayir, and this was the way to make sure the lesson stuck . . .

When Dauvid finally made his way to his aunt, she prepared him a meal with her own hands, as always after a beating. She stood over him until he'd drunk fresh listerblossom steep, and then, when Dauvid's breathing was easier, asked, "How was your year?"

"Stupid," the boy said fiercely. "Just . . . stupid."

She said nothing more, but when he asked a day or two later if he should take his little cousin to see the pups in the kennel, she said he could later on—Young Stalgrid was spending harvest season with his grandpa to keep him out of the way of the work.

Chapter Two

DURING Convocation that year, Goatkick Noth's certainties about the world underwent a change.

Goatkick was half a year away from promotion. He would be the first Noth to serve as royal staff, and every single year since he was twelve, he'd served the Jarls at Convocation thinking, *Maybe my family will be one of them. Maybe while I'm alive, even.* Because despite the old, old songs about how honor and glory were bound up in how wide and free you could ride, how many days you could gallop until you found enemies who did not bow out of your way, everybody knew *real* glory was in owning land. You had your own castle, and when you rode, it was *your* land under your horse's hooves, not everybody else's. You had a bench at Convocation, and you spoke for all your people. You *led* people instead of *being* people.

The second way to honor and glory was through being a hero in war.

For two and a half years he'd smoldered in silence about how Noddy Toraca had dishonored him and his fellow King's Runners-in-Training by sending them home right on the eve of the most glorious battle of the war! Like they were all babies or cowards!

It was a terrible struggle not to spit when Toraca's name was mentioned, especially when the king and the Harski-aldna went on about what a hero Noddy Toraca had been. Goatkick and his friends ranted in private about all the ways they could have won glory, like by catching up the banner and leading the charge after Noddy and Hawkeye fell.

Goatkick had quietly dropped that one when his cousin in the horsetails had let him try riding with a lance when he went home for a visit ("home" being wherever Uncle Horsepiss was garrisoned, ever since Grandpa Noth was killed in the first big pirate attack) just before spring the year after the battle.

All right, so he wouldn't have even been able to pick up a lance on the battlefield, much less gallop to the charge, without falling right off the horse. But he could have done *something* heroic! He could have run the crucial message . . . well, except that Sundog Tlennen's uncle Hanther, who'd been up on the cliffs with Cama One-Eye's men, had come to Convocation last year as an escort for the Jarl of Cassad. He'd told the boys that after the battle in the pass had started nobody had time for any messages until after the Venn surrendered and slunk away, the cowards.

That third Convocation brought Buck Marlo-Vayir for his first royal city visit since the battle. The senior Runners-in-Training were on duty as aides to the King's Runners assigned to welcome all the Jarls and see to it that they got to their rooms and everything was right. Goatkick, as a new senior, was experiencing his first turn as an aide. When the trumpets announced a Jarl riding toward the gates, a look-out shouted the banner's owner down to the alcove just off the tower, where the boys waited out of the winter wind. The aides for that Jarl scrambled down to the royal stable yard just inside the castle gate.

The first glimpse of the Marlo-Vayir banner caused a great crowd to assemble, not just from the castle folk and the guard, but the main street was lined with people cheering Buck as he rode in. He grinned at everybody, looking good in his specially made saddle with its strap across his leg stump, securing his balance.

Goatkick had seen a few one-legged men, but no one missing both a leg and an arm. He looked away, ashamed when Buck-Jarl twisted around like a worm on a hook in order to get down off his horse. Then his Runner was there with a wooden crutch, and Buck hopped like some kind of weird old bird, his short horsetail bobbing at each step. Goatkick followed uneasily, thinking, *He's a hero, all right, but he doesn't look like one.*

His uneasiness stayed with him until everyone assembled for the First Day oaths. While the Jarls got into rank order (Buck hopping and clacking) they sang the "Hymn to the Beginning," with drums in the gallery. Goatkick felt good again, reveling in Marlovan strength, courage, and victory.

But after the old song came that slow, sad one that made the skin on the back of his neck hurt. The one they called the "Lament," about the heroes of Castle Andahi.

Some of the voices changed. Buck's strong, not-very-tuneful baritone went husky, and Goatkick looked his way. Buck no longer sang with that lifted chin of pride, but with a sorrow like Goatkick had seen in the Jarl of Khani-Vayir's face when he delivered Noddy's stupid armband letter.

Well, Buck Marlo-Vayir had nothing to do with the glory of Andahi. Goatkick could barely force himself to look at the one who did—the *little child,* the *girl*—who hadn't been sent to safety like the King's Runners-in-Training. Oh, no. They'd given her a *command,* and let her stay right in the midst of the action! Ten years old, and Goatkick was sent home at near sixteen! And then what happened? Cama gave her a name that none of Goatkick's friends could bring themselves to use. And Inda-Harskialdna himself gave her one of those toff earrings!

Jealousy wrenched Goatkick. He shot a glare at Han Tlen, the stinking, strutting brat, there at the end of the line where the twelve-year-olds always stood. He expected to find her smirking with pride (Goatkick knew *he* would have been, as was only right) but his hands felt icy when he saw her face squeezed like a raisin, and tears bouncing down the front of her tunic. Her skinny body jerked with her effort not to make any noise.

What?

Goatkick lifted his head, and dared a peek at the Harskialdna, whom the boys would do anything to please. The high point of their week was when Inda himself trained them in the double-knife fighting, which those strutting horsetails no longer got, ha ha! Inda-Harskialdna was a true hero, and maybe that was it, true heroes didn't have feelings, because usually Inda just stood there with all those scars on his face, not looking happy or sad or much of anything. Goatkick and the others had talked endlessly about that day in the tent before Inda smashed half the army in a knife fight without even breaking a sweat. He'd talked about pirate fights, and wearing no chain mail in battle, and those scars like it was Restday in the city. Heroes didn't have feelings.

But when Goatkick stood on tiptoe to peer over several heads at Inda, he was amazed. Inda had that same long upper lip and thin-pressed mouth, the same faint lines at the corner of his eyes as Buck—like he was *sick*.

What was going on here? You *did* feel the glory when you looked at Buck and Inda, and Cama One-Eye when he'd been here, tougher than steel. Your heart got a lift right inside your chest, and you yearned to be as brave, as true, to lead a victory, to *win*. But right now not a single face looked the way you expected a hero to look: proud.

"Did ya see her blubbing?" one of the boys asked later, when they met up on the roof above the bakehouse, which was their hideout in every season but summer. "Like a baby!"

In the last year or so, one boy had gone missing from these sessions: Slacker (so named because he was always the first one up in mornings) Tlen. They all knew it was because *Captain Han* was a sort of cousin, and everybody knew you didn't rip at kin unless they'd rabbitted, or snowballed, or something deserving. The girl hadn't broken a single rule, she never talked, much less strutted, and she hadn't snitched during the first spring when some of them had sort of given her some of the stings that after all everybody more or less had to endure.

Sundog Tlennen jerked up a shoulder. "Well, she did lose her whole family. That song is about how they all died."

"Arms cut off? Eyes poked out? Yeah," someone muttered, trying to get away from the image of his own family dying like that.

Goatkick snarled, "Was only Liet-Jarlan got killed that way."

"How d'ya *know* they all didn't get the same? Just because Rad didn't see it."

"Yeah. I mean they all got killed. By the Venn. Sure none o' the Venn said, oops, no bad death for you! Here, turn around, I'll make it nice and quick."

The session ended in the usual muttering about what they'd do if they ever caught any Venn, that's for sure, and they slunk off again.

Downstairs, Branid Algara-Vayir strode through the halls looking for Inda. He'd been trying to find him for the entire week he'd been here, but Inda was always surrounded by people.

He had no idea that Inda's own personal staff was on watch, warning Inda when Branid was around.

Inda carried on with his duties, slipping away whenever he overheard Branid's irritating voice—too high and too loud—somehow sounding both bragging and fretful as he gave unnecessary orders to servants or tried to attach himself to the Jarls as they went off to meals.

But Branid was determined. He bullied, whined, and bribed his way into finding out Inda's customary paths until at last he cornered him down in the stables.

"Cousin Inda!" Branid yelled, enjoying how heads turned all over. "Cousin Inda," he said again, reveling in not having to append 'Harskialdna' to his name. "Heyo, you're impossible to find. Commanding any wars?"

Inda forced himself to respond politely as he mentally sorted excuses for getting away.

Branid sidled a look around. "I need to talk to you privately."

Inda gave up. "Come on, let's go see the academy. No one will be there and we can talk without ears."

Branid turned out his hands in a semblance of indifference, trying to hide his intense curiosity about the place he'd heard about but had never set foot in.

Within a hundred paces beyond the first arch Inda got that sick-gut sense that he'd made a mistake. Branid looked around with his lip curled, his voice full of scorn. "Look how worn those buildings are! I'd thrash the house staff with my own hand for that kind of neglect at home, I assure you. Are those willow toys in that barrel really practice weapons? Why, we were using steel at home, remember?"

Only on the sneak, Inda thought, but he resisted saying it. Why should he have to defend the academy to Branid? He finally cut through it all. "What did you want to say?"

But now that he'd been offered his chance, Branid hesitated, his shoulders coming up in the familiar slinking hunch that made Inda grit his teeth.

Would it really have made any difference if Cousin Branid had come to the academy to be trained? Inda had only been there two years. Maybe Branid would have found friends. Or allies . . . Inda sensed that Branid would have joined up with Kepa and Lassad. Would *that* have been any improvement?

Inda stopped, gazing around at the weather-and-boy battered equipment, the plain buildings. *Maybe Branid would have thought so. Mates . . . friends . . . allies. It's here that men make their true alliances, not at home.* Uneasy—he knew he needed to think about that—he said, "Well, shabby as it is, I assure you your son will learn to love it."

Branid scowled. "That's why I wanted to talk to you. Dannor made me promise. She won't have children unless they can inherit. What good is it to send my son here if he's not a laef? Dannor says a prince and princess can't have their sons be mere Rider or dragoon captains, it insults our rank. And I'm supposed to remind you that if *your* son is raised here, how's he ever going to know anything about Choraed Elgaer?"

Inda thought he'd reached the limit of discomfort, but this question stabbed even harder. "I don't know," he said finally. "Same way men appointed to new positions get accustomed. It's the king's will, d'you see? If you want a change, you must talk to him."

They walked back in silence.

Goatkick was still ruminating on rank, heroes, and ruby earrings when he went to Piwum Harbor for his home visit just before spring.

He was never quite sure how it happened, but somehow he got singled out from the tumble of cousins by Ma Noth herself. She sat him down in the alcove where she worked on hand-smoothing a new bow, and said, "Talk."

Out it all came, in a disjointed morass of self-serving excuses, empty threats, and a headlong cry, "Why did they put that girl in with us?"

Ma Noth pointed a calloused, gnarled finger at him. "Why not? Ye know she earned it, or the queen wouldn'ta put her there. And they need good Runners. Ye know too many died."

"But a girl!"

"So? Ye don't think she's tough enough? After what she did up north? And, I wager my chitlins, being fed a steady helpin' o'horse-apple biscuits by y' young hounds ever since, what ye call 'stings.' But she seems to be sticking to the saddle."

"What if they start making *us* stay on the walls, and send girls out to ride?" When his aunt cackled so hard she dropped her bow, he said defensively, "They could, you know!" And, in a grumble, "I hate change."

She cackled again. "If there wasn't change, I'd be scrapin' fish scales off me granny's fisher. And you'd be scrapin' out stalls! It's 'change' only when ye didn't want it, but 'bettering' if you do." She attacked her bow.

He was still fuming over that a month later, as spring shoots fuzzed the plains below the royal castle. During the past couple of weeks the cold winds still blowing out of the east had stopped freezing his nose and ears to ache at first blast, and the air even felt almost warm once the sun was up. Goatkick had decided that Auntie Noth was wrong, though she meant well. Change was good when you'd *earned* it. Like a promotion.

The problem there was, he couldn't find any reason to say that Han Tlen hadn't earned her place next to the hawk-nosed Fera-Vayir brat (named Pirate-Prow because of his connection to Inda-Harskialdna's mother) as second-year Runners-in-Training.

That morning he was on duty as third Runner outside the king's government office; only staff was allowed inside, hearing the king's business. But the Runners-in-Training were responsible for greeting any newcomers who made it this far and sorting out their business, often directing them to the guilds or heralds or guards.

A mud-splashed foreigner in a shaggy coat appeared at the top of the stairs, yawned gapingly, then plunged forward, a husky boy of sixteen walking just behind. The boy was clearly sweat-sticky with nerves, big as he was.

The first two duty Runners were gone. Goatkick was the senior Runner-in-Training over fourteen-year-old Pirate-Prow and Han Tlen. He'd been talking to Pirate-Prow so he didn't have to talk to the girl.

"You have business with the Harvaldar?" he said to the newcomers.

Of course they did, or they wouldn't have been passed by the sentries at the gate, or the lower level Runners. But Goatkick and his mates were the last gate to the king and many was the privately expressed hope that they might discover an assassin among the few foreigners ever sent this far.

"Message from Queen Wisthia," the stranger with the shaggy wool coat said in careful Iascan. Then a jerk of a mittened thumb toward the boy just behind him. "Man along the border given me room and board if I bring his son to your King's Shield."

The boy wrenched his hands together, then muttered in Marlovan, "Harskialdna told my dad. At Lindeth. To send me when I turned sixteen." In a lower voice, tremulous with his awareness of his own temerity, "I want to go for a guard."

Well, that was easy enough. "If you wait right here, when the door opens, that means the king is ready for whatever's out here." Goatkick motioned to Pirate-Prow. "Fera-Vayir, you take this fellow over to guard-side, to the watch captain."

Their footsteps vanished, then the red-eyed messenger swayed. "Huh." He yawned so fiercely that Goatkick and Han felt that jaw-hinge, back-of-the-tongue gape of sympathy. "How long is the wait?" the man rasped. And yawned again.

"Don't know. Some days, all morning, some—"

"The ambassador didn't say 'in his hands,' so I can trust you, can't I? Right outside his door? I don't think I can wait without falling over. We got caught by a snow storm east of the river, and haven't had a bite for almost two days."

Goatkick hesitated, eyeing Han Tlen, who stood against the wall, gaze down at the scuffed toes of her boots. He could send the stranger off with her. No one would say anything. Hand-delivering important messages was as cherished a privilege as drumming the second gallop at Restday Drum for the entire castle. When you got to hand-deliver messages inside the office you often got to watch the king open them, and hear him talk about important stuff.

Goatkick was going to give the messenger to Han. He knew she'd obey. But the turmoil inside him every time he saw her had changed to something closer to guilt than to the old resentment, though he couldn't explain why.

And so he snarled at her, "You stay here with the message. I'm going to see to this fellow." He smacked the message into her chest.

Han hastily clutched it, then looked up, startled. She'd been in training long enough to understand the unspoken privileges; her face drained of color, then flushed to the tips of her ears.

Goatkick plunged past. "Heyo! Come along, Runner. Don't sleep on the wall there."

He stalked down the hall, the stranger plodding wearily after.

Han held the weather-worn, heavy sealed packet tightly against her body, wondering if this was another sting. One of the big Runners-in-Training surely lurked somewhere to lure her away from her post on a false duty, so she'd get beaten. She planted her feet, clenched her jaw, and hugged the bulky message, determined to stay right there until that door opened, even if the entire Venn army galloped down the hall. Even if it took a year.

She'd scarcely had time to imagine trying to protect her charge against a horde with winged helms, like she had seen in the pass, when Vedrid opened the door to let one of the staff Runners out. As the man strode past, Vedrid smiled at Han. "What have you there?"

She croaked, "Messenger from Wisthia-Queen."

"The king's mother? The border passes are open early this year, it seems. Come inside."

The word "mother" still hurt, but Han was so relieved to discharge this important duty (and to the king!) she felt it less than usual.

Evred had heard his mother's name, which evoked a brief image of her watchful face, the expression of her eyes—so loving, but sometimes inexplicably perplexed.

That blurred into a vivid image of Tau, who lived with her now. How strange that was.

He cast an absent smile at Han before dismissing her, and turned the bulky packet over in his hand. Someone had wrapped it in several layers of thick paper, and there was something inside.

Evred pulled his knife and slit the seals, noting that they did not seem to have been disturbed.

The letter was written neatly in Old Sartoran. Evred grimaced. He'd never read it fluently, though he'd come close many years ago, during his command at Ala Larkadhe. But he hadn't had the time since.

He bent over the heavy paper, puzzling out the letters and realized that the actual language was new Sartoran, just framed in the ancient lettering.

It was quite short.

> *Evred: I am here in Bren, name and reputation having preceded me. That means I am surrounded by Estral Mardrics. Queen Wisthia assures me the accompanying (assuming it reaches you) is what mages call "clean"—meaning guaranteed to be uncorrupted. Let me know when you have it, and I will assay a more particular report. Here's how you make the magic work . . .*

Below the instructions he'd signed his name in the language of his ancestors, *Taumad Dei*.

Estral Mardric? Evred recovered the name: the murderer of Flash Arveas. She'd been a spy for the Resistance under the guise of an Idayagan poet. Why would Tau bring her name up? *Because he is surrounded by spies.*

Evred poked at the paper-wrapped object and discovered a slim golden case. He grimaced, feeling world politics stoop from the mountainous border and dive at him like a hawk on the hunt.

Chapter Three

JUST before midnight, Fulla Durasnir stood on the highest tower of Saeborc contemplating the meaning of words.

Overhead the first thunderstorm of the year crackled, hissed, and roared. His extremities were slowly going from painful shivering to numb, but that did not matter because he was shortly about to step off into ... what?

Millennia ago, *a walk to the far shore* meant putting the old into a shallow boat and sending it into the winter ice. The early Venn sent their dead heroes out in burning boats, and the old and weak into the winter darkness, in order to make place for the strong. That custom persisted even after they settled, spread, and encountered the Sartorans, who called their practices barbaric.

The practice persisted until a king, wise as well as strong, discovered on getting old that the juices of life, though thinned, still ran. He also discovered that some elderly folks had vanished to the south rather than freezing to death—and some wily oldsters had even managed, with willing co-operation from their families, to take some of their wealth with them. This discovery gave an ironic twist to the expression "walk to the far shore." A self-proclaimed exile was not an outcast, especially if they cast their wealth and wit with them, to the eventual benefit of Venn's enemies.

The wise old king appealed to hearts as well as to heads when he spoke of the wisdom of age balancing the strength of the young. As his son was impetuous and arrogant, no one was in any hurry to see him inherit, and so the custom of the winter ice ended with him when he died peacefully in bed. But traces of the grim legacy lingered in idiom and song. Fulla Durasnir's mother had said when he was young, *Down at the taproot of Venn thinking is the concept of the undiscovered country on that far shore, the dark sea between being death.*

As Durasnir contemplated stepping off the tower into the unseen waters crashing far below, he wondered if going a-viking had been his ancestors' way of going to war against death.

While he meditated, his wife Brun sat at her table six flights below, checking her list. She'd spent two days personally overseeing the delivery and stowage of Fulla's belongings aboard *Cormorant,* so that Erkric's minions couldn't introduce spiderwebs into them; the old captain's cabin, now that Rajnir and his entourage were established across the stern suite, had been inspected by one of the ship's trusted navigators.

Something was wrong, despite her care. Instinct had been prodding at her all day. Lacking an identifiable cause, she'd decided that something had to be missing from Fulla's sea gear. She bent over her list yet again as, outside her door, Dag Ulaffa paused after the long climb to the Oneli Stalna's rooms, midway up Saeborc. Ulaffa leaned against the wall with a hand pressed against his side. *Climbs are not for the old,* he thought wearily. But this entire life was not for the old.

Despite the cold his brow and upper lip were slick with sweat. That and the pain in his side were not good signs, he knew. He must not drop dead. *Must* not! He tapped at the door, and when the servant brought him into the warm chamber where Brun Durasnir sat at the desk, he sank wearily into the guest chair.

"I went out on . . ." He gestured wearily upward, toward the towers. "Fulla is up on your tower."

"He's on board the *Cormorant.* Or at the chart house—"

Ulaffa made a negating motion, and swiped a hand across his eyes. "Saw him. When I. Went outside to talk with Agel."

Brun's mouth whitened. *Here* was her something wrong.

Leaving the dag to recover in the guest chair, she ran out, heedless of cape or gloves, and propelled herself up the last spiral of steps, her skirts bunched in her fists. *If he dares to leap off the tower . . . I'll murder him myself!*

Oh, that makes such good sense, she thought with the hilarity of desperation. She dashed into the bastion, thrust shoulder to the door, and saw her husband poised at the edge of a crenellation, staring into the blackness below.

"Fulla!" Brun shouted with all her strength.

The wind snatched it away, but Fulla Durasnir's head turned.

Their eyes met.

Reluctantly—Brun could feel the effort Fulla made— he stepped back. Just a little, as wind screamed around the stones, and rain slanted in stinging spears.

Not for Brun the heart's cry, *How could you do this to me, to your son?* He would obliterate himself despite them, he would do it to protect them, he would do it because all honor and meaning had gone from his life.

"I deny you this luxury." Her voice rose above the shriek of the wind.

Durasnir's head dropped back, his anguish illuminated in the glare of lightning. When the long rumble of thunder died away, he said, "I cannot bring myself to speak to the empty shell of a king. He's the living, breathing emblem of the emptiness this kingdom has become. And I lent myself to it, with my forcing you into that pretence when we arrived home."

"I was glad to—" A gust of wind belled her skirt like sailcloth and nearly blew her off the wall. Durasnir lunged forward to catch her, but his numb hands only slid over her, unable to grasp.

So he threw himself on her. They crashed onto the tower stones in a clumsy tangle of limbs.

Durasnir levered himself painfully up, and they helped each other regain their feet. "You, unlike the king, have volition," Brun gasped, fear sharpening her voice. "Use it."

"I was so doing." Durasnir leaned his head down so it almost touched hers. His tone was dry, too bleak for humor. "When I chose to end a life that mocks everything I swore to uphold."

Brun clawed her hair out of her eyes. "This is not a good death. It is a coward's death."

He bowed his head; she'd only told him what he already knew. *So try again, woman.* "Fulla. Your death on the eve of launch will bring nothing but disaster for us all."

"There is no path out of Rainorec, Brun. At most I hoped my death might postpone it. Long enough that someone stronger, smarter, might prevail."

"That's stupid." Brun grimaced. *Wrong again.* "No, that's exhaustion. Fulla, this last year would have ruined a man of twenty. If you've slept at all these past two weeks, it was not in our bed."

He lifted a hand, which could have meant anything.

"Dag Ulaffa reminded us just after Rajnir's coronation that what little meaning is left is in *our* hands. Can't you see? The fleet *will* launch come morning's tide. Your death will not halt it because Erkric needs to get the king away. And we've all conspired to keep knowledge of Rajnir's empty head from the people because we know that the streets will run with blood if anyone finds out." She paused, and slowly Durasnir turned toward the tower edge, staring out.

"Maybe . . ." He did not finish the thought.

Maybe it was time to unleash the Rainorec. She knew he was thinking it: how could life become worse than it was?

It's worse for you because you are bearing all the pain that everyone would feel if we were engulfed in civil war. "You say you hoped someone smarter would lead, but that will not happen because Erkric would control the promotions."

Fulla had stilled. He was listening.

So she babbled on, telling him nothing new—some of it he'd told her—but she had to anchor him back in this world. "That fool Dyalf Balandir would lead the pack of wolves. He thinks being young, handsome, and first-born son of an old House entitles him not just to be your second in command, but to anything. Loc would try again, despite what happened to his brother. Because of it. Lefsan would try to regain their old influence. Hadna House is always conspiring. They're raised that way. Don't you see? If they find out about Rajnir, then at least five, probably seven, Houses would throw all their treasure and men into securing the city, after talking themselves into thinking it's for Drenskar and the Golden Tree."

Durasnir had not moved.

Brun tucked her hands up under her armpits. "So far, you have managed to prevent seven Houses from tearing one another apart, right down to their thralls. And you know they would do that. How has that betrayed your vows?"

Durasnir said slowly, "The fleet is not ready, except in outward form. Like Rajnir, it is a semblance. Half the new ships are cobbled together with unseasoned wood. Their holds are crammed with old men forced back into service, or very young men—some scarcely men—with little or no training because the Houses were forced to call to service far more than they could afford. Erkric knows it. Brun, I would swear an oath before the Tree he was gloating over it. Does he want us to fail?"

"No. Oh, it takes no penetration to assume he wants you wearing yourself to death. He may even hope that you will take that unseasoned navy to battle, because he wants you to call upon him for magical help. He can figure as savior of the kingdom. And gain the power he craves. Gain immortality through Norsunder."

Durasnir's shoulders dropped; that release of tension signaled she'd won.

She said, "I know the circumstances are terrible. I know Erkric blocked the promotion of the right men and put forward the wrong ones, all to strengthen his control. But the Oneli look to you to lead them."

Durasnir said to the unseen, hissing sea, "I cannot escape the fact that we are going to a war we never should fight."

"The Oneli will go whether you are there or not," Brun said. "It is up to you. *You*, Fulla. To see that a semblance of honor remains, a living twig caught in the deluge. You must replant the tree, because poor Rajnir cannot. His ability has been taken away along with his life."

Durasnir lifted his head, and peered into her anxious face. "Do you believe that Drenskar exists?"

"I believe," she said steadily.

"And I believe . . . in you. I'm sorry, Brun." He fumbled for the latch of the door.

They walked together down the mossy steps and to their rooms, where he sank into the chair Ulaffa had vacated; the dag was gone.

Brun ordered dry clothing and some warm spice milk for Fulla to drink, then went to change her own sodden clothing. *Why did he shut me out?* No, that was the wrong question, because she knew the answer. He'd talked himself into thinking he'd spare her the pain he was in. *What is it about honor that makes men think they must hide their pain?* She paused at the door behind which slumbered her seven-year-old son Halvir. *What can I say to Halvir as he grows to teach him that honor is not just earned by bearing pain or giving it to enemies, but by preventing it?*

One of the most famous poems in the long history of the Land of the Venn was written by a poet shivering on the heights of the tenth tower the morning after Fulla Durasnir nearly walked off Saeborc's heights.

Despite his numbing nose and toes, the poet captured in singing phrases the sight of the ancient Banner of the Tree belling in the wind like the sails of the great *drakans* filling Twelve Towers Harbor.

With a skirr of wings a flock of seabirds jetted upward from the rocks below the pier as the royal party paced out to the flagship. Once again, the king was going a-viking, a phrase so long unused it resonated down to the bone with portent and power.

The poem is justly famed for its guesses about what the king thought that day—such a range nearly everyone could at least imagine, if not feel, what the poet wrote. The poet never knew that the handsome king pacing so slowly down the dock behind the banner, and before his military leaders, remembered nothing about that day. His mind was locked in a strange space surrounded by fragmented mirrors and windows. Inside the prison of his mind he turned and turned, straining to catch the glimpse of an eye, a hand, catch the whisper of a word, or even part of a word, and put them together into meaning.

Despite wind and rain people lined all the towers and walls, singing mightily, young ardent voices mixing with the croak of oldsters as King Rajnir, dressed in white and gold, stepped up the ramp into the *Cormorant,* and after a soft word from Erkric, gave the signal to set sail.

The loosened courses snapped home, filled with wind, and the king's flagship sailed slowly out to sea, pulling the flagships of the Battlegroups after him, and after that—in order—the chief warships of all the subordinate groups.

Here were the Oneli, Lords of the Sea, Firstborn of the Venn. For the first time in generations all four great fleets were together: Eastern, Western, Northern, and Southern.

As the mighty armada began to sail away to the south, Durasnir forced himself to turn to Rajnir. He made his obeisance and said, "May I signal the captains to assemble, my king?"

Erkric contemplated Durasnir's haggard face above the rich pinky-gold gleam of his copper torc. The Oneli sea lord had aged, too, the stiff-necked reprobate. With the king's speaking nine words—"The Golden Tree will again go a-viking to glory"—Erkric had worked Fulla Durasnir right down to the bone—the Oneli Stalna, his House, and the eleven other Houses. Try causing trouble now! The Twelve Houses were beggared and would be for several years to come, but they had met the king's demand for ships and men.

The king.

Erkric whispered the word that would release Rajnir to speak his assent.

"Make it so, Oneli Stalna my Commander," Rajnir said.

Durasnir made his obeisance to the king, then walked across the deck to speak to the signal ensign. Then he vanished down the causeway to the old captain's cabin where he now lived.

Nine Erama Krona stood at silent guard surrounding the king and the Dag of the Venn. Durasnir's own Drenga guard must take second station amidships; Erkric narrowly watched as Durasnir passed the former Drenga captain, Byoren Henga, at his post. As always, no sign passed between the Oneli sea lord and his once favored captain.

Erkric could not comprehend that relationship at all, and it made him restless and angry. He still had no one inside Durasnir's House, due to the vigilance of that woman Brun. With Henga's surprising demotion after the invasion, he'd thought he had a perfect opportunity to get ears inside Durasnir's command. But the Dag's interviews with Henga had produced utterly nothing.

Former Captain Henga was certainly brave, and an excellent commander. Erkric caused Rajnir to award him a gold arm torc for the left arm, the sign of honor in battle, for his speed and effectiveness in breaking Andahi Castle for the invasion. It was a waste of gold; Henga never wore it.

Bone stupid, Erkric thought and swept the fleet with his glass. Away from all the prying eyes and interfering fools in Twelve Towers! Away to glory and power.

"The king goes a-viking to glory," Rajnir said.

Startled, Erkric lowered the glass. He peered into Rajnir's face, which was reassuringly blank. Maybe Rajnir heard one of the signal words in the deck chatter.

Time to go inside the cabin anyway, for the captains would soon be arriving.

Erkric had Rajnir settled to a long meal when the horns began blatting the captains' longboats: *Petrel, Auk, Katawake,* and *Blackgull* in the lead.

On the king's orders, Erkric was now part of all military meetings. When the last Battlegroup captain sat on his bench around the long table, winged helm on his knee, Durasnir lifted his gaze from the chart of the western coast of Drael.

"Here is our plan, as approved by the king." His face and voice were as expressive as wood. "We will land at Nathur and spend the winter there in training and in reinforcing our *drakans.* Drenga Captain Vringir will board each of you with specifics, the better to be prepared when we do land. Questions?"

"Why don't we go straight to Halia?" the new Battlegroup Chief asked with a smirking glance toward Erkric.

Several of the older captains stirred. Whatever their political leanings, they all knew that Balandir had no experience. Yet he'd been promoted over all their heads to Battlegroup Chief, the rank directly behind Durasnir—which Seigmad of the *Petrel* should have had.

Erkric was silent. He almost never spoke at military meetings. Half the time he didn't listen. He was there for two reasons: to make certain that Rajnir's orders were carried out and to remind them all that magic would strengthen their efforts in war.

"Not until we've secured the strait," Durasnir said. "As you are perhaps aware, we carry no Hilda."

A couple older men chuckled, and Balandir flushed then sat back, one fist on his thigh, his other hand absently stroking the scaling engraved on his copper torc.

To reinforce his point, Durasnir continued on to tell them what they already knew, what Balandir should have known. "Commander Talkar remains in Goerael, where the king has placed him as interim governor over our lands there. When we have secured the strait, and assured lines of the supplies we will need, the king has spoken of recommencing our efforts in Halia."

Seigmad showed his disgust at Balandir's stupidity by returning abruptly to the former subject, as if Balandir's interjection did not exist. "So our first launch will be against Llyenthur, I take it?"

"Yes. We'll make certain of the little harbor at Granthan, then proceed to Llyenthur Harbor, which we will retake and establish as our mid-strait base." Durasnir brushed his fingers over the carefully drawn scattering of rocky islands off the gaping fish-mouth of Llyenthur Harbor. "If Llyenthur is going to resist, it will probably be here, and not at Granthan. That's where I'd take my stand. They can hide some of their fleet behind the islands, and the rest up the river, which we can't navigate, as some of you remember when we were stationed there. Currents are against ships with deep draught."

"Take us in the back when we're busy with the islands," Seigmad said.

"Exactly. We will offer Llyenthur peace—and the old terms—and if they refuse, we will smash them so thoroughly that the rest of the strait will think the better of our offer." And to young Balandir, who now sat with his strong arms crossed, his handsome brow furrowed, "A peaceful resumption of the strait leaves us the stronger for when we take up matters again with the Marlovans, yes?"

No one had any objection to that.

The captains left again, in strict order of rank.

Chapter Four

EVRED left the scroll-case in his desk.

Though he could not see it, sometimes he heard it rattle when he shut the drawer. Every reminder unsettled him, as if any words he might write and send by magic would diminish his control over events. He knew that magic was not the cause, or the single cause—he'd been using his father's locket since 3912. He had learned through his reading that resistance to change could be defined as fear of loss of control. That was a lifelong battle for him.

Besides, it would create an avalanche of new work to monitor all the military or money-related communication if he opened the border to the guilds.

So . . . he would think about it on the morrow.

Next week.

After the academy was settled for the season.

After he and Inda finished their review of the dragoon training, now that Inda insisted that dragoons as well as the King's Runners should learn the Fox drills . . .

After the Summer Games.

After Inda took the dragoons into the plains of Hesea to drill with the new training.

After Convocation.

And so the sun rolled on its daily courses toward the north and then back again, every day rising higher in the sky. Evred had learned to hold as tightly to moments of peace as he did to his semblance of control.

There were even spikes of euphoria, such as when he observed the academy boys going to and from activities, how generally happy they seemed. Even Gand had noticed it. Not that there weren't problems, but the problems were fewer, and smaller, than before Inda had come. More secret happiness when Inda brought up the old topics of discussion at dinner, just like when they were boys. *Where did the idea of honor come from? How did tradition turn into law?*

Outwardly, the kingdom flourished for the first time in ten years. The harbor cities were a fair way to being rebuilt at last. Evred's gratitude was the more intense for how little he trusted the sensation.

Convocation came and went in an orderly manner. Again Horsebutt Tya-Vayir conducted himself with uncharacteristic cooperation. Evred still did not trust that. Once or twice he caught himself wondering if Horsebutt had somehow got hold of magical cases. If one person could get them, why not another? *There is no sign of conspiracy. I will not invent one.*

I am not insane.

As the new year's winter days at last gave way to a late spring the first sign of the passes opening was a mud and travel-stained courier from the east bringing two letters. By chance Han Tlen had drawn office duty again, but this year she was in charge of a thirteen-year-old and a twelve-year-old; Goatkick had been promoted and was at that moment laboring through a late snowdrift with messages to Parayid Harbor.

Han had grown into a weedy, gangling colt of a girl with a quick grin. Inda, Tdor, and the royal couple had all noticed how sometime during the past year she'd gone from isolation to becoming the mascot of the King's Runners-in-Training.

"Shall I take it?" Han asked the messenger.

"I'm to put it in your king's hands," the messenger said.

"It won't be long," Han said in her careful Sartoran. "Then you'll get something hot to drink."

When Evred's door opened, Han stood by so that the messenger could hand the king his packet, as he'd promised. That done, Han sent the twelve-year-old to take the messenger downstairs for refreshments.

Evred shut his door again. He sent the duty Runner on an errand, ensuring he was alone. His heart hammered, but he would not postpone whatever lay therein.

From Wisthia to Evred:

> *My dear son. Only a Dei could leave his role as the lover and decorative house steward of a famed player and return as a diplomat and leader of aristocratic fashion. My house is now the place everyone in royal circles must be. Prince Kavna, a dear young man, practically lives here, and Princess Kliessin takes care to grace us with her presence at least once a week. I give large parties every night, all the details seen to by Tau—it was after meeting him on his tour as new king last autumn that your cousin Valdon doubled my ambassadorial allowance.*
>
> *Tau's success surprises me. I believe there is more to it than his golden hair, black velvet and lace, or his skilled conversation. Most have conversation, and many have beauty, but they do not come near his popularity. Part of it could be his reputation, and also his famous name, but the truth lies closer, I believe, to the fact that he has no ambition. Taumad is no Sarmord Dei, and people do sense such things.*
>
> *The result is we hear everything. I will leave it to Taumad to make his report, and once again I will pay the enormous sum to hire someone to risk his life traveling across the mountains. Yes, that is a hint. I will be more forthcoming if I need not rely on a year of back-and-forth travel (and how trustworthy are the mountain passes anyway?) but you must do your part and communicate.*

Sarmord? Kingmaker, Evred translated. Adamas of the Black Sword had also been called "Adamas Dei Sarmord."

Taumad Dei. Once Evred had likened the tightly intertwined pain and pleasure of Inda's straight-on gaze to gazing into the sun. Tau's sudden laugh, his touch, affected

Evred the same way; the discovery that Tau was a direct descendant of Adamas Dei was like discovering that the sun had fallen out of the sky and burned directly outside the door.

Evred opened Tau's letter which, like Wisthia's, was written with Sartoran lettering, but unlike hers was in the Marlovan language.

> *Since half a year has passed between the time I thought my letter and gift would reach you and now, I'm not certain if my messenger was waylaid or you tossed the scroll-case into the nearest horse pond. I even had a wager going with myself. The benefit of betting against yourself is that you never have to pay up.*
>
> *So here's my second try, with entirely frivolous chat, that I trust you will pass on to our mutual friend Estral.*

Estral? The only person Evred knew with that name was the Idayagan assassin who'd posed as a poet. Friend?

> *Just after I sent you the gift, I continued my search for the best foreign food. Alas for our trade! My shipment of pickled cucumbers was bought at a better price by the Zhaer Ban brothers...*

Evred frowned, and reread the letter. Was Taumad drunk when he wrote that?

Of course he would not go to the expense of sending a drunken scrawl on a six-month journey—and this was no scrawl. *Pickled?*

Pickles. *The vinegar-stinking Venn*—

He read the words more slowly. Estral Mardric, pickles—then he flushed at the obviousness of what he had missed. When he was ten years old, his father had encouraged his studies in Sartoran by telling him, *The easiest diplomatic code begins with a personal synecdoche, and once you know its context, you can determine the real meaning of seemingly innocent messages.*

So, if the pickled cucumbers were the Venn, and highest price was either betrayal or death, what did bringing in the Zhaer Ban brothers mean? They were the biggest saddlers

in the royal city, their main building on the river a stone's
throw from the castle. Were they traitors?

No, of course not. Evred had known the old man all
his life; the oldest son had volunteered as a Rider during
Tlennen-Harvaldar's first call for war. What was wrong
with them? Or was he thinking about it all wrong? House
on the river—on the water—northeast corner of the river,
just inside the eastern wall . . .

Water. If you looked at the map and substituted the
river for, say, the strait, then the brothers' saddlery was
located approximately in the same place as Ymar. Or the
Port of Jaro.

Evred set the letter down. Why was the Port of Jaro important? Yes. The winter before last, Barend had sent him
a note after delivering the gold to Queen Wisthia. He'd
added a single line that the Fox Banner Fleet was sailing
with a newly-formed alliance to turf the Venn out of Jaro.
Evred had not heard directly from Barend since. He knew
his cousin was safe, as Barend had sent a verbal message by
some traders to Cama last year, with two items of news: his
locket was lost, but they'd won their sea battle.

All right, then let the saddlery stand for Ymar.

Evred turned back to the letter.

> . . . *Celebrations lasted until the first snow. Since
> then there have been messages crossing the river in all
> directions. Since your mother's folk have no horse in
> this race, their coast being the playground of Sartoran
> wastrels, your mother's domicile is deemed neutral ter-
> ritory. I sit around like "stage furniture—palace scene"
> and listen sympathetically to every envoy, toff, and
> Idayagan poet who comes here to drink our spiced
> punch and complain about the others, each waiting to
> see who tries to build a new bakery on the river. Every-
> one agrees that it ought to be done.*
>
> *The new Ymaran master baker feels that as his
> shop was chief victim in the fires several years ago, he
> should form a River Eatery, with workers supplied by
> everyone else. Paid for by everyone else. His neighbor
> to the north feels they should head it, as their buck-
> ets were principal in putting out the most recent fire.
> (Though the gossip is that Cousin Barend and his*

*band of wastrels carried the most water.) The locals
believe that their position in the middle of the river
makes them the best choice—but suddenly there are
new players in the game, the envoys from the old
tower, now that they've given up the pickle trade. And
of course the dish-makers want everything.*

*So. I stand ready to represent you in the seeking of
the perfect food, but what is your preference?*

If "dish-makers" was a crude swipe at the platter-faced
Chwahir, then Evred understood it well enough: every government along the strait wanted it patrolled but didn't trust
the others and didn't want to pay for the force necessary
for patrol. Meanwhile, rumors had it the Venn were going
to return.

He walked to his open window, and stared down at the
academy. Clashes, clangs, and boys' voices echoed from the
distant practice yards. He thought he caught Inda's laugh
among those braying teenage honks. That sharp bark was
Honeyboy Tya-Vayir. Inda had said, "I'm going to make
Honeyboy captain on a game. He'll never be Cama, but
he's not Horsebutt, either. Let him have his chance."

Evred rejoiced at Inda's every success, but each reflection brought him hard against the fact that everyone, men
and boys, was loyal to Inda. He did not resent it. He couldn't.
Call it wariness, left over from boyhood. The familiar wariness lay inside Evred like a curled fist; what Evred resented
was his own readiness for that fist to tighten to rage. He
made himself breathe slowly until it loosened while he contemplated how Inda had never in his life tried to command
loyalty. People just turned to him to lead them. And all his
own loyalty was given to Evred. There was no king in the
world who had a better shield arm.

Insane, Taumad had said once. Evred counted breaths
again. He was *not* insane. He could not let himself become
insane; he did not have that comfort.

Six days later Evred received a locket note from the
Runner who had replaced Nightingale Toraca at the Nob.
The first bit of news was the report from fishers sighting
the massing of Venn warships at Nathur, the southernmost
Venn base on Drael.

The second piece of news: *A woman we believe is Signi*

the Venn landed at the Nob from a trade ship. She set out alone down the south road.

Over the following days, as Signi jolted and swayed in a coffee wagon along the narrow Olaran coastal road leading to Lindeth Harbor, Evred considered his response. His first reaction had been anger: the massing of the Venn above Halia and her reappearance could not be coincidence.

But that did not mean she returned as a spy. He owed Signi the Venn the opportunity to explain herself. So he sent Kened to meet her with a mount. If she was not going to transfer by magic, but intended to travel overland to the royal city for some reason, at least she would not have to walk all the way south.

Half a year passed. Iasca Leror was too busy with everyday pursuits to notice until once again the long autumn twilight layered over the sky in bands of color. Harvest time was here. It was Restday when Dauvid Tya-Vayir reached home after his long journey from the academy.

Uncle Stalgrid seemed shorter, somehow, his jowls more fleshy, his brow more pinched as he shouted orders at the men laying the new roof on the stable. On their approach he turned sharply, his face tightening into suspicion.

All along the journey Dauvid had envisioned telling his uncle how he'd commanded two cub overnights, but the words dried up at the sight of that suspicion. No welcome, just suspicion. It was as if the world split somehow, and Honeyboy fell out of one world, becoming Dauvid in his uncle's smaller world, where everything that happened was somebody's fault if Uncle Stalgrid hadn't ordered it. Where everyone was a claphair or a coward or a slacker or a spy.

And so when his uncle said, "Well? Don't just stand there. We have work to do. Give me your report. What did they do to you this year?" Dauvid said, "Nothing."

"As well." Stalgrid Tya-Vayir snorted. "Lick their boots, get through the seven years. Then they'll leave us alone, until I'm forced to send the boy." And when Dauvid did not answer, Stalgrid motioned impatiently. "Get up there. Next time it will be your task to reset the roof, until such time as that idiot Montrei-Vayir in the royal city is willing to pay out for a mage as he promised."

It was not until much later that Dauvid trod wearily into

the castle. Everyone worked on Restday in Tya-Vayir if Uncle Stalgrid was in one of his moods.

Aunt Hibern, Aunt Imand's mate, was waiting for Dauvid. She greeted him kindly, asked if he was hungry, then brought him to his aunt. She was down at the summer bake house on the hill above the lakeshore. They'd rebuilt it that summer, Dauvid saw. She gave him a quick smile, and a searching gaze as she said, "We're still trying to learn its ways."

Dauvid opened his hand. His mother was now Head Baker, and his earliest chores had been kneading, before he got so big Uncle put him to train with the Riders, then chose him to be the new Randael.

"What did you learn this year?" Aunt Imand asked.

"I learned . . ." He hadn't meant to say, but Aunt Imand had never slapped him for saying the wrong thing. He'd discovered at the academy that nobody except Inda-Harskialdna wanted to hear what he was thinking. He got along better with the boys when he was quiet, and he had figured out why. It was because of all that time he'd spent trying to force the other boys see the world the way Uncle saw it.

So the words burst out of him. "If there's a young horse, Uncle sees the old nag it might be. There's a man, and Uncle sees a coward or a claphair. Everybody is, um, oh, smaller, for Uncle Stalgrid." He looked up, not having said that much to anyone since the last time he was sent to the Harskialdna in trouble—and he had only got in trouble once, early in spring.

"Go on," Aunt Imand said.

It felt good to talk. "I had a good year, and Uncle wants me to have a bad year, because he didn't order it. Because he doesn't like Headmaster Gand or the Harskialdna-Dal or the king. But I like being Honeyboy now." He groped, reaching into air as if he'd find the right words to grip onto. "When I'm Honeyboy, I'm *there*. And I led the cubs. Twice! It was good."

"When you're Honeyboy, you see the world everyone else sees. Welcome to it." Imand brushed a strand of hair off his forehead.

"What do I do?" he cried. "Try to change Uncle? Am I a coward to stay silent?"

"No. We all tried to change him, but he wants the world to be his way. The way his father and grandfather tried to force it to be."

"Why?"

Imand shook her braids back and wiped her brow. "I don't know. I grew up with them all, and I—well, here's something I learned. Your great-great-grandfather was a powerful warrior. It says so not just in our songs, but in all the songs. But a good warrior isn't always a good man. See?"

Dauvid shifted from foot to foot. "So what do I do?"

"What we all do. Say what he wants to hear, because he's the Jarl. And he works hard for Tya-Vayir, in his way. But we do what must be done in our own way."

Dauvid thumped his hand to his chest, and took more confident steps into this new world, which included other worlds, made by other people. And later, when Aunt Imand asked him to help Little Stalgrid with his first riding lessons, he went to do his best to teach that big world, the one that included everyone, to the little boy.

Evred sat back at his desk, wondering if he should risk a Fire Stick or just pull on his winter gloves when someone tapped at the door. Relieved at the interruption, he opened it himself, to discover Tesar, Hadand's personal Runner outside. Tesar's broad face was superficially impassive, but the corners of her mouth and the glisten of her eyes belied suppressed emotion.

"Hadand-Edli requests an interview," she said.

Hadand never interrupted him unless there was cause. He locked away Tau's last letter, then rushed down the long hall to the queen's suite.

The bow women on guard all grinned as they saluted.

Evred's heart thumped. He found Tdor and Hadand standing by the window in Hadand's bedchamber. "Hadand?"

Her eyes widened as she laid a hand over her belly. "It's been three weeks past when I ought to have had the monthly course," she said. "And there are other changes in my body, but I never thought—I didn't dare to—I ignored them. The healer says that I should stop drinking gerda." She gave an unsteady laugh. "Which is as well because as soon as I make myself choke it down, up it comes again. Evred, we will be parents next summer."

Later he was not certain what he said, or even how he got out of the room. Elation was so fierce he couldn't breathe for a time, so he retreated to his office, where he stood at the window staring sightlessly over the academy roofs.

Change.

He was going to be a father. Maybe a girl, the one he'd promised to Cama. A son, a future king? Joy twisted into dread. *Do not be like me, my son. Or my brother. Or my uncle. Maybe I should stay distant after all, leave you to Inda. Except I want you to be as much like my father as is possible. He was a great king.*

The next day, he faced his Guild Council.

They faced him. After six years of struggle to maintain a semblance of order despite what had seemed unending threat and disaster, the more observant of the guild leaders had learned to recognize the king's mood by little signs. Evred-Harvaldar was at all times reserved, even austere, far more than his father at the same age, the oldest maintained.

But today there was that about the set of his shoulders, the lift to his eyelids that made his eyes seem very green, the way he used his hands instead of hiding them, that caused the council to sit up a little straighter, or lean forward. The atmosphere, usually businesslike, sometimes tense, was now charged with expectation.

"I have established an envoy in Bren. He and my mother, who is ambassador for my Adrani cousin, have begun to form trade contacts."

Some cautious nods. None of this was new. The oldest sat still, waiting.

"I've been advised to open the way for you to exchange communication with your particular guilds in Bren, and through them, the rest of the world. This is a break with Marlovan tradition—"

His words were lost in the exclamations that no one could hold back. The council recovered themselves very quickly, but that was enough. Evred had his answer.

As soon as he was free again he wrote a short letter to Tau, reporting the gist of the council meeting. What else

should he write? He hesitated over his news. No, he would
wait for appearance of the child.

So he folded the paper, put it in the case, spoke the magic
words. When he opened the case again, the note was gone:
gone in an instant, and not carried step by step overland, to
reach Bren in half a year.

Change.

The next morning, Tdor kissed Inda and sent him off to his
weekly drill with the Runners-in-Training. She wasn't certain why she wanted to be alone for what she was about to
do, but it felt right. Maybe because most every other woman
who drank gerda seemed to take it in stride, or laugh a little
then got on with their lives.

But Tdor had always wanted to know what was coming next, she liked to prepare, and though even her closest
companions had sometimes teased her a little, she loved
little rituals.

Noren entered the bedroom, bearing a tray with a steaming red clay pot. Noren knew what was about to happen—
she and Tdor knew everything about each other. That was
why Tdor wrote unnecessary letters to Fareas-Iofre during
winter and summer, sending them back via Noren just so
Noren could see Whipstick.

"Here's the boiled water." Noren set the tray down.

"A pinch in the cup," Tdor said, quoting the healer.

She picked up the little ceramic jar painted around
the rim with a fairly exact replica of gerda in flower. She
broke the beeswax seal and lifted the lid. A pungent smell
emerged, not quite like what she'd smelled in Hadand's
chambers. It was somehow both sharper and sweeter, in a
vegetable way she could not define.

She dipped her fingers into the powder and dropped the
gold-green fragments into a shallow Marlovan dish. Noren
poured the boiled water carefully over it. Now it began to
smell familiar.

Noren glanced from the dissolving powder to Tdor
and laid down the wooden stir-stick they usually used for
mulled wine. Then she went out.

Tdor sniffed the aroma curling off the steep in slow
writhing vapors. She stirred, and when she could see the
bottom of the cup, picked it up with both hands and took a

cautious sip. Sharp and tart, not sweet. The healer had said many preferred to chew the root, bitter as it was. The taste was distinctive, not particularly good, but bearable. Far better than willow-bark steep.

She drank it all down, hot as it was, ignoring the sting on tongue and mouth. She wanted to feel the warmth spreading through her body. *This is how you begin to make a baby,* she thought. So very, very strange an idea! From one into two. Love made you and the one you loved two in one. Friend-love made you part of twos, and threes, and fours, part of kin-circles, part of a kingdom. And now she would become a two with a tiny being inside her body.

Joy tingled through her nerves, leaving her breathless. She sat there, cup in hands, until the sensation gradually diminished into the sweet ache of tenderness, but it did not go away. When she realized it would never go away—*never*—this was the love Fareas-Iofre had talked about, and it was here, for her—she got up, walked into the bedroom, pulled her knife from her sleeve and made another notch on the trunk.

Then she went downstairs to work.

As harvest time passed, fitful winds veered across the plains from the snowy mountains to the east, sending dry leaves skittering through the streets of the royal city.

Inda took his sentry walk early in order to escape a dousing from the dark line of clouds sweeping down. Tdor, newly arrived from the queen's side, joined him.

He was scarcely aware of the signal trumpet note announcing a King's Runner returning. They'd just reached the sentry walk over main gate when Inda stopped, staring downward at a small female form riding next to Kened, one of Evred's Runners, as they approached.

Inda drew his breath in sharply. "Signi?"

He took off, running past sentries who whirled around to stare. Inda ran like a boy, skidding at corners, leaping down the stairs six at a time, his coat skirts flapping behind him. Tdor could scarcely keep up with him. It was a long run; Kened and Signi had just passed through the castle gates into the royal stable yard when Inda and Tdor clattered down the residence's south tower.

Inda's face flushed with joy as he flung his arms around

Signi. She put her arms around him, but held her hands away from his back, gloved fingers spread. They clung together, rocking and laughing.

Tdor stood to one side, her emotions swooping and diving. A step at her shoulder brought her attention up. She was startled to discover Evred there.

Signi looked over Inda's shoulders, straight into Evred's eyes. This was no inscrutable mage, hiding behind her dance gestures. She looked older, and thinner, and frail, somehow, and her expression below a white scar on her forehead was troubled. He gazed back, perplexed.

How many kinds of love are there? Tdor thought. *Love is all around us, free as the air. Like trust, you have to give it before you can expect it back.* Her heart filled with the joy of Inda's happiness.

Evred said to Signi, "Welcome."

The tension smoothed from Signi's brow, but not the pain; Tdor and Evred realized that the puckers were lines formed there since they had seen the Venn dag last.

Signi knew what it meant for Evred to come all this way himself, instead of ordering her summoned to him. "Thank you, Harvaldar-Dal."

"I have received reports that your countrymen enter the strait," Evred said. "I ask only if they are on their way here."

Signi bowed her head. "I am an outcast, an exile. But I believe they sail down the strait to the east. And I am not to remain here: I await orders to carry on with the old plan, to give our navigation to Sartor. That way must be cleared by others first."

Evred opened his hand, and Tdor said, "Come on in, let's get you settled. It's almost time for Restday drum, and then a good, hot supper. We kept it waiting against the rain yonder."

Once Restday drum was over, the three of them ate alone in the Harskialdna suite. Evred sent a Runner to say that he would dine with Hadand.

At first Inda was as happy as Tdor had ever seen him, but that heedless cheer did not last. The dinner conversation was awkward, Inda's questions resulting in soft, smiling answers of "It can wait," after which Signi asked after people she knew. But those being few, she ran out quickly. Tdor hated her own stupid comments about weather, crops—inane questions, as she fumbled to fill the silences she could not account for. Signi's accent was strong again, making it difficult for Tdor to understand her.

The meal ended at last, Tdor thinking wistfully of those easy days around the campfire after they left Tenthen almost four years before. Remembering how gracefully Signi had left Inda to Tdor on her wedding, and on their first day of travel, Tdor excused herself to go visit Hadand. Maybe the two of them would be more comfortable if they had time alone.

"Signi is back," Tdor told Hadand, whom she found lying down in her bedchamber, her stomach too unsettled for her usual long day of work.

Hadand's eyes widened. "Inda's happy?"

"Well, he was at first. But just before I left, he was doing this." Tdor mimicked the distinctive grimace Inda gave when something was wrong.

A quiet knock they both recognized caused Tdor to get up again. Evred entered, followed by a pair of Runners bringing dinner for himself and Tdor and a pot of steeped ginger root for Hadand.

Tdor left them and walked slowly back to the Harskialdna chamber, wondering what the other two had decided about sleeping arrangements. She was surprised to find Inda lurking inside the main room.

"I was about to come looking for you," he said in a rumbling not-quite-whisper. "She's down at the baths. Tdor, I don't know what to do. There's . . . her voice." Inda grimaced. "I don't know how to explain it. There's *pain* in her words. It wasn't there before. It gripes me." He rubbed the back of his neck.

"Did she say what delayed her?"

"Not really. Just she can't do magic anymore. She didn't say why, or where she went when she vanished from the south. Just said, 'It can wait.' "

"I thought that meant wait until I was out of the room."

Inda rubbed his hands up his face and over his head. "No, she never does things like that. I think it means she just doesn't want to talk about whatever happened. That change in her voice—she kept those gloves on, did you notice? Something happened." Inda's eyes narrowed, then he turned away, staring sightlessly at the wall. Tdor waited, and when he turned back, he said, "What should I do?"

"Hold her," Tdor said, pressing her forehead against his, until she felt his brow untense. "If she's in pain, then hold her. Love her. Everything else will sort itself out."

Chapter Five

THE year 3919 was called "The Year Without a Spring" until forty-four years later, when the Great Frost peaked the cycle of long, cold winters.

On land that year, when the sky finally cleared, those most observant kept part of their seed stock in reserve, despite the unconscionably late melt. They better withstood the destructive effects of the last (and most ferocious) winter blizzard that howled out of the east a month later, leaving the land abruptly steaming in summer.

On the seas, the customary spring fogs and rain as the wind and currents made their spiraling shift were replaced by spectacular thunderstorms. The Venn fleet (and after them, the cautious sea trade) sailed when at last they saw two days of clear sky in a row.

Those with long experience of the strait watched the skies with deep suspicion. They knew that an appearance of sudden summer usually brought on typhoons like those that often struck the vast oceans between western Goerael and eastern Drael.

The sun was a month short of midsummer when the Venn fleet reached Llyenthur's main harbor.

Oneli Stalna Hyarl Durasnir stood at the open scuttle as

he wrestled his baldric over his armor. He nibbled like a rabbit, testing the air with his front teeth. When he was a teenage ensign, he and his group once decided they'd emulate their ancestors by clenching a knife in their teeth during battle. They began with fighting drill. Durasnir didn't need more than a day to really hate the distinctive grit of metal against tooth enamel. Because they were young idiots, no one would admit what a spectacularly bad idea it was, and it had taken the inevitable sanguine disaster to end the experiment.

Ever since then, he defined that quality in the air before an oncoming storm as knife-in-the-teeth. The hot, still summer air tasted metallic, though not a cloud was visible anywhere in the strait, or northward above the uneven jut of low mountains inland of Llyenthur Harbor.

He adjusted the baldric and its knotted hangings before sliding his sword into the loops. The last sword fight he'd engaged in was right here in Llyenthur, decades ago.

He stepped out of the small cabin into the wardroom, where his ensigns waited with the rest of his gear. He lifted his arm so his ensign could affix his arm torcs. No embroidered ones for this interview, but the real ones, uncomfortable as they were. He had never believed his ancestors actually wore the things to fight in. His armor was polished mirror bright, his helm as well, the wings newly lacquered.

When he was satisfied with his appearance, he reported to the cabin, as required. Under the pretence that the king commanded this venture, Erkric not only read every order but must be apprised of all comings and goings. When approaching the doors to what had been his cabin for years, Durasnir always reminded himself of his promise to his wife. The war was going to happen. It was his job to limit the cost to the Venn.

The Erama Krona before the door silently parted. One guard permitted entrance to the outer, public chamber, where Durasnir's great table still sat. Rajnir sat in a kind of throne behind the chart table, strong sunlight through the stern windows highlighting the king's long pale hair, but otherwise throwing him into silhouette.

Durasnir made his obeisance to that shadowy figure. "My king, I depart to the parley. I also wish to advise you to order the fleet to make sea room. In my experience—"

"Yes, Oneli Stalna Commander." Erkric used the strictly

formal mode, without the "my." "We've had a nine of messages about storms so far today. As there are no clouds to be seen in all directions, we *can* keep watch over the inner islands and the estuary. The king has not changed his orders."

Durasnir once more made his obeisance, an empty gesture toward an empty vessel. He effaced himself, bypassing the silent guardians in white. No one ever addressed the Erama Krona. As for the Yaga Krona, he and Dag Ulaffa interacted as little as necessary in public.

Durasnir climbed down into the longboat. The light reflecting off metal and water was peculiarly penetrating, a white glare that seemed to dart through his eyes to the back of his head. He would have a kraken-sized headache by nightfall, he thought sourly as he peered through his glass toward the shore, where the parley flags hung limp in the still air above the harbormaster's tower.

As the crew lifted their oars on signal, Durasnir settled back, eyes closed against the winking glare off the choppy waves. A restless sea in still air that now tasted of rust.

His head panged. At least he could conduct this parley without the presence of that young idiot Dyalf Balandir. Erkric could not blame anyone else for the stupidity of his candidate for Battlegroup Chief, who should never have been made a captain. As the boat surged through the water, Durasnir thought back to the previous month, when they'd finally closed in on Granthan.

The small harbor at Llyenthur's western end had put up only a semblance of resistance. What could be anyone's motivation for what seemed afterward outright madness? Perhaps it was frustration at being balked of battle glory that caused Battlegroup Captain Hyarl Balandir to board a fisher with a band of nine of his personal guard without waiting for the Drenga.

Only someone whose desire for glory outweighed sense and experience could have failed to see how very poorly that "fisher" had disguised its habitual trade as a pirate.

Though Balandir would recover, it would take a while for the broken bones to knit. It was still impossible to know if the healers could repair his eye. As well the pirates had been taking their time about their fun; they hadn't begun on the second eye when the Drenga caught up.

The pirates were long dead and their ship burned before Durasnir arrived on inspection. No pirates left to question, leaving him puzzling over that peculiarity about eyes. Pirate tortures had been far too common in the bad days, including breaking the major bones of a commander and leaving him to die. But the knife games with eyes appeared to indicate deliberate intent.

The longboat crew rowed back under *Petrel*'s lee. Battlegroup Chief Seigmad climbed down.

Safe on the wrong side of the ship from *Cormorant* and Erkric's vigilant spyglass, Durasnir permitted himself a brief smile.

Seigmad settled next to Durasnir in the stern sheets and raised his glass.

As the longboat skimmed into the calmer waters of the inner harbor, the two commanders appraised the fleet lined up across the horizon, ready on signal to comb through the islands. They'd had to tack and tack again out in the strait for four weeks, waiting on a shift in the wind. Durasnir knew they'd lost any hope of surprise. Perhaps the weeks of dread would better serve them.

The *drakans* bobbed gently on the water, 324 warships plus his *Cormorant,* all stripped to fighting sail, the occasional wink and gleam of sun on steel from the rails and the mastheads. Beyond them, rank on rank dotting the horizon, the masts of the raiders. It was a daunting sight—one could be forgiven for surrendering without a strike to such a force.

"Everyone exactly on station," Seigmad said with satisfaction, then scowled skyward. "If only it didn't feel like a blow! Think these locals will give in?"

"No." Durasnir pointed at the hazy humps of islands off the western shore. "Their fleet will be hiding behind those and the rest up the harbor, where our draught is too deep to sail. Just like when I was here last." He sniffed. "If the coming storm doesn't hit first."

Seigmad gave a bark of laughter. "They talked of the stink of our spices. What stinks to me is their fear."

Except for the creak of wood and the quiet whoosh of oars too well handled to splash, there were no sounds. The two knew that a spiderweb lay over the longboat: whatever they said, Erkric would hear.

The main pier was visible now. A knot of people in gaudy dress awaited them at the end. They stood close together in the manner of people trying to hide uneasiness. The sun was merciless on their formal wear, which was long, cape-layered coats worn open over shorter personal coats of contrasting silk, embroidered vests, and paneled trousers. It seemed that in Llyenthur, embroidered shoes were now the fashion; of those gathered there, only one held himself with what Durasnir and Seigmad considered military bearing.

"Fat one toward the back."

"Just so."

As the longboat drew to the kelp-streaming, barnacle-dotted floating dock below the pier, Durasnir gazed up into those watching faces. They betrayed apprehension in widened pupils and compressed mouths, anger making bodies tight, and cheeks mottled with color that had little to do with the bright sun radiating directly onto their heads.

The little group stepped back as Durasnir's chosen Drenga guards mounted the stair from the dock to the pier and spread out, steel drawn, points down.

When they had satisfied themselves that no weapons were in sight, they parted, and Durasnir and Seigmad climbed up. A woman stepped forward. "We have prepared a place to hold the parley." The feathers in her upbraided hair looked limp. Seigmad wondered if these people had never heard of lacquer.

Durasnir motioned for them to lead the way.

Byoren Henga was on point; to him belonged the honor of dying first if the locals planned treachery. Durasnir contemplated the delegation while Seigmad assessed Henga's grip, his grim mood. Here was a man who longed for death, but he would take as many of the enemy with him as he could. Seigmad still could not quite fathom why Durasnir had demoted Henga after the Drenga captain's success at Andahi Castle in clearing the way for the failed invasion.

The harbormaster's building sat squarely athwart the land end of the main dock, encircled by boardwalk.

Henga and the guards ducked under the low doorway opening into the ground floor of the building. The room was empty of anything but a table and chairs, except for a steaming pot of something sitting on a sideboard next to some lemon cakes.

The last guard signaled the all clear, and the Venn commanders followed the others inside. Durasnir glanced around. He'd been stationed in Llyenthur for two years on his first cruise, before his brothers fought their duels and died. The carved panels of dragons and leaves that he remembered in this room, once the Oneli command center, had been hacked out and replaced with brick. The furnishings—the clean-lined curule chairs and the tables with rune-carved circular legs— were all gone. Someone had replaced them with rough-hewn tables and benches. Or maybe those had been brought specifically for this meeting as an oblique insult.

The delegates settled around the table after a series of nods and hand motions. The woman with the drooping feathers sat at one end, and the fat man with the military bearing stood behind her, his elbows out, hands on hips, his broad forehead beaded with sweat above heat-flushed cheeks.

"Would you like refreshment?" the woman asked.

The food was probably not poisoned. That was the swift way to martyrdom. Loaded with overpowering spices would merely be humiliating to the unwanted invaders. Durasnir made a negating motion.

"What do you want?" the man said, the civilities over.

Durasnir said, "We have returned, as you see. We will use this harbor as a base, but you will be free to carry on your trade under our regulation. For our part, we promise there will be no more alliance with pirates. They will not be tolerated in any waters we patrol."

"And in the future?"

"The future will take care of itself. We are concerned with the present. Either you make peace, or we will secure the harbor by force."

The woman with the feathers reddened, and a younger man looked down, his fists tight at his sides.

"Are my words unexpected?" Durasnir asked. "You must know that we hold Granthan, which was given the same message. Your people abandoned it after half a watch of resistance."

"And you destroyed the town," the fat man said, his jowls quivering with rage.

Durasnir said, "It was necessary in order to establish control. My orders are specific. If you surrender the harbor, we take over use of the primary buildings and leave the remainder in peace. Otherwise, we destroy all buildings, tunnels, passages—everything that constitutes what we consider a military threat. We will require local labor to rebuild according to our design."

"Peace!" the young man said, his voice husky with rage. "We heard what kind of peace you gave them over the water in Andahi, when they hauled their flag down."

"Chopping up little girls after putting out their eyes," the woman said, and spat on the floor near Durasnir's feet. "Go ahead," she declared, her voice thin and quavering. "Put mine out. Chop me up. For speaking my mind. I'd as soon it was now as later."

Seigmad's jaw sagged.

Durasnir flicked him a glance and tipped his head toward the door. Battle it was, then.

Seigmad followed, impatient to get far enough out of earshot of the locals (now heard vehemently arguing with one another) to demand an explanation. His impatience intensified when he caught a glance between Durasnir and Henga.

For five, ten strides, he controlled his impatience, then burst out, "*Little girls?* You never showed me the Andahi report. No, don't waste time telling me the report belongs to the Hilda as Captain Henga was under Talkar's command. Tell me this. Did Talkar break Henga or did you, and why?"

The thud of their heels on the warped dock timbers were the only sound; Durasnir peered under his hand. The white glare was nearly blinding, but he made out long ripples out on the water, its color a deep, almost startling green.

Seigmad waited for an answer.

"Erkric caused Talkar to commend Henga," Durasnir said finally. "I ordered Henga to choose an appropriate action after he confessed to me."

"That he murdered children?"

"No, but the world will always believe that." Durasnir lifted his voice. "Henga? Why did you choose demotion?"

The man was directly behind them, his gaze remote.

Was she a coward or a traitor to her people, this Jarlan?
Henga's wife had asked.

No. She defended her home to the last.

Did you give her a clean death?

*No. She went into warrior rage. She killed herself before
we were done with her, and cursed us with her dying breath.*

There were girls? Henga's daughter had demanded.
There were girls defending, and you killed them?

Yes. And he told them how.

"Drenskar," he said flatly, "requires one to respect one's
enemy. That means necessary strength against a worthy
foe."

Seigmad grimaced, head down. Henga was that rarity,
good at command on water and land, as Drenga must be.
Now thrown away. No, he'd thrown himself away. Seigmad
understood now. Henga had removed himself from command because in extremity, he had surrendered to blood-
lust when his foe had lost the power to resist.

Seigmad wondered which was worse, the demotion or the
memories.

They had nearly reached the end of the pier. "It'll take
us a week at least here," Seigmad said. "If not longer. It's
madness to expect us to take Nelsaiam and the north coast
this summer, much less attempt both sides of the strait."

The madness of Rainorec, Durasnir thought, remembering what Brun had said. *Erkric is rushing the Oneli into victory or death. The more of us who die, the easier it is for him
to put his dags in our place.*

He paused halfway down the barnacle-covered ladder
to the boat, then dropped the rest of the way. "Heh. Signal
flags."

Seigmad settled beside him, his joints protesting as he
slewed around. "Command to win sea room," he translated,
and clamped his mouth shut on the question, *Who got that
souleater Erkric to listen to sense?*

As the boat crew plied their oars, the two commanders
observed the expert shift of sail along that vast row, following which the ships turned, beautiful in profile against
the thickening white haze. All sails set, even studding sails
extending to either side, an impressive sight, or would be
impressive when the sagging sailcloth filled.

Seigmad wiped sweat out of his eyes and sat back, considering his words. If he looked sideways, he could catch the faint glimmer of magic along the gunwales, reminding him of the ever-present spiderwebs. "I don't understand that comment about surrender. The Marlovans never surrendered, everyone attests to that."

"Talkar, Henga, everyone reported that the women cut down their own flag in response to the offer of peaceful surrender. My guess is, Idayagans watching from the mountain heights above Andahi Castle misread the gesture. Thought it capitulation."

"Idayagans would have shit themselves if we'd hove up on the horizon when they held that castle." Seigmad chuckled.

"They certainly wouldn't have been able to surrender fast enough," Durasnir said as he lifted his glass to the mountain heights on either side of the river, then swept it over the terraced city below. He focused on the steady stream of inhabitants, many pulling small carts as they evacuated into the hills. The line wavered, some gesturing away toward the east. A few began to hasten back down again. Others stood around in knots, talking and gesticulating.

"Looks like a cross-sea getting up," Seigmad said as the first of a set of waves rolled toward them. The boat began rocking, sending up refreshing splashes of water.

Durasnir said to the crew, "Stretch out."

Not that they needed the reminder; the boat soon reached the *Petrel*, which promptly raised sail and tacked away on the fitful, hot gusts blowing out of the west, veering sharply south and then back again.

By the time Durasnir reached the *Cormorant*, the opaque white line all dreaded formed with deceptive slowness across the eastern horizon, thickening rapidly.

The sail crews had already taken in the jibs and studding sails. The maincourse came down as Durasnir clambered aboard, yelling, "Luff! Luff! Abandon the boat!" They'd just begun to ease off when the first wind hit, knocking the ship on its beam ends.

The main- and fore-topsails ripped free of the bolt-ropes edging them; several men were flung overboard, their cries unheard as the wind screamed, sleet flying horizontally with the force of arrows.

Crack! The foremast tipped slowly toward sudden mountainous seas, rigging snaking after. Durasnir grabbed up a hatchet, hacking madly at the tangle. For an endless time everyone on board fought to cut away the snarl of rigging and canvas and wood, then to get a scrap of sail on the maintop, enough to keep them up into the wind. They had lost sight of the others. They existed alone in lightning-flared blackness, sky, sea, storm all one ferocious vortex.

When the storm at last expended itself the next morning, leaving a white-foaming sea strewn with wreckage, Erkric emerged from the great cabin, his face blanched into extreme age.

"The king wishes us to take this harbor at once." His voice shook.

Durasnir had expected those orders. As the storm began to lose force, the sea dags had begun locating themselves and reporting in, the lists of damage appalling. Devastating as the storm had been on the Oneli, it would have been equally terrible on shore, and Durasnir doubted that Llyenthur would put up much of a fight. How many of their ships had been wrecked on the rocks of those islands they'd been hiding behind?

Then Erkric spoke again, and this time took Durasnir by surprise. "Once you have secured this harbor, the king wishes to establish a base here. You will send messages under white flag to Bren and Nelsaiam, giving them a year to surrender their harbors."

Durasnir gave the necessary orders, then retreated to his cabin. *Erkric must have been frightened by his first typhoon,* Durasnir thought, sitting down to wait for the first food and drink he'd had since the morning before the storm. He crossed his arms and laid his head down, falling immediately into a deep slumber.

Erkric prowled the deck, making and discarding plans. The storm was already forgotten. What frightened him had occurred before the storm hit, while Durasnir and Seigmad were en route from the parley.

All on his own, with no signal or sign, Rajnir had suddenly said, "I want the fleet to win sea room." And he had turned to Erkric, his blue eyes *aware.* "Order the signals, my Dag."

Chapter Six

ON a balcony one floor above the King's Saunter, the once-grand boardwalk sweeping in a grand arc along the inner harbor at Freeport, Nugget stood with a spyglass to her eye. "*Cocodu*'s warping back in," she called.

Footsteps pounded up the staircase from the bakery below. Pilvig appeared, her black eyes wide, round face flushed. "We're all ready."

Nugget squealed, a shrill, keening squeal that stopped the strollers below, causing most to laugh, some to shake heads, a few sourmouths to curse.

But most of the people in Freeport Harbor were in good moods, because today was Midsummer's Day. There'd been no spring this year, so Flower Day's Games had been postponed until now.

By the end of breakfast, one of Dhalshev's staff had run along the Saunter to each of the businesses, collecting donations for the favorite event: the gold bag run.

The time was set for noon, just as the tide would turn. Volunteer guards stood glowering along the docks floating on the water below the Saunter, protecting the rowboats waiting for the competing teams.

Mutt sat at the best table at the best tavern on the Saunter, observing with a combination of amazement and satisfaction the sweep of windows in a broad, semicircular bank. They slanted inward, emulating the stern windows of a captain's cabin as they overlooked the northern end of the Saunter, the main square, and the pier end of Freeport's main street. When the sun dropped westward toward the entrance to the harbor, sometimes it threw light reflections over the ceiling of the tavern, with its ancient painting of some night sky no one could figure out.

Mutt twisted his head: there was the betting book, and the ceramic pot with the money collected over the years from those who wrote a guess and bought in. Someday someone would identify that sky, and if they could find the one who'd guessed right, that person would get the pot.

Mutt remembered that pot, and the guess book, and the sky, from his very first day in Freeport. He had been so young he couldn't remember much from before then. Just cold, hunger, and this building, and the grown-ups chasing him out again when he tried to climb up and steal the pot.

He'd always meant to steal the pot, just because. He had even organized some of the other orphans at the doss down at the far end of the Saunter, where castoffs lived, if you didn't mind hard work for nothing more than a place to sleep and food to eat. Then Inda took him on. When he next returned to Freeport, the bet and the pot and the weird sky were just funny.

Now he was sitting here, a captain in his own right, member of the toughest independent fleet in the southern world. The indies and privateers gave place when he and his fellow captains in the Fox Banner Fleet sauntered the Saunter. Weird what life did to you. If you survived.

Just beyond the windows lay a brick terrace full of benches and tables; in good weather, those tables, with their vantage on the Octagon, the main pier, and the city square, were the place to be seen.

The *squeak-squeak-squeak* of wheels that spent too much time in the salt air broke Mutt's reverie.

"Beautiful, eh?" Mutt tipped his head toward *Cocodu,* his new command, alone there in the harbor.

Only a captain could see beauty in a ship wallowing under a single scrap of sail, otherwise bare poles glistening suspiciously, a bag dangling from the mainmast top.

Dasta leaned back in his wheelchair, smiling wistfully around his tavern. "Beautiful," he repeated.

He still had bad dreams about those days following the Venn attack. The list of dead, including old shipmates—Fox's angry voice offering someone a king's ransom if they could heal Dasta's backbone. "It late," an old woman quavered in heavily accented Dock Talk, as Dasta lay shivering and sweating in his bunk. "Much late, you here much late."

Dasta gazed in satisfaction at his tavern. A fighting ship captain needed at least one working leg. His legs were just there, unable to move, so Dasta had used his part of the treasure and bought the best tavern on Freedom Island.

His tavern. He liked tavern keeping, he'd discovered. He liked hearing the tales the captains brought in. The only thing that really hurt bad was a year ago spring, when Fox gave the orders to sail. He'd watched them all grin and hasten to pack up their gear, just like he'd once done. Then they'd sailed away, leaving him sitting on his newly bricked terrace.

He was glad to have them around now . . . except why *were* they here? Fox lounged around as if it were still winter.

"You know Nugget's going to compete?" Dasta asked.

Mutt grinned. "Why d'you think I sent *Cocodu* way out there to prepare? I knew she'd post her posse on the roofs to spy out whatever she could."

"That's exactly what they've been doing," Dasta said.

Nugget's headquarters was Dasta's second best room upstairs.

"Charge 'em double for being annoying." Mutt snickered.

They were all rich, or at least rich as mariners understood rich. Mutt was glad Dasta had bought this tavern, now his second home. Mutt even had a room of his own—he'd paid Dasta five years' rent, so no one would ever sleep in it or touch his few belongings. It was the idea of a home that he liked, a place always waiting for him whenever the tide brought him back.

Not that he would leave anything important there. His mind snapped to his share of the treasure, still stored on *Cocodu*. Mutt thought back to his promotion as captain right after the battle at Jaro, and Dasta lying in the bunk, shivering and sweating by turns as he whispered on and on in an effort to tell Mutt things a captain should know about *Cocodu*. Dasta had spent years tapping and twisting at all the bric-a-brac in the cabin, discovering new secret compartments over time. During his fits of wakefulness, he'd directed Mutt to most of them.

Made sense to keep one's stash there. If the ship went down, Mutt was likely to be going down with it. He still didn't know what to do with that much treasure anyway ... sometimes he wondered what Nugget would do with hers ... *Nugget*.

"I'm not surprised Nugget's going for it," Mutt said, watching that bag swinging against *Cocodu*'s mainmast. "It's not the gold. It's winning."

Dasta grunted. "She'll get it, too. She's been drilling her team out back of Lark."

"I know." Mutt grinned. "I bet against her. Just to make her mad."

Dasta chuckled, then made their old ship rat signal for "captain coming." "Fox given out any orders?" he asked Mutt.

Mutt shrugged and spread his hands. "You know how gabby he is." Sometimes he felt so tough, being a captain of a fast raffee with a wicked rep. The girls along the Saunter thought him something fine, that's for sure. But when Fox loomed up, silent as a cat, he felt like a ship rat again. "I don't know what he's up to. Nobody does. Know what else? I think Dhalshev hates him. Wishes we were gone."

Dasta snorted. "Always known *that*."

Above, from the balcony around the Octagon's top, Harbormaster Dhalshev watched the competitors shoving their way through the crowds to line up along the stone rail carved with a lyre motif.

Thick as the crowd was, everyone flowed around the single black-clad figure walking down the middle of the Saunter toward Dasta's Chart House, hand raised against the sun as Fox contemplated *Cocodu* being anchored stern-on.

Dhalshev eyed that lean, straight-backed figure. The only color about Fox at this distance was the ruby glinting in one ear and that bright red hair.

"Lookin' at Fox?" The deep, slightly husky voice belonged to Jeje, the single member of the Fox Banner Fleet permitted entry to the Octagon's command center at the very top.

"Is he always the center of attention?" Dhalshev asked, not taking his eyes away from Fox.

"I dunno. He's not popular, like, say, Mutt. Or Dasta. Or Eflis. I think people notice him just to stay out of his way."

Dasta or Eflis or you, Dhalshev thought, but didn't say it. You never knew with Jeje. She might get flustered, or she might turn that ferocious scowl onto you and vanish. "Why does he wear only one of those ruby earrings?" Dhalshev asked. "From what I understand of your tradition, he could wear two."

"He won't. And just laughs when anyone asks why." Jeje made a spitting motion, more habit than conviction.

"I'm certain I'd get the same nonanswer if I asked what his plans were."

"Heyo." Jeje leaned against the rail. "He's not going to take over Freedom, if that's where you're going."

He already runs it, Dhalshev thought wryly. Everyone deferred to Fox, everyone. Dhalshev maintained a carefully neutral affect toward him, something he didn't have to think about with anyone else, even the occasional pirate who sailed in. These latter obeyed Dhalshev's rules, or he could raise the harbor against the pirates. Pirates knew it, sailors knew it, merchants knew it.

Fox could order his fleet to take the harbor, and though the harbor might fight back, they'd lose. Harbor knew it, Fox Banner Fleet knew it. Dhalshev knew it.

Dhalshev knew Fox knew it.

The last gold bag team was in place along the wall now, the individuals jostling impatiently. Dhalshev waved to his signaler on duty, who blew the horn, and a shout rose below as the teams stampeded down the ramps to the floating docks. Gusts of laughter rose, and howls of encouragement or insult (or both), as people got shoved or tripped (or thrown) into the water. Boats launched, oars splashing hard. Boats rammed one another, tried to hook one another. Laughter and shouting rose to such a pitch the sea birds roosting on the slanting roofs flapped skyward, scolding.

"Here's a strange thing," Dhalshev said as he pinpointed

golden-haired Nugget below, her team skimming to cut off the fastest boat. "Even kings can't guarantee orderly transfer of power. Though most would like to. Especially the ones who took over."

"Kings." This time Jeje did spit, but out over the water below the rail. "Whyja bring up kings? Fox remind you of one?"

Dhalshev did not make the mistake of thinking that in any way complimentary.

Fox sauntered up the wide brick stair to Dasta's tavern, and crammed as the place was, sure enough, everyone got out of his way until he dropped down next to Dasta's chair at the best table. They could see the bay, the curve of the Saunter into the main street, and the Octagon—and they could be seen.

"No," Dhalshev said. "And yes. In all ways he'd make the most sense to replace me as harbormaster. But I don't want him for that very reason."

Jeje looked up, quick concern. "You're not abandoning Freeport? It's home!"

"No, no," Dhalshev said, patting the air. "But I wasn't young when I settled this place, nearly twenty years ago. Some days during winter, I wonder how much longer I'll get up those steps. I'd like to hand it off to someone who would maintain what I've made."

"And you don't know with Fox. Well, neither do we. He's got some plan in that brick head of his," Jeje exclaimed. "I just hate that. He smiles and I want to smack his face off. Last year the weather was just as bad, or almost, and we sailed anyway. Went after that villain Finna, the renegade Venn. Fox says it's the weather, why we haven't sailed by now, but I *know* he's waiting for something."

So that answered Dhalshev's main question. If Fox hadn't told Jeje, then he wasn't talking to anyone, except maybe Barend—but he was even more close-mouthed than Fox.

Out on the water, Nugget stood poised on the bow of her boat, bare feet balancing on the gunwales, her hand swinging her rope in a glittering circle.

Just as three boats converged on hers, she sent the rope shooting upward in a perfect arc, the hook catching on the upper shrouds. She leaped up, turning end over end as the rope wrapped round her legs; below, her crew whipped out spears from the boat bottom and turned on the attackers, sending two scurrying. One held its position, only to get a full pot of oil splattered over them.

"Nugget's got it," Jeje said. "Heh!"

"Not yet. She seems to be sitting there on the fore-masthead." Dhalshev rubbed his jaw, remembering Nugget's shrill voice when she was small, her limitless hunger for attention. "Is this demonstration to prove to the world she's as good as those with two arms?"

"Naw, she already did that long ago. Had to, the way Fox smacked her around until she fought back. I think it's 'cause Mutt got up her nose. Those two, they're either brother and sister—squabbling like 'em, I mean—or else lovers. Nobody knows which they'll be one day or the next, least of all them."

Dhalshev observed the furious scramble on the *Cocodu*'s deck. Splashes all around the rail caused whoops and shouts in the spectators; above, Nugget swung back and forth, bopping heads. As yet she hadn't hooked over to the mainmast to grab the bag, though the younger crew of the Fox Banner Fleet, who'd spent all last spring learning to fly about the upper masts, knew she could any time she wanted to.

"Didn't you sit her and Mutt down?" he asked, as one who'd ended up being in some wise a father to Nugget.

"I did. Year before last. Put 'em on stink-oil duty when we had that brush with the Venn off The Fangs. It worked—for a day. Until Nugget saw Fox in action."

"She hadn't seen that?"

"Of course she had! But between one time and another she'd woken up. All that one year, she flirted with Eflis, mostly trying to make Mutt mad, but also experimenting around. Then it was Fox she wanted, all because she liked the way he looked in battle."

Dhalshev laughed at the sheer unlikelihood.

"Brief. Very brief. But very intense."

Dhalshev grimaced. "I can't see those two hammock dancing."

"Neither could Fox, because it never happened. Intense on her part. He ignored her. The night we celebrated Sparrow's and Eflis' handfasting—this was last spring, just before we took on Finna—she tried walking into his cabin wearing nothing but her arm fringe on one shoulder and a jug of wine on the other."

Dhalshev was surprised into a hoot of laughter.

"He steered her right out and barred his door. Had half the fleet laughing. Older half. Younger ones fuming on her part, though she just pranced around in her skin and ended up with Mutt."

Dhalshev smiled.

"By the time we got done with that renegade Venn, they were fighting again." Jeje jerked up her chin. "Heyo. There goes the bag—Pilvig! I wonder if that's some kind of payback. Now, time to get ready for the wedding."

And she dashed out, leaving Dhalshev still without a clue why Fox kept the highly trained, battle-ready fleet in harbor. The weddings were an excuse, not a reason.

Chapter Seven

BY the time Mutt's crew had finished cleaning up the *Cocodu*'s deck (a spectacular mess) and had begun replacing all the grease-smeared standing rigging (worn, frayed stuff put up for the gold bag run), the King's Saunter was undergoing its festival transformation. Everywhere people hung up big colored rice-paper lanterns, most with tiny glowglobes inside, and the poorer emporia with little candles. The result was a galaxy of brilliance above tables loaded with refreshments.

Dasta had hired a group of musicians to play from the other end of the terrace. The younger girls had decorated the rail with garlands made with flowers raided from every garden a day's trudge from the harbor, with silk lilies donated by Lark Ascendant to eke out the ends.

Midsummer's Day was as popular as Flower Day for weddings; when there wasn't a Flower Day due to bad weather, all the weddings got saved up. The Fox Banner Fleet had two. As these involved three popular captains, the crews of most of the fleet crammed into the Chart House, dressed in their best—or their most colorful—and many had begun their celebratory drinking and dancing long before the wedding pairs appeared.

Eflis took in the drunks and slapped her thigh, laughing. Her hilarity was irresistible; even Sparrow, so still and serious, briefly smiled, the chimes braided in her hair tinkling sweetly at every step.

That sharp, bloody battle against the Venn had accelerated a number of changes in ship command as well as relationships.

Gillor had avoided entanglements with any one person her entire life, though she'd looked Fox's way ever since Gaffer Walic forced them on board as crew.

Looking Fox's way had become habit. After the Venn fight, when she had time to reflect on the long, nasty battle, she'd realized her worst worry was about Tcholan, who was her most frequent lover, and she hadn't spared Fox a thought at all, except irritation when *Death* hove up late to *Cocodu*'s rescue, the scuppers running with red after repelling two Venn boarder attacks.

Life was short and precious. Before they'd faced Finna last year, she and Tcholan had handfasted in secret. It had felt good to face battle with the prospect of something permanent in a life full of farewells.

So here they were, the four of them, all wearing wedding green and white. Off to the side stood the youngest two Marlovan orphans; Jeje had given the ship rats to Eflis to train after the battle, and to everyone's surprise, the two youngest and Eflis had bonded.

Eflis bent over the islands' official scribe—hired from Sartor to write Freedom Island contracts, as there was no recognized government. "Family name Zhavala. Eh? We're all agreed?" At a solemn nod from Sparrow and foot-hopping, happy grins from the tow-headed boy and girl now being officially adopted, the official smiled back, and wrote all their names down.

As the children each spoke their names (the boy with a slight tremor in his words) and watched their legal status take form, Eflis stared at them in amazement. She'd taken on children for years. Some stayed, some went, a few died. There were five of these Marlovan rats, all orphans from that battle out west, but somehow these two had become hers. Their happiness mattered. She didn't go to bed until she'd seen them asleep; she made certain they had clothes and food and had found herself wondering if she should put them to a tutor. When the boy stuttered, she knew he was anxious; if they hurt, so did she.

Sparrow's hands tightened. "We're a family," she whispered.

"Almost." The official held up her sved. "After the vows."

"All right! Let's go!" Eflis yelled, twirling around.

Eflis had chosen a magnificent gown of gold-edged lace over green silk; Sparrow wore layers of pale green moth-wing silk that floated in hypnotic swirls when she moved.

Gillor strode in, decked out in her usual swashbuckling trousers and puffy shirt, but the trousers were wedding green instead of blue-and-white striped. Tcholan wore a green shirt and white deck pants. He was proudest of the fine gold-stitched sash that Jeje had given him, bought when the fleet had touched at Sarendan's coast the previous autumn.

The four stood under the wedding arch of green boughs, each couple holding hands. They spoke their vows more or less together, Eflis' voice trembling with laughter when someone or other stumbled. The newlyweds kissed to a roar of approval from those crowded round, and bottles passed from hand to hand.

The Sartoran scribe flourished her hand a little as she affixed the sved and said the magic spell over it. The crowd roared in approval as each contract vanished with a faint glimmer of light, to be stored in the Guild Archive in Sartor.

The two families looked at one another with pride and delight.

Then Nugget, barely waiting for the formal part of the evening to be over, swung down from the painted ceiling and began a rope dance over everyone's heads.

The band began tapping and jingling in time, and people clapped as Nugget whirled and danced through the air in a way no one had ever seen before. The guests howled and cheered.

Dhalshev backed from the door, where he'd stood long enough to see the couples wed. He was about to walk on down the Saunter to the other weddings he'd been invited to when a gleam from high up brought his attention to the Octagon silhouetted against the stars. In one of the windows at the top someone flashed a deadlight: blink-blink pause, blink-blink.

Signal from headland.

Dhalshev elbowed through the crowd to gaze across the harbor toward the rounded hills that formed the mouth of the harbor. Nothing visible, naturally. He pushed past a couple of Tcholan's upper yardmen singing a bawdy song with their captain's name inserted for a pirate infamous for sexual adventures, then checked when the darkness intensified at his side.

Fox was there, dressed in black as always.

Instantly suspicious, Dhalshev asked, "You expecting someone?" He waved toward the distant headland.

"News only," Fox said.

Dhalshev was uneasy at winning that much from Fox. Something was amiss, all right. But it never did to ask. Instead, "I noticed your wedding pairs hired the scribe to make up treaties. That means they own something to be negotiated. You given your captains their ships?"

"No. Anything taken by us belongs to the fleet, which still belongs to Inda. That idea still holds them together, tenuous as it is. Except for Eflis. She came to us with her ships, and she adopted two of our ship rats."

Dhalshev was surprised to learn that much and reflected that the signal might signify news. And Fox wanted to be there to hear it. Give a little, get a little.

The surging, yelling bands of merrymakers in the square gave way as Dhalshev and Fox made their way to the stair to the Octagon. Dhalshev peered upward, one foot on the first step. The signals flashing overhead indicated someone coming in, awaiting permission to dock at the pier.

Dhalshev cursed his knees, then forced himself up the stairs three at a time. Fox was right behind him.

At the top, the young woman on signal duty met Dhalshev, eyes wide. "Three Khanerenth warships, flying truce flags at the foremast above the crown-and-clover. Can they dock on the pier?"

. . . and a price of a thousand golden royals for the person of former Admiral Garjath Dhalshev, living or dead. "Usual policy," Dhalshev said. "One in, others out."

Because of the Midsummer's Day Games, the pier had

been cleared, and all ships except *Cocodu* were anchored out in the middle harbor.

Dhalshev peered through his glass. By now the three big brigantines were visible, lanterns at foremast and mainmast, all stripped to fighting sail.

Dhalshev observed with deep appreciation the precision with which the topsails and jib vanished, then the mainsail, as the flagship rounded into the wind and drifted gently up against the dock. "Midsummer's Day. Is this timing a coincidence?" he asked as he started across the square toward the main pier.

Fox drawled, "Traditional day of weddings, treaties, beginnings? Hmmm."

Dhalshev cut him a sharp look, wondering if Fox intended to make trouble. Fox ignored it, his eyes on the expert way the flagship was moored, all sails beautifully furled. He didn't have to see the deck to know each rope was set to the precise degree he'd been trained to when he was a boy.

They were halfway down the pier when the first figure leaped over the rail to land, hands on knees. When the tall young man straightened up, Dhalshev's breath caught.

"Woof?"

Laughing, exclaiming random words of happiness, Woof Woltjen closed the distance and clasped his former admiral's arms.

"Where have you been?"

"Prison."

"What?"

Woof glanced up at the warship as the crew on duty boomed out a ramp.

Woof said quickly, "Admiral Mehayan and an envoy have the royal communications. When I left you to look for Nugget, I never got any farther than Sarendan. We got caught in a sweep. My accent betrayed me, and they put me in another prison as a Khanerenth spy."

Dhalshev cursed under his breath.

"Oh, it was just as bad as you think. They dosed me with kinthus, and of course I told them everything, including all your signals. At least I had the comfort of knowing that we—you—change them every three months, so what I told

them was long out of use. But then they used me as a game
token in their negotiations with Khanerenth because they
wanted some ranker back who'd been caught where he
shouldn't be. I never saw the fellow. If it was a fellow. Anyway, they shipped me back to Khanerenth, and once again,
I was under threat of death."

Dhalshev shook his head. "I wish I'd known."

"Well, I wished I could send a message. Over what felt
like the next ten years I was questioned by two dukes, one
herald-advocate, Admiral Mehayan, the count who got my
father's land, and finally the king. Had three interviews with
him. I could tell he didn't want to kill me, especially when
the count—my own cousin though to the third degree—
tried a little too hard to get me put out of the way. Then,
just days ago, came the news that the Venn are in the strait.
Took Llyenthur, right after a typhoon that smashed its way
up both coasts. The Venn sent a white flag to Bren saying
they had a year to surrender their harbors, or next year this
time the Venn will come in force and take 'em. Get this!
According to some fishers who ran cross-channel, they did
the same to Nelsaiam just on the other side of the strait."

Fox stilled. Dhalshev whistled softly.

Why didn't you tell me, Ramis? Fox thought. No answer.

Woof waved his hand toward the brigantine. "So suddenly our king concluded the peace treaty with Sarendan
that's been in negotiation for two or three years now, and
he declared amnesty for all the former adherents to the old
king who would swear fealty. And the next thing I know,
I'm on my way here with the admiral and this envoy with
Official Communications."

On deck, there was an orderly flurry as civilian and
military protocol were strictly observed. Dhalshev success-
fully recognized an attempt to compromise, blending the
old ways with the new—that is, new as of nearly twenty
years ago, when the present king took the place of his
predecessor.

Woof said softly as the two men boomed down the ramp,
"So I have my lands back. Rank if you return. I'll have you
know I'm no longer Woof." He grinned, his narrow face
wry in the brilliant light glowing from the Saunter. "*Lord*
Woof. Lord Walaf, that is." A mocking gesture toward the
brigantine.

Four men approached. In front, a smooth-faced man in fine civilian dress and a round-faced, balding man wearing the light blue coat with large gold buttons belonging to an admiral. A coat akin to one Dhalshev had folded away in his clothes chest, untouched for nearly twenty years.

"Mehayan!" he said, his hands behind him to avoid the doffing of an invisible hat of salute.

Admiral Mehayan had had strict instructions. He flicked his hand to his forehead and then out in the full doff. "Dhalshev. It is good to see you. May I present Lord Hamazhav?"

Dhalshev bowed, the old politenesses coming back to his tongue. They exchanged the proper words, suave as a meeting in a marble palace and not on the dock of an infamous privateer lair, as music and laughter drifted over the water.

"There is much to hear, I gather," Dhalshev said, gazing past the admiral's armed marines waiting at a respectful distance, and the pair of lieutenants Mehayan could use as messengers or as backup muscle, as needed. Dhalshev took in the clean, familiar lines of the second and third warships, which were floating at station midway between the inner harbor and the entrance.

Warships. The crews on board would not be sitting on their hands. And no doubt they were backed up by a fleet sitting outside the harbor.

He turned Fox's way to catch a slack-lidded glance, and Dhalshev knew that Fox could shoot one of those weird warbling arrows of his, and his fleet would be armed and ranged across the harbor before anyone could sail in.

Even if you didn't like the man, you had to admit he was useful. If on your side. Dhalshev laughed to himself as he led his surprising guests past the warehouses to the Octagon's stair, where he paused. "You really don't need the marines, Mehayan. Keep the boys, but down here. There's not enough room up there for us all. Woof, shall I send someone for Nugget?"

"She's here?" Woof asked, grinning, then he made a quick gesture. "We'd better talk first. It's enough to know she's fine. All the rest can wait a bit longer." He made an unobtrusive sign to the two lieutenants, whose faces betrayed quick grins before they stiffened into duty mode.

"Very well. Follow me, Admiral. My lord."

As Mehayan dismissed his marine guard to take up a stance on the dock midway between the ship and the Octagon, and waved the two lieutenants to stand down to informal mode, Hamazhav said to Fox with just a little too much hauteur, "I am Lord Hamazhav of Khanerenth, Royal Envoy. Who are you?"

"An interested observer," Fox replied.

Hamazhav swerved around at this piece of masterly near insolence. He took in Fox's lounging posture in the unrevealing black clothes, the polished hilts of knives at sleeves, waist, boot tops, and last, the ruby earring glowing evilly at one side of that steady gaze. Then he made an airy gesture and turned back again. The king had said to expect pirates, and here, it seemed, was his first.

Dhalshev tightened his jaw against a laugh and dismissed the urge to explain. Though he'd accepted this truce mission—and though Mehayan had once been a friend, twenty years of having a price on his head obviated the necessity to explain anything unless he so chose.

So they trooped up the stairs in silence, Hamazhav unable to resist a glance or two at that red-haired fellow. Was he really wearing a ruby earring? Yes. Could this possibly be Elgar the Fox?

Across the busy square, most of Fox's crew danced on Dasta's terrace, surrounding the wedding couples, but Barend lounged on the wall where he could see the Octagon balcony as well as the celebrants. All the captains had noted Fox heading up to the Octagon after a signal, even Gillor, Tcholan, and Eflis. They continued right on with their fun, but kept one another in sight. *Heyo, a merry thought.* Eflis laughed to herself. A fight on her wedding day would make it perfect.

When Dhalshev and the delegation reached the top, Mehayan visibly restrained himself from peering down at the fascinating harbor emporia, so colorfully lit. He turned his back to the broad windows. "Dhalshev, Lord Hamazhav here has the official documents, in a lot of fancy language. What it comes to is the king wants you back. You and your independents. If they join the navy, there will be full amnesty. Pay reinstated. Keep current rank. We can't be divided, not if the Venn are coming back on the attack. Word is, their entire fleet is in the strait. They won't be satisfied with just the strait. They're going to take every harbor on the continent. The kings in those parts apparently think they're a staging goal, not a final goal."

"And so?"

"And so the king will make you high admiral once again. You lead us. I know I can't go up against the Venn. All my experience has been in chasing pirates. You'll get your old lands back. Everything restored. More. It's all in that paper."

Dhalshev smiled. "I will peruse it, I promise. No hurry, today is a festival day. Permit me to offer you some wedding wine cup. The official part of the evening is now over. You are our guests. Woof, why don't you take those young men over to the Chart House for a drink."

Woof turned to the admiral, who stepped outside, waved in release to the two below, then returned. Woof ran down the stairs. The last thing he heard was Dhalshev saying, "Now, tell me about everyone I know. Who still lives?"

At the bottom of the steps, the two lieutenants waited for Woof, after having watched in fascination what looked like a lot of pirates dancing, singing, carousing.

"What goes, Woofie?" one asked.

"They're settling in to reminisce."

"Augh, if you get Mehayan started, he'll be at it all night. You know what he's like when he invites us to supper in the cabin."

"And a lesson at the end of every boring story!" the second one added around his friend's shoulder.

"Come on," Woof said, not without sympathy; though he'd only been invited once to dine at the admiral's table during their two weeks of travel, once had been enough. "I'll introduce you around."

The three started off, all still relieved at the unexpected outcome of a meeting they had dreaded for years. Woof clattered down the steps, thinking about the days he'd stood up there on the tower, remembering how inseparable they'd been as boys first sent to sea. How at first the three boys had ignored the revolution, believing it just a lot of adults ranting and raving until suddenly people started dying. Homes got taken away, people you knew went to prison. Or to execution.

Then Woof vanished with High Admiral Dhalshev after Lord Woltjen was put to death. The two middies had missed Woof, but what could they do, they'd asked him when they met up again. *We figured we'd work hard and keep to duty. But we always wondered what happened to you, Woofie.*

Yes, said the other. *We dreaded finding you on board some ship we had orders to stop and search for traitors.*

Woof had retorted, *Why d'you think I refused to sail all those years? I never wanted to find either of you at the other end of a sword.*

Now the two stood where they had never imagined setting foot. They were actually in that den of alluring pirate iniquity, Freeport Harbor. The harbor was astonishingly old-fashioned, with the tall windows and curlicues of their great-grandparents' day, but the pirates all looked like real pirates. Everywhere people wore an armory of weapons as they drank, sang bawdy songs, danced.

"Is Inda the Fox here?" one whispered, elbowing Woof.

"No. Other side of the continent. Fox is the one in black you saw at the Octagon."

One lieutenant whistled, and the other said, "That fellow looked tough enough to chew steel."

Woof wasn't listening. "There's my sister!" he exclaimed.

He pointed at a tall, slim girl dancing on a tabletop. She had Woof's narrow jaw, a snub nose, a cloud of sun-lightened hair flying around. She wore tight deck trousers and something billowy, with a swirling fringed shawl worn tied baldric-style over her shoulder and at her trim waist.

The two lieutenants were bewitched by her laugh, which was nothing like the courtly, well-bred titter they were used to at home. They were drawn by her grace, the way she danced on her toes all airy and free, unlike any of the orderly court dances.

"Nugget?" Woof called. "Nugget!"

The girl stopped, her eyes going wide. "Woof?"

She leaped over the heads of her circle of friends, landed with a quick step, and flung herself into Woof's arms. When they fell apart, breathless with laughter, she wiped her eyes with a slim, calloused palm and fingers. The dazzled lieutenants realized she didn't have a second hand.

"Where did you come from?" She took in the two in uniform, and her eyes widened even more. Then she whirled around and took in the ghostly outline of the warship at the dock. "Trouble?" Her expression changed fast.

"No. Truce."

Jeje had been sitting with Khajruat Swift, daughter of one-legged Captain Swift. Jeje was almost unfamiliar in that handsome silk robe—and hadn't she taken teasing over possessing such a thing! She and Khajruat Swift exchanged glances, and each came up to one of the lieutenants, slid an arm through one of theirs, and said a variation of, "Come on and meet the rest of the crew. And tell us all about what's going on in the outside world."

Woof and Nugget were left alone, except for Mutt standing just within earshot, on the other side of some roistering forecastlemen. Woof said, "We can have our name back. Our land. You can be Lady Waki Woltjen again."

Mutt turned away, bitterly thinking, *Lady Waki. What would a Lady Waki ever want with a fellow named Mutt who didn't learn how to read until he was old enough to grow a beard?*

"How fun!" Nugget bounced on her toes in the old way, then paused, head tipped. "What happens to whoever's got Dad's land now?"

"No one lives at our house. Our land got awarded to this cousin for turning Dad in."

"Is he evil?"

Woof rubbed his jaw. "I'd say not so much evil as greedy. He had a hand in Dad's death, and he sure tried to get me killed, but then, as the king pointed out in my first interview, to him, I'm a traitor and shouldn't be able to come back after being a pirate and take over land he's been governing."

Nugget crossed her arms. "Want a wager? They'll want me to marry this cousin, or his son. Make it all family again."

"Actually, they mentioned his daughter—the heir—for me. But all that can wait. It all depends on Dhalshev going back. Then he has to win against the Venn."

"The Venn are tough," she said, her smile vanishing. "We fought some of 'em in the strait. Remember Dasta? Nearly died. We lost a lot, Woof. More than we did at The Narrows,

I think." She eyed her brother. "Do you want to go back to
Khanerenth, marry this cousin, and be a land lord?"

He sighed. "Tell you true? Not sure. I never thought
about it before, but so much of how you have to live with
people is, oh, what you think they say when you're out of
the room. How it's different than what they say to you
when you're in it."

Nugget's face lifted. "Oh, yes. I always wanted to be famous," she admitted. "I longed to be the most interesting
girl in the room." When Woof snorted, she grinned ruefully, relieved to be able to talk true. "When I was little,
everybody here made me a pet. The rules for everybody
else weren't for me. I guess I thought that the rules in the
world would not be for me either, that I'd be the world's
pet. Ended the day that pirate thought I was just another
brat to kill. In a court kind of life, don't they lie a lot?" she
asked. "People acting like Tau. Remember him? He was so
handsome, but nobody ever knew what he really thought."

"That's exactly it." Woof looked around at the place
he'd loved most, now including the people he loved most.
"Heh. The fellows seem to be having a good time, so let's
sit down somewhere and you tell me about the pirate and
everything else."

Upstairs in the Octagon, the admiral, the envoy, and Dhalshev finished the reminiscences. The envoy was used to old
fellows maundering about the past while waiting for others
to come to the point, but he sensed it was not his place to
call them to business. The two admirals were uneasy, the
one knowing just how much trouble there would be back
home if the king's generosity were turned down, the other
knowing he'd been asked for more than he could give.

Mehayan finally rose, said he'd return on the morrow,
and left Dhalshev to peruse his royal invitation.

As soon as their footsteps had died away, Dhalshev
turned to Fox, who had sat just outside the circle, never
offering a word.

"Well? Sounds to me like desperation," Dhalshev said,
"if they want me, after twenty years out of command. What
do you make of their news?"

"How reliable is this man?"

"Mehayan used to be a stickler for precision. Probably

why he's at the top now. Wasn't for his flair for action. I'd say the news is pretty much whatever the king has, less their two weeks' sailing to us."

"A year to prepare." Fox drummed his fingers soundlessly on the chair arm. "Then the Venn attack Bren, which is central to sea trade for us. And on the other side Nelsaiam. Then, I suppose, a run down the strait. Secure it before winter. And the next year? This coast, right here." He pointed in the direction of Khanerenth.

"What about Nelsaiam? I don't know any more about it now than I did as admiral. I was never actually in the strait, except the very east end of the battle off Chwahirsland in '03." Dhalshev tipped his head toward the back wall, where he kept the chart of the strait. "Most of the northern side of the strait is still empty, as you can see. Inda promised me through Mutt that he would share what he learned, but that was before he vanished into the west."

"Inda and I did some poking around," Fox admitted. "But we didn't chart much beyond a few inlets on uninhabited shores. We kept away from settlements, though we did a lot of cross-country observation."

"What can you tell me?" Dhalshev asked neutrally. "You know Drael under Venn control has been hostile to us on the Sartoran side for time out of mind."

"Still is, Inda and I discovered. Nelsaiam is a huge bay. Think of it in shape as a fish-mouth five times the size of Llyenthur. Filled with reefs, treacherous islands, rocks just below water level. As you probably know, its people are long-ago descendants of the Venn. They were given self-governance generations ago. That bay is useless for sea trade—and Inda and I learned that the people there mostly trade over land, inside of Drael. My guess is, if the Venn want them back, it's because they want wood. If Nelsaiam fights, they'll be formidable."

"Will they ally with us, do you think?"

"No idea. What do you think will comprise your 'us'? I notice your admiral made no mention of the Chwahir, or Sarendan, for that matter, in his proposal of a grand alliance."

"Of course not. Chwahirsland has never acknowledged the new king. And you know what the result has been."

Fox grinned. Khanerenth's revolution had caused many

on both sides to turn to brigandage on the seas, and the coast of Chwahirsland had been a favorite target. He made a dismissive gesture. "As for the Venn, it surprises me they'd split their force. But then this entire venture surprises me."

"What troubles me is those thousand ships Mehayan said the Venn have. Even if they took damage in the typhoon, and then Venn have trouble getting enough wood to replace their masts and rebuild their hulls, a navy that size? Nobody can stop them. Nobody." Dhalshev stared down at his gnarled hands. He was closer to seventy than sixty, he knew he could not lead a fleet against even half the Venn. Was there such a dearth of commanders? No, that was not the question. Was there such a dearth of commanders that allies would accept?

He looked up. "What is Inda doing these days? Has he ever thought about going back to sea?"

Fox leaned back in his chair, arms crossed. "Don't think I can run a battle?"

Dhalshev was too deeply disturbed to hear Fox's sarcasm. "None of us can, not the size of a fleet to face all the Venn in the world. I don't see how anyone runs a battle that large, once you set it up. How could anyone possibly keep a thousand ships in sight?"

Fox lifted his chin. *So my instinct to stay was right. But why didn't I hear the news from you, Inda, first?* "They have to believe someone can command, is that it?" His chair crashed forward. "Maybe it's time to write to Inda again. Who knows? This time he might actually answer."

Chapter Eight

THE day after Midsummer, while the academy boys were out practicing for the Summer Games, Inda walked over to the stable with Gand, Olin, and half a dozen others, to be there when one of the mares foaled. He exchanged smiles of satisfaction with Olin and Lennad. They had four more foals due this week, but none from Clover's line, so far unmixed, all from the Nelkereth Plains to the east. The new one—they'd already picked her name, Wisp, for the puffball flowers that grew on the plains and blew apart in the wind—was handsome, long-legged, with intelligent eyes.

Wisp had just given voice to the distinctive chuckle of a newborn foal, a sound that made them all smile, when one of the castle girls appeared, panting. "Harskialdna-Dal." She waved her hands. "You're to come. The queen's giving birth."

Inda leaped over the foal struggling to her feet and took off for the residence.

In the queen's rooms, Runners cleaned everything up, and Signi dressed the baby herself, as Noren and Hadand's other personal Runners had no experience with babies. They

watched, frightened and entranced, as Signi gently rubbed
and patted the baby clean and dry, pulled on the waiting
nightgown, and laid the babe in the lap of his mother, a
towel beneath him. He would get his first diaper when the
cord dropped off.

Now everything was ready for visitors.

Evred entered with quiet step as soon as Tesar opened
the door. His son lay on Hadand's lap. He bent to kiss
Hadand, and then just touched his lips to the thin, veined
skin over the babe's fragile skull. "How are you?" he asked
Hadand.

"Tired. Sore. But fine." She smiled, still euphoric: even
the soreness was bearable now, though the healer had
warned her that that wouldn't last and not to get up too
fast.

She'd sent Evred a Runner just before dawn, and though
he'd offered to be there if she wished, she'd chosen to keep
only women at hand.

Hadand watched the new Sierlaef wriggle, his small
mouth working, dark blue eyes looking about vaguely as they
tried to find Mother's face. Evred moved behind Hadand
to the window, where he stood, hands behind his back, as he
struggled with equal parts joy and apprehension.

The women forgot his presence, so absorbed were they.
Hadand said to Tdor, "I so wanted him to be Tanrid. Evred
said traditions and expectations being what they are, he's
got to be Hastred."

"Hastred-Sierlaef," Tdor said experimentally. She would
have said more, but a surge of nausea dried her mouth.

"If we have a second boy, he can be either Tanrid or
Tlennen." Hadand turned her gaze back to her baby. "How
odd, to look at his face, and see Tanrid in the shape of his
forehead, but Evred in the shape of his chin." And then, in
a rush of words, "When we made our treaties, we always
talked about *a* baby. Now, he's *this* baby. He's a person. With
eyebrows like an uncle he'll never meet. Will this black hair
turn red? What will his life be like in the nursery? Will he be
friends with his future wife? While he was inside I thought
and thought. One thing I promised myself: If I have a girl,
there's nothing I can do about her being promised to Cama
and Starand's boy, but I'm going to raise her first. She can
see the boy when he comes to the academy. But Starand is

not going to get her claws on my daughter until she's old enough to learn some defenses."

Tdor shivered, overwhelmed by the strangeness of change, and love, and wonder. And the slow burn of nausea that had been steadily increasing for several days.

Even the nausea was forgotten when she imagined a daughter out of her own body going to Shendan at Darchelde, an idea once so alien.

"I have a question," Signi said.

She so seldom spoke that Hadand and Tdor said instantly—their words colliding—"Ask!"

"Is Hastred not the same name as Fnor and Buck's baby? Will that not be confusing if they are contemporaries in your training school?"

Hadand chuckled. "Likely they'll lose their given names by the time they're sheared. Fnor says already they're calling their boy Hot Rock, though it might not last the year. If my boy doesn't end up being 'the Sierlaef' like his uncle was, he might be Hasta, or he might end up with something like Wolfhound."

Signi said, "Ah! I had forgotten these other names such as Noddy, and Rat. They did not seem to mind them."

Tdor's stomach ceased bubbling. She leaned forward and stroked a finger gently over the baby's soft black fuzz. "Here's what the academy means. The spring before you came, Inda was riding around up north all winter. He almost killed himself riding home from Olara, just so he would not miss the first day of the academy, or the second day's shearing—when they cut the hair off the new boys."

Signi looked puzzled. Hadand sent her a brief smile, then went on contemplating the singular and exquisite beauty of her newborn son, already smarter and more handsome than any baby ever born.

"Let me try again." Tdor's nausea had definitely eased. She grinned. "If I have a son, I will pick his name very carefully, because names are important to families and alliances. Probably it will be Jarend, same as Inda's father, since Inda's now the oldest son. He might get a nickname at home. They usually do. But most nicknames don't get past the academy. Inda did, and so did Noddy. And Whipstick. But that's because the academy accepted those names. If they don't—if they give the boy a new one—that's what he'll be known as for the rest of his life, even if he lives another sixty years beyond his horsetail days."

"You changed my name from Sponge," Evred said.

Hadand smiled up at him. "True. But I am convinced it only took because you were a prince."

Tdor thought about the pleasure that stained Evred's face when Inda or Cama or Cherry-Stripe slipped and called him Sponge, and wondered if she dared to speak, then the door banged open, and Inda stumbled inside, breathing hard. His eyes widened when he saw the baby lying there in Hadand's lap. He pointed. "Boy?"

"Want to make sure?" Tdor asked, moving to lift the blanket, and all the women laughed at him as he blushed to the hairline.

"Well, they all look alike at that age," he protested.

"Don't tell me you never saw one at home," Tdor asked, laughing.

At home. Evred felt a spurt of annoyance as Inda said, "Who cares about babies when you're eight or ten? They don't do anything but shit and spit."

Evred's irritation extended to Inda not noticing that "at home," then snapped inward by habitual effort of will. "He's got black hair!" Inda exclaimed, and the women found that funny.

No one was aware of Signi, who slipped out of the room without anyone noticing.

It took no skill for her to leave. She was not truly a part of their lives, though they accepted her presence, even the shuttered young king, Evred. Inda treated her as he always had, his face lifting in welcome when he saw her. She had even found a measure of peace in telling him what had happened to her after she felt question in his touch, question that reached his face and voice. He had always been empathetic. That quality had first drawn her to him.

When Inda did not see her he was busy with his life, sometimes so busy that if she encountered him anywhere but in the Harskialdna suite, once he'd greeted her he forgot her presence in the room. Tdor's tranquil acceptance extended to the little courtesies, but Signi descried the difference between the thoughtful awareness that always included her, and actual belonging. Signi was not a part of Iasca Leror's work, and that was what defined the daily lives of Harvaldar, Gunvaer, Harskialdna, and Harandviar.

So Signi tried to make herself useful in little tasks to free Hadand and Tdor from their unending labors. She taught Old Sartoran and carried verbal messages and helped the healer. But others could have done all that. This was not Signi's home, and though she had a lover, and their time was precious beyond words, he was not her mate. When she left for Sartor to fulfill her vow—for someone must teach the world Venn navigation—he would not follow.

Will I wander the world and never find rest? No, that was self-pity. There had been a single time in her life when pity was justified. But she had survived the Beast.

Here is the truth. I am halfway between forty and fifty. The change of life will come soon.

Her steps led to the converted stable where Taumad's theater was located. The building had halted. The stage was still scarcely more than a raised platform with cushions for the front on the dirt floor, benches in the back. But people liked to come here and perform, or watch others perform. They seemed to revel in exactly the same thing over and over again, down to all forty verses of tedious war ballads, or stupid and obvious jokes that were not at all a surprise. The anticipation of them sent the audience into paroxysms of laughter.

She became aware of singing. The melody was familiar, and recognition was an inward blow: it was the lament she'd heard on the wind during the Marlovans' Convocation, when she walked the walls: the Andahi Lament. The melody belonged to old Sartor, with the Sartoran triplets replaced by the trumpet charge, but with just the middle note shifted to the minor mode in such a way as to change the chord to a compelling, poignant sound.

The singing did not come from the stage, but from the hackle-yard behind the spinners' warehouse adjacent to the theater.

Signi paused by the open door to the theater, which still smelled of horse. She closed her eyes. *Scutch, scutch, scutch,* sticks beat the flax straws in rhythm while the plaintive song ivy-bound the air. Signi kept her eyes shut, seeing the scutchers at home beating the flax that had been steeped since the summer before, the rotting vegetation

rinsed just before winter and the flax put in water with bluing. The women combed it after beating it, then repacked
it in barrels with more bluing to be laid out in the sun the
next summer.

The Marlovan women worked in the same way as had
the ancestors they shared with Signi, bending, stirring, and
shaking as they sang the Lament. First came the painful
story, but simply told, and then the shifting, triple-step melody over and over, a long series of names.

"We honor Liet-Jarlan Deheldegarthe,
oath-keeper, giving life and blood . . ."

When the Lament ended, the women's voices split
into groups of three and they began to sing the Lament in
round. If possible, it gained in beauty and in poignancy by
this interweaving of the melodic line.

This lament will be remembered, Signi thought, walking
into the theater, where sun shafting through holes in the
roof lit whirls of dust. *And so the women will be remembered.* The dust flurries brought her hands up in mimicry;
she slipped out of her shoes and leaped up onto the stage,
stretched carefully, and then took a cautious step or two in
dance mode, toes testing the smoothed boards.

Once before she had danced outside of the boundaries
of her own closed chamber, despite her vow never to do so
after she had been dismissed from the hel dancers. It was at
Tdor's wedding, because Tdor had asked.

She had believed until now that her body, twisted from
the cruelty of Erkric's torturer, must never dance again.
She did her daily exercises only to keep herself healthy. But
where there is life, there is hope, and the possibility of joy.
And she had always, always, expressed joy in dance.

She stretched up her arms, whirled as light as a wind-
scudding leaf, and leaped. She danced to the sweet-voiced
threnody on the bare stage in an empty horse barn, twirling and flitting in and out of the sunbeams and dust. First
she saluted those unknown women who had given life
and blood, though the battle had been against her own
people, who had also given their life and blood. People
who all should have been alive today, smiling at spring
growth, watching children grow. But love and loyalty had
demanded this sacrifice, each on the steel of the other.

What creatures we are, she thought and leaped high, twisting her body to express wonder and torment; the aches, the shortened steps, the gnarled pull where once she'd moved without effort were her own minor mode, because oh, the sharpness of paradox! *We make poems and music to celebrate beauty, and we train to kill, and call it art.*

Though dance provided no answers, she could gain peace in expressing the questions with each leap and turn and step, until the midday sun shone directly onto the stage. The unseen women ended their song, one by one, until only a single voice remained, light and tremulous as a bird call. Signi whirled, her hands fluttering upward until she stopped in the center of the beam of light, face and hands lifted toward the warmth of the sun.

A caught breath was the first sign that her reverie had not been private after all. She opened her eyes, but her vision was dazzled by the sun. All she could see were shadows.

She stepped out of the sunbeam to discover a crowd of Marlovans pressed against the back wall. All remained silent, no one quite sure what to do next.

She had been taught that dance was a gift, and so she gave her audience a tentative smile as she slid her feet back into her shoes. She discovered from the cold on her face that she'd been weeping, so she slipped between the people, who parted to let her pass.

Just before she reached the street, she heard a man say, "Who *is* she? Where do you learn *that?*"

And a girl stated with the assurance of the young, "Oh, she's obviously sent by Taumad the Runner. That's how they dance in Colend. Everyone knows *that.*"

Signi laughed to herself, and ran back to the castle to bathe and change her clothes.

When she reached the Harskialdna suite, she stopped in the doorway, her nerves wringing coldly.

While everyone had been busy in the queen's rooms, someone had laid before the door of Signi's bedchamber a sprig of milkweed.

The first sign.

Chapter Nine

GRADUALLY over that long winter Evred began writing short notes to Tau, at first strictly about guild matters. As the winter extended into spring, keeping most people inside—including the academy boys and the girls of the queen's training—Evred found himself with more free time.

So he wrote cautious letters, not only reporting on Inda's and Gand's invention of lessons to be done indoors (the throne room resounding to the clickety-clack of double-stick fighting, the Great Hall set up for lance evolutions) but asking questions about the etiquette of foreign courts. Tau exerted himself to be entertaining, passing on current gossip about people in high places.

Then summer arrived abruptly. Gand and Inda vanished with all the boys on an extended banner game.

The day after the Summer Games, Evred returned from a council meeting to get ready for the departure banquet for the Jarls who'd come to see their girls and boys compete. As had become habitual, he checked the scroll-case and found another letter from Tau:

    Evred, I think we're going to need Inda. His name is on everyone's lips. There's a royal frenzy down the entire

*strait clear to the east side. Spring brought Venn envoys
under the white flag with warnings that they're coming
back to take up where they left off. Their demand? Cede
control of the strait or every ship they encounter will
be sunk, and every harbor destroyed. The rumor insists
that Rajnir is in command himself, and he won't stop
until they control the entire southern continent. Everyone is asking where Elgar the Fox is, and will he come
fight the Venn as he once promised? Would you pass
this message to Inda and see what he says?*

Evred ripped the letter across, twisted it up, and dropped
it onto the hearth. He bent, struck a flame on the old
sparker, and waited until the note was ash, then walked out
of the government office, past his surprised Runners and
herald-scribes. The king had never done that before.

They shrugged and returned to work.

Evred checked his ring. Inda was over on the guard
side with Gand, supervising the shift of horsetails to their
two years of guard duty. Through a bank of open windows
Evred glimpsed yellow clouds of sun-powdered dust as the
boys lugged their gear over the sun-baked ground to their
new barracks. The heavy, humid air carried the nasal crack
of teenage laughter.

Evred stopped outside the Harskialdna suite. A female
Runner on duty at the door indicated Tdor, at least, was
inside.

Evred said, "Is Tdor ill?"

The young woman struck fist to heart. "Stomach."

Evred considered. "Has she left instructions not to be
disturbed?"

"*You* can go in, Harvaldar-Dal," the Runner replied,
eyes round. The king had never entered the suite before,
as far as she knew. "I'm just keeping out the girls coming
to complain."

Evred went in. The bedroom door was open, and Tdor's
pale, strained face turned his way. He trod quietly to the
door and assessed the slightly greenish cast to her pallid
cheeks. "Child-sickness, do you think?" he asked.

Tdor swallowed, her eyes closing. "I think so. I've
stopped thinking it too many of those old almonds after
supper or a peach past freshness."

"How long has this been going on?"

"About three weeks. Not bad at first, but in the past few days . . ." She swallowed, and winced. "Hadand will preside at the banquet." Her face flooded with color. "The healer said to stop drinking gerda. Good. I can't keep it down."

"The healer told Hadand when she felt like you do that the best thing is sleep and the next best is ginger-steep."

Tdor smiled. "I drank some. It did help. For a while." Her brow puckered. "Is there something?"

"Nothing that can't wait."

He closed the door soundlessly, and went to Tdor's office, empty as expected. Hadand was putting on her good robes for the banquet; the ring indicated Inda was still guard-side. Signi would be finishing her Old Sartoran tutoring session with the heralds-in-training.

Evred reached into the plain wooden chest behind the "Files and Piles" table and pulled out Inda's battered golden case, then opened it.

These things really could not be trusted: you had to know the particular spell to send a message, but anyone could open a case. Or at least this one. Evred had been checking it every few months, ever since he'd received that golden case from Tau. He'd sought out Inda's and opened it just to see if anyone could tamper with one.

That explained Evred's first breach of privacy. The ones after that . . . he called them necessity. And since Inda and Tdor had both forgotten about Inda's golden case, Evred was the only one who saw Fox's subsequent short, pungently funny letters, written in a small, neat scribal hand on tiny squares of fine rice paper. Nothing in them was of any military or political significance. The oldest and longest letter described the battle against the Venn off The Fangs; the most recent, and shortest, listed the marriages of persons unknown to Evred, the return of another faceless stranger called Woof, and had Inda heard that the Venn were in the strait? Everyone wanted to know if Inda was coming back to sea.

Evred opened the case, and there was a new letter, shorter than any:

> *Inda, if I get one more confidential note begging
> me to put you in touch with Chim, I'm going to have*

to defile your sacred soil myself to haul you to Bren.
Who carved "messenger" on my back?

The date was two days ago.

Evred folded the note along its original creases and tucked it back into the case. He'd already ordered the harbor commanders to reinforce their patrols with detachments of his dragoons, so there seemed nothing more to be done as yet, as far as Iasca Leror was concerned. The rest of the continent could look after itself. It had certainly done nothing to aid Iasca Leror when it was the target, he thought as he went back to get ready for the banquet.

After Evred left her, Tdor got up wearily, worried that something was amiss. Unfortunately, opening the door to the Harskialdna suite somehow brought a whiff of the fish in braised onions that was being carried to the dining room for the banquet.

Tdor reeled back, convulsed with dry heaves, and plopped in a heap on the floor. Inda arrived moments later, to find her still sitting there with the door Runner bent worriedly over her. The Runner pushed past him, saying, "I'll fetch more ginger-steep."

Inda's good mood vanished at the sight of Tdor's drawn, pale face. "Tdor?"

"It's a child," she said bluntly. "Has to be. I've never been sick like this in my life."

"Can you get up?"

"Every time I try, I get dizzy and the heaves."

Inda picked her up and carried her into the bedchamber. She stretched out on the bed and sighed in relief. Then she opened her eyes and smiled at the comical look on his face. "Inda?"

"Is it all right to be happy?" he asked, scratching his head. "I mean, you're sick. That's bad. But . . ." He flapped a hand. "You and me? A child? It sounds so, hoo! So strange."

Tdor laughed, then clapped her hand to her mouth. "Urp. No laughing. Oh, Inda." She collapsed back, halfway between tears and happiness. "Go get that dust off, and be both of us at the banquet. And when you come back, *don't* tell me about the food."

* * *

Evred's resolve lasted for another three months.

They'd just finished Restday drum in the guard parade ground adjacent to the women's area. Over the quiet years Tdor, Hadand, Evred, and Inda had developed a smooth routine as they distributed bread and wine respectively to their captains. These crossed back and forth handing it out as the male and female Guards, the Runners, the castle and stable folk drummed and sang together. After that everyone except those on watch rotation got an evening of liberty, trooping off in clumps to the city pleasure houses and eateries, and the four plus Signi trod upstairs to dine together.

Tdor sniffed, and said, "Braised fish! Oh, I am so glad to have my appetite back."

Inda said, "I still can't get the idea of a son into my head. I just don't think I'm old enough!" Then he made one of his sudden stops, causing everyone behind him to stumble, some muffling laughter. "How old *am* I, anyway?"

Tdor was going to tell him—she had never ceased secretly cherishing his Name Days—but Hadand chuckled. "There are plenty of fathers much younger than their midtwenties, Inda. Are you going to be like Peddler Antivad and declare that everyone else ages but you?"

"No! I just—"

Vedrid met them at the tower stair outside the Harskialdna suite, his demeanor formal. Inda fell silent.

"There is a ... person who wishes to speak with you, Harvaldar-Dal. And you, Harskialdna-Dal."

"Where'd you stash the body?" Inda asked.

A corner of Vedrid's mouth lifted, but he stayed in formal mode. "She came to the throne room."

"The throne room?" four voices repeated in variations of surprise and disbelief. No one used the throne room except for Convocation, royal weddings, memorials, or royal judgments with an execution directly following. The single exception had been spring, when it became part of the indoor academy.

"That's where the south side roaming patrol found her. And that's where she says she'll stay. She says she is from Lindeth Harbor." He added, "A Mistress Pim."

The high clerestory windows glowed with nearly horizontal rays of ochre light. The row of banners on the gallery walls gleamed and glittered with rare color. Standing before the throne gazing upward stood a stolid woman with a grim face and hair skinned back into a bun in the old Iascan style. This was Ryala, not her mother, who had retired from the business.

Evred, Hadand, and Inda were too familiar with the room to pay attention to the eerie lighting. Signi turned her gaze upward to see what it was that Ryala Pim studied so closely. When she identified the brown-stained, ripped blood red banner that had flown over Castle Andahi, the cold of winter ice ran through her veins.

War is nigh. And I cannot stay. Signi bowed her head and slipped out unnoticed by three of the four.

Evred ran up the dais, flanked by his wife and shield arm, who took stances at either side of the throne. Only Tdor remained on the floor, a little distance away, where she could see everyone, including Signi's quiet exit.

Pim stood stiffly, taking in the familiar faces of Marlovan king and war leader. In the fading light they looked even tougher and harder than they had seven years ago, when she'd glimpsed them last. She braced herself up. "You did fair by me once, the both of you. So I'm here, on behalf of the Fleet Guild," she said in her slow northern Iascan.

"The Fleet Guild?" Inda repeated.

She ducked her head in a half nod, half bow. "The Fleet Guild wanted to get a message to you, Indovun Algraveer. No one else would come into your land, so here I am."

Inda glanced at Evred, then said, "Your message is?"

"The Venn took Llyenthur and the western end of Drael. Last I heard, two months ago, they've settled in for winter. Right after the big typhoon raked the strait, they sent some bully boys in winged hats with a warning to Bren. Some say to the north side, too. To go back to the old ways, them ruling the seas. Tariffs and supplies paid them. Anyone surrenders, they *say* won't be touched." She pointed up at the bloody banner. "But we all know how well they keep their word. So Fleet Master Chim sent a message by magic transfer to our Fleet Guild desk, and I came here to ask you to go and defend Bren."

"I can't get our army raised and marched to Bren by summer," Inda stated.

"Nobody wants your army," she retorted, sharp with fear.

Evred raised his brows at her rudeness, but even in the fading light her face was blanched, anxious.

Pim went on less truculently, "They do want you to lead a fleet against the Venn. Like you once promised. Fleet Guild believes only you can do it, and Chim says Prince Kavnarac told him that other kingdoms in the east are saying the same thing."

"Me?"

"According to the prince, Khanerenth's king says he'll declare a full pardon if the Freedom Island independents sail under their former admiral, you know, at Freedom—"

"Dhalshev of Freedom Isles," Inda said. "I remember."

"Dhalshev says he is willing to lead Khanerenth under your command, independents and navy both." She snorted. "Despite Deliyeth of Everon's claims, we know who really won at The Fangs."

Inda send a puzzled look Evred's way. "I didn't know about any battle at The Fangs," Inda said in Marlovan.

Evred addressed Ryala Pim in Iascan. "Return on the morrow. We will have an answer then." He got to his feet and walked away, Inda following after exchanging a pained look with his wife.

Hadand signed to her Runner, who led the rigid woman off to be housed in the guest hall.

Out in the courtyard Inda turned to Evred. "Did Barend tell you about a battle off The Fangs?"

"This was a couple of years ago. My last direct communication with him, he reported only that a sea battle was imminent," Evred said. "He lost his locket during it. I subsequently found out that the Venn had retreated, and so trade was resuming. It did not seem pertinent to our affairs here to report any of that to you."

"I sure didn't think to ask." Inda grimaced. "I used to know everything going on in the southern seas. Now I'm behind, what, how many years since I came home?"

As they ran upstairs Inda thought back, trying to recover when he'd last heard any news of the Fox Banner Fleet. Then he remembered throwing his golden scroll-case into Tdor's fireplace in a fit of temper and reddened. It was his own fault.

Evred kicked the door to his private office shut. "The kingdoms along the strait are all in turmoil, according to Taumad. I haven't said anything to you or Hadand because their internal affairs are their own business. Just as they left the pirates and Venn to us a few years ago."

Inda turned out his hand. He didn't care about the matters of kings. It was the individuals he wanted to hear about, but he'd let time slide by without troubling himself to ask.

Evred went on, his manner tense. "It sounds like the kingdoms along the strait are far worse than Idayago was before we went north: kings conspiring against one another, secret deals and spies and lies, not just lurking in alleys but high in courts and palaces. My mother sees that as normal dealings. She even likes it, or at least the social side. Taumad finds it all amusing. I . . ." His voice suspended, and he stared out the window as the guards-in-training ran along the sentry ways, snapping alight the torches. He swung around to face Inda. "They're weak. Like the Idayagans were. Too busy squabbling with one another over who will pay for what, who gets what. The Venn will smash them."

Inda sighed. "Probably. But if they do, then they'll come after us. Especially since the plot against you failed."

"Against me?" Evred repeated.

"You already knew about it." Inda flicked his hand open. "Magic. Take away your brains. You remember. Well, Erkric was going for it, only in secret."

Evred controlled the recoil, but blood beat in his ears. "I thought that idea was hypothetical. That the threat ended when the Venn left."

Inda sighed, and smacked the edge of Evred's desk. "I didn't tell you because . . ." Another smack. "Well, the reason Signi disappeared is, Erkric blamed their problems on her. She got hunted down and put on trial. And tortured."

"I had no idea."

"I don't think she even wanted to tell me. But I saw her scars." Inda paused to get control of his own voice. Weird, how the very word *torture* brought a surge of anger—he wanted to smash something. He released his breath instead. "D'you see? The hunters that nabbed her were training to go after you next. Erkric's secret plan, so he could control you as well as their king. Her friends couldn't save her, but they made sure Erkric can't get you. You're protected by magic now. Long's you stay in this city."

Evred was far more adept at hiding anger. Magic, *how* he loathed it. There was no defense against so immoral and horrific a personal trespass. To take away someone's mind! It was worse than death. If he died, there would be another king; Hadand was strong enough to hold Iasca Leror for Hastred. *But if I am made into Erkric's puppet, forced to mouth out Erkric's commands . . .*

The horror was inexpressible.

When Evred spoke alarm burned through Inda's nerves. Evred only whispered in that deadly soft tone when he was in a cold rage.

"So we can be certain, then, that the Venn's next try against us will be the massive invasion." Torchlight from the windows gleamed in Evred's wide eyes, twin leaps of ruddy flame. The rest of him was in shadow: he did not clap on the glowglobe. "They want the strait so they can coordinate a large scale effort and aim everything they have at us. Probably in the very same plan you once outlined, and as much as we've recovered, we would never stand against that. There aren't enough of us." Then, in a less deadly tone, "Could you defend the strait?"

Inda sank down into one of Evred's wing back chairs. "I don't know. I doubt Bren's got enough ships, or they wouldn't be wanting me. But even if the fleet Jeje was training is still somewhere waiting for me—and I don't believe it, as I stopped paying them before the Venn attacked us here—sending indies, fishers, and privateers against well-drilled warships would not be like my old fleet fighting pirates. We counted on pirates not trusting one another enough to learn to fight together. That would not be true of the Venn."

Evred opened his hand. "So it's impossible, is what you are saying?"

"Depends on what sort of allies I'd get, and what I'd have at the center to build around. Don't know where Fox is with the Fox Banner Fleet—or if he'd respond."

"Center to build around." Evred paced along his torchlit windows, hands gripped tightly behind his back. "If your fleet with Savarend Montredavan-An was willing to become the core of a Marlovan navy . . . that would not break the treaty agreement. I would pay them. Do you think they would accept that?"

Inda whistled. "Fox'd have to decide for himself, but I suspect the others would go wherever there's pay. But how would I even find him? It would take years! Last I remember of my gold case is kicking it into Tdor's fireplace. Dunno if it exists, and if it does, if it even works."

"It does, and it does. Tdor rescued and kept it." And then, though it took an effort, "I have been reading the missives in it from time to time."

Evred knew he would have put to death without hesitation any man who had breached his own privacy in that way, and yet he had done it to Inda, the man he trusted most.

Inda leaned forward, and because Evred could not see his face—he had not wanted Inda seeing his—he clapped on the globe.

The light threw the shadows back. Though Evred had little appreciation of figurative language, Inda's thought processes had always reminded him of a running stream. Inda seemed clear as water, and yet, if you assumed you saw straight to the bottom, the illusion of the bent stick was a reminder of how easy it was to trick the eye. Inda was clear, he seemed to hide nothing, yet Evred could not predict Inda's reactions when it mattered most.

Inda groped impatiently. "Well, what was in it? I'll eat this desk if Jeje ever wrote me. And Tau lost his, as I recall him telling us. The only one who wrote back to me was Fox, and that was usually to jab at me."

"There were a few letters from him. Nothing that seemed important enough to interrupt your ongoing duties. Though the most recent one repeated gossip about the Venn. The letters are there—not many—when you want to read them."

Inda lunged out of the chair. This time Evred sat down, to be out of Inda's way as he prowled the perimeter of the crimson and gold rug. "So if I can find Fox , . ."

"Can you do it?" Evred said again.

Inda grunted, tapping the windowsill, the inner door latch, the desk, the wall, the top of a wingback chair, then circled around again. "Look, Sponge. Here's where I keep coming back. If they've got their entire fleet, why didn't they take the strait already? Why dig in at Llyenthur and send threats? Even if they took damage after that typhoon Ryala Pim mentioned, they'd still be stronger than anything . . ."

Evred waited.

Inda pounded the windowsill, the chair back, the windowsill, the chair back. "Rajnir. It's got to go back to Rajnir and Erkric and all that." He whirled around. "Where's my chart? Where's my—oh, yes. On the *Death*. Right. Right . . ."

Evred said finally, "Right what?"

Inda whirled around and paced back. "Ever since the Pim ships were attacked, when I was pigtail-age, I've fought the battle the enemy brought to me. Even the pirates. I figured we were close enough in force for me to have a chance. This battle, even if the Venn are weak, that weakness is relative, I've got to pick the ground, but is that enough?"

"The reports all mention three hundred ships. More. Isn't that what came against us?"

"They now have over three hundred *warships,* what they call the *drakans*. They'll have more like a thousand with the raiders and that."

"And you think them weakened in some way?"

Inda jabbed a finger toward the window. "Relative. *Something*'s wrong." He stopped abruptly. "I need Signi's deep sea navigation. If she plans to give it to Sartor, why not teach it to me first?"

Evred had no answer. Inda wouldn't have heard one if he'd spoken. He clutched his head, then exclaimed, "I have to write to Fox. Will you give me leave, if I do come up with a plan?"

"I could never deny you anything," Evred answered. And wished the words unsaid.

But Inda just laughed and rubbed his hands. "Then let's fetch out that scroll-case! I'll write to Fox and see if I have a fleet, or if it'll be just Chim and me in a jolly-boat waving the Fox banner and yipping as loud as we can."

Chapter Ten

THREE people did not sleep that night.

Inda's mind cascaded the familiar stream of images
and ideas, beginning with his dash up to the archives for
a continental map to recover current and wind patterns
while he waited for an answer from Fox.

Twice he stuck his head in Evred's door. The first time,
"Did they say Rajnir was with them, like when they came
against us?"

"I gained that impression. I do know from something I
read in the Ala Larkadhe archive about the Venn that the
Golden Tree banner only goes where the king is, or a prince
under the king's orders. Taumad mentioned once a thirdhand report of that banner being flown on the flagship."

The second time, "A Marlovan navy. Does that mean the
exile treaty will be set aside?"

Evred could not sleep until he had confronted the profoundly disturbing threat of Erkric stooping through the
skies and reaching magical talons to pluck him from the
once-regarded safety of his fortress to be used against his
own people. The Venn truly had become an evil empire, but
even so, he could not trust impulse and emotion. He had to

get control of his emotions. To think everything out, in the most methodical way.

Exile. Montredavan-Ans. "I will have to put the question of the Montredavan-An treaty to the Jarls at Convocation," Evred said.

Inda grunted and vanished.

He prowled around the Harskialdna suite. Tdor was asleep in the big bed. A ghost-hand squeezed Inda's heart when he looked at her still form, outlined by the knife of light through the cracked door. *I won't be here for my boy's birth,* he thought. He couldn't imagine having anything but a boy. Especially since a girl was supposed to go to Darchelde to marry Fox's son, a decision made long ago in accordance with some treaty. It had been a promise made to Inda's mother when she was forced to leave what had been her home to marry Inda's father. It had also been an implied insult to Montredavan-An ambition that the Algara-Vayir second son, and not the heir, would provide their treaty daughter ... and look what happened! No, the idea of a girl was too strange, her future too unclear.

Inda shook his head, closed the bedroom door, and saw the gleam of light below Signi's door. He tapped.

"Enter," she said.

On her desk lay a complicated map drawn on thick heralds' paper, with a webwork of interconnected lines laid over the outline of Drael and the Sartoran continents.

"Is that what I think it is?" He pointed. "I was just coming to ask if you'd teach me Venn navigation."

Her smile was crooked as she turned her ruined hand over in a graceful gesture, her wrist veins close to the surface of her white, puckered skin. "Our first big test is to draw an accurate map from memory." She touched the map. "A quick explanation, then questions, then the long explanation if you and I agree. This is what we call a mirror map. These mirror maps are easy to make. When I was a sea dag, we used them to check on our peers' positions. You can also ting anyone—"

"Ting? Is that like tigging lances?"

She smiled faintly, a smile more sad than merry. "Perhaps, but we use the image of a bell. If you tap a bell in a forest, people can follow the sound. You ting ships and map-dags either on ship or on shore. They ting you back. The mark shows up as a little magical glow." She whispered, and the paper filled with what looked like firefly dots all over the paper, clusters along the western end of Drael, and a mass off the fish-mouth of Llyenthur Harbor.

"That's the fleet at their latest ting," she said, then made a sign and the lights vanished.

Inda lunged forward, hands grabbing at air. "Wait!"

"No, first I must ask you to promise. If this forming alliances does choose you as leader. Will you promise me not to loose a slaughter?"

Inda flung his hands out wide. "D'you see, *that*'s my plan! What I figured is if Rajnir is going to battle himself, but he's . . ." He knocked his forehead with the heel of his hand. "It has to mean your Erkric keeps him close by, right? Because only he can control him, right? And he can't let anyone else know, right? I'll lay out a good battle plan. I've got some ideas, pending information from Chim. But the real plan is I go after Erkric myself."

Signi stilled, her face distraught.

"What is it? I won't go alone, I'll have a picked team to help ward off those fellows in white. Erkric's the cause of all the problems, right? So if they're gone, well, things can't get any worse, can they?"

Signi trembled. "Oh, Inda, you can't. Erkric is the most powerful dag of the Venn. You cannot challenge him to a *halmgac—*"

"A what?" Even as he spoke, Inda heard the familiar root for Marlovan *duel* in the unfamiliar word.

"It is old, very old. Forbidden now. At least, according to the old form, where they rowed away to an island and one returned. Some say that's where we get the notion of the far shore, though we have the far shore in so many meanings. . . . Is that something exclusive to us Venn? Or is it a part of human nature, to go from the group, or force one from the group, but what does that say about the group?"

There she went, in that soft voice, her gaze far beyond the limits of furnishing and walls. Inda loved those conversations, when one thing would lead to another, and then to another, often not resolving, questions netted to other questions as he and Signi and Tdor speculated about every subject under the sun.

But that was before time pressed him for answers. Time, and Evred. He sensed Evred waiting there in his office.

And Signi heard, or felt, or saw some subtle clue in Inda that brought her back. She squared her shoulders. Her tone shifted from wondering to brisk. "We still have duels. Anyway, too many were dying, and Drenskar, the . . . the honor of service, replaced it. But Inda, this is what's important. You cannot attack Dag Erkric, either alone or with your warriors, however well they are trained. His flagship will be filled with wards and traps."

Inda bumped gently against the table and frowned down at the map. "Well, so much for the easy way. We'll just make my other plan the real one. Signi, I can't promise how others will behave, you know that. But I can promise that my own orders will never include massacre or torture. Fight until they surrender or retreat. Then end it."

She trembled there on the opposite side of the desk, eyes half closed as she gazed down the path that he could never see. But he'd always sensed it. And so he waited.

Her gaze lifted and searched his, her brow tense with questions. "I think . . . I think I see the true path. And I believe you." She held herself tightly, then opened her eyes. "Here is how it works."

When Inda walked into Evred's office at dawn, he discovered the king there, and though glowglobes did not reveal time like candles, and Evred was scrupulously neat in his person, Inda sensed he had not slept.

"Your report?"

"Fox just wrote back. They're off the coast of Khanerenth, trying maneuvers with them, Dhalshev's independents, and some volunteers from Sarendan. It gives me half a year to get to Bren."

"If you leave after Convocation," Evred said, "you can ride north with Cama and a wing of dragoons. He's already started down with just a flight, but I can give him more. Was going to rotate some to the north anyway."

"But I—"

"Don't you think you will be a target? If I were the Venn, I'd be watching for you, especially if your name is on everyone's lips."

Inda looked surprised, then his brow cleared. "Right."

Evred rose from his wingback chair. The weak morning sun highlighted the tension sharpening the bones of his face. His voice was calm and deliberate, but Inda heard the strain of the old days at Andahi. "We've got almost four weeks until Convocation, and a lot to do before then."

The women took the news in characteristic ways: Hadand resigned to Inda's being sent off again, but busy with her son and her own enormous workload. Tdor's resignation was far sharper, driven by fear that she would never see him again, that the distant seas would swallow him, sped by Venn steel.

She held him tightly to her all the next night, and after he fell asleep she lay awake watching over him, with only the cold metallic disk of the moon to witness when she wept.

After supper the next night, when an early snow whirled in crazy patterns outside the windows, Signi sought Tdor out in her workroom that overlooked the white-quilted roofs of the queen's guard barracks.

"Do you have time to speak in private?" she asked in her accented Iascan. "About Inda," she added.

Tdor set aside her pen.

"I am here to beg of you a thing of terrible cost, I know, and it will be worse when you realize that I will then do a more terrible thing." Signi pressed her fingers against her lips, her eyes closing for a moment.

Tdor's curiosity chilled to fear. "Speak, Signi."

"I–I have reason to believe that when Inda leaves, I will probably get the signal I have waited for that will send me to Sartor."

"I assumed you'd go with him," Tdor said, not hiding her regret. "You're a ship dag, you are free to go."

Signi touched her fingertips together. "I am not free."

"What? Why?"

The mage looked worn and almost ill; Tdor realized she had not slept. "It is harder than I thought, this conversation. He goes north, to lead a war against my people. My path lies south. And after that . . . I do not know. Much depends on what occurs in the strait. But I do not believe I will ever return here."

Tdor slid her hands over the knife hilts in her sleeves.

Signi pressed her misshapen fingers against her lips

again; even the distortion of protracted pain had not taken away the neatness of her movements, grace without flourish. "My path seems to lead elsewhere. But I would have this one thing." She faced Tdor. "I would take with me a child of Inda's begetting, if I can." Her voice suspended. "My cycle was last week. I could this day begin to drink birth-herb."

Tdor said gently, "Should you not be discussing this matter with him? I don't see my place in it."

"Because I do not want him to know. That is what is so terrible, a moral trespass in both our cultures—all the cultures of the world. But I do not want him to worry about a child he will never see. *You* will know and make a place in the records, for I also know that secret children of those in power beget future problems. I will make certain we are together in the time of my cycle likeliest to make a girl."

Tdor signed agreement. Though no one had any control over if or when the Birth Spell worked (other than desire of a child) she'd been taught how, when conceiving children the ordinary way, girls most often resulted from mating before the egg white appeared, and boys that day, or a little after. Not always predictable, but as close as human endeavor could contrive.

"She will know wherefrom she comes, and you will have her name, Tadara Jazsha Sofar, in your family scrolls."

Tadara: a version of Tdor. A gesture of goodwill that would ramify through the future. Tdor had just enough vision to perceive it.

There was only one answer to be made to that. "So shall it be."

Signi placed her palms together in the gesture that Tdor had come to understand was akin to the fist to the heart. "If there is a thing I can do for you, who never asks anything for herself, I will."

Tdor breathed slowly, her palms damp despite the cold. "All right. If you truly mean that. I have a question, though I know you don't like to speak of battles. And I know this will probably sound frivolous, but, well, I've wondered all my life. Is it true you, um, see ghosts?"

Signi's face altered, her pupils huge. "It is part of our training, to see what is there."

"Supposedly there was a ghost at Inda's castle. I never

saw it. I never believed that ghosts were possible. I don't understand how, or even why, they could be. Were there really ghosts on that battlefield in the Andahi Pass?"

Signi walked to the window, staring out. The cold white light revealed light gray strands in her hair. Tdor sustained a little shock, and then Signi turned.

"Yes, I saw ghosts. How could I not? The sun was vanishing then, but in its last light they were there, like a mist rising, a light seen here," she touched her heart, "and here." A touch to her eyes. "As I watched, the mist wavered upward like smoke, taking human form all over the vale between the cliffs. Young men. Some as children. Bewildered, sad, angry, or lost, Venn and Marlovan together, their annihilation of one another forgotten." Her voice dropped, rough with empathetic grief. "And though the sun set, there came to pass a sense of light in that direction, west and north, and most turned and together drifted like smoke on the wind, vanishing through rock and brush and the fires being lit by the living. Some did linger, though there is no future in this world for their bodies conceived in joy, and fair by nature made, then desecrated by the violence of human will."

Tdor eased her gripped fingers knuckle by knuckle.

"By morning their number had dwindled, except for the rare ones who still drift about that place, seeking and seeking. What do they seek? That I cannot tell you. Whatever meaning our souls descry beyond our physical lives, the truth is, we the living cannot legislate eternity any more than we can the human heart."

"Thank you," Tdor said as Signi bowed, opening her hands in peace mode, and left.

And so that answers my question about ghosts, but where do they go? And if someone answers that, will there be another question behind it? And another behind that, and out, and out, beyond the world and light? Tdor remained where she was, suspended between tears and laughter and wonder.

Chapter Eleven

INDA was the only one surprised when the Jarls responded almost unanimously not to set aside the exile treaty.

Cama was disgusted, but he held his peace until Inda sat with him, Evred, Rat Cassad, Tuft Sindan-An (Rat and Tuft riding along with their brothers to Convocation after hearing a rumor that Inda was off to war again), and the Marlo-Vayir brothers at a private banquet at the end of New Year's First Day.

"I thought they'd vote the treaty rescinded," Inda said, looking around at his friends. "Here's Fox, going to war for us, and what's he get in return?"

Once the oaths were finished, Evred had done his best to speak in favor of relaxing the treaty so that the Montredavan-Ans could join Convocation, but he'd seen in the closed faces before he even asked for a raise of arms that the Jarls did not want the Montredavan-Ans among them again. No one knew them, but they knew their history: they were troublemakers, their sons would strut in the academy. Let them see that when Marlovans made treaties, they kept them. He didn't have to hear the individuals to know what was being thought.

"His family will be granted the command of our navy," Evred stated, bringing Inda back to the present. "I will invite the heir to be a King's Runner while he is an heir. And Hadand-Gunvaer suggested that their daughters be permitted to become heralds or royal scribes, if they choose, since part of the treaty forbade their marrying out."

Despite the universal approval ("More than generous!") Inda doubted that Fox would like any of that, but he had decided to deal with such discussions face-to-face. Fox had only asked him to come back and command a sea battle. The future—if they all survived—could be dealt with later.

Cama grinned. "Jarls might like Fox a whole lot better if he helps you bring Rajnir's head back, carried on a pole."

"Hear him!" Tuft roared, lifting his cup in both hands. "Inda-Harskialdna Sigun!"

That shout echoed the next day, when Evred addressed the assembled Jarls. "We have been at peace for five years, which means for five years I have refrained from making a war speech before we begin our own debates and judgment. But I am still a Harvaldar, and not a Sieraec, because we have all suspected that what we won at so dear a cost five years ago was a respite."

He paused for the curses and comments to die away.

"This year, we have been called to the north to defend the strait from the Venn invasion. Indevan-Harskialdna will command the defense, which will be made up of seagoing allies from all over the southern continent."

Cherry-Stripe leaped to his feet, fist in the air. "Inda-Harskialdna Sigun!"

"Inda-Harskialdna Sigun!"

"Death to the Venn!"

"Death to Rajnir!"

"Here are my orders. Indevan, I order you, before the eyes and ears of Convocation, to go north as my Voice and my Will. You shall defend the southern continent against the invaders."

He paused for the cheering, reveling in the ring of conviction in their shouts. Even Horsebutt yelled, fist in the air, "Death to the Venn!" They all knew that if the strait fell to the invaders, Halia would be next.

Evred smiled, triumph singing along his nerves. "There has never been a commander like Indevan," he said and

laughed at the louder shout the Jarls and brothers and
sons sent up, ringing against the stone. "He shall prevail,
and he shall secure the strait against all enemies, so I have
ordered." He used the old future-must-be modality, which
caused a frenzy of yipping, shouting, and drumming on
benches.

When he could be heard, he turned to Inda. "Indevan-
Harskialdna, I call upon you, so do you swear before me,
and before your peers convened?"

"So I do swear," Inda said, fist up in the air.

"Then ride to the north, *and victory*."

"Return in triumph! Rajnir's head on your sword!"
roared the irascible old Jarl of Jaya-Vayir.

"Rajnir's head!"

"Victory!"

"Inda-Harskialdna Sigun! Three times three!"

As the accolade reverberated against the walls, Evred
picked up the sword he'd set beside the throne, and Inda
drew his Harskialdna blade, once Evred's. They clashed the
blades together, sending up an arc of sparks.

Runners handed each another blade, and as the Runners-
in-Training above enthusiastically pounded out the galloping rhythm of the war dance, he and Evred flung down their
swords, east-west crossed north-south. Grinning at one another over the steel, they began to dance as a single body of
sound and voices and drums resonated through bones and
blood and nerves.

Inda walked downstairs with Cama the next morning.
Cama said, "We'll ride out soon as the sun is up. Good riding while this thaw is on. So you say your farewells today."

"Good." Inda endured another pang of impending parting. "About the thaw, not the farewells. I hate riding in snow.
Got enough of that coming home from the north last time."
As Cama uttered his growl of a laugh, Inda grimaced. "One
thing for certain. If I have to be organizing a lot of patrols
and so forth to guard the strait after we turf out the Venn,
at least nobody will expect me to be bringing home any
heads in bags."

Cama snorted another laugh.

"What is that with heads, anyway? And what would you

carry it in? A basket would leak, and who'd want the fellow's nose poking through the weave?"

Cama paused midstep to let out a guffaw, then wiped his eyes. "Wait till I tell Cherry-Stripe."

"I'm serious," Inda protested, hands on hips.

They sobered when Evred appeared, Hadand and Tdor behind him. Tdor's robes still hid the firm mound of her belly, but Inda had kissed that warm skin earlier in the morning, after feeling a faint flutter under his palm that she insisted was the babe moving, and not just her breakfast digesting.

Signi had said her good-byes in the Harskialdna suite, amid tears and tenderness, and an odd formality that Inda did not understand. *Some Venn thing,* he'd decided as he kissed her and grabbed up his gear bag.

Evred stepped aside when Inda would have clapped him on the shoulder. Inda turned away, remembering that Evred did not like being touched. That was fine. Inda still hated anyone touching his head unexpectedly.

So he kissed the little Sierlaef, who waved mittened hands, then Hadand, and last and most lingering, his wife.

Evred said, "You will speak with my Voice." He opened his palm. On it lay Hadand's locket.

He stretched the chain between his fingers, lifting it toward Inda's head. But then he clenched his fingers and tossed it instead.

Inda caught it, his mind already galloping into the future. "You'll use this thing when the baby is born, right?" He turned from Evred to Tdor.

"I promise," Evred said.

Inda looked up, but did not see Signi anywhere, only the faces of his friends among the Guards and Runners, all of whom saluted, fist to heart. Inda's throat tightened as his gaze lingered on the people he loved most. It hurt just as much to leave voluntarily as to be sent away; tears stung his eyes as he mounted up.

Cama gave the signal to ride out. They thundered through the gate, horns pealing from tower to tower where youngsters enthusiastically rang the bells. Inda wiped the tears away so they wouldn't freeze.

*   *   *

In Bren, Tau was just returning to Adrani House from a party.

As he mounted the stairs just inside the queen's suite, two voices blended with intimate laughter: Wisthia's and that of the baron she'd recently taken up with. He looked a lot like his nephew Prince Kavnarac and had a similar genial manner.

Tau paused, listening not to the words—they were too muffled to perceive—but to the qualitative change in voices that happiness made. How to characterize it? As always with difficult things, his senses mixed curiously. The sound tasted like wine, glimmered like polished gold in sunlight. When he told people that, they looked at him as if he'd gone mad.

He laughed when he thought back to the previous year's sober New Year's Week. *I've never been in love,* Wisthia had said before they departed for an obligatory royal party. *One of the fine things about adulthood is realizing you can have a good life without the emotional catastrophe. In fact, judging from the throes and woes I so often see around me, a better life.* There was nothing wrong with finding satisfaction in a life without a love-mate, but not half a year later this fellow had inherited his baronetcy and come to court. Within a week he and Wisthia had fallen for each other as hard as any two teenagers.

Tau clapped on his light and in the same movement brushed his fingers over his scroll-case though he didn't expect anything. Evred wrote very rarely and his messages were always short.

The tingle of a message startled him. He sat down abruptly, careless of his black brocade court clothes. From his golden case he extracted a thin scrap, written in Evred's fine scribal hand.

Inda is on his way north, after swearing before Convocation to restore order to the strait.

Tau tucked the note away, dismissing "restore order" as a surprising lapse into empty rhetoric on Evred's part. Why not write "to save Bren"? The most compelling thing was the realization that Evred had let Inda go.

He got up to report the news to Queen Wisthia, remembered that she had company, and waited until the next time they met alone.

"Evred sent Inda," Tau later reported. "With orders to 'restore order' in the strait. I hope that means we will be seeing Inda before spring is over." Tau shook his head. "You'd think someone would have got one of those transfer tokens to him so he could spend the winter and summer drilling instead of traveling."

Wisthia tipped her head. "Taumad. Do you really think any monarch will trust the famed Elgar the Fox with his force for longer than it will take to win a battle? No, don't protest about how long it takes to drill. I know that, though I wouldn't have before being forced to live among Marlovans as long as I did. I can assure you, Kliessin wants your Inda to walk in, lead Bren's navy to a spectacular victory, and then go home again. Preferably in a day."

"Well that won't happen," Tau retorted.

"No, and I'm afraid to find out what will." Wisthia began to pass, then halted and looked back. "What did Evred say? 'Restore order.' " Her expression was difficult to interpret. Then she smiled. "I do hope whatever happens, that young man comes here at some point. I confess to an almost overwhelming desire to meet him."

The world was made of silence and lay outside of time.

Language had failed Rajnir, and so he abandoned it, straining toward the ceiling of gray ice in hopes of another window. He cherished the last window, examining it minutely again and again as he reveled in sensory memory: how his lungs expanded of his own volition, without the constraint of the vile whisper. How heat pressed upon him so that sweat trickled down his brow into his ear, ran down his inner thigh. How the white silk squeaked when he moved his arms. The press of his loosely-laced armor under his arms when he arched his back.

He remembered *hearing* words. Not the vile whisper. He heard Uncle Fulla. He understood the words! *"My king." That is I! I am Rajnir!* He held onto the meaning of those words, saying them over—sensing a window—turned and turned until he found it, and there it was! He used his eyes—his eyelids lifted, and he reveled in the cold air on his eyeball, the itch along his lashes, because it was so very good to *feel!* He cherished the tearing of bright light. There was the table, with a chart on it. There were inward

slanting ship windows, with a green sea moving outside.
There *he* was, the vile whisperer, but giving orders to his
dags, and so Rajnir relished the cold flow of air against his
face, and the sweat inside his clothes. The expansion of
an indrawn breath, the shape of his own lips and jaw and
tongue. He moved them! His throat worked, and he spoke
words! *"I want the fleet to win sea room."* And when the
vile whisperer spun around, eyes and mouth three circles,
Rajnir thought, *I am king!* and said, *"Order the signals, my
Dag."* He said them! He thought the words, and his own
lips and tongue and breath shaped them! What pleasure,
what glory, to choose to speak and then to do it!

Then came the fight to hold onto movement, and meaning, but he could not shut out the vile whispers. Inexorably the ice built and built, shrouding him with numbing
cold until the window closed. Gone was volition, and
feeling, and hearing. Gone everything but floating in the
ice-bound silence, except when the whisper forced him to
stand, forced him to sit, forced him to speak a stream of
words whose meaning was gone as soon as the sound left
his lips.

So he cherished the memory of that window, of feeling
and being, again and again and again . . .

Then he felt another window. And a new voice, whispering *Rajnir*.

At first he let the whisper pass. Rajnir had no being, no
voice, no volition. Only memory.

Rajnir, come to the window.

That was not the vile whisperer. The vile whispers took
away the windows.

It took immense effort to remember how to turn. How
to look. How to listen. The new voice persisted: *Rajnir.
Come see. Come find me. Open your eyes.*

. . . to find a world within a world. He floated higher,
aware of the sensation of floating, of movement. Sunbeams
shot through the gray, and when he turned, there was the
deep blue immensity of the sky.

Rajnir. Open your eyes.

In his dream he had self again, and opened his eyes,
but he knew it was a dream, for he was in Ymar again, the
tower high above the port of Jaro. Higher than the clouds, a
cold wind blowing and blowing, and above the sky so bril-

liant and pure a blue it hurt to look, it hurt his skin to feel
the wind, it hurt his body to walk . . .

. . . and he tumbled out of the dream and into a room
he had never seen. He fell to his hands and knees, his
body thick and heavy, his breath sobbing in his throat. His
limbs trembled with the effort it took just to hold himself
on hands and knees in a crawl. His eyelids burned, but he
forced them open.

A small old woman with untidy gray-white hair knelt by
him. He remembered her, not who she was, only that he knew
her. Memory! It had become more precious than gold.

"Rajnir." Hers was the other voice! No longer a smooth
whisper inside the gray world but real, the cracked voice of an
old woman, hissing through real teeth and over a real tongue.
And so familiar, and so kind, calling and calling to bring him
out of the ice. "Come, wake up. We must speak."

He made a great effort and lifted his head again. Drew
in a breath of his own volition! "Uuuuuhhhhn." It was his
voice! His word!

"Rajnir, I am Brit Valda. I've created a hole in Erkric's
spells. We are in a bubble outside of time. It will not last,
the cost is so very great just for this much," she said quickly.
"Do you hear me? Do you understand?"

He shifted, sitting down abruptly. The stone floor was
cold and rough under his haunch. He ran his fingers over
the stones, loving the coarseness of the grit. "Where am I?"
His voice, his chosen words!

"You are in Llyenthur Harbor. You are in the old palace on the hill. Erkric has frozen you inside of spells, a terrible lock and interlock of spells, and when my own bubble
bursts, the spells await you again, I am desolate to admit.
We got you out once before, but then Erkric locked you in
again, far more securely than before. I want you to know
what is happening to you, so you can take the knowledge
inside when the waiting spells close around you again. And
know that I am fighting Erkric, and others are as well. We
will free you. I vow to you, my king. By twig and root. We
will free you."

"Spells," he whispered. "Is that the gray?"

"I don't know what you see. There are two sets of spells.
One binds your mind away from your body. Another set
binds your body to actions controlled by magical signals,

leaving you only the ability to eat, drink, and use the Waste Spell. Speak what you are constrained to speak, on signal." She touched his arm. He twitched, then stretched his arm out again. Oh, to be touched—and to choose it, and know it!

She seemed to understand, and ran her hand lightly over his shoulder, then up to his head. She stroked his hair, tender as a mother.

Rajnir's face crumpled. His chest ached with misery.

"Come. Come. You must regain your chair. Erkric must not know you moved."

He gasped, and strained to sit upright. Valda lent him all her spindly strength as he forced himself to rise. He could not resist swinging his arms, just to feel them swinging, and though his knees trembled with his effort to hold himself, he stomped once, twice, thrice.

Then collapsed into the chair. She flicked his hair smooth, his robe straight. Her clothes smelled musty with the thin sweat of the old. Her breath on his cheek whiffed of the spice-milk she'd drunk at dawn. He breathed deeply, gathering to him the evidence of another life, of existence, of his ability to command his own body, strange and heavy and weak as it was.

A faint blue light flickered, and the woman gasped in dismay. "Already my bubble wears! Rajnir, hear me. Erkric right now is back in Twelve Towers, stripping the old protections from your chambers and laying his Norsunder magic. But we will destroy that, too. Augh, it's fading."

"No," Rajnir begged. "No. Please, don't—"

The woman whispered, making signs, then shook her head in frustration. "I'm sorry," she whispered, tears gathering in her eyes. "I'm sorry."

The window vanished, and Rajnir tumbled back into the featureless, painless gray, then gradually lost the sense of tumbling. He floated again, in the world of ice. For a time he raged and wept, except he had no voice, no tears.

But he did have memory. And so he cherished the memory, revisiting each sight and smell and touch. Each word.

Even the ones she had whispered.

Fox: I'm on my way north.

The doors to the cabin slammed open to a whirl of frigid

blizzard winds as Barend stumbled in, recognizable only by his crimson knit cap and his pointed chin. Fox sprang up and kicked the door shut.

Barend flapped his arms, shedding wet snow in clumps.

"Thank you for bringing that inside," Fox said.

Barend was too cold, and too alarmed, to care. "There's a fleet hull up. All across the horizon. We near to sailed into the midst of 'em."

"Venn?" Fox asked sharply in total disbelief. Even the Venn couldn't sail directly into the winds, especially these vicious, steady winds straight out of the east, unhindered by any continent for months of sailing.

"Hard to see, but Pilvig swears they're Chwahir," Barend said.

"She'd know." Fox also knew what the Chwahir did to renegades they plucked off other ships. "She's the mate on deck this watch, eh? I'll come up. Relieve her."

Barend turned away as Fox reached for his winter gear. By the time he reached the captain's deck and looked around at the *Death* stripped to fighting sail, the foremost Chwahir could be made out through his glass by the ship rat shivering on lookout.

"Parley flag at the foremast!" he screeched.

Fox gestured to the mid at the signal flags. "Run up the 'parley agreed.' "

No one moved; a faint whiff of the smolder pots whipped down from the mizzenmast from an errant gust of wind. The blizzard was breaking up.

The Chwahir spilled wind, and the flagship waited for the *Death* to slide up on its lee and shiver sail so that the captains could look across at the opposite ship.

The Chwahir had also stripped to fighting sail, bow teams waiting in the tops.

The Chwahir captain stood abaft those tending the wheel, his manner attentive to someone on the poop deck, in the position of supreme command. Fox turned his attention to the small, still figure dressed all in black, just like him. He recognized that childish form—

Snapped his glass to his eye. "Thog?"

Thog daughter of Pirog lifted a thin, small hand in gesture. She spoke, but the wind took away her words. But there was no mistaking that invitation.

As soon as wind, water, and surging wood would permit, Fox climbed aboard the Chwahir flagship, the first non-Chwahir to do so, as far as he was aware. A swift glance revealed a deck much like any other: wind-scoured, everything orderly, round-faced, black-eyed Chwahir at their posts, looking even more alike in their severely plain hooded tunic-coats.

The rounder hulls sat better in the water than Fox's narrow-hulled racing ships. The forecastle was a true forecastle; that is, a raised structure off the main deck, as was the aft castle, the captain's deck where the ship was conned, and a poop up behind.

Fox was conducted by silent Chwahir into a plain cabin, furnished much like any other cabin, with a bolted central table, charts spread.

Thog looked exactly the same as Fox remembered. She'd always seemed about twelve years old, though she was Fox's age. As she came forward, the clear light of glow-globes showed tiny lines at the corners of her big, dark eyes and etched across her broad, tense forehead.

"What are you doing this far south?" Fox asked. "This armada I'm part of is—"

"I know its purpose, Fox," she said, in the same light, timbreless voice he'd heard in disturbing dreams for years. "I know you took command of the alliance between Sarendan and Khanerenth. My question to you: is it true that Inda comes back?"

"Why do you want to know?" he countered.

The brief compression of her lips might have been an attempt at a smile. "To unite against the common enemy. The Venn would love our shipyards, our cordage, and especially our sails. Our people, as laborers."

Fox did not deny it. Instead, he ventured another question. "What happened to you? I thought your laws were definite about runaways. Called them renegades."

"Our laws are definite about everything." Her Dock Talk was clipped, but clear. "Including the reward for defeat of enemies such as Boruin. Majarian. And the Brotherhood of Blood. We were given place in the navy. Uslar and I are now captains—our training with Inda stood us well. The new high admiral summoned me. He appointed me commander of our defense to fight under Inda Elgar the Fox."

Fox said, "Inda's on his way to Bren. If you can join us right away in sailing west now, we'll be able to touch at Jaro, talk to Ymar's people, then start for Bren—"

Thog raised a small hand and looked down at the deck.

"What?" Fox demanded. "Are you or aren't you joining us?"

"Yes. But not to defend Bren. My king's orders are specific. We will unite our forces with yours, under Inda's command, anywhere off our coast in a defensive effort. But we will not defend another kingdom." And when Fox crossed his arms, obviously preparing for a fairly hot retort, she said, "I suspect you will find the same will be said from Everon. They will not sail up the strait to defend Bren and leave their own coast undefended."

Fox held back a retort. Instinct insisted she was right. Further, it explained some of the hedging he'd been hearing that he'd attributed to the mushy rhetoric of diplomatic usage. "I never thought we'd have you Chwahir, but I confess I did think we'd have Everon and Ymar. Then we won't have enough ships, not against the Venn."

Thog's small chin came down. "No. Everyone knows that. Despite all their talk, they are all afraid."

"All right. I'll consult with the others. We do still have Inda coming to command us."

Thog smiled briefly. Then her serious gaze flicked to the chart. "Yes. And if we heard it, the Venn will have also. I hope Inda knows that."

"So do I." *Have they, Ramis?* Fox shook his head. "So do I."

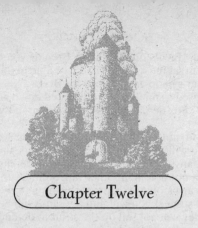

Chapter Twelve

THOSE mad or desperate enough to attempt it could make it through Andahi Pass during the winter. Horses were useless, as snow buried the trails and a false step could plunge one to the neck in muddy slush. Runners took the mounts to Ala Larkadhe as the rest started up a trail Cama had got to know very well in all weathers.

The pass itself was filled with icy snow and impossible for anyone but small animals to traverse. Cama, Inda, and their Honor Guard toiled up the rocky footpaths, often feeling cautiously at every step for black frost. The easiest part was crossing the lakes. Goats galloped daintily over the ice, drawing sleighs every which way, or a person could pole speedily over a well-smoothed track, balanced on a sled. A couple of days' hard rowing (or a day of nice sailing if the wind happened to be right) was reduced in winter to a brisk morning's slide.

Because they caught a stretch of days with blue sky overhead, they made it to the top of the pass quicker than a horse journey through the pass in spring; there were times when it would take eight weeks, because of frequent stops for blizzards.

Their spirits were high. The journey had ended most

days with campfire planning sessions for the defense of Bren, while Cama's dragoons paced a watchful double perimeter.

Cama knew little about the sea, but he was willing to learn. Mindful of the fact that he might be called on one day to defend the north coast against another invasion, he pestered Inda tirelessly with questions: Why did the wind change? How could the current flow one way and the wind another? Which way did you point the boat when the big waves came at you? Inda helped him to translate maritime conditions into land equivalents.

So each night they sat on rocks by the fire, drawing with sticks in the snow as they discussed different ideas. A few of the dragoons listened in, offering heroic and dashing notions, most of which were useless, but Inda didn't tell them that. How best to use the islands off the harbor was the main topic of debate, Inda trying to look at the problem backward: What would the Venn be expecting the defenders to do?

"Break their line through the middle," Cama kept saying.

Inda and Cama both had heard that the Venn invariably lined up across the horizon before they invaded. "I've got to break it from all directions," Inda often said, hoping that enough discussion would furnish a great idea.

Cama's usual retort was a reminder such as, "Tough to manage when you're stuck with line-of-sight and the damned Venn aren't."

Back around they'd go, talking in circles.

Inda hadn't heard from Fox for weeks, so he was glad when he felt the tap of magic early that last morning as they were trudging up the trail (kept clear by the beacon teams) to the highest beacon house. From here it would be mostly sledding downhill.

Inda took out the scroll-case as camp was set up. His sudden, heated cursing froze everyone and startled one of the Runners into dropping the Fire Sticks into the snow.

Inda seldom swore, but he made up for it now. The dragoons resumed making camp, a few of them mentally stowing away some of that incomprehensible nautical invective for future need.

Cama appeared, slinging his pack onto a rock. "Bad news?"

"The worst." Inda handed Fox's note to Cama, who angled it toward the fire, frowning to bring his one eye into focus in spite of the flickering flames.

Inda, I'm on the way to get you, but it's just me and my four fastest. There will be no defense of Bren unless King Galadrin wants to sic the half of his navy caught inside the blockade on whatever Durasnir brings over. Details when I see you. Suffice it to say, kings are afraid to leave their shores undefended. Negotiations prolonged until it was too late to reach Bren by summer. They all want to fight at The Fangs, which at least does make military sense.

"And the Venn know it," Inda said, sighing.

"They know Bren as well, don't they?" Cama observed.

"Yeah." Inda dropped onto a huge flat rock. Since he'd left the royal city he'd fought against a vague sense of having finally overreached himself. Planning, being prepared, thinking about everything was supposed to banish that sense. "Better report to Evred."

Inda worked his right arm, which ached dully, took out the tiny roll of paper and the field pen screwed into an ink-well. Laboriously he reported in as few words as possible, sent the message, then looked up. Cama was still waiting.

"Listen, Inda. Now that we've reached the top, and there's no chance of any ears but the night birds, I talked to Shoofly Senegad here." Cama clapped a tough, sturdy dragoon on one broad shoulder, a man in his midthirties with white-puckered sword scars on his face. "He looks enough like you. Pretty much your size. Hair more or less the same." He flicked the unruly brown horsetail hanging down Shoofly's back. "Got slashed fighting pirates with Hawkeye at the Nob. And he was with Hawkeye at Andahi, too, so he's already got one earring, you see?"

Senegad yanked up his wooly cap and displayed his earring for any doubters. His mates grinned. Some saluted him in friendly mockery.

"Crossing our kingdom, I think you were safe. Up in Idayago? You know how it's been for me. For you, we should add in Venn spies and assassins. They've got to know you're coming." Cama smacked Senegad on the shoulder. "We'll put Shoofly in chain mail and surround him with fellows, shields at the ready. He's gonna wear two earrings, see, and he'll ride behind the banner. Make a lot of noise, hand out orders right and left, look like a Harskialdna."

"I'll take the second earring out again, soon's it's safe," Senegad said modestly, though every dragoon there knew old Shoofly'd be bragging about that earlobe hole for the rest of his life. If he survived the ruse.

"It'll be like me'n you when we covered for the gold wagons. You get into your sea gear, like you were wearing when I first saw you at Cherry-Stripe's, before the war. No one would've thought you one of us. You slip on by. Fox gonna be here soon?"

"No. Sounds like he got delayed with whatever those negotiations were," Inda said, fighting impatience. Well, nothing for it. "I'll get myself to Trad Varadhe alone then. Hire onto a trader going east, let Fox know. That'll save time." He turned to Shoofly, then gestured to the Twins. "Jaya and Lith here will shield you, since I can't take Runners to sea. But you sure you don't mind being a target?"

"It'll be fun, being you," Senegad said. He had a deep, rusty-sounding voice. "I'll make these slackers sweat." A thumb jerked at his companions. "Order floggings all around, maybe get 'em to build me a castle or two."

The dragoons broke into laughter. This was just their kind of humor. So strange, Inda thought, how on land or sea people would work double-tides, and risk their lives, to hoodwink an enemy. These fellows obviously looked forward to long and grueling rides in winter weather in hopes of being spotted by some spy. But . . .

Inda realized they were all staring and forced a grin. He didn't want to say, "But Senegad is *old*. I'm midway in my twenties!" Inda rarely looked into a mirror and then only to make certain his clothes weren't awry, or stained, so he had no notion how his experiences had planed the youth from his face.

He turned out his hands. "Sounds like our plan."

After a heart-pounding, bone-rattling thrill of a descent through the mountains—tough dragoons whooping like boys—Cama and his Honor Guard marched past Twisted Pine down the switchback carved into the massive landslide above Castle Andahi. Behind the crimson eagle banner, bright against the snowy expanse, marched a broad-shouldered, heavy-chested, scar-faced man wearing two ruby earrings. He was seen later on the sentry walks, waving his hands and pointing as if placing mighty armies for future battles.

King's Runners Ramond Jaya and Ramond Lith were unhappy at being ordered to remain behind. Until Shoofly's ruse was put in force, they'd assumed they would accompany Inda out to sea among the pirates and far-flung navies. But Inda was adamant: everyone recognized them now, and they had to protect the fake Harskialdna.

He could see how disappointed they were. He liked them very much. But he hadn't grown up with them. He didn't talk about experiences they'd never shared. The truth was, he was relieved when he set out alone.

Nobody paid any heed to a fellow in sloppy sailing clothes and an old sock cap beneath which hung a scruffy four-strand sailor braid. He wore an old knit muffler that only showed the tip of his nose as he hitched a ride on a wagon going from Castle Andahi to Trad Varadhe.

A couple weeks later, Inda shuffled forward in line at the new harbormaster's warehouse-cum-office at Trad Varadhe as the false Harskialdna and his pack of Guards rode, jingling with martial ardor, down the middle of the road.

The false Harskialdna marched around inspecting the new castle foundations and the partial walls, then kept his men standing about all afternoon, watching the slow process of pouring molten bronze through the openings between the clay core and cope of what would be a great bell. Trad Varadhe's castle bell had not lasted fifteen years. Made by the Marlovans to their own pattern the year they took Idayago, it had been melted by the Venn soon after their invasion. They took the bronze with them when they retreated.

While that was going on, Inda stood outside a glazier's shop, transfixed by a process he'd never witnessed before. He watched so long that he nearly missed his tide. A sudden shower recalled the here and now, and he loped down to the dock, paid three times the going rate to be rowed out to the brig called *Leaping Fish,* and under the scowl of his new captain, went below to stow his gear in the crew's cabin.

He dug his hand down into his gear bag, closed his fingers around a golden scroll-case, and whispered a transfer spell. Then he thumbed it open. The note he'd prepared— *Fox, I've just left Trad Varadhe*—had vanished.

He hung his bag on its hook just below the hammock assigned him and went to work.

The Sarendan trader *Leaping Fish* had endured the worst trade voyage ever.

They'd left in 3911 with a hold full of second-tier Sartoran leaf. Pirates, Venn, and finally storms dumped them on the Idayagan beach just in time to discover that the Venn were about to invade. They'd spent the summer dismantling the caravel and hiding it. By that time the Venn had come and gone, but when the captain took a party up into the mountain pine forest above Ghael to find a replacement foremast (fallen, of course—everyone knew the Sartoran Wood Guild would get you if you chopped one down and turn you into a tree or worse, a rock) he found the mountains full of other scavengers.

When they finally located what they needed on an isolated mountaintop and lugged it down, it was to discover from the captain's unhappy, abandoned brother-in-law that the his remaining crew had succumbed to greed and sold off the ship's timbers for triple the price. After the Marlovans got rid of the Venn, the new Jarl had offered abandoned farm plots to anyone who farmed them for a year. Half the former crew promptly retired to take up life as landsmen. The others pocketed their gains and signed on to other ships as trade started up again.

After several years of labor, the captain had a new ship. Until the winter of 3920, sailors were plentiful and cheap. But the rumor that the Venn had come back and were prowling the strait made it suddenly difficult to hire anyone without promising stiff pay. He arranged on credit to carry the new island coffee east, but it seemed like any profit he made was going to go straight to the crew.

Then at the hiring dock below the harbormaster's new house at Trad Varadhe, he got a single break in the long chain of disasters: a sailor obviously trained at all stations who accepted the first (low) pay he offered, without negotiation. The captain had almost chased him off, thinking him a criminal or a drunkard or worse, but desperation prompted him to hire the fellow on trial.

The fellow started off badly by almost missing the tide. He wasn't much to look at—a shortish, scarred sailor, his Dock Talk Iascan accented. He wore a kerchief round his head, but he had a long sailor-braid, which was what had convinced the captain to accept him as genuine.

A lot of former pirates wore kerchiefs to hide the holes in their ears, but the captain had been a privateer in his early days and could overlook such things—as long as he didn't see any pirate behavior.

He didn't. The newcomer was strong and hard-working, experienced, and even abstemious. Within a few days he was promoted to third mate.

Watching Idayago's shore retreat at last, the captain relaxed. So it was late winter, and the current and the air against them: they could tack and tack eastward, every tack taking them farther from Idayago and closer to home. If they saw anything with a curved prow on the horizon, they'd just dive inland and hide in one of the many inlets.

As they were trying to get around the hump of land between Idayago and Bren, storm after storm blew them back faster than they could sail. They spent a couple of weeks in a cove until the weather relented enough for them to poke out.

And that was when the lookout bellowed from the masthead, "Hai deck! Sail hull down on the horizon, right off the bow!"

Everyone went about their tasks, there being a rough sea and a brisk wind. But when the lookout squeaked, "Them's *pirates*!" everyone who had a glass dropped what they were doing and snapped them out.

"All hands! All hands to the sails!" The captain plunged among them, bawling and cuffing right and left. "We'll have to turn tail and run back to Idayago," he shouted, sick to the heart.

The third mate appeared at his elbow. "Uh, no, you won't."

"What?"

"I know those ships," the mate said. "It's all right, nothing will happen." He added awkwardly, "They're coming for me."

"What?" The captain did not wait for an answer, but gave the order to hold course. It wasn't like they could outrun the chasers anyway.

The wind-backed pirate dashed up like a stooping raptor. The trading brig's crew watched with a mixture of admiration and envy as the trysail, a low, wicked-looking black-sided vessel, flashed its sails. The way came off it, leaving it rocking on the wintry gray sea. Far in the misty distance, they made out another ship—from the outline, a raffee. Obviously another pirate.

The third mate had vanished and now reappeared on deck. His kerchief was gone, revealing *two* ruby hoops in his ears, and the captain put together the clues at last. "You with Elgar the Fox?"

His former third mate grinned as the black ship's gig tossed over the waves toward them. "Whoever I am," he said, "here's some advice. If you don't want to be caught in a Venn sea battle, you keep going straight east, don't stop, don't speak to any other ship—keep 'em below the horizon if you can. Understand?"

The fellow with the rubies tossed his gear down into the gig and vaulted over the side.

As the gig splashed its way back to the black pirate ship, the captain said to his second mate, "They can't be pirates."

The brother-in-law scanned that black-sided, rake-masted trysail from topgallants to hull, then cocked his head. "What makes you think that, against all evidence of m'own eyes?"

"What pirate would scamp his pay?" the captain asked, not without satisfaction. "That fellow worked all this time, never collected a flim."

The brother-in-law chewed the inside of his lip as he watched the boat hoist aboard the trysail, and then—just as promised—the sails dropped, sheeted home, and filled. As the ship made an elegant arc and tacked away, he grunted. "Maybe. Here's what I think. Less we know about that there black ship, and that fellow with the rubies, the better.

We've had a gut-fill of adventure. Let's take his advice and stay mum."

Inda and the gig crew were soaked through and shivering as they clambered aboard the *Death*. Barend shouted, "Light out to windward!" Then, a wide grin in his triangular face, eyes crescents of mirth, "Heyo, Inda."

The enormous din of filling sails caused Inda to throw back his head. Exhilaration rushed through him at the sight of *Death*'s complicated geometry of shrouds, standing and running rigging, the curves of the now-taut sails sheeting home, and he laughed for pleasure. The ship surged as it began to go about; the wintry light over the bow, the sound and smells were so familiar, but so much had changed.

Inda's reverie broke when Fox sauntered toward him, boot heels loud on the deck boards, the fringes on his fighting kerchief flagging in the wind. He drawled in Marlovan, "You going to stand there all day holding that bag like Peddler Antivad in the stone spell?"

Inda looked at his dunnage as if surprised to discover it there, clutched in his left hand. "Oh." He followed Fox aft along the companionway. Most of the faces were new, but not all. There were women among them of course. Inda drew in a breath, appreciating the sight of women in bright, tight clothing, all in taut shape. Why weren't there any women in the dragoons, he wondered wistfully.

"Lorm! Good to see you. Cooking for *Death* now, instead of *Cocodu*?"

"I go back and forth," said tall, somber-faced Lorm, cook aboard the pirate when Inda led his mutiny. "Trainin' the youngsters now." Lorm's somberness eased a little. "Good to see you with us, Inda."

"Captains in Freeport are beginning to pay smacking good sums for one of Lorm's trained cooks," Fox said, smiling.

Inda was still scanning the crew. "Where's Fibi the Delf?"

"Died at The Fangs," Barend said from abaft the wheel.

"Did you send word to the Delfs to let them know?"

"Soon's we landed." Barend's fingers flicked in salute.

Inda felt stupid. Of course they knew Delf clan customs.

He wondered why he had asked such a stupid question, then thought, *It's Fox's fleet. But I'm acting like it's mine.*

Barend looked Fox's way. "Signal all captains soon's they're in sight?"

"Yes." Fox made an ironic gesture toward the cabin and led the way inside. A new rat brought in flat-bottomed cups of whiskey-laced hot wine, ordered as soon as the brig was hull up. She turned curious eyes to the famous Elgar the Fox, then sped back to her mates crowded along the companionway below. "He's got the two earrings, but he's short!"

"He's not short, he's medium," said a mid, one of Cama's orphans, now a seasoned sailor. "You easterners don't know nothin'."

In the cabin, Inda took in the etched silver tray resting on a blackwood sideboard inlaid with golden lily patterns and the beautiful golden gondola lamp swinging overhead.

None of these furnishings were familiar. Even the cabin itself seemed altered in dimension. Inda dropped his dunnage on a side chest carved with cranes in flight and squelched onto the adjacent bench, concentrating on the inward-curving lines to the cabin. Yes, it had changed.

Well, so have I.

"So what happened? Why is there no defense of Bren?"

Fox said, "The allies were afraid to leave their own coasts open to one another, though they blamed the Venn out loud, and the Chwahir in secret. Oh, and Deliyeth has her own crazy notions. Finally the Khanerenth diplomat got them to agree that The Fangs is more defensible. Especially as we wouldn't have the Chwahir in support anywhere else but off their own coast."

Inda clapped his hands on his knees. "Fangs is better than Bren, actually. Just where I'd pick, if I could pick the ground."

"Which the Venn are sure to realize." Fox dropped into his chair next to the desk, poured out two cups, and sipped his wine, amused by Inda's abstracted air. When the silence had lengthened, Fox broke it. "Were you in Andahi?"

Inda blinked, the sudden onslaught of memory breaking like dreams. He looked up, wondering if that was Fox's way of asking how Cama and Ndand were. He'd heard about how well they'd all got along. "Didn't poke my nose in the castle," he said. "Slipped on by, while a fellow pretended to be me. In case of either Venn or Idayagan assassins."

"Some," Fox drawled, "might call the Idayagans would-be rescuers of their invaded kingdom. Never mind, don't waste the breath arguing over what's already occurred. But Venn assassins? I will wager this entire fleet that Erkric would love to get hold of you for some of his Norsundrian spell-casting."

"Dags. Magic. I forgot about that." Inda grimaced as he pulled a cloth-wrapped roll from his gear bag. "Weird, when you consider that they came close to trying a snatch on Evred. But he gives the orders at home, not me. What use would it be grabbing me and turning me into a puppet, since my orders come from the king?"

"Those of us who know you would twig to it in a heartbeat," Fox said. "Making me wonder how many secretly cooperated with Erkric up there in the cold northlands, if he really has taken over the king's mind as you said." He pointed to the scroll-case.

"Signi told me that Erkric kept isolating Rajnir, one person at a time. Starting when he was young."

Fox drummed his fingers on the desk. "Perhaps. So, have you come up with a plan?"

"Did nothing else but, these past two or three weeks. One thing I've learned is, people expect *the* plan. Not *a* plan."

"You're talking about leadership."

Inda waggled a hand, and then began to peel off the cloth wrappings around the roll. "I think leadership is mostly in people's heads. Most want to follow if they're not sure of a win. Want to lead only if they know they'll win. Against the Venn? They want me to lead. I've got to have *the* plan. D'you see?"

Fox shook with silent laughter. "Is this an abrogation of your position as hero?"

"It's me telling you I have *a* plan, and unless you have anything better, you're going to help me convince whoever we get as allies that it's *the* plan. Because here's what I've been finding in my reading. The other half of leadership is believing their leader is so good they make it true." He finished unwrapping his rolled chart and looked around. His vague expression turned to a frown of perplexity as he indicated the handsome carved desk built into the bulkhead. "This thing is fine, but where's the old chart table?"

"Forward wardroom. So what you're telling me is that you have more than one plan?"

"Yes. One's got to stay secret. Only you and me and Barend'll know. Jeje, if she's here."

"You don't trust your former mates?" Fox's brows slanted upward.

"I don't trust anyone who might be listening in on 'em," Inda retorted. "In the old days, I knew every face. Now I won't. And like you said, there are spies all around. Probably in every single one of the allied fleets waiting for us."

"Except maybe the Chwahir. I can't imagine Thog being that remiss."

"Thog? You saw her again?"

"Yes. She's got a sizable force for us to use at The Fangs."

"Thog." Inda shook his head. "I guess I'll think about that later. Back to my plan. It's the easiest way. One's public, the other secret."

"Very well. What is that?"

"Signi made a chart showing Venn navigation." Inda leaned against Fox's fine desk and carefully unrolled Signi's mirror chart.

Fox studied the lines propagating out in spokes from certain harbor cities, crossing the axes from other cities in a bewildering grid of diamond shapes. He set aside his empty cup then placed a finger on The Narrows, midway between the land bridge that almost connected the Toaran continent to the Halian. He put another finger on the Nob, and slowly brought the fingers up the drawn lines bisecting each location until they reached a city he'd never heard of, halfway up the west coast of Drael.

Inda pointed at the map. "We can't use it to navigate. If we use their 'ting' as they call it, it bounces back to all the other dags, making us appear as a dot on their maps and charts."

Fox whistled softly. "We don't need it to navigate, we just need to see them. This chart will get us back through the Venn blockade. We had to wait for a storm to come this way." He looked up. "But how do we judge where we are in reference to these dots of light?"

"Like always. Line of sight with one another and with landmarks. But once we know where they are in reference to our landmarks, we'll be able to avoid them." Inda plopped down on a bench, looked around, and whistled. "You raided some castles?"

"All legitimate pirate loot." Fox's smile was twisted. "By the way, you are ruining Captain Finna's bench. Get out of those clothes."

Inda got up, peered down at the bench inlaid with light wood carved in the form of stylized cranes, and bordered by old runes. "You attacked a Venn?"

"Venn pirate. Just setting up his empire over in Fire Islands, as his countrymen have abandoned that part of the world. I believe he was demoted, or cast ashore, or whatever it is the Venn call it. So he was helping himself to their leavings."

Inda had begun to shiver, his right shoulder sending shards of white lightning up into his skull.

"Hot water in the bath through there," Fox said, recognizing that old look of pain in Inda's tightened jaw and thinned lips. "I got a duplicate of Walic's pool given to me in gratitude when we took care of a pirate problem off the tip of Toar a couple years back." He extended his hand toward the bulkhead behind Inda.

"I thought the cabin was smaller." Inda's teeth chattered as he shed his clothes.

He grabbed dry drawers and trousers from his bag and soon settled into the bath kept hot and clean by magic. The aches and pain receded, leaving him able to breathe deeply. Fox bent over the navigation chart, trying to comprehend the logic behind its design, as they conversed through the open door and he brought Inda up on who was where. Inda gave a deep sigh at the news about Dasta.

When Fox was done catching him up, Inda forced himself out of the warm bath. He dried off fast, and pulled on the clothes he'd brought into the bath chamber. "Listen. I'm to tell you that Evred offers to make the fleet a Marlovan navy."

"Does he, now?" Fox said. "Putting me under whose orders?"

Inda had expected derision. "Mine." He rapidly fingered his hair into his sailor braid.

Fox snorted. "And you are his military Herskalt. What does the King command, O Voice?"

"Establish order in the strait." Inda rummaged in his sea bag for a shirt.

Fox laughed at the locket swinging against Inda's chest. "So your keeper has you on a short chain, eh?"

Inda shrugged. "Reminds me. Better let him know I'm here."

Chapter Thirteen

EVRED Montrei-Vayir hated change, but had come to terms with the fact that he could not always control it. He also hated war, though he accepted all the talk of glory and bravery. Bravery was necessary to face the brutality of war, and glory was the reward the survivors gained for their risk. So the flags and the songs and the precedence bound the people together with pride into kinship.

His reluctant conclusion was that war brought out the best in some people. But that was no reason to seek war. All winter long, whenever he could get a few moments free, he delved into the archives for the reasons people chose to go to war when there was no imminent attack. Most of what he found was self-serving, but here and there he discovered reluctance, regret for possible loss, and most of all, overriding need.

He wrote back and forth to Tau, asking questions about the various kings and their policies, particularly those on the strait. Everyone, it seemed, wanted precedence—just to make certain no one else got it, if for other reason. Ymar wanted it because they saw themselves as first among victims, deserving the highest reward. And the Chwahir just always wanted land.

Everyone wanted precedence, but no one was willing to sail to Bren because they didn't trust one another.

Everyone wanted Inda to reappear in his Elgar the Fox guise and fix the problem. After all his reading and writing and meditation, Evred began to comprehend that the "problem" transcended the Venn threat.

What they really wanted was someone strong enough to reestablish order.

And Inda was the one to do it.

The rightness of this vision—the Marlovans guaranteeing order—seized Evred so viscerally that his emotions swooped all winter between the heights of a moral conviction, at last, at long last, and the abyssal fear that Inda would die trying to save the wayward, indifferent kingdoms of the Sartoran continent from the evil Dag of the Venn. Every reminder of Erkric's thwarted plan to capture and ensorcel Evred's own mind, to force him to betray his people in service of the Venn, infuriated him all over again.

Inda *must* prevail. For the sake not just of Evred, but every man in the army, every woman and child and horse and dog in Iasca Leror, Inda must bring peace to the southern world. It was no mere military goal, but a moral imperative.

And so, when Inda wrote at last, just before spring, saying that he was now onboard his old flagship—and corroborating everything Tau had said—Evred neatly wrote out the orders he'd thought about so carefully.

Fox left Inda to make a tour of the deck. Barend appeared, having just finished his watch. "Come into the wardroom. I've got some eats waiting there."

They dropped down a deck and entered the wardroom to find two trays of steaming food that smelled wonderful.

They'd just finished when Inda sat up abruptly. "Ho. There's the locket. I wish Evred trusted the scroll-cases. It's not just you can use a bigger paper, but these things, it's like someone's poking me in the ribs from inside."

"Hated that," Barend commented, as a couple of shipmates wandered in to begin their recreation watch, one pulling cards and markers from a worn little bag.

Inda thumbed the locket open and retrieved the neatly

trimmed strip of paper. A few moments after, "Read it." He extended Evred's note.

Barend sighed. "How about you read it to me? Truth is, I don't do so well with letters that small. Though Evred writes much clearer than most."

"What about them?" Inda tipped his head toward the three at the other end of the wardroom.

"Don't speak Marlovan."

"Right," Inda said after a moment—the three were bent in low-voiced conversation punctuated by the clatter of markers.

He lowered his own voice. " 'When you have cleared the strait, you will clear the harbors of the strait and establish peace through regular patrols. Give all safe passage, fair trade. No favorites, no secret alliances, no double deals.' And on the back, he put, 'If the kingdoms want to fight each other, let them do it at their borders on land.' " Inda looked up expectantly.

Barend shrugged. "Sounds clear enough. If what you say about us being a navy is right, well, it gives us something to do after the Venn are gone."

Inda rubbed his scar hard, the way he always did when he wanted his brain to work better. Only rubbing his scar didn't help him understand his hesitation. So he turned out his hands. "First thing is clearing the strait."

Barend's laugh sounded like a rusty hinge. "I'd call that a big enough first thing."

"I'll tell Fox about the orders afterward. Maybe by then he'll be more used to the idea of being a Marlovan again."

"He's always been a Marlovan." Barend lifted a bony shoulder. "But an exiled one. I don't know that he'd make an oath to Evred."

"Hadn't thought of that."

More shipmates clumped in then, and the galley crew started bringing in trays of food.

A day and a half later, they'd caught up with the rest of the ships Fox had chosen to sweep the coast in search of Inda's brig.

The *Vixen* reached them first. Jeje scrambled up the sides of *Death* and charged up the companionway, a short, solid figure before whom all gave way.

She grabbed Inda in a crushing hug and lifted him clear off the deck.

"Augh," Inda squawked. "Can't breathe!" He gave Jeje a smacking kiss, which made her blush deep red as several of the younger crew hooted with laughter.

"When you've finished your touching reunion," Fox drawled, "you might join me before the rest show up to pull Inda into five equal pieces."

"Huh." Jeje flipped up the back of her hand at Fox, but followed him into the cabin, as did Inda, still rubbing his chest. Barend, grinning, shut the door behind them and quietly moved around the cabin closing the scuttles.

Inda sat on Finna's bench, elbows on knees. Fox moved to the desk so he could view everyone.

"This is just for us four. Here's the real plan," Inda said, leaning forward. "I am going to go after Erkric and Rajnir myself. Jeje, that's where you come in. I'm going to strut around on the *Death* and practice maneuvers soon's we find the allies. When it comes time for actual battle, I sneak onto some ship no one knows—"

Barend raised his brows to find Fox staring at him, eyes wide. Fox let out a low whistle.

Inda flicked his gaze from one to the other. "What?"

Jeje looked mutinous, distrusting Fox's grin. Except Barend was grinning, too.

"What would you say," Fox drawled, "if I could give you a ship with all kinds of magic all over it? A Venn ship? An old Venn ship, belonging to one of their kings?"

Inda sat up on his bench. "Venn?"

Barend grinned. "Here's a hint. Black sails?"

"You got Ramis' *Knife?*" Inda asked in disbelief.

"On the south side of Ghost Island. While we were loading the treasure ships, I took Barend over in a boat to see it, just to make certain I wasn't dreaming. Or crazy."

Barend shook his head slowly. "It's there, all right. And it feels . . . strange. Magic all over it."

"You saw Ramis?" Inda asked, distracted. "I thought he was dead!"

"I don't really know what dead means in Norsunder." Fox lifted a hand. "If anything. But he gave me that ship. Said we might find it useful."

Inda rocked back and forth, eyes half closed.

"It's probably got more of those magic things than any-thing Erkric has," Barend offered. "Weird. How do you think Ramis knew Inda would use it?"

Inda snorted and opened his eyes. "He didn't. Because I won't."

"What?" the other three said together.

"First of all, I wouldn't trust anything a Norsundrian 'gave' us," Inda said. "Second, think about it. Pretend the magic wasn't in question. Try to see me sailing a black-sailed Venn ship toward their world armada. Even if there's magic protecting it somehow—and I don't trust that at all—wouldn't that be like painting a target on my chest?"

Fox grimaced ruefully. "Yes."

Inda dug his fingers into his right shoulder, craning his neck. "Well, maybe my plan is just as obvious. Still, if they *think* I'm on that thing . . . well, if my plan is to work, I need to be on the sneak. But, say we split off a feint attack and put the *Knife* at the lead?"

Barend wheezed with laughter. Fox frowned.

Inda snapped his fingers. "That's it. Use their expecta-tions against 'em." He carefully opened Signi's mirror chart and knelt on the deck to spread it, one knee and one palm holding it down. Barend crouched down to put his hand on a third corner and set an empty mug on the fourth.

"So my feint is lined along the south coast, west of the Fangs. Right here, just east of Danai, the headquarters at that old pirate lair we cleaned out after we smashed Bo-ruin. And the rest in line at The Fangs, just as they'll prob-ably expect. If we could just flank the Venn as they attack our main force, and I'm in something unknown, small, unwatched—"

Fox leaned back. "I see what you're thinking. Good plan if we had enough ships to mount two attacks. But we don't."

"Then we'll just have to make it look like two attacks. We'll put Ramis' *Knife* at the front of a feint. Durasnir'll take one look at that thing, straight from their ancestors, and he's got to think I'm on it, at the head of us all."

Jeje waved at Inda. "So you're really on the *Vixen?* If you want us to be an unknown fisher, I kept that terrible old sail."

"Good." Inda moved his knee and the mug, and the chart

rustled back into its roll. "Barend, will you take *Skimit* and while the east wind is strong, go fetch the *Knife?* If you lay on every stitch of sail, you might possibly get there before the winds change."

"Then every stitch of sail coming back. Got it," Barend said. "Well, I've always wanted to see how fast I could race the strait, and *Skimit*'s the one to do it. We've rebuilt it twice to make it faster."

"Fox, you give him your gold case so he stays in touch."

Barend rubbed his hands and got to his feet. "Can I pick my crew?" Inda and Fox both turned up their hands, noted the other doing it, and Fox looked sardonic.

Barend eyed them, then said, "Be gone by next watch."

As he left, the halloo, "Boat ho!" came through the open door.

"Captains are here." Inda rapped the table with his knuckles. "Remember, no one knows about my *Vixen* plan or about the Danai feint or the *Knife*. If there are spies in the fleet, as we suspect, then it's best to have everyone think we're all going to be at The Fangs, inverted arrow-heads as our tactical innovation. We can pick our feint right before the attack and have them get into position at the last moment."

When Jeje signified agreement, Fox opened the cabin door.

Gillor, Tcholan, and Eflis were delighted to see Inda again. Tough, lean Mutt colored with intense pleasure, looking like a boy again when Inda clapped him on the back so hard his eyes watered. "Good to see you with your own ship," Inda said. "Sorry it's Dasta's, but Dasta must be glad it's you."

Mutt did not try to untangle that any more than the others did, just nodded emphatically as they settled around the big table, which Fox had some of the rats bring back in.

Lorm made up special a jug of the delicious cranberry drink Barend had introduced, which was a mixture of water conditioned with yeast and sugar stirred into the juices of cranberries and lime. Add to that a dash of fiery distilled corn-whiskey, and the cold vanished at the first sip.

The Fox Banner Fleet captains drank with appreciation. Inda, as usual, could have been drinking marsh water for all he seemed to notice as he indicated Signi's chart.

"Here's what I heard." Inda leaned forward, gathering their attention with his earnest gaze. "The Venn promised to come thundering down on Bren by midsummer if they don't agree to terms."

"Same with Nelsaiam," Fox put in. "We got that from several sources."

"So here's my question. What have you heard? Why so slow? Why not sweep the entire strait last year?"

"They couldn't rebuild the damaged ships with what they'd get at Llyenthur." Tcholan's white teeth flashed in his dark face as he laughed. "My new carpenter comes from there. Said Llyenthur's like everyone else, pledged years ahead in trying to rebuild their navy, soon as the Venn disappeared a few years ago. There won't have been an extra stick or spar by the time the Venn got in there, even before the typhoon swept the harbor clean out to sea."

Inda tapped a rhythm on his thigh. "Then the Venn warships might be fished and frapped. That would explain why you slipped their blockade so easily."

"Maybe. But even if their ships are bundles of twigs, they'll be disciplined and drilled."

"So here's what I want to do. Jeje, you've got to run ahead. Slip through the blockade and stop at Bren. Tell Chim what's been decided. If they want to fight, it's up to them to run a land battle on their own, or else they can slip the rest of their navy out after you. Send 'em to The Fangs to reinforce the allies."

Jeje rubbed her jaw. "That means they're leaving the harbor to the Venn."

"The Venn are going to take it anyway, right? So Bren's harbor will be occupied for a time, but we hope no more than a month or two. Supposedly, if they surrender the harbor, the Venn won't wreck it."

Jeje shrugged. She'd been deeply unhappy about Bren being left to its own devices ever since she learned that no one from the east coast was going to risk entering the strait on Bren's behalf.

"I've got to take my stand at The Fangs if I'm to make it all work."

Gillor frowned at the map. "They have to know how many ships everyone's got since they lost control before."

"Yes," Inda said. "And also, every harbor's got to be full of their spies. Can't be helped."

"How we gonna avoid the Venn blockade when we go down the strait?" Mutt asked.

Inda spread the chart open. He whispered the spell Signi had taught him, and the captains bent in to gaze avidly at the glowing lights on the chart still clustered in orderly manner around Llyenthur Harbor and westward of there in precise triangles. "What you see is where all the Venn ships are right now. Since we'll never use it to ting them—never mind what that means—they'll never see us. But you cannot mention this thing to anyone outside this cabin, not even to one another. Are we agreed?" He picked up the mug, tasted it, and whistled. "Hoo, that's good. Have I had that before?"

After Evred wrote to Inda, he wrote to Tau with the addition:

> *Our trade is established. I would like you to ask my mother to oversee it. Your skills will be necessary to Inda in the execution of his orders once there is peace.*

Tau frowned, wishing that he had not helped himself quite so generously to Princess Kliessin's famed Flower Day Wine Cup.

Squaring himself at his desk, he read more slowly. Inda-Harskialdna was ordered to build the fleet he'd been asked by outlanders to build, defeat the Venn, and then take control of the strait in the name of justice and peace.

Tau got up and moved restlessly around his study. Sounded fine, but what was the truth he sensed underlying these words? The problem was "truth" was not a single discrete item, like a desk. Truth and love, two of the most important words to human beings, and among the most difficult to define. He'd never been able to define love in words, and hadn't needed to. Jeje was always first to mind, but close behind was Inda—without any component of sexual desire—and Evred with a large component of desire, but friendship tentative at best due to Evred's profound difficulties with trust. And there they came full circle: Evred trusted Inda to establish peace and wanted Tau to aid him.

But what did that really mean?

He knew he should wait, but he also knew he would not sleep until he'd written. So he dipped his pen, and pulled a cut square of scroll-case paper from the little case.

> *Evred: Your goal sounds worthy, but if I am to wield words as weapons, I need to be on firm ground. Did I just mix metaphors? Blame Princess Kliessin's Wine Cup. Please tell me precisely what you mean by "establish order."*

As always, it took a day or two for a reply. Evred was far too reserved to write spontaneously, at least to Tau.

> *How can the words be made more clear? In Sartoran:* inaugurate harmony. *It seems logical to assume that if the southern world looks to Inda to establish order, they must look to him to maintain it—first in the strait, and then in the harbors. He has sworn before the Jarls to achieve this order, for the good of the southern world. Of all people, Inda will be most scrupulous about establishing our laws and justice, no difference between their people and ours. Everyone under the same law.*

Tau sat back, stunned. "Under the same laws?"

He's ordering Inda to take control of the strait in the name of Iasca Leror.

Tau dashed out and nearly ran into one of Queen Wisthia's house runners. "Two messengers from the harbor, my lord," the girl said to Tau.

He forced himself to stop and even to smile. On Tau's arrival, Wisthia had said, *I have instructed the servants to address you as Lord Taumad Dei and to introduce you as the same.*

Lord of what? he'd exclaimed, imagining what Jeje would say. *I'm not lord of anything.*

If you were ten years younger, I would send you to the archive to write down just how many overlapping grants-for-heirs-in-perpetuity your family, in all branches, has had of courtesy titles. Just because you don't place value on a social advantage, I trust you will not throw one away if people insist on granting it to you. Not if you expect to succeed in the world of diplomacy, which is one layered in symbol and hidden meaning.

Wisthia appeared right behind the servant and dismissed the girl with a touch and a soft word. "Taumad? You appear to be in a trance." And when Tau's gaze snapped upward, "When you look like that, you had better speak to me before going anywhere."

"It's Evred." Tau handed her the letter.

When she'd read it through, she tapped it against her palm, her compressed mouth and wide, intense gaze sharpening her resemblance to Evred.

"He means for Inda to take control of the strait," Tau said in Sartoran, testing the words. "Doesn't he?"

In answer, Wisthia thrust him inside her chamber and shut the door with her own hands. "The timing is ill," she said. Then added under her breath, more to herself than to Tau, "I'm afraid it was inevitable."

"The timing is ill with half the city evacuating?" Tau tipped his head toward the window.

"No, I consider that a removal of problems, but I don't have to concern myself with Bren's interrupted trade and revenue. I mean the tension between the princess and the prince is already considerable. How much will it worsen and threaten our own trade?"

Tau made a polite gesture of regret. Despite the social attempts to maintain civilized flow of discourse, all winter long everyone felt the pressure of negotiations going on far away. Bren wanted its supposed allies to come to its defense; the supposed allies did not want to risk their navies in the strait so far from home; Prince Kavna had championed the maritime alliance as Bren's only hope, and Princess Kliessin did not trust any of them to come to Bren's defense.

Now, Inda was coming to the rescue of the alliance, if not directly to Bren's defense . . .

And he was bringing a new threat.

"What do you intend to do?" Wisthia asked.

Tau sighed. "Not quite certain. I know Evred as well as Evred lets anyone know him. He wants Inda to actually

take the strait by military force and govern it, but he really
is motivated by good intentions."

"And, being a Marlovan, he would not be able to see
that even a benevolent tyranny is still a tyranny." Wisthia
pursed her lips. "All right. There's no time for more, not
that we can do much. As it happens, Guild Fleet Master
Chim just sent word that Jeje's vessel entered the harbor."

"Jeje," Tau whispered.

"You had better stir about your business," Wisthia responded, seeing his anticipation in his tense hand gripping
the door latch. "But listen to me first."

Tau let his hand fall.

"The Venn constitute the biggest problem before us now.
Evred's intentions will have to wait. So you have time and
your wits. Evred expects you to explain him to the world.
It could be that you are called upon to explain the world
to him."

"But I did," Tau protested. And winced when the next
thought occurred. "I wonder if I'm in some wise to blame?
I've been trying to be entertaining with my reports . . .
maybe exaggerating some of the worst qualities of our fellow diplomats."

"If they didn't have those worst qualities, you wouldn't
be able to exaggerate them," Wisthia said. "I will reflect a
little, then attempt to write to Evred myself."

Tau dug in his pocket and handed her the gold case.
"Then you should take this." When she hesitated, he said,
"If Evred wants to communicate with me, or I with him,
Inda surely has some means."

Wisthia accepted the case. Tau smiled and then gave in
to impulse and kissed her.

It was a chaste kiss, from a son to a mother. Wisthia colored, laughed, and patted Tau's cheek. "Go on."

He whirled his caped coat around his shoulders and left
with light step, thinking, *Jeje is here.*

Behind, Wisthia closed herself in her room. So much
to say, and she could give in to impulse and satisfy herself
with pages of reasoned prose, but how much of it would he
read? Motherhood had taught her that no matter what you
say, your children don't always hear it, and then they don't
always heed what they hear.

Keep it short, she decided.

Still, it took a night and a day of crumpled attempts before she satisfied herself enough to copy out her message in fair:

> *Evred, my beloved son. No one knows better than I how conscientious you have always been about doing your duty as you perceive it. Let me remind you of a lesson the great Connar Landis wrote: that a king is as good as his word, but a great king knows how to admit to a mistake and finds a way to fix it. If you wish to communicate with me, you have only to write. Taumad has given me this scroll-case, as he knows Inda will have some means of communicating with you.*
> *Your loving mother,*
> *Wisthia*

She put it in the case, did the magic, and it was gone.

Chapter Fourteen

THE *Vixen* lowered sail and anchored near the main dock, a rare privilege. Tau elbowed his way through the small crowd gathered. When Jeje hopped up on the dock, brown and solid and inexpressibly dear, Tau gave a strangled sob of laughter. She looked up, a big grin slashed across her face, and hurled herself into his arms.

They kissed with desperate, gasping passion, right there on the pier, for a few white-hot, ecstatic moments oblivious to the cheers and hoots of sailors, dock-workers, guards, and everyone else around. He hugged her closer because he couldn't get enough of her smooth skin, her silky short hair that smelled of the sea, of her solid warmth. His knees weakened with tenderness at the growl like a hunting cat deep in her chest. No, it was a *purr*.

Then she pushed away enough to let a little air between them. "Put that gaff away for later. In my hammock."

Tau let her go, laughing unsteadily. "Where's Inda?"

"He's on the *Death*. Coming as fast as they can. *Vixen* is still the fastest thing on the water, save only *Skimit*. And that's gone somewhere else." She jabbed her thumb into the cold east wind. "Inda sent me here ahead, since I lost my gold case thing." Her gaze took in his beautiful, fashionable clothes, then strayed back to her scout cutter.

"So did I. Mine went overboard the winter after the war." Tau caressed her cheek. "No, I am not going to become a duke."

Jeje smiled up at him, but her brow stayed furrowed. "I was just afraid you'd get mixed up with kings and, you know, like it." She indicated his caped coat. "Here, let's go talk to Chim, and . . . whee-*yoo*! Bren took an even bigger beating than Danai, if this is from that storm last year. They lost the entire rope walk."

Tau indicated the half-deserted wharf with new storefronts here and there, and piles of brick and stone awaiting rebuilding projects that had been abandoned because of the expected attack. "The people got this end of the harbor sandbagged pretty well. We could feel it coming. But the west end got swept clean."

"The ghost yards, where the poor live," Jeje said grimly.

"Well, no one lives there now. The point is the winds were stronger there, and it sits lower. By the time the guards got down to the waterfront, it was too dangerous to approach. The waves were breaking halfway to Fish-Spine Alley. Your old tavern vanished in the first wave. They're rebuilding closer to Schooner Hill."

Over the noise of caulking hammers, sails flapping, bells, the thump of goods being loaded and unloaded, and the halloo of marine voices, Jeje heard clattering and banging in the distance. She hoped some of her old friends had employment and a place to live. But Tau had never known those people, so she just said, "Glad we missed that storm. You and me will catch up soon's I deliver Inda's messages to Chim."

"I'll get my gear and meet you there."

Jeje gripped his wrist. "You're coming back with me?"

"Yes." He smiled wryly. "My career as a trade envoy is over, at least for now."

Wisthia was in conference when he arrived. He left his chambers scrupulously neat, his trunks of good clothing labeled and awaiting paid movers to stow, his papers all burned. He was dressed in his old deck clothes, though the shirt was too tight, the inevitable result of crossing Iasca

Leror as Inda's sparring partner and the strenuous exercise he'd performed since, though he hadn't sparred; *Fox will no doubt amend that with bone-crushing vigor,* he was thinking as he shut his door.

There was his hostess. "You're ready to go?"

Tau said, "You'll find a letter of apology for Princess Kliessin on my desk. It's a good letter. Has three references to current plays, and I threw in some Old Sartoran allusions when describing her generosity and kindness, not to mention yours. Which is quite appreciated, by the way. I thank you for everything."

"Fare well," Wisthia said.

He hoisted his gear bag over his shoulder, spoke to each servant (handing them a handsome vail) and then left.

He hitched his gear bag more securely as a cold, wet wind straight off the water buffeted him on Dock Street. How much did traffic block winds, he wondered, looking around the mostly empty street. Even in winter, under ordinary circumstances, it was usually thronged.

He reached the Fleet Guild building to find it ringed with guards. Not just the city guard, but the fellows in burnt orange with the tall hats: Royal Guards.

They passed him through. Tau entered to find yet more guards, and wide-eyed workers behind the counters self-consciously doing their jobs. The guard captain somewhat ironically waved Tau upstairs to Chim's office, where he found Princess Kliessin herself seated in Chim's chair, Chim and Jeje standing in front of the desk. There were no guards in the room, just the two posted outside the door.

They shut Tau in, and he heard them take up stance outside the office.

"I should think you could afford a better chair than this," Kliessin said to Chim, thumping the arm with her fist. "There is no comfortable way to sit."

"Makes me work faster, yer highness," Chim said.

Kliessin gave a proper princess sniff, then turned on Tau. "And here's our envoy. What's your excuse, my lord?"

"Excuse for what, your highness?" Tau bowed as if he still wore his velvets, his manner formal.

"For being here, in those clothes."

"I am going to join Inda's fleet," he said, as if that ought to be obvious.

"Which is going where?" Kliessin had been extremely angry ever since the discovery that the so-called Sartoran Alliance was abandoning Bren. Tau had not been present when the foreign diplomats were forced to admit the truth to her, after weeks of sumptuous parties and compliment-thick hedging; Wisthia had encouraged him to stay home, emphasizing to all that he had nothing to do with the decision.

"Who ordered you to leave? That horse-riding king over the mountains?"

He felt the weight of all three gazes. *Explain Evred to the world* ... "Evred-Harvaldar directed me to serve as Inda's aide."

Kliessin struck the battered chair arm with her palm. "Excellent. So tell me exactly what that means. Do you speak for the Marlovan king, or for your Inda, or both?"

Tau grimaced. "I can't speak for Inda as I have not yet seen him. It's been several years since we had any communication."

"You're beginning to sound like those damned sugar-mouths from Everon and the rest."

"I really haven't."

"He hasn't," Jeje cut in. "He doesn't even know what I just told you, about Inda saying you should surrender if you have to, but postpone and delay and argue as much as you can beforehand."

"Inda said that?" Tau asked Jeje.

"Yep. Says don't waste lives. Stick it a few months until we sweep the strait clean of 'em." Jeje faced the princess. "Your other ambassadors ought to have told you by now that the alliance is gathering at The Fangs."

"I have been informed about this putative alliance," Kliessin said, her expression wry. "But so far, all it's done is sail around somewhere east and talk. No one sees fit to actually aid us. And yet they want my little navy to reinforce them."

"Inda says that's our strongest position, at The Fangs," Jeje stated.

"Which brings me to him. What concessions does your Inda expect from us?"

"Nothing." Jeje shrugged, her indifference plain.

Kliessin turned to Tau, who was, as she expected, as unreadable as he was beautiful. "And? You'll just tell me again that you haven't seen Inda." She sighed. "Look, I know you two mean well, or we would not be here so comfortably. You, Jeje sa Jeje, I know are as politically naive as it's possible to be. Lord Taumad, you are not. But I have respected your good intentions, so let's not fence words. This is what I want. If your Inda Elgar steps on my dock, then within a watch he had better swear before my father or brother or me that he will not attempt any interference with my kingdom whatsoever, and that his authority over my navy—*my* navy, not his—extends only to the end of this conflict with the Venn."

Tau's chest had gone tight. He met her steady gaze, flicked a sideways look at Jeje, whose expression was uneasy, and wily old Chim pursed his lips.

"Inda is not coming ashore," Chim said. "Sailing straight past, Jeje sez. Got to get east as fast as he can. With us or without us. I say 'we' because that was always my purpose, to command the Guild Fleet. The five guilds have put together their fleet, and though ye took some of 'em, yer highness, there are still Guild ships from Ymar, Everon, and our other signatories gathering out at The Fangs. One thing I do know, it's gonna take every ship we can find to confront them damn vinegar-pisses."

"And Elgar the Fox is to lead this armada." Kliessin spoke slowly, her eyes narrowed. "Guild Mistress Perran thinks he's risking his life for nothing more than goodwill. The Everoneth believe he wants to establish a seagoing empire. I want to know the truth."

And a lie came to Tau's lips, easy and mild after months of diplomatic dodges, "Inda won't want to touch land. He knows how threatened everyone feels, how ambivalent about his past."

Kliessin's brow, a straight dark line unexpectedly like Jeje's, lifted, then furrowed. "How do you know that? You just told me you haven't had communication with him in years."

"No. But I know him."

Jeje nodded slowly. "It's true. Inda never wanted anything to do with any kings. Except that Marlovan one. On account of them being friends when they were little."

Kliessin smacked her hands down on the chair arms

again, but this time with an air of decision. "All right. Will you two swear to me that you will carry this message to him, just as I spoke it?"

Jeje shrugged again. "Sure. But it's a waste of time, he doesn't want anything to do with—"

"Lord Taumad?" the princess cut across Jeje.

Diplomacy was like a play in real life, Tau had once told Evred. He could hear the echo of his own voice, sickening in its careless self-satisfaction. *Diplomacy is like a play. I'm good at plays.*

"I promise to carry your words to Inda exactly as spoken." And there was the thrill of danger, of risk. Tau recognized it with a weird amalgam of excitement and self-hatred. *Human beings love the hunt* an old Colendi play observed through the character of a drawling duke. *And what is better to hunt than the hunter?*

Kliessin sat back. "Then you may go. Chim, you'll take my message to High Admiral Brasvac. Verbal orders. I'll have nothing in writing, because officially my father is too ill to consider the Venn proposal, and I am going to twist and hedge and dance as hard as I can to put off committing myself, exactly as Indavun Algraveer requested." Her smile was sour. "His orders happen to coincide with my plans. So far. I want to preserve lives, and livelihood. If the biggest city in the kingdom was not this harbor, who knows what we might have done?"

Tau bowed.

"So. Hurry along. Set sail. Carry your messages. I'll wait for an assurance either in person or in his own writing from your commander stating his agreement to my terms." Kliessin thumped her fist on the arm of the chair. "But if he walks on my shore without it, I'll order my Guard to shoot him where he stands."

Jeje had not forgotten how good sex with Tau was, but somehow it was even better than she'd remembered.

Most of her encounters were romps with paid professionals, and recently the occasional night with a friend who, like her, enjoyed an undemanding encounter. Once the passion was spent it stayed spent, and with dawn they returned to work, untroubled by emotional tangles.

Tau made her body feel like silk spun out in gleaming

threads. She opened her eyes, loving the sight of him lying at her side, the reflection from the water below her open stern windows spangling him with early morning golden sunlight. Was it his training or her passion that made it so much better with Tau? Probably both. Somehow she found that funny, and shook with silent laughter, which for some reason made her eyes sting. *Not* tears! She hated tears, but had no defenses, not even a name, for tenderness.

To get rid of the tightness in her throat, she lifted her head to peer out the stern windows just behind her elbow. The open stern windows.

Her mood veered wildly, this time the laughter stayed laughter and bubbled up inside her chest. They must have given the night watch quite a performance! She snickered. A soft noise that woke Tau.

The sight of his long eyelashes lifting hollowed her out inside. "Happy?" His voice was low and husky, and inflamed her so much that she attacked him again.

Presently they lay side by side, weary but content. "Teach me those tricks," she said drowsily.

"Gladly. Jeje, I cannot express how much I missed you."

You could have seen me a year ago. More, she thought, but she wouldn't say it. Nevertheless his antennae were as fine as a butterfly's; he began, without her having to ask, to tell her his adventures since their last parting.

It took a long time, because he omitted nothing except Evred's final command. He knew how she would respond and anyway first they must survive the Venn.

Besides, Jeje had no interest in politics. "Huh." She rolled over, her fingers playing with the ruby earring he'd replaced in his ear. She was glad the diamond was gone. "I can almost feel sorry for that cousin of yours."

Tau chuckled. "This might be the first time Lord Yaskandar Dei has ever been pitied."

"Pity for one heartbeat, maybe. Typical of a 'risto! Waits for someone to give him something to do with his life, instead of going out and finding it. Like us. Well, like me." Jeje patted the bulkhead.

"And me. My family name may be famous, but it did not suddenly bestow land and wealth on me," he said, smiling. "The title is what they call a courtesy." He quirked an ironic brow.

Jeje had no interest in titles. "Why'd that queen of Sartor go insane?"

"I don't know that she's insane, but crazed . . . perhaps. My mother told me her story years ago. The queen, when a princess, was spoiled beyond belief. She was famed for her temper, but of course everyone around her just smiled and accepted it. Then one day she destroyed some ancient treasure for a frivolous reason, and in anger her father put her to work as a laborer. She ended up rebuilding a house, stone and wood, and the experience was so satisfying that it changed her for life. When he died she declared that all aristocrats would provide service in the same way, and the more they resisted, the more determined she became."

Jeje puffed a laugh. "They almost sound like . . . like people."

"Under the armor, symbolic and not, we're all frangible. The queen also found comfort in physical labor when mentally wrestling with questions of political agency, and so her favorite method of resolving problems was forced on all others. She never married, never had a child. Her heir is reputed to be the most successful hypocrite in court."

"And so when this Queen Servitude dies, they'll all go right back to their old ways."

"Probably. Anyway, Yaska might have stayed, but my cousin Joret thinks he was thwarted in love."

"Love," Jeje repeated, throwing her head back on the pillow. The sun had risen enough to shine off the water, sending light patterns to writhe on the ceiling of her dear ship. Love. How she loved *Vixen!* And Tau. But in such different ways.

Again he seemed to divine her thoughts. "People ridicule the Colendi for having thirty verbs for types of love and twice as many nouns. But communication is important to them, and that means everyone agreeing on how important words are defined."

Jeje stirred. "Except that everybody says the Colendi hide meanings behind other meanings, which hide more meanings, until they say red and everyone thinks they really mean green." Tau laughed, shaking his head, and she went on. "Love. Yes. Last night I was thinking it's so clear just how much Inda hates going back to war again, but here he is, doing it for love of his homela—Tau, what is it? What did I say?"

Tau got up, his face turned away as he collected his things and moved toward the fresh water to wash up. She waited for an answer until she realized that there wasn't going to be one.

Chapter Fifteen

*S*HIVERING with cold, Brit Valda stumbled as quickly as she dared into the cave high in the desolate mountains above Searn at the south end of Mearsies, straining every nerve for sign of betrayal. The rustle and flitter of bats overhead made her stoop, arms over her head. The creatures squeaked then were gone, leaving her alone. She sensed it, smelled it.

She flung herself past the first turn, scraping her shin on a stone. Biting back a cry of anguish, she pulled a small glowglobe from her filthy robe and whispered over it, ignoring the tears of pain. The shadows vanished, leaving her in a crevasse with water trickling down from above and flowing away in a shallow stream to disappear beneath the rubble behind her. She yanked up her robe to examine the bark on her throbbing shin. A scrape; she ignored it and surveyed the cave.

Humans had lived here some time ago: there was a ceramic pot, a rough stone ledge too regular to be natural. The cave might even have been made comfortable, she thought, ducking below the slanting ceiling. That argued a place chosen, not run to, a retreat and not a mere hideaway.

She hoped that meant that the ancient map it had taken one of her dags four months to find had been marked true.

She trailed the fingers of her free hand over the stone. Other hands had touched here, enough to blunt the roughness of the stone, but long ago. Another promising sign.

Heartened, she stooped through the small, angled hole which widened into a domed chamber. Animals had lived here more recently; there were two nests. The bats appeared to make their home in an adjacent chamber.

Various sized openings gaped darkly here and there. Valda walked by each, listening, breathing, feeling the air. Faint—ever so faint—came the sound she listened for, though it seemed to reach past her ears into her head. It was a little like singing, midway between human voices and the wind.

She could not yet determine which tunnel led to the Selenseh Reidian, but she knew the mystery was nigh: "selen" was Sartoran for harmony, "se" of, "rei" as a prefix could mean bright but also sun-touched, and "dian" was stone in the plural. Why "dian," which contained the word "di"—day—she did not know, as "dan" was also a word for stone, but she'd learned that the Sartorans built meanings inside of meanings in their words.

The map seemed to be true. She hoped that meant the claims about the Selenseh Reidian were true—that they were pools of magical power, perhaps even loci for the mysterious beings native to this world. She pushed into the tunnel in which she sensed the subaudible thrum of magic and walked on for what seemed a long time. But there was no way to gauge time, or even direction. Very different from the tunnels of home, with their brilliant mosaics and carvings, so that you always knew where you were, and the currents of subtly scented air blown by ancient magics gave one a sensory connection to time. Here she felt stranger by the moment, as if she walked and walked yet the world became more still around her, all sense of motion and change diminishing.

A glow, like a summer sunset through a prism, was her only warning. She'd braced for the appearance of powerful Sartoran gatekeepers to demand an accounting. She was alone.

Alone in an immeasurable space filled with glowing

crystals of every imaginable hue. Crystals, diamonds, perhaps some other stone altogether. She had no name for the patterned complexity of facets reflecting and refracting their own light. The intensity as well as the spectrum of that light dazzled her eyes, making her feel warm, a little giddy, the air too pure to breathe; she knew she was only perceiving a fragment of the phenomenon here.

She fell to her knees, her chest heaving. Laugh or sob, she was overwhelmed, and yet aware that, at least for now, all her hurts had gone away.

But she must not stay. She could not use this chamber of stones; she would not risk defiling what she instinctively felt was consecrated space.

She forced herself to step out again, though the longing to return was sharp. But clear thought returned with even a little distance, and she did not need to test the space to know that whatever magic she did would be untraceable relative to the powerful presence here.

She laid her transfer tokens upon the ground in a wide circle, so that if any two mages arrived at the same time they would not try to share the same space and impel one another violently into the stone walls.

She said aloud, in Sartoran, "I promise my purpose is peaceful, though I know my people have been proscribed by the Sartoran Mage Council."

No answer.

Hoping she did not summon her diminishing group to their deaths, she whispered the contact spell over and over, touching each token.

Ulaffa arrived first, looking impossibly old and frail, his once plump body diminished almost as much as Valda's own. "Erkric is about to give the signal for the war fleets to depart," he gasped. "I cannot stay."

Valda said, "I just returned from Twelve Towers. King Rajnir's chambers are free of the Norsunder wards again."

Ulaffa's frizzy hair floated around the dome of his head as he smiled. "Again? Erkric was furious the last two times. I cannot begin to tell you how enraged. He's not sleeping, feels conspirators all around him—"

"As there are," Valda said. "Good. Let him fear. So long as *you* are safe."

Ulaffa smiled sadly. "He has assigned me to Seigmad,

just in case I might be tempted to sympathize with Durasnir. But Byarin holds fast. He complains of Durasnir most bitterly all the time. Unfair watches, too slow and old, sleeps too much, drinks dark beer on duty. Erkric cherishes every slander."

Valda gave a sharp bark of laughter. "Tell me about the conspiracies. I overheard some young dags-in-training talking, when I was in the royal chambers. They thought the chambers empty, and safe of spiderwebs, poor heedless children. If I had not just removed all the wards! Never mind. The report was that Nanni Balandir had been killed by that terrible stone magic," Valda said.

Ulaffa made the sign of Rainorec. "Yes, but not by Erkric. It was Yatar. Nanni was adamant that Signi Sofar had become a Seer, and she would not act against—" He waved a hand as if to push aside the subject. "There is no time. Erkric has taken Yatar to be his assistant night and day. Under his eye. The others have been placed under threat of a stone spell if they use the Norsunder magic except when ordered, and he won't give them access to any more of those spells. That means his responsibilities just grow. I cannot stay, Brit. Tell me this: Is Signi safe?"

Valda thought of Signi, visibly pregnant, sitting unnoticed among the beginner or unambitious mages who renewed Fire Stick spells. Two months of tedium earned enough pay for a modest year's living, and furnished all the gossip out of Sartor's capital. "She is in Western Sartor, serving as a Fire Stick Mage."

Ulaffa smiled. "Good, useful work, and so many of them, her traces will be buried by all the other efforts. Even if he had time to seek, Erkric could never find her there." He made a sign and vanished.

Presently Dag Anchan appeared, barefooted, wearing the coarse midden-brown clothing and iron torc of a thrall. She was a young woman, her hands rough and red from daily labors in the laundry.

She straightened up, looked around, and breathed deeply. "Oh." She clasped her work-roughened hands to tug ineffectually at the iron torc circling her throat. "Oh, it feels good in here."

"What can you report on the king?"

"I've only been able to get near enough to put the spindle through twice," Anchan said, her blue eyes tired. Then she gave a quick, triumphant smile. "But I felt it work, and Dag Erkric has stationed even more Guards around the king's chambers."

"You are the main reason we are met here," Valda said. "Do you have the spindle?"

"Of course." Anchan's humor died away. "If I am caught, I can plunge it into my own heart. Better that than what he does to people."

From her robe she pulled a sharp-pointed silk spindle which Valda took into her own hands. She'd prepared layers of spells to make this task easier. They were far harder to hold, but she'd gained practice in the past three years. She layered the spells on, casting them to overpower Erkric's evil shroud of magic lying over the king's living space. These spells did not remove the mind-magic, alas, but they did remove the terrible protective spells that kept the king isolated.

"I am going to try to get near the king again," Valda said. "But you know Erkric must first be at a safe distance. Now, I just finished removing all his work at Twelve Towers, and I left my signature over everything. As soon as he finds out, I trust he will transfer back and feel sufficiently threatened to commence replacing all his wards yet again. Maybe he'll take more time and lay some traps. It will keep him busy and at a distance from Llyenthur."

"Dangerous," Anchan said.

"But I do not intend to go back. We are all running out of strength, and time. Our efforts must be concentrated on the coming battle."

Anchan bowed her head, took the spindle back, and slid it into her clothes. She vanished back to the laundry at Llyenthur, leaving Valda leaning against the wall, forearms across her middle as she recovered from the effects of the magic. Even that was easier to bear here, leaving her to wonder if anyone would ever know of Anchan's heroism. Not many would have the strength and conviction to wear the iron torc of a thrall and labor ceaselessly in the laundry wherever the fleet went just to gain access to the king's chambers.

The next one to appear was tall, massive Dag Byarin, attached by Erkric to spy on Oneli Stalna Durasnir.

"We're about to leave," Byarin said. "I dare not stay but a moment." Passing his hand over his eyes, he drew a deep breath, then said rapidly, "It has been terrible. Oneli Stalna Durasnir has had little success in getting wood. There isn't any. So the war fleets sail as is. Erkric drives him mercilessly." An inward jolt—some private signal—and he whispered and vanished.

You, too, feel the strain, Abyarn Erkric. Our efforts must be everything, or nothing.

After a time, Valda realized her last two transfer tokens were not going to bring anyone. She made her way slowly out, tears of grief cold on her face as she mourned dags Audir and Falki. She hoped their deaths had been quick.

In Llyenthur Harbor, the remnants of the Southern Fleet not on blockade duty lay with anchors atrip, the *drakans* on station in ranks of nine across the inner harbor, sail crews motionless at sheets and halyards, awaiting orders.

Much farther out, the North and East War fleets were just visible hull down, awaiting their signal to sail. The West Fleet was only present symbolically: in reality they were strung out in orderly patrols all the way to Nathur, the raiders forming a search net to stop and question every ship they could catch at the west end of the strait.

Oneli Stalna Durasnir worked hard on controlling his fury as he finished climbing the long switchback brick-patterned stair cut into the palisade leading to the manse that had once belonged to a prince. That prince had been replaced by the Venn governor when the area fell to the conquerors, who redesigned and rebuilt the house. On the departure of the Venn the house was taken over by a self-proclaimed duke as Llyenthur declared itself part of a new kingdom. The duke—some said a former thief—had vacated in haste, leaving the harbor to the delegation of the guild Durasnir had met the day of the typhoon.

Now the manse—in the process of being expanded to a palace—was the king's royal headquarters, guarded at every door and hall by silent white-clad Erama Krona. The number of Guards was double what the king required for his own prestige at home. Because the locals had caused no difficulties whatsoever, Durasnir wondered if Valda was having any success against Erkric. He had heard nothing from her for an entire year, but he judged from Erkric's increasing tension that the silent war in the magical realm paralleled the military efforts.

In silent resistance to Erkric's magic, Durasnir refused to use transfer tokens. So he was rowed in, had to walk down the long pier, across the wharf, and up the switch-back stairs.

It gave him time to think and to get a grip on his emotions. He knew he would lose this contest, but his own sense of justice—his determination to do everything he could to preserve the lives of those under his command—required him to make the attempt.

He reached the doors.

Durasnir was waved through into the circular chamber that had been converted to a throne room. Curved windows were cut to let in the strong southern light. The banner of the Golden Tree hung from the domed ceiling.

The senior captains were all there, winged helms under their arms. At his approach they moved to either side in strict rank order. Durasnir stood alone before the king, who sat on the throne, his magnificent robes hiding how fleshy he'd become. His gaze, as ever, was blank. Durasnir noted, then regretfully dismissed, the faint sheen of sweat across the king's brow. He had tried to descry signs of intelligence there over the past year, coming to the reluctant conclusion he was fooling only himself. Maybe Rajnir's clothing was too heavy for the warm weather.

Durasnir's attention turned to the tall, white-haired Dag of the Venn standing beside the throne.

Erkric certainly looked old and tired, but Durasnir had checked his own mirror before dressing in formal clothes to receive the order for departure. He felt, and looked, ten years aged since the shattered navy limped into Llyenthur Harbor the summer before.

Dag Erkric watched Durasnir approach, morosely pleased at the tension to be seen in the commander's face. Erkric was too old to be constantly forced to cheat himself of sleep. He could win extra time by chewing roasted coffee beans from the islands, but his hands shook and his heart labored. More bitter than the taste of the beans was the silence from Norsunder. He was so close, so very close, to winning. He just needed one more spell, one that would get him rest beyond time. No, two spells. He needed the ability to place spy spells without physical proximity. Durasnir's treacherous duplicity was evident in how diligently he guarded his scroll-case and how bland his conversations were within the reach of magical ears.

It was also evident in how, more and more frequently, he spoke directly to Erkric and not to the king on his throne, even when Rajnir had asked the question.

Erkric watched Durasnir narrowly. And yes, Durasnir's gaze briefly touched the king, then went diffuse as he addressed the air somewhere between Rajnir and the Dag. "The Oneli is ready to depart, O my king. I request your consideration for my continuing Captain Seigmad as Battlegroup Chief."

"But I am fully recovered," Balandir protested, stepping forward. "Oneli Stalna Commander." He sketched the obeisance impatiently to Durasnir, then turned to Rajnir. Erkric was aware, and bitterly so, that he was rewarding the man for his stupidity. But only for now, only until he gained control. "I admit the one eye is blurred." Balandir touched the healed eye, which was marred across the surface by discernable lines. The healed scars gave his handsome face a wicked cast, one Balandir had secretly come to admire, now that the pain was gone. His own cronies certainly deferred to him.

He squared his shoulders and deepened his voice. "My good eye sees straight and far. Surely what I suffered in the service of Ydrasal and our Golden Path has earned me the right to resume my command."

Rajnir twitched. Durasnir, facing him, was the only one who noticed, but he shifted his attention back to the circle of faces on either side of the king: Never before had he seen so clearly who had experience of battle at sea and who did not.

"Captain Hyarl Balandir," Durasnir said. "Your survival is most welcome to all, but surviving wounds even as grievous as yours does not prepare you for command." *You should not have been taken in the first place.* "Except for this one small engagement at Granthan, you do not have the experience I deem requisite."

Balandir's three cronies mirrored his anger and objection. The rest looked relieved and resigned.

Rajnir flinched, distracting Durasnir for just a heartbeat. "Captain Seigmad is experienced with the conditions and tactics we will find there. Moreso than I, in fact, which is why I am sending him to Nelsaiam while I deal with Bren."

Dag Erkric began smoothly, "We all admire your reasoning, Oneli Stalna my Commander," as at his side his fingers began to twist in one of the signs—

Rajnir spoke. "Make it so." His voice was hoarse, strained. "O. Oneli. Stalna . . . my Commander. Make . . ."

Erkric's fist tightened, his whispered a word, and Rajnir stiffened, his eyes going blind again.

Durasnir spoke swiftly, before Erkric could force the king into negative utterance. Judging from the chalky color of the dag's face, he was as surprised as anyone.

"Then may we have permission to depart, O my king?"

This time it was the flat voice. "Make it so."

Durasnir began his obeisance, but Erkric, angered and unsettled, hurried into speech. He'd meant to think this plan over a little longer, make certain all was secure. But now he needed a grip on Durasnir, because something was wrong with this cursed house. Treachery from within or old magic from previous tenants? Twice, now, the king had spoken unaccountably.

"The king was asking me just this morning, Stalna Commander Durasnir. Is not your son Halvir ten this year?"

Durasnir stilled, the only reaction the dilation of his pupils. "Yes, Dag Erkric."

Erkric heard his breathing, now. *Oh yes, you are afraid. Good.* It was past time to make Durasnir's suspicion work against himself and not the kingdom, for once. "Would it not be a gesture of gratitude toward our Oneli Stalna, O my king, if you were to bring Halvir Durasnir here to begin his training under royal auspices?" Erkric said to Rajnir, making the gesture for the agreement speech.

Rajnir stirred, and said, "Make it so, my Dag."

Durasnir gripped himself hard, not even breathing as he bowed. "I thank you, my king." The words were drier than the picked bones on Sinnaborc's roof.

As Durasnir led the captains out, Erkric peered down at the king, examining him closely. His gaze was opaque, and he'd given the right responses. So . . . what had happened?

There were far too many anomalies. It was time for the

king to shift to the safety of the ship Erkric had been preparing. No more *Cormorant* or access to Durasnir. This would be a magical command center, the king's safety the given reason. If they launched soon, he could get Rajnir into the middle of the strait, and when Bren and Nelsaiam had fallen, the fleet would unite and sweep down the rest of the strait.

Meanwhile, since he had to return to Twelve Towers anyway, he might as well begin to collect Rajnir's future companions and start preparing their minds for obedience.

Fox and Inda got used to handing off Inda's scroll-case when either of them took a sleep watch. They overlapped their watches at drill time and otherwise divided running the ship.

Within a week, Inda had so regained the rhythm of ship life that sometimes it seemed his life in Iasca Leror had receded to a dream. But sudden reminders would catch him up again: a laugh that sounded like Hadand, the smell of toasted bread that reminded him of sharing a snack with Tdor after a late summer night doing the sentry walk rounds together.

Tdor's face was no longer the child's face he'd seen all his early years. Now he saw her grown up, her level gaze, her thin lips with just a hint of smile.

Evred and the Jarls at Convocation.

Evred's orders. Thinking of those always drove him restlessly back into the stream of tasks awaiting his attention. And it always was a stream.

Then one day, just as the east wind was dying for the year, Inda felt the tap of the scroll-case.

He set down the spyglass and thumbed it open. In a crabbed hand, Barend had written:

> *I've got the Knife. Track the Venn for me.*

Inda obediently went to the map, did the spell, then wrote back, *No Venn near Ghost Islands. Nearest off Nathur.*

When Fox appeared and Inda handed off the case, he told him about Barend's note. Fox said, "He's making sure no Venn see that prow on the horizon."

They added Barend's location to their various chalk marks building on the secondary chart.

Durasnir did not relax his rigid hold until he had been rowed back to the *Cormorant*. He climbed aboard, turned what he thought was an impassive face to the flag ensign, who stepped back, then flushed. Somewhere far in the back of his head, a nasty voice howled in manic laughter. Durasnir said, "Signal fleet. Make sail."

The ensign sprang away, his relief plain.

Seigmad's *Petrel* at the head of North and East broke out in sail first, the winds being so light that studding sails were raised low and high, creating great pyramids of taut curved beauty. Durasnir usually loved the sight of the fleet under way at last, especially in full sail, but now he was far too angry.

And afraid.

As distance grew between Llyenthur Harbor and Durasnir's Battlegroups, he worked to regain control. He was not without allies and there was nothing he could do at this time. His scroll-case was compromised, his ship was covered with spiderwebs. But Dag Byarin was on his side. Brit Valda was still alive, working unseen. And back in Twelve Towers, Brun would be vigilant.

He stepped to the deck and looked around, testing the air, which was hazy, a fitful breeze mostly out of the south making small waves. The summer winds were nigh.

He watched the sails bloom above, studding sails fully extended to both sides. As the ship began sliding through the water at a genial, regular roll, he turned to the unending tasks, intending to keep himself so busy he would not think about Halvir or remember dead Vatta.

Chapter Sixteen

Evred: We're nearing Danai. On the mirror chart
V. Battlegroup crossing twd. Bren. No sign of Chim or
Bren navy astern.

EVRED had bent over a lamp so closely to see Inda's
tiny letters, which had bled through to the other side of
the paper, that his fingers began to singe. He snapped fingers and papers away from the lengthened flame. "Astern."
Didn't that mean behind?

Kened's quick knock at his inner chamber door brought
him into the outer office. "Latest dispatch from Vedrid,"
Kened said. "And Gand awaits you."

Evred opened the window, though the air was still frosty,
and read Vedrid's report as a shrill "Yip-yip-yip!" rose from
the distant field.

I reached Parayid. Spoke to the garrison commander.
Traders all report trouble with Toaran pirates. They are
not coming up The Narrows, but sailing along the Land
Bridge. Some think there are pirate coves there.

Evred looked up. "I want my fastest Runners, one to

each Jarl. They are to send two flights of Riders apiece in rotation to support my dragoons on the coast. Send Gand in."

Kened struck fist to chest, and dashed through the door, mentally sorting the King's Runners. He was shorthanded again—everyone in motion—maybe the seniors could be trusted with this run. Capn'n Han could make the long Lindeth run—she was fast, trustworthy, and hadn't had any home leave. So she could be granted some time . . .

Gand entered, each year more grizzled, the hard lines in his face more furrowed, but otherwise as tough as ever. "Problem, Harvaldar-Dal?" He saluted, then with the same hand, jerked his thumb after Kened.

"Pirates. Maybe. Again. From the western seas, this time. The coastal Jarls will see to it. How was the first day muster?" Evred asked, tipping his head toward the window, and the sound of boys yipping enthusiastically.

"No trouble." Gand's tone said *As expected.* And because Evred waited, he added, "A few messages sent along with the Rider Captains bringing boys. You could name who would send them, and what they'd say, and be right: will there be the same rigor, will there be problems with Inda gone, and of course from Horsebutt, will things at last go back to traditional toughness, or will be boys be cosseted through another year? I can send the letters up if you like. I kept 'em in case."

Evred turned out his palm. "No need."

"Would you like to be at the shearing? We can hold it any time that suits you."

Evred's gesture was more emphatic, flat-handed negation. "No." He frowned at the window, then said slowly, "I want to know if Inda's absence will affect the academy."

Gand regarded the king with surprise, wondering what lay behind the question. Evred was never easy to second-guess at any time—it had been that way even when he was a twelve-year-old scrub.

"Inda's absence will not be a disaster, if that's what you are thinking," Gand said. "The academy has never been better in my lifetime. When I look carefully at the records, I suspect it has never reached the excellence of the present."

"Better skills?"

"Partly that. Yes. Certainly that. But the spirit, or temper, has changed. Surely you have noticed?"

"Yes. But I did not know if that's just the human conviction that whatever our generation does must be the best."

"When I was a horsetail, public canings were so frequent we had a schedule, Firstday of every month. The year after your father came to the throne, there were two duels to the death. I was out in the field then, as you know. But we all heard. One of them was the only son of my captain. Ten years after your father came to the throne, there were three Jarls' sons caned for drunkenness on duty, a hundred apiece, and you remember what it was like under your uncle. We haven't had a public caning since your second year as king, when Haucvad was running the gambling circle out of the stable. Last year we did not have *any* caning. The masters still wear their canes in their belts as habit, but at year's end four of them had never taken them out. No rules have changed. Yet without exerting himself in any perceivable way, Inda casts a very long shadow."

"Thank you," Evred said, his tone noncommittal.

Gand saluted and left, thinking the matter over. Everything he had said was true, yet he suspected the masters would be somewhat relieved to be free of Inda's long shadow for a year. They didn't resent Inda—they knew he hated the boys going behind the masters' backs in their efforts to cajole him. What they resented was how the boys would do anything to gain Inda's attention, and in Gand's opinion, a year free of it would do boys and masters a world of good. Especially Lassad.

Gand was as protective of his masters as he was of the boys, weaknesses notwithstanding. He was not certain how much of Lassad's little digs at Inda in front of the older boys were conscious. "Oh, well, if *Inda-Harskialdna* says so, far be it from the likes of me to disagree!" or "If Inda orders it, of course you'll leap to obey, but in case you've forgotten the rest of the masters . . ." Maybe they were the result of Lassad's anxious, relentless internal measure of himself against those he admired.

So Gand smiled as he returned to the academy, leaving Evred thoughtful, distracted, and as busy as he could contrive. He tried not to think about the locket shifting inside his clothing. He restrained himself from writing just to cause Inda to write back. The locket was a terrible vessel for communication; Evred wished now that he'd not been so adamant in holding out against the scroll-cases.

The weather was balmy when the horns played the triplet for a prince: Algara-Vayir. Surely that would not be Inda's cousin Branid, whose business it soon would be to reinforce his harbors. Evred paused, pen in the air. Then he smiled inwardly when he remembered Hadand had invited her mother for a visit to meet one grandchild and attend the birth of another.

Tdor's spirits lifted at the appearance of the woman she regarded as mother. Though she'd exchanged letters a couple of times a year with her own mother, they'd never been close. Fareas-Iofre looked smaller and grayer and thinner than Tdor had remembered, but calm as always, tender with little Hastred, and a welcome presence at the dinner table. She brought a stack of books her sister had sent from Sartor that she thought Evred might want to see, all about the changes in language in different areas of the world.

If only Inda could be there! Tdor was aware of herself as happy, but it was conditional happiness, because every time she sat down to eat, or lay down to sleep, or stepped into a room she had shared with Inda, she thought about him. If she could find a way to send him all the strength in her body, so that he could withstand whatever threatened him, she would have.

She'd left the sheet and quilt on the bed as long as she could, because they retained his smell, until her own had overborne it. Things ... rooms ... home. How much of "home" is bound up in people as well as places? With Fareas-Iofre in the royal city, she almost had all those who meant most to her. No, she didn't have Whipstick, or her old friend Liet, now married to one of the Riders with a little daughter.

After a few days, Fareas-Iofre settled into their lives as if she'd always lived there.

As well. Hadand was ill in the mornings again, and Tdor had slowed so much that Fareas-Iofre took on the Gunvaer work, familiar from eight years before. On the third morning of Fareas-Iofre's visit, Tdor oversaw the introduction of a new set of fifteen-year-old girls, but she was impatient

with her own lumbering gait. Especially when twinges and
jabs made her gasp—the baby must be larger than a two-
year-old to kick so hard!

As Tdor trudged up the stairs after an exceptionally
long, trying day, her back aching at every step, she thought
wistfully about Tenthen Castle, which was maybe a quarter
the size of this castle. She still missed Tenthen, though she
knew she would hate living there with Dannor and Branid.
She'd become accustomed to the royal city, and she loved
working with the girls and knew they responded to her just
by the way that they quieted when she entered a crowded
room. She saw respect in their faces, even these days when
she waddled, as her hip bones had a disconcerting habit of
shifting in and out of their sockets.

The prospect of dinner alone with Fareas buoyed her.
What a relief, to be able to talk about such things again,
without being afraid she'd hurt Hadand or Evred. Hadand
had already gone to bed, and Evred was in a long meeting
with the Guild Council and harbor representatives.

But when Tdor finally reached her suite, it was to discover that her stomach had closed. She hadn't eaten all
day, but the prospect of food was not appealing. She was
overheated, uncomfortable, the suite was stuffy. *Summer's
coming too soon*, she thought as she trundled up into the
alcoves to open the few west windows. Then she propped
the doors open in hopes of getting air into the windowless
middle chamber.

As she opened the door to the small room that Signi had
lived in, she caught a faint whiff of Signi's personal scent,
which had always reminded her a little of clove wine. Tdor
missed Signi. Not the deep and unending worry that wound
about Inda through waking and sleeping, but it was strong
enough to make Tdor's throat tighten.

She leaned in the doorway and stared at the empty bed
frame, knowing she would be glad if Inda returned and
found Signi there. *Life is so fragile,* she thought. *And so is
happiness. Signi, I hope you are safe, wherever you are, and
I hope you find your way back to us.*

She wiped her eyes, wondering why her emotions were
so like a spring storm, as she shuffled back to the central
room. It had gained furniture, but nothing was ever going
to mask its strange shape unless it was rebuilt, and Tdor

knew Inda would never ask Evred to do that. The girls had made mats for her and Inda as gifts, and Evred had given them a fine new table after the crown debts were paid. Maybe hangings? Yes. If Dannor could organize a tapestry-making, why couldn't Tdor? Only where did you begin ... and when?

Fareas-Iofre had settled neatly at the table, uncovering the dishes. Tdor lowered herself to her mat, feeling more ungainly than ever. Stupid mats! She shifted her legs in a futile effort to make herself more comfortable. She would not whine, even to herself. "Is a sense of home bound up in childhood memories?" she asked.

Fareas tipped her head, the exact same way Inda did when he was thoughtful. "I think it can be in some. But then a sense of home varies so much from person to person."

"Was Tenthen your home, or Darchelde, or Fera-Vayir?"

"Darchelde. Until I realized that it was more habit than conviction, oh, about the time all of you were in your teens. I realized I wouldn't go back if it was offered." Fareas smiled, her cheeks dimpling. "Part of that was knowing if I went back, nothing would be the same. Some of my sense of home was bound up in my companions, who had all changed as much as I had."

A sharp twinge in Tdor's back caused her to grimace and lean forward. "Is mother love the same for everybody? Does it sometimes not come?"

Fareas smiled into Tdor's anxious face—the same anxious expression Tdor had shown at age five when she worried about whether dogs got their feelings hurt if people called them ugly.

"Motherhood is unconditional love forever, for most," Fareas said. "Not for all. But I think it's safe to say for most, at least in the beginning. And most of the time, the child mirrors it right back."

Tdor endured another twinge at the base of her spine. Could it be—no. Hadand had said you felt your lower belly muscles pull. This pain was all in her lower back, a more intense version of what she felt at the end of a long day on her feet.

"But if you raise them well, that singular love for you erodes in the child and spreads to other people. Other things. The child—I will say a son, as others raise our girls—a boy has to change if he's to survive. So he looks away from you to friends, and boys at the academy, and lovers, and then to those he gathers around him and to whom he owes allegiance."

Another pang, much sharper this time. Tdor's pelvic bones glowed with pain, causing a spring of sweat on her forehead. *I already love my baby as fiercely as one can love.* "How can you bear it? Their turning away, I mean?" she asked, though she knew it was foolish, that time and-gradual change made everything bearable, or how could people survive?

"Because *your* love will never change. You take whatever the children give you and cherish it, and if the children go away, you cherish your memories." Fareas's eyes narrowed. "Tdor, are you feeling birth pangs?"

"No. It's my lower back." Tdor drew in a deep, shaky breath. "But oh, it hurts." A cramp seized her lower parts in an iron vise, and a gush of warm wetness spread under her. "Uh oh." She strangled a laugh. "Send for Noren?"

As it happened Tdor's body had done most of its work already, so the baby made his appearance before Noren even got there, though she came at a braid-flapping run. Fareas and the young Runner on door duty (now practiced with Hastred-Sierlaef) cleaned and dressed him. Once Tdor had seen her son, kissed and held him, submitted to being cleaned up, she dropped into a profoundly deep sleep.

Fareas smiled down at her, suspecting how long Tdor had been quietly feeling discomfort. Like Inda, Tdor rarely acknowledged physical ills. *I did not raise them that way,* she thought, holding the babe close; *I taught them to be sensible, to heed the body's needs.*

She wondered as she took little Jarend up into the window alcove and sat upon the stone seat, if she'd modeled that behavior, all unknowing. She looked down at the newborn, who had turned his face toward the light. He blinked, staring in that disconcertingly opaque way of babies new to the world, and a rush of emotion seized Fareas, the ache in arms and chest that for her defined the powerful upwelling of love.

But this is not my baby, she thought. *I will not see him grow. I will always love him, but to him I will only be a dis-*

tant old granddam, possibly of some utility but certainly of no interest.

His arm wiggled, the delicate fingers opening and closing. She bent close and nuzzled Inda's boy softly, pressing kisses all over his face. He responded immediately, his head jerking as he tried to see her.

I will pour love into you while I can, she thought. *Even if you never know it's my love, I trust it will pool inside you, adding to the well that you will draw on someday when it is your turn to give.*

Chapter Seventeen

Jarend-Laef Algara-Vayir, next Adaluin of Choraed Elgaer, was born yesterday. Your mother is here with Tdor. Name Day celebration tonight.

INDA looked up from the slip of paper in his hand, happiness making him giddy. A son, a Jarend! Oh, to be home again.

But he wasn't. He was the Harskialdna, with this battle between him and any chance of ever getting home again. He tucked the note into his pocket to reread later and bent over the mirror chart.

He noted with a neat chalk mark the landmark the lookout had just spotted. Now they could orient themselves with reference to the sizable detachment of Venn crossing toward Bren behind them, and could in turn report Barend's approximate position with reference to the Venn, when he wrote to ask next, as he'd already done twice.

"I wish we had eyes in Bren," Inda muttered to the map, his hand sliding to the locket swinging inside his shirt. Could he write Evred for more details? Except what would he ask? *I just want to go home.*

Fox walked into the cabin then. "On your feet," he said,

and Inda grinned. Drill really was better with Fox, Inda had discovered. It was worth the occasional numbness and tingles down his arm from his right shoulder to get the best workout he'd ever had.

Fox's brows rose at the sight of Inda's hand gripping that locket round his neck. "Are you really bound to Evred Montrei-Vayir that tight?"

Inda dropped his hand and mumbled something too low to catch under the sound of the rain and the working of the ship. But Fox got the gist in the words "wife" and "son."

Inda's tone was resigned, not reproachful. As he vanished out the cabin door, Fox paused, annoyed with himself. He was never going to shift Inda from that unswerving loyalty; maybe his gibes were strengthening it.

He followed Inda out and said, "You've been leading left-handed. That a whim?"

Inda looked up, blinking the fine rain out of his face. His shoulders dropped just enough for Fox to see that they'd been braced. Yes, it was time to leave the subject of Evred Montrei-Vayir back in Iasca Leror. Inda had not brought it up since his arrival and his relay of the Marlovan fleet idea. Fox was disgusted with himself.

Inda flexed his right hand, hesitant to talk about it. What was the use? He hated whining. "Catches sometimes."

"Maybe we should have a little left-handed drill, eh?"

Over the next few days, as the variable winds shifted gradually north and more west, Durasnir hoped Seigmad had better winds on the other side of the strait.

A day outside of Bren, Durasnir had drawn in his blockade and all waited on station as the *Cormorant* lookout reported the scout *Cormorant White* sighted, just where expected.

Durasnir had hot spice-milk and fresh food waiting, knowing from days of old that returning scouts liked coming back to food from home.

Rain plunketed against the sails overhead and spattered the deck, damping down the seas as the craft rounded to under the lee of the flagship. The two scouts, dressed in the manner of Bren sailors, clambered aboard. They were young, nondescript, and Durasnir trusted them; their (spoken) orders had been to only use scroll-cases under dire need, so he awaited their report. Erkric would probably be hearing it at the same time Durasnir did, but at least there would be no tampering with spoken words the way Erkric could tamper with scroll-cases.

The scouts tramped into the cabin that Durasnir had to himself again, shedding water at every step.

Byarin sat at his desk, apparently busy with dispatches, his bulk hunched over the work. He flicked a look Durasnir's way and nodded minutely: Erkric had ordered Byarin to place a spiderweb. As expected.

"I assume I will find a remnant of the Brennish navy waiting for us in the harbor, Scout Adin?" Durasnir asked for the sake of the spiderweb. His blockade had been almost criminally inadequate—yet another proof of how ill-prepared this venture was.

"Not even that. The last of them slipped out during a thunderstorm a couple weeks ago," Adin said, not hiding his regret. He, too, knew the blockade had been stretched too thin and that its movements had been fairly well reported by the swarm of Brennish fishers.

But others could use fishers as spies.

"Walfga followed them in his boat."

That meant Hegir was still aboard one of the Bren naval ships as a forecastleman. Again, no magical communication. Walfga was Hegir's contact or rescue, as needed.

"So it's surrender, then." Durasnir had figured on that when no one sailed up the strait to reinforce Bren. However, no one knew what sort of mad plan Elgar the Fox—whoever was using the guise—might risk.

Durasnir looked up, and the two scouts were startled by the bitterness in his face. But his voice was neutral as he said, "Was Indevan Algara-Vayir among those who slipped in and out?"

"No. But rumors were consistent about the rest of Bren's navy sailing east to meet him." Adin studied his commander, then ventured a question. "No one of ours in Idayago, where Algara-Vayir was reported last?"

"No."

They understood one another: Erkric had sent dag "military aides" to capture the famed Marlovan commander. The spies had reported failure—Indevan Algara-Vayir was

constantly surrounded by at least a hundred of his followers until the day he just vanished.

Durasnir didn't have to say anything. They all knew that
dags were mostly useless in war, in spite of those rumored
death spells.

"What can you tell me about Bren's available wood?"

"Not a stick but what's been claimed. Their prince and
princess have been fighting over who should get precedence. The navy got its share during winter, in preparation
for defense against us, and sailed with it. Guilds have all the
rest against rebuilding after the typhoon damage."

Durasnir dismissed the scouts and began issuing orders
for a peaceful entry to the harbor.

A day later his ships ranged in the vast line just beyond
the outermost island of the bay. The long, martial skyline
looked impressive, and as the ships would be hull down
from the spyglass of the inner island lookout, no details
of fished masts and repaired spars should be visible to the
Bren.

Durasnir sailed to the inner harbor accompanied by his
elite squadron of nine warships, every one precisely on station, the *Cormorant* observing flag etiquette.

Prince Kavna, watching from the highest tower of the
palace on the eastern ridge, lowered his glass when his
scroll-case tapped. He said to Kliessin a moment later,
"Dalm on Island Point says they're hull down."

"What does that mean?" Kliessin asked impatiently.

"It means they're far enough out so he can't see details.
So we can't see what kind of shape they're in."

Kliessin turned on her brother, anger and fear spiking
her irritation. "They could be patched with paper and still
thrash us."

Kavna knew how worried she was, and what a terrible
position she was in. Their father had always promised he'd
step down from the throne before he got too old to think
on his feet ... but he hadn't. His mind wandered back to
his youth these days; one never knew what year he thought
he was in.

Kavna said, "If Durasnir's in bad shape, he's going to
want wood. Look, there's only nine of them coming in. He
expects surrender."

Kliessin twitched a shoulder impatiently. "Well, we expected spies reporting to him. I just wonder if he's also got 'em with Chim."

"I don't think with Chim," Kavna said. "Those people all know one another. In the navy? Maybe."

Kliessin chewed her lip. "So he knows we're going to surrender, and he probably knows where all our wood is."

She wished once again that the Venn would attack on land so they could bring their guard down out of the hills on them from behind. Bren's long, successful history of defending its borders depended on knowing every hill, cave, grotto, and stream. On the ocean, everyone could see everything.

And as a young girl, she had seen these same ships, or ones just like them, sail in triumph through the wreckage of their old fleet to dock at the king's pier. She had hated ships and the sea ever since.

"I'm going to try to stall." She gripped her hands together until her rings pinched her flesh. "If that shit Durasnir wants to see Papa again, let him listen to the stories about court fifty years ago."

Durasnir reached the palace precisely at noon and was ushered to the most formal hall, which seemed largely unchanged from his last visit in the company of his son Vatta.

Kliessin's first sight of the tall warrior in gleaming silver and gold armor and the winged helm threw her back nearly twenty years. The memory just made her angrier.

Durasnir took in the sword-backed princess in her stiff brocade glittering with gems, her hair twisted up in a complicated knot behind the golden circlet she wore banding her head, and knew that he'd read the signals correctly.

The Bren guards had lined the main road, as if to herd the Venn along. Weapons at the ready, but no word of attack. No word at all, challenging or friendly. As if he and his Drenga Honor Guard were wild beasts.

Durasnir slowed his step incrementally, waiting for the princess to speak. Old King Galadrin was not present, though Durasnir knew he lived. Prince Kavnarac stood at his sister's shoulder, also dressed in a brocade robe stiff with gems. Durasnir did not remember seeing him when he negotiated the previous treaty; Kavnarac would have been a small boy then. And as always happened—like bumping a bruise—the words "small boy" brought back images of Vatta's face as he had looked around this marble room . . . *Halvir in Erkric's grip?*

He must concentrate. Within a few heartbeats, it became clear that Princess Kliessin was not going to speak first. She might stand there until the sun fell out of the sky, but she would not speak first, underscoring that he was an invader.

All right, he was an invader. "Princess Kliessin," he said in Sartoran. "Or is it queen?"

"My father," she replied coldly, "sits in his chamber, counting peanuts. You may visit him and view him if you wish. We cannot make any decisions until he regains cognizance of his surroundings, which he does from time to time."

Once my people would have forced him to sail for the far shore, Durasnir thought. *Mercy or expedience? Was Brun merciful when she bound me to life?*

He set that aside. "I am aware that you effectively rule this kingdom, therefore this stalling ploy is ineffective. You know by now that we keep our word—"

"What word," she cut in, her voice thin, "did you give those Marlovan children out west?"

"Is it children, now?" Durasnir retorted. *Brun's mercy . . . Brun, be as vigilant over Halvir as you were over me. I hope to better end.* "That castle was full of warriors, who happened to be women and girls. Trained. Probably better than these fellows in the orange I see all around me, judging from the way some of them hold their weapons. The women refused our offer of peaceful surrender and fought to the last. Are you prepared to fight to the last? Because if you are, we are likewise prepared, and can commence at any moment."

Her gown shimmered as her hands flexed, then she said, "No. My commitment is to preserving the lives of our people."

"Then my men will stand down. I will assign a captain to supervise the harbor. You will be given a list of our requirements as tribute, and once those are met, you will carry on your trade unmolested. But supervised through our headquarters."

"And if we don't meet your demands?"

"We will take what we need," he said, the pain from his

head shooting down through his jaw. "I encourage you not to put me to that trouble."

"Inda."

Fox rarely used that tone, quick and serious.

His partner lifted his hands and stepped away, freeing Inda to roll to his feet. He'd been demonstrating how to turn a defensive fall into an attack as he conducted the drill on the forecastle under the swaying light of lanterns. It was supposed to be Fox's sleep watch. Inda wasn't surprised to find Fox still awake.

Inda motioned the ship rats back to double-stick drill and trotted aft to the cabin, working his right shoulder absently. Double-stick drill seldom bothered it, not like grappling or sword work. But that fall hurt. He knew how to land—why did falls on his right side send those lightning bolts up through him like that?

As soon as Inda reached the cabin Fox slammed the door. From the still air, Inda knew the scuttles had been closed. "Something wrong with Barend?"

"No. He's fine. Reached this headland." Fox touched a chalk mark on their chart. "Look here." Fox walked to the desk, where he had the mirror chart spread out and pinned down.

As Inda watched, Fox whispered the words and made the pass. The lights glowed, as usual: patrols along the north side of the strait, a few in the south, neatly spaced, what they called a search net. Rigid lines representing ships on station just above Bren.

But Nelsaiam's bay showed complicated clusters, some of them blurred. "So the Venn attacked Nelsaiam," Inda said. "So? We can't see what Nelsaiam is doing and the dots don't make sense."

"They do when you make a pass every other glass," Fox said. "And now, look here." He pulled from his desk a sheaf of papers covered with splotches. "This is their progress," he said, throwing the sheets down one at a time. "I figured out what the blurs are, they have to be double tings from various ships. Over a watch, they'd cover enough distance to blur here, and if I compare them against all these intersecting lines, I can see not only the direction of the fastest ships, but their approximate speed." He sat back in triumph.

Inda bent over the papers, looking more closely. "So . . . we can guess what the enemy is doing."

"More than that. If you assume tactics along the Venn patterns—see on this paper, I put what I think are the Nelsaiam ships in red dots—then it makes even more sense."

Inda whistled. "We're getting a lesson in what they'll bring against us."

"It's not as good as being there, but it's better than anything else."

Inda grinned, then slapped his hand down. "Wait. How often are you doing it? What if the magic wears out?"

Fox grimaced. "I hadn't thought of that. Did Dag Signi tell you there was a limit?"

"No, we didn't talk about it. But I can't imagine the magic on that thing is limitless. Every pass probably was laid down with a spell, and I don't know how many times she did that."

"Do you think watching the evolution of this battle worth the risk?" Fox asked.

Inda frowned down at the sheaf of papers. "We need to learn, but we also need to know when they're coming at us. And how." He rapped his knuckles on the desk as he studied the spread of papers.

"D'you see it? They're breaking and reforming in triangles. I think the raiders are interlocking with the capital ships. If so, they're tight."

Inda sighed. "Watch the battle. I think that's most important. If the magic runs out, we'll have to scout 'em the old way. It's not like their coming is any surprise."

"Soon as it slows, I'll go back to once a watch. And when it's done, back to once a day."

Brun had only a heartbeat's warning when her front chamber thrall entered, her face pale.

Alarm burned through Brun. "Fricca?"

"The Dag of all the Venn. In the Tree room. For you, Vra Oneli Stalna."

Alarm chilled into dread. Brun carefully stoppered her ink, wondering who would next touch her desk, and what they would make of her translation as she rolled up the scroll and set it neatly on the rack. How would Erkric put her to death—or was he merely going to steal her mind?

While her trembling hands moved to neaten the desk in a frantic but futile effort to postpone whatever horror awaited, she tried to calm herself.

Finally the shock wore off enough for her to realize that calm was not going to happen until she knew the worst.

"Oh Fulla, I trust it is not about you," she breathed out as she twitched her plain, spring-green-dyed work over-robe into flatness, swiped an errant strand of hair behind her ear, then marched toward her own formal parlor. How terrible, when an enemy enters your citadel and, with merely the sound of his step, erases your boundaries of safety.

Erkric looked up from the Tree candelabra, which she kept burning.

"Nine candles, Vra Durasnir?" he asked. He looked old and worn, but his pouchy eyes were both aware and very angry.

Her gaze slid from his to the Durasnir Tree. "Nine seemed sufficient when the king himself goes sailing," she said evenly. She would never tell him the truth: that she lit nine every morning, hoping that their light would somehow add brightness to Fulla's path in the same way that Signi Sofar's face had reflected brightness when she raised her eyes to the Great Tree at her trial.

Erkric's gaze was that of an angry man, but his manner was not angry. He smiled, humorless but complacent. Uneasy, off balance, Brun said, "Would you care for refreshment? I can ring for spice-milk, or anything you like."

"Your hospitality is most welcome." He gestured in peace mode. "But my time is limited. The king sent me by magic transfer to see to state affairs both big and small. I have dealt with the large ones, and now it is time for the small, the most pleasant saved for last. It seems that he wishes to form a group of promising youths from the Houses, to be trained during our triumphant journey. He has chosen your son Halvir, as a future Oneli commander. Halvir will form part of the king's household on the royal ship."

Royal ship. He did not say the Cormorant, *Fulla's flagship.*

Brun's heart gave one sharp lurch, then thumped against her breastbone. "Halvir is only ten, just beginning his studies. He—he is not ready for so great a responsibility—"

"He will have tutors aboard ship," Erkric countered

smoothly. "I am prepared to depart now. He only needs a few things to wear, otherwise everything will be provided."

Erkric is taking Halvir. His complacence was now comprehensible. Brun knew Halvir was in danger, and she also knew there was absolutely nothing she could do. Erkric had caught her by surprise so that she could not send the boy away and make excuses.

And Fulla could not have warned her, if he even knew. Erkric had control of every means of magical communication.

"I will fetch him." The words seemed to scrape her dry, constricted throat. Knowing that whatever she said would be remembered by this evil man, and maybe even visited upon the boy, she forced an obeisance, and the formal words, "The king does honor to our House." Though the words were such a mockery she nearly choked.

Outside the door she leaned against the wall, and for one overwhelming moment she wished to be with Fulla on the tower again, only this time she would let him escape and jump after him herself. Life had become a succession of horrors, and now the worst: the evil one was taking Halvir.

No. Not the worst. Where there is life, there must be hope. You counseled Fulla to take courage. It is now your turn. Do not prove yourself to be a hypocrite.

She straightened her spine and forced her trembling legs to take her down the back stair to her son's rooms, bright with mosaics depicting dragons at play, and animals rarely seen in this part of the world. Ancient runes glinted, gold-painted, around the walls just under the patterned ceiling, bright in the light of the crystal globes full of gathered sunlight: Brun did not subject her children to a window.

Halvir knelt at his table, busy with paint pots. His tutor—a young scribe on his first assignment—was in the act of hanging up a painting to dry. They looked up in surprise, their voices colliding, "Vra?" "Mama?"

She walked forward. Made her mouth form a semblance of a smile at the tutor. "Scribe Niart, would you bid Halvir's chamber thrall to pack his clothing? His winter gear ... hold. Is it not summer down there at this time? Summer gear."

Niart made his bow and left.

Brun put her hands on either side of Halvir's face. His

wide eyes, so blue like Fulla's, raised to hers in question. She gazed hungrily at his sweet young face, his brow like Brun's own mother's, mouth and chin just beginning to emerge from the roundness of childhood with Fulla's strength. No rancor in that face, no slyness. Intelligent and good.

So Vatta had been, dead at sixteen.

Her eyes shuttered but the tears came anyway, and Halvir said, "Mama?"

She firmed her lips, and her voice. "The king has sent for you. You—and boys from other Houses will go to the Oneli—"

"I get to go a-viking?"

"Perhaps. Halvir, listen. Drenskar requires you always tell the truth."

He resisted the impulse to kick the rug with his toes. Why was he being jawed now? Hadn't he heard that at least ninety-nine times a day since he was born?

His mother bent, her hands sliding down to his shoulders to hold him steady, her lips just above his hair, her voice soft, quick, and trembling. "These days . . . when one wishes to survive . . . it is wise to offer the truth only to those you trust. Answer with as little truth as duty requires where you do not trust."

Halvir sighed. "I *know,* Mama. Will I get to see the king?"

"You will indeed." Erkric spoke from the doorway.

Brun forced herself not to jump, but her fingers tightened on Halvir's shoulders, making him wince. It was such a trespass, to enter the private chambers unasked. But who could deny the Dag of all the Venn?

Halvir kept himself from running around and yelling for joy only because he'd been taught to behave in the presence of strangers.

"Would you like to attend the king?" Dag Erkric asked, his smile broad.

Halvir recognized the Dag of all the Venn. He was tall, and old, and people acted afraid of him. He knew his parents didn't like him, but he didn't know why. But the throb in his shoulders from his mother's tightened fingers, her tense face, the big smile below eyes that didn't smile, all warned Halvir to be careful. More grown-up stuff he just didn't understand.

Halvir bowed, hands in peace mode. "Yes, O Dag," he said.

The Dag gestured for Halvir to follow. When the travel bag of clothes was brought by the silent chamber thrall, the Dag said, "Can you carry that yourself?"

"Of course! I'm strong," Halvir protested, and clutched the bag against his body. He looked up in triumph at his mother, who mouthed the word "Remember!"

Then magic ripped Halvir out of the world and stuffed him back in.

He staggered and dropped the bag. "Leave it, Halvir," the Dag said. "The chamber thralls will see to it. Come within and meet King Rajnir. We'll show you your chambers. And as soon as word reaches us of the success at Bren or Nelsaiam, you and I and the king will take sail."

Chapter Eighteen

THE change in the winds sped the Fox Banner Fleet the last distance to the narrowest point in the strait. As expected, they were spotted by lurking fishers, both of whom were identified. So Inda and Fox were pleased when they raised all sail and raced off to report to the waiting allies.

The *Death* and its consorts arrived on a summery early morning within sight of the outermost of the gigantic rock teeth called The Fangs, white-splashed with guano as a hundred varieties of sea birds circled in dizzying patterns overhead. This rock was at the southwesternmost reach of The Fangs, just above the border between Chwahirsland and Danara. Not far beyond, two small ships had been stationed as sentinels; when the Fox Banner Fleet hove to on the horizon, signals went out in all directions, spyglasses winked and gleamed in the strong light, sails jerked up and filled in the summer breezes as ships began to converge.

Inda stood at the rail, staring out at a whale blowing a spout in the distance, the sun sparking rainbows through the spray. The scuttles were open all over the ship; from belowdeck came the voices of a pair of mids who should have been working. Inda was thrown back in memory to his mid days when he heard them arguing over whether the spouting was a pattern indicating communication, or art, or just fun.

Fox sauntered up and leaned on the rail next to Inda. "You want to sail around and inspect?"

The voices below stopped. Brisk sounds of cleaning commenced.

Inda said, "No. Let 'em see me here. Me on the *Death*, like we planned. Get that fixed good in their minds."

"You're still determined on this idiocy?"

Inda sighed, staring down at the foaming wake. "We'll talk up our line and the inverted arrow. Get a count of what we have."

Fox turned away to instruct the youngster tending the signals, then returned, and while everyone was busy, said in a low voice, "I think Nelsaiam has fallen. If I'm reading the lights correctly, the Venn lost about eighteen—no telling what size—and somewhere around fifty of them have not moved since the last ting. I'd call that severe damage, if nothing more."

"I wonder how many Nelsaiam sent against them."

"I tried to get a sense of it, but couldn't. Maybe if I'd been reading them longer, or more frequently. My assumption about speed designating raiders might also be wrong."

Inda half raised a hand. "We learned plenty."

Fox lifted a shoulder, then said, "Barend just wrote demanding another sighting. When did he turn so faint-hearted?"

Inda grinned. "Maybe he thinks Ramis will come hunting his blood if he loses the *Knife* to some random raider out shirking duty. We didn't send enough hands with him to fight two ships, just to sail them."

"True. Well, I'm off to do his sighting, then roll up the mirror chart and hide it before the first of your visitors arrives." Fox sauntered away, and a few moments later Inda heard his voice making some pungent observations about the set of the topsails before he vanished back into the cabin.

Inda raised his glass, sweeping it slowly over the hazy, glinting waters, as though he could cause more ships to spring into view just by will. *I hope there are a lot more than I'm seeing.*

By midday the haze had lifted, and the captains' flagships rocked on a sparkling blue sea under a bright summer sky, flags jerking up and down foremasts by exasperated crews as the strait captains signaled back and forth about who had precedence.

The *Vixen,* its distinctive tall, curved mainsail belled taut, reached the *Death* first. Just after the scout hove up under the *Death*'s lee, Nugget yelled up, "Inda! Inda! Look who's here!"

Inda shot up on deck. Fox, who was now at the wheel where he could watch everything, snorted in a mix of amusement and irritation when a tall, splendid man appeared behind the folding mainsail, golden hair burnished in the sun.

"Tau!" Inda yelled as Taumad leaped across to the main-chains and vaulted over the rail moments later. "I didn't know you were coming. I thought you were doing trade talk in Bren for Evred."

"My envoy days are done. Or nearly. But we'll discuss that later."

Inda was so glad to see Tau again he heard one word in three. Fox considered that "or nearly" but said nothing.

"Then if you're mine, you can go back to being my eyes and ears. Like you were before. Explain these alliance people to me." Inda's scarred face reddened, taking everyone by surprise as he added, "And you have to remind me when I'm slurping my soup."

Tau laughed and extended a hand toward the ships out on the clear sea-green water, some having raised sail to approach, others in the process of booming down captains' gigs and boats. The *Vixen* had moved downwind, and Nugget was just climbing up the side of *Cocodu.*

"You're Inda the Fox," Tau said. "If you slurp soup, they all will slurp soup if they think it will make them win. Here they come to satisfy themselves that you still exist."

Inda turned from Tau to Jeje and back. "You've been here a few days, right? What am I coming into, here?"

Jeje said, "The weirdest is Thog. The nastiest is that Deli-yeth. She looks, and acts, like she expects us to squat and piss on her deck."

Inda sighed. "Then that's where you go first, Tau. See

if you can win over Deliyeth. So we don't have any north coast allies?"

"What we have is all under Deliyeth." Jeje made a spitting motion toward the rail and laughed in surprise. "Heyo, here come all the easterners, looks like in a bunch."

"Who are they?"

"First ones first. I see the Sarendan flag in the front boat. You probably remember Taz-Enja—"

"Who?"

"Nugget remembers." Jeje ducked out of the way as a sail party clattered by, carrying rolls of lighter summer sail to the shrouds to be handed up to the masthead.

From over *Cocodu* a cable's length away came Nugget's angry voice, "What's this *Lady* Waki this, *Lady* Waki that? Mutt! When have I ever called myself Lady Waki, you rat-faced bun-stuffer?"

Jeje raised her voice. "When we first left Freedom to go after Boruin. Taz-Enja was captain of a Sarendan warship chasing that pirate, I forget his name, had the big barrel of distilled liquor in the cabin. Gave us the fire-ship idea. Taz-Enja remembers you and Nugget."

"All I remember is a cabin boy sticking his tongue out at Nugget, and she wanted to wave her knives to threaten the entire warship."

"Well, that cabin boy's a chief lieutenant—next thing to a captain—and Taz-Enja's an admiral of their navy now. But they're not here as a navy."

"They're not?" Inda turned from Jeje to *Cocodu*, where one high female and one young man's cracking voice exchanged insults in at least three languages.

"No. Inda, don't pay any attention to Mutt and Nugget, they always argue like that. Then they'll end up in his hammock, or hers. Listen! The Sarendan king married the daughter of the Venn prince who used to rule Geranda. This was before the old geezer died and the Venn took off for home. But for whatever reason makes sense to kings and their like, Sarendan can't officially get into this battle, so he let Taz-Enja raise a volunteer fleet for what they're calling maneuvers." Jeje snorted. "Bren's sent a high admiral, Dhalshev is called a *flag* admiral, but Taz-Enja is to be called just 'commander.' Their people aren't wearing their green navy tunics, since it's volunteer duty. They got themselves what they think is pirate clothes. You're gonna laugh, but don't do it in front of them. We've got almost their entire fleet. Saving the most senior warships, which are staying close to their coast on patrol."

"I don't care if they're naked," Inda said. "They'll know something of fleet maneuvers."

"So do the Chwahir. That is, they know how to read a signal and stay on station. But they are slow as logs. Anyway, I think you'll like Mehayan of Khanerenth. I've only talked to him twice, but Dhalshev and Chim both like him—"

"Chim!"

"He's sailing with the Brens, and, um, he's got a surprise. But he'll tell you that, and I promised—well, see that brigantine with the raked masts just brailing up abaft the Chwahir? That's High Admiral Brasvac. I think he might be some kind of cousin of Prince Kavna. They talk a lot alike."

"Boat ho!"

Jeje faded back as the newcomer's crew hooked on.

The rest of the day, Inda received a succession of captains. First the higher ranks, but as the *Death* did not signal a desist, several other captains had themselves rowed over so they could meet the infamous Elgar the Fox in person. Both Foxes, because there was the tall redhead as well as the short one with the scars.

Inda welcomed them all and patiently explained his line-with-inverted-arrowhead idea over and over, figuring the word would pass the faster.

At the end of a long day the last of the boats rowed back, the three captains sharing it filled with Lorm's good whiskey-laced punch as they talked over their conversation (and the good advice they'd bestowed on Inda Elgar) before returning to tell it all over again to their crews.

Just after sunset, Inda, tired and hungry (he had not drunk a drop of the punch) left the cabin to walk on deck with Jeje. She'd stayed to furnish names and backgrounds. Tau remained in the background, listening.

Inda said, "So that just leaves Chim, and whatever his surprise is, and I still haven't seen these Ymarans and Everoneth—"

"On deck. Signal!"

Inda poked his had out the cabin door, peering upward. "Who?"

" 'Captain Deliyeth invites Elgar alone, or requests permission to bring party.' "

Jeje snorted. "It's an insult! She's all but saying she doesn't trust you. What can one of her parties do if we really wanted to kill her?"

"Jeje, if you're going to make that face around her—and by the way, does she get a special title? High, or flag, or crown, or—"

"She's their commander, but she expected *us* to only call her captain. Tau says it's reverse snobbery." Jeje grinned unrepentantly. "I'm leaving. Sun's about gone. My guess is this is your last visit of the day, and you don't need me for it. Eflis and I worked up some night drills for the schooners and scouts while we were waiting for you. It's your idea, only smaller. For taking on raiders."

Inda lifted a hand, and she left. He yelled for the watch mid and they both began neatening up the cabin, which still had a few cups lying around. As the girl carefully carried away a tray full of crockery, Inda cast a look around, satisfied that things looked shipshape.

Captain Deliyeth had waited all afternoon for the Fox Banner Fleet to signal her. They'd held court instead, like the pirate emperors she suspected them to be.

When the sun had slid most of the way down the western sky she decided that sitting around waiting for a signal and asking herself questions was even more useless than cadging thirdhand gossip from others. She had never shirked her duty, no matter how unpleasant.

It was time to go call on the pirate king.

She chose her biggest, strongest, toughest marines. She knew they could hardly take a stand against the entire crew of the pirate ship, but she wanted visual evidence of just how much she distrusted the chosen leader of the alliance.

She had her gig crew row her over as she sat in the sternsheets, straight-backed and silent, perforce requiring her company to remain silent.

She eyed the long, low trysail as they neared, not admitting even to herself how interested she was to set foot on board the infamous black-sided *Death*.

The ship was clean, everything neat, in fact neater than

the ships of some of their allies. She glimpsed that sneering redhead Fox at the wheel, but she did not acknowledge him, nor did he do anything but lean his arms between the spokes and smile that hateful smile of his.

The cabin was surprisingly beautiful—but of course pirates would have their pick of the world's treasures, since they never actually paid for anything.

Inda Elgar was younger than she'd thought, though scarred, the top of his head even with her eyes. Unlike his red-haired captain, he dressed like a deckhand. He even had bare feet, though they were far lighter a brown than the rest of his visible skin. "Sit down, please," he said.

She took her time motioning her marines into place, sat down on a carved bench that had probably been looted from a monarch, and said without any preamble, "You are the one who murdered Count Wafri."

Inda Elgar's face blanched, then flushed a deep red that made his scars stand out palely. At first she thought that a reaction of guilt, except for the downward turn to his mouth. That was pain.

Inda had expected trouble, but not that. "I didn't kill him," Inda said finally, when he knew his voice wouldn't bleat. But he was unsettled enough to burst out, "Why don't you people believe that? And would you blame me if I had? He used to torture your people for sport! He assassinated your queen—he–he–he bragged about it to me."

He sounded outraged! Deliyeth jerked her hand up, waving aside his words. "So you say, so you say. But his lordship was well loved in Ymar. He was the new king's own cousin, from a long-respected family. Whereas about you, what do we hear? Everywhere, blood and death. Burning and destruction. With my own eyes I saw what you did to Limros Palace."

Inda gritted his teeth.

"We're told you even allied with Norsunder to get rid of your rivals in the Brotherhood of Blood! Who can stand against you?"

Inda twisted away and worked to calm down, wiping his sweaty face. Just the thought of Wafri made his joints flare in memory-echo. "I did not ally with Norsunder. And I didn't make that rift."

"The *Venn* all believed you made it!" She pressed her

hands against her forehead. "They said so in the hearing of—"

"Damn the Venn! Ramis made that rift."

"How can you expect me to believe you? We've heard witnesses who saw your fire ships, saw you burn pirates. Heard from traders about you walking about Ghost Island like old friends with the Norsundrian Ramis—"

Inda resolutely stayed silent. No one had ever called him a liar before; there was a disturbing sense that every word he spoke somehow twisted in the air, turning into some other word before it reached her ears.

She hesitated, unsettled by his glumness. Fox's insolence, his sarcastic drawl, that she expected from pirates. Of course, Elgar's reaction could be a sham, or maybe even guilt to have his crimes spoken out loud. Obviously none of those other bootlicks had dared.

She squared herself to duty. "And next thing we hear, you've made yourself the Marlovan king's right-hand man, though you'd been exiled for killing a boy ten years before. How many of your countrymen did you also kill to make that jump in rank? Not that I care anything about the horse barbarians. You can kill all of them you like, since that seems to be what they like doing to other people. Here's my question, what is to stop you from taking all our ships and people, and once the Venn are gone forever, just stepping in and taking their place yourself?" She thumped the bench she sat on. "Is this going to be your throne, Emperor Inda Elgar the First?"

Inda stared back at her. "You don't know the truth about me. But I've also learned that people who don't want to see the truth won't." He pressed the heels of his hands into his eyes, then flung out his hands. "I promised people I would lead an alliance against the Venn. If you don't want an alliance, then there's nothing to talk about. If you do, let's just lay out the conditions and proceed from there." And when she did not get up to leave, "How many ships do you have, and what types?"

When she departed a short time later, Fox was waiting. He'd positioned himself at the wheel, where he could keep an eye on the comings and goings, and hear everything in the cabin below through the open scuttles.

He summoned the mate of the watch to take his place,

and went down to the cabin, where he found Inda alone, prowling around from object to object, touching them sightlessly the way he did when he was thinking, or upset.

"I heard that," Fox said. "She's a damned fool."

Inda looked up, and for a moment all the old pain was there, bleak and stark. "Wafri." He expelled the word like a curse. Then rubbed his hands over his head. "How can they see escaping from a torturer as being destructive?"

"Probably has to do with setting the treasure room at Limros Palace on fire."

"I did not!"

"Inda, *you and I* nearly caught fire, we stood there so long, watching Wafri's stuff burn."

"I did not burn anyone's treasures. I remember that damned day clear as—" Inda's voice tightened. "I remember the rope—and you pulling me up. I remember walking. My ribs hurt, I remember that much."

Fox studied Inda uneasily. "You don't remember the eggs in the boots?"

"That wasn't us, that was a story from when I was a boy. Dogpiss Noth and Dancing Nderga. I must have told you that story, and you mixed it up with—" Inda frowned. "Wait. Wait. I remember the stairs. I slipped on some water somebody threw. There was fire. We were laughing. Did I have a basket of eggs, or is that a dream?" He shook his head. "I do remember shooting from the wall. But not burning anybody's treasure."

Inda had hunched over in the old way, as if he was seventeen again, and Fox reflected on how physical scars might heal, but the emotional ones could linger through one's life. "I remember you nailed more of those Limros guards in knees and elbows than I did," he said.

Inda's face eased. "I was always a better shot than you, even if I couldn't beat you on the deck. Did you ever lose a fight?"

Fox laughed soundlessly. "Once," he said. "Once."

Inda scarcely heard. He got up and roamed restlessly about the cabin, touching things in absent pattern. "Fox, listen. She was the last of them. I asked everybody how many ships they had on hand, and I've kept a running tally in my head. We don't have enough."

"What do you want to do?"

"Since the Venn are coming, we don't really have a choice, do we? Well, we were outnumbered in Andahi, too. And I do have my plan. So I'm going to start right in working."

"How do you want to do that?"

"I'm going to put 'em through maneuvers until they're tight, fast, know how to watch one another, and don't have to be sitting on signals. You drill 'em on their decks. If you can get some of their boarding crews trained to our composite bows, good, because they're so much handier in the tops. But if you can't, train 'em to use what they've got."

"Done."

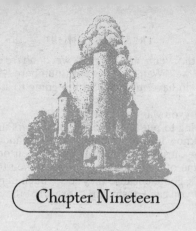

Chapter Nineteen

AT first, Halvir Durasnir found Llyenthur Harbor interesting. But that did not last long.

He would have loved to run up and down those zigzag steps below the palace on the hilltop, especially in the warm air. They almost never had warm air at home in Twelve Towers, and definitely no zigzag flights of stairs. Through the window he'd seen boys his age, some of them going to the fishers, or to the harbor shops where they prenticed, and some helping the workers busy on the expansion, but at first he was forbidden to go near the scaffolding, and then he could not go outside at all.

Instead, he had to sit in the king's outer chamber, being absolutely quiet so that he would not disturb the king at meditation. And all he was permitted to do was practice his runes until he felt like his head was stuffed with armor quilting. Like he was six, not ten!

So after too many boring days, all exactly alike, when the Dag came in and told him to follow the king to the royal ship, Halvir leaped up. At last he'd get to do something! He'd be sailing with the Oneli! And best of all, he'd get to see his father, who he knew commanded the Oneli flagship.

One by one his hopes were smashed. The Erama Krona closed in like moving white pillars, with the harbor duty Drenga as outer perimeter, so Halvir only saw armed men, between whom were mere glimpses of people, of dock, of water. The Erama Krona carried the king in a thronelike conveyance, but he did not talk to anyone. He did not even look around.

Then—*finally*—the ship they got onto was just a converted raider, no cut booms or anything. Not the *Cormorant*. There was a sail crew, but no Drenga, only Erama Krona, silent as always, plus a lot of sober-faced dags in blue. Halvir felt the fuzzy tingle of magic as he and the king were led straight below to a big cabin in the middle deck and Halvir got pushed beyond that into a tiny oddly-shaped cabin that he figured had to be in the forepeak. Halvir didn't even get to stay with the king, not that the king had ever spoken to him once past that first "Welcome, Halvir." And he'd said that as if he were asleep.

Halvir's new quarters were clean, with two small scuttles, a narrow bunk, and on the opposite side a tiny desk below a glowglobe. Several scrolls sat on the desk, and paper, and ink, and pens.

Lessons. Halvir groaned. He so wanted to climb the rigging, and talk to people, and *see* something. Where were the other boys he was supposed to be learning with? He'd even be glad to see that sniveling Fald Hadna.

He was shut in and told to sleep or read a scroll. The ship rocked and rocked, and then he felt the jerk and lift and roll that meant they were under way. He waited, stomach growling. He knew better than to complain. It was a little frightening, being under the watchful eyes of those silent Erama Krona, who (everyone knew) would kill you if you as much as talked to the king without his asking you a question first.

It was dark when he woke and peeked through the scuttle just overhead. He felt cranky and stiff as he climbed off the bunk and straightened out his clothes. Then the door opened, an ensign brought in some warm spice-milk and food, which made Halvir feel better.

But then Dag Erkric himself summoned him. "Now, Halvir," he said. "Tell me, who do you think are the smartest boys your age?"

What did adults mean by smart? The ones the adults told you to act like, or ones you liked to play with? Ones who thought up the best games? Andr Loc was funny, but he was always in trouble. Maybe better not mention him.

"Fald Hadna?" Halvir asked. Adults always held him up as the example of a good boy, though he was a sneak and a serpent-tongue.

"You think carefully before you speak," Dag Erkric observed, his gaze steady.

Halvir looked down, fighting against the fidgets. He couldn't define why he felt uneasy, he just wished he could get away.

So how was he to answer? The Dag smiled. "That is a very good trait."

All right, so far at least there weren't trouble questions, like, "Why are you so undisciplined?" There was no right answer to *that* question.

Dag Erkric said, "Get your pens and ink and paper, Halvir. You are to sit at this desk while I work at protecting the king and the ship by magic. You must sit very still and not disturb me, for this is difficult magic I must cast. You are to write out all your runes, taking especial care with them."

Halvir bit off a protest that he knew his runes. He obeyed, but as he sat down to the tedious task, he wished he had another boy to talk to.

Instead, here he was, with the king somewhere, and all those silent Erama Krona. He was so very glad he was an heir, so he would never be asked to join *them*. The grown-ups all said it was a great honor if a second son or a cousin of an heir was invited to the Erama Krona, but who would want to be taken away from his family for years and go through the terrible training he heard about? The big boys once told Halvir and his friends that the Erama Krona candidates had their balls cut off, but his mother had said that was only in the olden days and they hadn't done that for centuries. But still. You couldn't be in a family until your twenty years of service were over and you were fifty. Who wanted to *live* at fifty? Well . . . Mother would be fifty next year, and she was alive . . . and maybe . . .

As Dag Erkric's voice droned softly in the background, whispering spells over and over, Halvir blinked at his rune, and tried to remember where his mind had been wandering. Odd how sometimes it got really hard to think.

In the palace courtyard, Dag Anchan straightened up wearily. She fought the impulse to tug that disgusting iron torc around her neck. She knew it would not choke her. Iron did not change size. It was the idea of it, the heaviness of it, that made her feel choked.

She stretched her back and regarded the lines of sheets adjacent the racks of shirts, drawers, and socks, all spread out in readiness for the rising sun. Down here in the south, laundry could usually be sun dried at least once a week during most of the year. Even in winter, she was assured by a local woman, there were plenty of sunny days this close to the middle of the world.

At home the laundry was above the baking rooms, which kept the air warm and dry. Mages kept the glowglobes intense, which required almost as much work as the cleaning and cranking through the wringer.

Anchan was *finished*. Not just for the day, but for good. She looked around at the people who'd been her companions, some for three years, others since her arrival in Llyenthur. Most were justice thralls, their crimes petty, except for the Laundry Chief, who was a born thrall. All but one were young. The older woman's thieving made no sense. Anchan suspected from her odd comments that the woman saw the world through a broken window and needed a healer good with troubled minds. It would not happen, not with Erkric sending the best healers on the warships.

The court was warm. The new sun radiated off the stones, burning her bare toes a little. She walked head-bent toward the thrall gate. As always, the few people she passed avoided looking at her, as if thralldom would defile them if their gazes touched. Could she blame them? No. She'd expected to find no lover during her rare free moments—she'd grown up hearing people say in a disparaging tone, *She'd have sex with thralls,* or *He couldn't get anyone but a thrall in his bed.* Long, long ago thralls could not say no. Now, people despised you if you slept with thralls. She had discovered that she couldn't bear the thought of intimacy with any of these people by whom she sat at meals, whose breathing she heard from their sleeping alcoves when she was off duty.

Now she could leave. It would even be easy. No one noticed thralls unless they did an unthralllike thing. The small traces of her magic would vanish before Erkric or any of his minions could be bothered to examine the space. Everyone would assume her time was done. So she rolled the sleep-mat, stashed it neatly under the narrow sleeping platform. She folded the ugly, rough brown thrall tunic and placed it on the barren shelf for the next poor soul assigned to this minuscule alcove. She put on her blue dag robe, wriggling all over just to feel the fine linsey-woolsey again. Then she pulled her transfer token from where she had wedged it between the join of the sleep platform and the wall.

Light, air, and space ripped apart the world and reassembled it; she staggered as noise buffeted her. The glare of sunlight dazzled her eyes. Two small, firm hands gripped her just above the elbows to steady her.

"Come. Sit," Valda said, looking older and thinner, her wild hair more white than gray. "Why are you here? Disaster? One word will do."

"No." Shuffle, shuffle, something hard bumped the backs of Anchan's knees, and she sat gratefully, then opened her eyes. "The fleet left. No laundry thralls taken aboard the mage ship."

"Mage ship? Dag Erkric is not on the *Cormorant?*"

"It is still at Bren, last I heard. Yesterday Erkric took his prisoners and his chosen Erama Krona to the raider *Cliffdiver.*"

"Prisoners? King Rajnir and—"

"And Oneli Stalna Durasnir's son Halvir."

Valda gasped. "So that's why the scribes and archivists . . . I did not know."

"No one knew. But what's this about the scribes? Is my mother involved?"

"Oh, yes. Your father has learned how to remove the Norsunder wards from the king's chambers. As for the scribes—oh, we can talk about it later. Now I know why they are angered—it must be on Brun Durasnir's behalf. Tell me more!"

"The Dag brought Halvir back from Twelve Towers

when he returned. I did not risk a message because he came back in an ice-storm temper, increasing wards everywhere as soon as he recovered from the transfer. We learned he intends to gather a coterie of dedicated young men to serve the king."

"All bespelled," Valda whispered. "This is terrible."

"He began the bindings on the boy as soon as he laid his wards. I discovered it after three days had passed, and in my horror, that very night I spindled them. I could not bear a child being . . ." Anchan bowed her head. "I believe I acted in error for that next day, Dag Erkric announced the king's decision to join the fleet, and they were closed off from contact while everything was readied. Now he's got both of them on that ship, out of our reach."

"This is terrible, terrible." Brit Valda perched on the bench like an untidy bird, rubbing her gnarled hands absently over her bony knees.

"Where am I?" Anchan asked, looking down at her scrub-worn hands, which right now looked older than Valda's.

"You are in the north of Sartor."

"Are these mages?" Anchan asked, looking about as she fingered the torc still around her neck. "Can you remove this thing?" Then she remembered the whispers about Valda's birth and her face heated.

"They would think it merely an ornament, here," Valda assured her with a crooked smile, then reached up behind Anchan and murmured the unlock spell. The torc fell into Anchan's lap. "They don't have thralls, either born or criminal. Judgments are handled other ways."

So Anchan pocketed the torc and took in her surroundings. She was in a square of what appeared to be a village or town, leafy trees at each corner dappling the bricks with shade. The houses displayed the broad windows she'd discovered were typical of the south. Most houses were built to one or two levels. The extravagance of wide windows was enhanced further with flower-potted balconies; from some of the open windows came the rhythmic drone of the spell for Fire Stick renewal. The summer sun shone warm as well as bright, so far in the south, and the air was quite hot. Anchan took in the rich, unfamiliar scents and smiled. She was free again, wearing the blue she'd earned. She'd even come to like short hair, light and free of trouble in this warm climate.

Valda said briskly, "Are you recovered? Your transfer magic is safely disseminated. We can sit a few moments longer, then get you a good meal. We'll put in some work as trade, but first, finish your report. Did Erkric say where he planned to take the king?"

"Once the Oneli win the strait he will transfer to Jaro for the winter."

Valda touched her fingertips together. "I honor you for three years of heroic work. But you are not finished with danger. Here is my report for you. Nelsaiam fell to us, but at a sharp cost. Seigmad collapsed in a calenture near the end of the battle, and there was some struggle over who would take command. Battlegroup Captain Hyarl Dyalf Balandir wished to reassert himself as Battlegroup Chief, but his Battlegroup was at the edge of events, and I'm told he had no idea what to do besides waving his fist and shouting to attack. Captain Baltar of the *Katawake* assumed the command until Battlegroup Chief Seigmad woke."

"Good."

"But while that was occurring, Dag Yatar commenced using magic against the enemy. He said at the king's own command. And they claim the spells turned the tide of battle."

"What spells?" Anchan felt sick.

"Some kind of fire that pulls heat out of the air while the spell lasts. They put the magic on fire arrows before the Drenga shoot them. These fires are not doused easily. There is also the stone-inside-objects spell, though Byarin reports difficulties. One must have stones at hand, and it takes time to make the spell and assess the exact position of the enemy in order to transfer the stone inside them. They did kill a few people, and shocked many more, but far more of the stones fell uselessly and rolled around the enemy decks. Some were even pitched back by enemies adept at the use of lines."

"So Erkric will have dags training in the future to use magic spells such as these," Anchan said in disgust.

"Unless we ward those spells from the start, so that they fail, and they are seen to fail. That is why I am here in this town full of mages. I am making warding tokens, and no one can trace me with the air full of magic. Here is your new assignment. Byarin begged me for a dag who is not assigned a ship, for Erkric is keeping close watch on all sea dags. We need someone of whose presence he is unaware. You are going to spend the next month slipping from ship to ship and wedging a token on each vessel."

Anchan laughed and rubbed her hands. She had volunteered for the thrall duty partly because she wanted to spare the older dags the work, but also because she'd hoped it would bring adventure. It had only brought the worst kind of danger: unceasing threat amid wearying labor, and a slow, inexorable erosion of spirit.

"You'll have all the *drakans* to ward. Once they are done, the raiders as you and I can. But the *drakans* first."

"How long do we have?"

"Byarin says that they figure on two months at the outside before they reach the confederation of ships forming up at the east end of the strait. Ulaffa believes Erkric intends to make his demonstration of magic's power after he contrives Durasnir's death. He's been asking too many questions about the various captains, and conducting personal interviews with them, on various pretexts."

Anchan gasped.

"Come. We'll eat, work, and you will go to Ulaffa via Byarin, the first load of my ward tokens in your pockets."

They rose and Valda walked briskly across the square toward the long, low whitewashed building from which the chanting drifted. Then she stopped, pointing to the other side of the square, where two broad streets converged.

Anchan turned, puzzled. The traffic was the usual carts and walkers and horseback riders, brightly-clothed people of all ages and degrees, many carrying baskets, some with food that sent savory drifts on the summer air: pepper, citrus, many types of flower, baking pastry.

"The bench." Valda chuckled.

Anchan had swept her gaze past the row of old people seated on a bench in front of a trellis over which climbed a flowering vine. The old people were just sitting there, some enjoying the sun, others chatting. Anchan realized that this pleasant, dull scene fascinated Valda.

The Sea Dag Chief said, "I hope soon to be able to spend

my old age seated on a sunny bench, watching people go about their lives. Oh, how I cherish that thought!"

"You're not old," Anchan exclaimed, though she knew it a lie. Valda's sagging face, her knobby hands and prominent veins, her nest of mostly white hair, had long lost any remaining trace of youth. But Anchan did not lie with the intent to lie. The impulse was to underscore her belief in Valda's strength, vitality, her keen intelligence.

Valda laughed silently, then said, "I am old, but the word to me means familiar, comfortable. Accustomed after long and venerable use. Not dilapidated and useless."

"Old or not, I trust you will gain your peaceful bench in the sun," Anchan said sincerely, thinking, *You've earned it, ten times over. But you'll never do it. We'll find you dead at your desk, pen at hand. I hope it will be many years yet, for our own sakes, as well as yours.*

"Halvir."

Halvir squirmed—and couldn't move.

In the dream he'd been falling through the air, falling and falling. He fell with people, and houses, and ships, all spinning slowly end over end. His limbs sank down, heavier and heavier, and he didn't know why he fell, and he didn't feel pain. He wanted to cry but he couldn't do even that. He just fell.

"Halvir."

He opened his eyes. Was he awake? Real awake, not waking inside of another dream? He'd had so many wakenings, but they were just more dreams, slipping from one to the next before he fell yet again, down and down into white clouds.

This time his eyes stung, though he could not see anything. Wait. Wait. Was that a chink of light, down there? He'd go see—but he couldn't move.

He wriggled a little, then with increasing desperation. His arms and legs, his middle—someone had tied him to a chair!

He opened his eyes so wide they hurt, but he couldn't see anything except that faint line of light. But this wasn't another dream, it wasn't! Panic rose inside his throat, almost choking him. Why would he be tied up?

"Halvir."

He struggled to get enough breath to scream, but he couldn't breathe, they'd taken away his eyes and ears and his breath—

"Halvir."

The whisper broke the panic long enough for him to suck in a breath to yell—

"You must be silent, Halvir. You must not be heard."

Halvir gasped and struggled to contain the hard-edged sobs that cut the inside of his chest, wanting out.

"Halvir. Do you hear me? Whisper back."

"Yes." His voice squeaked.

"Good boy. Good boy. Listen. You are on a ship called the *Cliffdiver*. We are sailing with the Oneli."

"My father?" Halvir went cold all over. "Where is my father?"

"Be still. Be silent. Halvir, you are called upon to do a man's work. Can you manage that?"

Halvir straightened up as best he could, though his clothes were twisted and itchy in awful places. His mouth felt dry and horrible. His hair tickled his cheeks and neck, like it hadn't been combed in days. But he could do a man's work, oh, yes, he could. "I will," he whispered.

"Good boy. Before I can tell you more, I must know you can pass a test."

"How can I? I'm tied up."

"This is a test of endurance, not of action. You must pretend to be asleep when Dag Erkric comes back in. Or when Dag Yatar comes in to make us take food and drink. Because you are not alone. There are two of us in here."

"Why?"

"That will come. First, you must pass the test. If they think you are awake, you will·get more of the bad magic that makes you dream. Do you want that?"

"No!"

"Then heed what I say. Pretend, be asleep, do what they tell you when they whisper. You'll feel the dreams come on again. Do not fight, for I can take them away again."

"Who are you?" Halvir asked.

There was no answer, only the rocking of the ship and the soft sound of water sloshing against the hull.

Chapter Twenty

INDA clambered from *Vixen*'s heaving deck to *Death*'s rail. His right hand tingled, his grip slid on the slimy main chains. He used his left hand to propel him the rest of the way, cursing under his breath.

A cold wind blew out of the northwest. Some of those who'd survived the bad typhoon cast quick looks skyward. Inda was soaked through to the skin, cold, hungry, and exasperated from the covert squabbling between the independents and the Khanerenth navy. "Why'd you signal? Venn on their way, now?" he asked in Marlovan, barely audible over the drum of rain on the deck. "We expected that."

Fox said from the cabin door, "You did not expect this."

Ten swift strides and they were inside the cabin. Inda wiped his sodden sleeve over his face, blinking away the rain, then looked down at the mirror chart as Fox whispered, waved—

—And there, in the middle of the otherwise empty sea at The Fangs, was a single glow. Fox said, "That is, we always expected spies, but now we're looking at proof."

Inda tried to whistle, but his lips were too numb. So he cursed instead.

"At least one," Fox drawled.

"Right. This one is able to ting."

"Could be one of the fishers who sails around selling fresh garden supplies from either coast. He probably sails around with all those others bringing us fresh food, and collects reports from spies on our warships. How many fishers do we have supplying us?"

"Several hundred. More appearing every day."

They contemplated that, then Fox dropped onto the bench. "What do you want to do?"

"You don't think Deliyeth is purposefully hiding Venn spies? Look how close to Drael that dot is. Ymaran coast closest."

Fox lifted a shoulder. "Unlikely. She hates the Venn even more than she hates us, or she wouldn't be here."

Inda thumped his big toe lightly against the table leg. "It'll be impossible to find that ship or boat, since we don't have any reference." The little light sat there seemingly alone, east of The Fangs, but in truth it lay somewhere in the middle of Inda's alliance fleet. "Counting us as well as getting an earful of all orders and reports being passed up and down the lines."

Fox's smile was nasty. "So we will create new reports to pass on."

Inda gave a crack of laughter and went to beg Lorm for something hot to eat, still not aware that Lorm kept a corner of his galley just for Inda, who showed up at odd times day and night. There was always something hot for Inda when he actually remembered to take a meal.

As maneuvers improved, and abilities of captains and ships took shape in Inda's mind, he held discussions with Taz-Enja, Mehayan, and especially with Dhalshev, but as yet Fleet Master Chim had not visited him.

Bren's High Admiral Brasvac had himself rowed over to the *Death* to clarify some points—and to nose around, Inda suspected, from the way the man's eyes took in every aspect of the cabin. The Bren high admiral did not mention Chim.

But after a week or so of meetings aboard the high admiral's flagship, Inda became increasingly aware of the occasional hesitancies, the careful wording of the Bren officers. The way they'd check one another after someone said

something about leadership, command, and related subjects. They weren't unfriendly or even wary, like Deliyeth's
closest associates. They were just . . . secretive. He decided
it was time to tour Bren's ships with an eye to possible
improvements.

He did it systematically, pausing to exchange friendly
chatter with everyone. When at last he ran Chim down,
the irascible old Fleet Master awaited him on the biggest
brigantine, the one they always kept in the center of their
flotilla.

The weather had turned ugly, a threatening summer
storm damping the gray seas as the flotilla practiced maneuvers in an unstated but determined effort to get their
speed to match that of the Khanerenth navy, which was exerting itself to match the speed and versatility of the Fox
Banner Fleet.

Despite the heavy, splatting drops, and the low, uneven
crashes of thunder, Chim drew Inda out to the forecastle.

There, he pointed to a large, smiling second mate dressed
in the light brown and burnt orange of Bren's navy. "That
there's Prince Kavna, who insisted on being with us. Only
reason Princess Kliessin agreed is that she wants an eye she
can trust watching me as well as their cousin Brasvac."

"I thought the admiral looked familiar." Inda grinned.

"I didn't know you ever saw Prince Kavna."

"Not to talk to. But he was on his yacht the day I rowed
in to report to you and Mistress Perran, before we sailed
west. We went a stone's toss away from the yacht, so I could
see all the gild work. The rowers were proud of it, and proud
of him. Where's that yacht, is it here?"

"Oh, I'm sure Venn've got it. We didn't bring it. Thought
it would be a target. Listen, Inda, Brasvac and the captains
were forbidden by the princess to tell you who Kavna was.
But he's doing well. Serves a watch. Messes with the mates,
eats what they eat. Knows a sheet from a line, so don't think
he'd go buy a chart o' Sartor from a Venn."

Inda grunted a laugh. He hadn't heard that expression
since his Freeport Harbor days. On the surface it had meant
someone stupid enough to buy a detailed chart of one
shore on another continent, instead of getting it local—and
cheaper. It was the "cheaper" aspect that Tau had explained
once while they were sitting in the rigging, fletching arrows.

Only the rich were arrogant enough (and stupid enough) to wave off cost if they wanted something right away, instead of waiting like anyone else.

"If he's doing well, then why is he pretending to be a second mate?" Inda asked, hating what he knew would be the answer. Better to get it said. He hated all the sidled looks and sneaking around worse.

They used Sartoran, which Chim spoke better than Dock Talk. A gust of bitter wind made Inda's right shoulder feel as if someone was sticking cold icicles into it; Chim's hip felt the same, but they both were too experienced with shipboard lack of privacy, and so they moved all the way to the bow as tiny missiles of hail bombarded them.

They hunched their backs to the wind, pulling their collars up to protect their ears from the hail. Chim said, "You oughta know how it is with lords and princes. I hear it's the same everywhere. If they got power, they get cosseted. If they don't, they get scragged. Seldom the fair start the ordinary hand gets. He said he doesn't have real experience, so he didn't want to be a captain. Not and have everyone double-checking every order behind his back."

"And so you told me about him to protect him? Or scrag him? Or leave him alone?"

"He's always been on the side o' the sailors."

Inda knew that already, and he knew that Chim knew. So he'd asked the wrong question. Ah. "Nothing was official because ... they think I might take him hostage? Is what you're saying related to that message Princess Kliessin sent about me making some treaty or they'll shoot me on sight?"

"Mmm." Chim squinted out at the gray-green rollers stretching away to the steel-gray sky. A flicker had caught his eye. As he and Inda watched, three silver porpoises and three mers shot up out of the water, the silver-skinned mers clapping hail with their hands. For a moment the six were suspended against the gray of sea and sky, porpoise mouths grinning, mer mouths open in silent laughter. "Do they even have voices?" Chim asked.

"You're asking if they're human. Sometimes I wonder what being human means," Inda responded.

Six graceful arcs, six dives and they were gone. The waves chopped and foamed, hiding where they'd been.

Inda turned his head, still waiting for an answer.

"You Marlovans have a rep," Chim said slowly.

"Yes, or you wouldn't have sent Ryala Pim to get me, and I wouldn't be here talking to you. I'd be at home, getting ready to ride out with the boys to the banner game."

Chim turned his way, his old eyes acute. "That was me who sent Mistress Pim, and you might say my own rep rests on my decision. Oh, they know you're good. None better. But the fact is, some are uneasy, and I don't just mean old Bitterweed Deliyeth. They afear they might fight alongside you to get rid of the Venn, just to find that they've been replaced by another tyrant."

"Tyrant!" Inda snorted. "I don't want to—" He frowned. "Do you mean Evred-Harvaldar, our king? Evred is no Erkric."

"He's a distant king, and people want him to stay distant," Chim said.

Inda stared. "But we're here because your kings all along the strait, both sides, were never strong enough to keep out either the Venn or pirates. I'm here to do both, and ensure peaceful trade."

"Good. Peaceful trade is good." Chim thumped Inda on the shoulder. "But first we have to win."

> *Scout Frun to Oneli Stalna Durasnir: just sighted off headland at west end of Hanbria a flotilla of ships at extreme range. They look like Delfin Islander ovals—sharp prow, narrow stern, broad midships.*

Erkric stared down at the paper. *Delfs?* This far east? It was a direct flouting of the orders he'd had Rajnir issue to the islanders two years before: *No trade with Sartor.* Well, they'd pay for their temerity, but it would have to wait.

Erkric waved the paper gently in the hot, still air, and forced himself to relax. His stomach griped all the time, his blood rushed in his ears. So much treachery all around him! Proof over and over, that nobody could be trusted. All people were thralls, they just did not know it. All of humanity required an iron collar for its own good. So when he chose his thralls to carry out his will, he limited their access to knowledge, he assigned tasks according to ability, he used weakness to determine his thralls' reward.

He needed *time*. But when one did not have it, one was forced to number tasks in order of need. Twelve Towers and the vanishing wards could sink down the list: good as it would be to arrive home triumphant to a fortress he knew was utterly secure, it would have to wait on the victory.

A victory achieved after Durasnir's glorious death—and the rescue of the fleet by magic. These Delfs might make it unnecessary to have to plan that on top of all else . . . number your tasks . . .

He smiled. It was wonderful when human greed and ambition could serve him without his having to exert himself.

He methodically shredded the dispatch and flung it out the stern window to tumble in the foaming wake. Once again, proving that thoroughness always paid off, tedious as it was to deflect every military dispatch to his desk first.

When Halvir was smaller, one midsummer the bigger boys asked him to be the dead hero on a shield for a ballad enactment. It was strange to shut his eyes and pretend he was dead while others picked him up and posed his hands and feet and twitched his clothes into place.

It was like that when the Dag came in and whispered words that made Halvir tingle from magic, then said, "Eat. Drink." The only thing they left him able to do for himself was to use the Waste Spell. Otherwise, they moved him around, then put him down on the bed, or sometimes back in the chair.

And then came the whispering again, and that feeling like snow falling inside his head, covering everything. Even his thoughts.

But he submitted, because it was a test. He never moved, or made a noise, or even opened his eyes. He knew he was being tested, and that meant he could pretend it was a game, like the big boys played. Then everything was bearable. So he did a good job, just like when he was the hero on the shield, and Rigi Hafnir and the others gave him berry tarts with extra sweetened cream afterward.

The snow piled and piled until he fell into dreams again, falling and falling . . .

"Halvir."

This time when he woke up, he only panicked a little.

He lay flat on a bunk. He had a light blanket holding him down, not sashes. They had not tied him up again!

"Halvir, can you rise?"

Halvir sat up slowly. His head pounded, forcing him back down. When the pounding and nausea died away, he sat up more slowly, trying to sneak upright before the hammer inside his head noticed. It only tapped.

"I'm sitting up," Halvir whispered at last. "But I don't know where I am. I can't see. Where are you?"

"Other side of the room. I can't get up, not without difficulty."

"Who are you?"

"Rajnir."

The sun exploded behind Halvir's eyes. He almost yelled, but controlled himself, then whispered, "You can't be. You said we're prisoners. The king can't be a prisoner."

The voice made a noise that sounded kind of like a bleat, and the hairs prickled on the back of Halvir's neck. Was that a laugh or a cry? "Yet I am. Now, I need you to do something for me. I order it." The voice changed on the command word, and then came what almost sounded like a real laugh, but angry.

"Command me, O my king," Halvir said, just like in ballads. At least he knew what he was supposed to say!

"Feel your way to the trunk below and behind where you lie."

Halvir got to his hands and knees. He waited until the pounding his rising caused died away again. Then he got a sense of the roll of the ship. Somebody had taken away his shoes and socks. He slid his legs over and felt for the deck with his toes. He eased down until he crouched on the deck, which smelled of brine and old wood. The smell was comforting.

He felt his way. Bunk. Chair bolted down. Bulkhead. Little table. Oh, was this it? His fingers encountered an enormous trunk, metal at the corners, the surface deeply carved. He ran his fingers over it, finding runes, and a long, undulating dragon. Ships, a sun . . .

"Find it?"

Halvir jerked guiltily. "I think so, O my king." He scrabbled for the latch. The lid did not want to come up. He

braced himself against the side of the lid, and muscled it up.
"It's heavy."

"That's the one. Feel down inside. Should be in the front.
Wrapped in silk, and then velvet, are my weapons. There
is a long knife. It has a *drakan*-head hilt. Bring me that
knife."

Weapons? Halvir's eager fingers touched, felt, sorted,
wormed down until they encountered the right shape.

He took the knife in its wrappings—the steel was horribly sharp—to the deck, and he felt his way back along his
bunk. "Where are you, O my king?"

"This way. This way. This way." The slow words guided
him past a huge table, more trunks, another table, benches,
a big chair. Beyond that, another bunk. It smelled sharp,
like old sweat and stale food. Halvir wrinkled his nose, then
breathed through his mouth as he felt his way up. When
his spidering fingers encountered a warm shape in silk, he
snatched his hand back.

"There you are. Now, give me the knife."

The velvet came away, the silk slithered to the deck with
a soft chuff. Halvir felt with one hand until he encountered
a man's hand, warm, damp. The king's hand! He guided the
knife into it.

"You had better get back to your bunk, because when
they find me, I do not want you blamed."

"I don't understand, O my king."

The king did not answer, because he was determined to
act fast. He'd thought it all out. The single choice he had left
was death and through that, and only that, could he defeat
the enemy, which was not the Marlovans, nor Norsunder,
nor the greedy Houses. Erkric had become The Enemy, and
Rajnir would deny him the kingship.

But . . . his arms wouldn't hold him.

He grunted, his heart beating hard from the unaccus-
tomed effort and from the knowledge of what his mind
willed. The heart wanted to beat, but was helpless to save
itself. *I will . . .*

But at last will was denied him, or the physical act of will.
"Halvir," he gasped, falling back. "Halvir. Take the knife."

Halvir knelt on the deck. By the sounds the king was
struggling, like in wrestling, but nobody else was in the cabin

with them. Halvir reached with tentative fingers, fumbling in the disordered bedding until he found the knife lying loose in the king's fingers, as the king lay panting, his breath rasping in his throat.

"I tried to lift myself. So I can fall on it. But I can't hold myself up . . . Halvir. Take the knife."

Halvir's own heart began to thump. "I have it, o my king."

"Here." The king's fingers bumped his, then dropped, rose, swept his hand upward. Halvir jerked the knife back, afraid the sharpened edges would encounter the king and hurt him. "Here," the king said impatiently.

When Halvir cautiously extended the knife again, the king pushed the knife point across his body until it rested, a sharp prickle, just below his rib cage. Halvir was standing on his toes now, half leaning on the king's bunk.

"Jump up here, so you can use downward force. And make it fast, boy. I have it positioned. All you have to do is push it past my ribs, straight into my heart."

"No," Halvir cried, and fell back, the knife clattering to the deck.

Both froze, listening. The only sounds were the water along the hull, *whish-whish,* and the graunch of the mast at one end of the cabin, reaching down to the keelson several decks below.

The king said, "Halvir. I *have* to die. It's the only way to defeat Erkric. If he does not have a body to control as puppet, he is exposed."

"No," Halvir squeaked.

"They won't blame you. Oh, Erkric will, but I am convinced your father knows. He has not looked me in the face since we came home from Halia. He knows, I tell you; he'll save you. And I think Ulaffa knows as well, though I cannot be sure they aren't all in on it. But your father . . . I trust him to do what's right. He always did what was right. Even when I didn't. He would tell you now to help me do my duty and defeat Erkric."

"No," Halvir whispered.

"I command you, boy."

Halvir rose, then fell back, tears burning his eyes. His chest heaved, his head throbbed sickeningly. "I can't."

"I tell you, no blame will attach to you once your father finds out."

"I . . . can't. Do that."

Rajnir cursed him until Halvir's squeaking, half-suppressed sobs forced him to get control.

Halvir also fought to get control. Should he do what the king said? Oh, but push a knife into him? *The king?* The idea filled him with such terror and wretchedness his chest couldn't contain the pain, and he buried his face in the side of the bunk, sobbing desolately.

When he had to stop in order to breathe, he realized the bunk shook, and he heard the king making odd, creaky breathing noises.

"What a king," Rajnir breathed at last, his voice tremulous, his consonants thick, and Halvir gulped, aching with desolation. "What a king! I haven't even power over one obstinate boy. Halvir. Why do you not obey? Do you not realize I could have you flying the blood eagle on Sinnaborc for flouting my will?"

Rajnir considered the absurdity of his words, and uttered another creak, far too strangled a noise, and too bitter, to be laughter.

"I can't," Halvir squeaked.

"Why not?"

Water splashed the hull, wood creaked, before Halvir said in a whisper, "My mother will hate me."

"Explain that."

Halvir thought he *had* explained. He groped for words just as he'd groped with his fingers in the dark cabin, his mind bumping from horror to disbelief and sadness and fear, and anger, too.

But the king was waiting. "My mother says never harm an unarmed person. My mother says you take a knife to an enemy. And he has to have a weapon. She says war has rules, and the first one is that one. She says, Drenskar is not just the glory of winning battle, it is in keeping our oaths. To you."

"But if I command you—"

"Not to kill you. I'm supposed to protect you." The young voice quavered, but the tone was steady.

Rajnir forced his breathing to slow. He had no strength, and little will. *I am en-thralled.*

Erkric had reduced him to a thrall even lower than his own thralls, who at least could choose to move. All choice had been taken from him except for this one thing. He must die, for the good of a kingdom he had never ruled in actuality, not for so long as a heartbeat. How ironic, that his single true order would be his own death?

"Halvir. If I die, you can get out. The kingdom will be free."

"I think you should escape," Halvir said. After all, wasn't that what the big boys always said in the games? If the enemy gets you, your duty is to escape.

"I've tried. I can't even move anymore. The flesh hangs from my bones. It's been too long since they permitted me to stand. It's why I can't get myself positioned to fall on my own knife."

Halvir's insides pinched at the roughness in the king's voice, hinting at emotions bigger and darker than this stuffy, smelly dark cabin. But Halvir knew what to do. "*I* can move," he said. Wasn't that his part in the games? "I will find a way for us to escape."

Joy hollowed Rajnir's heart, just for a moment.

"You can't."

"Sure I can. I can move. When it's dark. I'm good at hide-and-find!"

Rajnir let himself feel again the fierce triumph he'd experienced when he was able to put together Valda's spells from the inside one layer at a time. Fierce, and bitter. If the boy could find a way to the deck, then Rajnir could get himself over the rail—and drown.

He just would not tell Halvir that.

He said, "I can take the spells off us. But it requires a long time. I cannot measure the time, because I am doing the magic from within. And as I've only learned it relatively recently, I have not been able to move to explore, so I don't know what magic is warding the cabin."

"If they don't tie us up again, I can check," Halvir said.

"They seem to have laid aside the bindings as too much trouble, since we have never moved. We must take care to sustain that belief."

"We can do that." Halvir spoke with the confidence of ten years.

"Your brother was like you."

"Vatta?" Halvir said the name cautiously.

"Yes."

"Tell me about him? Mama and Papa never do. They grieve for him, though it's been a long time. Grandmamma told me so."

Rajnir felt his way mentally to a new conviction: he must gather some measure of strength to try to protect the boy. His kingdom had dwindled to one human being outside himself. Maybe he could keep the vows Erkric put in his mouth.

Or he could die trying. *Thrall.*

I will not let myself be en-thralled. "Let me tell you about Vatta. He was the best of us, though he wasn't a Breseng boy." Rajnir lifted his arms. His breath shortened, his belly jiggled, his muscles trembled. His arms dropped, but then he made another attempt. *Nine-and-ninety times. Each day. You just have to make it to the ship's rail.* "He wasn't a Breseng boy, being our age . . . though he was our age . . . Dyalf Balandir was the worst of us. That is, he was the hand-somest, everyone said that, but he was slow at lessons, and mean . . . He thought he'd be picked for king, see." Breathe, breathe, breathe. "The Balandirs all thought they were the next house for kingship . . . They acted as if they already had it. But Vatta . . . he was smart. I studied long at nights, just to try to keep up, and I pretended that I'd look at a book and remember it, like he did . . ."

Chapter Twenty-one

LAUGHTER gusted from the open scuttles of *Co-codu*'s wardroom. Back in the bad old days of Gaffer Walic, this wardroom had been made large enough for the captain to fit his entire crew inside when he wanted to demonstrate his power on some hapless crewmate. The blood-soaked deck had been planed and stained by Inda when he first took it from the pirates. That never quite removed the discolorations, so Inda had put down some of the fine rugs from Bermund to hide them, later replaced by marquetry when Dasta became captain. Mutt added to this spacious, pleasant atmosphere his youth and popularity, drawing the more dashing captains from the independents—Khanerenth, and Sarendan—to meet here most often when they were not on maneuvers.

Everon's and Ymar's captains were forbidden to mix with raffish privateers (may as well call them pirates given leave by rapacious kings, Deliyeth insisted) and the Chwahir were forbidden to mix with anyone at all. The older captains, especially those sticklers for the strict decorum of rank, clumped together aboard Admiral Mehayan's brigantine.

Tau had wholly failed at the task Inda had asked of him:

to try to win over Deliyeth. On their first meeting, he'd seen in her dismissive head-to-toe scan and stiffened posture, the way her chin twitched back in mute affront, that his looks, clothing, even his smile marked him as untrustworthy. And the struggling conversation afterward, during which she became steadily more truculent, affirmed it.

So he'd made himself useful in other ways, one of which was volunteering to help Mutt's cook when all these gigs began rowing or sailing over to *Cocodu*. This gathering soon became a regular occurrence in the evenings after maneuvers, as the alliance stood off and on just east of The Fangs in what soon became known as "polishing the teeth." (The boring sameness of tack and tack again was deemed excellent practice for the younger members of the various crews, who came to thoroughly loathe the night watches.)

Cocodu's new cook, Nilat, had been trained by Lorm, which was another draw. The Khanerenth and Sarendan captains, well stocked by regular provision ships sailing up and down the coast to and from home, often brought food and drink as donations. Nilat turned them into delicacies.

As Tau helped, he listened. People talked about the alliance and how they perceived its divisions. No one questioned the leadership of Fox and Inda, not even Deliyeth. The two commanders were like sun and moon, as one stayed on *Death*'s deck, spyglass to hand, rotations of signal flag youths on duty as he directed ship maneuvers. Fox sailed around overseeing repel-boarder defenses and tactical ploys. The big Khanerenth brigantines served as the enemy, as everyone agreed they were most like the Venn in size. They thoroughly enjoyed attacking other ships; the allies liked repelling them as much as they hated trying to repel Fox's own crews, who were far tougher.

Fox also conducted the hand-to-hand training. He was not any more popular than his hand-picked boarder crews, but after several not-quite-friendly challenges the word spread faster than fire that he was the best fighter on any ship, and so the smartest shut up, listened, learned. The rest complained but did what they were told. When the gossip touched on Fox, Tau was amused by the drop in tone, the attitude reserved for the ally who could thrash you without effort. You only scorned the ally you considered under your protection.

As the days slipped past, Tau gauged the spread of the lies that Inda had told Tau in private to expect, meant to be passed to the Venn via the unidentified spies. The Chwahir were leaving; Elgar the Fox was now a prince of Khaner-enth; the Chwahir were staying, first line in the defense; Finna of Fire Island, the renegade Venn pirate, was alive and allying with the Fox Banner Fleet; the Chwahir army was secretly on the march across Drael to attack the Venn homeland while its entire navy was busy at The Fangs.

Then came the breezy afternoon several fishers were spotted by the alliance patrols at the western perimeter. They were stopped, questioned, escorted along the coast of Chwahirsland to the easternmost point, and told to keep going south. They insisted that the Venn were out in a mas-sive line stretching from the north coast of the Sartoran continent to the south coast of Drael. They were sweeping everything before them, taking any ship they caught.

Fox and Inda already knew from Signi's chart that the massive line was fact. Now they could release the news and attribute it to the fishers.

Tau watched the effect ripple through the alliance over the next few days. *The Venn are a month away.* Drills tight-ened, ships no longer peeled off if they thought the weather hid them or it was past dark. The determination that Inda had met on his arrival was back.

Late one afternoon, Inda called off general maneuvers due to a series of lightning-punctuated black squalls.

Jeje signaled to the smaller vessels. They would carry right on with their own drills. Their tactics required line of sight, so the bad weather was a perfect test.

Since Tau's station would not be on *Vixen* in the final battle (Inda wanted Tau on one of the capital ships, in case there was negotiation to be handled), she dropped Tau at *Cocodu.* From the number of gigs bumping in its wake, it was clear that the storms were an excuse for merrymaking.

Tau climbed up behind a work party of mids busy taking laundry down. "Oh *won't* they nag if it's damp or stiff," one boy groused, so indignant his honking teen voice cracked. "Tougher they are, the more finicky. You think Angel Face is bad, you haven't heard Fox!"

The complainer couldn't see the violent gestures his wide-eyed mates made to hush him up, as his load was piled to his tipped-back chin. "You'd think a black shirt, you just throw it anywhere, dries in the sun, put it on, but ohhhhh no! Got to be just so, he's worse than a guild-master. Worse than a baron—"

Vividly remembering his own mid days, and Norsh's heavy hand with a rope's end, Tau said kindly, "Here, let me show you some tricks I learned back in my laundry duty days. Makes it so much easier . . ."

Caught flat, the boy was morally obliged to listen, so for the third time, Tau explained snapping, airing, and shaping clothes before they were quite dry, and the best way to hot-press, ending with a hint about fresh herbs in the trunk. Then he took mercy on the mids, left them to their press below, and climbed up to the galley.

The harassed cook welcomed him with relief. "Take these in?" Nilat wiped her brow. "They're eating like a pack of wolves in the wardroom."

Holding the tray of freshly-baked shrimp biscuits, Tau eased past the lashed-down barrels in the companionway, and paused when he heard Fox's drawl.

". . . when I was on board with Thog daughter of Pirog. Discipline is tight. She gives a command—no more than a few words—and everything's carried out without talk. No yelling. Threats. No negotiation and backchat, like our indies and you Khanerenth bravos."

Laughter and jibes followed, the sharp, hard, too-loud laughter that had little to do with hilarity, and everything to do with tension.

"Captain through fear! That's the way," an independent roared.

Then Mutt said, "Oh, Thog isn't so bad. Just a little strange."

"Not so bad!" the independent shouted, with an eye to his audience. "Not so bad! Why, she only awards fifty lashes instead of five hundred if you forget to salute!"

"I've heard that about those Chwahir," declared a young Sarendan captain dressed in purple with antique lace. She rolled her eyes. "Flogging's their idea of deck-rec."

"I don't believe that," Gillor said. "Not about Thog. I shared a cabin with her for a year. She never once talked about floggings."

Tau carried the food into the crowded wardroom, its

heavy, humid air thick with the scents of ale, wine, food, and too many people.

"Believe it." Taz-Enja was older, but he enjoyed the younger set. Now, however, his tone was sober. "Every village in Chwahirsland has a whipping post. Floggings seem to be the main entertainment. Either that or flayings."

"That's what they do to pirates."

"And it's the sentence for treason." Taz-Enja raised his glass, drank off the last of the cold spice punch, and plunked the glass onto the tray that Tau carried around to collect the dirty dishes. "They've got books full of laws under the heading of 'treason.' I can't tell you how many runaways from Chwahirsland end up on our shores. Better a life as a beggar or work slub, no family or connections, then flayed at the post."

When the expressions of disgust died down, peg-legged Swift protested, "They say that about the Marlovans, too. But I've met a few of 'em since The Narrows opened up. Told me it's all exaggeration. Only floggings you get are in the army, and that's just a touch-up, what we in Toar call My Lord's Decorum, to remind you of duty. That was our way in the old days, before the takeover at home."

Fox drawled, "For Iasca Leror, the truly entertaining floggings are mostly confined to the upper ranks."

"Upper ranks?" Gillor asked, then turned her head and smiled. "Oh, thanks, Tau. Here's my cup. I'm done."

Fox lifted a shoulder. "Bigger responsibility, bigger sticks. Er, stakes." He mimed snapping a stick over someone's back.

Amid the guffaws Gillor yelped, "Why, if I lived *there* and they tried to promote *me*, I'd skip to the hills!"

After the laughter, Fox said, "They only do it for cowardice, treason, or not obeying orders. Do not imagine I approve of their government. Far from it. But if you make yourself familiar with our history, you'll find that flogging to death the commander who does not obey orders is how the recent kings forced hierarchy and a semblance of order onto notoriously independent clans."

Fox drawled when he was angry, or with intent. Tau lifted his tray. Their gazes met over the beaten silver.

Tau kept turning, and walked out to dunk the dirty dishes in the magic bucket and hang the cups on the hooks to dry. The plates got stacked on the rack. He performed these tasks mechanically; when he left again, he was not surprised to find Fox waiting in the lee with the *Death's* gig.

Tau sighed as he leaped over the rail and dropped into the gig. He settled to the tiller as Fox stepped the mast and raised the sail.

The breeze was hot and fitful, the low, uniform ceiling of cotton-puff clouds like a lid on the humid heat. Thunder was on the way again.

Tau's head ached a little; he'd been avoiding Fox's hints, but he could not deny the persistent sense of dread. So it was time to address the matter. "And then what?"

Fox did not ask what Tau was talking about, which was in itself an answer. He sat against the high rail, rope in hand, as the gig heeled hard. His profile was grim. "You really think Inda is going to win?" he asked at last.

Tau braced, the tiller shuddering faintly. The wind had risen to wet gusts, churning up the water. Clouds fast obscured the emerging stars. "I think people so desperately want to believe Inda will lead us to success that they'll strive to make it happen. I've gone from ship to ship, I've watched him with them. I think his secret plan—which is madness—makes him feel he has an edge. He sounds convinced, and if he's convinced, they're convinced. *He's never lost a battle.* That's what they say to one another. I've tried to count up how many versions I've heard. Had to stop because of how word order works in different tongues." Tau lifted his hand in the Marlovan manner, signifying, *it could be.* Then dropped it. "Say he wins. And then what?"

Fox hauled the sail taut, sending them bumping over the cresting waves. "You tell me."

"If he carries out Evred's orders to take the strait and enforce peace and order, will your fleet follow him? They like their independence, it seems to me."

Fox snorted. "If Inda wins, they'll do anything for him. Even the new ones."

Tau regripped the vibrating tiller as the surging sea sucked at it, and raised his voice. "What about you? Going to follow Inda to carry forth Marlovan glory?"

Fox spat over the side.

Tau waited. He'd guessed about his connection to the

Deis when in Bren, after hearing gossip about the Sartoran branch of the family. But the connection to the Montredavan-Ans had taken him by surprise.

He'd sensed Fox had figured pretty much from the beginning who Tau was, having known more of the old story. That would explain a good deal of his instant antipathy, besides his teenage jealousy of Tau's influence with Inda: he and Fox were both in some wise outcasts, but Tau's was of a sort easier to bear than the deliberate cruelty of the treaty forced on Fox's family. Nobody had exiled the Deis—far from it. Fox surely had to be hearing the "Lord Taumad Dei" foolery that the diplomats were slinging around in order to bolster their own prestige, as it established his. Tau had not expected the slightest change in Fox's attitude when they met again, but in subtle ways something fundamental *had* changed with Fox. Tau knew better than to assume it had anything whatsoever to do with him. But it was there, or they never would have been actually conversing for the first time.

So he waited.

They neared the *Death,* which was surging on the rolling sea, curses rising from the painting party suspended over the side. They'd been in the process of repainting the weatherworn black halfway down the larboard side, working fast as the weather began to change. But not fast enough. As rain splotched the wet paint, they hoisted themselves to the deck and helped the sail crew double-reef the topsail.

Fox peered at the swinging lanterns, the sails, and then turned back to Tau, who was barely visible in the rapidly closing dark. Fox loosened the sail, so the way came instantly off the boat, and they sat there on the rising sea, plunging and tossing.

Fox stepped aft and crouched down within an arm's length of Tau, ignoring the packets of spray washing over the rail. "If he loses, then we're done with the question. But if he wins ... he's still under orders. If Inda doesn't carry out those orders, do you think he'll do the smart thing, like Dhalshev did, and avoid the legal grief?"

"Legal grief"—a horrific understatement, if Fox had told the truth to the merrymakers on *Cocodu.* Tau knew it was true: it took no more than a dozen heartbeats to look back over his memories of his time as a personal Runner and all the wry references to what happened if a Marlovan did not obey orders.

Fox moved away to tighten the sail; the conversation was over.

A huge wave crashed over the gunwale as Tau steered them under the *Death*'s lee. The boom crew was at hand, ready to pull up the gig.

Fox went to the cabin to change, and Tau, soaked to the skin, climbed to the masthead to watch the storm and think. The air was warm, and he did not mind the wind and water; in a sense they kept him anchored to reality as he considered Fox's words, which he knew were not a gift. Or a confidence. They were a responsibility—more like a burden. Fox had figured out Inda's orders, but for whatever reason had decided he could do nothing about them.

Tau was still at the masthead when the storm blew past, leaving the rigging to drip unmusically as stars glittered overhead. He was still there at the midnight watch change, as a new young mate tramped assiduously around the deck, clapping his arms to his sides and singing tunelessly.

He was still there when the sun rose and the new watch emerged from below, relaxed and sleep-heavy as they began, one by one, dousing the deck lanterns.

He went below to find an unused hammock, and get some sleep. He had a plan. If "Lord Taumad Dei" actually had any prestige, it was time to use that, and his skills, to fashion a peace treaty. If he got all the coastal governments to agree, that would remove the necessity for Evred's orders. Inda is released, Evred gets his order and trade—everybody wins.

Right?

Chapter Twenty-two

W HILE Fox and Tau took the boat from *Cocodu* to *Death,* Inda stood in Thog's austere cabin. Inda had just called off the drill, but not because of the coming storm in spite of what everyone thought.

For a moment they faced one another, Thog braced, and Inda regarded her stiff, slight figure, her intense black gaze. Just so had she regarded him the last time they had faced each other alone, after she had set fire to a ship full of pirates in order to burn them alive.

All right, easy things first, Inda thought. "Thog, you're not going to be grabbing any of our crew, are you? Pilvig— usually so steady—won't take a day watch, and we've got others who are afraid you'll send a party over at night to snatch 'em off the decks and drag 'em back to Chwahirsland to be put to death for running."

He hadn't expected a smile. Thog never smiled. But he had expected reasonable assurance.

He did not get it. "Actually, I am under orders to retrieve our people."

"And beat them to death? What use is that?"

"Warning to our own, mostly, but as it happens, we would not have to do that. A flogging, certainly. Laws must be seen to be obeyed and consequences dealt out impartially. But nothing more than a week's stiff back and then they have a place. We need trained people, in truth."

"How do I protect my crew from being taken against their will?"

Thog studied Inda from her dense black eyes, then said slowly, "If we do not see a Chwahir we have no reason to act."

Pilvig and the others will have to wear kerchiefs, Inda thought. *Dress like Brens or Ymarans. Don't let Thog see Chwahir.* He could see the effort Thog made, and he knew he would not get that much from her peers. "Thog, I don't understand your customs, and I need to. Or it's no use. This alliance isn't going to work unless you can be straight with me."

He'd thought her pale and tense, but her face blanched to the color of paper. "I just conceded. Though we need the people back. And I obey your orders," she said.

"Sure." Inda kicked his bare toes against the back of a bench bolted to the deck. "You do. I know that. And I know you can't tell me where the rest of your navy is. I'm glad to have you and the ships you did bring. But you aren't telling me why your ships are slow. Riding low. Why you have to hide the fact that you have the equivalent of three or four crews stuffed down there. Everyone's speculating—they're too experienced not to notice—and they assume bad faith, that you aren't hiding fighting crew from the Venn, but from *us.* Like you mean to take some ally ships. How can I counter that when I don't know your reasons?"

"I'm under orders—" Thog began.

"We're all under orders. And some of the rulers are so worried about their people obeying orders that they're here in various guises." A tangential thought flickered—*Evred's orders*—and Inda's chin came up. But he remembered that Evred had no stake whatever except peaceful trade. He certainly did not want more land.

So Inda shook his head impatiently, ignoring the pang, and when a stuttering crash of thunder had rumbled away, he said, "I can't figure out where to put you. Deliyeth hates my guts, and she only came aboard me once, but when I toured her ships she showed me everything from keelson to topmasts herself, in hopes of wringing extra speed and versatility out of 'em. So nobody thinks she's gonna swarm us from the hidden coast here with a new flotilla and send a hold full of fighters over the rails to attack us in the night. Nobody wants to sail near you, because they think you're going to attack 'em instead of the Venn."

"I would never do that to you," Thog was stung into exclaiming.

Inda sighed. "I know you've got your loyalties. We all do. All I'm saying is, for this mission, I need to know what you've got, what I can expect in battle. Nothing else."

Thog pressed her thin fingers to her face, then turned. "These ships. Are all we've got." Her whisper was so low Inda almost did not hear her.

"I understand that's your command," Inda said impatiently.

Thog took a step nearer. He could hear her breathing, see how her fingers trembled. "You don't understand, Inda. This *is* our navy. All of it."

The storm had shifted to cold north winds and clattering, roaring bombardments of hail when Inda clambered aboard the *Death,* soaked and shivering, his teeth chattering, his left fingers dug into his right shoulder.

Fox waved the wand that transferred heat magic over the bath and pointed silently to the alcove.

Inda left a trail of icy clothes that Fox picked up. When Fox poked his head into the bath alcove, Inda's blue lips had warmed to a plum color.

"You were with the Chwahir?" Fox restrained his impatience. "Did you tell Thog that they're even slower than they were at Jaro? What's Thog's problem?"

As he spoke, Fox felt the tap of the scroll-case against his leg. He slid his hand into his pocket, but just held the case: it could only be Barend, pestering them yet again for soundings.

Inda rubbed soap into his scalp, then ducked below the surface. When he splashed up again, he said, "What I'm about to say can't go beyond you."

Fox shut the cabin door, snapped the scuttles shut, then came back as Inda surged out of the bath, groping for his towel. His muffled voice emerged, "We have every fighting ship they've got."

Fox snapped his fingers. "We've been running the wrong dog all along, if she's telling the truth. If that's true, then why this years-long war with Khanerenth, which comes down to their refusal to recognize the Khanerenth change of government?"

Inda paused in the act of toweling his hair. "Because they dared not risk acknowledging a king after a violent revolution when they've been having the same problems."

"Civil war?"

"Bad one, Thog says. And I believe it, because everyone at home knows there's nothing worse than Marlovan fighting Marlovan."

Fox uttered a bitter laugh.

"We don't know how many of their own ships they've destroyed in fighting each other, but we don't need to. Thog's got her holds crammed with warriors, so if the Venn do their dismast and raid, they can spring out and fight to take over the Venn ships. That's their secret orders, to board and take wounded Venn ships. The older admirals, lacking ships, are all back on land, organizing the entire country for defense if the Venn do break us and invade."

"And they will invade," Fox said. "The best canvas and cordage in the world comes from the Chwahir."

"So I'll train the Chwahir to maneuver, and everyone can laugh at their slowness. But when the time comes, our fast ships go in front to harry, and the Chwahir are our dragoons, to dismount and fight hand-to-hand when the Venn try to take ships. We'll let the Chwahir take them."

"Done." Fox flicked the scroll-case open and moved toward the mirror chart. Barend's frequent demands for position sightings had become an irritation. What did he think they were doing, playing with the map all day?

Inda had expected the same, so he was not surprised by Fox's frown. But when Fox snapped the paper closer to his eyes, and then moved to the nearest and strongest light to reread it with his nose almost on the letters, Inda impatiently yanked on his dry clothes. "What? What?"

Fox held out the paper, his eyes wide and sea-green in the bright light. "Barend's here. At Boruin's old lair east o'

Danai. And he's got the entire Delfin Islands fleet with him, a hundred strong."

"Yip—" Inda clapped both hands over his mouth, his face reddening.

Fox laughed softly. "He wants to know if they should join up now, and start maneuvering with us."

"No. No! Don't you *see?* That's our feint! There are so many, we might even fool the Venn into thinking *we're* the feint. The Venn see all those Delfs in a line, led by the *Knife,* one of their own ships?"

"Shit," Fox exclaimed. "You're right."

"Unless our spy ventures south and spots 'em. I can't believe a hundred ships got down the coast without being noticed. I mean, I see why Barend wanted soundings so often—they must have sailed hull down off the coast . . . but . . ." Inda realized he was babbling, and sprang to the map.

Fox was already there. "The spy is in the same place, somewhere that way." He lifted his chin to the northwest. "I wonder if he's getting ready to break for their lines. Probably under cover of a storm."

"Give me paper." Inda flung himself onto the chair.

> *Barend: stay put. Practice combing, then breaking into threes. We are standing on and off just east of The Fangs, which will break their arrowhead for us. If we get any southing on that wind, you're going to be our surprise attack. Then when they shift, we'll hit them on the flank.*

"Did you do exactly as I said?" Dag Byarin asked Anchan. His eyes were ringed with dark flesh, his lips cracked.

She bit back a snappish reply. "Yes. I took the extra tokens as you said. I matched ship to token as directed." She couldn't help adding, "I got Valda's tokens on the entire fleet, in case you have forgotten."

Dag Byarin rubbed his eyes. "I know, Anchan. Forgive me. But you *must* not make an error with these tokens of mine." His voice was so bleak, he looked so exhausted, she forbore questioning what sort of magic lay over his tokens.

Besides, she should not be there—she risked discovery

every time she spoke. The spell of invisibility was hardly that. Even magic cannot make a thing exist and yet not exist. But it could draw the eye away, if you made the spell that blurred the air before you, and kept quiet.

Enough of it and her head throbbed. She had used it a great deal when passing from ship to ship in order to lodge one of Valda's magical tokens on each, in a place vigilant sailors would not notice. Inexorably the magic, and the need to keep alert at all times, had sapped her strength.

So she said, "Your tokens are now in place, and each as you desired. My next task?"

Byarin rubbed his eyes again, and her nerves chilled when she saw that he was weeping. But he visibly gathered himself, and said, "Go down to the hold, here in the flagship. Ulaffa has made a place. You will see the rune on the bulkhead, past which is a tiny alcove. Rest. Eat. Next task is the battle, and Valda wants you rested and ready."

"Who doesn't know about Prince Kavna being with us?" Tau asked Jeje as the *Vixen* raced toward the rendezvous under a high west wind. He was putting the finishing touches on a fine courtly outfit he'd borrowed in pieces from various people through the fleet.

"The Venn?" Jeje loved seeing him sitting there on the capstan, his needle flashing in the sunlight, the metal scarcely less bright than his gold-touched hair in the wind. She'd thought the borrowed tunic-vest and shirt and trousers looked fine, but Tau had tutted, taken them off, tweaked and cut here and there, resewing until the fabric draped just so, and now it all fitted as if he'd been born in the clothes.

Tau smiled as he threaded his needle. "The Venn were probably the first to know when he set sail."

He was applying to the umber-dyed linen tunic-vest a thin satin-stitch edging of color Jeje couldn't put a name to but reminded her of the eastern sky just before the sun rose. That was in place of the gold thread he'd considered garish.

"Inda's not supposed to know, except he does know," Jeje said. Despite her impatience with courtly custom and clothing, she deeply appreciated the twisty thinking. "And Kavna knows Inda knows."

"Kavna has wanted to meet Inda ever since you and I were living in Bren."

"I remember. Heh! Kavna knows that Inda knows but Inda pretends he doesn't know, I guess so that Deliyeth can think it's a secret, except I know her gig crew knows Inda's been there. We all sat under the flagship scuttles, passing some iced wine back and forth while the captains were up on deck brangling over who got the 'honor' of being first in the line against the Venn."

"Speaking of Deliyeth," Tau murmured, tying off his thread. "You *don't* know about their king. Got it?"

"I see nothing, hear nothing!" Jeje said in a deep, flat voice.

Deliyeth stared through her stern windows at the approaching Sarendan flotilla. "I don't believe it. We're forming a battle line with ships full of merrymakers?"

Tau plucked the slim, gold-chased spyglass from the pocket of his long, Colendi paneled silk overtunic of palest mauve. There in the lead was Taz-Enja on his splendid brigantine. He stood squarely on the captain's deck, a broad-brimmed hat shading his eyes. The wind fingered through the cluster of curled plumes in his hat. His clothes were bright in the sun—a silk shirt of violet, belted by a crimson sash with gold tassels. The widest-hemmed deck trousers Tau had ever seen rippled in the wind. Taz-Enja, whatever his age, had a good butt and fine upper legs, turning them to account in the tight upper portion of those absurd trousers, and the even more absurd high heeled, tassel-topped boots.

Tau heard a soft chuckle on his other side.

"What is the purpose, Lord Taumad?" asked Ymar's new king.

He was just Tau's age, a slim fellow beautifully turned out in sober-hued pearl gray cambric and linen, his brown hair worn short around his ears, which emphasized his round face and slightly protuberant eyes. Those eyes would be a mark of pride, Tau had learned during his stay at his mother's: the royal family of Sartor, the Landises, tended to come out with frog eyes according to generations of portraits, no matter who they mated with. The frog eyes also appeared when they married out, silent testament to the highest royal connections.

If we lose, the Venn will kill me anyway, he had said when first introduced to Tau, his smile rueful. *I may as well go in the free air and not smothered in some dungeon.*

"They're dressed like pirates." Captain Deliyeth's voice thinned with suppressed vehemence and disgust.

The king said softly, not lowering his glass, "Green and yellow brocade? Do pirates really wear such things?"

"Some do. They like to be noticed, they like sumptuous fabrics. And fashion . . . is adaptable," Tau said, hand open. He liked that Marlovan gesture. Everyone seemed to comprehend it without him having to commit himself to words that he might later wish unsaid.

The king's shoulders shook with half-suppressed laughter. "So is the pirate clothing a challenge to the Venn?" he asked at last.

Tau said, "In some wise. I suspect it's also a way to bolster their own courage."

"By acting like pirates?" Deliyeth asked, snapping her glass to, and pacing to the binnacle to put it down.

The king turned an enquiring look to Tau, who said, "Not like real pirates. Who tend to be just as sneaky, nasty, and untrustworthy as Captain Deliyeth believes them to be. Cowardly, sometimes: most of the pirates I have encountered only took action when they knew they could win. But once they were cornered, they fought savagely, because they knew there would be no mercy."

"It could be that some admire their freedom from the constraint of law," the king said. "So I've been told."

"Yes, and their freedom from responsibility. A man gains a sum in a city, he puts it into his work, his home. Maybe in a trip for his loved ones. A pirate spends it on pleasures."

"And crimson shirts. Is that what Elgar the Fox does?" the king asked with a glance at Deliyeth.

She watched the Sarendan ships tacking into place, then brailing and reefing to match speed with the rest. But she was too still; Tau knew she was listening. "He's not a pirate. He fights pirates. And for a while, spent money like a pirate—but on ships, not clothes. Then he went home to his responsibilities. He's married now, with a home and a new little son."

The king's mouth rounded in an unspoken "Oh."

"He's here because he felt responsible." *Because his king ordered—later, later.* "He was asked to keep an old promise he made. He's here to keep it."

The king still held the glass to his eye. "So tell me. *Why* is he keeping his promise? Does Elgar the Fox intend to take his turn on a throne?"

"What he wants," Tau said, practiced by now, "is everyone to agree on harmony in the strait. Trade guaranteed by all."

"I want that," the king said.

"Would you sign a treaty to that effect?" Tau asked as he tracked a low-flying sea bird.

"Would anyone else?" the king retorted mildly, watching the nearest ship put its helm down and turn in its length. "Beautiful maneuver. Pirates or not."

Late the following night, at the other end of the fleet, Inda, Fox, and Prince Kavna stood alone on the foredeck of the admiral's flagship.

"What are you trying to do?" Inda said. "I don't have enough ships to send you safely back of the line. Why are you here?"

"You can leave responsibility for my survival to me," Kavna stated. Even in the weak light his heavy face was grim. Determined. "As far as you are concerned, I am a second mate, so put this vessel where we can best function." And, at Inda's hesitation, he said in a low voice, "They invaded your land last time. This time it's mine they are invading. I have to be here."

"You are more liability than aid." Fox lounged behind them, indicating the firelit line with one lazy hand. "What do you think will happen to your shipmates if they go home without you?"

In the ruddy light Kavna's face was stubbornly desperate. "Nothing," he said. "Nothing. My sister made that clear when I left. I'm nothing but a spare anyway."

Kavna looked out to sea, then back. He jammed a hand in his pocket and brought out a scroll-case. "My father woke up enough to abdicate. My sister is now queen. She'll have chosen a consort within another year and probably have an heir within a short time after that. If she doesn't send me off to marry some princess for treaty purposes, I will stay at sea—which suits her just fine."

He lifted his gaze to the firelit faces before him. Their expressions were characteristic: Fox's grimly amused, Inda's troubled and oddly distant.

Kavna said, "First we all have to survive. And that means you put us where we can fight best."

Chapter Twenty-three

"... AND there's nothing more to address to Battlegroup tactics. Keep your eye on your flag, and if your sea dags begin performing magic on the orders of the Dag of the Venn, stay out of their way."

The captains murmured and shifted a little on the fine benches set below the carved bulkheads in the captains' wardroom aboard the *Cormorant*.

Dyalf Balandir tried to shut out Old Man Durasnir's voice, thinking: *Why do these doddering old fools hold on to command so long? They like power too much, that's why.*

"So my remarks are confined to that observation about the dags. Stay out of their way. We have been ordered to heed the fact that their purpose is no longer confined to navigation. If an ensign is put in charge of a dag's ting charts, do not demur."

In the old days, they put the old men in their boats, pushed them out to sea, and set fire to them. Why can't we do that now? If only Beigun wasn't so afraid to take what is ours by right, we could have burned old Seigmad a month ago. Look at him!

Balandir glared from his one good eye at Seigmad, half of whose face sagged. The old man looked terrible, sitting like a lump there on his bench, left arm dangling. *What a commander to inspire the younger men,* Balandir thought scornfully.

Durasnir noted who was paying attention and who not. He tightened his middle in order to add force to his voice, though it took more energy than he had to spare.

"Here is where we stand. According to the count Scout Walfga relayed yesterday, they have gained no more capital ships, which gives them just under two hundred to the two hundred forty we have with us now. We've got roughly equal numbers of smaller rated ships, or they have a few nines more. One Battlegroup has left Nelsaiam as reinforcement, though without their Drenga complement. Their Drenga remain in Nelsaiam, on the king's order . . ."

Balandir slowly turned his head. Unfortunately, he couldn't sneak looks any more, but a captain—once and future Battlegroup Chief, one time a Breseng youth and then an heir—should not *have* to sit here sneaking peeks like a scolded ensign.

". . . and your orders are clear. If any ship from Khanerenth, Sarendan, or Bren surrenders, you will treat them politely. You'll know them immediately, because they'll fling their weapons down or flap white flags or even kerchiefs at you. You will treat them with politeness, because they have complicated rules of honor which suffice to shift the conflict to theoretical, and the side with the best manners gains the moral high ground."

Several captains shifted, and a couple of the older captains chuckled. "It's true," someone muttered.

And you old men can dance around with those eastern cowards, Balandir thought.

Beigun sent Balandir a fast look and a smirk: oh yes. The younger men would go where assigned—madness not to— but they could burn through the idiots until they reached the Fox Banner Fleet. Everyone knew what they looked like: outright pirates. That's where the real glory promised to be.

". . . if the Chwahir try to offer surrender, be aware of a ruse. They fight to the finish, the Chwahir. Always. If one surrenders, he will be flayed if sent home."

Another stir and a grimace.

Balandir thought, *Slowbellies all. Ugly old tubs, but we need the wood. Ugly, and easy wins.*

"And finally, the leaders. We are told that the king has offered rank and land to anyone who brings the head of Elgar the Fox. Either of 'em," Durasnir corrected. "I've seen the one. He's quite short, scar-faced, brown hair. Broad through the chest. Fights like a berserker, as effective as the demons of ancient lore. You will have heard stories from Andahi Pass. Those do not exaggerate, for I was a witness. The other is tall, red-haired, dressed in black, and reports claim he is as formidable, or nearly. I suggest you shoot them if you can. Questions?"

"Does the king sail with you?" Seigmad asked the question most were thinking.

Durasnir looked down, then up. "I have not been told. I will assume unless instructed otherwise that he remains aboard the mage ship—"

"—for his own protection." Dag Erkric spoke from the door, his voice rusty with exhaustion, but his sunken eyes were quick and alert. "The banner will fly at the head mast of the flagship when you launch toward attack and victory, I am enjoined to inform you."

Durasnir said, "And my son?"

Erkric smiled. "At the king's side, the place of honor, O my Oneli Stalna."

"Phew. When is the last time you changed the king's linens, Uncle?"

"Less than a week!" said Dag Yatar to his nephew.

"It smells more like a year."

"Why? All he does is sleep."

"Must get hot in here during the day. Did you work an Air Funnel Spell? I notice the scuttles are closed."

"The Dag's requirements." Yatar dragged the ensorcelled bucket over, loathing this thrall duty. At least it was the king, though these past months had proved that royal flesh was exactly like any other flesh in the most mundane regards. "Why go to the fatigue of creating an air funnel when they won't notice? It's not as if they'll smother, not in a leaky ship."

The other thing that made this duty bearable were Erkric's spells that lifted the king and turned him. Yatar could not imagine how much magic had been expended, though he was grateful. It must be akin to the spells that enabled those winged folk up in the mountains above Sartor to fly.

"You done with the boy yet? You could help me get these robes over him. Even when he's like this—" He indicated the king motionless in the air. "—he's become so fat . . ."

"Why do we have to dress him in the whites?"

"The Dag said the Oneli might expect to see him out there under the banner when they form the line before the attack. Ulaffa says he thinks it will be tomorrow. Maybe even tonight."

A sigh. "Can't come too soon. I'll be glad to settle in Jaro again. Best quarters we ever had. Far nicer than home, though it doesn't do to say."

Yatar snorted. By the Dag's order they'd been committing far more crimes against their oaths than belittling cold, frozen, storm-ridden Twelve Towers with its scarce two months of near summer weather.

Yatar and his nephew—promoted to dag just last year by Erkric himself—finished, one dipping Rajnir's long yellow hair in the ensorcelled bucket and then combing it smooth, the other painstakingly making certain the glorious long white brocade tunic over the heavy pure white linen shirt were all wrinkle free and smooth.

The magic spell was reversed, which gently laid the king back onto the freshened bed. Then the Yatars layered another nine of the Mind-shroud Spells over boy and king, according to their orders from Erkric, who'd said, *We don't know how long the spells last. There can never be enough.* He was still harried by those unexpected, and unexplained, breaks, which at least had not been repeated.

The two dags left.

Rajnir had got much faster at removing the spells from the inside. In fact, he was probably the only mage (mage in a very limited sense, but he was one) who could perform magic mentally, without the aid of the mnemonics and gestures that enabled the human mind to "hold" magic then link what they thought of as spells. Few could manage that for little spells, but Rajnir had become adept at very complex, dangerous magic out of enforced necessity and sustained will.

He had learned to remove the spells from himself first. He'd made the mistake of wakening the boy first, to discover (or rediscover) just how thin was a boy's veneer of bravado. When the last shroud dissipated, the first sounds he heard were Halvir's sobs. He'd thought the king dead.

Rajnir brought himself out from the magic shroud, then Halvir. The boy yawned, and then came the rustling noises of his stretching. "Should be night watch now," he whispered. "Want me to check?"

"Please."

Another memory recovered, the elastic strength of boyhood. Halvir had a clear enemy, a secret, a companion to share the secret with, and a goal. His mood was sunny, he even laughed over the humiliation of being controlled by magic.

"I wiggled my toes and fingers a little, and they don't notice," Halvir whispered in triumph.

"Don't test them," Rajnir warned. "I did, and look what's happened to me."

He could hear Halvir's shrug and did not elaborate. As Halvir crawled to the door and felt for magic—and yet again did not find it—Rajnir reflected on that humiliation.

He did not, and would not, burden the boy with the horror of control of his own body being taken from him. At first commanded to eat meals meant for an active man, he'd slowly but inexorably become fat, for there were no more sessions with his Erama Krona training masters. There was no more sex, there was no more walking just to feel the sun and wind. When Erkric returned after months away and found out how fat the king had become, they'd starved him. There were days and days when all he was permitted to eat (ordered to eat, under control of the shroud) was a single orange. Or a single biscuit. A chicken wing.

His flesh still hung from his bones. But he could lift his arms, and if he bent his legs first, he could lift those, too. And he could turn over, though mustering that much effort turned the bed into a damp nest of sweat.

I made myself thrall to Erkric, until brought to my duty by a boy who still believes that a king is still a king.

So while Halvir fingered the door open just a crack, and then rolled the tiny piece of wood he'd scratched from the decking and molded to a round shape, Rajnir exercised grimly, lifting legs and arms over and over.

Halvir flicked his piece of wood through the crack in the door . . . and the Erama Krona did not start.

He'd learned when he was a small boy aboard the *Cormorant*, that if a single noise occurred where the prince was, the Erama Krona were alert. They moved with unnerving smoothness to cover one another and Prince Rajnir as they investigated. Even something as inconsequential as a mouse scuttling across the deck.

Halvir hadn't admitted that the boys had loosed mice a few times, just to see what happened. Halvir had been little then, but he remembered it. That had been the first secret the bigger boys had ever included him in on. It was a good memory, how they'd collapsed in writhing, red-faced heaps in their effort to keep from laughing out loud. That was until the Erama Krona somehow caught them. The beating the big boys got was fearful indeed. Halvir remembered that, too.

So when he'd first tried opening the door and found the expected Erama Krona outside—and then a lee lurch during a thunderstorm sent a piece of something tumbling about the outer cabin, and they hadn't reacted—it hadn't taken long to figure out that the dags were shrouding the Erama Krona. When he shared his observation with the king, Rajnir said, "The dags're taking risks. They must be overreached. They don't tie us up anymore, and they must be shrouding the Erama Krona so they don't have to explain their actions coming and going."

Halvir agreed, shivering with delight. He and the king had become conspirators, and because he was with the king, he was doing right.

Three . . . four . . . five . . . The Erama Krona guards did not even twitch.

So the boy crept between them, feeling his way along the perimeter of the cabin rather than making for the swinging bar of light from the hatch above.

As drips of water plopped down from the working of the rolling ship, he eased along a companionway, practiced after years of hide-and-seek games, and scouted out his next hidey-hole before he snaked from the one he was in.

He had yet to make it to the top deck. Too many people

around. From the way they all moved and talked, only the ones on the deck below had the shrouding spells, so he had to be extra careful.

But he'd learned things. He'd learned that they were soon to be in battle, and that the two dags would be on Battlegroup captains' decks to do magic. He'd learned that Dag Erkric would be back.

The ship rose steeply, causing Halvir to wedge himself between a barrel and a bulkhead. The plunge the other way almost threw him down the companionway.

The bell ringing hard for "all hands" sent Halvir scrambling below again. He eased back into the room, and then, reluctantly, climbed onto his bed. How he hated that bed! But the king had convinced him that it was safest to be in place, as they never had much warning when the Enemy were approaching.

"Made it almost to the galley, O my king," Halvir said.

Rajnir had tried to get the boy to drop protocol, but Halvir had been so uncomfortable at the idea of saying "Rajnir," it was clear that whatever remained of conventional response to rank was comforting.

It had nothing to do with Rajnir's worth. He knew that. All that time for thought had brought him to many disquieting truths, beginning with the conviction that the distancing of protocol—so necessary to make the king seem greater than human—was the opposite of friendship, or indeed, of any kind of real communication. He'd so missed the friendship he'd enjoyed as a boy before he was singled out by Erkric to be heir that he'd participated in the lethally false friendship of Count Wafri. Rajnir had plenty of time to review memories and to see where he had accepted Wafri's skill at the pretence of friendship, his combination of flattery and demand for intimacy, just the way he'd accepted Erkric's smooth explanations for all the disasters that had singled Rajnir out for kingship. He'd believed because he'd wanted those things to be true, not from conviction, but because life was easier that way. But when he wanted to act like a prince, and exert his authority . . . *I don't like that fellow Wafri,* Vatta had said. *He smiles too much.*

I want us all to be friends. They do things differently in Ymar. I want him to be one of us.

He hates us.

No he doesn't. You don't trust him because you don't like him. You don't like Ymarans.

That day when the Chwahir closed on their ship. The smell of the wind, the color of the light on Vatta's face. Wafri's as he grinned across the cabin. "I thought you boys swore to protect your prince?" he said, laughing softly.

Rajnir remembered Vatta paused—the way he looked from Wafri to Rajnir and back—then picked up his sword and was gone. He left before Rajnir could say, *The Erama Krona will do that.* Rajnir had wanted to impress Wafri with Vatta's loyalty, his prowess.

He wondered if Halvir looked like Vatta, but did not dare turn his head when the dags brought light in, and in the dark, he could not see and did not ask. He did not demand the trappings of friendship with Halvir—a king ordering companionship. Instead, he fumbled tentatively toward communication by sharing memories, by listening, debate even—he never insisted he was right because he was king. He shared jokes.

The truth Rajnir had to accept: he had never been the smartest or most able. He was only the most amiable and lazy.

Now he had to make amends, or he betrayed Vatta and everyone else who had died to make him king.

"Where were we?" Rajnir asked. He remembered very well what they'd been saying before the last interruption, the exact words. That was one thing he'd won from all that time imprisoned inside his head. He could remember a magic spell if he just heard it once. And he could recall every detail of his memories. He revisited them over and over.

But if he asked where they were, the boy could pick the subject of their discourse.

"You left off telling me about the time you and Sefni Loc and my brother loosed the spiders down the Balandir sleep-chamber air vent."

"Ah yes. First we had to catch the spiders . . ."

Chapter Twenty-four

INDA sailed in the *Death* up and down the forming line. Each flotilla worked hard to wear and tack on station, conscious of observant eyes on neighboring bows and taffrails. A summer storm rolled away to the northeast, leaving clear sky and a strong wind out of the southwest.

Just where Inda wanted it. Wasn't the advantage an east wind would give, but this time of year, there was no east wind. A southwest wind gave neither line the advantage. Only Barend's surprise would do that.

The captains of the alliance watched Inda grinning on his captain's deck as the *Death* slid goose-winged past them on this last inspection, the trysail's black sides shining with new paint, sails expertly handled. Inda passed close enough so he could yell encouragements to each captain.

"Remind your small ships to travel in packs of three, whatever they attack!"

"Stay in line!"

And, most often, "We can take 'em! Stay in formation and we can take 'em!"

His grin, his excitement, was more convincing than all the words. He *knew* something, they felt it. It was easy enough to translate that into: he knew he would win. He never lost a battle.

When he'd finished sailing down the line, the *Death* began to beat close-hauled back to the central position.

Inda found Fox laughing quietly in the cabin as he waved his hand over the mirror chart. "And there goes our spy, straight west in the storm." His finger moved toward the line of glowing dots nearing The Fangs. "If the wind just stays with that southing . . ." He brushed his fingers over the rocky coast of Danara, where Barend and his fleet of Delfin Islanders had been practicing maneuvers in one of the bays guarded by a squadron of Chwahir personally appointed by Thog.

Fox looked up. "Thog kept the secret or the Venn would be broken into two wings by now."

Inda was still relieved that he'd had his talk with Thog before the inevitable sighting of Barend's surprise off the Chwahir coast. "The Chwahir kept our secret and we kept theirs. Are we done?" A memory, the dinner aboard *Cocodu* for the Fox Banner Fleet captains, Gillor at one end looking grim, Tcholan and Khajruat Swift either too formal or too smirky at the other end. Later in the evening, just before Inda was going to leave, Gillor at the rail, her face invisible in the darkness, her voice low with regret, *I never should have married. I don't have it in me to stay true to one man. I told myself it was all right for me to stray. It was always quick, I always come back. But when I found him and Khajruat playing hammock dance—and I like to fight alongside her!—I wanted to kill them both, so I knew it was time to slip cable and run.* Inda tipped his head toward Tcholan's *Wind's Kiss*, with Gillor's *Rapier* abaft, exactly on station. "They'll be all right?"

"They're my tightest captains, them and Eflis, and they're used to working together." Fox made what was meant to be a lazy gesture, but his hands betrayed his tension. "They'll dissolve their marriage contract when we get back to Freedom. Go right back to business as usual." He sat back. "So . . . we are done."

They regarded one another, Fox tired from too many nights of wakefulness. He was momentarily distracted by Pilvig moving past the open door as she put her boarder-repel team through a rigorous drill in spite of the weather; her crimson trousers and long yellow kerchief were distractions in themselves, especially on a crew member who had always dressed to be unobtrusive.

Then he wiped a loose strand of his wet hair impatiently off his brow as he tried to recall the long chain of reasoning he'd put together while handling the tricky navigation himself as the *Death* threaded through the line.

He gave up trying to find a last, compelling bit of reasoning, and said, "Inda, I hate this plan."

Inda turned out his hands. "There's precedent for it, I figured that out. Signi mentioned some custom the Venn have. Hel—hal—"

"*Halmgac.* The duel on the far shore." Fox flipped up the back of his hand in the direction of the Venn. "I should be fighting such a thing. Not you. That arm of yours is . . ." He made a violent warding gesture. "Doesn't matter. That soul-sucker Erkric will be damned certain you won't ever get the chance to come at him with sword or knife, Inda."

"Surprise is still on my side," Inda said, thinking: *And if I lose, everyone's in the right place, you heading the fleet, Tau to make peace after.* But he knew better than to give Fox orders. Fox knew what Evred wanted. "Let Barend strike first, right?"

"I'll hold our line back until he says they're engaged." Fox brandished the scroll-case, speaking the obvious because of the tension in Inda's face, the near hopelessness of his plan. Of all their positions.

Inda rocked back and forth, shoulders tight. "If Durasnir thinks that the Delfs are the main line—since they have to know we're short, compared to them—If he gets them turned south, and then you hit—"

"Then in the confusion, you've got your best chance." Fox pointed toward the mirror chart, did the spell, and waved. The Venn advanced in their arrowhead, everyone beautifully on station. That would change to a line as soon as the enemy spotted Inda's allies hull down on the horizon. "Remember, they'll cluster tightest around the commander. That's been consistent. So that's where you will find Rajnir and the Dag. At least you've got Jeje navigating."

Inda snapped the chart into a roll and slid it into its covers. "If anybody can get me in and out, it's Jeje."

He tucked the chart into his waiting gear, then he made a slow tour around the deck, and once full dark had fallen, while Fox conducted an unnecessary drill aft, he got his bag and slipped over the forecastle rail to where the *Vixen* had slipped under *Death*'s lee.

Jeje waited for him to appear. She was silent, grim. She'd refused to say farewell to Tau, because it felt too final. Now she regretted her decision with a sick conviction that they would never see one another again.

Inda went straight below. Jeje could feel in the minute jerks and thumps of the deck under her bare feet Inda's movements as he set up the mirror chart where the old chart used to be.

On deck, Nugget stood poised at the jib, her silhouette stark against *Cocodu*'s enormous, faintly glowing mainsail as *Vixen* and *Death* drew apart. Her head gradually turned as *Cocodu* dwindled behind *Death*.

Jeje did not have to reach for her glass to know that Mutt was over there on the captain's deck trying to make out *Vixen*—and Nugget. *Too many farewells, or what should have been farewells. We didn't have that problem in the old days*, she thought, and then cursed as she swung the tiller.

The *Vixen* headed straight out to sea. When Inda could not find any running lights anywhere on the horizon, he came up on deck. He and Jeje squinted up at the stars, and Jeje brought her chin down in a short nod: there were enough to guide by, along with the distant rough line of the Chwahir coast far to the south. They began beating up into the wind.

"We'll be riding in on Barend's flank," Inda said. "Let Loos take the tiller. I want you to watch this chart. See how the dots move. You'd better get a sense of it, because you'll be guiding us when things get hot."

"Right," said Jeje. *Something to do. Then I won't be thinking of all the things I didn't do.* "Right." She poked Inda in the chest. "Your eyes are redder than a couple of berries. Go get some sleep."

"I'm not—" He was taken by a sudden, violent yawn, then grinned. "Well. Maybe we should all swap off, watch by watch."

"Great idea," Jeje said. "You first."

Inda shucked his clothes and crawled into her bunk,

kicking aside the quilt and pulling the sheet over him. The air was too warm for quilts. He was ordering in his mind the things to do during the midnight watch when he fell straight down into sleep.

And did not waken until light teased his eyelids, reddish sparkles from sun striking the waves outside the stern window.

Sun. He opened his eyes. Jeje crouched over the map almost in arm's reach. Her profile was absorbed—narrow jaw, dark eyes under heavy, expressive brows. Inda lay looking up at her. Strange, how Jeje had seemed unchanged since they were ship rats aboard the *Pim Ryala*, but he could see tiny shadows at the corners of her eyes, her mouth. Not yet lines, but they would be. What was she, almost thirty?

She'd ripped the sleeves off her old shirt, which was soft from years of washings. Jeje was the only person Inda knew who had less interest in clothing than he. Her brown arms were bare, the skin smooth, muscles sleek as a mountain cat's. A rush of emotion warmed him, partly erotic as he lay in this bunk with Jeje's scent on sheets and pillow. But far stronger was the hollowing of tenderness, intensified by his heartbeat—steady, just a little fast—in his ears. A fight was nigh.

Jeje looked up, her dark brows quirked.

"You were supposed to wake me," Inda said.

"You were snoring away so nice, it seemed a shame to yank you out of your dreams."

"Jeje, you need to be rested as much as I do."

"What are you going to do, kick me out of the battle?" she retorted. "I've been in more ship fights than you, Inda. I know when I need rest, which isn't now." She grinned and pointed. "Or you got something else in mind?"

Inda's face heated. "That's me in the morning."

Jeje chuckled. "I love the way men are made."

Inda was too embarrassed to say how much he liked the way women were made, so he busied himself disentangling from the bedding.

Jeje laughed again, more softly. She'd never had any attraction to Inda. He'd always been too young, and by the time he'd finally reached the age of awareness, he'd slid firmly into "brother" in her mind. But loyalty was strong, and so she said, "If you want to, what with the battle, well, here I am."

He blushed even more. "Naw."

"Then finish getting those clothes on and come look at this thing, there's something odd going on. The lights smear, kind of."

"Are we running out of magic?" Inda fastened the shank on his trousers and thrashed impatiently into his shirt, ignoring the smell of stale sweat as he bent his attention to the mirror chart.

A small spur of relief eased the vise gripping the back of his neck when he saw that the magic was as bright as ever. But when Jeje made the wave twice, there was an odd effect.

"Do it again."

A blurring of the dots radiated out in a complication of rings, a little like the intersecting of raindrops early on in a storm, when the smooth face of water was patterned by ringing ripples.

"They're tinging often," Inda said, as the raindrop pattern shifted into meaning. "Maybe ten times each turn of the glass. They must do that just before battle."

Jeje brought her chin down, a decisive gesture. "There's something else I'm seeing."

"What?"

She narrowed her eyes, chewed her lower lip, then said, "I'm not going to yap. Not yet. Because I'm not sure I'm right. But I'm going to keep watching. Why don't you go up on deck and do whatever you were going to do? Loos spotted the Delfs, by the by, just after dawn. They should even be hull up by now."

Inda grabbed the dipper from the ensorcelled bucket and took a drink, mostly so the water would clean the inside of his mouth. As he left the tiny cabin Viac Fisher said, "Inda. Eat this," and thrust a biscuit stuffed with greens and cheese into his hand.

Inda gulped down the food as he climbed up the hatch to the deck. He'd do some warm-ups soon as he scanned sea, sky, wind.

"Inda look at that!" Nugget held out her spyglass. " 'Bout four points off." She kicked up a foot just larboard of the direction of the bow and wiggled her toes.

She was at the mainsail, so Inda went forward, laughing at the ugly old moss-splotched, patched sail that Jeje had saved from the old days. Nets and barrels sat about on the deck—they'd taken on the guise of a worn old fisher.

Inda propped his bare foot on the rail and leaned his elbow on his knee to steady his hand. When the glass encountered Ramis' *Knife,* he gasped.

It was an extraordinarily beautiful ship—a three master rigged for square sail. Black sails, a pure black that seemed to swallow light, but Inda only glanced at them. Drawing his attention was the prow, seen before as the anonymous upward curve of Venn *drakans.* But now the ship wore its dragon-head prow. Even at this distance, the carving was fantastic, as if a dragon had flown out of ancient days and frozen there, horns extended at an aggressive angle from a lean open-jawed skull.

"Where'd he get that dragon head? I don't remember that," Inda said.

Loos sidled a look around—as if Venn spies had sneaked through the water and were listening in. "My granddam used to tell us our ancestors put the heads on before a big battle. Taking years to carve 'em, they didn't sail with 'em everyday, like. They don't even have the dragon heads anymore." He laughed, deep in his throat, almost a growl, then spat over the side. "That thing'll make 'em piss their pants."

Inda noticed a twinkling abaft the dragon-prow: someone waving something red. He put glass to eye. "Heh. There's Barend. Pull us under their lee."

In these light airs, with the *Vixen* fighting up into the wind, it would take a while, so Inda went below again, the dragon head clear in mind. *Why didn't you warn me about Wafri, Ramis?* he thought. Three most dangerous enemies, Ramis had told him once: Durasnir, Rajnir, and Erkric.

Because Wafri wasn't a danger until my stupid decision to go ashore myself.

So here he was, choosing to go after Erkric, Rajnir, *and* Durasnir, all by himself. Another stupid decision? Or had Ramis somehow known it would happen and sent his *drakan*-ship, complete to the thousand-year-old war prow?

How would he *know?*

Probably the same way Ramis could make a line between sky and sea and shove six ships through. It all seemed to come back to Norsunder, and Erkric's willingness to use Norsundrian magic. Inda felt itchy and restless thinking about it. Too many questions unresolved.

He dropped down onto the bunk, and the locket shifted under his shirt.

Evred. That reminded Inda of the series of bad dreams he'd had just before dawn, inchoate images of home, the Jarls shouting *Inda-Harskialdna Sigun* as blood dripped down the walls from a row of the heads of enemies Inda had cut down ... He jerked up again, his head pounding. He dug out pen and paper, used his wrist knife to cut a thin slip of the paper, then sat back, trying to find the right words.

He would rather have not thought about the aftermath of battle. He might not be there to see it. But if he was ... if he was ...

He sighed. Busy as he'd been, he never saw Captain Deliyeth's wary, suspicious face without remembering her accusation. Then there was the request for a treaty letter that Princess Kliessin of Bren was expecting. It sounded reasonable ... except Evred was right.

Inda remembered the harbors during his boyhood, the shrugs people gave to widespread corruption, the harsh consequences to the sudden change of kingship in Khanerenth, and he knew Evred was right about that.

Inda had seen Idayago during his winter visit, and Cama proudly pointed out how the place had improved since his arrival. People had waved at him, stopped to talk to him— not all the Idayagans hated the Marlovans. So Evred had been right there, too.

And finally, Evred had given him orders at Convocation. If all the Jarls felt it was right to extend Marlovan law down the strait, well, then, it had to be right.

So why did he have bad dreams? Oh, he knew why. He had only to think of Deliyeth, and her scorn for his pirate throne.

Pirate empire.

He reached for his paper and ink.

Evred: Battle soon. If I am here after, Everon and Ymar don't want us. They think I'm going to create an empire and crown myself Inda the First.

*   *   *

On the other side of the continent, the midnight watch was two turns of the glass away.

Evred felt the tap of the locket. He forced his hands to stay still, and his body to relax, as the guests at his banquet table chattered on. He tried to subdue his irritation, but he wondered when this banquet would end. It was far too hot to be sitting in the heavy wine fumes over the remains of a meal he had not wanted to eat.

Fareas-Iofre turned his way. "When did it begin?"

"Did what?" he was forced to ask, after a quick search of his mind for echoes of conversation. There were none—he'd been shutting them all out.

Fareas-Iofre's brows rose, but her expression was concerned, understanding. She extended her hand toward Tdor. "That knife-throwing contest between the best of your big boys and the best of the girls. I know we did not do that in my day. Though I must say, I enjoyed it very much."

Hadand laughed unsteadily, her face shiny with high color and the heat. "Tanrid and I started it."

Tdor saw in the flicker of Fareas' eyelids, the thinning of her lips, the dart to the heart of grief that never went away, and it was instinct to leap from there to *How will I bear it if my child dies young*? She closed her eyes, struggling against this new and terrible emotion, the fear of losing a child. *Get hold of yourself,* Tdor scolded inwardly. *Nothing has happened. My babe is safe.*

"I never really knew Tanrid," Hadand went on reminiscently. "Though that day was a good one."

"I remember hearing about that day." Fareas-Iofre smiled. "You wrote to me about it, and Tanrid told me when he got home. How proud he was of that display, and of Anderle-Harskialdna's singling him out for praise. Well, Anderle was the Sierandael then, before the war in the north. You didn't tell me you added that competition to the games."

"We had to." Hadand chuckled. "The girls would have mutinied else."

"And it's been good, because when we win . . ." Tdor laughed, giddy with relief to see Fareas' smile. *You do recover. She has Inda back again. She has grandchildren to love.* "When the girls win, the horsetails always get serious about their knife work the next year."

The girls sitting nearby drummed their hands on the table in triumph. The horsetails reacted with blushes and elbow-digs at sisters and future wives.

The hilarity was not unanimous, Hadand saw. Evred had that headache strain in his forehead, and she remembered him saying the day before that Inda would be in his ship battle any time.

"Well, let us sing the 'Hymn to the Beginning' over our last toast, and then everyone can get some rest." Hadand held up her wine goblet in both hands. "Tomorrow will likely be very hot. You should get as early a start as you can."

Evred found the patience to finish the song, and the toast, and then he walked around the table, saying individual farewells to fathers, boys, and girls. Then he slipped away, grateful to Hadand, who lingered after giving him only one glance—as always, they communicated without words.

The moment he was alone in the hallway, he read Inda's note. They don't want us? What had that to do with anything? Of course corrupt governments did not want anyone interfering with their corruption!

It has to be battle pressure, Evred thought and forced himself not to run to his rooms, which were comparatively cool, and were definitely quiet. As he walked, he composed his answer.

He wrote two drafts, and when he was satisfied, copied it all onto a tiny paper.

He was just folding it to send when a quiet, tentative knock sounded at the door. Tdor's knock. Since he'd waved off the duty Runner so he could be alone, Evred answered it, and as expected, found Tdor.

She said, "Is the sea battle starting?"

"It is imminent."

Tdor looked away, then back. "Will you do something for me?"

Evred said immediately, "Of course."

To his surprise, she held out a small square of blank paper. "Send that to him, please? When it's time. I know he'll write to you, when it begins."

"I will, if you wish. But do you not want to write a message on this paper?"

Tdor looked down. "I know it probably sounds stupid. But I kissed it. So did Hadand. Hastred and Jarend slobbered on it. That's why I didn't fold it. Still damp." She pointed. "I think—I want Inda to have it."

"I promise," Evred said. "Just before the battle starts."

She left. He carefully laid the paper on his desk, then sent his note.

At The Fangs, the *Vixen* began to round under the *Knife*'s lee. How beautiful the Venn *drakan* was! The patterns of leaves on the pale gold oak rails had sharpened into clarity when Inda felt the tap of the locket.

Inda gauged the distance between the two ships, then thumbed out the message. The handwriting was tiny but clear and painstaking.

> *Inda: Now is the time to demonstrate even-handed law that is not the whim of greedy, petty monarchs who won't bestir themselves to defend their own kingdoms. You might have to show force because that's what they have come to understand. But you will have proven yourself. They will welcome the peace that only you can bring.*

Chapter Twenty-five

HORNS blatted down the Oneli south flank.

Oneli Stalna Durasnir blinked against the sun as he peered through his glass toward the signal flags on the nearest raider sailing as sentinel. Enemy in sight.

He lowered his glass, his gaze falling on the Dag of all the Venn, who stood at the rail with his own glass.

Whatever's happening, he knows about it. Durasnir held his breath, determined to master the hot rage that demanded utterance.

An ensign dashed up to report, "Fleet coming from the south. Sentinel counts say nine nines, Delfin warships. Red flags at the foremast."

The rage flared into blinding fury. "Why did we not know about these before?" Durasnir addressed the ensign, whose face blanched.

The only sounds were the creak of masts, the rattle of blocks, the wash of the sea down the sides of the ship. The ensign was not at fault. Durasnir knew his scouts were not either; a fast glance Dag Erkric's way revealed patently false surprise on the old man's face. *He knew.* Durasnir turned his attention outward as he got control of his anger.

The airs were too light for the cut booms to gain much force: unless the wind picked up, this would be a bitter, bloody, yardarm-to-yardarm battle.

And Dag Erkric knew about this fleet of Delfs.

Durasnir swung around, goaded at last beyond endurance.

"May I remind you of the king's orders?" Dag Erkric asked, smooth and calm. "Shall I summon the dags to service?"

Durasnir jolted to a stop, knowing how very close he'd come to betrayal. It was not Rajnir's fault that he had no mind. And now was not the time to destroy what semblance of unity his people had.

He was aware of every pair of ears listening, every pair of eyes watching. They were shortly to go into battle. He must not dishearten or confuse his people; the accusations had to wait. Erkric wanted Durasnir to request the aid of the dags.

That would happen only when Durasnir was dead.

"I believe the Oneli are capable of handling this turn of events." Durasnir's tone tightened spines and shoulders all over the deck, but the Dag's smile deepened at the corners.

"Hull up—*ho!*" the lookout called, the last word wrung inadvertently.

Durasnir had his most trusted lookouts on duty, so this sidestep from the rigidity of proper response caused every eyeglass on the deck to swing out to sea.

And when Dag Erkric hissed, a long painful inward breath, almost a gasp, Durasnir's nerves chilled. He made out the shape of the foremost ship: the black-sailed *drakan Knife,* once before seen. Only then it had not worn a ten-century-old dragon-head, relic of a fabled king.

Erkric had not known about *that.*

"The Norsundrian must be in command." Erkric's voice was husky with terror. "We must turn aside—the battle is here!"

Durasnir said, "It's a feint."

"What?" Erkric gasped.

Durasnir paused again. This time the words he wished to utter were "Permit me to command," but he knew they would only sound petulant. And in the larger sense, Erkric *was* in command—of the Venn kingdom. Durasnir's power was strictly confined to the Oneli's conduct of the battle.

No one had even asked why the king was not among them as they engaged the enemy at last.

Durasnir said, "While I find it difficult to believe that we were incompetent enough not to notice the approach of this force, I find it impossible to believe that we would not have perceived a larger one. We know what lies to the east and how many. Despite the surprising appearance of the *Knife* leading these Delfs, this is a feint, intended to send us into confusion by causing us to change course, so that their main line—what we *know* to be their main line—can strike on the flank. They want us sailing at our weakest, nearly up into the wind."

He saw comprehension in the sailors. Erkric was impossible to read, save the vein beating in his temple revealing that he was as angry as Durasnir. Maybe angrier.

"We will be straitened now, but not unduly, for our discipline is the greater." Durasnir said it loud enough for the entire deck to hear. And then he gave the command for two Battlegroups to detach, with all their raiders and cutters, to deal with the newcomers: the main force would stay on course.

From the *Vixen,* hidden in the midst of the cluster of small boats and light schooners that had accumulated, Inda watched the Venn put helm down, rise tacks and sheets.

How beautifully they stayed in their own length! Despite the lazy summer airs, the warships were as quick as their cutters.

The entire fleet had staggered when they saw the *Knife.* Inda could almost feel the tremors through their command: the conviction that they had been tricked. *I can't believe Barend kept the Delfs completely unseen by the Venn,* he thought. *Either the Venn are incompetent or they've got their own command problems.* Didn't take much to guess which.

As the sun slanted westward, the cluster of curious small craft on the extreme edge of the Delfs slid nearer to the Venn, *Vixen* among them. The detachment was clearer now and it was not the entire Oneli, but just a few Battlegroups.

Well, Inda had not really expected to fool Durasnir so easily. He settled into *Vixen*'s bow, glass pressed to his eye, appreciating the beauty of ships sailing toward battle. He wondered if a charge across the plains looked as glorious as these graceful craft with studding sails extended like wings, as the arched prows plunged through the waters, sending white lace fans feathering down the sides. Inda's memories of his single land battle were vivid, but included nothing of beauty, only the stink of sweat, the grunts from men laboring to kill, struggling to survive—the blood-splattering chaos of hand-to-hand fighting between sky-high cliffs.

The blood and stink would come soon enough. The Venn and Delf ships closed and met, perfect order vanishing as they curved round one another, seeking the advantage to close, grapple, and board. From this distance it looked like a game, the ships and crew like dolls. You could not see blood at a distance, or hear cries of pain.

The sun hung just above the water on the western horizon, creating a trail of golden spangles. *Is that the image that lies behind the Venn Golden Path?* The darkening east began to glow with the false dawn of burning ships: several Delfs. No Venn.

Then the Venn horns blatted like a herd of attack beasts: in perfect line, red flags at the foremast, Fox's fleet had begun to engage the main force.

"All right, time for us to leave the fishers," Inda said.

Jeje rammed the tiller over, Loos shifted the mainsail. The *Vixen* nosed away from the relative safety of the watching fishers and headed straight for the Venn.

Aboard the *Cormorant,* all hands stood at battle stations. Erkric prowled the windward rail of the captain's deck, with Yatar and his nephew at either side. Erkric only waited for full dark, so he could transfer to the *Cliffdiver* and give the order for the dags to commence the magic attacks. He'd thought to wait for the height of battle, but he was already so confused that he knew he would not recognize the height, and Durasnir, watching the ting chart and receiving a constant stream of reports, was so detached Erkric could not call himself ignored. But Durasnir was making no effort whatsoever to translate the arcane military language into clarity.

Erkric watched the west, waiting for the stars to appear,

and brooded about the *Knife*. He'd tried several spells against it, each warded. Who was on that thing?

Erkric gave a fleeting thought to the Yaga Krona below; Ulaffa and Byarin were sufficient to hold the *Cormorant*. Dull and slow both, but obedient.

Though Erkric dismissed the Yaga Krona from his attention, they were very aware of him.

As soon as the horns blew for the attack, Ulaffa and Byarin locked the cabin door, left a trusted young dag outside to give warning, and Ulaffa placed a transfer token on the deck.

Moments later Valda appeared. Anchan crept out of hiding, practiced by now. Valda staggered from transfer-reaction, to be caught up by Byarin's powerful grip. He guided her to a chair.

"Never mind me. Go now, Byarin."

Anchan turned from one to the other. "Is there—may I help? I—"

At the sudden bleakness in Byarin's square, heavy face, she was taken aback. He opened a case, brought out a long knife with a dragon-head hilt, and then he took the token that Anchan had brought from Valda. And vanished in a faint glitter, sending a puff of air to ruffle overheated faces and damp hair.

Ulaffa said, "Not all of them?"

"All the ones who learned the Norsunder magic."

Anchan turned from one to the other. "What is it?"

Valda and Ulaffa ignored her. Valda said, "They cannot be permitted to live with that knowledge. It must die. Now. Before it is used again. You saw how the temptation is impossible to resist."

Everyone remembered what had happened to Nanni Balandir. Ulaffa bowed, hands together, fingertips down in grief mode.

Anchan thought, *He's going to kill the dags with that dagger. Those were the special tokens I laid down—identifying ships' dags who had been trained in the Norsunder magic.* Horror constricted her throat.

Valda turned to Anchan, looking old and sad. "Now, prepare to help me spell the wards in your tokens. It's time for you to bring up the ward against Dag Erkric's magics we've laid on my tokens."

Anchan dared a question. "You do not want to do that?"
It would seem the triumphant culmination of all their
work.

Valda's smile was rueful—pained. "I have a ship to find
and to ward as invisible, if I am right." She added in a low,
tired voice, "And if I am wrong, I want the blame to be only
mine."

In the middle deck of the *Cliffdiver,* Halvir said, as he had
a dozen times since the first horn, "Now?"

And Rajnir finally said, "Now."

He rolled to the edge of the bunk. He was still dressed in
his pure white silk and brocade garb, the kingly robes he'd
worn to the coronation he did not remember. But no one
had come for him: the people no longer expected him to
appear, and the Yatars were apparently too busy to come
and change him into more comfortable clothing.

The robes would be suitable to die in.

With an effort he sat, sustained the dizziness, and then
he and the boy made their way to the door. He motioned to
Halvir to check the Erama Krona with his wooden ball . . .

And they did not move or blink.

"This way to the deck," Halvir whispered. "We'll have
to go slow."

Rajnir almost laughed. "Slow indeed," he breathed.

Gradually the *Vixen* drew closer and closer to the Venn
ships.

"Douse our lights."

Jeje gave Loos the tiller; Inda took the mainsail.

The scuttles below snapped shut. As Viac quietly snuffed
the lanterns on deck, Loos guided by starlight.

Jeje returned, after having satisfied herself with a peek
at the mirror map in the light of a shaded candle. Loos took
the mainsail and Inda shifted position to scan. His fighting
shirt rippled in the breeze, which made the locket thump
against his chest. Locket!

He set aside his glass to pull out the small roll of paper
in his pocket, and the tiny steel quill that corked a little
inkbottle. He tore off a piece and wrote, *It's started.*

He crammed it into the locket, the ink still wet, and sent
it. Then he dove into the cabin and dug out his gear. He'd

just finished pulling his fighting shirt over his strapped-on weapons when the tap of the locket alerted him. He thumbed out Evred's message, which was largely blank. Surprised, he looked at the tiny writing at the bottom: *I promised Tdor I would send this. She, Hadand, your mother, and the babies pressed kisses for you on this paper.*

Inda tucked the paper back into the locket and finished his last task: strapping on his wrist guard. He flexed his hand. Already his wrist ached clear up into his shoulder, and he hadn't even lifted a weapon yet. He shook his head then ran up on deck.

There he found his tiny crew gripping their weapons, silent and braced to fight to the death. Not one of them, including Inda, expected to survive this plan: Nugget wept silently on the masthead. Until this moment she'd been exhilarated, anticipating triumph, because now she was with Inda. She was following orders. But as she stared up at the looming ship, she thought for the very first time, *We can't win against one of these.* And hard on that thought, *Inda knows it.*

Tears burned her eyes as she peered down at Inda on the deck, one hand digging hard into the muscles of his shoulder as he so often did. *He knows we can't win.* Grief made her chest hurt, and she held her breath so she wouldn't sob. Grief gave way to anger as she turned her eyes up to that ship. All right. So Inda wouldn't win. She clutched her knife and her belaying pin under her armpit. *But they won't get us easy.*

Jeje and the Fishers stood poised, ready to maneuver: they would have to be faster than the Venn to survive long enough to reach that flagship. What would happen then . . . the brothers whispered alternate plans, and Jeje gripped the tiller, sensing each minute change in water and wind.

The first *drakans* drew closer and closer . . . and no challenge. No horns. No one ran along the rails waving weapons, no one in the tops so much as looked down. Inda and his crew could see the Venn crouched there, longbows strung, arrows slack in fingers ready to tighten at a moment's notice, as a massive *drakan* drew ever nearer, then the prow arched overhead and . . . past, followed by the towering sails of the foremast, the mainsails, and the mizzen . . . until they gazed in blank amazement at the stern, with the ship's

name spelled in runes and a stylized seabird painted below
the name.

Inda did not want to say aloud the words they were all
thinking. It was as if speaking would burst the peculiar bubble of invisibility that seemed to surround them.

But as they passed between two more *drakans*, and
again between another pair, and the vigilant Venn did
not so much as look down, it gradually became clear that
somehow the *Vixen* really *had* become invisible.

There was no one to ask how. They had only to keep on,
sailing past rank on rank, close-hauled as only the *Vixen*
could sail, almost straight into the wind, Jeje brooding on
the astonishment in Inda's face. *He thought we'd be dead
by now.*

Past more and more until there was a space between
ships, too deliberate to be accident—open water between
the Oneli and a ring of raiders on guard, so the raiders had
clear sight and room to maneuver.

Inda swept his glass back and forth until he was sure. In
the very center of the raiders he made out the taller masts of
the command *drakans*. And central to those, a *drakan* slightly
bigger than the others with a stylized cormorant painted on
its stern. As the *Vixen* slanted toward that central formation,
Inda and his crew gazed silently at the ships' tops bristling
with archers and at the rails, cut booms at the ready.

The fiery rim of the sun sank behind them, leaving
a dense blue sky that brought Joret Dei's eyes to Inda's
mind, and from Joret his thoughts snapped to Tdor, and
Signi. High across that pure blue sky drifted downy wisps
of a startling pink.

Peace above and war below. Inda swept the glass around
the ocean, until he got dizzy; he looked more slowly, facing
the fact that Rajnir's navy was far more formidable than he
had anticipated. Rich sunset color, gold and ruddy rose and
deep blue, painted the two converging fleets with spectacular highlights.

"Loos. Where are your weapons?" Inda murmured without taking his eye from the glass.

"Right here. I'm sweatin' so bad, don't fit right. Figured
I'd wait until they're comin' right at us."

Inda checked his own wrist straps. Yep. Sweaty. But snug
anyway. They'd have to replace Loos' gear. "Viac?"

"Ready-o."

"Nugget?"

"Ready."

Inda didn't ask Jeje. He could hear her readiness in her breathing; she was thinking, *You expected to die, or wanted to die, Inda?* Then she shrugged irritably as the signal passed down the Venn to light up. That kind of question was for Tau.

Swift darts of golden color winked across the horizon and gathered into patterns of golden running lights, a heart-lifting sight that reminded Inda of Signi saying sadly once, *Why is it we cherish as beautiful so many deadly things?*

Behind them, the Delfs chewed into the *drakans*. Arrows arced back and forth, most of the high ones erupting in tongues of bright flame as each side tried to come at the others from the best angle for boarding and carrying. The light winds, intermittently strengthened by gusts from all directions—promising bad weather—rendered the pace of battle stately with deliberate cruelty. Over the water carried the groaning cracks of ships sliding alongside ships, the crashing topple of masts, and above all the shouts and cries of warriors swarming from ship to ship.

Inda leaned out, trying to see how the Delfs were doing to the southwest, when Jeje called, "Inda!"

A cold, wet gust of wind from the northeast ruffled their faces and belled the sail, sending the *Vixen* surging over the next wave.

Viac Fisher said, "See that?" He stood at the jib sail lines in trousers, boots, vest, two knife sheaths strapped to his bare arms, weapons at his waist, as he pointed eastward into the night. The stars were vanishing slowly: gathering clouds. "That storm wind's backing our line. Fox is raking their line with fire arrows."

"Make that halyard fast and take the tiller, Loos. I'm going back to that mirror chart," Jeje said. "I want to see these stinkers on the paper."

Inda fingered out his note with his left hand as he swung his glass across the Venn fleet and then back. The others were all intent forward. Had Signi also kissed it? Inda pressed the paper to his lips, but all he tasted was the rice-rag of the paper and the salt in the air. He kissed it again, feeling the briefest sense of proximity of the people who loved him, whom he loved.

Why wasn't Signi's name among the others? Inda suspected that was because he sailed to war, against her people. There was nothing either of them could say. Better no communication than false words.

Grief, regret, cut cruelly. Inda thrust his kissed paper into a pocket and swung around, scanning the line of enemy ships.

"Inda! You've got to see this," Jeje called from her cabin.

"What is it?"

Jeje said in a low, urgent voice, "I saw it yesterday, but didn't think it meant much: the tings aren't random, they ring out from the center. Now I know that the center is the command ships."

"So?" Inda shrugged.

"So nothing, I thought, just like you. But I checked again, because the closer we got, the more that center blurred. Thought it odd. Listen, Inda. The flagship isn't the only one sending out the ting commands. I've got the flagship pegged by sight on the mirror chart." She had poked up through the hatch. Visible only as a silhouette, she jabbed her finger toward the central defensive formation.

"There can't be two commands." Inda frowned. Instinct insisted something was amiss, though he couldn't define what. "Is the magic fading?"

Inda turned his glass south. More ships on fire, under the peaceful glimmer of stars above.

"The other command ship has to be there—three points off the weather bow."

"There's nothing there. Just a lone raider," Nugget called softly from the lookout.

Inda sighed. So much for a miraculous occurrence, like on Andahi. "Probably just a backup for communication disaster."

Jeje said, disappointed, "Guess I was wrong."

Chapter Twenty-six

"WHAT if the mers get us?" Halvir whispered.

Rajnir leaned heavily on the boy's shoulder. He tried not to—he could feel the boy's light bones bending—but as soon as he shifted his weight to his own feet, his knees trembled. "If they get us, they get us," he whispered, already out of breath. "But I don't think they will. All this fire. Splinters. They must be far below, watching."

"Watching the battle? Like it's a ballad act?" Halvir's wide blue eyes showed twin reflections of fire from distant ship battles.

Rajnir said bitterly, "If they're human still, would they not love to watch a war?" He gripped the rail. "Now. Over, onto the mainchains—"

It was dark enough.

Erkric gestured to Yatar and his nephew, gathered his strength, and transferred. That left the two to perform their own transfers, which they did.

When the three had recovered, Erkric had glanced quickly around the *Cliffdiver*'s deck. The Erama Krona stood like motionless pillars, given wide berth by the crew. Because all Venn grew up knowing that you never approach or address the Erama Krona on duty, no one had noticed they were shrouded.

The sailors were mostly aft, ensigns tending the ting chart and sending their own tings, as Erkric had commanded through the king. If Durasnir went up in a blaze, Erkric would instantly be able to take command.

Erkric motioned the Yatars close. "The forces are well engaged. Let's loose the magic now. Give both sides a demonstration of power. Yatar, you contact the mages. I'll finish preparation of my gift to Elgar the Fox."

The plunge into the water was shocking cold, sending bubbles tickling up Rajnir's flesh. He opened his eyes, catching a glimpse of his white robe billowing before a sharp sting made him squinch his eyelids closed and kick hard, striving upward for air.

He broke the surface, gasping. Damn, damn! It was supposed to be easy to drown, or was that in ice water? Two small, cold hands closed on his wrist, and in the weak light reflected from the torches of the raider slipping farther and farther away, Rajnir made out Halvir's round face, yellow hair plastered to his boyish skull, his eyes wide with fear and anxiousness.

"Come, O my king," the boy gasped, then coughed. "Come, you can float if you turn over. I will guide you. We'll swim for my father's ship—it's that one over there."

Rajnir assented aloud, even as he schooled himself to fight instinct, to sink, to shed this meaningless life.

Erkric braced himself against the rail, closed his eyes, and began putting together the spells he'd already prepared. This was a volatile, dangerous accumulation of spells, but—

"... O my Dag."

The interruption became more insistent, and a brief, bitter heat puffed as Erkric lost one of the spells. "What is it, Yatar?"

"There is no return contact." The man held out his scroll-case, which should have the blue glows of acknowledgments on it. There were none. The case was dark, except for the faint beat of rosy fire reflected on the gold edging.

"That's impossible," Erkric whispered.

The two stared back at him. He'd chosen them because they were obedient, not because they were intelligent.

"Try again." He mentally held the Fire Spell, though it was taxing. But he'd got used to these constant interruptions.

Yatar whispered the control spells, tapping his scroll-case for each message: three, four . . . nine. Each of the nine caused a brief yellow-white glow of a magical contact.

The three stood there, looking down at the case. And not one blue light glowed in it.

Where were the dags with the Norsunder magic?

Erkric whirled. Dag Byarin aboard the *Cormorant* was one of them—where was his spell? Was it possible he . . .

Disbelief turned into a vast unease. "Check on the king," Erkric snapped, though he hardly knew why.

But when the nephew returned moments later, his face stricken, Erkric knew his instinct had been right.

"He's gone. So is the boy."

"Unshroud the Erama Krona. They will search—and die if they've lost him," Erkric promised.

Within a short time the Erama Krona, armed with brilliant glowglobes, began a methodical search of the ship. And when they came back, the leader saying, "There is no sign of the king—" Erkric knew he'd been betrayed. He whirled around, aimed the half prepared spell at the flagship, and transferred it.

"Die, traitor!" he screamed, as blue fire erupted along the rails of the *Cormorant* and sheeted up to the sails.

The crew of the *Cliffdiver* stared, thrilled and appalled, at the gigantic conflagration—except for the Erama Krona, whose single thought was their life's purpose: guarding the king.

"Here, Dag Erkric," one cried, pointing toward the water a distance away. The light from the flagship's fire radiated out, revealing two swimming figures drifting on the current. "Men overboard!"

A weird tearing sound, and a smell of bitter gases from deep beneath the ground were the only warning to those aboard the *Cormorant*. Hot wind scoured the ship, knocking everyone off their feet, leaving them gasping from the stench; all around fire blazed and crackled with terrifying suddenness.

"Magic attack—" Valda croaked, sneezing violently, and

then heat and a glaring, searing light punched through the scuttles and knocked the dags to the wardroom deck.

Stars burst across Valda's eyes as her chin smacked the wood. She shoved herself up, knowing what had happened—what to do—mostly driven by instinct and a maddened desire to fight. She flung her hands up, fingers cupped toward the sky, and whispered the words to draw water. Magic hummed through the reeking, smoky air, bringing a mass of water in a sheer wave, up, up, high over the side, to smash across the upper deck. Then she scrambled to her feet, ignoring the blood running from her cuts, and hastened up the ladder to the weather deck.

Steam rose everywhere. The writhing figures caught by the flames fell into the surging, swirling water. Some looked stunned, others horribly burned and dying; those who had not been near the starboard rail forced shocked minds to think, terrified bodies to act, and formed bucket teams, under Durasnir's roared stream of orders.

Valda braced her trembling body in the frame of the dripping hatchway, and brought another spout up and over the burning mainmast, sending up billows of hissing steam.

Durasnir appeared and plucked her up from the hatchway as if she'd been a child. He set her against the rail. "Thank you for saving our lives." He coughed, nearly breathless. "But look. All those glowglobes. What is happening on the *Cliffdiver*?"

Loos and Viac hauled the sails breaking taut in the light airs as they floated slowly toward the big ship keeping a respectful distance from the lone raider.

"Want light?" Viac asked.

"Stay dark," Inda said, glass pressed to his eye. "Whatever is keeping them from seeing us, well, let's not test it."

"Here," Loos called from the tiller. "What's that? Someone is overboard. No, there, a finger abaft the beam."

Inda had turned toward the flagship. "Lee of the raider," Jeje muttered. "I see 'em."

Now boats were frantically being lifted from the hoists. Someone very important indeed was overboard, judging from the frenzied action aboard the raider.

Inda had just spotted the two struggling figures in the water when the air filled with a strange hiss. Light and wind tore wildly against nature, and the Venn flagship gouted upward in flame, as if it had been doused with oil, except no oil-doused fireship ever flamed blue-white like that.

The Venn guarding the flagship all put helms down and hauled wind, some of them nearly dismasting one another in their haste to put water between them and that terrible conflagration.

Whoosh, whoosh, water slid down the sides of the *Vixen* as they closed on the two figures in the water; it seemed the larger one was sinking, the smaller one tugging desperately at lengths of fabric.

"Here, grab this line," Viac yelled. "And you—hey-o, is that a boy?" He dove overboard, pulling the line after him, which he tied around the weakly struggling man as the boy gasped and sobbed, clinging to Viac's arm.

Inda and Loos hauled the man aboard, as Viac climbed after, the boy tucked under one arm. They set the man on the deck and Inda freed the line. The man looked like a beached sea lion dressed in slick white silk with streaming cornsilk hair. He sat awkwardly on the deck, next to the small boy who crouched, knot-jointed, near the mast.

The man seemed to have difficulty staying upright; in the few moments Inda and the crew eyed him, he sagged against the mast. In the orange light of the burning flagship, he coughed up seawater, his teeth chattering.

The boy bent over him, asking a question over and over in what sounded to Inda and the Fisher brothers like Venn.

While the shadowy figures stared down at him, Rajnir fought against the bitterness and humiliation of defeat—this time by his own body. The revolting taste of seawater, the sting, the suffocating sense of sinking in water—he had not been able to command his will sufficiently to drown, especially with the boy tugging so desperately at him to keep him on the surface. He had never imagined that he would be plucked from the water by a random fishing boat. His eyes stung as he blinked up at three male figures.

He said in Sartoran, as Jeje dropped a blanket around him: "You are?"

"Indevan Algara-Vayir," Inda said—and grimaced. Too late.

Rajnir's eyes widened. "Impossible. You are on the black-sided pirate—"

Inda said in Sartoran, without turning his head, "Who's in command? That raider, or the big warship on fire?"

"I cannot say."

"Can't or won't?" Inda grimaced. "Who are you, anyway?"

The boy struggled up, shivering violently. "H—he's K—k—king Rajnir of the V—v—enn. And y—you won't touch him. W—w—without g—going through me!"

"You forgot your sword," Jeje said in her flat-accented Sartoran, and dropped a blanket around the boy.

From the *Cliffdiver,* Erkric had watched in head-pounding amazement as Rajnir's enormous white form seemed to rise out of the water, then he realized what had happened: there was a ship out there with a Sight-warding Spell on it!

He peered at the water, and yes, there was a wake behind what seemed to be a smear in the darkness.

Impatiently he muttered the antidote to discover a scruffy fishing smack of some kind. The fishers—no uniform clothing—finished plucking a small figure out of the water, then bent over their rescues, as if they were not surrounded by warships.

Where had this fisher come from?

A magically warded fisher—

Betrayed again!

He whirled around, and jabbed a finger at the duty captain of the Erama Krona, who was still trying to comprehend how it could be possible to mislay the king when he and his men had been vigilant.

"Give me your five best men. No, three," Erkric amended. He knew the limits of his strength: he could not transfer six people, and anyway, could three or four fishers resist three Erama Krona? They could not.

As the three were motioned aside, Erkric added, "Kill them all for betraying the king." He waved at the open-mouthed crew, the two shocked dags.

And the Erama Krona, used to obeying Erkric, and assuming that the crew was part of the treachery that had led to the disappearance of the king, got to work.

On the *Vixen,* Rajnir and his rescuers were startled by a sudden outburst of screams from the raider. Inda snapped up his glass. "Those fellows in white seem to be—"

Air buffeted Inda's face, and on *Vixen*'s foredeck a flicker of weird greenish light resolved into four figures.

Erkric staggered, pointed, yelled "Kill them!"

Loos Fisher was at the mainsail. He had a single heartbeat to remember his weapons lying just two paces away as the men in white attacked.

In the moment it took Inda to rip his knives free, the first man decapitated Loos Fisher in a single blow, then bore down on Inda. Viac Fisher abandoned the jib sheets and attacked the Venn who had killed his brother. As they grappled furiously, Inda was left facing two Erama Krona, one gripping the huge double ax of old stories, the other a sword. They closed. Light, sound, sensation spun into a blur of noise and motion. A lightning strike of agony from his right shoulder blanked Inda: habit carried him into a rolling dive that ended in a heap. The ax-wielder lay bleeding from several wounds, Inda's right-hand knife in his chest.

Inda sprawled on the deck, half-dazed, his right arm icy-cold and motionless as he stared up at two still figures. His back to the mast, a tall silver-haired old man held Jeje against him with a knife at her throat.

Her own knives were buried in the last two Erama Krona.

Near the waggling tiller, Viac stood with a knife at Rajnir's throat, tears tracking down his face. Cowering in the bow was the little boy.

Erkric said, "Surrender the king, or she dies."

Viac did not move. Jeje shaped the word, "No."

Inda said, "Why should we believe you?"

Erkric smiled, a thin, nasty smile that everyone there—including Rajnir—could see in the glow of the distant fires.

A rope squeaked.

Inda and Viac knew the sound and stilled. Erkric did not know the sound. As he flexed his arm to cut the woman's throat, Nugget swooped down from above. She cracked him on the side of the head with her belaying pin.

Jeje drove her elbow into the Dag's midsection, and her heel hooked up to smash against his kneecap.

The Dag staggered, and Jeje wrenched free. He groped blindly, then raised a hand toward Jeje, fingers gathering an eerie greenish-yellow glow. Inda's own rage propelled him forward; before the Dag could finish his spell Inda ripped his wristguard barbs toward the Dag's throat in a backhand swipe. Erkric raised an arm just enough to keep Inda's blades from causing instant death, but one barb ripped deep enough to cause blood to spurt. Erkric howled in rage as he clapped his hand to his neck, unable to concentrate on the Killing Spell—

A flicker of cold light snapped everyone's attention to a tall, slender young woman whose dark eyes reflected the fires of the burning ships. Her firelit smile was vivid with malice.

Erkric had fallen to his knees, blood welling between the gnarled fingers pressed to his throat. "Yeres! S–save me!"

The woman looked down at the silver-haired man, hands on her hips, head at an arch angle. "You misuse what we gave you so unwisely."

The Dag uttered in a hoarse voice, "I can win. Here— take them all—there's Rajnir. Heal me—give me *time* . . ."

"*More* power? My dear, my dear. Did you not heed my brother when he told you that destructive magic must never be used defensively, only to take? And what do you have to offer us? A fat, brainless king and a bunch of fishers?" She kicked Viac's Erama Krona with Nugget's knife sticking up from his back. "Not even one of your famous fighters to play with!"

Inda's vision smeared weirdly. He felt a hot line down the back of his shoulder, and realized he had not completely escaped that ax. He said to the woman, "Did he promise his soul to you in return for some kind of magic?"

She gave the scruffy fisher an indifferent glance; was that face familiar? No. "I love the quaint way you people put things. To answer your question: useless as he appears, the Dag is ours, alive *or* dead."

Yeres uttered a soft laugh as the Dag sagged, his eyes wide and full of horror. She looked around contemptuously at the slovenly deck full of barrels and broken nets, the disgraceful sail, the small crew of scruffy fisher folk—

one dead, three wounded, one missing an arm—and gestured casually. A thousand moth-wings of dark converged on the Dag, coalescing into lightless emptiness, and then he and the woman vanished, leaving a brief sough of bone-scraping wind.

Chapter Twenty-seven

INDA struggled to his feet, the most pressing desire in his shocked, pain-hazed mind to retrieve Loos' head and return it somehow to its body. He would not leave Loos lying there so obscenely.

Then the air flickered again, and another woman appeared, this one old, wearing a ragged, stained blue robe that threw Inda straight back to the other side of the strait several years ago when he first captured Dag Signi.

"Where is Erkric?" she demanded, looking about, hands raised. Her fingers glowed faintly green.

"Dead," Jeje croaked.

"Gone," Inda added.

"Probably both," Nugget put in, swinging down and alighting on the deck. She kicked free of her rope, belaying pin half raised. "Some woman came. Was she really from Norsunder?" She turned to Inda, who just lifted a shoulder.

"Was she named?" the old woman asked, leaning against the water scuttle to recover from the transfer.

"Yeres." Nugget stared at her in fascination, as the woman hissed in shock. "Who are you?"

Valda struggled to make sense of things, to think ahead.

"My name is Brit Valda. I am—was—Chief of the Venn Sea Dags. Who are you? Your accent is eastern."

"Nugget Woltjen," Nugget said proudly, thinking, *We're alive! We're alive!* "And that's Inda Elgar, you may have heard of, and—"

Inda smacked his one good hand over his face. "Nugget. These are *Venn*." Though without much force, since he'd already told Rajnir who he was.

"Oh." Nugget blushed, then swung around, still dizzy with euphoria. Nothing seemed real, they were actually alive! "Why didn't that Yeres take you to Norsunder, Inda? They must want you more than anybody!"

"She didn't know who I am." Inda slowly retrieved his weapons, though his right arm dangled.

"I thought they knew everything," Nugget chattered on. "Had eyes everywhere. She certainly knew to come here to get that damned Erkric."

Damned indeed. Valda was dizzy, her body throbbing with pain. She almost laughed, until she painfully turned to make certain Rajnir was safe, and discovered the knife still held at the king's neck, the man holding the knife stark-eyed with fury.

"Erkric had granted her immediate access to him," Valda said, working to keep her voice calm. Reasonable. "That would be part of his bargain. Even Norsunder has its laws and limits. Though not enough of them." Her voice cracked, and she struggled to be heard, to be clear, though black spots drifted across her vision as she faced Inda. "As for you, she must believe you aboard your black flagship."

"That was what everyone was supposed to think," Inda admitted.

The little woman's eyes were bird bright in the fire reflections. "Signi has spoken of you."

"Signi," Inda repeated, and addressed Rajnir, still in Viac's grip. "I'm supposed to bring back your head." He closed his eyes, breathed in deeply. "You don't look like you could fight a duel any better than I could right now."

"Worse," Rajnir wheezed, wincing against the press of the knife. "Worse."

Inda would never cut anyone's head off. He'd had little inclination before, but the sight of poor Loos lying nearby hardened that conviction. Inda studied the sorry, sodden form of the Venn king. He was just as reluctant to plunge a knife into a man who couldn't stand without aid; he did not want to give Viac the signal he knew Viac badly craved.

So negotiate.

"Viac. Ease enough to let him talk." Inda's right hand had gone numb, so he pawed the air with his left. "I want the war to end."

Rajnir's chin lifted. In the beating firelight, his gaze was steady. "So do I. But I don't know how much control I have over calling a halt." His voice was hoarse as Viac's grip was murderously tight.

"I can help with that," Valda said briskly.

Inda cut his eyes toward Viac and lifted his chin.

Viac relaxed his grip on Rajnir, who sagged to the deck. "I do not want this war," Rajnir repeated, then lifted his head, giving Valda a long, somber stare. "End it. If you can."

Viac put away his knife and turned his back to them all. He staggered; only then did his mates realize he'd taken several bad wounds in fighting the Erama Krona who had killed his brother.

As Viac bent to straighten his brother's limbs, Jeje said to Nugget, "Nice work."

Inda flicked a look at Nugget, whose eyes were too wide, her cheeks flushed. He knew that state, the weird, unreal hilarity after a battle—and how suddenly reality, and grief, would sink in the invisible knife. "Not bad for one hand, eh?"

Nugget beamed. "I saved you both, didn't I?"

"Yes, you did."

Nugget turned to Viac, bent over Loos, and her triumph faltered, but she squared up and followed Jeje's lead in retrieving their blades.

Valda knelt by Rajnir, reassured herself that he was materially unhurt, then spotted Halvir still huddled in the bow.

"Bandages," Jeje said and ducked below, hand pressed to her bleeding neck.

Valda turned back to Inda, her hands on her knees, as Inda waved his knife toward the battle fires scattered all around the horizon. He had promised Signi to limit the slaughter. Now he had to try to keep his word. "Let's end it."

Valda cleared her throat, tightening her body in an effort to gather her dwindling strength. "Here comes the *Cormorant*. Durasnir is on his way."

Inda peered under one hand. The flagship's fires had been doused, the sails shifted. The *drakan* began its turn, and catching one of the rising eastern gusts, picked up speed with each surge.

"If you will permit, we need to agree on a story," Valda went on. "Everyone saves face, and you, Indevan Algara-Vayir, gain enough moral advantage so that Durasnir is not forced to order you all put to death." Her voice thinned with grief. "There has been enough killing. Not just against your armada, but right here, Venn versus Venn." She passed tense fingers over her face. "And so. We will all claim that you fought the *halmgac* with Dag Erkric, just after he treacherously turned on King Rajnir. In return, King Rajnir promised a truce, and granted you safe passage. Does that agree with you, O my king?"

Rajnir's voice rasped. "Better words have not been put in my mouth."

Valda's breath hissed sharply.

Inda tapped his numb arm. "Will anyone believe that? Me, against a mage? Even an old one?"

"You forget your reputation," Valda said. "They will believe it. Perhaps some are less credulous than others, but those latter will see how it is to everyone's advantage to cooperate."

Halvir had ventured cautiously forward. Now that the threat was over, thrill and curiosity replaced fear and dread. He was still weak from days of darkness and little exercise followed by that horrible struggle in the water when he fought to keep the king from sinking, but natural ebullience caused him to turn to Inda—after a long, fascinated gaze at poor Loos's head. "Are you really Elgar the Fox?" he asked in passable Sartoran.

"Well, one of 'em," Inda said, then looked up. "Jeje? You all right?"

Jeje paused as she wrapped some bandage cloth carefully around her throat. "Probably looks worse than it is.

He wasn't strong enough to cut deep, the old shit." She pointed at the dead Venn. "*Those* fellows were *fast.*"

Valda said, "They had just emerged from two magical spells, not just one. Or they would have been faster."

Inda half raised a hand, about to protest this slight against his crew, but the expressions in the king's and boy's faces made him pause. Maybe there was some kind of reassurance going on here—a restoring of balance, of self-worth. He remembered what he'd felt like when he'd escaped Wafri, and Fox saying something like, *You and I are the two most wanted fighting men in this half of the world . . .* Fox ordinarily never talked flash. But Inda had remembered that, over and over, in the bad days directly after his escape from Limros Palace.

Then the *drakan* flagship bore up, the enormous prow arching overhead. Despite the scorch marks and sails being replaced by crew in the rigging, the rail was lined with archers, at their head Oneli Stalna Durasnir, whom Inda instantly recognized.

Brit Valda walked forward, hands raised. "The king has declared a truce," she called, her old voice quavering and thin, but carrying.

Durasnir spoke a word, and all the arrows lifted skyward. Still nocked, but not aimed.

Durasnir stared down, amazed to recognize the young Marlovan Harskialdna from the cliffs above Andahi Pass. Then his heart flooded with visible relief when he saw his son, alive and unhurt.

"Came to fight your Dag in a duel," Inda called up.

"Dag Erkric is dead, after turning his hand against me," Rajnir said, hoarse but clear. *Sentient.* "Norsunder claimed him after he lost the *halmgac.*"

A swift murmur hummed through the Venn, and Durasnir motioned for a bosun's chair to be lowered to the *Vixen* as Jeje kept the tiller steady.

The king was soon aboard his flagship again, a sorry figure with his loose flesh ill-concealed in his sodden white silk and brocade. But his eyes, for the first time in years, were clear and aware.

"We could win it," Durasnir said, amazed to see comprehension in Rajnir's gaze. Uncertain how to proceed. "It's tight, but we could win. Their discipline will break, and—"

"And what then, Oneli Stalna my commander?" Rajnir said, in a private voice. "And then eternal vigilance, while the likes of Count Wafri plot behind our backs? Where is the glory in killing other people to take their land, then having to fight more when they try to defend their livelihood?"

Durasnir wondered if he dreamed, to hear his most secret thoughts spoken aloud, and by Rajnir, of all the people in the world. He said with care, "It has always been our way."

"As I lay there waiting for Erkric to use my body to enforce his actions, and my voice to speak his words, I began to wonder what it might be like if others came to take our homeland away because they had need of fish and cold weather and stone. No longer do I find Wafri so very wrong."

Durasnir pressed his hands together in peace mode.

Rajnir lifted his voice. "I declare this war at an end. We will return and rebuild our homeland."

Durasnir paced to his signal ensign. White, gold, white, the flags jerked up and up on the fire-scarred mast. Another ensign, his puffed cheeks purple, blew steadily on his horn, *"Blaaap, blaaap, blaaap . . . blaaap, blaaap, blaaap!"* which caused ships to disengage where they could, and draw together into the great arrowhead, as the signal radiated outward from ship to ship.

The bosun's chair was lowered for Halvir. Durasnir called to Inda, "Is the man called Ramis aboard the *Sinna-Drakan?* The ship you call the *Knife?*"

"I don't think so." Once again, Durasnir looked down into that scarred face, the wide brown eyes narrowed and alert, as the young man added, "Did he take it from you people?"

"I do not believe there is a simple answer to that," Durasnir responded, as if they were not at opposing sides in a battle, one in a scout, the other in a half-burned flagship with nine-and-ninety arrows aimed down from the mastheads. It seemed important: Durasnir intuited presence, as if more listened than were in view.

Durasnir had once seen the *drakan* the southerners called the *Knife,* at the very end of the pirate battle at The Narrows, on the other side of the world. Ghosts had prowled that deck, ghosts with long tangled hair, and long mustaches, old short swords and battle-axes to hand. Yet the ghost of the fabled king who had built the *Sun Dragon* had not been among them. Instead, Ramis stood before the whipstaff where the golden-torced ghost should have been ... "It sailed away. Our skalts insist it sailed out of time," Durasnir said when the two ships began to draw apart.

Indevan Algara-Vayir did not betray surprise, or doubt, or the smirk of secret knowledge. Just a sober tip of the head, then he turned away, the pain in his step unmistakable.

Halvir was set on the deck. He ran down the companionway, and now he reached his father at last, and lifted his arms. Durasnir gathered him up, and thin as the boy was— no more than flesh-covered bones—crushed him heart to heart.

Valda transferred herself to the deck just behind him. When she'd recovered, Durasnir said over Halvir's head, "*Cliffdiver?*"

"They are all dead," she said softly. "Erkric must have ordered the Erama Krona to murder the entire crew, including the Yatars. Then they turned their blades on themselves." She gestured to her middle. "For they had lost the king. I think we should burn it as is, let no hand further desecrate those murdered by Erkric's evil will, for they kept faith as best they could with their vows."

"It will be done," Durasnir said, gesturing to the duty officer to relay the order.

And so, Yatar, you regain honor in your death. You will have to decide if it is justice or mercy. Valda paced behind the ensigns helping the king into the cabin. The healer came forward, but when the king made a dismissive gesture, the healer turned Valda's way. "My cuts are superficial," she said.

Rajnir said, "Clear out." The healer flushed, but it had been so long since the king had addressed him, he did not know how to respond except to make a full obeisance and withdraw.

It was so strange to hear the king speaking again, strange and almost unnerving—everyone felt that way, and saw their own reaction in the others. The ensigns filed out, closing the cabin door behind them, leaving Rajnir on his throne, and Valda standing before him.

"I need to know." He made no attempt to hide his bitterness. "Are you now my voice?"

"No," she stated. "No. If you wish an adviser until you regain the present day, you should ask someone you trust. I recommend Fulla Durasnir, who is not a dag. I recommend—but do not tell you—to place Dag Ulaffa in charge of the dags. It's probably a forlorn hope that the terrible magic Erkric discovered can all be destroyed. Knowledge of any kind, once it's loose, is difficult to contain."

Rajnir sighed, leaning back. "Thank you for that. But is there some reward you want? Everyone wants something."

"I want peace." Her voice shook. "I would love an end to war, and the craving for war. We have already taken steps to make it more difficult for any more invasions: you should know this, O my king, there are some of us who sent a dag to share our navigation secrets with Sartor. So I think the Death Spells could be lifted from our sea dags. But again, I recommend. It is your decision."

"If giving our navigation to the world is not a betrayal, it is at least a judgment against us. But I accept it as our due. What about your reward? I keep hearing a 'but' in your voice."

Valda clasped her hands. "I do not want riches, and you cannot give me youth. If you were to give me a reward, it must be large, or none at all. So large . . . that you might not be able to compass it."

"Speak your mind."

"It is no less than this: that we set aside one of our oldest customs, the born thrall."

To Valda's surprise, Rajnir began to laugh. He shook all over, shading his eyes with one hand, and she frowned in affront until she realized that he was weeping.

"Oh, yes," he said finally. "Oh, yes."

As dawn's light smeared the east under the incoming oppression of heavy cloud, Inda's mood was low.

The *Vixen* emerged into the widening gap between the Venn and the alliance. Viac stayed at his post, but his tight breathing prickled Inda's nerves. They'd Disappeared Loos as soon as the last Venn ship vanished hull down, all of them together while the sail flapped and the scout rocked on the increasing waves.

Then Jeje passed out her small store of bandages—and ripped cloth when she ran out. They set sail again in the strengthening wind, heading straight toward the faint gray in the east under a cloud-blackened sky as to the north, the Venn pulled together into an arrowhead, also sailing east.

Not all ships disengaged from battle. Inda spotted distant clusters of winking lights emphasized by tiny glimmers of arcing flame as embattled ships fought to take the other ship, or to kill, or just to see the enemy burn.

But most of the hard-pressed alliance moved in a mass southward, some in formation as they paralleled the Venn, others in chaotic swarms as their captains tried to figure out what was happening. Why had the Venn abandoned their lines of attack and pulled back into the arrow? Was it time for the terrible magic attacks everyone had warned about?

Vixen was alone—and when the capital ships saw it, with its white flag at the foremast, signals flew out: *commander in view.*

When Vixen rounded to under *Death*'s lee, Fox himself appeared at the rail, his expression changing from a hard expectancy to relief, and then amazement. "Why are they back in the . . . You did it?" Then, in blatant disbelief, "You did it!" He gestured for hands to leap down to the *Vixen*'s aid.

"No, no, let me be," Jeje snarled. "Take Viac. He's covered with cuts. No, Loos died. Yes. Nugget? You go aboard *Death,* so I can get *Vixen* cleaned up."

Fox shut them out. "Inda, want a lift?"

"Of course not." Inda made himself leap up the side at something like his old pace, though he could only hang on with his left hand.

It took all his remaining strength to walk into the cabin, stared at by the entire crew. Somewhere in the distance he was briefly aware of Nugget talking rapidly. Fox lingered behind Inda, listening to the gist of things, practiced after years at sorting Nugget's enthusiastic embellishments.

Inda flopped onto the bed, arms out, one leg hanging over the side.

"You really fought hand-to-hand with Erkric?" Fox

asked as he took a seat where he could keep an eye down the deck through the open door.

"Naw. But that's what we're telling everyone." Inda grimaced. "Did Nugget say she bopped Erkric on the head?"

"She claims that you defeated him, after a terrific one-handed battle, one of the twenty or thirty Erama Krona having buried his ax in your back first. The ax, I gather, is true." He pointed to Jeje's good cotton-silk ship-visiting shirt, ripped and twisted around Inda's chest and shoulder.

Inda gave a short but succinct report.

Fox listened in silence, then said, "Brit Valda ... and your Dag Signi. It never ceases to amaze me, how you manage to find just the right person at the right time, alwa sympathetic to your cause."

"I didn't plan for any of that. I just ..."

"Just went on a suicide mission, because it was the only way out of an impossible situation. I know. It seems to me you've done that before. At Andahi, from what I hear. At The Narrows, from what I saw. The day we took Co-codu from Gaffer Walic. Each time you were the means of change, yet you would have failed but for these other people who saw in you their salvation."

"It's not me, it's them." Inda sighed. "They do what they're going to. I didn't have anything to do with Dag Valda. Never saw her before in my life. Ramis, same thing, at The Narrows. And at Andahi Erkric and Durasnir called the cease. No friends to me."

"The day you took Dag Signi, you set this day up. I would have kept her a prisoner, you set her free. Made her a partisan. And she made this Valda a partisan. Erkric's action at Andahi is tougher to explain, but do you see how it all connects?"

"Tdor would have it all humans are connected—now and through time—though we don't see the knots. What we did today is important to something going on in, say, Colend, though none of us know it. We might never. And that will be important to somebody in Toar ..." Inda was taken by a fierce yawn.

"Yes, everything will matter later." Fox looked amused. "Go to sleep. No, stay there. I'd have to change the bedding anyway, I can smell you from here. Sleep, and I'll deal with the detritus. There's bound to be plenty."

Inda could not have moved if all the Venn had charged the ship with fire and sword. Every bone and sinew loosened. Even his right arm had ceased to ache—had ceased to feel. With each breath he sank down and down, past scraps of memory, and down farther into infinitely yielding oblivion.

Fox tossed the blanket over Inda. He could feel the roll and pitch of the ship changing. That storm was near and would probably bring cold air.

He went out on deck, fighting his own fatigue. Despite the rain he did a sweep, and was not surprised to spot one of the Ymaran ships' stern boats skipping over the waves, its sail quivering in the rising wind, Taumad at the tiller.

Tau rounded to abaft the *Vixen* and leaped across to reunite with Jeje. Fox shifted his attention elsewhere, dismissing them from his mind; when he turned away from his attempt to descry the Chwahir and the eastern flotillas in the thick slant of gray rain to the southeast, he was surprised to find Tau on the companionway.

"Ymar is in a panic." Tau gestured northward, to where distant, fading twinkles indicated the Fleet Guild ships. He continued in Marlovan, "I promised to get a report. Saw *Vixen*. Where's Inda?"

"Asleep. Report? As you can see, we took little damage."

Tau's station aboard Deliyeth's flagship at the alliance's northern wing, closest to their homeland, had prevented him from seeing anything southward.

"Delfs engaged hard on the south flank, driving the Venn back toward their own force," Fox said, leaning on the rail. "As for us, we had the wind, and the speed, so we harassed their front lines with fire arrows, trying to draw their lines apart enough for the Chwahir to engage ship to ship . . ."

He gave Tau a rapid report of a battle that lost immediacy with every successive heartbeat. The rain sheeted at a wind-driven slant; the cold drops felt good after so long a stretch of sultry summer. But the rain was the first hint of winter on its inexorable way and the shifting of the winds and current to the east.

Ready for Inda to sweep back down the strait, Fox thought.

He'd finished his report. They stood at the rail, heedless of the rain. Fox permitted himself to consider the future for the first time.

There was the pleasure of survival. Amazement, too. But that was already fading, leaving anger and frustration at Evred Montrei-Vayir's typical, rock-solid Montrei-Vayir greed, which would get his boyhood friend killed after all. Probably not in battle. Fox suspected the entire strait would melt away before Inda's combined force. Maybe some would fight desperately against their old friend. And though Inda would win those fights, the day he stood over Chim's bleeding body would kill him, too, in all the ways that mattered most.

But freely given loyalty never meant anything to the Montrei-Vayirs in days of old, Fox thought. Only gaining the crown, and land, and more land, until they ruled all of Halia now.

And what is my place in all that? Will I be pulled back under the Montrei-Vayir rein as head of their navy?

Tau had been speaking. Fox caught the end: ". . . and on my way here I noticed that the military are all on station, the trade volunteers in a knot."

Fox snorted. "The navies all know this business is far from over. What do you want to wager as soon as yon Ymarans find out that Rajnir ended the battle they'll think they're done, let's go home, and who gets to sit where at the banquet?"

Tau gave a soft laugh. "I think they're more concerned about the coast of Drael."

Fox said, "My guess is that Durasnir will keep the Oneli moving. He has to know that every man, woman, child, and dog that has a stick to wave or teeth to bite will be ranged along the Ymaran coast right this moment, waiting to fight the first Venn to set foot in Jaro."

"You would be right," Tau said, thinking of what the king had let slip.

"Venn are probably on their way to Geranda. They must still have some ties there."

"Trade agreement. The last governor was cousin of the previous Venn king. Daughter married the king of Sarendan, and now there's some kind of interim government until their second child grows up."

Fox said skeptically, "Won't there be trouble if Durasnir just takes what he wants? That's not trade."

Tau grinned. "If the regency is smart, they'll close their eyes and see Durasnir's back that much quicker."

Fox snapped up his hand, palm out. "So they refit and resupply there. Inda will ride their tail to make sure Durasnir keeps going. If the Venn round the southern tip of Toar before the ice sets in, then we're rid of them."

Tau sat on the rail, turning his face up into the rain. After two days of no sleep, it felt good—soothing and bracing. "So, how did Inda manage it this time?"

Fox gave an even shorter version of Inda's report, ending with, "So Rajnir ordered them to go home."

"Just like at Andahi." Tau whistled a low note.

"Only this time, the fellow actually has his mind."

"As well." Tau peered seaward in the strengthening light. "My guess is, he's going to need it."

At first Durasnir was so busy with the most needed repairs on his ship, the necessity of proper death rites for the many who had been killed by Erkric, and the reorganization of the fleet, that he did not have time to do more than smile at Halvir, who stayed resolutely close to his side, tired as he was.

Halvir understood he could not interrupt the flow of dispatches, and so he remained a breathing, wide-eyed shadow, watching everyone and everything. Durasnir was inclined to assign him to an ensign, if nothing else to free him to be able to speak without reserve to his most trusted aides. But within moments of the boy's falling asleep on Durasnir's own bed, Halvir dropped into nightmare, thrashing and crying out. Durasnir dropped a pile of reports and stalked to the inner cabin to sit with Halvir, though the press of urgent decisions was just about overwhelming.

The imperative triple knock of the Erama Krona was the only warning Durasnir had, then in came the tension-heightened Erama Krona, clearly deeply disturbed over the summary slaughter of their number aboard the *Cliff-diver*. There was no one to tell the truth of events but the king, and they could not question the king.

The three thoroughly checked the cabin, each noting

Durasnir sitting empty-handed beside his bunk where Halvir lay loose-limbed in the reckless slumber of childhood, as his father slowly stroked his bright hair.

When the cabin was deemed safe Rajnir entered, leaning on a cane, and dropped into the chair Durasnir had just risen from, as it was the only one there. "Nightmares?" he asked, indicating Halvir.

"Yes, O my king. It seems to comfort him, my sitting here."

"Go right ahead, sit with him there." Rajnir indicated the bunk. "I will tell you about our conversations, presently. Suffice it to say that my first order to him, he would not obey."

"What was that, O my king?" Durasnir's neck tightened.

"To kill me."

Durasnir's hand stilled, cupped over Halvir's head.

"I ordered him to kill me. He wouldn't do it because his mother's lessons in Drenskar were specific about how the unarmed and helpless were to be treated. Even," Rajnir sighed the word, "kings."

"I do not know what to say."

"There is nothing to say about that. Tell me instead, did you trust Dag Byarin?"

"I heard they found him dead. I am sorry."

"You have been too busy to hear that he took his own life. With a dragon knife, has to be centuries old. I have no idea where he got it, he not being related to any Houses except in the third or fourth degree. And isn't it forbidden for any but House descendants to carry their ancestors' dragon knives?" Rajnir waved wearily. "Yet another senseless custom broken."

Durasnir bowed his head. "I did trust Byarin, though he purported to be Erkric's spy."

"So the dual role was successful. I would have given him the highest honors for his courage. Listen to this. The pattern of blood on his robe was odd enough for them to undress him partly, to discover that he had carved the rune for justice in his own flesh before he fell on that knife." Rajnir shifted. He was desperately uncomfortable. But he was determined to regain a semblance of his old self, and so he ignored the aches and pains. "His death must be related to

Erkric's murders in some way. You know that Erkric was killing all witnesses, there at the end?"

"Tell me what happened, O my king."

"I will tell you what happened on board the Marlovan's scout. The rest—like my conversations with Halvir—can wait." And he gave an unvarnished account of the truth. Then of Valda's exhortation at the end. He finished, "I told her I might tell you, if I so chose. No more secrets."

Durasnir touched his hands in peace mode. "I'm glad I did not know. It made things . . . simpler, at the time."

Rajnir said, "I haven't seen your dispatches yet—"

"I will bring them myself for you to examine any time you wish, O my king."

"—but I suspect the worst carnage was caused among ourselves. I hope that is at an end. I gave Ulaffa a free hand to deal with the dags. I know they are keeping secrets, most resulting from Erkric's duplicity. My question is, why? How did that come to pass? He was so wise . . . so good a dag. So devoted to the Golden Path."

Durasnir had been considering how to edit his reply, out of long habit. Then he realized that editing replies for Rajnir had become everyone's habit, and perhaps that was why it had been so easy to isolate him. If that was true, how much did Durasnir unwittingly contribute over time to Erkric's plan?

"You must examine all my papers and ask any question you wish of me," he said, bowing deeply.

Rajnir leaned back, sweat running down his face from his long day of exertion. "Thank you, Uncle Fulla. Thank you."

Rajnir began the next morning, laboring up the hatch by himself to watch the new mainmast stepped with the last precious spar. He stood for a time, then sat in a chair brought by the Erama Krona. When the shrouds were rattled down, he returned to the command cabin to read more dispatches, often stopping the duty ensigns to ask questions. Elementary questions. Then he invited Halvir to join him, and as the day turned into a succession of days, they read together, exercised together, and talked about all manner of things, from ancient history to speculation about the day's dinner.

Durasnir was so glad to see Rajnir alive, and so relieved to have Halvir restored safely, and he was so busy with the stream of damage reports, replacements, and promotions, that he failed to notice the tight mouths and covert glances from Captain Hyarl Dyalf Balandir and his set of friends.

There was only one all-captains gathering. Durasnir called it as soon as the fleet had sunk Drael behind them, and the alliance ships dwindled in undisciplined clumps to match pace with the Venn from afar.

This was a short meeting. Durasnir asked each Battle-group captain or chief to report on the state of his command, then Durasnir said, "We are sailing for Geranda to refit." He used the king's verbal mode, so no one could question him. At least publicly. "We will wait there until all ships are sound and the detachment at Nelsaiam catches up. Then we sail for home."

Two captains had died during the engagement with the Delfs, so there were two field promotions to confirm. Nine new sea dags were assigned to the captains who had discovered their dags dead in a welter of blood, no evidence of the culprit anywhere. Durasnir dismissed them and turned away, glad to have that over: he was still longing for real rest.

Under cover of a fog bank two days later, Balandir and his captains met in a gig between two of their ships: though no one was listening to spiderwebs anymore, all were in the habit of avoiding them.

Balandir said, "You notice that Seigmad is still drooling, yet Durasnir deems him fit to act as Battlegroup Chief."

He paused for the expected disgust, and then said, "Life is going to change, under a fat seal of a king with the mind of a small boy. Agar reports he spends most of his time reading history scrolls with Durasnir's son, except when he's been asking questions like what the basic signal flags mean."

The others laughed, then waited. They all knew something more interesting than the fat king and old Seigmad was on Balandir's mind.

"May as well call Durasnir king. Why plan to sire sons for the next Breseng? Even if Rajnir finally marries and declares a Breseng, it doesn't take scouts to see that Durasnir now holds all the power, and will be choosing the heir."

Mutters of agreement.

"So here's my plan. And if you haven't the courage, say so now. Our orders are to sail for Geranda, which we were forced to leave when our mindless king first led us west to lose the war against the Marlovans. The nominal ruler is, by treaty, a princess ten years old. The island is held in her name by another old fool. All decisions made weeks away, in Sarendan. I think we should take it back." He smiled.

"How?"

"When the fleet sails . . . we stay."

The others considered this temerity. One of them would not dare, but all of them? Would Durasnir turn around and fight them? No, not with the fleet limping as bad as it was.

Balandir tapped the gunwale. "We take Geranda, throw out Sarendan, and we've got ourselves the beginnings of a new kingdom. We," he tapped his chest, "will be the only ones to go a-viking."

Chapter Twenty-eight

WHEN Evred appeared on the sentry walk that had become Hadand's and Tdor's favorite observation place, the queen and her Harandviar were startled. Evred never interrupted the girls' training, any more than they would have interrupted the boys'.

Below, Mistress Gand became aware of the girls' attention turning upward and her voice sharpened. "Leap of the Deer! Reverse! Crouch of the Cat!"

The girls snapped to focus as Hadand and Tdor took in Evred's rare, broad smile. Hadand thought, *Inda did it, he beat the Venn,* and Tdor thought, *Inda's alive.*

"Inda broke the Venn," Evred said slowly, each word giving him pleasure. "They are running east."

Hadand crowed, then caught sight of Tdor's profile. Tdor's joy was far more tentative, and Hadand knew why. "Will he be home by Convocation, do you think?"

Evred nodded at the girls below. "Excellent form. I still have little notion how long it takes for ships to travel from one point to another, though Barend and Inda have tried repeatedly to educate me. Understanding must come with experience, as in most things. But he has only fulfilled part of his orders."

Hadand had never seen the ocean, and the ship talk had bored her into private daydreams. "Oh, yes," she said, making a hand signal to Mistress Gand. "He's got to bring peace to all those ports. Well, I trust it will be soon."

Neither of them noticed Tdor's closed eyes.

Most of the alliance turned southward to follow in the wake of the Venn, but not all.

The day they sailed past the last reaches of Ymar, Tau asked Jeje to take him to the ancient Venn *drakan Knife,* which still had its dragon-head on the prow.

"That's the way we found it," Barend told Tau when he came aboard. "It fits on underneath that gold collar thing with all the carving."

"I believe it's called a torc," Tau said. "And those are runes."

Barend shrugged. "The hands are afraid to touch it. They say the ship is full of magic—you can feel it everywhere—and they're afraid something will happen to them."

"Leave it," Tau said. "I came because the king of Ymar wants to tour this vessel before he turns toward home."

Barend's broad, high brow wrinkled. "Home? First one to slink off, eh?"

"I expected it." Tau gave his rueful smile. "So I want to get a start on Inda's work and see if I can get Ymar to set his kingly name to a treaty."

Barend wheezed a laugh. "Do what you want. There's plenty of space below. Just, my suggestion is, if you want the toffs in a good mood, you get Lorm over here to cook for you. Tancla is a ready fist with his double-staff on deck, but he has no talent in the galley."

"I was thinking the same thing." Tau was still smiling, but with anticipation. It was time to commence his plan. "If I can persuade Mutt not to lynch me."

Lorm had never chosen the sea; he'd been taken by the pirate Gaffer Walic after his entire family was slaughtered before his eyes. When Inda led the mutiny against Walic, Lorm had stayed to cook for him, partly from gratitude, and partly because he could not bear to return to Sarendan and his memories.

But time and experience can wear the sharp pain of grief to poignant dreams and the ache of sudden memory, especially when someone new comes into one's life. Lorm was married again, to Nilat, a fellow cook. Neither of them was young. They agreed that it was time to retire from the sea and start up an inn, as soon as this venture was over. In the meantime, Nilat (who had ambitions) assured her husband, if it became known that Lorm had cooked for crowned heads, what would that do for future business?

The king of Ymar came aboard, intensely curious, sat down to a meal fit for a Colendi, enjoyed an agreeable evening with Tau. Their friendship had swiftly flared to attraction, making the conduct of treaty business a matter of affection as well as good will.

"Well, that's one," Tau said to Barend on the foredeck the next morning, gently waving his treaty, as the king had himself rowed away into the pearlescent dawn.

Barend grunted. "Inda know what you're doing?"

"No. And only Inda would fail to notice," Tau added. "Do you really think he will mind, if I can get them all to agree to something that is of mutual benefit to all?"

Barend considered, then flipped the back of his hand in the general direction of Drael. "Don't ask me about politics. I don't even want to know about those at home." He walked aft to make certain that the new ship rats Inda had rotated over did not mar the gilding when they stretched out lines to hang laundry.

The next person to arrive was the urbane Lord Hamazhav of Khanerenth. Tau knew him by sight, but little beyond that; the reverse was not true.

"Well met, my lord. The rumor is that you concluded a peace treaty with Ymar before his departure," said the diplomat from Khanerenth.

Tau was about to exclaim at the extraordinary speed of rumor, until he readjusted to courtier mode. One of the most obvious tricks of the diplomat was to invent rumor on the spot in order to delve at a guessed truth.

"I have indeed, my lord." Tau made an inviting gesture, one suited more to marble palaces than to the deck of a ship, even one from ancient Venn. "Would you like a tour, refreshment, or both?"

Lord Hamazhav smiled. In one genial welcome this decorative young Dei with the mysterious background had managed to imply ownership of this even more mysterious vessel. In just the same airy way, he had (without once using Inda's name) assumed the authority to negotiate treaties. "Both," Hamazhav said as Tau opened the door to the cabin. "And a glimpse of yon treaty, if I may. What did you and the king decide?"

"Of course all depends on others' agreement, but it's simple: noninterference, and custom and trade pricing to be handled through the Fleet Guild, which has managed to become a respectable body, at least in the strait."

Lord Hamazhav bent over the extraordinary twisted tree candelabra that sat in the middle of an equally amazing carved table. "In my experience, treaties are a balance between goodwill and necessity. The goodwill I see about me . . ." He gestured vaguely.

And the necessity? Tau was about to recklessly commit Evred, but he hesitated. Before Fox's conversation about Marlovan law, and the penalty for not obeying orders, he might have done it. But he knew that he was obeying Evred only in one regard yet countering him directly in another.

"That can be established," Tau said smoothly, hiding the accelerated beat of his heart. Once again, the enticing thrill of danger and risk made him laugh, and his entire being seemed to expand. "When Inda joins us."

"Ah, yes," Lord Hamazhav murmured, deeply appreciating the sudden poise of Tau's body, the distant golden gaze. The attraction of the Deis was said to be wicked—like forbidden magic. *With this one, rumor understated truth.* "Life will be interesting indeed when your Inda joins us."

It would be untrue to say that as the days slid into weeks, Inda was unaware of the steady succession of gigs and longboats going to and from the *Knife.* He saw, and in a sense knew that Tau was hosting gatherings, but Inda was too busy to pay much heed.

His first problem was keeping the fleet together as they shadowed the Venn, who sailed straight to Geranda, as Fox had predicted.

The rest of the fleet was loud in resenting the summary departure of the Ymarans while Deliyeth remained, with

her Everoneth and Fleet Guild ships. She'd promised Bren's
Fleet Guild she'd stay until they disbanded, but she argued
with every single order until she agreed on its utility. By
the time the fleet saw the Venn reach Geranda, everyone
was thoroughly sick of Deliyeth and her unswerving moral
superiority.

The second problem was the refit of the Delfs.

The Chwahir offered to donate good canvas and cordage, but not a stick or spar. Everyone agreed that the Delfs
had taken the brunt of the battle, that they'd saved the
Chwahir, but the Chwahir were adamant.

Inda knew why the Chwahir refused—and kept the
secret—but the strained relations between Delfs, eastern
alliance, and Chwahir became more strained until Inda
conceived the idea of dividing the Delfs between the Star
Islands and Freedom Islands in order to refit. As the Star
Islands, like the Fire Islands, had repeatedly been preserved from pirates by the independents out of Freedom,
Dhalshev agreed that this was a good compromise. He
would simply tell his port authorities to boost charges to
certain nationals in order to recompense the island harbor
shipwrights. He knew they would agree or risk losing the
protection of the independents.

And so Inda returned to Freeport at last.

It felt very strange to sail between the familiar head-
lands into Freeport Harbor again, after so many years
away. *Death* was given pride of place alongside the pier,
so as soon as the graunching shudder of the hull easing up
against the pier had ended, he leaped down to the warped
boards, along with most of his old companions, and from
that moment his life became a whirl of fragmented greetings, questions half answered, and remembered faces
among the throng of new.

Delfin Islanders were notoriously proud and prickly.
Knowing what they were owed, Inda offered the last group
of them berths ashore if they wished, either at Mistress
Lind's Lark Ascendant pleasure house, or Dasta's Chart
House. Though he had yet to see Dasta, he knew he could
work that much out.

When the Delfs almost to a man and woman opted enthusiastically for the pleasure house (and made it clear

they expected their stay to be guaranteed) Inda took Barend aside. "How are we going to pay for that? You got any of that treasure left?"

Barend laughed silently. "You leave that to me. Already talked to Dhalshev. We're going to squeeze the two kings through their admirals and that soft-talking fellow Hamazhav." He pointed a thin hand in the direction of Sarendan and Khanerenth.

Before the Saunter lit up for an evening's entertainment the like of which had seldom been seen in Freeport Harbor, Inda caught a glimpse of Lord Hamazhav being escorted up to the Octagon, Barend on one side, Dhalshev on the other, Mehayan and Tau walking behind, all laughing at something Tau said.

Inda walked the last of the Delfs to the Lark Ascendant and paid his respects to the proprietor, Mistress Lind.

Now they were all settled. The Delf ships at Star and Fire islands were probably already heaved down and halfway to being rebuilt; Inda hoped that the Venn were the same over on Geranda, so that they would sail east and out of his life.

Everything organized, everything in train . . . and the sense of pressure building in the back of his mind had increased to an iron grip on his neck. He had not had a moment to himself since the day he woke up in *Death*'s cabin to Fox saying, *Here's your breakfast. I've given the orders to follow the Venn. There are twelve gigs in our stern wake, full of messengers from captains who insist on speaking to you. I figure the Delfs have first claim.*

Inda ran back down the trail he'd known so well as a boy. The harbor was full of allies, and despite the cold wind bringing a promise of rain, nobody seemed to have anything to do except walk around yapping. He dodged through the thick crowd on the main street, ignoring the questions thrown his way—"You Elgar the Fox?" "Where'd ya get the scars?" "Is it true you really . . ." "How did you kill . . ."

Is it true? The truth is . . .

A hand like a steel trap closed on the scruff of his shirt and yanked him stumbling through a back doorway.

Inda looked up irritably, left hand scrambling for his

knife hilt and encountering the damn sling. Then his hand dropped. "Fox?"

"This way." Fox's hard mouth curled faintly as the crowd melted back to a circle of staring faces.

The questions started up behind as Fox led Inda through the Chart House's kitchen. Inda caught a glimpse of the main room as a server hip-bumped the service door open and swung two trays through. The crowds were even thicker than the street and the Saunter, the noise a skull-thumping roar.

Fox pulled Inda through the kitchen and down a narrow, warp-boarded hallway, up some very narrow stairs with a ramp built over half—a series of block-and-tackle ropes above—and into a room that overlooked the Saunter.

The casements swung closed, cutting the noise from a roar to a hum. The windows and the door were controlled by another ingenious series of ropes and pulleys put together with sail blocks. Inda's gaze followed the control rope to the end dangling near Dasta's hand.

Dasta grinned. "Inda!" He looked older, his face thinned. He spun his chair, hand extended toward a table. "Here's supper, waiting."

Inda sank onto a bench and reached for a foam-topped mug of beer, then took in the others: all the Fox Banner Fleet captains.

Inda's stomach closed. He set the beer down. *It's here,* he thought. *It's here. They're waiting for the command.*

"Finally," Jeje exclaimed, digging into her braised fish surrounded by seasoned peas and rice. "That's the last of the Delfs, right, Inda? What's next? I've scarcely seen you for weeks."

"I've been surrounded by people for weeks. Everybody yapping at once." He looked down at the beer. *And I let them so I wouldn't have to think about what's next.* Then he looked up, and though he knew he had to give the command, once again he hedged. "It's strange, how many people want to yap about things that don't matter, but for some reason they think I should hear it."

From his post by the window, Fox snorted. The reflection of the colored lights from the Saunter outlined his profile and shone in his red hair. "They all want a piece of your attention." He waved a lazy hand toward the window. "Maybe yapping at you borrows some of your importance."

"True." Eflis chuckled. "And when you're out o' sight, they want to yap *about* you."

At Inda's grimace, the others laughed. Inda noticed with relief that Gillor and Tcholan sat companionably side by side—just like the old days. Somehow not being married anymore had resolved their problems. How strange people were! If Tdor ended their marriage . . .

From the cherished memory of Tdor's steady gaze, her beloved face, to a swift and unwanted series of images: Evred's orders. Convocation and *Bring back Rajnir's head!* Deliyeth and her empire.

Inda grimaced and shifted in his chair. The impulse to drum, to move, made him jerk; his right arm still did not respond, and he was hemmed in by chairs and benches wedged against one another around the small table. *Give the command.* Reluctance almost froze his tongue, and once again his thoughts jinked sideways. "If they think so much of me, then why pester me?" he asked, resisting the deep itch to kick the table leg. "They don't do that to Fox."

"You're accessible," Eflis said. "He's not."

"And now you know why," Fox said, then his chin lifted. "Hold hard. Signal." He peered up at the Octagon.

Dasta sat up straight. "Double blinks? Message from the headland?"

"No, it's the summons for Dhalshev. I thought he was up there."

"He and Tau were taking the toffs off to the *Swan* for a victory dinner."

"*Swan?* Oh, yes, Kavna's yacht." Inda remembered the beautiful craft floating in Bren Harbor's pride of place. "Someone sailed it here?"

Jeje grinned. "Some old mates of mine, from the Lower Deck tavern in Bren Harbor. The oldsters the navy wouldn't have. They couldn't stand the idea of the Venn getting the prince's yacht, so they hijacked it and brought it here. The prince has it back last I saw, and he was offering Lorm and his wife mountains of gold to come cook on it."

As the others laughed heartily, Fox pushed away from the window. "I think I'll go see what's what." He left.

Dasta sat back. "While he's out, I want to hear about

everything, from the time you reached The Fangs to the battle. Your part, too." He pointed at Jeje.

That was easier. Though when they neared the end, Inda discovered Jeje watching him, and he watched her for clues as he wondered which version to tell. Inda did not really know Khajruat Swift, who had taken her father's place as the commander of their three ships—they'd only met once, before the pirate battle at The Narrows. He had never seen the new captain of Fangras' wall-eyed *Blue Star*. How much could he trust them?

Just as Inda said, "We saw lights on the raider deck, and so we—"

Fox slammed in. "On your feet." He jerked a thumb over his shoulder. "Taz-Enja and his people are already buttoning into their green jackets. Sarendan has been called to war."

"What?" several asked at once.

"The Venn are back," Jeje exclaimed. "I never trusted that silver-haired Durasnir fellow! He looked like he chews ice to warm up in the mornings."

Fox made a flat-handed swipe to cut her off. "Durasnir's gone east. Except for at least two Battlegroups, and maybe more. Soon as the Oneli departed, this Dyalf Balandir killed off the old regent and his officials, secured the mostly empty garrisons, and took the harbor. Declared himself the new king." His teeth showed in a smile. "Far's Sarendan is concerned, he's a pirate."

Dyalf Balandir had talked himself into believing that he was reclaiming the glorious heritage of the Venn.

At least, so he said in the letter he sent through the dispatch relay, as soon as Durasnir wrote to ask why he and his Battlegroup were not on station.

Durasnir read the paper, then set it aside for a moment. The previous dispatch had reported that Battlegroup Chief Seigmad (whose mind remained clear, despite his difficulties in speaking) had asked for a spice-milk, picked it up, looked surprised, then fell over dead.

Regret was sharp, but Durasnir knew his old friend would have chosen just such a death: quick, probably as painless as such things ever are, and in service. He picked up the report, and left the cabin. From the positions of the

Erama Krona, he knew that Rajnir had climbed into the main top once again. Probably with Halvir.

A signal ensign hovered, waiting to be sent aloft, but Durasnir dismissed him with a gesture. Thinking that he could use the time as well as the effort, he climbed up.

The weather had turned cold, the sea gray-green, the wind brisk. It had been far too long since Durasnir had been aloft: he could not immediately recall the last time.

Two faces turned his way when he swung down from the shrouds. He hated how breathless he was and tried to hide it as he looked down at the game of ticky-bones. Rajnir had played the strategy game with Vatta, Durasnir remembered, and waited for the heart-seize of memory.

When it had passed, he made his obeisance. "Two reports. First, Battlegroup Chief Seigmad is dead. Whom do you want as Battlegroup Chief?"

"Whom do you recommend?" Rajnir asked.

"Baltar. He acted for Seigmad at Nelsaiam and acquitted himself well."

"I think I remember him—long nose, a squint. His ship, the *Katawake*."

"Yes."

"Make it so."

Durasnir acknowledged, then offered the paper to Rajnir.

The king cast his eyes down the page. Then he sat back. "Did you expect something of the sort? I did."

Durasnir was forced to make a sign of negation. "I admit I did not."

"You've been busy," Rajnir said. "And you were not meant to see what he did behind your head. But I could see. He had so denied me any authority that despite his empty words of allegiance, even when Erkric's spell was gone he went on in exactly the same way before my eyes."

Durasnir gazed out to sea, upset by his own blindness.

Halvir gazed unhappily at the deep furrows in his father's face. He hated it when his father looked so old and tired. But he said nothing. The king had trusted him with yet another secret: *You are so like your brother, who was once my greatest friend. And he really was a friend. I've decided there will be no more Breseng, and covert wars over boys who are chosen to forward others' goals. Nor will I have a son, for who's to say what he will be like? You are going to be my heir, but no one will know until you are old enough to hold the kingdom if they kill me over it.*

Rajnir said, "You cannot foresee everything, Uncle Fulla. Nor can I. Except this: I wish Battlegroup Captain Hyarl Balandir joy of his encounter with Elgar the Fox."

Chapter Twenty-nine

LOW drifts of smoke rolled slowly across the wharf to blend into the pall dissipating westward, out to sea. Crews on board ships had finished dousing fires and now faced the task of repair. In the harbor, the previous day's truce had required both sides to withdraw from the long, low harbor headman's buildings that Pilvig, two of her friends from the *Sable,* and some adventurous young Delfs had attacked and liberated in a short, vicious skirmish.

Pilvig had known about the tunnels underground.

The Venn hadn't.

The locals crept out cautiously during the night and set up a bucket brigade since the wintry wind for once did not bring rain. But at dawn, when the Venn rowed to the wharf again, the locals vanished, leaving the buildings to smolder. They'd have to be rebuilt anyhow.

Dyalf Balandir motioned his captains to wait on one side of the wharf and strolled out to the center alone to meet Elgar the Fox.

Once he'd secured Geranda after a disappointingly easy fight, he'd made what he considered a brilliant strategic decision—to take the Fire Islands to assure himself a first line of defense—but who could have known the damn harbor would be full of Delfs busy refitting?

They were not only root stubborn, but he knew they somehow communicated with one another over the world. It was legendary how what happened to one Delf at the northern reaches of Drael was soon known to the Delfs south of Sartor, though the Venn were the sole masters of deep sea navigation.

He set fire to their ships at once. Vastly outnumbered, they vanished into the thickly forested hills—which were a lot like the thickly forested hills of their own islands. He was still trying to hunt them out of hiding when the rest of them appeared hull up on the horizon, along with Sarendan, Khanerenth, and the Fox Banner Fleet. His scouts had vanished without a trace.

A day's battle and heavy losses had caused Balandir to make what he considered his brilliant tactical decision. He sent Beigun (who had begun to annoy him with his constant questioning and arguing) with a truce flag to demand that Elgar the Fox face him in a halmgac duel. At dawn. Only they wouldn't row away to one of the islands, they'd settle things right here, before all witnesses, on the broad wharf at the end of the short pier inside the bay.

The sun had just risen, barely warming the bitter winter air. Balandir stood alone, knowing his carefully picked Honor Guard was at the ready in case of pirate treachery, his Battlegroup captains nearby to function as witnesses.

He watched his breath freeze and fall and resisted the impulse to stamp. He had warmed up his muscles with the ship's armor chief well before dawn. His sword was loose in his baldric; he'd left behind his winged helm with its new gold torc twisted about it as a crown. He'd decided after a single practice that the winged helms were terrible to fight in, and these barbarians would not know what a crowned helm signified anyway.

A host of small boats drifted over the water from around the black-sided ship on the opposite side of the bay. Beigun's boat was in the lead. He moored it, climbed up, gave Balandir an indecipherable look, then retreated to stand with the other captains.

So Beigun had returned alive, much to Balandir's surprise, and behind him strolled a tall figure dressed entirely in black, except for the wink of silver in a belt buckle. The low northern sun, a pale silver disk, outlined the man from behind while keeping his face in shadow. His hair glowed an unpleasant red.

Balandir said, "I said Elgar the Fox." He'd spoken in Venn; he began to search his mind for the words in Sartoran when the enemy spoke in Venn.

"You've got Fox. There are more than one of us. It happens to be my watch." Fox's accent was strong, but he was understandable.

Balandir snapped, "I knew that." Then, feeling he'd somehow lost a step, he snarled, "Where's the scar-faced short one?"

"As well you have only me," Fox retorted. "He only faces kings and Norsundrians. I may not be as good at fighting, but I am far more merciful."

A rustle and whisper behind Balandir caused him to jerk around. He bit back a command to *shut up!* and confined himself to a glare.

"Get your sword," Balandir said, drawing his.

Fox crossed his arms and tipped his head. "Don't need one."

Balandir wasted no more time. He roared, charged, swung—and found himself attacking air. The man in black snapped his hands out, blades gripped in each. Balandir swung again, with all his strength. The whirling knives came at him, and he died before he hit the wharf boards.

Fox looked past him to the still captains, who were divided between stunned disbelief and grim anticipation of what that black-sided ship would signal next.

Fox said, "The rest of you may wait here for Sarendan's representative, who will land shortly. If you don't come to an agreement by midday, we'll use you for target practice."

"That was almost fun," Fox said a short time later, as he walked into *Cocodu*'s wardroom and stamped to warm up his numb toes.

Death was under repairs, it having been the target of Balandir's primary raider packs. Though Inda was still a formidable warrior even without the use of his right arm, Fox and Barend had seen after the battle how much such effort pained him. Inda was asleep when the Venn appeared under the truce flag demanding a duel. Fox and Barend privately settled their response, and just before dawn, when Inda woke Fox reported the news as he strapped on his knives, adding, "You took *Vixen* against Rajnir and Erkric, and I didn't squawk."

"Yes, you did," Inda said, laughing a little.

Fox shrugged. "So squawk. But now it's my turn." And he'd left before Inda could finish getting dressed.

Now he was back.

"I thought Venn were better trained than that." Inda waved his spy glass. "He was a big enough fellow. What happened?"

"Oh, he'd had the rudiments of good training, but my guess is, he'd never had a serious bout in his life. Probably thought any enemy would consider himself to be privileged to be killed by so exalted a fellow. He was arrogant right up until he was surprised." Fox saw Barend sitting at the table, then his eyes narrowed. "There a reason it's just us?" *Us three Marlovans,* he meant.

The wardroom door opened, and Tau entered. "Jeje and Eflis have everybody on the *Sable* for the victory party, except a nominal deck watch." He tipped his chin up toward the weather deck.

Fox dropped down on the bench, hands on his knees. "Inda?"

Inda got up and prowled around the enormous room. His restlessness seemed to fill the space, large as it was, and somehow magnified the outer sounds, making them distinct: the wash of water down the hull, the creak of masts, and through the far doors, in the captain's cabin, a high female voice.

"... and when have you ever heard me tell anyone my name is Waki? When, Mutt? Name once."

"Almost everybody's at the party," Fox murmured.

Inda paused midstride. "What's the problem with those two now?"

"Nugget's become the toast of those young fellows in the Khanerenth navy." Tau opened his hands out. "The ones with titles."

"So? He's got all the young female mates after him."

Tau said, "But Nugget likes to share. Mutt does not."

Inda shook his head, his shoulders, waved his left hand, then resumed his prowl. "Our other alliance captains. Ev-

erything was fine until yesterday. Everyone agreed we'd
use Gillor's and Tcholan's plan—they'd fought at Fire Island longest, had charted this bay—"

The low and high voices had tangled, fast and angry, then
abruptly Mutt's voice rose, distinct: he had to be standing at
the door to the captain's cabin. ". . . as long as it suits you.
But when you're tired of us, you can go off to your damned
castle and be Lady Waki. I hate that!"

Inda began to rub his hand over his face, wincing when
he encountered a pair of cuts, and an enormous bruise on
his cheekbone. "Should I say something? No." He hit the
table with his hand, then moved on, touching bunk, bulkhead, table, opposite bulkhead, and around again. "Everything was fine. Then we launch the attack. That's fine, too,
though it got mighty hot when they hit us with those six
raiders. Have to remember that formation—two inside trying to board, four outside laying down arrows."

Tau thought, *Why didn't I ever notice that before, how
Inda touches things in a pattern?* But he hadn't done it for a
long time. Since the days right before the battle at Andahi.

Barend whistled under his breath. "Worst fight we've
been in since the tussle at Jaro."

"Well, with the Delfs coming out of the hills, like we figured they would, we got them bottled. Just like we thought.
Right?" He paused, all made motions of agreement. "So
here's this fellow wants a duel, Fox, you go off, but ever since
the sun came up and I walked out on deck, our allies've been
watching me with their glasses. Not you and that Venn fellow on the wharf. Me. Why?" He turned around, rapped the
hull, the table, the back of a chair, his right arm in its sling
knocking against his ribs; the pattern was drawing in. "Last
night when I rowed around to look at damage, they were *all*
watching me. I mean the hands put down buckets to stare. Is
it because I took a couple of cuts, they think I turned soft?"

"No." Fox snorted, amused at the vastness of Inda's
understatement. A couple of cuts indeed. "They all think
you're invincible. Even with one arm hanging. Even if you
had no arms." He flashed a brief grin. "The Venn, too," he
added, thinking of the idiocy he'd spouted on the wharf
and the glum conviction in those watching faces. Then his
humor vanished. "They were all waiting for you to pick up
Balandir's crown. Still are."

Inda sighed. "That's why you're here right now."

Nugget's voice rose, more and more shrill. "... and you really think I could just walk in, and those court people would welcome me? When I don't know their customs, or their dances, or their clothes, or even their words for things? Mutt, you're a bigger snob than Nilat!"

A door slammed.

"How'd Nilat get into that?" Barend asked.

Inda cut a fast glance his way. "She says she won't cook for any but crowned heads anymore." He turned to Fox. "I told you Evred's orders." He self-consciously touched the locket through his clothes.

Scorn burned in Fox's gut, but he kept his vow. It was easy to see that, much as Inda was in pain from the fight outside the harbor, the internal pain was worse. "It's up to you, Inda. Either way you decide. So what have you decided? Are we here to plan how to take the strait?"

"I already know how to do that," Inda said impatiently, dropping into a chair. The others watched him wince as he carefully touched the right side of his face with his left hand. "But ... what they've all been saying. Deliyeth thinks I want to start an empire. Chim says Queen Kliessin thinks Evred's going to take her throne away. Thog ..." He turned, mouth compressed, then turned back, as though he could not sit still despite the evident headache. "But I'm ordered to bring peace to the strait. I take the harbors, and they all have the same laws. Same as our harbors at home. Which are doing well, everyone says so. How do I get them to see that, without a fight? I don't want to fight Chim—not even Deliyeth."

Tau thought, *It's time.* "Inda, I think I have a compromise."

Inda's sudden hope was a startling contrast to his previous tension. "You wrote to Evred?"

Tau's anticipation, his confidence, faltered at the intensity of Inda's hope. "No. I left my golden case with Evred's mother. It seemed the right thing to do at the time." He flicked his fingers out, toward the rest of the fleet. "I've been talking to everyone, trying to find compromises. I have two signed treaties—Ymar and Danara, though they recognize that no one has countersigned. But it's a step in the process, a preliminary promise of commitment. The rest of them await your presence at a formal meeting."

Inda said, "So they agree to our patrols? Our laws?"

Tau said slowly, "No. To mutual peace, yes. To guarantee freedom of trade, yes. But they do not want overlords."

Inda's gaze went distant, and his hand moved absently to the locket inside his shirt. Then he blinked and looked up. "Fox, I'm under orders."

"I know." Fox kept a tight grip on himself. "That's why I'm not arguing. You decide. We'll back you."

Barend turned his thumb up, gaze on his hands.

They all felt it, how Evred Montrei-Vayir's will had become a presence among them. One his cousin and lifetime ally, one his sworn Shield Arm and boyhood friend, one his lover, one his potential maritime commander—all of them in one sense or another under his command.

Tau began to knead Inda's tense neck muscles. "You don't have to decide today, Inda. We've got plenty of sailing time ahead. Let's meet with the others, and you can hear what they have to say."

"Evred-Harvaldar Sigun!"

"Indevan-Harskialdna Sigun!"

The roar of the Jarls from the throne room sent a few winter birds flapping skyward, past Fareas-Iofre, who was taking her daily walk on the castle wall.

The air was so cold she shivered inside her woolen robes and the scarf wrapped to her ears and nose. When she encountered another female form, she would have passed on by, but the woman veered toward her, so she stopped.

"How is Hadand?" It was Mistress Gand.

"Sleeping. He came faster this time."

"A he?" Mistress Gand asked, and cracked a laugh. "No wonder the king is down there getting the wolves to howl."

"There was a ship victory," Fareas said.

Mistress Gand gave her a squint-eyed look. "Your boy turfed some more Venn, or pirates, or pirates and Venn?" She grunted. "Have to say he's done well. And at least so far, no harm to *us*. Though I was angry."

Fareas had known about Mistress Gand's anger for years. It had been an unspoken wall between them—not that they'd ever been friends as girls. Fareas had come to the queen's training as the betrothed of a Montredavan-An, which had divided her off from most of the rest.

The "us" referred to women. Inda had broken his promise to Hadand by teaching Evred the women's Odni. And Hadand had carried on training Evred after Inda's exile. Two of Fareas' children had thus contravened generations of careful training, which had caused anger in some, and a bracing for trouble in others.

Fareas suspected that the mention now, after so many years of silence, was a kind of forgiveness, or at least acceptance. Her children had certainly proved their loyalty, all three of them.

But it didn't do to say. So she initiated a conversation, for the first time. "There are three boys in the nursery now." She smiled at the thought of tiny, newborn Tanrid, of the bright, bright red hair. And though many insisted you could not possibly tell which hand a child would favor for years, she was convinced that he would reach for the world with his left.

"Three boys," Mistress Gand said. "It's time and enough for some girls, eh?"

A hard, double-reef topsail east wind drove the alliance back toward The Fangs at a speed that would have been exhilarating except for the blizzard obscuring all but the pale greenish waves crashing over the bow.

The weather had been so bad there had been only two ship visits since their departure from Fire Island. Already their numbers were diminished as Taz-Enja was ordered home. For Sarendan, the adventure was over. Their interest in the strait was limited to the old trade route that followed all the ports around the great Sartoran continent. If necessary, they could venture through the windy ice islands of the south below Sartor. They preferred the strait, but it was not crucial. For the rest, the strait was vital.

During the long series of storms Inda exchanged notes with Evred via the slow, painful method of the lockets. Slow because, though Evred never failed to answer him instantly, most of the time that first answer was some variation on *Permit me to consider the question.* The second note might be half a day later, sometimes two or three, always written in tiny, careful lettering that Inda had to hold directly under a glowglobe to read.

"What's Evred said?" Tau asked Inda every day.

After the first note, Tau realized that Evred had not—and would not—greet the prospect of his treaty with instant approval. His confidence in having found a solution twisted into self-mockery.

As the fleet sailed inexorably west on the harsh east wind, the self-mockery at his assumption that he could civilize a king twisted into anxiety.

There came an afternoon when snow fell steadily on the deck and Inda sat backward on a chair next to the ceramic stone with its Fire Stick, rocking back and forth. "Any news from Evred?" Tau asked, brushing snow off his arms. "I was just aboard Kavna's *Swan*."

No need to say what the subject of the talk had been.

"I hate these little pieces of paper," Inda muttered without looking up, his forehead bumping the chair back, bump, bump, bump. "Everything you say, and Dhalshev says, and Kavna says, makes sense. But I can't seem to get it right for Evred."

"Let me try," Tau said, after a protracted pause.

He hated the way Inda's face eased, but he said nothing more, just sat down and pulled paper over. Someone had already added a drop of whiskey to the ink to keep it liquid; Tau warmed his fingers over the lamp as he considered what to say.

He rewrote his words in several drafts to explain clearly but succinctly that he had put together a treaty in which the signatories would agree to freedom of trade for all—including Iasca Leror—and no sovereignty in the strait. Instead, the waters were to be guarded by all.

After the last draft, he lined out all the claims about how this was the first such treaty in history—a white stone to mark the history of peaceful relations—all the words the diplomats and princes and captains used to one another. Tau could too easily envision Evred's disbelief, his silent derision at what he'd dismiss as empty oratory. Evred Montrei-Vayir understood the dynamic of human relations within one context: force.

Sighing, Tau threw the carefully written square into the fire, and wrote out the treaty stipulations once more, ending it with these words: *This document is unprecedented, and while high-flown hyperbole decorates the mutual compliments, there is a truth all acknowledge: the power of goodwill. All including Inda. He's fought beside these people and believes in their goodwill.*

He gave it to Inda, who sent it unread.

There was no answer that night—but who knew what time it was on the other side of the world?

There was no answer the next day.

Three more days passed. Inda went about his usual tasks, but Tau's anxiety increased as he avoided all his old friends outside the Fox Banner Fleet.

"What is wrong?" Jeje finally asked, after he'd been restlessly prowling around *Vixen,* getting in the way of Viac and the new mate he was training.

"Let's go below," Tau said.

Jeje's dark brow rose. When they'd shut themselves into the cabin, he said, "Evred ordered Inda to take control of the strait. The Marlovans will run it."

Jeje shrugged. "So? Makes sense to me. You know he'd do a good job."

"Jeje. Think back to your single meeting with Princess Kliessin. Now queen. Multiply her words by every king along both coasts, but add double for Kliessin because Bren Harbor is also their capital. Anyone who runs that harbor effectively runs the kingdom."

Jeje's brow now drew down into a glower. "So she'd have Inda shot. Why? Because he'd do a better job running things than she would? That's just why I hate kings. And that goes for queens." She sighed. "I also hate politics."

Tau gazed at her, his lips shaping the first words—*Inda's life depends on his obedience*—then he hesitated. Inda had not told Jeje, he'd not told anyone outside of Fox, Barend, and himself about Evred's orders.

"This matter is all politics," Tau said slowly and waited for her to ask how. Or why. Or what could be done. He wanted badly to talk about it, and with Jeje he knew he'd get sympathy for his own dilemma. But he needed insight, not sympathy. Though Jeje left him far behind when she talked about sea tactics and strategy, she had never evinced much interest in land history, and none in the doings of kings.

Jeje gave a loud sigh. "Spare me." She made a spitting motion. "They're all idiots. Politics is another word for idiocy." Her scowl turned into a squint as she peered out the steamy stern window. "Besides, Inda's signaling for you."

Their private signals were flown from the mizzenmast. Tau climbed into the gig and despite the choppy gray seas throwing up packets of icy water, scudded from *Vixen* to *Death*.

He had to wait until Inda was finished overseeing bow training, and then a visit from Woof, then at last Tau was alone with Inda, who held out a slip of paper.

Evred had written only: *Who is to enforce this treaty?*

Tau grimaced. So much for the power of goodwill. He sat Inda's table and wrote, *The alliance in common will guard the treaty, details to be agreed on through negotiation.*

"Here, send that," he said to Inda, after twisting the paper.

Inda shrugged, tucked it into the locket, and sent it. "Now, let's go down to the galley. Lorm's got food waiting."

It was a long day and night before Evred wrote back to Tau.

> *The way they allied in common to defend Bren? Inda may sign your treaty if he deems the wording true to my orders. But he is also under orders to guarantee peace with the force he has raised.*

Tau read it through three times, then sat down unheeding as Inda, Fox, and a couple of the other captains pored over the charts of the eastern end of Land of the Chwahir, which were dangerously vague: the Chwahir would not permit foreigners to chart them. "Stay away from the rock teeth, then there's no danger," Thog had said, which was the same thing Chwahir had been saying for centuries.

Tau gazed at the back of Fox's head as he and Barend carefully measured distances, then he looked back at Evred's note. Tau now understood why Fox had retired from the discussions. Either Inda carried out Evred's orders and subjected the strait to Marlovan peace—which anyone could see Inda was reluctant to do now that he'd realized what that entailed—or else Inda returned home and faced the consequences of not obeying orders.

An intolerable choice.

He reached for paper, despite the sickening inward conviction that all his work was for nothing. He had failed of his most important purpose: to save Inda this choice. Evred would never see outside of his Marlovan convictions.

If reason would not prevail, might not there be one last principle to try, the bonds of loyalty? That was part of the Marlovan code. Surely Evred would understand the breaking of trust . . . no, he couldn't put it that way, because Evred would not be able to separate trust from obedience.

Tau could not rest or even eat until he handed Inda one last tightly folded paper, in which he'd written in Old Sartoran, *Don't force Inda to fight his friends*.

Inda shoved it into the locket and sent it off, then returned to Barend, and overseeing a drill of the new ship rats they'd taken on at Freeport and at Fire Island.

Chapter Thirty

TDOR looked up from her desk when Hadand entered, and laughed as she extended her mittened fingers over the lamp to warm them. "Imand writes that Honeyboy is trying to teach Little Stalgrid to—" Her words stuttered to a stop when Hadand came into the light, her eyes wide, her mouth pressed into a thin line. Tdor rose up on her knees, dropping the letter onto the desk. "What's wrong?"

"Evred requested our help," Hadand said.

"Our help?" Tdor repeated, looking around wildly for enemies, fire, some threat as she followed Hadand to the door.

"It's Inda," Hadand whispered on an exhaling breath.

Tdor's neck chilled. "I thought the Venn were defeated. They are back?"

Hadand just gave her head an impatient shake, so Tdor schooled herself to silence as they dashed out. Despite Hadand's shortness, she had a very long stride when she wanted to move fast, and Tdor had to stretch out to match her pace.

They passed the king's suite without a check and headed toward the government annex at the south end of the royal castle. Tdor realized she hadn't seen Evred for days. *Once it was our habit to all dine together,* she thought as they ran down the steps. *When did we do that last? When Inda was here.* Then Signi had left, and Tdor and Hadand had formed the habit of eating together in the nursery, where they could watch the babies at play, or at sleep (Tdor had never imagined the fascination of watching a baby sleep), and talk over their day.

They reached Evred's public office, and Tdor's right fist came up ready for a salute but Hadand opened the door to a room occupied only by her mother.

Fareas-Iofre sat next to Evred's high desk. She looked like a small graying wren, perched straight-backed and uncomfortable in the massive raptor chair as she bent over tiny scraps of paper, lit by three branches of half-burned candles, and one of the hallway glowglobes resting on a folded cloth.

She looked up and rubbed her eyes. "These are nearly impossible to read. I don't think Inda picked up a pen all the years he was gone."

"He didn't." Tdor gazed down at the desk in astonishment. "What are all these paper bits?"

Hadand pointed. "Inda and Evred. Inda seems to be having trouble with his orders, and Evred doesn't know why." She touched a smaller pile of rumpled papers. "*These* are from Tau. It looks like he's trying to—" She frowned.

Tdor bent closer. Tau's fine handwriting was clear, but . . . she looked up in horror. "They're discussing orders—matters of import—with these little scraps of paper? These are even smaller than the ones we used with the scroll-cases! Why don't they use those, at least?"

Hadand sighed. "Evred didn't trust the scroll-cases because there was some evidence that Dag Erkric of the Venn had tampered with them right before the Andahi battle. The lockets go all the way back to his father, and they never failed." She turned up her palm. "Evred asked me to find a way to explain himself more clearly."

"To Inda and Tau?" Tdor asked. "I still don't understand what the problem is."

"This longer one here is from Cama." Fareas-Iofre's brown gaze flicked from Hadand to Tdor. "Evred wrote to him yesterday," she said.

"They begin here." Hadand indicated the row of Inda papers. "This one first."

Tdor sighed, wishing Evred used a regular desk so she could sit on a cushion. She hitched herself onto the edge of the desk.

After puzzling over several of Inda's scraps, Tdor said, "Do we have what Evred wrote?"

Hadand had leaned forward, elbows on the desk, head in her hands, Tau's close-written first note before her. She lifted her head. "No. But he said he just keeps repeating his orders: take the strait, establish our rules over all equally, promise to patrol and enforce fairness."

Tdor struggled against a new horror. "He can't think there's some, some *plot* going on. Not Inda!"

"Not Tau," Hadand said in a low voice.

"Read them all," Fareas said. "Ask questions after."

Tdor flushed and bent over the little paper again, puzzling out each smeared, quick-writ word in Inda's sloppy but dear handwriting. Once she surreptitiously kissed a paper before she set it aside, touching what she knew he had once touched. But as she worked her way through the carefully preserved scraps, her questions did not go away. They only intensified, causing more questions, like streams branching from a river.

When she'd read Tau's last, written in Old Sartoran— *Don't force Inda to fight his friends*—she looked up to find the other two waiting.

Hadand said, "You're the best at explaining things so others understand."

Tdor flushed at the unexpected compliment, then turned Fareas' way. "But whatever I know was taught me by you. When you said to us as girls that explaining things was like jumping from horse to horse in the field games: you wait and match the rhythms of both and then it's easy. If you don't match rhythms, you fall off."

Hadand leaned back, smiling wryly. "But I was the best at horse jumping, so obviously I'm not seeing something."

Fareas said, "Tdor has always heard the way others use words, so she could explain things to people using their own words and ways."

Hadand was about to protest, then tipped her head, considering. "No, you're right." She grinned. "I tend to just hand out orders, if I get impatient. Maybe that's why the girls love you best, Tdor." Then, more seriously, "So what do you think?"

As Tdor's hesitation lengthened, the only sound was snow patting at the window. The air in the room had stilled, the candle flames elongating with barely a flicker.

Tdor said tentatively, "This is really important."

Hadand flung out her hands. "Everything we do is important!"

Fareas squared the little piles with neat movements. "Everything you do is important here. This matter touches on lives in other lands."

Hadand sighed. "Exactly. We're bringing them peace. Well, we already brought them peace. Inda's to see to its being kept."

Tdor watched Fareas' fingers smoothing the papers, like stroking a crying babe. "But . . . I think what Tau is saying is that they don't want our laws, or our patrols."

Hadand sighed. "Yes, Tau's treaty. Why did he do that? I just can't believe that Tau wants to become some sort of king. Is that why Evred is so angry? It doesn't seem like Tau."

Fareas touched Tau's first note. "If he's stating the truth, he claims no authority whatsoever. In this agreement between all these other monarchs, there would be no authority in the strait."

Hadand sighed even louder. "That's what I don't get. There has to be an authority. People need one. Or you get the Venn, or pirates, or someone else turfing you out of your own homes, killing your people, and taking your things."

Tdor hugged her arms against her body. Once, when she was about nine, she'd taken a Rider's horse out, thinking she'd get a faster gallop than the girls had on the older training mounts. She got a gallop all right, but she couldn't control the animal, who was used to a man in the saddle, not a small girl who could barely stay on. The speed had not been exhilarating but frightening.

She felt that way now, only worse, because of the strain across Fareas' brow. If this were a simple matter of finding the right words, why could she feel the tension in the air?

They think you can explain. So explain. "Tau . . . seems to think that they can agree not to have an authority. And

Inda doesn't want to fight his allies to make them follow his orders."

"But you *can't* not have an authority. That's what Evred doesn't comprehend about their so-called treaty, which sounds just mad. He explained it to me this morning over breakfast. This is why he turned to Cama." Hadand flicked Cama's note, written in a strong block hand. "Who's reminding us of what Idayago and the north was like before we got there—the nobles squabbling, the king building castles and ignoring the pass because he wanted the Olarans to pay for road-clearing. The Olarans ignoring it because they wanted Idayago to pay, according to some long-ago treaty that everyone had otherwise ignored. Lindeth Harbor charging three times the rates of the Nob, because no one liked trading at the Nob and then having to hire wagons for the long road down, past all the old robber caves. In those days, full of robbers, unless you hired a lot of guards."

Tdor glanced down at the much-folded paper. Candlelight glowed on one thin strip, Cama's bold lettering standing out: *Tell Inda he gets tough with a few, the rest fall into line, just like he saw when he was here*. She looked up. "I think . . . I think Tau's treaty is suggesting a new thing."

"But the new thing makes no *sense*. What's more important, Inda swore before Convocation," Hadand stated, shrugging. "Wisthia-Queen said once that we Marlovans don't know anything about how politics in other kingdoms work, and I saw the truth of that in Anaeran-Adrani. Evred's been learning about foreign politics, Tau was helping with that. Inda's never known anything about 'em. Not even ours! But he swore before Convocation that he would bring Marlovan peace and fair laws to the entire strait. And one of our laws is when you're under orders, you carry them out. Even Inda knows that. If we don't all obey the laws, from king to cottager, then we end up like the north, waiting for someone stronger to ride in to the attack."

Tdor said slowly, "I think Inda and Tau want Evred to change his mind."

"Yes," Fareas said.

Hadand's eyes widened. "But that's impossible. Evred's given the orders—which he and Inda discussed for days before Convocation, I remember that much. Then they swore together before the Jarls! If, if, oh, there was some great

king known for fairness along the strait, who promised his
own fair laws and the force to keep them, I could see Evred
changing the orders. But there is *nothing!* Just this silly idea
that everyone *knows* doesn't work or why are there kings
in the first place?"

Before Tdor could answer the door opened, and Evred
stepped in. Shock fired along her nerves. So rarely had she
seen Evred angry, but those times had been nothing to how
very angry he looked now.

Hadand moved from his chair as he walked past Tdor
to the desk. "We're done with the envoys." He sank down.
"I figured out what these Toarans really want, which is the
secret of our steel."

"So we lose those harbors for trade?" Hadand asked,
leaving Tdor feeling as if she were making her way over
unfamiliar river ice. She had so little idea what was going
on outside of her own duties.

Evred pinched his fingers tightly to the bridge of his
nose. "We'll go with the Delfs, even if it means paying more.
At least their demands are straightforward." He dropped
his hands. "Well? What do I say to Taumad to make myself
clear?"

Fareas had drooped her gaze to the papers on the desk,
her hands gripped inside her sleeves; Hadand said, "I'd just
send Cama's note."

It was then that Tdor understood the sense of Hadand's
earlier words. She was not there to try to convince Evred
to change his mind. He knew his mind. He believed his decision to be the right one, and he'd sworn it before all his
Jarls.

In those moments he looked past her to address Hadand
about the audience he'd just finished, she realized that what
she'd taken to be anger was a tension so severe it looked
like anger. But when he was angry, he whispered. His voice
right now was flat with pain.

He needs us to help him explain himself to Inda and Tau.
The import of that felt like a burden of stone, and the desperate importance of that communication was yet another
great block of stone, and the consequences of failure a
block so massive that its weight seemed to crush mind and
spirit. *Is this what being king is like every day?*

Evred turned Tdor's way, and she braced herself to meet

that pain-flat gaze. "I need ... more time to understand," she said, because he was waiting, though she hated the inadequacy.

"There isn't time." He flat-handed the words away. "Here *or* there." An indrawn breath—they heard it. "Have you descried something that I misapprehended? There has to be a reason they keep writing all these words about this empty treaty."

Hadand turned toward the door. Evred's pain hurt her, as it always did, though she fought against it. But she was tired, everyone's duty seemed clear, and Inda's willful blindness irked her as much as the silent conspiracy to preserve it. Despite all the trouble that had caused. "If nothing else, remind my idiot brother to keep his word of honor," she said and walked out.

Tdor said something—later she never remembered what—and found herself with Fareas-Iofre outside of her own suite. She did not remember walking there.

"I believe I will go visit my Fera-Vayir relations," Fareas said. "It is time."

It was then that Tdor really understood not just the price of kingship, but the price Inda would have to pay if he did not obey. And his mother, dauntless all these years, could not bear to be there to see him pay it.

Inda signaled the *Vixen* the next day. When Tau climbed aboard to the sound of creaking ropes and masts as the ship rats skylarked overhead, Inda waved at him from the cabin.

As soon as Tau shut the door Inda said with an odd expression, more pained than rueful, "What did you say to Evred? He told me to explain to you what honor means, beginning with how we always keep our vows. Phew!"

"Well, I tried," Tau said, hating the futility of his words—of weeks of effort.

He rowed himself back to *Vixen*.

Fox watched him leave. Wasn't hard to figure out what had happened. Next morning he was alone on deck with Barend just before the dawn watch change. They'd both checked sky, sea, and sails, before Barend was ready to take command, and Fox to rouse the morning watch for drill before he retired. "Your cousin," he said, "seems determined to force Inda to succeed where the Venn failed."

Barend squinted his way. "In what?"

"Conquering the world."

Barend was silent a long time, then turned his squint skyward. "We brought Inda to it. Whatever happens, I'll back him."

$$\text{Chapter Thirty-one}$$

KHANERENTH still rode with the alliance.

Aboard the Khanerenth flagship, the conversation was superficially about customs, kingdoms, accords—finding the meaning of words in other languages—but the real subject was who was going to find out what Indevan Algara-Vayir, their unbeatable commander, was going to do next. Until then, Inda had always been open (if not blunt) about what was on his mind. The two times they'd seen him since everyone sailed away from Geranda he'd not only been evasive, but uncomfortable to a disturbing degree. So everyone turned to Lord Taumad Dei for explanation, but all they got were vague assurances and expert deflection through questions about their own thoughts on matters—they'd leave, having lengthily aired their views, and not realize until they reached their ships that, yet again, they had no idea what Inda was going to do next.

Mehayan and Hamazhav wrote to their king, asking permission to leave the alliance. Both were told variations of, *Stay with Elgar at least as far as the Chwahir coast and make sure they sail on into the strait. We don't want you arriving home just to discover the rest of them entering our harbors next season, swords at the ready.*

"Altruism," Dhalshev said to Mehayan, "is what we all claim at the treaty table. It's expected. We cloak naked self-interest in a wish to serve others, mix it with a modicum of goodwill, and then hope to find a balance."

Mehayan leaned over to freshen their wine cups, first with the good blue wine from Gyrn, and then with the mulling rod. It hissed, filling the cabin with the heady aromas of hot spice. "That is so, that is so." He laid the rod back on the grill above the Fire Stick in the cabin's ceramic furnace.

"Lord Taumad, despite his silver tongue and golden looks, is one of us," Hamazhav observed, lifting his glass in salute.

Dhalshev said, "Inda is one of the only two people I've ever met who I think of as altruists. Though maybe I don't understand what that really means."

Hamazhav raised his brows. Mehayan uttered a barking laugh. "I'll know if you and I mean the same thing if you tell me your second one."

"Jeje sa Jeje. My first real talk with her, she told me how to defend the island. She could have taken my map to Inda. I saw her evaluate it in a single glance. I couldn't have stopped them—I was hard pressed between you, the Fire Island rats of the time, and the remnants of the Brotherhood."

The others chuckled appreciatively.

"I have yet to converse with him alone," Hamazhav murmured. "He is quite elusive for so uncouth a figure. Yet everything I hear paints a picture of an old hero, a paragon."

"A paragon with no manners." Mehayan barked another laugh. "Eats like a dog at his dish, ignores the table's prominent person, and converses on Old Sartoran verse forms with the least important person at table without comprehending the insult handed to the rest." .

Everyone laughed, Dhalshev included, though ruefully. He had been caught napping; sometime, somewhere, he'd been selected. Now they were waiting for him to realize it.

"Here's my question about altruistic claims of peace and goodwill." Mehayan stirred his forefinger around the top of his wine, then licked the spices off. "How do you enforce goodwill?"

"I don't know, but as soon as this damn snowstorm lifts, I mean to row myself over and find out," Dhalshev said, capitulating. At least they hadn't brought up his social familiarity with pirates.

Between two storms, a grand captain's barge rowed over to the _Death_ from the Khanerenth flag and up climbed Dhalshev, Harbormaster of Freedom Islands.

The ice-numbing wind made Dhalshev feel his age. He was going to retire soon, now that he'd survived what he'd expected to be a spectacularly bloody end. But he had two missions: the one he'd been sent on and his own. _Altruism,_ he thought, laughing to himself as he climbed aboard the black-sided pirate ship.

He'd half expected to be turned away, or at most to gain the ear of one or the other of their Elgars. He did not expect to find himself shut into that splendid, kingly cabin with all three of the Marlovans, though he could see in Barend's averted face, his purposeless sketching on a tutor's slate, how reluctant he was to be there.

So they had expected him, then. Dhalshev abandoned the careful chain of conversational gambits, and said, "Where are you going next? I've two purposes. My first is a thought to Freedom Islands' future. Even a bricklayer wants to hand off his domain, small as it is, to someone who will build the way he did."

Inda turned over his good hand, and Fox said, "Though she'd kill me if she heard me say it, you could not do better than Jeje sa Jeje."

"I had been thinking of her." Dhalshev sat back, pleased to find agreement so far. "If she weren't so fierce in her antipathy to any type of authority, I would have asked her the year Woof vanished."

"Keep at her. She'll settle to it." Fox was amused at the patent relief in Dhalshev's face. No use in reminding him that if Fox had wanted to run the Freedom Islands federation, he would have been doing so by now. They both knew it. "Freeport is her home. She'd fight to keep it safe, and if you put it that way to her—harbormaster is one way of fighting to keep it safe—she might even listen. Eventually."

Dhalshev signed his agreement, then said in the same affable tone, "The talk of peace and harmony and guaranteed trade is all good, but the question you've been avoiding is, _whose_ peace?"

"Mine," Inda said, thinking, *Here it is at last*. And then, quoting Evred, "The same way I came to Bren's rescue last year. When no one else would."

Dhalshev said, "You came because you were asked." He got to his feet. "We've had a good relationship, and you are owed a debt of gratitude. The thing about gratitude is, when one tries to convert it into either money or blood it vanishes."

Inda leaned forward, his expression earnest, his shoulders tense. "What if I don't want money, or blood, just guaranteed peace?"

Dhalshev looked around the cabin, then back at Inda. "Did Idayago and Olara and Telaer Cassadas down in the south of Halia a couple centuries ago ever ask the Marlovans to come in and guarantee peace, once the dead were Disappeared? For that matter, did the Iascans?"

He opened the cabin door and left.

Inda rubbed his hand over his face. "I don't know what to say to that."

Barend was drawing a battle between two ships, rapping the chalk against the slate as he made fire arrows arcing back and forth. He did not look up.

Fox gave him an exasperated glance. "You're going to have to figure out what to say, because we're going to spot Chwahirsland on the horizon soon. Thog's going to want to know if you're going to pass them by . . . or not."

"I wouldn't attack the Chwahir even if I was ready to attack anybody," Inda said crossly, circling the cabin, fist pounding lightly on the chair back, table, bulkheads. "They'd have to come last. Bren first, and the rest would follow. Bren won't want to fight—you held them off with five ships I remember Jeje telling me."

"They had almost no navy then, just the ten capital ships the Venn had left them from the old days," Fox reminded him. "And most of them weren't in the harbor. But even so, we can take 'em. If that's what you really want."

"I don't want to *take* anybody! Except maybe the pirates Evred said are nosing around our coast. That's where we should be, is protecting our own . . ." Inda stopped. Those words were treason.

He saw in Fox's derisive gaze, and Barend's sober face, that they were thinking the same thing.

From outside came a muffled "Boat ho!"

Fox moved to the cabin door, then looked back. "Since the weather has briefly lifted, they might all be on the way over. Listen, Inda, I'll back you, whatever you decide. I don't mind being a Marlovan navy, especially if my hypothetical son will get outside Darchelde for a time. But if you take the strait, it's going to mean a lifetime of keeping it."

Fox opened the door as footsteps approached, and in walked Thog. Barend picked up his chalk and slate and slunk out. Fox closed the door behind them both.

"No, I'm not going to attack Chwahirsland," Inda said irritably.

A corner of Thog's mouth lifted faintly. "I did not think you would do that. Not you." She tipped her head toward the stern, indicating the rest of the alliance. "They seem to think I will attack them."

"They don't understand you," Inda mumbled, his face going hot and cold.

Thog turned over her calloused hand. "I don't understand Pilvig, who hides even now if she sees me, though she must know she will not be taken back. I understand dressing by others' custom—that was our agreement—but those purple trousers, and all those ribbons! Is this piratical dress the back of the hand to me?"

"She likes dressing that way. The brighter the better, she said. Do all Chwahir dress in the colors of rock and mud?"

Thog turned to face the stern windows, through which the snow fell softly, making lacy patterns on the pale sea before melting. "At home, you do not want to stand out."

"It's amazing anyone stays," Inda said. "All I hear is bad rumors."

"They say the same about your people. Yet we have good times. Our music is not like anything you have ever heard. They liken it to what the Morvende do, with chords and complicated beats, underground. Echoes. We . . . hum, because words are not always safe."

Inda had never heard that much from Thog. "Go on."

She seemed to withdraw again, and turned her back on the window. "We want to perform a work that people will point to, and say our name. A thing we make, or a thing we do."

Inda was fascinated by her wide, blinkless stare. "What will you do?"

"Be a great commander," she said in a whisper.

Inda's perceptions swooped, as if a hatch had opened below him. *She's going to fight a war.*

Maybe conflict between the Chwahir and their neighbors was inescapable—ineluctable. But that might not happen for years. Decades. Much as he'd love the expediency, Thog was not a justification for Evred's war. *Evred's war.* Even those thoughts were treason.

"Fare well," she said. And left as quietly as she had come.

Not long after the Chwahir sailed off, Lord Hamazhav arrived in his most formal clothing to offer to sign Lord Taumad Dei's treaty in the name of his king.

Prince Kavna was present, as well as Captain Deliyeth, as representative for Everon, Ymar, and the north shore Fleet Guild. Tau hosted a magnificent party aboard the *Knife,* and on the surface everyone was full of goodwill and laughter . . . but they all knew that Inda had not signed.

Nevertheless, the Khanerenth navy tacked back toward The Fangs and southward, Dhalshev and some of the independents with him. Most of the rest had chosen to follow Elgar the Fox, in hopes of adventure or treasure—maybe both.

By the end of the two months it took to ride the east winds up the strait to Bren, Kavna had met with Inda a dozen times, mostly aboard the *Knife,* a setting resonant with gravitas. Kavna was friendly, smiling, appreciative, full of questions about all of Inda's experiences—but he would not agree to anything but the Dei Treaty, which declared that no one had sovereignty over the strait.

And so, at this impasse, they neared Bren's cluster of islands. Inda knew he was watched as he continued to conduct drills. On the surface, friendliness and ship visits . . . underneath, covert ship visits to find out what he'd said, what orders he might have given in secret, to avoid surprise.

The last couple of days, Inda prowled around the deck of the *Death* restlessly. There was no avoiding the truth: all the questions had come down to a conflict of will. Not between nations, but between Evred-Harvaldar and his Harskialdna.

Inda understood that in Evred's mind, the matter was simple: the Harvaldar had issued orders. Inda had sworn to obey them.

For Inda, nothing was simple—if it ever had been. He'd always made his own orders, until he met Evred again and swore to become Harskialdna because of course they would want the same thing: the good of Iasca Leror.

Inda had lost the conviction that these orders were for anyone's good. But he'd sworn to obey them.

The day before the island cluster of Bren was expected to rise on the horizon, Tau hunted over the ship for Inda, and found him out on the bow again, shivering and staring into the wintry green sea, as snow clouds sailed overhead toward the west. And home.

"Inda."

Inda turned.

Tau gestured aft. "Chim is here. Insists on talking to you. And the rest are awaiting orders."

Inda started down the gangway.

"Fox and Barend are holding him on the captain's deck, and I have food coming into the cabin. You are to eat, if necessary at knifepoint. The demands can wait."

"They can't." *That's why I can't eat.*

Inda did not remember walking into the cabin, or sitting down. He was going over another conversation with Evred in his head, one he'd had a thousand times already, when he jumped at a knock. Tau opened the door, took a tray away from someone. He set the tray down and then stood with his back to the cabin door. "Eat."

Inda wearily picked up his knife. "You may as well tell Chim for me that I can't sign your treaty. Evred has given as far as he will."

"Eat."

Tau waited until Inda had reluctantly shoved a few bites of rice into his mouth. It was well-cooked food, rice balls with spiced cabbage and fish braised in wine, but Inda didn't taste it, he wasn't even aware of it; as Tau watched in silent comprehension, Inda's gaze went diffuse, and there he was, isolated again.

Tau would not presume to claim kinship. His sense of failure was acute but it was entirely personal. And he was not going to be called upon to pay the price of that failure. Inda was, if the Harskialdna did not carry out Evred's will.

Tau suspected Inda was not aware of how every time that locket signaled a new message from Evred asking for report on his progress, he jerked as if jabbed with a knife.

Inda rocked gently on his chair, spoon halfway to his lips. "The Chwahir were angry that I didn't take Rajnir," he said, gazing down at the fast-congealing food. "Did you know that? Kavna told me yesterday. Thog never told me. He said Deliyeth was also angry. If we had cut Rajnir into pieces, would that resolve anything?"

"No. They all wanted to see him suffer, preferably in some protracted execution. As if that would make restitution for the past twenty years."

Inda dropped his spoon, and reached with his left hand to massage his right wrist. After weeks of cautious effort and Tau's kneadings, he'd regained some feeling and limited movement, but if he twisted certain ways, his shoulder tingled and the limb went numb.

"I can work on that after you eat."

Inda sighed. "Before or after I talk to whoever's waiting?"

"Inda, I failed to explain the allies' reasoning to Evred, so I've tried to stay out of what I believe is the unconscionable decision facing you. But I think . . . I think I have to explain to you their viewpoint, just once. First, what do you want to do?"

What do you want? Inda heard not his friend Taumad, but Ramis of the *Knife,* and he looked up, quick, wary, to meet Tau's steady gaze. Light glowed in patterns up the cabin walls, and across Tau's face, revealing the tension Tau would rather have hidden.

I want to go home.

The memory faded; Inda shook his head. "It doesn't matter what I want. I am honor-bound to speak with the King's Voice. But they don't want what I am ordered to give."

"From you, they want one thing: freedom."

Inda sat back. "Freedom. They say it, but I don't understand. What kind of freedom is it if Durasnir turns around

and comes back? Or if Nelsaiam decides they want both
sides of the strait? Or some new pirate appears? My presence here is proof they can't protect themselves."

Tau waved a hand in dismissal. "But none of those are
real threats right now. The real threat that they see before
them is embodied in you: your unbeatable Marlovans. They
are very ready to be afraid of *you*."

"Me?" Inda thumbed his temples, though that did nothing for the headache that never went away. "Tau, I don't
want to fight them." The words burst out of him. "When
we started, we fought pirates. Then the Venn. Until I saw
them face-to-face, they were an easy enemy—"

Tau said quickly, "—and then you see them as individuals. Someone's brother. Cousin. Mate. But they're trying to
kill you, so you carry on because you want to stay alive."

Inda pressed his hands over his eyes. "But these are my
allies. My friends," he whispered.

Tap of the locket.

Inda dropped his hands and thumbed the locket open,
the old pain and weariness back in his face. He read the
note in silence, then crushed it in his good hand, murmuring, "He's waiting for me to take Bren Harbor. And I speak
with his Voice."

Tau sighed. "You're about to mouth out all his argu-
ments again, like a loyal Shield Arm. Barend and even Fox
are Marlovan enough to shrug and abide by Evred's orders, whatever they think of them. Maybe Barend regards
them as reasonable, understandable, practical." Tau held
out his hands. "To these people you are about to see—or
to conquer—you speak with your *own* voice. You won the
battle, you have their respect. You have their ear. Your king
is nothing but a far figure. A *threat*."

Inda winced, as though in pain. "You don't
understand."

"I think I do. A little. But I do not face your choice. Listen, Inda, I promised them I'd present their words so you'd
understand them, because it all comes down to how people
make sense of the world. The way they do, and the Marlovan way, are fundamentally different."

Inda sat back. "The evil empire, that's what Deliyeth
said. But they all see us that way, right?" He hit his chest.
"Now that's the way they see me."

"No—"

"But they do." His voice was high and raw. "I don't blame them for not trusting me. All I'm good at is killing. Maybe it's true, and I am evil."

"Inda—"

"But it's true. They think Evred is evil. So I must be too. Isn't it so, Tau? Then I have to be evil, or else I agree with them, and what does that leave me, sworn to obey an evil king who's been my friend all my life? But he's not evil. He's not."

Tau thought bitterly, *As well I'm getting used to failure. Because I've failed Evred, and I've failed Inda, too.* But even under the deluge, he would try to fashion a roof. "Finish up those rice balls, will you? I want to work on that shoulder."

"No." Inda stared down at the knife on the table, rocking; Tau wondered if the rhythm was Inda's heartbeat. "No," Inda said, almost inaudible. "Send Chim down."

Tau left to find Chim, angrier with himself than with Inda's obduracy.

Moments later, Inda was still rocking and staring down at his knife when the old man limped in, his gimpy gait expertly timed to the roll of the ship.

Chim rubbed his jaw. Inda looked like someone had gutted him, and he'd only now found it out. But not far off was an angry queen, and business was business. "Well, Inda, we'll be landing soon. What's going to happen?"

Inda looked up. *Evil chooses to do evil. I won't choose evil, I won't rip the net.* "First, tell me in your own words why they won't accept me guaranteeing peace, as I've been ordered."

"Free strait," Chim said. "Means we guarantee peace as a group, sorry and sodden as we are as an alliance. We have to learn sometime. But one thing we all agree on: no more overlords." Chim pointed through the scuttle. "What that means right now is, I go off this here vessel either with a piece o' paper, in which case everybody smiles and breaks out the eats, or else I go off and pick up me boarding blade." He switched from Sartoran to Dock Talk. "And yez loose yer boys and girls against us. Yez haveta cut me down first, and Kavna next. Cuz I ain't gonna stand aside."

Chim wiped his sweaty hands down his trousers, acutely

aware of the creak of wood, the wash of water down the hull, the distant cry of the mate on watch demanding an adjustment to sail trim, as he watched Inda hunched there, elbows on the table, forehead bumping his clasped fists.

Then Inda gave a long sigh, straightened up, and pulled a copy of the treaty from among the charts on the table. He read slowly, "*There shall be no power dominant in the strait. Any who claim dominance will be declared treaty-breakers, and the rest of the signatories have the right to rise against said treaty-breakers.* That's really aimed at me, isn't it?"

Chim's mouth worked, his chin lifted. "Or the Chwahir. Or Nelsaiam, across the way. Deliyeth is supposed to go north to them, everyone agreed. Did you know that?"

"No. No one told me."

"Then she goes to Llyenthur. I guess you can speak for the Idayagans, eh?" Chim's gaze was acute. His voice lowered to a rumble. "Reason I'm here instead o' Kavna, I'd like to be assured there won't be no cost to you. Not after all you did for us. Because unless I miss my guess, and I know I didn't, you'd be goin' direct against your king. And nobody has ever talked about Marlovan mercy. So what," he persisted, "is the personal cost to you for this here treaty?"

Inda looked away, then back. "Nothing I haven't required men without number to pay."

The Dei Treaty was written out fair before the ships passed the inner island.

Evred, they want their freedom. That includes from us as overlords.

They will be free from attack, from interference by their neighbors' greed, Inda! We will guarantee impartial peace. Make them see it.

I can't. I don't see it myself, not a peace that begins with me cutting old Chim down on his own dock.

Along the harbor stood warriors in burnt orange, but they were not armed for war. They were an Honor Guard.

Tap, went the locket.

Kavna, proud, happy, tired, introduced to Inda his sister, Queen Kliessin, who was impressive in glittering gems and brocade. She was amazed to find the infamous Elgar the Fox a fellow younger than she, and about her height, who dressed like an old deckhand, one arm in a sling. The only proof she had that he was really Elgar the Fox was the ruby earrings at his ears—and the deference everyone gave him, though she would swear he did not even notice. His one good hand brushed occasionally against his chest as he stood there where the royal pier adjoined the wharf, looking weary and absent while the signatories signed then made self-conscious speeches (hoping someone was writing them down) in celebration of a true Historic Moment.

Now intensely curious, Queen Kliessin said, "Commander Algraveer. To celebrate this occasion, please honor me with your presence at a banquet."

Kavna said cheerfully, "They've been cooking for days, Inda. I found out all your favorite dishes from Lorm."

"No," Inda said, his gaze bleak. *Tap,* went the locket. "I have to set sail for home."

He was rowed back to his ship as snow began to fall.

On the ebb of the tide the Fox Banner Fleet set sail, the deck crews busy and everyone else below. Inda was far forward, on the bow, curtained by soft white snow as he stared down into the dark waters. When the locket tapped again, he yanked it from around his neck and flung it far out into the sea.

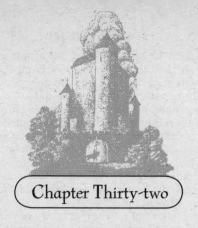

Chapter Thirty-two

A S far as the world knew, Elgar the Fox sailed west to
fight pirates infesting the west coast of Halia off The
Narrows.

It would actually be true—for the red-haired Elgar.

Fox enjoyed fighting pirates. So he would do it for a time,
building a navy for his homeland. Not because he cared a
whit for that homeland, but someday he would return, and
he wanted a child of his to be able to get a foothold in the
life of the kingdom again. He had his own work to do, a
private project already begun in the black-and-gold bound
book he kept locked in a private cabinet.

Until then he would equip and train a navy: as the more
independent of the Fox Banner Fleet tired of regular patrols and returned to Freedom, or moved on, he'd replace
them with Iascans and any Marlovans who felt no lure of
the plains.

Much as he would have liked to keep Inda by his side,
there was no stopping him. Or defending him in Iasca Ler-
or's royal city—Fox knew his own presence would just about
guarantee Evred Montrei-Vayir's ire. Though he did not say
anything to Inda, he hoped his own cooperative spirit would
in some measure mitigate what he knew lay ahead.

And so it was just Barend and Inda who disembarked from Jeje's *Vixen* on the Tradheval coast of Idayago at the beginning of spring. Overhead curved a sky of pure deep blue, the air cold after sleet had blown through. No one was around to witness the quiet farewells. "Fox says you're not staying with the navy. Where will you go?" Inda asked, after giving Jeje a hard, lingering hug.

Jeje shrugged, her mind on the tide. "Oh, I'm staying with the fleet. I just don't want to be part of any navy. I'll help Fox fight pirates until I can't stand his tongue anymore, then I'm going back to Freedom Isles. Promised Dhalshev I would. I like fighting pirates. It's good work. I also like Freedom." She grinned. "Come see us soon as you can."

Inda remembered what Dhalshev had told him about convincing Jeje to be his replacement. He turned to Tau. "What shall I tell them? Will you be back?"

Tau could not speak for a long moment. He had fought a silent battle alongside Inda, but because he was powerless to help, he would not burden Inda with the intensity of his regret.

"Kiss Hadand for me," Tau said, his voice husky.

Inda lifted his dunnage, Barend hefted his, and they began trudging up the beach toward the newly rebuilt castle they could see on the rise behind the harbor, a little way north of their stretch of beach.

Jeje's grin vanished as she and Tau pushed the boat back into the last of the ebb. They worked in silence to step the mast, Jeje frowning back occasionally. Finally, when they were midway between shore and ship, she said, "That hug. It felt like . . . like forever. Did he say anything like that to you?"

Tau seemed absorbed in the exact set of the sail. She was just beginning to feel irked when he gave her a quick smile. "No," he said. "Want the tiller?"

Cama's outer perimeter riders spotted the two shabby sailors not long after they'd trudged up the long, white, marshy beach to the road.

"We're here to see the Jarl," Inda said.

The riders betrayed surprise at hearing accent-free Marlovan from sailors, but no questions were asked. They carried the two back to the castle, where Cama had been

spending the winter in order to get to know his newborn
son. His expression, when he recognized the arrivals, went
from surprise and delight to a narrow, considering gaze.

That night they sat in Cama's private room. His wife
Starand—unaware of the identity of the two weather-worn
sailors her husband had welcomed, stalked away to her own
concerns—though that would not stop her, in later days,
from bragging out of her husband's hearing of the night
she had entertained so famous a pair. Cama's First Runner,
who recognized them as fast as Cama had, quietly saw to it
that no one came near.

Over food and spiced wine, at Cama's encouragement,
Inda began with his sea journey and the naval battle. Cama
frowned in concentration as Inda used game markers to
illustrate marine strategy and tactics, as he always had an
interest in the craft of war. But his interest intensified as
Inda came to the matter of most import: his refusal to carry
out his subsequent orders.

Inda's narrative was hopelessly tangled, plunging into
the past as he attempted to define political motivations.
Cama said little, as was his way. Finally Inda's voice hoars-
ened, and he shook his head. "And so I gave the orders for
Fox to cruise the strait, and our coast as well. But he won't
interfere with harbor affairs beyond our border."

Cama looked grim. "And so you came back."

Inda shook his head. "I had to. I brought the treaty I
signed in Evred's name. If he wants to flog me to death as a
traitor, well, that will be bad, but at least it'll be over. I can't
be an exile again, for the rest of my life."

Cama's breath spewed out. "Inda, what do you expect
Evred to do? You disobeyed an order. Not just one made
in private, but sworn before Convocation."

"I know."

"And so your sense of honor requires that Evred put
you to death? Do you have any idea what the cost of that
will be, and you think going off to one of your pirate hide-
outs would be worse?"

Inda rubbed his hand over his face. "All the honors
Sponge gave me. I made an oath. I can't throw it all over,
like it doesn't mean anything."

Cama hesitated, his one eye flicking Barend's way.

Barend stretched, uttering a dry laugh. "The King of

Ymar, and Prince Kavna, and that lord fellow all told me in private they were going to name these waters the Elgar Strait, now that the Venn are gone."

"That'll last a month," Inda retorted, unimpressed.

Cama wondered why Barend had said that, then dismissed it as irrelevant. It was plain that Inda still did not know about Evred's personal devotion, and the world still seemed to be colluding to hide it from Inda's finding out. Here he was, the bloodiest-handed commander left standing after years of war. Yet he was in some ways still the boy they'd all bunked with in the scrub barracks under Master Gand's stern eye, nearly twenty years ago.

"I'll have to send a Runner to Evred," Cama said finally, giving up.

Inda held up his scarred hand, the knuckles gnarled. A gold ring glinted on one finger, disconcertingly fine. "You may as well spare the man and the horse. Evred always knows where I am."

It was a full three months later that Rat Cassad, sent by Evred on special duty, met them at the ancient Marlovan inn at Hesea Spring, where the three great roads converged.

Inda and Barend arrived on hired mounts to find Cassad pennons planted out front, and Cassad waiting inside, with a host of armsmen.

Cassad looked the two tired travelers over, their shabby sea clothing, Inda's arm in a sling, no weapons in sight, and waved off his armsmen.

"Drink," he said, pushing mugs of ale toward them. He added, as they thirstily downed the good home ale, "My Runners spotted you days ago. Truth is, I don't really know if I'm an Honor Guard or a Watch Guard."

Inda's smile faded. "I will not interfere with whatever orders Evred has given you," he said bleakly.

Cassad sighed. "You are an idiot, Inda. At first he thought you were dead. The locket didn't work. But the ring still moved—and he thought—" His eyes met Barend's, and he faltered. "Well, never mind. He's waiting."

Evred was on the watch long before dawn the next day. He shut the doors against everyone, even his wife, and stood glass in hand at the window of his office at the archive, which was closer to the main gate than his private office at the residence, which overlooked the academy. For months he had fought his way through the entire range of human emotions, taking both sides of imagined conversations, but nothing prepared him for the sight, at last, of the thin figure, arm in a sling, face shockingly like his father's, that rode in the midst of Cassad's armsmen late that morning.

The banners and the horns signaled the approach of Cassad. Evred had not told his people to expect the Harskialdna, and Rat had not sent Gallopers ahead.

He watched the riders until they reached the gates, watched the morning light reflect in Inda's eyes as he lifted his head to study the walls. Studied every detail, from the untidy sailor's queue and the gold-mounted rubies Inda still wore in his ears to the long, dusty unlaced shirt, vest, deck trousers, mocs. There was no sign of the Marlovan about him, though he rode like one; Evred was still pondering that when they rode in the gates and vanished from view.

Vedrid was waiting in the stable.

Inda raised a hand in greeting, then said under his breath, "Well, what's it to be? The garrison prison again for me?"

Vedrid turned up his palm. "He's waiting."

Barend dismounted.

Vedrid said to him, "Alone."

Barend didn't make any overt threat, but his stance shifted, both hands within reach of weapons. "I'm going with him. It's why I'm here."

Vedrid struck his fist over his heart. "As you will, Barend-Dal."

Barend grinned. "You mean on my head be the fire."

Vedrid did not smile back. There was far too much tension spreading through the castle with the news that the Harskialdna was back.

Vedrid was about to offer Inda the chance to visit his rooms and dress properly, then he hesitated at even that. His orders had been exact. "Come with me," was all he said.

The two followed him upstairs and down silent halls, past watching guards. At last the door opened, and there was Evred, wearing his old gray riding coat, booted feet planted on the great crimson rug, hands behind his back, his face an unsettling reminder of his father and his uncle.

Evred nodded dismissal to Vedrid, then turned his head, brows raised. "Barend?"

"Whatever happens to him happens to me." Barend raised a thin hand, palm out, as Inda pulled from his gear the carefully wrapped copy of the treaty. "You may's well know that I signed that treaty, too, as trade envoy."

Evred winced, looked away, then back. "Leave, Barend. Nothing is going to happen now. Just leave us alone."

Barend turned from one to the other, and when Inda tipped his head toward the door he gave a slight shrug. After a last, speculative glance at his cousin, he went out, and shut the door softly behind him.

Chapter Thirty-three

INDA brushed his good hand down his sailor's togs. "Sorry about the ship gear. I handed off my coat to the fellow pretending to be me before I left. Didn't want to borrow any coming down here, things being how they are."

Evred pressed his fingers to the bridge of his nose but the drum and surge of heart and blood would not go away. "Inda. You know what our law is."

"Yes."

"You know why we have that law."

"Yes."

"You know that to show favoritism is to show weakness, and you can name every Jarl who will be panting at the gate in hopes I'll open the way to compromise."

"Yes." Inda's voice was so low, and tired. "Yes, Evred, I'll stand up against the wall. Or if you're going to flay me at the post, then do it. I won't argue. I know what I did. Please. Just do it."

"I do not want to do it," Evred retorted with barely suppressed violence.

Inda recoiled a step. Never had he heard that tone in Evred's voice. Then he thought, *I earned it.*

Evred didn't see the reaction. He paced the room. Too

easy to superimpose Inda's face over that of Hawkeye's father, almost ten years ago, dying at the post one flesh-ripping cut of the whip at a time.

Evred had spent his entire kingship proving his strength and determination to the Jarls, underscoring that no one stood outside the law. And here was Inda, ready to submit. His old friends would submit, but he could envision the censure in their eyes. None would interfere, or it would have happened by now. One of Evred's many nightmares in recent weeks had been of waking to an army of Inda's friends riding at his back. Except that Inda would not have permitted that to happen.

The only ones who would take pleasure in the proceedings would be Horsebutt and old Ola-Vayir and his cronies, and that not because of any sense of justice, but entirely because they wanted to see Evred in humiliation and defeat over the disgraced Harskialdna he'd promoted above them all.

And all because of the Marlovan oath binding one's honor to obedience to orders, the oath that Anderle Montrei-Vayir, Evred's own ancestor, had made law.

Evred knew the justifications, but he'd also dug in the records back far enough that he could not avoid the truth: his ancestor had made that oath law because he had broken trust when he stabbed Savarend Montredavan-An in the back.

Evred whirled around. "Inda, you swore before Convocation to be my Harskialdna. To serve as my Voice. And you accepted my order before the entire Convocation."

"Yes." Inda spoke to the floor. "But I came to see that the order was wrong."

The white lightning of rage stilled Evred—he did not even breathe. But the battle for self-control was as old as he was. When he trusted himself to speak, "So Taumad Dei talked you into that?"

Inda looked up. "No. That is, I'd already come to that conclusion before we talked. Tau stayed out of it, after those notes he sent to you. I think he figured out the cost if you didn't agree to his treaty." A thumb toward the open window and great parade ground below, where Hawkeye Yvana-Vayir's father had died the death of treason. From beyond floated the voices of boys at training, calling "Yip! Yip! Yip!"

Inda lifted his head, listening, and then turned away from the window, his expression bleak. "I tried to explain to you, but those little pieces of paper—I never was any good at writing—"

"Explain it to me now."

Inda groped left-handed in the air, then began the old pacing, though limping in a way painful to watch, his right arm dangling because it didn't seem proper to have it in the sling. "It's Tdor's net. That's how I think of it."

"I am not calling Tdor to defend herself." Evred flicked out his hand.

Inda's face whitened.

Evred took a swift step toward him, and then whirled away, and paced to the window. "That was an attempt at humor. Forgive me. The matter is entirely between us, Harvaldar and Harskialdna." He turned his head. "Whatever happens, at no time will your family suffer, you have my promise on that."

Inda sighed. "It's right for my life to be forfeit. There was a day . . ." He stared into the distance. "I told you about my conversation with Ramis of the *Knife*. But in general. I don't remember telling you what he said just before he sent me away. I didn't pay that much attention at the time. I was seventeen or so, I thought I knew what I was doing. And why."

He paused, and Evred said, "Go on."

Inda closed his eyes. *"Consider how many of our kings and heroes define honor by the worthiness of their enemies. Things will only change when we define honor by our works."* He opened his eyes again. "That might not be every word, but it's the gist of it. By our works. Just before I took ship again. I was in the north, wearing civ. Stocking cap on. No one saw these damn rubies. No one knew who I was. The wind was right, so I knew we'd sail on the tide, but I saw a glassmaker. I stood there outside his window all afternoon. Just watching him make a goblet." His gaze went diffuse, his words slowed to a rumble in his chest. "He *made* things. I've never made anything in my life. Other than a couple of shirts. For myself. When I was a ship rat. I've just destroyed things. People. Ships. Land, if you count what a battle does to the ground. Maybe there's some unseen court of justice somewhere that will be satisfied if I bleed my life out on those stones down there." He hooked his thumb back toward the parade ground. "All I could see was that the alliance had come to trust me. High to low. Even Deliyeth, when I kept to my word. It was a net of mutual trust, d'you see? It was strong enough for them to follow me into battle against the Venn, though we were outnumbered."

Inda paused, looked up, then down, and back to Evred, and again, his gaze was too painful to meet. Evred walked to the window, and closed his eyes as he listened.

"If I took those harbors, I'd spend the rest of my life killing people to keep 'em. Not just strangers, coming at me with a sword. People I knew. Fought alongside. Who didn't want us ruling them, while I forced them to it. I'd probably win because we're stronger, but I'd lose their trust forever."

"Their convenience—their *trust,* as you say—took precedence over mine, over the trust of your peers at Convocation?"

Inda sighed. "Don't you see? To the Jarls those other kingdoms don't matter. They don't care about the strait. Most of them couldn't name a single kingdom along there if you asked. They wanted me to win glory, and they would never understand that our glory to the people on the other side of the continent was . . . was . . . was the beginning of an evil empire to replace the Venn."

Evil empire. Where had Evred heard that phrase? Vedrid, years ago. *My mother, too, telling me that in the eyes of the world, I was wrong.*

Wrong. Could he be wrong? He'd read enough of Sartoran history to discover what people thought of the circular thinking of some kings: the king could not be wrong because he was the king.

His father had said that the people had to be able to trust the king to hear the truth. So what was the truth here? Evred knew he was not evil. He made no decision for his personal pleasure. Everything he did was for the kingdom.

And Inda had broken his oath.

Anger burned through Evred, and he felt the words form—the words that would lead, inexorably, to Inda ending up against that post, bleeding out his life in the sands that should have soaked up Rajnir's cursed blood. Again that twist deep inside, the distortion of the sexual urge he had never permitted himself to express before Inda.

He struggled to control it, to reach for reason. He was poised on the knife edge. "I have to keep my promises," Evred began, feeling the pull of will, of his own righteousness . . . then paused at the prod of memory. *Promises . . .* The words *I promise.*

Where he spoke them: the road to Andahi, spring of 3914. Standing in the mud, staring at Jeje sa Jeje's defiant face. What had he said? *If I am ever angry enough to throw a kingdom at Inda . . . I promise I will halt long enough to summon you to defend him.*

Evred stilled. He had made a promise.

Instinct prompted him to dismiss it. But as clear as the memory of that promise were Jeje's reasons for the promise: she hated kings because their personal emotions could be made political with the wave of a hand. She had expected Evred to betray Inda on kingly whim.

Aside from the profound stupidity of that assumption about kingly whim, *was* his anger really personal? Yes— and no. It was a question of treason, which was political, but the treason had been committed by the man Evred trusted most. That was personal.

He would not send for Jeje sa Jeje. But the brief, bleak flicker of near humor that accompanied the image of keeping the entire kingdom awaiting the arrival of one short black-browed pirate woman, enabled him one more time to grip his emotions, just enough to control them. That control would eventually exact a cost in nightmares and sleeplessness, but for now, he could think.

Fact: Inda had refused a royal command, though he had sworn before the entire kingdom, twice, to obey the king in all things.

Fact: Inda had never changed in the way that mattered most. If Inda did not believe what he said was right, he wouldn't say it. And he trusted the king enough to expect him to listen.

Evred had been staring at Inda all this time, but only now became aware of it, and for the very first time he met Inda's brown gaze straight on. Inda glared straight back at him, not in anger, or the same kind of anger. It was too full of pain for that: in hot anger, the kind that destroys, you don't feel pain. You give it.

Evred had seen that pain once before, and though the world had changed since that day so long ago in the prison on the other side of the castle, he could still remember Inda's face in the torchlight, sick, miserable, but honest and steady, and Evred heard himself whispering, *On my honor, on my soul, you will have justice.*

Evred said abruptly, "Sit down. You look terrible."

Inda sank down into one of the great raptor chairs, and gave a long sigh.

Evred paced to the door then back to the window. He glanced over his shoulder. "Did you also imagine conversations with me, over and over?"

"Every night. Since I threw that locket overboard." Inda lifted his hand, then dropped it. "I was angry—I couldn't get the words right to explain."

Evred gripped his hands together, then flung them apart. "I won't waste breath with the subject of disobeying orders. It smacks of my uncle, sticking to form, without ever acknowledging meaning. Do you realize that what you have done, and why, makes a wrong of everything my forefathers have done? Everything I have done?"

"Everything," Inda said, "I have done."

Evred made a negating gesture. "Do they really see us as the enemy?"

"They were ready to."

Evred said, "You never saw my father's records. Among his papers were captured Idayagan treaties, secret agreements, letters, coded and uncoded: their king was weak, bribing and threatening by turns, the lords squabbling with one another. Ineffective, all of them, but there was no peace. Not until we came and forced it on them."

"Forced it on them," Inda repeated. "I don't pretend to understand kingship. But is it really peace if people don't choose it?"

Evred paced again, then said, "I see the moral necessity for the strong to protect the weak."

"Yes."

"Even when one of the reasons the weak are weak is that they don't know how to protect themselves, they can't

because they are too greedy, too short-sighted, too indo-
lent to stir outside of their immediate desires. They don't
see danger until it overtakes them. By being vigilant to the
threat of danger we protect them."

Inda said, tiredly, "They'd say they have to choose that
protection or it's still the use of force. Under whatever
guise."

"But they did ask us to protect them. You and I were
both here when that Pim woman came on their behalf with
her petition."

"Yes, and then they trusted us to go away again. That's
their definition of an alliance. Band together for the common good, and when the work is done, return home. One
party doesn't take the place of the former threat as a new
enemy."

"*Are* we enemies?"

"The enemy *I* recognize is the one who comes at me
with a knife." Inda opened his left hand. "Other than that,
I—" He looked down at his feet. "I don't know."

"Enemy." Evred paced again. "When I make a mistake,
lives end." Again he thought of Jeje and turned away, as if
to leave her image behind. "Did you know that the women
have almost a secret language? Not just different slang, like
us saying, when we part with lovers, that we leave them
at the stable, and they say that they put them out to mar-
ket? A secret language, made up of Old Sartoran glyphs,
partly. My father tried to tell me once, but I didn't reflect
on it until I stumbled on old records, in my aunt's hand, that
Hadand had transferred to the archive."

Inda dangled his hands between his knees, head forward. "I never knew Ndara-Harandviar. But Hadand?
How could you find someone more loyal?"

"I couldn't. Yet there they are, busy trying to find out the
secrets of magic, and writing back and forth, not just to one
another, but to Joret over the mountains, and apparently
even farther afield." Evred rubbed his chin. "Did Cama tell
you that Starand got hold of his scroll-case? This was just
at the end of winter, she was bored, and wanted to whine
to Hadand. Too easy to imagine her reading all my notes
to Cama, and reporting what I said to Ola-Vayir. I called
all the scroll-cases in and destroyed them." Evred made
a negating motion. "I don't mean to imply that that idiot

Starand is at all typical of the women. I came to the conclusion that the best of them are loyal to an ideal kingdom, and to individual kings when they are deemed to represent that ideal."

Inda thought, *Signi and Valda were just the same, loyal to an ideal.*

"It sounds good, doesn't it? But what if the ideal is impossible? What if it's seen as evil, like the Venn ideal that their glory and honor required them to conquer the world?"

Inda sighed.

"I'm tempted to burn the last of the lockets, too. Everyone will be on an equal basis, relying on Runners. Same we've done for generations past."

Inda thought, *It's not equal, and nothing is ever the same. Runners can be killed, messages taken. And someone, somewhere, is going to find their way back to magic.*

Evred was watching closely, and as always, Inda was unaware of what showed in his face. Evred took a step toward him again, and this time stood squarely on the crimson rug, where his father and brother had bled out their lives. "Inda, do you think I have become my uncle, seeing shadows as enemies?"

Inda frowned at the carpet worked with its golden eagles. Then he looked up, his mouth wry. "Seems to me that *I* have become the enemy."

And there they were, back to the first fact: that the sworn Harskialdna had refused to obey an order of the king. Probably the most important order ever given, one that was meant—Evred still believed it—to establish peace, at last, over this half of the continent.

Inda had refused.

Evred paced a third time. Inda had explained everything. Evred could just comprehend what Inda saw as a moral imperative . . . and he could comprehend it because . . . swift images flitted through his mind: Taumad's refusal to make an oath he could not believe in. Jeje sa Jeje's stubborn hatred of kings because they were human, but could wield inhuman power. The freely given loyalty that Inda never asked for, and others never defined because Inda had become a leader without ever having had ambition.

Against Inda? The iron-hard Marlovan rule: you obey orders or die.

Evred turned around, and stared into Inda's scarred, tired face. The steady gaze, the resignation in the line of his mouth, Evred could feel as viscerally as if he'd been there how terrible the choice had been for Inda, out in the middle of the strait on his pirate ship: choosing between moral right and Marlovan law.

Between moral right and me.

Evred whirled away, but he could not outpace that one. *If there is a choice, it's between right and . . .*

Wrong.

Here was the truth. On his side he had the absolute right of Marlovan law, and the absolute power to enforce it. His people would not rise against his execution of justice, nor would his Sier Danas. Inda would walk to the post and pay the price of treason because he had chosen moral right over all.

Twisting the knife was the personal betrayal and its result: Inda's choosing what he saw as moral right over Marlovan law meant that Evred could no longer trust him.

As he had so many times over the past weeks, he addressed the memory of Tau in his private room at the end of that summer. *Am I insane?*

"Go home, Inda." He did not turn, but gazed sightlessly through the window. "Pack up your things and go home."

As soon as the words were out, he wanted to lunge after them, to grab them out of the air again. But then he saw the impact in Inda's face, and there was no going back.

He must protect what he had left.

And so he spoke rapidly, as the ideas came. "You will even go home as Adaluin, because the piece of news I had waiting for you was Branid's death. It happened just after New Year's. I'd saved the news so that I could consult you on whether or not Whipstick should be promoted to Adaluin, or you had another man in mind."

"Branid? Dead?" Inda repeated witlessly, thinking: *I'm to live? I can go home?* Tears leaked from his eyes, unheeded.

Evred turned away from those tears. "You owe me something, I think."

"What? Anything I—" Inda stopped, because *anything*

was no longer true. He'd had anything as a choice, there out on the water.

Evred said dryly, "This next Convocation, you are going to stand up and lie. How many know you threw the locket away?"

"Only Tau. And Barend. Most didn't even know I had it. Oh. And Cama—"

"You may leave Cama to me. You will tell the Jarls that your orders changed and that you signed the treaty in my name. I am going to approve this thing, whatever it says, which means there is no treason, therefore there is no need for war." Evred picked up the rolled scroll, and cast it down on the desk. "I will write to my mother, and ask her to propagate my agreement through the world. We will leave the strait to itself. Our ships will attend to our shores."

Inda wiped his coat sleeve across his eyes.

Evred walked again, everything falling into place. "Yes, and because there is no more need for war, there is no more need for a Harskialdna. Or for a Harvaldar. I will become Evred-Sieraec, and the Convocation will be, no doubt, relieved to return to five year oaths, except those who have displeased me. I will put my cousin Badger Yvana-Vayir in as Sierandael, and confirm Beaver as Jarl of Yvana-Vayir. Badger has discovered a taste for military command, and we might as well make my experience a custom: future kings, and their Shield Arms, will serve two years at Ala Larkadhe, just like I did, and Badger after me."

"So . . . I'm to go home."

Home. They both heard it, how Inda said "home," and for a moment Evred did not see Inda sitting there, cradling his useless right arm, face tight with pain, lined from months of unspoken tension. Memory forced him back to the pass above Ala Larkadhe, strike, smash, the exquisite bliss, so deep, so fierce, watching unleashed strength, grace, skill, hewing Venn warriors into blood-spewing wreckage. The insight, just touched at the moment of release, and fought ever since: Was this, then, the driving desire behind my forefathers? The pleasure of commanding the kill?

See, Taumad, I am not insane.

"Go," Evred said, though anguish made it nearly impossible to speak. But he had once promised justice. Not love nor lust nor ambition would gainsay that promise.

He forced himself to speak, though it took all the strength he had remaining. "Go home. Take up your life, Indevan-Adaluin. Of Choraed Elgaer."

Evred could not forbear watching hungrily for a sign of regret, but Inda's reaction was, though soundless, too un-mistakable for that: release.

Inda saluted and walked out, leaving Evred alone.

Tdor waited in the Harskialdna suite, her whole body tight with anxiety, which flared into terror when she saw the tears on Inda's cheeks.

"We're going home." Inda walked into her arms, and she sobbed in relief as they hugged. Then she felt his head turn. "Where is Signi?"

"She is gone. She got the call, and she had to leave."

He stilled against her. "Is she coming back?"

"She said she would not."

He murmured into Tdor's hair, "I'll miss her."

"I will, too." Tdor's gratitude and affection for Signi poured through her, intensifying her gratitude to have Inda home and safe. She prepared to say more, to even break her promise if Inda should ask about a child, but he didn't. He wouldn't, she realized—it would never occur to him. *I will tell my daughter,* Tdor thought. *When she is grown.* So instead, "Before she left for Sartor she gave us a pre-cious gift, which she wrote out herself, a book of magic fundamentals."

Inda thought of Evred's recent words, and pursed his lips, then loosened his grip on Tdor.

She observed his change of expression, and guessed correctly at his thought. "Hadand sent it to Shendan Mon-tredavan-An, where it can stay until such a time as magic studies are acceptable in Iasca Leror. Signi promised to speak on our behalf before the council."

Inda noted that she had not said they were not using it, and he thought of women's secrets, then dismissed the matter with an internal shrug. It was his sister's affair. He knew she would never do anything that would harm the kingdom.

"Show me our son," Inda said, and together they walked into the nursery and looked down at the napping babe, their fingers intertwined tightly. Then they walked out, and he glanced around with a vague air. "There isn't much here I want to keep. Most belongs to the king. Can you be ready to leave in the morning?"

"Watch me." She grinned.

For the rest of the day and evening Evred kept busy with constant affairs, but his ears were always on the alert for Inda's step, for his voice. He found himself pausing in the middle of a task to arrange his words taking Inda back as Sierandael, or even as Harskialdna, whichever one he wanted.

But when he returned to his rooms shortly before the midnight watch, he found a gold ring sitting on his desk.

He was still sitting there, turning the ring on his fingers, when Hadand knocked a long time later.

"I saw your lights burning," she said.

He made an effort to gesture welcome.

She entered softly, but instead of stopping just inside the door, she came around the desk and stood a pace or two out of reach, looking down into his face with those eyes so like Inda's, yet unlike. He looked away, unable to speak.

"Did you have to send them to Choraed Elgaer?" she asked softly.

Evred had meant to keep silence, but the words wrung out of him, "He broke his promise. I can't get past that." And in a stronger voice, "He could have stayed. If he asked. But he wants to go home. Home being Choraed Elgaer. Not our home."

Hadand came a step closer. "Yes. I thought I was the only one who saw that. How they both ..." She made a gesture. "But there's something else you should remember. Inda has broken two promises in his life. The orders for the strait was the second one."

Evred looked up sharply.

"When he taught you the Odni. And I broke a promise to teach you when he was gone. Should we regret those things?"

Evred sat back. Hadand waited.

"Except a couple of scuffles from those fools at Ala Larkadhe I never did have to defend myself," he said finally. "Others have always defended me." He looked up.

"Go on," she said.

He dropped the ring, and laid his hands flat on the table,

still and tense. "Those lessons . . . from you both. First made me see that change was possible. It took me a long time to understand that."

She leaned down and covered his hand with hers. "I was never going to tell you," she said, "but I've changed my mind. I am in love with you, Evred Montrei-Vayir, in all the ways known to human beings. I never wanted to tell you because I didn't want you to feel my love as a burden. But at the same time, I saw that you loved my brother in all the ways known to human beings."

His fingers stirred, but she held them in her warm, firm grip. "No. Hear me. Then if you like we will never discuss it again. I tell you because I do not want you to feel alone. We both know what it is to have the love we love most not love us the same way in return. Just in the way they can."

Chapter Thirty-four

THE courtyard at Tenthen was deserted, unswept. Inda and Tdor looked around warily. As Inda dismounted Whipstick Noth emerged from the stable doors, his old coat sun-bleached and worn. "You've sailed home? Or is this a liberty stop?" he asked Inda.

From behind stable hands emerged, looking up at Inda and Tdor with ambivalent faces.

Inda's question about the lack of perimeter riders died. He lifted Jarend down from Tdor's arms so Tdor could dismount. Then he and Tdor followed Whipstick inside, as the Twins (both of whom had chosen to stay with Inda, and Evred had granted permission) took charge of the cavalcade. Inda was disturbed at how worn and neglected everything seemed.

Whipstick waved them into the watch command office adjacent to the Rider barracks.

Inda shut the door, then set his brown-haired little son down. "This is young Jarend. The next one," he added, "will be Kendred."

Whipstick's hard face creased as he knelt down. For a moment he and the child studied one another, Jarend sucking his thumb, Whipstick smiling. Then he looked up. "Your boy's Shield Arm will be named for my brother?"

Inda opened his hand. "I just hope he won't put eggs in the Riders' shoes. Now, I know what happened—Branid's dead, something to do with pirates—but I don't know the details."

"We had Toaran pirates nosing up the coast out of The Narrows, so the king ordered us to reinforce the harbors from our own Riders. Some pirates tried a run at Parayid, came as far as Piwum. My dad and his dragoons drove 'em off. I'd been doing the border rides, but at the prospect of action, Branid insisted on taking command." Whipstick grimaced, then looked over both shoulders to make sure no one overheard. "My dad ignored him. Branid's orders didn't make sense once things got hot down at the wharf one night, when they tried to land in secret. But. Well. You can see the official report, but if you want to know what I think, I think the men scragged him," he said in a low voice. "Not those pirates, who were drunken fools. Looking for easy pickings, rumor probably still out that we have no water defense. Dad and I thought it better, all things considered, not to investigate closely. You might feel different, I know."

Inda gestured vaguely, his face pained. Then he looked around. "Why is the house so deserted?"

"It's because *She's* still here."

"Dannor?"

Whipstick's weather-lined face soured.

"Tell us," Tdor said.

Whipstick's bony shoulders lifted. "For a while it was all right. Branid did his best, by his lights. Then the fights began, when they started giving clashing orders. She was so high-handed and contradictory people started going to your mother to get orders, or to complain. When *She* found out, they'd get punished, or *She'd* get back at 'em some way."

Tdor said to Inda, "That's why Hadand invited Fareas-Iofre to the royal city. But she didn't tell me the truth—she didn't want me worrying about Tenthen. Your mother finally did, before she left for Fera-Vayir."

Inda thumbed his jaw scar.

Whipstick said, "When Fareas-Iofre left us—and I don't blame her—most of our best people packed off, saying they'd as soon work the fields, if Fera-Vayir would take them. We've barely got enough left to take care of the animals and work the land. We don't have enough Riders. Which is why I'm here. When spring came, I sent a Runner around to everyone. Said if there was a problem, send a message to me. I've been waiting for Evred-Harvaldar to make a decision about who he wanted as Adaluin."

Tdor's arms were crossed, her fingertips just touching her knife hilts. "So Dannor has been in command?"

Whipstick turned out his hands. "She's got rank. No one to say her nay."

"Until now." Inda turned to Tdor. "You want to do it or shall I?"

Tdor smiled. "This part of house defense," she said, "is mine."

The men laughed. Young Jarend laughed, too, just because the adults laughed, and he waved his much-gnawed carved wooden horse.

Inda took Whipstick's thin, strong shoulders between his hands. "I'm home for good."

Whipstick did not answer, but his sudden smile was sufficient. And he began to give his report on the state of Choraed Elgaer.

Presently a clatter echoed up the stone walls of the courtyard. Inda and Whipstick halted in the middle of their discussion of the castle horses and leaped to the window. A golden lamp lay on the flagstones. Then from above a golden tray arced out. *Clang!*

"No, *you* listen to *me*," came Tdor's furious voice, clear on the summer air. Neither Inda nor Whipstick had ever heard her angry before. "Gold trays? Gold trays when the stable looks worse than horse shit waiting for a wand? Silk hangings, with the garden overgrown? No, Dannor, there is *no* excuse! I am the Iofre now. This place is going to be clean, and orderly, and drilled, by Restday. And you are going to lead every single work party. Either that, or you can go home to Tya-Vayir."

Upstairs in the enormous prince's suite—what once had been the Adaluin's rooms in the olden days—the two women faced one another. Dannor flushed, fingers fumbling at her bare wrists. She'd stopped wearing her knives ages ago.

Tdor flicked hers out. "You really want to fight me?" she asked with interest. "Oh, please do. I'll wait. Get your knives."

Dannor had not drilled for at least two years, and it showed. Tdor looked fit, tough, and the long face Dannor had always thought boring and bovine was slashed by a very angry grin.

"I hate this place anyway. It couldn't be more dull," Dannor snapped and whirled around. "Go on, it's all yours to sweep and mop. It'll take me a few days to ready my things—"

Tdor still had that grin of rage, her thin cheeks pale except for two flushed spots below her eyes, making them seem unnaturally bright. "Here, I'll help." She reached for the nearest table, swept up its decorative items, marched to the open window, and flung them out.

Dannor gasped as Tdor stalked around the room, picking up and throwing all the gold and silver candlesticks, plates, cups, treasure boxes, straight out the window. Her arm was strong and her aim true.

When she reached for the first ceramic vase, Dannor waved her hands. "No! No! I'll get my clothes ready. We'll ride out today, if you'll just send the rest."

"Fair enough."

Tdor marched out, and each servant she saw got a list of orders.

Inda and Whipstick moved to the outer door in happy expectancy. Before long Dannor appeared, golden braids disheveled, robe crooked. She sent a brooding look behind her as she clutched two baskets from which colored silk draggled. Her First Runner carried an enormous woven basket stacked high with small inlaid jewelry boxes.

Within a short time the two reappeared on horseback, and the former Iofre and her servant vanished up the north road, to be followed very soon by two or three of her own toadies, whom the castle people promptly turned on and drove out.

Tdor walked across the courtyard toward the men, the flush of triumph fading into regret and even guilt.

"I should not have flung her things out the window," she admitted. "We could have worked something out—if she'd done *anything*. Even her tapestry is unfinished. It looks like she abandoned it years ago."

"She did. The day she hooked Branid into marriage," Whipstick said.

"Well, I put the people to work. Either they leave or get used to new orders." Tdor wiped a damp strand of brown hair off her forehead. "I may as well pitch in. I'm not sleeping in any room that smells of her attar of roses, and my old room is full of spiderwebs. Faugh!" She whisked herself off.

Whipstick bent to pick up Jarend, who was still chewing on his wooden horse. Hoisting the boy up onto his shoulder, he said, "I'll get him set up in the heir's rooms, why don't I?"

The next spring, Tdor-Iofre send a letter over the mountain to Queen Joret of Anaeran-Adrani, her foster sister.

She caught Joret up on Inda's last Convocation, where he was confirmed as Adaluin, and granted the lifelong accolade that his father had had: he was no longer required to ride to Convocation unless he had business to present. Evred then sent Inda home with a barrel of the same root brew supplied to the academy boys' tavern, Daggers Drawn. Evred knew that Inda would never have thought to ask the Tenthen brewer to make it, so the barrel was for him to match.

By the next year, another child was on the way, and the Algara-Vayirs and the steady trickle of returning people were busy restoring Castle Tenthen and its lands to their former state.

I also am delighted to report that Inda is finally showing some effect due to that healer that his mother's sister sent from Sartor. She's a strange sort, just sitting for a time, eyes, closed, finger just touching here and there, but what she said about Inda's arm—that he must have had a badly healed break long ago and it just got worse over the years—seems to have been true. Her magic spells make her sleep for a week, and then it takes months to see any effect, but Inda drills with Whipstick and the men again, and he goes out

*and swings a sword with Jarend, who is already mad
for dogs, horses, and steel, as are most of the boys.*

Evred did not destroy the lockets. He and Barend wore the
last two, so that Evred had a pair of eyes on Savarend Montredavan-An, with whom he never communicated directly.

Barend had no idea how Fox would respond when, one
day, he emerged from the cabin aboard *Death* and walked
up to Fox on the captain's deck. "Your father is dead," he
said.

Fox squinted out to sea against the sun spangles, so still
that for a long moment Barend wondered if he'd heard.
He was considering whether or not to repeat himself when
Fox spoke.

"Let me off near Marlovar River basin. I don't want to
be shot."

Two months later, a crew rowed him ashore. He'd forbidden Barend to tell anyone, knowing that the change in
command would little affect the routine that had adapted
easily from fleet to navy. Fox loathed the idea of parties and
foolish talk, he just wanted to disappear.

So it was a quiet departure. The fleet sailed away, and
Fox watched them go, suspecting that Barend's announcement would be accepted with a shrug, and maybe some
muttered insults from the lazier crew on how life might get
easier. He never knew how many regretted his departure
in the sense that, with him, the great days of adventure had
passed on.

Fox turned his back on the sea, laughed as he hitched
his gear over his shoulder, and walked up the low, marshy
beach toward the riverside, where he remembered the old
road had been in his boyhood.

He wondered how long before perimeter riders spotted
him, whether they would be Marth-Davan or King's Riders, or if peacetime had caused them to slacken.

By noon the Riders appeared on a distant ridge, crimson
banner waving. When they reached him and he identified
himself, he discovered that he'd been expected. Proof of
Evred Montrei-Vayir's efficiency, Fox thought, and at last
he permitted himself to turn his thoughts toward home.

He expected a welcome from his sister. The question
was really Marend, whom he'd left as a bitter, angry teen.

They'd just begun messing around in the way teens did, and he distinctly recalled a lot of wild talk about never having a son to echo his own meaningless life, and how angry she'd got at being reduced to part of his meaninglessness. When she'd turfed him out of her bed, he'd departed that day, cutting his leave a week short.

Such drama! And hugely funny from this distance ... funny and sad, when he considered how long it had taken him to realize he'd been training all the girls in the Fox Banner Fleet to be Marend and Shendan.

They were all there when he arrived home at last, a welcome that befitted a Jarl, even one who had never done a stroke of work or had even communicated with them. But the same strange loyalty that brought him back had operated on them, too. He found his father's rooms swept out, fresh linens on the bed, no trace of the maudlin, defeated stench of sour wine anywhere.

Marend and his mother were pleasant but wary. Shendan kept cracking jokes as they conducted him over the castle, explaining what had been done in the stables, the gardens, the land.

Finally they ended up in the main hall, with the beautiful mosaic of the screaming eagle worked in obsidian and gold. The doors to old Savarend's throne room were closed; that room had long been gutted, leaving only its enormous fireplace, and the enormous carved stone table with its raptor feet where once the king and his new Jarls had gathered. Irony still loured in the air.

Fox leaned against the doors, arms crossed as he regarded the three women. "Well?"

"Well what?" his mother retorted. "You're here, you must know what's expected of you."

"How long do you intend to remain?" Marend asked, her brows lifted.

"Evred is not the monster his grandfather was," Shendan said. "He's let me in and out of their castle and pretended not to notice. But I guess you know that, you saw Inda afterward. Odd!" She laughed, and shook her head. Her hair in the lantern light was as bright as it had been in childhood; by day Fox would discover that it was sunbleached to the color of straw. Shen often led the perimeter riders on the inside of the border. She added, "If you have a son, Hadand said he can go be a Runner. I hope you won't get sniffy, think it some insult."

Fox smiled. "Contrary. A King's Runner is a way inside."

Shendan laughed, flipped her hand, and took off. Fox was back at last, and she'd get time to pester him for tales of his adventures later, probably after she'd got some drink into him.

The Jarlan cut a glance from her son to her prospective daughter-in-law, then found something to do, leaving the two together.

They walked away, heads down, listening to the other rather than looking: they'd both become too good at masking their expressions. "And so? What's my place?" Marend said.

"I thought that was pretty clear," Fox said. "If nothing else was. The question from my end would be, what is my place?"

Marend said, "All right. If we marry, I'll be the next Jarlan, which gives me my proper rank in everyone's eyes. If we have a son, then everything carries on. I know you might not want that—"

"I was seventeen when I said what I said. I hope I can be forgiven the pugnacious wisdom of seventeen."

Marend laughed, wrung her hands, then smiled, her first genuine smile. "This is harder than I'd expected. Well, if you are willing to carry on, then you should know this about me: I've a life mate. Keth, now the miller. We've got a daughter, born two years ago. We were always agreed that I'd marry you, and if need be, move back upstairs, even. But he has first place in my bed."

Fox found these simple words unsettling. He had never expected Marend to suspend her life. Presented with the evidence, he discovered he had to redefine their relationship. But she did not seem unwilling, or even unfriendly.

"We'll all adapt," he said. "There's time."

Chapter Thirty-five

THE following spring, after the passes cleared, a Runner carried a letter to Queen Joret from Tdor:

> *Inda has begun making the rounds of Choraed El-gaer himself. The people seem happier to see him, and Whipstick's life is easier, especially since Hadand gave me permission to promote Noren to be my Randviar so she and Whipstick could marry.*
>
> *Inda stopped in Piwum to see the Noths, where he got news of our fleet. Barend Montrei-Vayir is now the commander, because Fox Montredavan-An—that is, Savarend-Jarl, now his father is dead—has returned to Darchelde and married Marend Jaya-Vayir.*
>
> *After New Year's Week Cherry-Stripe and Mran came south to deliver their dear little Rialden themselves. She wept for a week, and then, quite suddenly, she and my little Hadand began to babble away, as if they made up another tongue. Jarend treats them both like puppies . . .*

Though Tdor remained fond of her former foster sister, it had been years since they had seen one another, and the fondness was based on memory of shared experience, rather than immediate. So Tdor did not share everything, like how relieved the castle people were when Inda decided to ride the border. Not that they didn't love him. The problem was, they loved him too much to tell him how terrible were his attempts to work alongside them at tasks for which he was not trained—and how he got in the way when he meant to aid in the planting, based on imperfect boyhood memory of how things had been done.

There was one good thing Dannor did, though she abandoned it as soon as she gained her goal of marriage and a title. That is the tapestry. Inda absolutely loathes it—insists the fellow in the center is a strutting snowball—but it looks quite splendid, and once the weavers returned, they taught me how to help.

We've been working at it during the cold nights, and making good progress.

A year or so after that, her letter was less joyful.

I can only bear the thought of my darling little Hadand going north to Darchelde because my precious Kendred has been born. He is so like Inda, he laughed almost from the first week; Inda fell in love at once, though he had another one of those sudden springs of tears when he first cupped his hand round Kendred's head. "It's fuzzy," he said. "Like duck's down." Then he looked up and there were the tears, and he lifted his curved hand. "Noddy did this. Before the battle. Talking about his boy. I didn't know what it meant."

How can joy bring such sudden pain? Does pain ever bring joy? Anyway, I have been trying to overcome my own little sorrow at the prospect of losing Hadand. It does help, as Fareas-Iofre once promised me, that I know Shendan, and I know she will love Hadand as I love her, and my daughter's life there will be good, betrothed to Marend's new little son. My Hadand will even learn magic, from Signi's book.

Inda halted his line when he drew even with the captain of

the Darchelde perimeter patrol. He started to speak, then squinted. "Basna? That you?"

The captain grinned. "I think you're mistaking me for my cousin Mardred? Er, he would have been Basna Tvei, back at the academy."

Inda laughed aloud. "You look like him. What I remember." He hefted a squarely built child with tousled brown hair escaping a knit cap, whom he had been carrying at his hip. "I'm here to bring my daughter to Darchelde."

Captain Basna hesitated. The standing orders had been the same for years: no one to cross the border, except for betrothal home visits, and the fetching and delivery was done by Runners. It had been a generation since there'd been betrothal home visits, so had anything changed?

Inda said, "If you let us pass I'll write to the king myself." Thus taking responsibility for the breach of rules.

Basna saluted, fist to chest, and then reddened, because the scar-faced man with the ruby earrings was no longer a Harskialdna. But the rest of the men had also saluted. In a way, Indevan-Adaluin would always be Inda-Harskialdna.

The Riders watched as the Algara-Vayir Guard rode into the forbidden Montredavan-An territory, their gear jingling, the green-and-silver owl banner lifting in the wind.

Inda was intensely interested in seeing Darchelde again, after all these years. He'd discovered that on returning to places as an adult they usually diminished in size, as if memory reversed one's growth. But Darchelde was just as magnificent as he had remembered, as large as the residence side of the royal castle, its design with its broach archways far more pleasing to the eye. Black-and-gold banners flew on the many towers. The sentries were mostly women.

Inda had not seen an outer perimeter as the road dipped into forest before emerging on the rise before the castle, but he doubted the Montredavan-Ans had been caught by surprise. And it was Fox himself who strolled out of the iron-studded doorway at the top of the double sweep of stairs as Inda's party rode into the great court.

Fox looked exactly the same as ever, dressed entirely in black, no hint of Marlovan clothing except in the high blackweave riding boots they all wore, knife hilts winking at the tops.

"Inda," he said, brows slanting up.

Inda braced for a comment about being let off the leash, but Fox just issued a few brief orders and got the Guard moving in one direction, horses led by the rein, and Hadand's small baggage with Tdor's Runner, who'd come along to see to the child's care, in the other.

Marend then appeared—Fox's wife. She exchanged a glance with Fox, a look that communicated without words, her expression amused, faintly sardonic, then kind when she bent down to little Hadand, who clung to Inda's trousers with one fist, her other thumb in her mouth.

Marend was a distant cousin of Inda's, but despite her Jaya-Vayir glossy black hair and black eyes, her demeanor was Montredavan-An. She addressed the shrinking child in a soft voice, and a few moments later, when Shendan appeared, carrying a year-old red-haired baby, Hadand loosened her death grip on Inda. She stared with interest at the baby.

The women soon coaxed her away, Inda handing to Marend Tdor's thick letter packet full of notes about the two-year-old's habits, likes, and dislikes.

Then Fox took Inda away to offer a tour. It was an easy day, ending up in Fox's lair. "Was my father's tower, you probably remember. When I was a boy all I could think about was the wretched stench of sour wine. But now . . ." He stood at the door in the round room, permitting Inda to look through the ring of arched windows.

The tower was the highest of the eight, which were not uniform in size. The view was spectacular. Inda turned in a slow circle, gazing at the depth of forest gradually giving way to winding river, silver in the westering sun, the purple hazed mountains southward, the mellow plains stretching away in the north. And in the west, he thought he caught the faintest glint of the sea.

Inda loved Tenthen Castle, and the land around it. But this vista was far more dramatic, making Inda wonder if beauty was a matter of contrasts as well as reach.

Then Fox drawled, "I resent even the possibility of functioning as someone's errand boy, but when Ramis gave me the *Knife*, he told me to ask what you promised Noddy Toraca when he died."

Fox knew it was a mistake to bring up the past, but only

in a sense: he had a purpose. To hide that purpose, he had to sting Inda into response. He knew from old that Inda, pressed to remember, would go silent and brood. But the name Ramis was sure to bring a response, especially when one of Inda's boyhood companions was mentioned in the same breath.

"I couldn't hear him well," Inda said finally. "I think it was 'No more' or maybe 'No war.' 'No more' makes more sense—he was in terrible pain. Anyway, I promised him. What else could I do?"

Fox let his breath trickle out. He remembered Ramis saying, *What Toraca said was* no more war. *You decide if you want to tell Indevan: I tell you so you will understand what I offer.*

"Ramis. Strange to hear that name again." Inda waved a hand, then moved along the windows, tapping absently on the window seats.

Fox knew he only had a day or two at most, and there was no guarantee he could lure Inda back again, unless the remainder of the visit was pleasant. So he said, "You know I'm mewed up here. Can't go anywhere. So it amuses me to delve into mysteries like Ramis, and other aspects of experience."

Inda stopped pacing. "What experience?"

"Ours. Right now, though, yours, but only because I've been trying to figure out whether the academy is our biggest advantage, or our worst curse."

Now he had Inda's complete attention. *Worrying about that, too, eh, Inda?*

"Tell me this. You have to realize by now that if you'd taken that beating back when you were a scrub, you would have become the academy's hero. Your brother Tanrid would have seen to that, if he'd had to thrash his way through the horsetail barracks."

Inda rubbed his fingers over his old jaw scar. "True."

"So. Knowing what you do, if you could go back. Would you take that beating?"

"That's a strange question."

"But an important one, when you ponder how much we're trained to idealize violence."

Inda dropped onto one of the window seats. "I don't know." He looked up with the old considering expression.

"I guess the pain wouldn't have been much worse than the broken ribs. Well, maybe. Not that I cared about pain— well, of course I did. Hated it. Anyone in his right mind hates it."

"But you never flinched from it."

"Well, that was true until Wafri had me. I still flinch if someone reaches toward my head from the sides." Inda gestured at the periphery of his vision. "Or touches my hair when I'm not expecting it." He whooshed out his breath. "It was the humiliation more than the pain. No, that's wrong too. I would have taken that, if I'd thought I'd earned it. What I couldn't stick was how standing up for that beating would mean that I was guilty. But I hadn't done wrong. So . . . no, I wouldn't." He grimaced. "Are you saying I should have, so I could have become a hero? That's disgusting. Besides, Evred's uncle would have turfed me out of the academy no matter what I did."

"Disgusting." Inda was still politically naive, after all his experience. But this was one of the reasons Fox liked Inda—maybe it was a partial explanation of his popularity.

Fox went on to ask about some of Inda's innovations at the academy, and on that subject Inda was ready to talk. Much as he loved being home, he did miss the academy. From there he slid into his own experiences during his scrub years. Fox sat and listened, and they dined there; when Inda yawned and wandered downstairs to sleep, Fox sat up through the night writing down everything Inda had said.

Inda left the following morning, downcast at the sound of Hadand's shrieks as he rode away. Tdor had warned him. *We all went through it, every woman you know. Shen will love her . . . and when she comes home next year, she'll cry to leave them.* But it only made him feel marginally better—and that not until he'd got beyond hearing those desolate wails.

When he reached the border again, and had waved to the patrol, he sent one of his Runners to the royal city. Evred had written to him a couple of times; Inda had never liked writing letters at any time, but during that excruciating period when he was arguing with Evred via tiny pieces of paper, he'd developed a real antipathy to it. So he only wrote, *I took our Hadand to Darchelde. Fox and I talked about the academy, no war plans.*

There were no repercussions from Inda's breach of the

rules, and so, the next year, Inda detoured from the summer ride of the Choraed Elgaer border to fetch Hadand home for her Name Day month.

The evening was warm. Fox invited Inda to sit up on the highest battlement, looking west at the setting sun as they reminisced, passing a pitcher of cold beer back and forth.

The beer, the splendid view, and Fox's carefully casual questions gradually loosened Inda's tongue.

The spring following:

> *Joret: Fareas-Iofre has returned to live with us, but she insists that she is senior woman only in name, and that the only work she wants to do is tutor grandchildren. As to the children, this summer Ndara Cassad comes to us for Kendred. It will be good to have two little girls again . . .*

The years passed.

Tdor had a new habit, watching Inda's training sessions with Jarend, Kendred, Whipstick's Tanrid, and the other castle boys. They so often ended up with dust flying as Inda and his sons wrestled until Inda lay laughing in the dirt, the boys leaping on his stomach with no discipline whatsoever. Tdor could not explain even to herself the dizzying, sharp-edged elation the sight gave her. But sometimes the bliss was so intense it made her weep.

Inda began to look forward to his yearly visits with Fox, when he detoured off his route to fetch his daughter. Their talks ranged over reading, experience, speculation about the rest of the world.

One night, after talking about sailing, Inda said, "Do you miss the sea?"

"Yes," Fox said. "I intend to go back."

"To the navy?"

"No. From anything I hear, Barend is doing fine—and very few of the people we knew are left. I will stay here until my son is grown. He can take over the limited functions as Jarl—give him something to do. I'll leave Marend to her mate. She and her miller have been tolerant, but I'm more like an embarrassing relation than a part of the family after all my time away."

"So where will you go?"

Fox smiled. "You have to ask? That black ship is waiting for me. I will sail it around the world."

"You mean Ramis' *Knife?* Or, what did Durasnir call it, the *Sun-Dragon?*"

"*Sinna-Drakan.* That's its old name. I've renamed it."

"What?"

"Can't you guess?" Fox gave Inda his old, toothy smile. *"Treason."*

In Choraed Elgaer the seasons blended into years, good years overall, though there were the usual droughts and castle repairs and patrols to be made, roads to be maintained, and coastal vigilance kept up. And there were days when Inda thrashed and cried out in his sleep, and went around silent for a time afterward, and days when his joints hurt him, gradually more of them in winter.

Bringing us at last to a spring day fifteen years after they rode home from the royal city. New growth greened hills and trees, the sheep were lambing, and earlier that week the castle children had at last been released to run out to play.

That was the day the King's Herskalt appeared in the court with Kendred's longed-for invitation to the academy. The sturdy, brown-haired boy ran outside yipping to brag to the castle boys, leaving his father to read the letter sent by the king.

There were still occasional letters from Evred, always friendly, always about kingdom affairs, for Inda never again attended Convocation. Each spring he'd say, "Next year" but by the time autumn came, there was always some important reason keeping him at home. He did travel up to witness Jarend's Games every year, after he left Darchelde. When he reached the royal city he was immediately surrounded by his old cronies. They'd exchange news and reminisce amid much laughter. Inda never told anyone how much it always hurt, that first sight of the royal city on the horizon—he couldn't even explain it to himself. Nothing bad ever happened . . . but the pain was still there. Just like the nightmares that had never gone away.

Inda smiled down at the letter, then shook his head. "It feels like it was a hundred years ago when we were scrubs."

Then he went inside to continue getting ready for his spring ride.

That night, Tdor woke up to the sudden sound of rain and discovered that she was alone in bed.

Her mood turned from unease to acute worry when she could not find Inda. Not in the stable, or his rooms, or Whipstick's office, or even out in the court. Her random checks became a methodical search, bottom to top, until at last, on the western wall, she found a figure lit by one of the magically burning torches—one of the many quiet gifts Signi had left behind on her single visit to Tenthen. She ran forward, and there she found Inda kneeling on the stone in the steady rain, arms wrapped tightly around himself, body shaking with noiseless grief.

Tdor flung herself down at his side, rain thrumming in her face. "Inda. My dear one. Is there danger? What is amiss?"

He turned away. "No, no. I'm sorry. I'm just being a fool."

"Tell me."

Inda shook his head. "I hate to load my ghosts onto you."

"Ghosts!"

Inda shook his head. "It's memory ghosts, not the ones that walk around."

"Tell me." She added with some asperity, "As for burdens, not knowing is far worse, because then I'm left wondering."

He blinked rain away and looked into her face. "I'm sorry, Tdor. I don't mean to be a burden. You know I'd do anything to rid myself of nightmares. This one was worse than the usual, that's all."

"We share," she said, desperate to be understood, to not tread wrong. "If you can, tell me."

"It was Dogpiss. I saw him, so real. Falling away, and I can't reach his hand, and his eyes—I can still see them now, and it's been what, thirty years? He's falling, and I can't catch him. I didn't catch him, and he died. The Harskialdna was right to blame me—"

"Inda. It's just not true."

He dug his palm-heels into his eyes. "How many people have died because of me? I cannot count them all, though

I relive those battles, nightmare after nightmare. What will happen to Kenda when he goes to the academy? The other boys all fight Jarend, just because he's my son. He doesn't tell me, but I know."

Tdor said slowly, "Jarend reminds me of Tanrid. He just shrugs those things off. Hadand invited him over for Rest-day as an excuse, after the healer reported he'd cracked a rib that first year. We didn't tell you because it was Hastred Marlo-Vayir, the one they call Hot Rock. We didn't want you and Buck angry with the boys, or with each other." When she felt Inda's slight shrug of understanding, she went on. "Jarend told her he figures he has to be tougher than the other boys if he's going to be tough on an enemy."

Inda sighed. "Kenda isn't like that."

"He will be popular because he makes everyone laugh. And Jarend will watch out for him there just as he does here. Inda, please see the truth, not your night fears. There is no more Anderle-Harskialdna, no more Venn threat. The academy runs exactly the way you yourself fashioned it. Hadand says that Evred will not consider the slightest alteration from what you did, because Gand says it's the best it's ever been, ever and ever."

Inda let his breath out, and shifted, wincing. She recognized that there was pain in his joints, probably from sitting in the cold rain on the hard stone. She rose, taking his wrists and pulling him to his feet. His fingers wound tightly in hers as he said, "But don't you see? Evred and I, we designed it all to make them ready for war. Hot Rock and Jarend fighting, they're practicing for killing enemies. Is it true that he who spends his life getting ready finally goes looking?"

"They emphasize defense. You've heard Jarend when he comes home. Defense, just like you said back then. There is no plan for any wars; Hadand would have told me."

Inda leaned his forehead against her collarbone as rain drummed on them both. She wound her long arms around him and held him against her, willing the grief away.

After a time, "You know what Evred wrote to me?" Inda lifted his head, and it was clear he was quoting exactly. "*You remember your first day back, when you took me to Daggers Drawn? There is a new tradition. I had not known until Hastred brought it to my attention. That table you and I sat at is now reserved for the horsetail commander who wins*" *the Banner Game flag, along with his riding captains. The honor the boys perceive there is not mine, but yours . . . "*

Inda leaned his head on her shoulder. "I know he meant it well. But I can't stop thinking of Dogpiss, and I wonder why we measure glory by the pain of death."

Tdor said, "Come, Inda. Come inside and rest. Our boys are safe. They will not ride to war, because the kingdom is at peace. Jarend and Hot Rock are not enemies. Kenda will make friends with the other sons at the academy, friends for life. We have raised them well, to be fair, to value what is good in one another, to respect hard work of any kind. There is peace, Inda. You brought it. Evred keeps it. Come. Come inside, where it's warm."

Inda came obediently, and they walked inside, where it was quiet, smelling of herb-candles, and down past the nursery rooms where once they had slept and now the children were sleeping.

On the landing Inda paused, looking at Jarend's room, once his brother's, and he said, his expression uneasy, "When trouble does come, it will rise first at the academy. We all thought the Fox banner stood for glory, but what if glory is just another word for damnation?"

He was rocking again. Tdor's throat hurt with grief. "Inda, never forget that you gave us peace when it would have been so easy to go on fighting, on and on. Come to bed."

They reached the bedroom, and Inda sighed, massaging his shoulder. Tdor's eyes stung as she helped him out of his wet clothing and into dry, and then made him sit down so she could towel the wet out of his hair and comb it smooth again. She brushed slowly, gently, and her reward was to see the tension slowly smooth from his brow, and he ceased shivering.

"Ah, beloved," he murmured, his fingers caressing the faint lines in her brow, tracing the shadows at the sides of her lips. "How beautiful you are."

She couldn't help a chortle.

Inda heard the unsteadiness in her attempt at laughter, the disbelief, and beneath it, question.

"Joret was never beautiful to me," he said. "Not ugly, either. She was just Joret. Pleased the eye, but beauty, it strikes you right here." He closed a fist lightly and thumped it against his breast bone. "Joret was art. Tau was art. But to me, you were always beautiful. Before I really knew what beauty was. It was your face I saw when I was away. Awake and in dreams."

She laughed again, even more unsteadily, but he heard the genuine humor there, then she wound her fingers in his wet hair, bumped up against him, and said, "Prove it."

And he did. They loved with passion and with tenderness and with laughter, and when they were too tired to love again, he lay beside her, listening to her breathing, and said, "You make me happy. Don't say I do that for you, not when I yelp at night, and whine about my arm, and any beauty I ever had was long lost with all these scars. Do I do anything for you?"

"Everybody is beautiful. Life is beauty. Especially the young. But you?" She grinned, and nipped him on the ear. "You make me burn."

He grinned like a boy again and hugged her tight.

Presently he fell asleep, and this time stayed that way; his face looked peaceful, outlined by the soft golden glow from the torchlight on the walls. His grip on her had loosened.

So she slipped from the bed, ignoring the cold air, and knelt down by her trunk.

I cannot take away our painful memories, she thought as she unsheathed her knife. *And maybe we humans need to remember the pain, to help us learn not to cause it. But there are things I can give to Inda. Each day's small triumphs, moments of laughter. Little stories shared, they will add up and up, into a life of contentment. His greatness was in knowing when to empty his hands of steel and death. Mine shall be in filling his hands with life.*

She carved another notch to honor her vow.

Afterword

The King Who Was an Emperor

IN the days between Hadand's sudden death after her horse slipped on black ice, and the magnificent memorial bonfire attended by what appeared to be the entire royal city, all bearing torches, Evred made a decision.

Directly after the bonfire, he walked between his sons from the parade ground, which had not been big enough to hold all who wished to be there. The wintry air glowed with a fiery river of torches, creating a semblance of day as people streamed back through the tunnel and the castle courtyard to the city, many still singing.

Here and there echoed the laughter of the young; Evred shook away irritation. They had showed their respect by their appearance despite the shocking cold so late in the season. Evred could imagine Hadand's twisted smile, were she here. Just weeks ago she'd said, after yet another of their daughter-by-marriage's hall-ringing tantrums as she broke with another hapless lover, *I finally figured out Fabern Ola-Vayir's purpose in our lives. She's living proof that though we can educate the younger generation, we can even command them, we cannot control their lives, much as we think we'd do a better job of it.*

He lifted his gaze to Hastred's tall, dark-haired profile at one side. The ruddy torchlight made him seem older than he was. The heirs were past their wild youth, born early to their parents, a result of those desperate years when Evred was afraid there would be no more heirs left to the kingdom.

On his other side, red-haired Tanrid gave his father his lopsided smile, then made a move in the direction of the stable. He was so seldom still.

"Bide a moment," Evred said, and his sons paused, Tanrid mid-stride. "Come with me. I've something to discuss."

They walked in silence. It was a companionable silence, but still a silence. Evred had long accustomed himself to the fact that he had nothing in common with either of his sons. Tanrid could not read, though he was a dashing Sierandael—Evred thought with pride of Tanrid's leading of the restless younger generation to Ghael, where they rid the border mountains of infestations of brigands that had begun preying on the increase in trade. But when Tanrid was at home, he stuttered as much as had the Uncle Aldren he'd never met. Tanrid's academy name had been Jabber. Evred had hated the cruelty of that, though Tanrid never seemed to mind, except when Fabern sneered it. Hadand talked Evred out of his first impulse, which was to forbid it. By the time Tanrid was a horsetail the name had shortened to Jab, and now in the songs about the Ghael Hills routing of brigands he figured as Jab the Sword-swinger.

There were no songs about Hastred-Sierlaef, who was worthy and dutiful and hard-working. Hastred was only interested in horses during his rare leisure moments.

Evred led the way to his study, seldom used during winter any more. The kingdom had been quiet for so long that Evred had been spending more of his winter in the archives, organizing the family papers, annotating them, translating the Iascan archives into Marlovan. The days of using Marlovan only in the field were over. It was a good language, what matter that it used another tongue's lettering? He'd learned that that was more common than not.

"Father?" Hastred said, as Tanrid shifted about restlessly.

Evred broke the reverie he hadn't realized he'd fallen into, and said, "I have decided to lay aside the crown."

Hastred's straight brows were as dark as his hair. His

coloring was so like his grandfather Tlennen, yet his features unlike. He did not look pleased, or angry. He knew how much work that meant, but he had always squared to whatever task he was set, with a methodical exactitude that had astounded his tutors in the schoolroom. He liked lists, and order. Ruling all of Halia would just require a bigger set of lists. Evred could almost read his thoughts as Hastred's abstract gaze moved slowly over the crimson rug on the floor to the desk.

Tanrid whistled softly, for once standing still. His gaze shifted between them, and Evred saw his unspoken question, a need for reassurance. "I am not falling on my sword, I just think it is time. Tanrid, you have been Sierandael ever since you left the academy, so nothing will change for you, except that your orders will now come from your brother, as is proper. Hastred, you have sat beside me in council, at Convocation, and in here, since you left the academy. You will know what to do."

"When?" Hastred asked.

"Tomorrow," Evred said.

"Oh." Hastred did not know what to think. His father had always seemed ageless, strong as a tree. Hastred had been content with the quiet rhythm of their lives when Fabern was elsewhere. He liked quiet, and order. The first shock of his life had been his mother's death; here was another shock, that his father would go away. "Where will you go?"

"To the north."

Hastred struggled to accept, to comprehend. He had grown up knowing that some things just were, you had to accept them, and live around them. Like the prospect of being married to Fabern Ola-Vayir, accomplished a few years ago.

"Vedrid is arranging things," Evred said, watching comprehension work its way into Hastred's expression. Comprehension and decision. First the little things, then the cascade that would build to the greater ones. He must go away, leaving Hastred the freedom to make them. "Vedrid will ride with me; the other Runners I leave to you. The Jarls would hate riding back to another Convocation in the worst winter we've had since I was young, so I suggest you summon them to make their vows at midsummer, like I did." Evred caught himself. *I am no longer king.* "But do as you think best. I want to depart quietly. I would rather you tell no one until after I am gone."

"It shall be as you wish, Father," Hastred said.

He and Tanrid turned toward one another uncertainly. There was no custom for this moment. Most Marlovan kings had died by violence, only one by old age. Evred sensed constraint as Tanrid faced the window, fingers tapping nervously at his thigh, and Hastred looked down at the rug. All three knew that the moment she discovered she would be Gunvaer in fact, Fabern would be up in the royal suite, ordering the women to pull apart Hadand's rooms to be reorganized to her satisfaction.

And of course she would have the right.

Evred embraced his sons there in his study, then left them alone to talk it out in what would be the new king's room. He walked back to the royal suite, which seemed larger and emptier than ever.

He still had his old academy coat, though it had gone so threadbare he had laid it aside some years ago, saving it for an occasion he then could not quite define. He would wear it again on the morrow.

He looked around at his few personal possessions. The magic rings he had given to his sons; Hastred and Tanrid seemed to like knowing where the other was. On the mantel in his private chamber he still had the carved box that had once held his horsetail clasp. Since then he'd stored in the box his few treasures, mainly a ribbon-tied roll of Inda's letters. There were a couple of scraps left from his boyhood days, and there at the bottom Tau's last letter, written in Old Sartoran: *Don't force Inda to fight his friends.* How many times had he written answers to that in his mind, to reject them in the light of day?

Evred took the box down and laid it on the fire.

It had not quite burned away when there was a quick knock at the door. One he recognized. "Enter," he called.

In came his cherished daughter-in-law, Liet. For years everyone had exclaimed over Fabern's beauty—so much like her father Cama—but Evred had only seen the Ola-Vayir calculation in her eyes, the smirk of meanness that had appeared when she was scarcely able to speak.

Liet was tall, with the Toraca sloped shoulders, her large

ears pushed forward by heavy braids. She looked so much like her father, Nightingale—and sometimes there were echoes of Noddy in her face—that her appearance transcended trite terms like beauty, in Evred's eyes.

"Papa-Evred," she said. "I smelled something odd out in the hall."

"Merely some tidying." He rose, dusting ash from his knees. "I told Hastred and Tanrid, and now I tell you: I am laying aside the crown."

Her eyes widened, then her brow crimped with unhappiness. "What will you do?"

"I plan to ride north."

She bit her lip, but as always, did not remonstrate. "I was writing to Ki," she said. Evred thought of his daughter Tdor-Kialen, living up in the north with Cama's son. How much she resembled her mother!

"I waited to add in about the memorial. I think the news will hurt less, when I tell her all the good things people said about Mama-Hadand. Will you be going that far?"

"I don't know," Evred said slowly.

"It's all right. I'd planned to send my letter with—oh, it doesn't matter, I just thought—oh, Papa-Evred, I will miss you." She opened her arms, and he hugged her wordlessly. As he looked down at the neat parting in her brown hair, he thought, *You will be Gunvaer in all but name, and you will be as good as you have proven to be a good Harandviar, young as you are.* But such things were better left unsaid.

He and Vedrid departed at dawn the next day, and Hastred kept his word: there were no bells, no trumpets, though the sentries on the walls, men and women, saluted when they saw the king riding. He saluted them back, meeting eyes with grave deliberation. They would find out after he was gone that the gesture was a farewell.

He had not realized how melancholy he had felt until the royal city sank behind him, leaving crackling snow lying in broad, pale blue layers all the way to the horizon. It was good to be riding again. How many years since he had taken to horse? Since the desperate days he rode beside Inda to defend the kingdom.

The terrible winter was ending at last when he reached the outskirts of Ala Larkadhe. When he approached the castle, he was pleased to see alert guards. He and Vedrid rode with no markings on their coats, so again there was no fanfare.

Word had gone ahead, of course—they had shared an inn with a few of Hastred's Runners—so Evred's arrival was quiet, his welcome by the new commander genuine, though he could see that they were uneasy. No one was quite sure how to behave around a king who was not a king.

When he was done with the expected interview and meal, at last they left him alone, assuming he was going to one of the guest chambers to rest. His heartbeat drummed as he trod the back corridors of the castle to the white tower. He had hoped that time and a peaceful approach would once again grant him access to the Morvende archive, where he had hoped to live out his days in peaceful study.

But when he crossed the well-remembered landing and laid his hand to the door, he found it closed.

He stood there on the landing, head bowed. When he had got control of the almost devastating disappointment, he realized he was not alone: from behind came the rustle of cambric and silk, then a quiet step. He breathed a long familiar scent, a little like sage and wild thyme.

He turned.

Taumad Dei stepped out from the archway adjacent. "I caught ship when I got word about Hadand, and landed last week at Lindeth. I thought you might come here." He stretched out his hand. "Your work is done, and well done. Whatever the Morvende think."

Evred made the old flat-handed gesture of negation on the word "Morvende." Then faced Tau. "There are many things I regret. Most I made peace with. But this one I cannot, how I disclaimed your honor in that treaty you made."

"But you accepted it anyway." Tau smiled. Age had only refined his splendid features. His golden hair had lightened to silver. "You did right by your Marlovans and by the rest of the world at the last, and I know what that cost you. You gave us peace." He stretched out his other hand. "So now it's my turn to give a gift. Are you ready to see the world?"

Evred drew in a slow breath, and the tension left him as he lifted his own hand. "Yes." Their fingers closed and tightened. "Show me the world," Evred said.

Characters and Ships in
TREASON'S SHORE

MARLOVANS

Algara-Vayir Family
Jarend, Adaluin (prince)

Fareas Fera-Vayir, Iofre (princess)

Tanrid, Laef (heir), killed by secret order of Sierlaef, 3910

Joret Dei, betrothed to Tanrid, then to Inda, married Prince Valdon na Shagal of the Adranis

Hadand, betrothed to Sierlaef, married Evred-Harvaldar and became Gunvaer (queen)

Indevan, ("Inda"), future Randael, exiled nine years, appointed Evred's Harskialdna, eventually Adaluin

Branid, son of former Randviar Marend, two generations previous, became Adaluin after Jarend

Arveas Family (now Arveas-Andahi)
Kendred, ("Dewlap"), former Cavalry Captain, Jarl of Olara, died defending Sala Varadhe Castle in the Venn War

Liet Tlen, Jarlan, died defending Andahi Castle in the Venn War

Tlennen, ("Flash") Randael, died by the hand of a spy in the Venn war

Ndand, Jarlan, daughter of a guardswoman, so "of Tlen" or just Arveas, wife of Flash,

Kethadrend, ("Keth"), much younger brother of Flash, now future Jarl, name changed to Arveas-Andahi

Gdir Tlen, once Keth's betrothed, killed by Idayagans in the Venn War

Radran, baker's son, survived the Venn attack

Hadand Tlen, ("Captain Han"), survived the Venn attack

Lnand, cook's apprentice, survived the Venn attack

Haldred Mon-Davar, ("Hal") (brother Moon), survived the Venn attack

Ingrid Tlennen, serving as interim Randviar until the Andahi girls grow up.

Cassad Family

Senrid, Jarl

Ivandred, Randael

Ndara, second cousin to Jarl, married to Anderle-Harskialdna

Tanrid, Laef

Carleas Ndarga, betrothed—later wife—to Tanrid, the heir

Jarend, ("Rattooth" or more commonly "Rat"), future Randael

Kialen, intended Harandviar to Evred-Laef Montrei-Vayir, took her own life after the Hesea Hills Conspiracy

Mran, grand-daughter of Ivandred Cassad, brother to Jarl, married to Landred Marlo-Vayir

Idayago-Vayir (see Camarend Tya-vayir)

Jaya-Vayir Family

Camarend, ("Horseshoe"), Jarl

Manther, Laef, died at Ghael Hills battle in 3907

Marend, (betrothed to Savarend Montredavan-An ("Fox")

Ivandred, ("Vanda"), new heir

Retren, cousin to Vanda, now to be his Randael

Khani-Vayir Family

Nadran, Jarl

Nadran Toraca, ("Noddy Turtle"), Randael to his cousin Nadran, killed in the Venn war

Indevan, ("Inda"), Noddy's son

Branid Toraca, ("Nightingale"), Noddy's brother, married to Hild Sindan

Marlo-Vayir Family

Aldren, ("Buck"), Jarl

Landred, ("Cherry-Stripe"), Randael

Fnor, Jarlan to Buck

Mran, Randviar to Cherry-Stripe

Camrid, ("Scrapper"), former Randael to Hasta—Buck and Cherry-Stripe's uncle

Hastred, ("Hasta"), former Jarl of Marlo-Vayir

Hastred, ("Hot Rock"), Buck and Fnor's son, future Jarl

Indevan, ("Buttertub"), Cherry-Stripe's son, future Randael

Rialden, Cherry-Stripe and Mran's daughter, sent to Algara-Vayirs at age two, will be future Iofre

Marth-Davan Family

Tdor, Iofre, wife of Inda Algara-Vayir

Ramond, cousin to Tdor, future Jarl (deceased)

Ander, ("Mouse"), cousin to Tdor, Jarl

Montredavan-An Family:

Savarend, Jarl

Lineas Sindan-An, Jarlan, cousin to Tlennen Montrei-Vayir

Savarend, ("Fox"), heir; Inda's second in command of Fox Banner Fleet, also captain of *Death*

Shendan, ("Shen") Fox's sister, old friend to Tdor and Hadand from queen's training days

Marend Jaya-Vayir, Fox's betrothed, later wife

Montrei-Vayir family

Tlennen, former king, Evred's father, died by assassination

Anderle, former Harskialdna, or Marlovan Shield Arm during wartime, died by assassination

Ndara Cassad, former Harandviar—in charge of queen's training and royal guardswomen, murdered by her spouse just before he was assassinated

Tdiran, former king's sister, died in riding accident, married to Jarl of Yvana-Vayir

Wisthia Shagal, former queen, retired to Adrani homeland on death of husband Tlennen; appointed ambassador to Bren

Aldren, royal heir (Sierlaef), died by assassination

Evred, ("Sponge"), Harvaldar (king), intended at birth as future Shield Arm (Varlaef) but became king on father's and brother's assassination)

Barend, son of Anderle and Ndara—cousin to Aldren and Evred—interim Harskialdna, also shipmaster for Fox Banner Fleet at sea, later Cammander of Navy

Noth Family

Dauvid, ("Horsepiss"), King's Dragoon Captain, later interim Randael to Algara-Vayirs, then defender of Fera-Vayir Harbor)

Senrid, ("Whipstick"), future dragoon captain, promoted Randael to Algara-Vayirs

Kendred, ("Dogpiss"), included in first Tvei class—died in academy accident summer 3905)

Flatfoot and Goatkick Noth, sons of Horsepiss' brother, Flatfoot personal runner to Whipstick, Goatkick runner-in-training for King's Runners

Tya-Vayir Family

Stalgrid, ("Horsebutt"), Jarl

Imand Sindan-An, Jarlan

Dannor, ("Mudface") married to Aldren ("Hawkeye") Yvana-Vayir, then to Branid Algara-Vayir

Camarend, ("Cama"), Randael, later Jarl of Idayago, new name, Idayago-Vayir; his wife Starand ("Honeytongue") Ola-Vayir

Hibern, Imand's mate and First Runner

Dauvid, ("Honeyboy"), new Randael

Stalgrid, heir to Horsebutt

Yvana-Vayir Family

Anderle, ("Hawkeye"), heir, Jarl after father's execution for treason, killed in the Venn war

Tdiran Montrei-Vayir, Hawkeye's mother, sister to Tlennen-Harvaldar, died in riding accident

Dannor Tya-Vayir, ("Mudface"), wife to Hawkeye

Camrid, ("Mad Gallop"), Hawkeye's father, Jarl who led

an attempted coup, regicide, died a traitor's death at the post

Tlennen and Haldred, ("Badger and Beaver"), twins, sharing Jarlate

Fala, potter, (life mate to Hawkeye)

Dei Family

Joret Dei, betrothed to Tanrid Algara-Vayir, then to Inda, married Prince Valdon na Shagal of the Adranis

Taumad Dei, aka Taumad Daraen, once Inda's chief Runner, later diplomat

Saris Dei aka Saris Elend aka Sarias Daraen, owner of the Golden Butterfly pleasure house in Parayid Harbor before being taken by pirates

Yaskandar Dei, distant cousin to Joret and Tau (Sartoran branch of the family)

Chief Runners

Jened Sindan, Captain of Tlennen-Harvaldar's Runners—and his life mate—died defending Evred at Ala Larkadhe

Vedrid Basna, First Runner to Evred-Harvaldar

Ramond Jaya and Ramond Lith, ("the Twins" or "Twin Ain and Twin Tvei"), Inda's Personal Runners (one short and dark, the other tall and fair)

Branid Toraca, ("Nightingale"), chief personal runner to Evred

Kened, one of Evred's Runners

Tesar, chief personal runner to Hadand-Gunvaer

Hatha, one of the King's Runners, perforce made into a healer for lack of same

Fiam, Inda's steward-in-training

Chelis, youngest of Fareas-Iofre's personal runners

Noren, Tdor's personal Runner

"Flatfoot" Noth, Whipstick Noth's personal runner (and his cousin)

Hened Dunrend ("Dun the Carpenter"), a King's Runner, related to Captain Sindan, Inda's bodyguard aboard the Pim ships, unknown as a Marlovan to Inda until after Dun's death

OTHERS

Ramond Fijirad, one of Inda's scrub mates, now a dragoon
captain

Tdiran-Randviar, Randviar (defending woman commander)
at Ala Larkadhe, appointed Randviar for life

"Tuft" Sindan-An, one of Evred's and Inda's Tvei companions, a hero of the Andahi Pass Battle.

"Shoofly" Senegad, an Yvana-Vayir dragoon later reas-
signed to Cama—poses as Inda

DENIZENS OF THE NOB, HARBOR AT TIP OF
OLARAN PENINSULA

Harbormaster Sholf

Nangel, chief scribe to Sholf

Skandar Mardric, head of Resistance

Rend Dalloran, ("Dallo"), innkeeper, part of Resistance

DENIZENS OF FREEDOM ISLANDS

Commander Garjath Dhalshev, formerly Admiral of Khanerenth Navy, now harbor master of independents in
Freeport Harbor

Walaf Woltjen ("Woof"), his assistant

Waki Woltjen ("Nugget"), Woof's sister, crews on Inda's
ships

Lorenda, proprietor of a cordage shop

Mistress Lind, proprietor of the Lark Ascendant pleasure
house

DENIZENS OF BREN

Mistress Perran, chosen as Fleet Guild mistress. She's also
Mistress of the Bren Coopers' Guild.

Fleet Master Chim, supposed to command the fleet once it
was raised and trained, but actually invented the sailors'
own method of communications.

Friends at *Lower Deck Tavern*: Haelec, proprietor, Jeje
hires Thess and her son Palnas, Nathad, Marn the old
lady, Japsar, Col

Mistress Rosebud, proprietor of Wisteria House—pleasure
   house offering music and pantomime
Eris, daughter of playwright, a musician
Kerrem, waiter friend of Tau's, also a musician
Denja Arrad, actor nicknamed "The Comet"
Royal Family: Galadrin, King of Bren; Kliessin, Crown
   Princess of Bren, later queen; Kavnarac, ("Kavna,")
   Prince of Bren
Captain Wenald, a beached captain kept chained to a pi-
   rate galley eight years
Tald Brasvac, high admiral of Bren navy

ADRANIS

Martan Shagal, king of Anaeran-Adrani
Nalais, queen of Anaeran-Adrani
Valdon Shagal, crown prince
Randon Shagal, cousin to Valdon
Ored Elsaraen, Duke of Elsaraen
Lord Jasil, retired ambassador to Sartor, replaced by Lady
   Fansara Bantas
Tirthia Shagal, princess of Anaeran-Adrani several genera-
   tions before, famed for her beauty and wit

VENN

Rajnir, King of the Venn
Erkric, Abyarn: Dag, Rajnir's principle mage
Durasnir, Fulla: Hyarl, and Oneli Commander of the Venn
   Fleet (Stalna), flagship *Cormorant*
Vatta Durasnir, son of Fulla Durasnir, died at sixteen in
   Rajnir's sea battle against the Chwahir
Brun Durasnir, wife to Fulla Durasnir, her title "Vra Stalna"
   or wife of commander, a higher title than Vra Hyarl
Halvir, second son of Fulla Durasnir, held captive by Er-
   kric with King Rajnir

Military
Gairad, Battlegroup Captain directly under Durasnir
Seigmad, Chief Battlegroup Captain, later Battlegroup
   Chief, wife Vra Seigmad, flagship *Petrel*

Talkar, Hilda Commander of the South, Rajnir's army commander

Balandir, Nanni, Senior Dag, once part of King's Household

Balandir, Dyalf, Hyarl, briefly Battle Group Chief, captain of warship *Graygull*

Baltar, new Battlegroup Chief, of the *Katawake*

Hrad, Battle Chief in charge of the southern portion of the Venn invasion, replaced by Vringir when Hrad died during Lindeth invasion

Henga, Drenga Captain (sea-marines, under orders of Hilda once on shore), at Arveas Castle, later a guard captain

Oneli Coast Scouts: Adin, Hegir and Walfga

Dags

Jazsha Signi Sofar, sea dag, captured by Inda when sent on secret mission to Sartor, Inda's lover

Valda, Brit, Chief Sea Dag, head of secret ring of dags resisting Dag Erkric

Ulaffa, Fulk: Yaga Krona Chief (head of prince's mage protectors)

Other dags: Mekki, on Pass, under stone spell for one hundred sixty years

Anchan—pretends to be a thrall to aid the cause against Erkric

Audir and Falki—sea dags killed by Erkric

Egal—House dag

Byarin—sea dag attached to Commander Durasnir

Yatar (and nephew) assistants to Erkric

MISCELLAENOUS CHARACTERS

Lord Annold Limros, Count of Wafri (county in Ymar), who captured Inda and tortured him to try to force him to fight the Venn

Flek Gelbeann, once a merchant captain, new guild master of Lindeth Harbor

Zek the ropemaker, Lindeth Harbor, one of Mardric's Resistance

Retham the ironmonger, Lindeth Harbor, one of Mardric's Resistance

Paulan Ebetim, an Idayagan Resistance leader
Captain Ramis the One-eyed, of the *Knife*
Mistress Resvaes, from the Mage Council of Sartor
Lael Lirendi, new king of Colend
Lissais Landis, heir to throne of Sartor
Danden Sharl ("The Brainsmasher"), held Pirate Island before Ramis freed it

ALLIES IN STRAIT BATTLE

Admiral Thog daughter of Pirog out of Chwahirsland
Admiral Taz-Enja of Sarendan, detached duty
Admiral Mehayan of Khanerenth
Fleet Master Chim of Bren, head of the Fleet Guild
Captain Marn Deliyeth of Everon
Prince Kavnarac (Kavna), titular head of Bren navy

INDA'S SHIPS AND CREW

Blue Star, out of Sarendan, captain Fangras
Cocodu, raffee, (once *Coco* under Gaffer Walic), captain Dasta, later captain Mutt
Death, trysail (once *Spear* under Boruin), captain Fox Montredavan-An; cook Jarad Filic Lorm, (also cooks for *Cocodu*), wife Nilat
Rapier, raffee, captain Gillor
Rippler, small schooner
Sable, big schooner, captain Eflis Zhavala, Sparrow first mate
Skimit, small schooner, sometimes captained by Fibi the Delf
Swift, brig converted to raffee, captain Swift, his daughter Khajruat first mate, then later captain, when Swift is a kind of mascot-commodore,
Vixen, scout cutter, master Jeje sa Jeje, usually crewed by Fisher brothers Loos and Viac, second mate Nugget
Wind's Kiss, trysail, captain Tcholan

PIRATE SHIPS (REFERENCED FROM PAST ADVENTURES)

Sea-King, captain Halliff (died in pirate battles)

Coco, captain Gaffer Walic, first mate Varodif, second mate Gutless, taken by Inda, renamed *Cocodu*

Bloodfire, captain Ganan Marshig, commander of the Brotherhood of Blood (taken beyond rift into Norsunder)

Spear, captain Boruin Death-Hand, first mate Majarian, taken by Inda, renamed *Death*

Brass Dancer, captain Dal Raskan (defeated by Inda, ship exploded in alcohol fumes

Widowmaker, captain Emis Chaul, defeated by Ramis of the *Knife*

Princess, raffee, captain Scarf, taken by Fox's fleet, Gillor new captain, renamed *Rapier*

Wind's Kiss, trysail, taken by Fox and Banner fleet off Toar, Tcholan new captain

Knife, three-masted, square-sailed *drakan*, kept outside time for at least two thousand years. Sailed by Captain Ramis, then left at Ghost Island

Sherwood Smith
Inda

"A powerful beginning to a very promising series by a writer who is making her bid to be a major fantasist. By the time I finished, I was so captured by this book that it lingered for days afterward. I had lived inside these characters, inside this world, and I was unwilling to let go of it. That, I think, is the mark of a major work of fiction…you owe it to yourself to read *Inda*." —Orson Scott Card

INDA
978-0-7564-0422-2

THE FOX
978-0-7564-0483-3

KING'S SHIELD
978-0-7564-0500-7

TREASON'S SHORE
978-0-7564-0573-1 (hardcover)
978-0-7564-0634-9
(paperback)

To Order Call: 1-800-788-6262
www.dawbooks.com

DAW 110

Violette Malan

The Novels of Dhulyn and Parno:
"Believable characters and graceful storytelling."
—*Library Journal*

"Fantasy fans should brace themselves:
the world is about to discover Violette Malan."
—*The Barnes & Noble Review*

THE SLEEPING GOD
978-0-7564-0484-0

THE SOLDIER KING
978-0-7564-0569-4

THE STORM WITCH
978-0-7564-0574-8

and new in trade paperback:

PATH OF THE SUN
978-0-7564-0638-7

To Order Call: 1-800-788-6262
www.dawbooks.com

Tad Williams

SHADOWMARCH

SHADOWMARCH
978-0-7564-0359-6

SHADOWPLAY
978-0-7564-0544-1

SHADOWRISE
978-0-7564-0549-6

And coming November 2010:

SHADOWHEART
978-0-7564-0640-0

"Bestseller Williams once again delivers a sweeping spell-binder full of mystical wonder." —*Publishers Weekly*

"Williams creates an endlessly fascinating and magic-filled realm filled with a profusion of memorable characters and just as many intriguing plots and subplots.... Arguably his most accomplished work to date."
—*The Barnes & Noble Review*

To Order Call: 1-800-788-6262
www.dawbooks.com

DAW 47

Tad Williams

THE WAR OF THE FLOWERS

"A masterpiece of fairytale worldbuilding."
—*Locus*

"Williams's imagination is boundless."
—*Publishers Weekly*
(Starred Review)

"A great introduction to an accomplished and
ambitious fantasist."
—*San Francisco Chronicle*

"An addictive world ... masterfully plays with
the tropes and traditions of
generations of fantasy writers."
—*Salon*

"A very elaborate and fully realized setting for
adventure, intrigue, and more
than an occasional chill."
—*Science Fiction Chronicle*

978-0-7564-0181-8
To Order Call: 1-800-788-6262
www.dawbooks.com

DAW 45

John Marco
The Bronze Knight

"A sprawling tale of military battles, personal and political intrigue, magic, and star-crossed love set against a richly detailed land of warring kingdoms and hidden magic."
—*Library Journal*

THE EYES OF GOD
978-0-7564-0096-1

THE DEVIL'S ARMOR
978-0-7564-0203-4

THE SWORD OF ANGELS
978-0-7564-0360-X

"Marco's characters are complex and multidimensional, and his seemingly simple story is a rich, complex exposition of high fantasy with an underlying brutal reality. This brutality is punctuated with Marco's skill as a military writer...the battle scenes are massive in scale while remaining rich in exquisite, personal detail."
—Amazon.com review

To Order Call: 1-800-788-6262
www.dawbooks.com

Patrick Rothfuss

THE NAME OF THE WIND
The Kingkiller Chronicle: Day One

"It is a rare and great pleasure to come on somebody writing not only with the kind of accuracy of language that seems to me absolutely essential to fantasy-making, but with real music in the words as well.... Oh, joy!" —Ursula K. Le Guin

"Amazon.com's Best of the Year...So Far Pick for 2007: Full of music, magic, love, and loss, Patrick Rothfuss's vivid and engaging debut fantasy knocked our socks off." —Amazon.com

"One of the best stories told in any medium in a decade. Shelve it beside *The Lord of the Rings* ...and look forward to the day when it's mentioned in the same breath, perhaps as first among equals." —*The Onion*

"[Rothfuss is] the great new fantasy writer we've been waiting for, and this is an astonishing book." —Orson Scott Card

ISBN: 978-0-7564-0474-1

To Order Call: 1-800-788-6262
www.dawbooks.com